SHE SHIVERED WITH DELICIOUS PLEASURE

I will stop him before it is too late, she thought. But almost as quickly as the thought was born, it faded in a wave of trembling passion. She was aware that he had unfastened the bodice of her dress. She felt the gentle September breeze breathe on her hot flesh. Even then she could not release herself from the bondage of his kiss.

Again she opened her mouth to tell him to stop, but no words came as the web of desire tightened around her. Longing had become need. He raised himself to look deeply into her eyes. It was as though he could read her thoughts and knew she would not—could not—deny him.

MAURA

MARILYN GRANBECK

MAURA

A JOVE/HBJ BOOK

**for Bob,
whose faith inspires**

Printed in the United States of America

Library of Congress Catalog Card Number: 78-71583

First Jove/HBJ edition published May 1979

Jove/HBJ books are published by Jove Publications, Inc.
(Harcourt Brace Jovanovich), 757 Third Avenue, New York,
NY 10017

There may be heaven; there must be hell;
Meantime, there is our earth here. . . .
—Robert Browning
Time's Revenge

PROLOGUE

New York City, November 1848

"Maura Katy Sullivan, you're a she-devil in the flesh!" Patrick Sullivan's roaring laughter was caught by the crisp winter winds and whirled away in a gust of mist that eddied up from the Hudson River far below. He hunched forward on the flat saddle and kicked the bay horse gently to urge more speed.

"Come on, boy, don't let her beat us this time!"

The two horses thundered along the wooded palisade, manes whipping and tails flying. In the lead, Maura looked back as the distance between them lengthened.

"You won't catch me today, Father!" she yelled. She concentrated her attention on the cliff path where they had raced so many times before. She rode like the wind itself, free and wild, born of the elements and unwilling to be trapped by physical boundaries. The pert green riding hat slithered askew and slipped from her amber curls to hang about her neck by its veiling. The wind whipped her hair and sent clinging red tendrils across her cheeks as she glanced back. Her father was gaining. The powerful bay was a magnificent animal that could outdistance her own mare in the right circumstances, but the mare's spirit matched her own.

She leaned close to the chestnut's ear. "Don't let me down, Blarney, we must win!"

The mare's ears lay flat and its nostrils quivered. Bits of rock and frozen dust flew from under the pounding hooves. The rider and horse were one, with a single purpose.

Ahead the path narrowed and disappeared around a sharp outcropping of rock with leafless trees overhanging it like misty shadows. It was not wide enough for two horsemen and Maura knew that whoever reached the bend first

7

would force the other to drop back. There had been a time when her father was always first, but in the last few years she had bested him as often as she'd lost.

She clutched the reins. "We will win, we will win, Blarney!" She kept up a steady crooning as if her voice could coax more speed from the straining horse. With a sidelong glance she saw that her father was abreast of her now, his face wreathed in a wide grin that foreshadowed victory.

"'Tis no wonder that no man has asked you for his wife!" he shouted. "You'd drive him crazy with your challenging ways and need to win!"

Her cheeks stung with the bite of the wind. "I thought no man was good enough for the only daughter of Patrick Sullivan!"

She heard his laughter and the retort, "You'll find one, you'll find one, never fear."

She peered at him as the chestnut's mane whipped her face. It was the first time he'd said such a thing; she'd had suitors, but sooner or later turned them all away. Not one had come up to her expectations. She valued her freedom and longed for something far beyond the dullness of marriage. She preferred riding and sailing with her father—and her brother, until James had gone to Pittsburgh to establish a branch of the expanding Sullivan Company.

She lifted her chin and concentrated on the race. The bend was only a few yards distant and the mare was keeping step with the big bay horse. She would reach the bend a step ahead! Laughing, she slapped the mare's neck.

"We'll do it, Blarney, this time we'll win!"

Then they were at the narrow passage where the path fell away on one side to the sheer palisades and the rocks below. Maura turned in triumph to claim her victory and saw to her horror that her father was not drawing back to allow her to negotiate the narrow turn. The bay was pressing pell mell, forcing its way close, trying to round the turn without slackening its pace.

Suddenly Patrick Sullivan's laughter subsided as he saw that he had called the daring maneuver too close. Reining quickly, he tried to slow the racing bay, but the animal was caught in its own momentum.

"Father!" Maura screamed, "draw back!" She kicked the mare desperately in a furious effort to make way, but the heavier bay was already stumbling at the dizzy edge of the precipice.

Patrick cried out but the sound was lost in the frightened cries of the horse. Its back legs thrashed powerfully, but the loose rocks and shale gave way with a terrible rumble like distant thunder.

Through the turn, Maura slowed the chestnut and slid from the saddle. She ran back along the path, choking off the sobs that rose in her throat as the screams of the falling horse echoed in her brain. The wind bit at her cheeks where tears spilled, and chilled her flesh. Her heart tore at her chest in a torment of fear, and a cry keened from her lips unheard.

"Father! Father!"

She reached the bend and clutched at a sharp projection of rock to steady herself. Even before she looked over the precipice, the fear swelled into guilt and pain that turned her mouth brassy, then erupted into horror as she looked down.

Her father lay like a discarded rag doll on the rocks below, still as death.

CHAPTER ONE

New York City, September 1849

A vagrant wind ruffled the dark surface of the East River and made the green-gold leaves of beech trees along Water Street twinkle. It stirred the amber curls that framed Maura Sullivan's face as she sat in the carriage. She had pulled off the wide-brimmed straw hat, and the sprigged dimity gown was damp against her waist and bosom despite the cool breeze.

She stilled an impatient, tapping foot so she would not call attention to herself and be badgered into explaining her lack of interest in the day's outing. She would have preferred staying home, but her mother wouldn't hear of it. This was, after all, a Sullivan Company picnic, and it was fitting that the owners grace the festivities with their presence.

The coach turned from the cobblestoned street onto the low road that followed the shoreline. South of Catherine Street, the waterfront was a crowded maze of wharves, docks and warehouses where great sailing ships and steamers forged a lifeline to the burgeoning city. Maura thought longingly of the childhood rides along the river she'd shared with her father. Now the secluded paths had been devoured by the city's expanding population that already exceeded half a million. Suburbs had been swallowed up so that now one had to ride clear past Thirty-fourth Street to find open spaces or country retreats.

New York was no longer the quiet little city it had once been. It was a crowded metropolis full of bustle, noise and splendor. It was the city her father had always envisioned with pride.

"Before the turn of the century, New York will be built all the way north to Harlem, mark my words," Patrick had

11

boasted, puffing his chest proudly. "It will be the grandest metropolis this side of the ocean."

"I suppose Patrick Sullivan has arranged with the Almighty to be on hand to see it," Maura had teased.

He shook his head of unruly red hair. "No, but there'll be Sullivan coaches on every street. And maybe a redheaded grandson to carry on when I'm gone and you and your brother are too doddering to manage the Sullivan enterprises anymore," he'd added with a knowing wink.

Maura gazed through the lacy trees across the hazy greensward and the silvery blue river. So much of the joy of life seemed gone with her father's passing. It had been almost a year, but she still missed him with an aching loneliness. They'd been so close, shared so much. . . .

She glimpsed a cluster of gaily decorated sailboats tied near a red buoy marking the starting line for the regatta. In past years, she had eagerly looked forward to the annual regatta and picnic, but it was not the same without her father. The races had lost none of their excitement, but her enthusiasm was dampened by the thought of spending the afternoon in the company of her stepfather and stepbrother.

Stepfather! How she hated the word! To her, Pelham Turk was the man her mother had married, nothing more, and though he made a dutiful show of affection in both public and private, she sensed that she meant as little to him as he did to her. She was a necessary corollary of the marriage and a cause of considerable annoyance to him because she would not grovel and cater to him as he expected.

Early on he had taken her aside. "It is not my intention to take your father's place in your life, Maura, but I hope we can become good friends and that you will come to me with any problems or worries you have. I shall always endeavor to help. It has been a long time since Braxton and I have enjoyed warmth and comfort in our home life. I assure you we are looking forward to becoming a close family now, as I know your dear mother wishes."

Even the thought of Braxton Turk made her shudder inwardly, and she darted a glance at him. Could she despise a man more? Her stepbrother was a toad. It was beyond her imagination how any girl could enjoy closeness with him, even if she were tormented by loneliness! Maura

12

thought about the young men who had courted her. Any of them was more charming than Braxton, though she'd found none who suited her for more than a few casual outings. She had avoided all of them since her father's death. She was still immersed in grief and guilt over the tragic accident, and she used her mourning to shield herself from dull, stuffy suitors who bored her beyond words. But even in utter despair, she would never consider any kind of liaison with Braxton!

And it was Braxton who had, in a way, driven her from the beloved Sullivan Carriage Company. Before her father's death, she'd spent many hours there, watching and learning, interested in the business that was so dear to all the Sullivans. But Pelham treated her like a child. He humored her but firmly prevented her from delving into any company affairs. Braxton managed to appear at her side the moment she entered the factory, and to follow her about, until at last she abandoned the visits in disgust. She wished James would return to take command, but the new boatworks in Pittsburgh demanded his full attention. Shocked and grieved, he'd returned for their father's funeral. When Maura wept and blamed herself for the race that resulted in the tragic accident, he'd kissed away her tears and admonished her sternly.

"Father never would have listened to such talk, nor will I. You were doing what you both loved best, and there's no guilt to be borne on anyone's shoulders. Now hold up your head like a Sullivan. Mother will need your strength."

"You're not going away again!"

"I must. Our first paddlewheeler is already on the ways. To delay the work would mean a huge loss that would give our competitors an edge I've fought hard to gain. With river traffic growing so fast there are half a dozen boatyards ready to scoop up contracts if I don't meet our schedule."

"But with Father gone, you must manage the company here!" Maura said.

James smiled gently. "I have to finish what I've begun."

She smothered a sigh. It would do no good to coax. He would never abandon a goal he had set for himself. Hadn't he stubbornly insisted on the Pittsburgh venture despite Patrick's objection that there was enough work in New York

13

to keep them busy? There were fortunes to be made on the river, James said. Sullivan Company boats would make them, just as it had led the carriage industry for so many years. Maura suspected her brother's love for the river played a large part in his eagerness for the new project. For a number of years, he'd maintained a small boatyard on the riverbank below the factory. With a minimum of cost and labor, he turned out the finest quality sloops, yawls and ketches. In a very short time, the Sullivan name on a boat became a trademark of distinction. Earlier in the year, James had gone to Pittsburgh to study a new steam engine that was being developed. When he returned with visions of opening a Sullivan boatyard there, Patrick agreed to let him return and build that dream. James had taken with him Jeb MacDonald, a Sullivan employee who knew as much about building boats as any man on the face of the earth. Together they would select and train men to staff the boatyard and operate it at the high standards the Sullivan Company name stood for.

"I've put Duggan Quinn in charge of the carriage factory," James told her. "He's a good man and he's trustworthy. Father set great store by him."

James stayed long enough to see the young foreman take charge. Then with the promise that Maura and his mother would come to Pittsburgh for the inaugural trip of the first Sullivan Company riverboat, he was gone again.

Now, less than ten months later, everything had changed because their mother had married Pelham Turk.

Maura gazed at the river and vowed not to think of Pelham today. And if she were to find some measure of enjoyment in the afternoon, she would have to avoid Braxton like the plague.

Maura's mother had worried all morning lest it rain and spoil the day. Now she was peering from the carriage toward the persistent mass of gray clouds that seemed anchored to the horizon.

Pelham lifted one hand from the silver-headed cane propped before him and patted her hand. "It will not rain today, Francine. I have absolutely forbidden it."

She gave him a tiny smile.

How like Pelham, Maura thought, as she glanced at the line of clouds. She would enjoy seeing a downpour, just to

14

spite him. No, she must not wish such a thing. A shower would spoil the day for too many people.

"It hasn't rained on one of our regattas in more than five years," her mother said mildly. "I hope it won't today."

Braxton squinted at the sky. "The morning clouds have all but dispersed. The afternoon will be fair and pleasant, don't you think, Maura?"

"I'm sure it will." She barely glanced at him and wished they would get off the foolish subject.

But Braxton was determined to draw her into conversation. He leaned against the red velvet cushion and regarded her with an amused smile. She always felt as though he were peering deep inside her, trying to read her most private thoughts. It infuriated her, and she suspected that the fact that she had told him so caused him to continue the practice.

"I'm looking forward to the day, Maura. You and I have not enjoyed a sail together as yet." His dark eyes smoldered with hidden light, and he touched a finger to his small mustache

Like the hero in a melodrama at Mitchell's Olympic Theatre, Maura thought. He was a tall man, slender and wide-shouldered. Women considered him handsome but to Maura he was repellent. His dark hair and eyes gave him a sinister look, and she could not tolerate the caressing softness in his voice.

"No, we have not," she said as calmly as she could. She had no desire to sit beside him in a sailboat or any place else.

"I think you will be amazed at my skill. I've enjoyed the river extensively this year, though never in quite such charming company." He smiled at Francine, who colored a bit and turned her gaze away from her stepson.

She disliked Braxton and knew that Maura's feelings were much stronger than her own. A mother could not help but notice the looks that passed between them, or the lust in Braxton's eyes when his gaze followed Maura across a room. How could she have been so wrong about Pelham and his son? She regretted her hasty marriage and wished there were some way she could undo it, but that was impossible. It was Maura to whom her heart went out. Bereaved so suddenly of a loving father, now Maura had to contend

15

with Pelham's hypocritical manner and Braxton's too-warm interest. Francine had spoken to Pelham about his son, but he'd chided her for being a foolish, overprotective mother. Braxton meant no harm; it was only that he had an appreciative eye for beauty and a brotherly interest in his stepsister. Braxton wanted to be sure Maura was escorted properly and began enjoying herself again. She was too young to stay in mourning. And the Sullivans—or rather the Turks—had to uphold their place as leaders of New York society. It was expected that they would open the season with their annual pre-Thanksgiving ball, and naturally Maura would be invited to the Vanderbilts' gala Christmas affair. Young William Henry Vanderbilt had called on Maura several times these past months. Pelham declared it was time for Maura to come out of her self-imposed solitude. Patrick was dead and buried. Life must go on.

Francine said no more, but she watched her stepson fearfully and prayed that her husband was right. Looking at Braxton now, she felt a shiver of apprehension. The hunger in his eyes as he watched Maura terrified her.

Maura would have ignored Braxton's remark except that he made a point of eliciting an answer. "It's a pity we haven't had time to sail together before this," he went on, "Still, autumn is beautiful on the river. Perhaps we can manage an outing before the season is over. I haven't been to Peekskill this year. We might sail up one day."

His hand fell carelessly to the seat between them, and Maura felt the surreptitious pressure of his fingers at her skirt. She drew away in revulsion but disguised the act by smoothing her dimity skirt.

"Perhaps," she said without enthusiasm. Her tone brought a sharp look from her stepfather, but she did not care. She would not be embarrassed into making plans she had no intention of keeping. She gazed steadily at the riverfront as the horses clip-clopped along.

The regatta had been initiated by her father a decade earlier for the employees of the Sullivan Carriage Company and Boatworks. The Sullivan Company was the largest of its kind in the nation, and Patrick prided himself on the devotion of his employees. The regatta was only one of the many ways he showed his appreciation for their loyalty.

Maura had many pleasant memories of past regattas

with her parents and brother. James . . . how she wished he were here. It was more than three months since his last letter. There had been a few hasty notes from him after his return to Pittsburgh; they were filled with news of the progress of the steamboat, which would be named the *Patrick*. James was obsessed with the boat and with his dream, and he had time for nothing else. He had not even come home at the news of their mother's remarriage or Pelham's taking over the factory. He could be infuriating! Of late, Maura's letters to him were filled with sharp rebukes, but even these had not elicited a reply. Her annoyance was beginning to be tinged with anxiety. She closed her eyes. The regatta would not be the same without James and Father.

The driver slowed as the carriage approached the private jetty where the Sullivan boats were moored. It was in a cove halfway between the Sullivan factory and the busy commerce of Peck's Slip and Roosevelt's wharf, yet it seemed almost isolated from the bustle of the city. It was an oasis of green grass and drooping willow trees on New York's busy waterfront.

Most of the boats had already gone out into the Sound. White sails were bright against the gray-blue sky, and colorful banners trailed in the freshening breeze. A group of people waited on the dock; all eyes turned to the landau as the driver reined in. A scarlet-coated footman jumped down to open the door.

Pelham glanced over the assemblage of faces. The top executives and foremen of the company were awaiting his arrival to signal the official start of the festivities. Pelham smiled and climbed down with surprising grace in spite of the stiff leg that necessitated the cane. Then he turned to assist Francine.

Maura watched her mother climb from the carriage. She looked paler than usual and more frail, Maura thought. The realization brought a wrench of pity. She worried about her mother's health, which had deteriorated since her remarriage. It was as if living with Pelham demanded too much of her strength. For weeks after her father's death, Maura had retreated into solitude as a balm for guilt and depression. She shut out the steady stream of people who came to offer condolences, and she had shut out her mother as well. Lost in grief, Maura had not realized how

17

frequently Pelham Turk came to the house or that his visits were anything other than routine business. As one of the lawyers for the Sullivan enterprises, it was natural that he offer what assistance he could. But romance—! How could Mother be so gullible and stupid? Pelham wanted the prestige and power of the Sullivan name and money. Marrying Patrick's widow was the easiest way to get it.

Maura curbed her angry thoughts. Poor Mother. Only a few weeks after the small, private wedding, she'd taken ill with a cold that developed into pneumonia. She lay near death's door through March and April. It was not until summer that she was able to be up and about. Even then her strength never returned completely. She tired much too easily despite her protests that she felt fine. Dr. Holmes saw her regularly, but the old man seemed unaware that his patient's condition was deteriorating slowly.

Francine clung to her husband's arm as friends came forward to greet her.

"You look lovely," Nancy Rothingwell declared, fluttering a white lace fan in front of her plump face. Theodore Rothingwell, the Sullivan Company's office manager, murmured and bent over Francine's hand.

Pelham waved and boomed greetings with forced camaraderie. Someone said, "Mrs. Turk, it's nice to see you again."

"It's been much too long since you honored the factory with a visit," Stuart Rider declared.

"I plan to come one day soon," Francine said, offering slender white fingers to the company's accountant.

Maura lifted the yellow and blue skirt. Braxton was on his feet instantly to reach for her arm. When she drew away, quick anger flashed in his eyes. She gave the footman her hand to let him help her down. She turned away and busied herself with her gloves so she would not have to look at Braxton.

Pelham had arranged for a closed launch, since his wife complained that the wind chilled her no matter how warm the sun. Rothingwell and his wife, as well as several other executives, would ride in the launch with them, while the young people sailed a small cutter to the middle of the river. Braxton and Maura would host that group. Two other sailboats would carry other employees, each skippered by one of the foremen. Maura knew it was useless for her to request passage in one of the smaller boats. She was expected to remember her place, and *that* was in the main vessel with Braxton, who seemed impervious to her feelings for him. How she wished he would find another object for his attentions! But she'd seen the glint in his eyes when she drew away from him, and she had the uncomfortable feeling it foreshadowed an increased effort on his part to include her, no matter how, in his coterie of admiring females.

Braxton fell in step as they walked toward the river, his dark eyes mocking. "It will be a memorable day," he said, glancing about as if he'd had something to do with its creation. "I'm looking forward to spending it with you." He deftly slipped his hand under her arm. "May I have the pleasure of escorting you along the quay?"

She felt his warm breath too close, and turned her head resolutely. She concentrated on the river and refused to give him the satisfaction of seeing her squirm. She'd told him in no uncertain terms how she despised him, yet in public he took advantage of her at every opportunity.

They descended the grassy slope to the pier that jutted into the lapping water. Seeing the river brought a flood of memories. As a child she had sailed with her father, learned to take the tiller and thrilled to the power of the wind in the billowing sails. They had raced or sailed where the wind took them, father and daughter in companionable contentment. Maura felt the sting of tears; she missed him more than she cared to admit.

Theodore Rothingwell said, "The boats are gathered at the starting buoy awaiting our arrival." He motioned to the boatman standing in the prow of the launch, and the man barked a command. Two sailors came forward to assist passengers aboard.

"How's the betting?" Braxton inquired. "Is there a favorite?"

"The *Thistle,* I expect, though some think *Triton* has the best chance."

Maura stepped forward as her mother was helped over the passenger bridge to the launch. Francine clutched her reticule and glanced about. Maura smiled encouragingly.

Others boarded, the Rothingwells, meticulously proper

19

in dress, Stuart Rider and his dumpy sister, Martha, two colorless people who nodded at every word uttered by Pelham Turk, and lastly David Walton, the purchasing agent, and his pretty wife, Corinne.

Braxton was chatting with two men at the quay. "I'll take the *Sea Spirit*," he said, claiming the smallest and fastest of the sailboats for himself. "Duggan can skipper the *Misty Dawn* and *Aurora* is up for grabs. Let the women choose their own boats and skippers," he said with a rakish smile around the group. There was a fluttering of smiles and a lowering of lashes. They would all choose to ride with him, given the chance. After all, the son of the company owner was a prize. Covert glances slid past Maura, and no one spoke.

Maura twirled the white straw hat and lifted her chin. "In that case, Braxton, I choose to go in the *Misty Dawn*," she said boldly. For a moment, the look of disbelief on his face delighted her. She went on: "It has always been my favorite. Father always permitted me to take the tiller." She smiled engagingly at Duggan Quinn. He looked surprised but nodded. Though relegated to a position as plant foreman by Pelham, Duggan had stayed on. Maura thought him very good-looking, though too arrogant for his own good. She had heard many tales of his exploits with women, and though they were little more than gossip, she fancied they must hold an underlying truth. He always had a ready smile and a soft word for the girls, and his strong face, with sapphire-blue eyes and dark brows under an unruly head of black curls, drew females to him like bees to flowers. Patrick Sullivan had been fond of the young man and had respected his ability. Duggan Quinn moved up quickly in the plant, and her father had often consulted him on new ideas and procedures. He'd brought him to the house several times and when Maura ventured into the library after the business discussions ended, she'd flirted with Duggan and tried to engage him in small talk. He had been maddeningly aloof, as though remembering his place as an employee, and he persisted in calling her Miss Sullivan. His indifference seemed to spur her own interest, and the frank appraisal in Quinn's eyes made her determined to conquer his polite disregard.

She had seen him only very briefly since Pelham had

taken over. Now she gazed at him with the smile still lingering on her lips. His eyes were as blue as the sea on a shadowy day but with hidden lights that mirrored her challenge.

"It would be my pleasure to turn the tiller over to you, Miss Sullivan," he said. His voice carried a hint of brogue, and his gaze never left her.

"Then it's settled," she said, looking at Braxton. His face was suffused with anger and his mouth was tight.

A blond girl tossed her head and glared at Duggan. "What about me, Duggan? You did invite me—"

"May I claim you as my first mate, Lacy?" Braxton said quickly.

Lacy Marsh smiled triumphantly. "It would be a pleasure, Braxton, an absolute pleasure." She shot an icy glance at Duggan. "You don't mind, Duggan?"

Quinn smiled wryly and made a mock bow in Braxton's direction. "Not at all. I'm sure you will enjoy the *Sea Spirit.*"

Lacy's eyes flashed dangerously. Maura hid a smile. Lacy was the niece of the Rothingwells, and a very ambitious young lady. A year or two Maura's senior, Lacy had tired of her small Pennsylvania hometown and coaxed her mother to allow her to visit her aunt and uncle in New York. The visit had extended to six months, and Lacy showed no indication of leaving. She had golden-brown eyes that were markedly feline, especially when she cast them at one of the handsome young men who competed to attend her. It was gossiped that she was often in the company of Duggan Quinn. Maura had seen them together several times, including the party Pelham gave to celebrate his marriage to Francine, and once when she chanced to see them strolling along Broadway, apparently having come from the theater. They'd been laughing and whispering with heads close, and Lacy clung to his arm in a very possessive manner.

Now Lacy slipped her arm through Braxton's just as readily. She said in a breathy voice. "No matter how secure they are, these rickety bridges terrify me."

Maura thought Lacy's professed fear unlikely as the girl set a foot daintily on the wooden ramp spanning the space between the pier and the gently bobbing sailboat. Braxton was close behind, his arm sliding easily about her slim waist in a protective manner. With a cold glance at Maura, he turned his attention completely to Lacy.

Maura brought down the brim of the hat to hide her smile. Pelham would be furious when he discovered her in the boat with Duggan instead of with his son, but she was immune to his displeasure.

"Give me your hand, Miss Sullivan." Duggan Quinn was watching her and a smile played at the corners of his mouth. "Let me help you aboard."

"Thank you." She grasped Duggan's extended hand and was helped over the board planks into the boat. When he stepped back, she settled herself in the stern sheets, pulling off her gloves and tucking them into her reticule.

Four others came aboard, Amos and Samantha Whittington, and Madison Ufford and Sally Gorham. Both Amos and Madison worked in the company as clerks and had joined in the annual regatta celebration for several years. The fact that they willingly left the skippering of the vessel to a relative newcomer was a mark of the respect they bore Duggan Quinn.

The *Misty Dawn* was a twenty-foot yawl, slightly smaller than the *Sea Spirit*. It did not have the same speed, but it handled exceedingly well. It was rigged like the larger cutter, with two masts and fore and aft sails. Maura had sailed both vessels, and though the *Sea Spirit* was a trifle more handy, she knew the *Dawn* was a sturdy, pleasurable boat for an outing.

"Cast off the lines," Duggan ordered, and the men on the quay quickly tossed them aboard. Duggan swung the tiller over, looking up at the sails being lifted to the peak by Madison and Amos. The wind caught them and the yawl glided off into the stream.

Raising her face, Maura inhaled the spray-laden breeze. For a time she forgot everything but the sense of freedom sailing gave her. The boat heeled and they were sailing with the wind abeam on the starboard side. A dozen other boats glided by like a gaggle of silent geese, and Duggan swung the tiller to follow. In a moment they were running free with the wind on the quarter, cutting through the silvery water with lacy spray blowing along the port side.

Duggan studied Maura covertly. He'd been surprised at

her sudden announcement that she would sail with him instead of with Braxton, and he had not missed the quick spark of anger in the other man's eyes. The girl had spunk, he credited her with that. Perhaps too much for her own good. Braxton would not take the rebuff lightly. He would find a way to get back at her, as he did anyone who crossed him. The men at the factory stayed clear of him as much as possible.

His thoughts turned inward. If only Patrick Sullivan had not tumbled to his death in that foolish riding accident. His passing was a loss to many, Duggan among them. Patrick had been like a father to him as well as a friend and employer. The older man had given him a position of trust and a promising future with the company. Duggan had been pleased by Patrick's faith and worked with a zeal that matched Sullivan's own. They had talked about a partnership. Only a week before his death, Patrick had given Duggan a copy of a letter he planned to send to James discussing the move. James had not received the letter before the funeral, but Duggan's word and his knowledge of the business had been sufficient for James to put him in charge. The partnership would come as soon as the Pittsburgh venture was assured.

But before Duggan knew it, Francine Sullivan had remarried. It was a shock to everyone. Patrick hardly cold in his grave, and a sharp-talking, quick-dealing lawyer convinced her she needed his protection. How could she abide a miserable excuse of a man like Turk after knowing Patrick's strength for so long?

When Turk took over the factory, angry pride made Duggan confront him openly with Patrick's letter. Pelham read it, then locked it in the office safe, stating that he would study it and establish its validity. Duggan had never seen it again, and Pelham denied the conversation had ever taken place. *Ah, Patrick, we were both foolish not to legalize the pact immediately!* He'd written James but received no answer.

In spite of this, Duggan could not leave Maura and her mother to Pelham Turk's high-handed ways—or to Braxton, who was a scoundrel if one ever drew a breath. There were plenty of stories about young Turk's affairs with women. Now that his father had married into the Sullivan

23

fortune, Braxton was sought after by every unwed female in the city—and some of the married ones as well. Duggan's blood rose every time he saw the covetous glances Braxton gave Maura. He'd like to beat the bastard to a pulp.

Seeing Maura now, Duggan knew she held no love for her newly acquired stepbrother. She despised him, and Duggan felt a wave of pleasure at recognizing that truth. She was a comely one, and he'd been attracted to her from first sight, but he would give no man cause to say he used a romance with Maura to gain Patrick's benediction. He would make his own way in the world first, then give the red-headed lass the attention she deserved. He'd kept silent, but he spent many restless nights alone in his room thinking of her.

The yawl neared the center of the river where the current swirled gray-blue water past the bow in undulating waves. He was so absorbed in his thoughts, he forgot all but the power of the tiller under his hand. A man drew strength from the river or the sea, just as he did from his work and accomplishments.

He turned as Maura spoke at his side.

"I shall hold you to your promise, Mr. Quinn." Her smile was breathtaking and Duggan forced his voice to be steady.

"I've not forgotten, Miss Sullivan." He slid around to make room for her on the seat. Her slim hand grasped the tiller, which he did not release until he was sure she was settled. Her challenging gray eyes met his until he drew his hand away, letting his fingers brush hers lightly.

Maura felt a shock of pleasure but grew uncomfortable under Duggan's gaze. She averted her face, tossing her head so the wind whipped her hair back and cooled her suddenly warm cheeks.

"Thank you," she said, glancing up at the mainsail. The wind had slackened a trifle; it could be fluky, like a balky horse that couldn't make up its mind whether or not to pull a wagon. She studied the river traffic, then eased the tiller slightly. The boat wanted to run before the wind and she had to keep it on course. The *Sea Spirit* was ahead of them. She saw Braxton glance back, then send the boat almost directly across the *Misty Dawn*'s bow.

"What the devil—" Duggan exclaimed.

She felt a surge of anger at the stupidity of Braxton's jealousy. She knew he was trying to prove his sailing skill by daring maneuvers, even if they endangered everyone on board both boats. She saw a small tic of irritation working at the corner of Duggan's mouth.

She knew he was itching to take the tiller back, and she gripped it till her fingers were almost numb with the pressure. The cutter was far ahead, setting a straight course for the buoy where it would tie up. The *Aurora* was astern; it had fallen back and now moved slowly in a line parallel with the riverbank. At a jetty farther downriver, a squat black barge sent a hoarse whistle toot into the quiet afternoon.

Braxton glanced back again at the *Misty Dawn*, then the *Sea Spirit*'s jib filled as he sent her across the *Dawn*'s bow once more. Maura shouted to Amos and Madison to spill the wind. They jumped to the sheets as Duggan growled, "The damn fool—" His hand reached for the tiller, but Maura refused to relinquish it. Her eyes danced with fury as she signaled to let the sails fill again and brought the tiller over.

"I am capable of outsailing Braxton Turk, Mr. Quinn." She lifted her chin defiantly.

Duggan considered forcing the issue but thought better of it. Instead he sat back and folded his arms in a relaxed position. "Can you now, Miss Sullivan? Well, you are in command."

His smile annoyed her, but she was too pleased with her victory to give it another thought. Suddenly she had no time to do more than gasp as Braxton brought the *Sea Spirit* across their bow again. She heard his triumphant laugh.

She quickly turned to port and the *Dawn* heeled and threw up white spray. She saw Braxton's expression change; he was frowning now that she'd evaded him and was reaching on the *Spirit*. The Whittingtons and Madison and Sally looked nervous as they glanced at her. They clearly wished Duggan would take charge, but no one voiced the opinion. Under her pink bonnet, Samantha Whittington was pale and her fingers sought her husband's hand for reassurance.

Maura dismissed them from her thoughts. She had

enough to concern herself with keeping the *Misty Dawn* aright, trying to anticipate Braxton's next move. If she could get ahead of him all would be well, but the *Dawn* was not a fast enough sailor. And judging by his expression, Braxton was determined to remain in the lead. Once more he steered across their bow, this time barely missing the jib. Maura held steady despite the wash that rocked the *Dawn*. For a dozen seconds the wind died. The sails flapped before filling again, but they had lost a boat's length.

Samantha dabbed nervously at her face with a lace handkerchief. Duggan muttered under his breath. Maura leaned on the tiller. The *Dawn* began to run before the wind, scudding along like a thoroughbred. Measuring the distances with her eyes, Maura realized that she would never catch the *Spirit*.

But easy victory was not enough for Braxton. With a glance back, he slid the tiller across and brought the *Sea Spirit* about on the port tack. The move was so unexpected and uncalled for that Maura gasped. She reacted instantly by changing course as quickly as possible, but Braxton had not given her room to maneuver. She half rose from the seat to shift her weight and help bring the boat about sharply.

"Watch out!" Madison Ufford grabbed the gunwale as Sally Gorham threw her arms about him and screamed.

Duggan swore and let go of the boom line. The sail swung free, luffing in the wind, but it was too late. With a rending crunch, the *Misty Dawn* crashed into the stern of the *Sea Spirit*. The force pitched Maura against the gunwale where she seemed to hang suspended for a moment before toppling into the river.

The cold water took her breath away as she struggled to the surface. The dress, its light fabric suddenly heavy and dragging in the pull of the water, clawed at her legs, and the high-buttoned white kid shoes were lead weights. But her fury surpassed all else. Braxton had deliberately tried to make a fool of her! Sputtering, she broke the surface and spat water. She was aware of a splash nearby, then of strong hands grabbing her and holding her up.

"Easy, Miss Sullivan, easy . . ."

Duggan had an iron grip on her, one arm crossing her

bosom and holding her securely to his chest as he swam with the other. She tried to free herself and swim under her own power.

"I am capable—" She struggled, but he held her fast.

"Easy, Maura . . . easy . . ."

She was aware of the commotion aboard the *Misty Dawn*, which was drifting lazily now. Braxton was trying to bring the *Sea Spirit* around to rescue them, but Duggan ignored its approach and headed for the *Dawn*. Madison and Amos reached over the gunwale to grab Maura as Duggan boosted her up.

"Balance the weight," Quinn yelled to the women. "Move to the other side!"

Pale and frightened, they did his bidding. They watched as Maura was lifted from the water into the boat. Samantha was close to tears, and her hands clutched each other nervously.

"Is she all right? Oh, Amos—"

"Hush, dear, see to her while we take Mr. Quinn on."

The men turned their efforts to pulling Duggan over the side. Maura tried to sit up as Sally wiped the water from her face.

"Oh, Maura, are you all right?" Samantha fretted.

Maura's answer was lost in a fit of coughing. She'd swallowed water in the sudden dunking. Then Duggan bent over her and lifted her head. He looked at her with concern.

"I'm all right," she managed to say before coughing again.

He raised her to a sitting position, his arm warm against her wet body despite the soaking he too had received. "You'll breathe easier if you can sit up." His hands were incredibly gentle as he settled her back against his knee. "Is that better?"

She nodded. Her dress was sodden, clinging to her body like a caressing touch. Her hair was a tangled mass at her neck, the careful chignon and curls gone. She felt all eyes on her. Amos Whittington cleared his throat and looked away from the wet, clinging gown.

A shout made them look up. The *Sea Spirit* had come alongside. One of the men in the boat grabbed for the *Misty Dawn*'s hull.

27

"All hands safe?" Braxton called.

Fury swept Maura. They were safe, but no thanks to *him*. She contemplated feigning injury just to frighten him, but her pride would not permit such deceit. She struggled up. Duggan made a motion to restrain her, then when he saw it was no use, helped her to her feet. He stepped aside and let her face Braxton across the interval of the two boats.

"You deliberately cut across my bow!" Maura shouted.

"It was an accident—" Braxton looked flustered. "I misjudged the distance."

The lie infuriated Maura but she held her tongue. It would do little good to engage in an argument. It was Braxton's word against hers, no matter how many witnesses there were. Besides, none of the others would be comfortable in taking sides. They were all dependent on the Sullivan Company for their livelihood, and both she and Braxton were considered too important to anger. Privately they would believe what they wanted, but none would be foolhardy enough to speak out.

Duggan shifted position and said, "A good sailor does not misjudge critical distances, Mr. Turk. The *Misty Dawn* had the right of way."

Braxton's face darkened and his mouth worked angrily. "Are you calling me a liar?"

Duggan's expression did not change. "A fool would be more to the point."

Braxton exploded in a whoop of rage, sputtering when he was unable to find words. Maura was delighted by the unexpected support from Duggan, but he, too, was a fool to criticize Braxton openly. She did what she could to rescue him.

"You are very gallant, Mr. Quinn, and I thank you, but there is no purpose to be served by carrying on this argument. We'll both catch our death of cold, standing about with our teeth chattering." She glanced at Braxton. "If you will be good enough to move on, we'll deposit our passengers on the launch before returning to shore. You can make my excuses to your father."

Braxton had little choice but to call for the sails to be trimmed as one of the crew let go of the gunwale. The *Sea Spirit* drifted away.

In moments, the *Misty Dawn* was underway, with a dripping Duggan at the tiller. Samantha and Sally nervously tried to sop up the water puddled around Maura's feet, but the deck rags were soon soaked. Maura smiled to put them at ease. "No need to bother, it will dry quickly," she said.

"You're shivering—" Sally was solicitous. "Here, take my shawl."

The lace square was no use against the breeze, but Maura accepted it with a smile. "Thank you."

It took only a few minutes to reach the buoy where the launch was anchored. Duggan brought the *Misty Dawn* directly to the ladder where a sailor waited to grab a line. The accident had been noticed, and a crowd of concerned faces peered from the railing.

"Maura—!"

"I'm fine, Mother. Please don't worry."

"You're flushed."

"Excitement and the cool breeze. I'll go home to change."

"You'll miss the regatta."

"Only part. I'll be back before the fourth race, you'll see."

The Whittingtons, Madison Ufford and Sally Gorham were helped up to join the group on the deck of the launch.

"Sailor, accompany her and wait to bring her back," Pelham ordered the man on the ladder. The sailor nodded but before he could step into the sailboat, Duggan shoved off. The startled man had no choice but to release the line or be pulled into the water.

"I'll sail Miss Sullivan in," Duggan said. "And back when she's ready." He bowed in Pelham's direction as Maura took her seat and grabbed the boom line. Duggan settled at the tiller and brought the *Misty Dawn* about, to head for shore. He grinned as Maura trimmed the sails on the starboard tack.

She shook her head and answered his smile. "You have not endeared yourself to either of the Turks this morning, Mr. Quinn. I cannot make up my mind whether you are a brave man or a foolish one."

He tilted his head and met her gaze. "Braxton Turk is an idiot, if you'll pardon me, Miss Sullivan."

"I would think that after rescuing me from a watery grave you might call me Maura."

He laughed. "Watery grave? I think not, Maura. I'd wager you are an excellent swimmer as well as sailor."

"Then why did you dive in after me?"

"It seemed the proper thing to do, just in case." His eyes danced.

She knew he was teasing. "I wouldn't think you the type to worry about what is proper and what is not." She felt strangely exhilarated yet somewhat uncomfortable under his scrutiny. She was aware of her disheveled appearance, but he seemed not to notice. She brushed the limp wet hair from her neck and drew Sally's shawl about her shoulders.

"Then consider my gallantry a ploy to hold you in my arms," he said without a flicker of expression.

Color flooded her face. "In view of the situation, I shall overlook your bold rudeness."

He said nothing. The silence was more strained than the conversation. He was still watching her, but she dared not look at him. She concentrated on the line in her hands, glancing from time to time at the shore. Why *had* he rescued her? He could as easily have thrown her a life preserver. The boat was well equipped, a fact he knew. She had seen him take quick inventory of the flotation cushions as he came aboard.

She glanced at him sidelong as he concentrated on bringing the boat to the quay. She busied herself with the sail without waiting for instructions, and he nodded approval. When the *Misty Dawn* was secured, he followed her from the boat.

The astonished footman scrambled from the seat of the landau where he'd been gossiping over a pipe with the driver. Duggan handed Maura into the carriage and to her amazement, climbed in beside her.

He grinned. "I promised to see you home, and I shall do just that. To Meadowfield," he called to the driver, "and by the most direct route so Miss Sullivan does not take a chill." He settled back as the footman clambered to his seat and the horses responded to the slap of the reins.

Maura was annoyed at his manner, but she did not argue. He seemed unperturbed, and her annoyance swelled. He was an infuriating man who took liberties that should

30

be objectionable, yet she felt a strange excitement as though she shared some secret with him, a pact that pitted them against Braxton Turk.

When she was silent, he hid a smile. She was in a fair temper, and all the more beautiful for it. He had not believed it possible to feel such admiration—and desire—for her! When she had stood up to Turk, he'd revised his impression of her as a spoiled, willful child; he saw now that he had misunderstood her strength. There was a lot of her father in her, and that could not be bad.

The carriage went around a corner a bit too fast and Maura was pitched sideways. His arms caught her and held her as the carriage righted itself. Her smoky gray eyes went wide with surprise, then with something else that was far more suitable for a woman. Awareness, longing.

Duggan had only to move an inch so that his lips found hers. He kissed her with a desire that had been smoldering inside him since he first met her. For a moment she was unyielding, then her mouth was warm and eager under his. She seemed to melt against him, and the cool dampness vanished in an engulfing heat.

Maura was drawn into a maelstrom of emotion. A pulse throbbed in her temples and her breath fluttered. He was holding her so close, she could feel each ripple of his strong muscles, yet there was no pain, only intoxicating pleasure. She clung to him and her fingers strayed to the damp curls that lay against his neck. His hands moved over her waist, explored the curve of her breast. She wanted to pull away, to protest, but she was powerless against the rising tide of ecstasy.

Duggan was filled with longing. She was incredibly soft and warm, and he felt a stirring in his loins. With supreme effort, he released her mouth and drew back to gaze at her. Her eyes were closed and her glistening red lips were parted so he could see her even, white teeth. How easy it was to want her. He forced himself to release her gently.

She opened her eyes and her tongue moved across her lips sensuously. For an instant, he glimpsed desire in the deep pools of her eyes. Then she pulled back abruptly and lowered her gaze. Her hand was unsteady as she tugged at the wet dimity skirt. When she looked up, she was angry.

"You presume too much, Duggan Quinn!"

How like her to hide behind her temper and try to disguise the willingness her kiss betrayed.

At his smile, she looked away quickly. From the window, she saw that the carriage had already turned away from the river onto James Street. Ahead she could see the cool greenery of a small park enclosed by a low iron rail. They would be at Meadowfield in a few moments. She fussed with her skirt and tried to calm her emotions. She felt his steady gaze on her, and her heart raced erratically.

The carriage drew up before the three-story red-brick house at the corner of Batavia Lane. Before she could collect herself, Duggan reached across to unlatch the door and swung down easily. Maura gathered her skirt and swept past him, ignoring the hand he offered. He rushed ahead to open the high gate, where he grinned devilishly.

"I shall return for you in an hour's time," he said.

She swept past, cheeks flaming, without sparing him a glance, then rushed along the walk and up the front steps. She could not bear to be in his sight another minute!

CHAPTER TWO

Francine Sullivan took a stand on only one issue when she wed Pelham Turk. She would not move from Meadowfield. Patrick had brought her there as a bride, and she refused to consider any other home.

The house overlooked a pleasant little park with curved paths. Years ago, she had strolled there with other young mothers while their children played on the grass or frolicked under the towering oak trees. After twenty-five years, the neighborhood still maintained its friendly yet elite atmosphere. The houses were set well apart from each other, with gardens and private stables and alleys bordered by high hedges. The quadrangle surrounding the block-long park was a pleasant relief from the more densely populated areas of Greenwich Village and Washington Square to the west.

Meadowfield was set behind a high, wrought-iron fence that encompassed a flat lawn and several flower beds of bright-colored chrysanthemums. The house had a peaked roof and dormer windows; in front was a brownstone stoop with iron railings that ended in twin wrought-iron lamps. Two large sycamores shaded the front of the house. In the rear, a wide porch was covered with grapevines and a horse chestnut tree spread leafy arms over the yard and stable. The house was almost severe on the outside, with straight Georgian lines. It had been built when Patrick was starting out in business and marriage and had little money for frills. But over the years, as the company and marriage prospered, Francine had redecorated the interior until its style and luxuriousness reflected the Sullivans' place in the community. The rooms were high-ceilinged and painted in soft, warm colors or covered with embossed patterns of

French wallpaper. In the center of each arched ceiling was a chandelier of cut glass, imported from England. Matching lamps were fastened to wall brackets along the halls and stairs so that the house could glow bright as day at any time. Silver candelabra stood on the mantel and on the gleaming mahogany table and sideboard in the dining room. Across the hall on the lower floor, three sitting rooms could be opened into a large ballroom by means of hinged oak doors that slid into niches in the walls. The ballroom would hold two hundred guests—and often had—though Francine favored smaller, more intimate parties with close friends.

Maura heard the carriage pull away but she did not turn. She was still breathless from Duggan's kiss, and she imagined she could feel him watching her. As she reached the top step, the door opened. Hobson, the butler, who had been hired about the time of Maura's birth, took in her appearance without a flicker of an eyelash.

"Send Lenore to me at once," Maura said, rushing past and up the marble staircase. Her own room was at the rear of the house. It had been hers as a child and she steadfastly refused to consider any other.

She crossed the thick, wine-colored carpet and flung open the door. Her room was spacious and bright. The midday sun enhanced the luminous yellows and golds Maura had chosen for wallpaper, rugs and curtains. Dominating one wall was a four-poster teakwood bed with a tawny copper spread over a deep-brown dust ruffle. An armoire stood in a corner. There was a writing desk, a dressing table with mirror, and a comfortable chair upholstered in flowered cretonne. At one side, a dressing room hung with two long rows of gowns opened onto a lavatory which had recently been fitted with a built-in basin with a drain pipe that carried waste directly to a sewer trench outside.

Glimpsing herself in the mirror, Maura exclaimed in surprise. She looked like a drowned cat that had been rescued at its final moment of life, except that her cheeks were glowing with color and her eyes stared back at her with a luster she had never seen.

She turned from the glass and began unbuttoning the soggy dress. A moment later, the door opened and a plump, round-faced woman entered. She stifled a gasp.

"Maura! Whatever happened?"

"I fell in the river. Help me get out of this—" The wet cloth stuck to her flesh like seaweed.

Clucking, Lenore put nimble fingers to work releasing her mistress from the ruined dress. She rolled it into a ball and placed it on the washstand so it would not drip on the pale-gold carpet that covered the parquet floor.

"Here now, let me help." The servant unfastened the lacings of the petticoat. In a few minutes, Maura stood naked and Lenore was rubbing her dry with a large bath blanket brought from the lavatory.

"Your skin is like ice. Shall I light the fire?"

"No, I'm not cold." Maura hugged the blanket about her. "Have Amy fix me a cup of tea." She sat at the dressing table and stared at herself in the glass. She looked a sight, but Duggan had seen nothing amiss. The color rose in her cheeks as she thought of his kiss. Behind her, Lenore watched with a curious gaze.

"Please order the tea," Maura said to cover her embarrassment.

Lenore pulled a bell rope and waited at the door until a rosy-cheeked girl rushed up the stairs, then gave the order for tea. Maura was pulling a comb through her straggly, wet hair with a dismayed expression. She reached for a towel to rub it dry.

Lenore smiled indulgently. "As soon as you're warm and dressed, we'll curl it. It will only take a few minutes to have you looking pretty as a picture again. Here, let me dry it." She worked at the hair until it gleamed in the sun spilling through the window. "Keep that blanket around you or you'll catch your death. Now, I would like to hear how you came to fall in the river. I declare, if your poor father could see you—"

Maura did not take offense at the servant's manner. Lenore had been with the family longer than Maura herself. Hired as a housekeeper when Francine was awaiting her firstborn, Lenore had been nursemaid to James and, later, Maura. She had been companion and friend to Francine as a young bride, and a source of strength and comfort to her as a widow. She scolded and ordered children and mother about—for their own good, of course. She was a woman of strong opinions and temper, but she was as gentle as a

35

mother robin with her fledglings. Maura adored her, though she sometimes grew impatient with her.

Quickly, she told the story of Braxton's folly and her own subsequent tumble into the Sound. Lenore let the towel fall and picked up a hairbrush.

"Braxton Turk is an idiot!"

Maura laughed. "That's the second time today that someone has described him so aptly!"

Lenore looked mildly surprised. "Only two? And who might the other observant soul be?"

Maura's color heightened and Lenore looked at her with questioning eyes.

"One of the foremen."

"And does this wise man have a name?"

"Duggan Quinn."

"Ah."

"It was he who rescued me from the river. Jumped right in to pull me out."

"You could swim the river across if you'd a mind to, *and* back."

Maura fussed with the blanket. "Mr. Quinn had no way of knowing that. It was gallant of him to act so quickly."

"I see. Well, I've nothing but admiration for Mr. Quinn if he dared to call Braxton by his true colors. His father has given him his head too long. He should have been horsewhipped when he was a lad. Set him on the right path, I'll wager." Lenore did not hide her dislike for Braxton or Pelham. Only Francine's firm refusal to let the servant go kept her at Meadowfield when Pelham would have sent her packing.

"And to his face! I wish you could have heard it!" Maura launched into an excited description of the incident and of Braxton's rage, and of her own trip home, escorted by Duggan.

Lenore said nothing, but her look was knowing. She drew the silver-backed hairbrush through Maura's hair until it gleamed like burnished copper and was soft across her shoulders. Lenore twisted it into a loose rope, then went to the armoire and brought fresh undergarments and stockings.

"I suspect your dashing Irishman will be along shortly to

36

take you back to the regatta. Best we get you dressed and that hair curled."

"He's not *my* Irishman!" Her cheeks stained with color as her pulse quickened. Lenore stood beside the open doors of the dressing room waiting for Maura to choose a gown. In chemise and petticoat, Maura studied the dresses, pausing over one, only to return it and go on to another.

"It's only a picnic, child," Lenore scolded.

She settled at last on a green cambric that was tightly fitted over bosom and waist and fell in soft pleats about her hips. The neckline was rounded becomingly, with an edging of white lace that gave it femininity without frills. From the jewelry case on the dressing table, Lenore lifted a jade pendant in the shape of a heart. It enhanced the green of the gown and added glints to her smoky gray eyes. The pendant had been a gift from her father on her seventeenth birthday last year, the last birthday he'd shared with her.

Lenore's gaze softened lovingly but her voice was steady. "Now the hair. Come along. Maybe we can catch Amy before she starts up the stairs. That child is as slow as a Scotsman's hand to his purse." She took Maura's arm and ushered her downstairs, chattering the while.

On the lowest level of the house, the kitchen was a huge, sunny room that was always astir with activity. In addition to food preparation, the room served as a social hall for the servants, a place where they sat between duties to gossip or drink tea. It had been Maura's favorite place since she was a child and had come begging freshly baked cookies from Rose, the fat black cook who always had a smile and a cheerful word. On a huge woodstove in one corner, several pots steamed gently; a long butcher-block table held a tea tray on which Amy was just placing the steaming pot. She looked up as Maura and Lenore entered.

"Miss Maura will take her tea here," Lenore said. "Fetch the curling iron, Amy, so I can do her hair."

"Yes'm." The girl scurried away.

Maura settled in a cane-back chair where her maid could reach comfortably to the fire for the curling iron Amy brought. Lenore readied the tongs over the open fire where Rose lifted a lid and was preparing a thick cloth to wipe the hot metal before it was applied to Maura's hair. Maura fussed until Lenore told her to be still so she would not get burned; finally she settled down with her tea and thought about the regatta. She had not realized how eager she was to return to the river. A few hours ago, she had been anxious for the day to be over, anticipating only boredom. Now everything was changed. She should be angry with Duggan Quinn, but she could not still her excitement. When the doorbell sounded, she leaped from the chair.

Lenore quickly released the hair wound around the hot iron. "Land's sake, child, Hobson will get the door. Mr. Quinn will wait a minute or two without vanishing." Lenore patted the final curl in place. "Now just let me tie this ribbon—" Her fingers worked deftly. At last she stood back with an approving glance. "As pretty as a picture. No Irishman alive could help but think he's seeing a bit of Killarney. Off you go."

Hobson appeared at the door. "A gentleman, miss. Mr. Quinn says you are expecting him."

"Thank you, Hobson." Maura lifted her skirts and fairly flew upstairs until she reached the hall. Then she patted her curls, smoothed the green skirt, and slowed to a sedate walk.

Duggan was standing at the tall, leaded-glass window that overlooked the park. He turned as she came in, and his breath was fairly taken away. He'd never seen her more beautiful. Her hair was done differently, with fuller curls to halo her oval face. And the smoky eyes were tinged with green, or was it the dress and necklace that made them seem so? He'd never before noticed the tiny dimple at the corner of her mouth.

"The dunking in the river has caused no permanent damage, I see," he said. "I would not have believed anyone could be so lovely."

"You flatter me, Mr. Quinn," she said with no betrayal of her turmoil.

He looked amused. "I doubt that. You are accustomed to compliments." He had changed to dove-colored trousers and a blue jacket that deepened the shade of his eyes to a misty azure.

She was unable to tell if he were teasing or serious. Finally she answered in kind. "And you to giving them."

He chuckled. "Perhaps, but only when they are deserved." His gaze did not waver.

38

She looked away, disturbed in a pleasurable way. "Mother will be worried if I don't return soon."

"Then permit me . . ." He picked up a white, stiff-brimmed straw hat and offered his arm.

At the door, Lenore waited with a bonnet that matched Maura's gown. She studied Duggan Quinn openly, nodding approval. He'd been at Meadowfield before, and she made it her business to learn all she could about him because of the way he looked at Maura when he thought himself unobserved. Maura shot her a warning glance and descended the steps quickly.

"I took the liberty of sending the landau on," Duggan said. "I prefer driving my own rig. You don't mind?"

"Not at all. I enjoy a small carriage." She realized the remark sounded patronizing, but when she looked at him, he had not taken offense. He helped her into the buggy and climbed beside her to take the reins.

"I like a woman who doesn't put on airs," he said with a grin. He slapped the reins and the horse set out at a lazy walk.

He drove slowly around St. James Park, then turned north on Rutgers Street. The iron tires of the chaise clacked monotonously on the uneven cobblestones. Duggan glanced sidelong at Maura and hid a smile. She was pretending fascination with every house they passed, as though she had not seen them every day of her life. He was deliberately taking a longer route than the one along the waterfront; he wanted as much time alone with her as possible. After a bit he said, "How are matters since your mother's marriage, Maura?"

His earnest look surprised her. "Quite well, thank you." She didn't want to discuss her personal problems with Braxton, though Duggan probably surmised them.

"Forgive me. I don't mean to pry, but your father was my friend and I miss him sorely."

A sigh escaped her lips. "And I!" She gazed at the block-house that was left standing when an early palisade was moved north. It was a grain warehouse now, but it had stood vacant many years when Maura was a child. Sometimes on hot summer evenings, her father had taken James and her inside to explore its dim, damp interior. She still recalled her delectable shivers as he recounted stories of how as a lad he'd helped defend the city against Indian attacks. She was well into her childhood before she realized that he had invented the tales to amuse them. The only Indians Patrick had ever seen were those who wandered into the city to beg door to door along the busy shops of Broadway.

"The Sullivan Company is an important part of my life," Duggan said softly, bringing her from her reverie.

She faced him with a curious frown. "In what way?"

Surely if his job meant so much to him, he would not have jeopardized it by speaking so bluntly to Braxton. She wondered why Duggan had so meekly accepted his fate after Pelham usurped his authority at the factory. Was he content to be a laborer all his life? Or did he hope that when James returned he would promote him again? With time to think over his hasty outburst this morning, Duggan might be regretting his words and trying to get her to intervene on his behalf.

"Your father and I talked of the future." It sounded as if he were begging, and he changed the subject abruptly. "Is there any word from your brother?"

"We've heard nothing for several months. I know he's busy with the boatworks, but I'm afraid he doesn't consider how Mother worries. A letter from him would lift her spirits greatly."

"I'm sure you'll hear soon." But he was not. James had not answered his letters either. Duggan had even written Jeb MacDonald in an effort to learn what the devil was going on. Before Pelham ousted him, Duggan had been able to follow the progress of the Pittsburgh venture through the weekly reports sent to New York and from James' hastily scrawled notes. Expenses were high but the work was proceeding on schedule. James was confident about the success of the project. But that had been four months ago.

He realized Maura was watching him. He shifted his thoughts into more cheerful channels; he had no wish to cause her more worry than she already felt. "Your brother is right, you know," he said.

"In what way?"

"The rivers are major highways of the country. Goods can be shipped more quickly and at lower cost than by

40

wagon. The river trade is booming, and it's a wise man who sees his opportunity to be part of it."

She was silent as she recalled how James had expounded that idea time and again, until their father was convinced to finance the new venture. James had been as excited as a child with a new toy. He pored over plans for weeks before he and Jeb left for Pittsburgh. James had selected Pittsburgh because it was the mouth of the Ohio River, an industrial center that offered skilled workers and an inexhaustible supply of raw materials. And as a major river town, it would also supply ready cargo for the new Sullivan steamboats. But Patrick Sullivan had expected to be around to guide his son and extend a restraining hand if James' enthusiasm outweighed his good judgment.

"Both my father and brother realized that, Mr. Quinn. I'm sure James is succeeding in what he has set out to do."

That brought an amused smile from Duggan. "Are you always so sure of everything, Maura?"

"I know my mind and I know my brother. He is a strong person who does not give up easily." It was true, but she also knew that James had a stubborn streak that sometimes brought him to grief. Nevertheless she felt compelled to defend him. It was as though, by doing so, she reinforced her own armor against Duggan's keen insights.

"That is an admirable quality, to be sure."

He was laughing at her again. Maura's temper flared. Was he accustomed to women who agreed with everything he said as though he were some great oracle? How exasperating he was! She tightened her lips and turned to watch an ice wagon drawn by a plodding Percheron. The driver clamped a clay pipe between his yellowed teeth and squinted in search of ice cards in windows. Seeing one, he halted the horse. Instantly, half a dozen youngsters converged on the wagon. Grunting, the driver climbed down and brushed sawdust from one of the large blocks of ice in the wagon bed, then began to hack at it with a pick. Chips flew like sparks, and the children plucked them up and ran off sucking the cold treats.

At the corner of Catherine Street, Duggan turned the chaise toward the river. In the distance, a glimpse of the water appeared between the solid rows of houses. Clouds over the high coast of Brooklyn had settled to a thick bat-

41

ting of gray wool, but overhead the sun was bright. A brisk wind funneled along the narrow street and made Maura clutch her bonnet. Duggan glanced at her. Her chin was still tilted defiantly, and he did not break their silence. He had no desire to spoil a marvelous day in her company, but he wondered if she knew—or cared—how serious conditions were at the factory. He was sure she had more depth and strength of character than the willful, spoiled woman she had first appeared to be. Patrick had set great store in her . . . perhaps his own judgment was colored by that. She seemed to be hiding her head in the sand like one of those big, ungainly birds in Africa. Well, she would have to face the truth soon. The trouble would not vanish because she did not want to see it.

As they came out onto Water Street, Duggan reined in momentarily to let a heavy dray pass. The driver brushed the horses' flanks with a thin switch as he guided the wagon through a narrow space among the carts clustered near a tall-masted sailing ship. Seamen on its deck were cranking winches to lift nets of cargo aboard. A mate shouted and gestured, but the sound of his voice was lost in the clamor. Out on the river, a square-rigger loosed her sails, caught the billowing wind, and began to glide toward the channel around Governor's Island.

Duggan turned the chaise away from the hubbub, but the noise followed them until they reached the low road that led to Sullivan's Cove. Maura was still studying the river as though it demanded her full attention, but Duggan saw that the tightness at the corners of her mouth had eased. How beautiful she was—and how headstrong. Like Patrick.

Maura was aware of Duggan's scrutiny but she did not turn. He could be completely charming one minute and rude the next, and she was unsure of herself with him. If any other young man dared talk to her that way, she would have dismissed him without hesitation. Instead, she found herself wanting to know Duggan better. She gazed across the Sound to where the tall-masted clipper ship was vanishing in the distance. She regretted that she had not engaged Duggan in conversation instead of turning from him in pique. Now the ride was almost over.

As they approached the quay, Duggan glanced along the

line of carriages for a place to stop, then halted at a hitching post and swung himself down. After tying the reins through the iron ring, he gave his hand to Maura. Her fingers were cool in his rough palm.

They crossed the dock, and Duggan once again helped her into the *Misty Dawn,* tossed off the line, then expertly guided the boat out into the river. The soft, fluky winds of morning had built to a steady breeze from the southeast, and the *Misty Dawn* rode with puffed sails. Maura did not ask to take the tiller. She was content to watch him handle the craft. He sat with his face to the wind, his dark curly hair tousled, and his blue eyes squinting. From time to time, he glanced at her and she smiled. In spite of the bad start the day had taken, she was enjoying herself now.

In the middle of the Sound, a cheer rose as the racing boats rounded the final buoy. A foghorn bellowed and whistles tooted.

"We've missed the running of the sloops," Duggan said, studying the sails clustered near the judges' launch.

"Thanks to Braxton Turk," Maura replied with annoyance.

His face crinkled in a wry smile. "I have the feeling that young Turk does not take your fancy."

"I loathe him!" Maura shuddered involuntarily.

Duggan threw back his head and laughed. The sound caught in the wind and rolled in the wake of the boat.

"I see nothing humorous in my remark," she said stiffly.

He stopped laughing and gazed at her. "Nor I. 'Tis only that it delights me to hear such a candid opinion of that idiotic pup. He has not endeared himself to the men at the factory these past months. You'd know that if you had not suddenly taken to staying away instead of running a business that is rightfully yours."

She stared at him in amazement. "What I do is none of your concern!"

"But what Pelham and Braxton Turk do is," he answered with a matching touch of irritation. His blue eyes were diamond-hard. "Did you know that his father has put Braxton in charge of the shop? He has authority over every department and operation. He's caused more than one muddle with his stupidity, and he doesn't care a whit for

43

the men, only for his production schedule. Mark my words, there's going to be trouble."

Maura's anger was momentarily forgotten. "Trouble? What kind?"

"That's impossible to say, but when men are pushed too far, they break. The employees of the Sullivan Company are not accustomed to abuse at the hands of their employer. Your father was a fair man."

"I don't understand. Surely no man is struck or punished. These are not the Dark Ages, Mr. Quinn."

He cocked his head. "To be kept at their labors without relief from sunup to evening is abuse. Young Turk has been told to increase production and profit, and he does not care whom he sacrifices to do it. We've already lost four of our top craftsmen and a dozen laborers." He looked at her, and his mouth was a hard, thin line. "These men have been with the company many years. Starting over somewhere else isn't easy for them, but they prefer it to what the Sullivan Company has become these past months."

"They left because of unreasonable demands Braxton made?" She was astounded, and her cheeks flushed with a stain of guilt. She *had* avoided the factory because of her personal animosity for Braxton and Pelham. It had not occurred to her there might be trouble.

Duggan nodded slowly. "And they could abide no more of that devil's arrogance. He is not an easy man to deal with."

Maura felt a stirring uneasiness as Duggan watched her.

"If James came back, it would put a stop to the dissent," he said. "The men would like to see a Sullivan in charge."

Maura stared out over the gentle waves and did not answer. Her own irritation at James arose, but she would not air it in front of Duggan. It would only give him further cause to criticize and lay blame. Not a day went by that she didn't long for James' return. His cheerfulness would be a welcome change in the dreariness of Meadowfield with the Turks. But she had assumed that despite her dislike for her stepfather and stepbrother, they were capable of handling Sullivan Company affairs well. And she was sure James assumed the same, or he would not compound the sin of his absence by silence. *Why* didn't he write?

44

"*You* might show more interest in the factory to give the men hope that the entire operation has not been turned over to the Turks," Duggan said reprovingly.

Maura's face warmed and she lifted her chin defiantly. "It is not your place to tell me what to do!" she flared. His arrogance was unbelievable. How dare he—!

But he would not let the subject drop. "Must you always be so headstrong and quick-tempered?" He scowled and gripped the tiller so his knuckles were white. He wanted to shake her until she came to her senses. Didn't she see that Turk was ruining everything Patrick had worked so hard to build?

Her eyes sparked like bits of flint against stone. For a moment, he thought she was going to strike out at him. She shuddered as she controlled her fury, then drew her shoulders taut and turned away from his censuring gaze.

"Aren't you interested in what's going on?" he said.

Her chin rose again and a muscle at her jaw twitched, but she did not answer.

Duggan sighed. He'd get nowhere while she was in her present mood. He should have eased into the discussion with more tact, but his own temper was combustible where the Turks were concerned. Well, he could match her stubbornness. If she had no more respect than that for her father's memory, there was no use in talking to her.

He glanced along the line of anchored boats as he tacked across the wind. Instead of finding a vantage spot from which to view the races, he eased the *Misty Dawn* toward the launch. A flicker of surprise crossed Maura's face.

He smiled arrogantly. "Since my conversation disturbs you so greatly, I'm sure you prefer other company to mine. Besides, your mother will want to see for herself that you're all right."

Before she could answer, Duggan hailed the launch. A sailor scrambled down the ladder and grabbed the gunwale as Duggan brought the *Misty Dawn* against the landing platform.

Maura climbed out without a backward glance. Duggan's insolence was unbelievable! One minute he was kissing her as though she were the most captivating woman in the world, and the next he was putting her out of the boat as if she were baggage he'd been hired to transport! And

45

worse, he blamed her for her stepfather's misdeeds! Shaking with rage, she marched up the steps determined never to speak to him again.

The afternoon passed quickly, and when the races were over, the cups were presented on the deck of the judges' launch. Pelham did the honors, with Braxton and Lacy Marsh standing beside him when Maura refused to go. She sat with her mother on the sidelines, using the accident as her excuse for not being drawn into the circle of activity that was rightly hers.

In spite of her smoldering anger, she found herself watching for a glimpse of the *Misty Dawn,* but she could not pick it out of the crowd of boats headed for shore. Duggan's accusations haunted her, and she knew that her resentment stemmed partly from guilt. She *hadn't* shown an interest in company affairs since her father's death. For all she knew, every word Duggan said might be true. He was in a position to know better than she. Her father had faith in Duggan and James had entrusted the management of the plant to him. She'd be a fool to discount his opinion summarily. She wished now that she had drawn him out and listened to what he wanted to say. She knew absolutely nothing of what was happening at the factory.

Well, she would find out. She would visit the plant and see for herself if what Duggan said was so. And she would write James a sharp letter and demand that he come home at once to set matters right.

The picnic was held on a wooded bank of the river below the factory. Although the city had crowded around the rural setting Patrick Sullivan had chosen for his company, he'd steadfastly refused to turn over every inch of land to production. He'd set aside several acres on the hilly bank to be preserved in their original state. Paths had been laid out among the trees, and benches were set up where employees could enjoy occasional respite from the heat and noise of the forges and shops. A fringe of trees screened the park from the factory and boatyard and muted the sound of the city traffic.

For the annual picnic, pits were dug in a large grassy clearing for steaming clams, corn and potatoes. Kegs of beer that had been cooled for days in the ice house on

Catherine Street and that still had sawdust clinging to their damp staves were tapped. Men filed by, amid laughter and chattering, to fill their glasses. The women sat at long picnic tables, gossiping and keeping an eye on the children who raced around on the grass or rolled hoops along the paths. Everyone connected with the company, as well as many guests, came to the picnic, which officially welcomed autumn and marked the end of another successful year. Workmen, foremen and executives smiled at Maura as she escorted her mother to a pleasant, sunny spot sheltered from the breeze. There seemed to be no indication of the discontent Duggan had mentioned, and Maura began to wonder if his story was exaggerated.

She settled her mother comfortably with a glass of cold lemonade, then wandered away as soon as Pelham arrived. She was sure he'd heard Braxton's version of the accident by now. His angry scowl showed that she was considered at fault, not Braxton. Had Pelham also heard of Duggan's outburst? Yes, Braxton would go out of his way to even the score for Duggan's affront. Duggan had made an enemy.

There was no way to undo what had happened. Duggan had acted impulsively and would have to face the consequences. Perhaps it would teach him to guard his tongue. Guilt touched her cheeks with color. Duggan had been defending her, and it was she who had insisted on riding in the *Misty Dawn* instead of with Braxton. Still, it did not excuse Duggan for forgetting his place.

She took a path leading down toward the river and raised her face to the fresh breeze. She was not responsible for Duggan Quinn's actions. If he got in trouble, it was his own doing, and he would have to find his own way out. She didn't care what happened to him.

She stifled a gasp as Braxton stepped unexpectedly from behind a tree.

"I see you've recovered from your unfortunate accident," he said, with a smile that made her want to slap him.

Her neck corded, and anger was bitter on her tongue. "An accident caused by your malice!"

His face darkened. "It was a misjudgment. I don't like being accused of malice."

"And I do not like being made a fool of in front of my friends and employees!"

47

He ignored her outburst. "I'm very fond of you, Maura. I would never want to hurt you." He reached to take her arms. She pulled back but he gripped her tightly and forced her against his chest. The brass buttons on his blazer dug cruelly into her breasts. His breath was sour with the smell of spirits, and she averted her face.

"I've been attracted to you since I first met you," he said huskily. "Living in the same house with you is driving me mad, you must know that."

She pushed and tried to pry loose his grip. "Let me go!"

He laughed, and his fingers bit more cruelly into her flesh. There had scarcely been enough time for him to get drunk on beer. Had he been nipping at a bottle earlier? It was possible. More than once she had seen him under the influence of too much liquor. His grip was like iron. She twisted away again as he bent close, and she felt his hot breath on her cheek.

"You've teased and tormented me long enough. I will have you—"

She drew back a dainty-slippered foot and kicked as hard as she could. He yelped with surprise but did not release her. His face was hard.

"So you'd fight me?"

"I would kill you given the chance!" She took advantage of his momentary distraction and kicked again, catching him sharply just below the knee.

"Bitch!" He hopped back in pain. Maura tore away from his grip and turned to race up the path to the sanctuary of the crowded picnic grounds. She did not look back until she gained the crest of the hill. Braxton was still on the path, glaring after her, his face twisted with rage and mottled by the gloom beneath the thick oak.

She headed for the picnic area with a defiant toss of her head. Filled with loathing, she was determined to speak with her mother and Pelham about Braxton's odious behavior. She suppressed a shiver and forced herself to smile as Sally Gorham and Madison Ufford approached.

"Maura, I've been so worried about you," Sally declared with a quick smile. "Are you all right?"

"Yes, thank you. I'm fine."

"It's a shame you missed the races. They were quite exciting," Madison said.

"I saw the last two and the presentation of the cups." Maura changed the subject abruptly. "Tell me, Madison, are things going well at the factory since my father's death?"

The question took him by surprise. "Why yes, the company is prospering. Business is expanding steadily."

"And the workers? Is there dissatisfaction?" She could not shake Duggan's dire prediction from her mind.

He hesitated and arranged his face carefully. "I don't get in to the factory much. I assume everything is fine."

He was uncomfortable at being questioned and obviously did not want to speak against his employer. That in itself gave credence to Duggan's opinion. Maura didn't press the issue. Looking at Sally, she shifted the conversation into more innocuous channels. "Your shawl was soaked. I'll return it after it's laundered. You must come to tea one day next week. I hear that you and Madison are getting married soon."

Sally blushed prettily. "Next month."

Maura murmured appropriate congratulations, then took her leave saying, "I haven't had a bite to eat and I'm famished."

Madison said politely, "Can I get you a plate? The pits have been opened and the food is delicious."

"Thank you, no. I know you two would prefer to be alone." They protested vaguely, but Maura said good-bye and strolled toward the long benches that had been set upwind of the smoking fires. Her attention was immediately claimed by several young men who rushed to bring her food. She seated herself and tasted the delicate steamed clams, tiny ears of sweet corn bought only this morning at the farmer's market on Pearl Street, and firm new potatoes with thin skins roasted crisp. There were salads, tiny sandwiches, and hot cornbread that crumbled with each bite. The day on the river had given Maura an appetite. She ate heartily as she responded to remarks and questions, though she paid only scant attention to the people clustered around her. She'd been escorted on various outings by several of the young men—to a concert at Niblo's Garden, the opening of an amusing play at Mitchell's Olympic Theatre, and a performance at Palmo's Opera House. But for the most part, she found these suitors dull, pompous or stupid. She

49

rarely went out a second time with any of them, since there seemed to be a steady supply of eligible bachelors who requested her company.

A couple strolled near the table and the group fell silent. Maura glanced up and saw that it was Braxton and Lacy who had put a damper on the enthusiasm. It was obvious that the men were ill at ease in Braxton's presence. He glared as he noted the sudden dearth of conversation.

Lacy fluttered her eyelashes coquettishly. "My goodness! Look at this, one girl with so many young men all to herself! That's hardly fair, Maura."

Maura gave her an amused look and pretended to rise. "Would you care to take my seat?"

Lacy fluttered a handkerchief and held Braxton's arm. "Oh, I wouldn't think of it!"

Braxton was flushed and his cravat was awry. He looked like a schoolboy who'd been off kissing a maid behind a hedge. "What are you staring at?" he said peevishly.

Maura lifted one brow archly, not bothering to disguise her dislike. With another amused smile, she said, "I thought you were with Duggan Quinn, Lacy. I'm glad to see that Braxton is being so devoted."

"Duggan seemed fully occupied," Lacy snapped. "Or has he deserted you now too?"

One of the young men at the table muttered a comment that evoked a hastily smothered chuckle from the others. Braxton swung around and scowled at the group.

"They're getting up a ball game. Perhaps it would do some of you good to work off a bit of energy," he said nastily.

The men rose and moved off. Lacy plucked a tidbit from a plate. "Mmmm, steamed clams." She tasted it and made a pert face at Braxton. "They're delicious. Would you like one?"

He ignored her. "I haven't seen Quinn since the boats came in. He seems to have little loyalty to the company with regard to social affairs."

He seated himself across from Maura, while Lacy sat beside him. Her amber gaze touched Maura with animal wariness. She was flaunting Braxton's attention and kept glancing at him to be sure it was not diverted to Maura.

"We've been strolling down by the river," she said with a

50

suggestive smile. "It's cooler there. The air is so heavy today." She touched Braxton's arm with a possessive air. "Braxton's been telling me the most fascinating things. The company is positively flourishing under his papa's hand, but I'm sure you already know that. Uncle Theodore says Braxton is doing a wonderful job managing the factory."

Braxton smiled appreciatively but barely turned his head. His eyes stayed on Maura and seemed to glow like coals in the deep sockets of his face.

"I'm a man who gets what he wants," he said in a low voice.

Maura's expression did not flicker. With a cutting edge to her voice, she said, "There's so much involved in the manufacture of carriages, you must be incredibly clever to have mastered it all in such a short time."

"Don't be—" he began.

"Imagine a man who has never worked before," Maura continued in a mocking tone, "able to assume responsibility for an entire carriage factory!" She gave him a too-sweet smile. "How in the world do you find time for your own pursuits, Braxton?"

"He manages the factory magnificently," Lacy said with a defensive air.

He glanced at her with a flush of pleasure for her support. To Maura, he said with tight self-control, "It's a matter of priorities. And I have excellent assistance from men like Lacy's uncle and a few others." A tic of irritation pulled at the corner of his mouth. His eyes darted left and right as though he were wondering if anyone could overhear the conversation. "That offsets the obstacles put in my way by men like Duggan Quinn who have no vision."

Maura's irritation swelled. "Mr. Quinn worked closely with my father and brother. I hardly think he would do anything detrimental to the company." As she spoke, she wondered why she was defending Duggan, except that it gave her satisfaction to oppose Braxton for any reason.

"He's too obstinate for his own good."

"You mean his views differ from yours."

"He's a troublemaker who'll find himself out of a job if he doesn't stop trying to organize the men against our management." His voice rose and grew harsh. "He's been warned several times."

51

Maura's chest tightened with anger but she forced herself to smile. "I think I'd organize against you too if I were a worker."

Braxton glowered. He curled his hands into fists and his face flushed. Lacy glanced at him nervously, as though afraid he might turn violent. "Why don't we walk by the river again, Braxton?" she said quickly. "It's so pleasant there."

He got up and almost pulled her away.

Maura's gaze followed until they vanished beyond a thicket of young maples. She was relieved to be rid of their company. If only she could banish Braxton from her life as easily! Pushing away her plate, she rose. She should see how her mother was feeling—she often became overtired unless someone insisted she rest.

As she turned, she spotted Duggan leaning against a birch a few yards away. His hands were in his pockets, and there was a curious smile on his rough-hewn face.

"Thank you for coming to my defense."

"You were eavesdropping!"

He shrugged. "I couldn't help overhearing."

"It's the same thing!" Her anger returned in full force, fueled by the provocative smile on his handsome, angular face. She started to walk away. She was determined not to stand for any more of his arrogance nor waste time talking to him.

"Are you still looking for a battle?" His soft chuckle rippled. "It must be that Irish red hair."

She turned, ready to answer in kind, but he was staring down the path where Braxton and Lacy had disappeared. "So Braxton wants me to stop talking to the workers about his policies, eh?"

"Are you doing that?" The words were out before she realized he had piqued her curiosity and momentarily dispelled her anger.

He shrugged. "He sees it that way, and as a danger to him, I suppose. But I cannot stand by and see him throw away everything your family has built." He looked at her intently but without reproach.

How solemn his laughing eyes could become without warning. "Are you saying you have the good of the factory in mind?" she asked, still annoyed by his complete self-assurance and her own wavering doubts.

"Yes." He did not relinquish her gaze. "Do you believe me?"

She hesitated. "I suppose I do." Even though she knew few of the facts, she was ready to take his word against Braxton's. Duggan's manner was infuriating but also compelling, and she wanted to believe he was on her side.

"I'm not doing anything different from when your father was alive," he said.

"He would not organize his own workers against management."

"He had no need to. They were already united toward a single goal."

She studied his well-chiseled face and noted the firm line of his jaw. "You've spoken intimately of my father several times. How is it that I know so little of your friendship with him?"

He regarded her with a devilish smile. "I don't know why your father was silent, but I will gladly rectify the oversight if you will consent to go for a ride with me."

She'd vowed never to see him again, but she felt a peculiar quickening of her pulse. He was constantly challenging her and setting her to her heels. Did he think himself irresistible?

"I am expected to play hostess here," she said with a glance toward the crowded picnic tables.

"Do you always do what is expected of you?"

Her eyes flashed as she met his amused glance. She would not let him best her again. "No, as a matter of fact, I would enjoy a change of scene." She looked at the group around her mother and Pelham. She would not be missed, and there was no one here whom she wanted to spend the afternoon with. "A ride sounds like an excellent idea."

"Then come along. I've left the rig at the end of the path." He put his hand under her arm as casually as if they had been friends all their lives. An impulse to rebuke him sprang to her lips, but she bit it back. She was perfectly capable of handling Duggan Quinn, and she could hardly chastise him for acting like a gentleman. Besides, she was eager to hear about his friendship with her father.

They followed the river north past the sprawling Sullivan

Carriage and Boatworks. Maura gazed with pride at the impressive multistoried wooden buildings that housed the shops, offices and warehouses. How huge the company had grown since her early childhood! The Sullivan name as a hallmark in carriages had been built right here. There were eleven structures in all, plus the separate boatworks facilities at the water's edge. These were modest, but her father had been talking of expanding them. Steamboats . . . Cornelius Vanderbilt was the leading steamboat owner in the nation; Patrick had envisiond himself giving his friend the Commodore a run for his reputation. If James' venture in Pittsburgh were successful, they would expand the New York boatyard as well.

The city, too, had grown rapidly in the past few years. Maura was not as familiar with the area north of the factory as she was with the sector to the south. Here, brownstones and row houses crowded around imposing mansions that had once been country estates. The old Boston Post Road, closed now more than ten years with the advent of better highways and railroads, had once been the only passable route north. Now busy cobblestoned streets crisscrossed Manhattan with geometric precision as far north as Thirtieth Street. Some said the city was only in its adolescence, that someday it would reach well past Hell Gate. *Clear to Harlem*, her father had vowed.

"What brings a smile to your lips?" Duggan asked softly.

She hadn't been aware he was watching her. "I was thinking of my father." At Duggan's answering smile, she said, "Tell me about your friendship with him."

He did so, easily and comfortably, and his voice was nostalgic as he spoke of his first meeting with Patrick and of the friendship and understanding that had quickly bloomed between them.

"Perhaps it's the tie of Irish blood," he said with a wink. "He decided on the spot that I was trustworthy and hired me. I put a hand to every job in the factory, and he made me foreman in less than six months' time."

Maura's faith in her father overrode any doubts she might have of Duggan's competence. "He would not have done so unless you deserved it."

"I did everything in my power to make sure his faith was not misplaced. He was as close as a father to me, though

54

we were never aware of the difference in our ages. I miss him sorely since his passing, God rest his soul."

It startled her to hear the tenderness in his voice, the words that might have come from her own lips. When Duggan glanced at her, her eyes were misted with tears.

"I should not speak of things that bring a cloud of sadness over you. Forgive me. It's only that your father saw fit to share his dreams and plans with me. I cannot cast them aside as though they'd never been."

"I don't understand."

He worked the reins through his strong hands as he tried to find the right words. "Your father believed I could be an asset to the company and was planning to take me in as a partner."

"That's absurd!" she burst out in disbelief. "James will take over the entire company when he returns from Pittsburgh! It has always been a family business. My father would not relinquish any part of it to a hired hand!"

Duggan's eyes flashed dangerously and his neck corded. "Your father and brother valued my skills more than my pedigree."

Maura's cheeks flushed but she would not relent. "The fact remains that the Sullivan Company will always be in Sullivan hands."

A scowl etched his tanned brow as he regarded her with amused scorn. "It will be no simple task to convince Pelham Turk of that. He'll not overlook your mother's marriage vows and the rights they give him under the law."

Her chest tightened with pain. As often as she had silently condemned her mother for the foolish marriage and the havoc it had wreaked in their lives, she would not listen to Duggan's censure. "My mother cannot be blamed for succumbing to her loneliness," she said sharply.

Duggan heard the bitterness in her voice. She was not as placid about the arrangement as she would have him believe. If she hadn't already worried about Turk's influence and power in the Sullivan Company, she'd best do so now. Did she know how bad the situation at the factory was? Turk wasn't likely to discuss business with her, and she'd hardly set foot in the plant since her father's death. Did it mean so little to her?

"I blame no woman for seeking comfort in a man's arms,

but I think it can be done without throwing away everything she ever held important."

Maura whirled on him with blazing eyes. "So you are an expert on women as well as managing business affairs!"

"That I am," he said with a mocking grin.

She fumed at his arrogance and averted her flaming face. He was impossible. She regretted the impulse that had made her accept his invitation. No—she was glad she had come. She might have gone on thinking he was a pleasant young man who was worthy of attention because he professed friendship with her father. Well, she did not believe him for one moment, no matter what he said. He was an impossible, crude oaf! Did he think she would swoon at his charms like Lacy Marsh or the dozen other women whose names had been linked with his in gossip? If so, he was sadly mistaken.

When he spoke again his voice had softened, and the hint of Irish brogue in it brought a nostalgic memory of her father. "It's much too nice a day to spoil with quarreling. Let's enjoy our ride and say no more of things that put you in a temper." His grin was disarming.

Her mouth opened with a quick retort but she bit it back as she realized he was trying to make peace. She forced a smile and said sweetly, "I had begun to wonder if you had learned any gentlemanly manners in your vast experience and wisdom."

He grinned more widely. "It might surprise you, the manly things I have learned."

She blushed at the implication of his remark and averted her eyes. She would not flutter and stammer like a schoolgirl because of his boldness. He was no different from any other man, and he could be manipulated by feminine wiles. She would play his game, and she would beat him at it!

They rode past the ornately designed Waddel house on Thirty-seventh Street. Surrounded by a stone and iron fence, it stood like a castle in splendid isolation. A crenellated keep and five stone chimneys were outlined against the blue sky. The mullioned windows were shaded against the sun, while at the rear, a spacious greenhouse welcomed its rays through hundreds of glass panes screening a jungle of greenery.

The paved streets came to an end. Duggan took a road

that followed the river, dipping and rising with the contours of the land. A few suburban houses were scattered across the hills, and there was an occasional farmhouse set among brown fields ready for harvest. The road narrowed and wended through a copse of oak and beech trees that canopied it. The two of them seemed to be the only ones abroad in the sunny afternoon. The silence was broken only by the trilling of the birds and the steady clip-clop of the horse's hooves. The wind died to a gentle breeze and the day warmed, though milling clouds still hugged the skyline beyond Brooklyn.

Duggan guided the horse to a rough trail that wound toward the high riverbank. A startled squirrel scurried across a rock, then raced up the rough trunk of an oak as Duggan halted the carriage and looped the reins. Without a word, he climbed down and came around to hold out his hand to Maura.

She climbed down, smiling disarmingly. He seemed to know the spot well. Was it a favorite trysting place? How easily he assumed her willingness, as though it were his due. She hid a smile and walked beside him along a path that was barely discernible among the trees and brush. It brought them out to a grassy knoll that afforded a sweeping panorama of the river and Brooklyn.

"What a wonderful place!" Maura exclaimed with delight. It was the kind of spot she and her father used to seek for their outings, a calm oasis in the teeming metropolis.

He smiled and spread his jacket on the grass. Maura sat down, pulling off the green bonnet and lifting her face to the breeze as she hugged her knees to her chin and gazed at the tranquil scene. A lazy steamer seemed to drift with the current, and gulls wheeled and dived.

Duggan settled beside her; Maura smiled at him. "When I was a child, I used to dream that someday I would live in a magnificent home that overlooked the river. My father talked about building a house in Tarrytown one day."

"Yes, he told me."

That surprised her, and she gazed at him with curiosity.

"Your father and I talked about many things. We were friends." He spoke with such sincerity that Maura's breath caught. If her father had liked Duggan, could he be guilty

57

of the wicked intentions she had suspected him of possessing?

Duggan smiled. "You can still have the house if your heart is set on it."

She looked out across the river, unwilling to meet his gaze. "With Father gone, it seems unimportant. It was his dream more than mine. He would have built it long ago except that Mother would not hear of leaving St. James Park. I don't think she'll ever go."

"And you?"

She was aware of his scrutiny. "I shall marry one day and have a home of my own." Marriage was the furthest thing from her mind, but she would not admit that to Duggan Quinn. Somehow she had never envisioned herself anywhere but at Meadowfield, yet she was beginning to realize that to stay on with Braxton and Pelham was impossible.

"Ah, will you now?" His soft words were borne away on the whispering wind. When she looked at him, there was a curious mixture of wonder and laughter in his smile.

Annoyance curled inside her. "Do you think that so impossible, Mr. Quinn?" she said scornfully. "If my father spoke to you about so many personal things, I'm sure he must have told you that I do not lack for suitors."

"He told me."

The azure of his eyes deepened to the blue of a turbulent sea as his gaze touched her lingeringly, caressing her face and sweeping across the taut shoulders and bodice of the green gown.

Though her question had demanded an answer, Maura felt a flush of embarrassment that the two men had discussed her personal affairs. What had her father found in common with this brash, infuriating man?

"Then he must have also told you that I have already had several proposals of marriage from men of good family." She wanted to slash his pride and humiliate him.

"He told me that, too," he said with an easy smile. "But he did not have to tell me that you spurned them because you are waiting for a man who can match your spirit and tame your temper." The smile flashed in his eyes again.

Maura clenched her fists as a trembling fury shook her. "My temper is in no need of taming!"

"Is it not, now?" He laughed softly and held her eyes hypnotically. "Is it not?" he repeated.

Her heart skipped a measure and the blood roared in her head. Her mouth was dry when she tried to speak. "And if it were, it would not be a task for you!" Somehow the words came out a breathy whisper instead of the forceful condemnation she intended. He was deliberately goading her and trying to overpower her with the silver Irish tongue other women found so fascinating. She would show him she was not so easily conquered. She refused to relinquish his gaze.

He leaned closer until his face was only a breath away. His blue eyes became solemn, then demanding. Maura saw her face reflected in the depths of the dark pools. She wanted to pull back but could not move. She no longer heard the birds for the pounding pulse beat in her temples.

Duggan slid an arm about her waist and drew her to him. She felt his warm breath on her face and his muscled chest pressing against her breasts. Then his lips touched hers as gently as a leaf floating on a current. She was keenly aware of his arms around her, tight now so she could not move. She did not try. She would let him kiss her, and when he believed she was his willing slave, she would fling him away and laugh in his face.

Teasingly, she moved her lips under his and felt a quick fire spring into his kiss. His lips became urgent, and one hand stole to her neck and played at the soft curls nestled there. Then his tongue thrust past her lips and claimed her mouth fully. Her hammering heartbeat threatened to overwhelm her. His fingers were gentle as they traced a path along her throat and found the smooth neckline of the gown. When he touched the rounded rise of her bosom, a shock wave coursed through her. The intoxicating pressure of his mouth blotted out her protest. He eased her back to lie on the warm grass without giving up her lips. Her lashes fluttered and her eyes closed in an effort to escape the bold question she read in his look. Tingling trails of fire raced through her as his fingers captured the taut peak of her breast and set the nipple afire.

She had to pull away now and halt his advances, but she was paralyzed by a desire totally new to her. No man had ever touched her so intimately, no man had ever stirred a deep core of heat in her belly like this. She shivered with delicious pleasure.

I will stop him before it's too late. I will—

Almost as quickly as the thought was born, it ebbed in a wave of trembling passion evoked by the pressure of his body and the renewed ardor of his kiss. She was dimly aware that he was unfastening the bodice of her dress. She felt the cloth slip away from her shoulders, and the soothing September breeze breathed across her hot flesh. Even then she could not release herself from the bondage of his kiss.

Time was suspended in an eternity of longing so exquisite it left her breathless. His hand cupped her breast and he released her mouth so he could bend his lips to it. A fluttering sigh of agonized pleasure escaped Maura's lips as his tongue traced the rising contours of budding flesh. Her back arched and she moaned with frenzy as he pushed aside her skirt to stroke her thigh.

She struggled against the tide of sensuality his caresses roused. She wanted him as he wanted her, felt the pressure of his manhood against her thigh. It was a burning, unrelenting promise of fulfillment.

"No—" She tried to push his hand away, but she was pinned under his weight. She twisted and threaded her fingers into his unruly dark curls and forced his head up. He covered her lips instantly in a scalding kiss. His hand found the intimate joining of her thighs and sent a new warmth spreading through her.

"No . . . no . . ." But the words were only a whimpering sound in the cavern of his mouth. His tongue tormented her, his lips bruised and caressed. Maura's hand slipped from the web of his hair to stroke the warm flesh at his neck, holding him close in complete defiance of the screaming warning of her brain.

The last of her lacings were miraculously undone, and the gown fell away from her fevered flesh. Duggan's gentle hands trailed along her body until it quivered and arched. Then his shirt and trousers were swept away, and he drew her to the length of his nakedness. For a moment, she hovered on the brink of an abyss, every taut nerve echoing the wild alarm of her conscience while just as surely pushing her past the point of retreat. Overpowering heat consumed her as he moved over her slowly and she felt the hot, hard thrust of his passion. There was a brief instant of pain that was quickly washed away by a dizzying tide of awakened sensuality. Her breath exploded with a small sound in the still afternoon.

His movements, gentle at first, became more demanding. His embrace enfolded her and fused the heat of their bodies. Her fingers raked the hard muscles of his broad shoulders as the tingling excitement became a rampant flood. His hand slipped beneath her hips and pressed them tighter to him. His face blurred in the haze of sunshine and blue sky as the last of Maura's reserve was swept away. She welcomed his thrusts and met them with the intense, newborn instinct of her womanhood. Pleasure mounted until her mind whirled and she plunged headlong into its raging tide. His heartbeat thundered against her breasts and the incredible heat of his flesh scorched along the length of her until she thought she would faint with desire.

And then they were soaring into bliss, riding the crest of a wave so heady that Maura's senses reeled. Ecstasy burst like a dazzling comet and left her quivering.

She lay with eyes closed as she savored the wondrous new emotions that filled her. Duggan caressed her gently, still holding her close.

"Open your eyes," he said softly.

Her lashes fluttered and her gaze found the crystal pool of his. She looked away quickly as the first ripples of guilt assailed her. Duggan brushed her cheek with his lips.

"Here, look at me," he coaxed.

She turned her face and tried to pull out of his arms. She was angry at herself for giving in to him when it was to have been a game of wits and wills. She was angry, too, at his ready acceptance of her submission as if it were his due—so natural that it was not worthy of comment!

He drew her close again and murmured with his lips against her throat. "Maura . . ."

His skin was damp and smelled of the sweet autumn grass and verbena shave soap. She steeled herself and closed her mind to the whispered entreaty. More deeply disturbing than her conscience was the realization of how totally she had enjoyed his lovemaking.

"Tell me what you're thinking," he whispered.

61

When his hand traced the curve of her breast, she pulled away and sat up. Her mind was in a turmoil and it was impossible to define her emotions. She felt Duggan watching her.

"You're very solemn all of a sudden," he said, sitting up and reaching for his trousers.

She turned with a sharp answer on her tongue but faltered when she saw the gentle look on his face. She averted her gaze and busied herself with her dress. Her fingers fumbled at the lacings as Duggan rose and his shadow fell across her. She ignored his outstretched hand as she got to her feet.

"And silent, too," he said with a twinkle in his eye. "I would not think you the kind to be left speechless so easily."

She smoothed a curl that had fallen across her forehead. "Would you have me dance on the riverbank like a forest sprite?" she said at last to hide her confusion.

"It might be entertaining."

He was laughing at her again. She turned her back and looked at a lonely gull wheeling in widening circles over the gray river. She was regaining her composure, but her face was warm and she could still feel the inner trembling that was an aftermath of their lovemaking. Duggan came up behind her and slipped his hands down over her arms. It was like the ripple of an icy stream along her spine. His breath was sweet at her ear.

"You are an alluring woman, Maura. It would be easy to love you. . . ."

Maura's heart missed a beat. They had not talked of love, and she was not certain she wanted to. Was it part and parcel of his bold approach? To first torment a woman until she succumbed to his lying, devious ways, then speak casually of love as though it somehow righted the wrong he'd done?

When she did not turn, he whispered at her ear. "Have you heard the poem, 'For where there are Irish, there's loving and fighting'?"

She slipped from his grasp, picked up the green bonnet and pulled it over her disarrayed curls. "I think you made it up," she said without looking at him.

"No, I forget who said it, but I am not the first. It's true, too." He moved around to stand in front of her and waited until she looked up. "Love and fighting are often close kin. I'd fight for the chance to love you. I'd even fight you if necessary."

She tossed her head. "I do not want your love or your Irish poems. I can do quite well without either."

"Do without love? No woman can." He smiled beguilingly.

"I can do without yours." She set her chin and tried to match his confident air.

"Every Irishman is a reader of poetry, a drinker of ale and a man who loves a red-headed woman."

She snorted. "And a bit of a liar. I don't believe a word you say."

"Ah, but you want to." He challenged her with a knowing look.

Beneath the light banter, a note of seriousness had crept into his voice, and Maura felt a warm eddy of awareness in her core. She smoothed her dress so she would not have to look at him.

"Take me home," she said curtly. She took a step to pass him, but he blocked her path and took both her hands so he could peer at her from arm's length.

"Do you always run from things you don't want to face?"

"I am not running away!" She jerked free and started up the trail. Duggan swept up his blue jacket and snapped it to shake off the bits of grass clinging to it. He flung it over his shoulder and jogged along the path to catch up with her. He did not take her arm but walked beside her with long strides, pushing aside branches that dipped across their way. She stared steadfastly at the dappled sunshine that spilled across the path. His physical presence was almost overpowering, and though the air between them was charged, she said nothing.

At the carriage, he helped her over the wheel. She settled as far on the seat from him as possible. The magic of the interlude on the bank was passing, and her irritation was returning. Duggan had deliberately seduced her to prove himself capable of mastering her. He'd even declared beforehand that he thought her in need of taming. Oh! Fury churned in her breast. What a fool she'd been to give in to

63

a moment's weakness. She'd done exactly what he wanted her to do—and she was sure it had been his plan all along!

He tried several times to make conversation as they drove home, but Maura said nothing. At last he fell into a stony silence that matched hers. When they reached Meadowfield, she leaped down from the rig before he could fasten the reins. He watched her straight, stiff back as she marched up the steps and Hobson closed the door behind her.

CHAPTER THREE

The sky was gray and overcast when Maura woke after a restless night filled with disturbing dreams. The evening before she had fled to her room as soon as she reached home, feigning a headache so that she did not have to face her mother or the others who, she was sure, would be able to read her turmoil.

She stood at the window and stared at the yard where two grooms were hitching a gray to the carriage Pelham and Braxton used to commute to the factory. It was her custom to dress and descend to the morning room for breakfast, but today she rang for Lenore and ordered a tray. She'd heard Braxton come in late, stumbling on the stairs and muttering drunkenly as he struggled with the door of his room. He would be in a foul temper this morning and she had no desire to cross swords with him. And after the long picnic, she was certain her mother would be too tired to get up early. Francine stayed abed many mornings of late, dozing fitfully, and hoping to gain strength to see her through the day.

The carriage was taken around to the front as the hall clock struck eight. Pelham's voice rumbled in the hallway. "Braxton! Braxton, where the devil are you?"

There was a grunting sound, then Braxton's heavy steps on the stairs. A door closed, and a moment later Maura heard wheels on the cobblestones. She finished her coffee and crossed to her mother's room. As she expected, Francine was in bed. Her face was drawn with weariness, but she was awake.

Maura sat on the edge of the wide bed and took her mother's hand. "You've exhausted yourself. You should not have stayed out the entire day."

"The people expect us."

"Your health is more important, Mother." Maura's heart wrenched as she saw pain shadow her mother's face.

"It's only the storm. You know how I hate them. Pelham says there is a hurricane down the coast in the Carolinas. I hope it doesn't reach this far."

"They rarely do. You mustn't worry about it. We'll have some rain, but nothing more." She smiled reassuringly. "How are you feeling? Are you in pain?"

Francine let her gaze slide away. "No, I'm fine."

"I think you are not as well as you would have me believe. I see it in your face." She had come to discuss the factory, but her mother's obvious exhaustion drove all other concerns from her mind.

Francine bit her lip and tears formed in her eyes. Maura bent to kiss her cheek. "Mother, I worry about you. Perhaps we should have another physician. There are specialists—"

"Dr. Holmes is doing what he can."

"But another consultation can do no harm."

"Please, dear, I prefer Dr. Holmes."

Maura let the matter drop, though she was far from happy. Perhaps if she talked to the doctor herself . . .

"Can I get you anything?"

"I've had tea. I'd like to rest." Francine patted her daughter's hand and closed her eyes. She was utterly weary even though she had slept the night. It was as if she could never get enough rest these days, but she did not want to worry Maura. These talks eventually came around to other topics, mainly Pelham. Francine didn't care to talk about him now. Even thinking about him made the pain in her breast worse. How she missed Patrick! Her body heaved with a sigh, and she felt her daughter's lips touch her cheek again before Maura tiptoed from the room.

In her own room Maura dressed in a violet-colored linen suit with a tight-fitting jacket; dark piping edged the pointed collar and folded-back cuffs. Her mother was failing. It pained Maura each time she saw her and listened to her weak protestations. This morning, Maura had made a decision, a silent one, since it would upset her mother to know of it. She was going to visit Dr. Holmes and insist on his calling in another doctor. Once the appointment was made, her mother would not be able to change it, nor would Pelham be able to protest. She should have done it long ago, she knew, but now she would not wait a moment longer.

She fastened the frog closings on the jacket, smoothing the cloth over her breasts and tugging down the waist. She studied her image in the mirror as she settled a small black hat atop the loosely upswept hair she'd arranged for easy comfort. The hat sat forward at a becoming angle that emphasized the perfect oval of her face. Lenore came at her ring and was surprised to find her mistress ready to go out.

"You've not had a proper breakfast!"

"I am not hungry. The toast will hold me until noon."

"It's not right to starve your body. Mark my words, you'll make yourself ill. I'll have the cook fix eggs—"

"I've no time now. Bring my cloak and order a carriage."

Muttering, Lenore brought the wrap and placed it over Maura's shoulders. From the armoire she brought a black silk umbrella. "I'll not have you compounding your folly by getting soaked again." She forced the parasol on Maura.

Dr. Holmes' office gave an appearance of clutter, though his medical instruments and supplies were neatly placed in two large cabinets with shirred linen screening the glass doors. The desk was covered with papers. An ashtray held a blackened pipe. The smell of tobacco hung in the air. Holmes peered at Maura over the rims of spectacles perched halfway down his long, thin nose.

"Good morning, good morning. Your mother's not worse, I hope?" His brown eyes squinted.

"I don't know. That's what I've come about. She is vague when I question her on your medical findings."

The doctor fussed with the papers on the desk, rearranging them without straightening them. His hands were bony, with long fingers and large knuckles, and their motion was unceasing. She was distracted momentarily, then put her question directly.

"What is her problem, Dr. Holmes, and is she recovering?"

The brown eyes lighted on her. "I encouraged her to tell you."

"But she has not. What is it?" Maura was cold all at once and suppressed a shiver.

The fingers drummed a silent beat. "Her heart is weak. It is a condition of many years' standing but only recently serious enough to cause her discomfort."

She stared at him.

"Her pain is considerable. She is rarely free of it, but she has forbidden me to tell you. The condition grows steadily worse and—" He frowned and his gaze told her the seriousness of the prognosis.

"She is dying?" It was scarcely a whisper.

"There is no way she can be helped except to make her last days happy. That is why I respected her wishes in the matter of silence."

The office was quiet except for the dull thud of her heartbeat. Her mother was dying! Tears filled her eyes and she dabbed at them with a handkerchief. The doctor was silent until she spoke again.

"Does Pelham know?"

He nodded. "He came to me a short time after your father died. Since he was to make her his wife, I had an obligation to tell him."

"He came *before* they were wed?"

"Yes, a month or so. He had already asked for her hand, I assume. I hoped he would take her abroad. It might have helped, but there is no way of telling."

She would have avoided the bout of pneumonia that had undermined her strength so terribly.

"Would it help her to go away to a warm climate now?" Maura thought of her mother lying restless, depressed and exhausted, dreading the storm.

"That's difficult to say. It might lift her spirits, which certainly would be good medicine." He leaned forward and tented his fingers as he frowned. "Maura, I think it would do little good to tell your mother of this conversation. I cannot be less than honest with you. Anything that upsets your mother is bad for her, very bad."

"I see. Very well, I will not mention it. Thank you for the truth, Doctor." She touched the handkerchief to her eyes once more before stuffing it away and drawing on the black kid gloves. "I would feel much relieved if you would stop by to see her today, Dr. Holmes. I fear she overtaxed herself yesterday and is paying the penalty."

"Of course."

"Good-bye, then."

She walked from the office in a daze tinged with anger. On the brownstone stoop, she stood staring at the busy Broadway traffic. A hackney clattered past and pulled to the curb as a heavyset man in a black coat and beaver hat hailed it at the corner. Why hadn't Pelham told her? Why hadn't he taken her mother away so she could benefit from the sun and rest? He'd known all along, and he'd done nothing! She descended the steps slowly.

As the liveried footman helped her into the carriage, she said, "I wish to go to the factory."

He acknowledged the request with a bow, closed the door and climbed to take his place beside the driver. Then the carriage was moving along the street with a steady rhythm. Maura stared at the dim interior with its red velvet cushions and small side vases in which fresh flowers were placed each morning. Chrysanthemums, white and cold, like death.

The overcast turned to a steady drizzle by the time the carriage turned into Cherry Street, its iron tires rattling on the cobblestones. When the team headed for the main factory building, a boy ran from the gate shed, threw his weight to the doors that led inside, and waved as the coach drove through. The driver walked the horses into the vast shop, and the footman climbed down to open the door for Maura.

She paused with one foot on the tread. From the rear of the shop came the wonderful wood smells and the pounding of blacksmiths' hammers. Two young men carrying raw iron hoops that would soon be sweated onto wheels hurried toward the forge. One of them accidentally brushed a hanging lantern so it swayed back and forth. The youth gazed up at it with anxious eyes until it settled.

"A bit of sunshine you are on a gloomy day," a voice said. Maura smiled at Seth Rawlins, a factory hand who had worked for her father for many years. The big, grimy man wiped his hands on a rag before offering one to her. "Here, let me help you down, missy."

She grasped his hand without hesitation, lifting her skirt and stepping down. "Thank you, Seth."

"Will y'want me to wait, miss?" the coachman asked.

She nodded. "I won't be long."

Several other workers paused to greet her and were pleased when she remembered their names. Though she had not visited the factory lately, as a child she'd spent hundreds of happy hours running about with her brother, listening solemnly as their father told them about each process, and becoming acquainted with all the skilled workers like Seth Rawlins.

Seth was a wheelwright, one of a few men who were able to follow the exact specifications laid down for Sullivan Company wheels and to produce them expertly. Seth had explained to James and her how each spoke was fashioned separately with a drawshave yet matched every other spoke in shape and weight.

"Each one has t'be mortised into the hub so it can't be pulled out by anything less'n a team of mules. And the mortises got t'be cut just so. Lookee here." He had showed them how each spoke inclined slightly toward the center of the hub so that the wheel appeared to be pushed inward. "It's got to stand agin the force of goin' around fast curves. You take a wheel that ain't dished like this and she's likely to collapse on a curve, 'specially when it's hot summer."

"Why in the summertime?" James had demanded.

"If the wheel ain't made proper, the iron tire'll expand in the heat, but the spokes and fellies will shrink. The whole wheel will come apart, then cr-rash! The coach'll topple and ever'body inside will go tumblin' down the hill."

Seth had been younger then; now he was foreman in charge of the wrights and joiners. Maura accompanied him across the cavernous room, aware of his beaming pleasure at having her beside him. She paused to watch one of Seth's men bring a wheel to a forge where an iron tire had been heated cherry-red. With great dexterity, he lifted the glowing metal with tongs, slipped it over the wheel and, as the pungent smell of singed wood drifted to her, plunged the wheel into a vat of water. There was a loud sizzle and he lifted out the dripping wheel with the iron tire sweated on.

The stairs to the second floor were near the stacks of sorted and cured lumber at the end of the shop. The steps were of heavy wood, with a polished bannister and scraps of old carpet tacked to the treads. She pressed Seth's hand, then made her way up, lifting her skirts lightly.

Maura paused to gaze down at the busy shop room from the landing. At one end, two carriages were taking shape, their oval bodies complete and ready for paint. Behind them three others were in various stages of completion. On one, two men were installing the heavy leather braces that would provide a smooth ride. Another man was working on the brake mechanism of a second coach. There was no sign of Duggan Quinn, and Maura realized she had been looking for him. She inhaled the delicious smells of wood, leather and hot iron. The clang and clatter of tools and the vocies of men resounded in the big room. She loved the pungent smells and the warmth of the shops. Smiling, she went up into the hall where the offices were. As she closed the door, the sounds below were shut off. It was cooler here, and the smells of the shop did not permeate. The hall was paneled with gleaming cherry wood, and a rich burgundy Axminster carpet deadened the sound from below. Maura walked quickly to the suite of offices at the rear of the building.

She glanced through an open door and saw Amos Whittington in shirt-sleeves behind a walnut desk. The clerk was writing and scratching his head in concentration. When he glanced up, he got to his feet in surprise.

"Miss Sullivan! I didn't know you were coming."

"Nor did I until a few minutes ago, Amos." She entered the office. "Is my stepfather in?"

He nodded and glanced toward a door behind him. "Yes, but Braxton is with him." He came around the desk and drew up a straight-backed chair. "Won't you sit? Can I get you a cup of tea? I've got some brewing. It's a raw day."

"Yes, it is." She folded her skirts aside and sat. "I'd love some tea."

He went out, and she heard him in the next room. He came back in a few minutes with a cup, a small pitcher of milk and a bowl of sugar on a lacquered tray. He put it

71

where she could reach it easily and went around the desk again.

It was a large office, with filing cabinets at one end, a wall covered with pictures in glasses, and with two other desks that were unoccupied at the moment. Directly behind Amos' desk was a door with gold leaf lettering: PELHAM TURK, PRESIDENT.

"I think you'll enjoy the tea," Amos said. "It's an Indian variety Mrs. Whittington gets at a shop on Broome Street. We find it delicious."

As his voice faded, she became conscious of sounds from Pelham's office as if the occupants had moved closer to the door. The door clicked but did not open, and she heard Pelham say, "You are not to disrupt production, is that clear?"

She glanced at Amos, who looked away quickly and sat down to pick up his pen.

The two men apparently moved back into the room; Braxton's tone was angry and she could make out only a word here and there. " . . . other men as good . . . troublemaker . . . best for all of us . . ."

Amos cleared his throat and made an obvious attempt to hide his discomfort. "Is it still raining?"

"Yes, but I came in through the shops," she said, sipping the tea. "You're right, this is delicious."

Someone slammed a hard object in the next room. Pelham shouted, "I'll not have it, do you hear me? I'll not have it."

"And I'll not put up with contempt and mockery!" Braxton shouted in response. "While I'm in charge I demand respect and obedience. How in hell else will the men do as they're told?"

Pelham said something Maura did not catch. It drew a harsh laugh from his son.

"You don't have to contend with him face to face," Braxton said. "*I* have to deal with day-to-day problems, and there are a damned lot of them."

Maura finished the tea and slid the cup and saucer back onto the tray. Amos tried to smile but only managed to look more uncomfortable. It was amusing the way he sat staring, saying not a word in regard to the argument that raged behind the door.

Pelham's voice dropped, his tone conceding. The dialogue continued more quietly so that only a murmur reached them.

Amos let out his breath and said, "More tea?"

"No, thank you."

At that moment, the door opened and Braxton stepped into the outer office, a triumphant smile on his flushed face. He halted abruptly at sight of Maura.

"Well, this is a surprise. Have you come to see me?" There was irony in his voice.

A quick retort sprang to her lips, but she merely said, "I want to see your father."

Braxton's gaze flicked to Amos and back, then he shrugged. Without another word he crossed the room and went out.

Amos Whittington went to the lettered door and tapped.

"What the devil is it now?" Pelham thundered.

Amos slid the door open and peered inside. "Miss Sullivan to see you, sir."

"Maura? Show her in."

Pelham was seated behind the wide oak desk that had been her father's. Seeing him there brought a lump to Maura's throat. She noticed, too, that the floor had been recarpeted and several comfortable chairs added. Pelham did not deny himself luxury. She waited until Amos closed the door before she sat.

"This is a pleasant surprise, Maura. We missed your company at breakfast this morning, but then your mother was tired from the picnic, too. A long day. Thank heaven the rain held off."

"It is about Mother that I wish to speak with you."

He raised a dark eyebrow and leaned back to regard her, as he extracted a long, thin cigar from an ivory box on the desk. "Has your mother sent you to plead some cause?"

"She does not know I am here."

The eyebrow arched again.

"I have just come from Dr. Holmes' office. He has disclosed the seriousness of my mother's condition. Why was I not informed?"

Pelham pursed his lips, regarding her with a steady gaze. "I did not wish to worry you. It would have served no purpose."

"No purpose to know that my mother may die at any time? How could you be so cruel!"

"Your mother did not want you to know."

"My mother is more concerned with the welfare of others than she is with her own, else she would have insisted that she be allowed to winter in a warmer climate. Why did you not take her south instead of letting her remain in New York through the bitter cold? She would have been spared the bout of pneumonia that almost took her life and which has drained her strength to a dangerous level! I'll not have her put through such torture again. I insist that she go away before the weather turns cold!"

"Are you giving me orders?" His tone was mocking.

"I am stating facts. She cannot be permitted to jeopardize her life. She should not have spent the day exerting herself at the regatta and picnic yesterday. She should not—"

"I do not force her into these things. Really, Maura, you are acting like a child."

"I do not wish to lose my mother as well as my father!"

He stiffened visibly, and his gaze clouded. She went on recklessly. "I *demand* that a specialist be called in to see Mother, and I am going to arrange a cruise to southern waters as soon as possible. Florida, perhaps, or Cuba."

"*You* demand." He looked amused.

"It is my understanding that my father's will left his estate divided among Mother, James and myself. Surely we are not paupers who cannot afford a few comforts? I will use the money that is ours."

Pelham's face darkened. "Not paupers, indeed. But you must realize that money left idle does not grow. James has spent considerably more than was first estimated on the Pittsburgh venture. And I have found it necessary to invest capital in expansion here. Both the factory and the boatyard are turning out a larger quota each month."

She put a hand on the edge of the desk and refused to look away from his gaze. "Are you saying there is no money?"

"No such thing, not at all."

"Then you approve my idea?"

He was silent a moment. "If your mother wishes to

74

travel, it is with my blessing. I'm sure I can shift my responsibilities here—"

"There's no need. I shall accompany her and take care of her."

He bristled but said nothing. Maura rose and swept from the office without bidding him good-bye. Some of her anger had dissipated, and she felt a tremendous relief at the action she had taken. She would talk to Mother as soon as she got home, and they would make plans. There were perhaps four to six weeks of pleasant weather before the air took on the chill of winter. By then they would be away. A leisurely voyage would give them the opportunity to discuss business matters away from Pelham's watchful eye. Perhaps they could devise a plan to execute changes that would save the reputation of the company and retain valued craftsmen.

She started down to the carriage, her thoughts occupied with the pending trip. She came around the landing onto the open steps and halted as voices rose over the noise. Then all at once the hammering of the blacksmiths ceased, leaving a hollow quiet.

Duggan Quinn's voice was clear and icy. "You haven't got the authority to sack me."

She took another hesitant step. Duggan was standing near a coach body set on a frame. Braxton, his back to her, pointed a finger.

"You think not? You'll believe it when you're tossed out. And I'll see to it that you don't work in this city again."

"I take my orders from the Sullivans." Duggan's tone was curiously flat and cold. Even at the distance, Maura could see the dark anger in his eyes. His fists clenched ominously.

Braxton sputtered and turned to two workmen. "Here, you two, throw Quinn out of the factory!"

"Stay where you are," Duggan said to them. The two stared from Braxton to Duggan and back again, rooted to the spot.

Braxton raised his voice. "Do as I say, or you'll find yourselves out with him!"

Maura felt a rising anger that Braxton should take it on himself to fire a trained and capable worker because of personal animosity. She took several quick steps, then halted again as Duggan repeated his command to the workmen.

"Stay where you are!"

Braxton shouted to the two, who were glancing at each other in indecision.

Duggan moved, quick and agile as a cat, his fist raised. "If I'm to be tossed out like a lump of coal, then I'll have the pleasure of doing this first." He drove a fist into Braxton's face.

Braxton fell and there was a low rumble from the men gathered around. Maura stood transfixed, her mouth open to call out, yet no sound came. Pelham Turk would never be able to overlook such an act of insubordination—a direct attack on his son.

Braxton staggered to his feet, wiping away a splatter of blood from his chin. Cursing, he eyed Duggan with a malevolent stare. He seemed unaware of the silent men who had formed a ragged circle about them. It was a rare thing to view a fight between the owner's son and a top foreman. There'd be plenty to tell the wives this night.

Duggan had not moved; his face was flushed and his eyes were icy blue pools. The muscles in his jaw worked, but he said nothing as Braxton came toward him slowly.

Braxton gasped as he tried to get his wind back. "You're finished, Quinn, all finished."

Duggan circled as Braxton sidled toward him. "You may be the finished one."

Braxton snarled and moved with rattlesnake speed, flinging himself at Duggan with both fists flailing. He scored a blow on Duggan's cheek before he was fended off, then took another sharp blow to the shoulder that turned him half about. He swept his black hair away from his eyes and his mouth curled in a smirk. He made as if to run at Duggan, then with a swift, unexpected dart, he snatched up a length of heavy wood from a nearby shelf. A cry rose from the crowd as he whirled it in both hands and took a vicious swipe at Duggan, who jumped back out of reach.

"I knew I couldn't expect you to fight like a man."

Braxton's answer was to aim another swing at Duggan's knees. Duggan skipped away and came in past the club to land a teeth-jarring blow to Braxton's jaw. He followed it

76

with another to the ribs, then leaped back as Braxton thrust at him feebly before falling to both knees.

"You've had enough," Duggan said. "Put it down."

Braxton panted as he got up. His face was red and blotchy, his lips were pulled back in an ugly grimace. He swung the heavy bat with all his strength, but it sliced the air harmlessly. His breath expelled in a throaty grunt. The men in the circle whispered back and forth.

Quinn tried to kick the wood from Braxton's grasp, but the other was too quick, yanking it back, then shoving desperately. The end of the club rammed into Duggan's middle; he twisted away and gulped air. With a roar, Braxton jumped forward with the bat raised high above his head.

"Stop it!" Maura yelled. "Stop it this instant!"

No one seemed to hear her. Quinn slid aside so the wood whistled by him and, in the next instant, he slammed a powerful fist into Braxton's face. The sound of bone on bone was loud. The length of wood clattered to the floor as Braxton tottered and held his face with both hands.

Maura raced down the remaining steps. "Stop them at once!" Several workmen glanced around, surprised to see her, but no one pushed between the two fighters who were unaware of her presence. She would have run into the center of the little arena, but one of the men held her back. "Don't, Miss Sullivan—"

She started to push away the restraining hand, then saw that Braxton had gotten off the floor again. A hush fell on the crowd and she felt icy fingers curdle her insides. Braxton's lip curled and hate darkened his eyes as he raised an iron crowbar.

She pressed back against the wheel of the carriage. The coachman was on the box, gazing at the scene and oblivious to her plea. "Do something!" she begged.

A cry went up from the onlookers as Duggan jumped aside from another vicious swing, but this time Braxton was thrown off balance by the momentum of the heavy tool. It slipped from his grasp and crashed into a support pole. The lantern hanging there swayed and rocked. Before anyone could grab it, it smashed to the floor, spurting hot oil. Flames flashed with sudden fierceness in the sawdust and shavings.

A shout went up as men stomped the fire. Maura jumped to the iron step of the carriage. Duggan ran to a box of sand and was scooping it rapidly onto the spreading flames when Braxton attacked him again, pummeling with both fists. Maura screamed, but Braxton was a madman raining blows on Duggan's head and shoulders.

Duggan tried to contend with both the man and the fire. Others were flinging sand now too, but the fire seemed to eat it up. Flames crackled and caught one of the wooden walls and a support pole; smoke began to eddy and boil in the air. Quinn flung Braxton aside, shouting for someone to ring the fire alarm.

In the sudden rush, Maura was thrown into the coach. Tripped by her skirts, she fell to the floor with a jolt as the horses whinnied and reared. The coachman fought to get them under control, but at that moment, the clanging alarm bell pealed and the animals pranced in the harness again. The coach was yanked savagely, and Maura found herself pitched forward; the smoke seeping into the carriage half blinded her. She heard the coachman yell, and men shouted and swore. She had all she could do to keep from being slammed about and knocked unconscious. Finding a strap, she clung to it and braced her feet against the opposite side of the coach. The team was running madly, slewing about, then running again completely out of control.

She could scarcely breathe in the thickening smoke and heat; her chest was a knot of searing pain. She had to get out of the carriage! She groped for the handle of the door which had slammed shut, but the pitching of the coach increased in violence, and she clutched the strap again.

Then the coach came to a rocking halt as someone caught the horses. Maura struggled to sit up and grab for the door. The alarm bell was roaring steadily over the crackling of the fire. Through the smoke, she glimpsed pillars of flame shooting up toward the second story, fed by the tinder-dry wood stockpiled for use in coach bodies. All at once, several cans of lacquer exploded like cannons going off; the horses reared and the coach swayed dangerously. Maura was flung into a corner. Her head struck the door frame and her senses reeled. She felt the coach smash into something. The collision rattled her teeth, and she was pitched onto her face as the carriage tipped. A wheel was

78

gone, she knew. The thought filtered into her brain that now the team could be brought under control.

She stared with horrified eyes as a sheet of bright flame enveloped the side of the coach and curled inside. The horses screamed, then the greedy, fiery fingers were licking at the varnished interior and filling the carriage with acrid smoke. Each breath was agony. It was a struggle to think or to focus her eyes as she tried to force her body to respond. The heat was a living thing that immersed her in its furnace while long curls of orange flame ate at the plush cushions, singeing her brows and hair.

The door of the carriage jerked open with savage force. "Maura!" Duggan coughed and fanned at the thick smoke. "Are you in here?!"

"Duggan!" Her voice was faint and weak. Dizziness sparked colored dots before her eyes, and she beat at a crackling flame that caught her skirt.

"Grab my hand," Duggan said urgently. "Maura, do you hear me? Grab my hand!"

"I-I'm trying—" Her outstretched hand touched his fingertips. The coach was at an angle so she had to climb uphill. Waves of heat washed over her and she found it difficult to breathe. Then Duggan's strong hand closed around her wrist and he dragged her upward. Her head was whirling but she knew she must not lose consciousness. She had to help! She scrambled and found a foothold to raise herself. He pulled her through the opening as the carriage slipped dangerously and threatened to topple. She heard a shout close by and glimpsed figures trying to unhitch the two horses as Duggan set her on her feet.

"Are you all right? Can you walk?"

"Y-yes—" She felt dizzy, and putting a hand to her head, she found a bump the size of an egg that gave off waves of pain. She tottered when she tried to take a step.

Duggan wrapped his arms around her. An oven opened behind them as the coach exploded into a holocaust. Maura buried her face in his rough shirt as he pulled her along. Her throat was raw and she was gasping for breath. Heavy smoke was everywhere, screening the benches and equipment like fog on a winter night.

Her head ached, but the dizziness was passing. Duggan's grip was tight at her waist. He said, "This way."

They had taken only two steps when a huge timber fell directly across their path to send up a cloud of sparks and soot. He brushed a live coal from her dress and looked her over anxiously. "Come on." She held up her skirt as he led her around the timber. The smoke and flames were so thick she could barely make out his face, though he was only inches from her. Her eyes smarted and tears scalded her cheeks. She brushed at them as a spasm of coughing racked her. Her head was throbbing.

Duggan changed course abruptly at another fallen timber that suddenly flared. Over the roar of the inferno, the alarm was still clanging ominously. Duggan could no longer see the walls, but he knew that there was a door ahead. It was their only hope of escape, and he moved steadily toward it. Maura moved automatically, as if controlled by wires. She seemed dazed, and he prayed that her injury was not serious, but there was no time to examine it now. Any delay might prove fatal. A sliver of burning wood fell on his sleeve and he slapped it away. If only he could see in this blasted smoke . . .

An abrupt wall of fire barred their path. Maura cringed from the intense heat, but stood her ground at Duggan's side. Her faith in him was absolute; she could no longer recognize anything and had lost all sense of direction. The careening carriage had spun her about, and the wound on her head left her dazed. She felt blisters rising on the back of her hand and her eyes were swollen almost shut. The terrible smell of burning flesh mingled with the nauseating fumes of paint and varnish.

Duggan tugged her to the left as an agonized scream erupted behind them. It took Maura several seconds to realize it came from the horses. The wall before them began to fall in bits and pieces, cascading sparks and debris like a glowing waterfall. They jumped back, then hurried to extinguish sparks. Maura felt aflame inside as Duggan tugged at her so that she was forced to run. Then all at once there was cool, blessedly cool air!

She gulped hungrily and nearly choked on the sudden rush of air into her lungs. They were out of the building but still perilously close to the searing heat. Duggan was pulling her along, and with each step the heat diminished and the smoke thinned. The roar of the flames dulled and she became aware of other sounds. People yelled orders, bells and sirens shrilled; several firemen ran past trailing a snaking hose.

"Please, Duggan—" Her lungs were bursting and she was shaking with exhaustion. Her skirt tangled about her ankles and she could run no more. She tried to free herself from his grasp but he would not release her.

"The wall is going to collapse!" he shouted above the din.

She looked over her shoulder to see the huge expanse begin to buckle. Red-orange flames darted from cracks, then as an enormous maw of flame pushed the wall outward, acres of hissing sparks shot upward. The wall seemed to fall with incredible slowness; it crumpled and finally dropped to the ground with a roar and clouds of swirling smoke. Duggan lifted her into his arms and ran until they were clear.

Crowds had gathered and were rushing about or gaping helplessly. A horse and engine clanged past; firemen pumped water to the fat hoses with piston-like precision. Maura stared at the conflagration and knew that nothing could be done to save the main structure where the fire had begun. When Duggan knelt and put her down, she collapsed on the wet ground. She pressed her hands to her face to blot out the horror she was witnessing.

There was a gentle touch at her shoulder. "Are you all right?"

She looked up at Duggan's anxious, soot-streaked face. "Yes." Her hand went to her head, but he pulled it away gently.

"You've got a devilish bump. And your hands are burned." He turned her palms up; they were black with soot and had angry red welts where blisters were forming. He examined each carefully, his face tight. "They'll need some ointment, but the flesh is not charred."

The gentleness in his voice reminded her that he'd risked his life to save her, and she was overwhelmed with gratitude. He looked at her with a critical gaze, and his hand went to her hair. She raked her fingers through the stiff, singed ends.

"It will grow out. A good brushing to remove the soot and you will be as beautiful as ever." He spoke as though

81

their parting the day before had not been strained. Maura occupied herself with picking bits of ash from her skirt. The violet suit was ruined, spotted with holes and streaked with grime and ash. She realized that she was sitting on the wet ground with rain misting about her. Her shoes were wet and she could feel the dampness through the thickness of her skirt and petticoat.

She let Duggan help her up as she gazed at the fire. Tears welled in her eyes; she was watching the destruction of everything her father had worked so hard for.

"They may be able to save the other buildings," Duggan said. Four firemen pushed past with a line from a gooseneck engine, and he drew her out of the way. "I'll have someone take you home."

"I want to stay."

He drew her back as another fire engine pulled to the curb and men leaped to uncoil the hoses and begin pumping. He pushed a path through the crowd, and before she realized it, he had found a cab. When she repeated her refusal to leave, he shook his head firmly.

"It will serve no purpose for you to stay and worry. Go home. Warm and dry yourself. It would be a kindness if you were to break the news to your mother rather than let her hear it from someone else."

"Mother!" She must be kept from the shock! Maura sank to the cushion as Duggan closed the door. He called the destination to the driver and stepped back as the carriage pulled away. Behind him, the red glow of the fire outlined his figure in the misty rain.

CHAPTER FOUR

As the cab came into St. James Park, Maura saw the doctor's chaise in front of Meadowfield. She thanked heaven for the fortuitous timing. The news would be a harsh blow, for her mother had seen the factory built and watched it prosper over the years.

She alighted from the cab as soon as the driver halted and told him to wait as she ran up the steps. Hobson could scarcely contain his surprise at her disheveled appearance.

"Pay the driver, Hobson."

"Yes, miss."

"Is the doctor with my mother?"

"Yes, miss."

She was already on her way up. Lenore came along the upstairs hall as she reached the landing. The servant stared openmouthed.

"Holy Mother! You were in the fire?" Lenore reached for her mistress and held her at arm's length, inspecting her for damage, plucking at the ruined gown, touching the singed hair.

"You already know about it?"

"Bad news travels fast. The milk lad told the cook, and the servants' tongues were wagging the story in minutes." Her plump face clouded. "Your mother's taking the news hard. I sent for the doctor at once."

Maura felt a cold shiver along her spine as she recalled Dr. Holmes' warning. "I must go to her—"

"If she sees you like that, she'll have another attack. Best you change. Come along. Here, Daisy, fetch hot water and be quick about it." A maid in black with a white apron and fluted cap scampered down the stairs as Lenore drew Maura into the bedroom. By the time Daisy returned,

Maura had stripped off the ruined clothes and was wrapped in a warm robe. The girl poured the basin before Lenore shooed her out. Maura's mind was filled with concern for her mother. She asked a steady barrage of questions.

"What does the doctor say? Will she be all right? Oh, hurry, Lenore—here, give me the cloth."

She scrubbed her face, heedless of the stinging blisters on her hands. While she toweled herself, Lenore readied fresh chemise and petticoats and a comfortable brown dress of light wool. The day had grown chilly, and the fires had been lighted.

Despite her impatience, Lenore would not let her leave until an ungent was spread on every burn and her hair was brushed and arranged to hide the damaged ends.

"It would be cruel to rush in and frighten her," Lenore insisted. "She's had worry enough this day."

Maura stared in the glass at the servant who stood behind her. Lenore had not answered her questions, and she recognized that the woman was trying to protect her. Her heart felt icy as she turned to study Lenore's face.

"Is she worse?"

Lenore nodded reluctantly, her brown eyes brimming with tears. "The doctor is very worried."

Maura rushed across the hall to her mother's room. The doctor was sitting beside the bed where Francine lay like a pallid child, her eyes closed and her face severely strained.

The doctor glanced up. "The shock has been too great."

"Will she be all right?" She was filled with anguish at seeing her mother in so pitiful a condition. It was as though her own heart were wrung and bruised. She looked at the doctor hopefully, but he shook his head.

"I've done what I can. Her pulse is weak. It would be wise to send for her husband."

Numb, Maura spoke to Lenore, who had followed her into the bedroom. As the doctor rose, Maura sat beside her mother and took the thin, cold hand into her own. Francine's eyelids flickered open and her unfocused gaze roamed the room.

"I am here, Mother."

The blue eyes found her. "Maura . . ."

"Yes, Mother. Do not tire yourself. You must rest." It

was difficult to force words over her dry tongue. If only she could relieve the suffering!

Francine's lips moved soundlessly and a furrow appeared between her brows. Maura leaned close to catch the breathy words.

"Patrick . . ." Francine's eyes filled with tears. "All his work . . . the factory . . ." The tears overflowed.

Gently, Maura brushed them away. "It's not all lost, Mother. The damage can be repaired."

Francine's breath escaped like the fluttering of a hummingbird's wings. "It's too late. I've been a weak, foolish woman." Her gaze found her daughter's face. "Tell James to come home. I beg you, don't let your father's work be in vain." Her fingers gripped Maura's pitifully. "You must keep the company in the Sullivan name—promise me!"

Maura's heart wrenched. Now that it was too late, her mother saw the peril she had put them in by her hasty marriage. Why hadn't she considered it before Pelham became so firmly entrenched? Now Maura recalled Duggan's admonitions that *she* must do something. Her mother was demanding the same.

She took her mother's hand and pressed it to her lips, then tucked it under the coverlet. "I promise. Now rest and don't excite yourself. You need your strength so you will be well when James arrives." She kissed her mother and brushed a gray-streaked strand of hair from her brow. Francine's eyes closed wearily.

Maura went into the hall with the doctor. "Is there nothing you can do?"

"I have given her foxglove and carbonate of iron. I'll come again this evening, but don't hesitate to send word if I'm needed before then." He shifted the medical bag so he could grasp the railing as he descended the stairs.

She watched until Hobson closed the door behind the physician. He hadn't said it in so many words, but he was telling her that there was no hope. Her mother's life was to be measured in days, perhaps hours. She was filled with pity as she looked in again at her mother. How sad she was even in repose. Her life had crumbled around her, first losing the husband she adored and now the carriage factory. It was Patrick's name she had spoken, not Pelham's. Patrick and James . . . her mother's memories centered

85

around them, as her life had. Maura whispered instructions to the girl who had come to sit with her mistress.

"I'm to be called the moment she wakes."

The girl nodded as she took her place beside the sickbed.

In her room, Maura sat at the Chippendale desk near the window. The light was dim but she did not ring for the lamp to be lighted. Taking a quill, she dipped it and wrote:

Dear James,

How I wish you were here so we could talk as we did when we were young. I cannot understand why you have not written even a line to tell us of your progress. If you don't care about me, you should at least think of Mother.

And now it may be too late. I have just learned that she has a heart malady of long standing, and today she had a serious attack. The doctor despairs of her recovery. She is so weak, I too have given up hope. She sustained a terrible shock that has done her condition irreparable damage.

There has been a fire at the factory, and it is still raging as I write this. Much of our father's work is in ashes. Even if some of the buildings and the boatyard can be saved, it will be weeks before work can be resumed.

She heard voices in the hall. Putting aside the pen, she went to the door. Pelham was striding up the stairs, his cane thumping and his voice loud. "I'll tend to you later! I'll not abide inefficiency or laziness among my servants!"

A maid cowered at the foot of the stairs, too frightened to reply. Maura went to intercept her stepfather before he entered the bedroom. He was unmarked by the fire, except for a smudge of ash across his coat. The workers in the offices must have been alerted in plenty of time to escape.

"Lower your voice," Maura said testily. "My mother is very ill."

For a moment she thought he was going to rage at her, but he drew a deep breath and let it out slowly. "Forgive me, I am upset that I was not summoned sooner. Francine—?" His gaze went to the door of the bedroom.

"She is extremely weak, the doctor has little hope." Her

86

voice broke and she could not halt the sudden rush of tears.

Pelham's expression altered and he stepped toward her, a hand reaching to her shoulder in comfort. She drew away instinctively, and his eyes narrowed.

Maura did not notice. "The news of the fire was too much of a shock."

"You told her?" He looked incredulous.

"Not I. A careless word among the servants."

"I'll sack the lot of them!" His voice rose again.

Maura put a finger to her lips. "The harm is done and nothing will undo it. I only pray, sir, that we will make her final hours as pleasant as possible."

He scowled. "It is unnecessary to speak such admonitions, Maura. My wife's happiness and well-being are of the utmost importance to me."

"If that were true, why did you not concern yourself with her health and welfare before now?" She was carried away by grief and anger and spoke in a rush of words.

"We have been over this ground before. I will not be called to task for my actions, is that clear? You forget that Francine is my wife as well as your mother. Now, stand aside before I lose my temper!"

For a moment, she thought he was going to push her from his path. Then he stepped past and entered the bedroom with a cold glance in her direction. Before the door closed Maura glimpsed her mother still sleeping in the wide bed. A crash of thunder foretold a reawakening of the storm. Too late she recalled she had not asked Pelham about the damage from the fire, nor had he raised the subject.

Back in her room, she stared through the window as the glistening trees bent under the wind and rain. Huge puddles dotted the yard. Paths turned muddy where the horses and carriages had crossed from stable to street. She strained to hear the sound of fire bells, but there was nothing but the steady drum of the rain on the glass and an occasional rumble of thunder. She returned to the letter to James.

We have not had word from you for several months. Both Mother and I worry, though Pelham as-

87

sures us it is only because you are busy with work. But now I implore you to come home immediately. I cannot live at Meadowfield with Pelham and Braxton, who are strangers to me. I have heard disturbing stories of changes they have made at the company.

She stared at the paper and bit her lip. They were nothing more than rumors, but after the incident between Braxton and Duggan that preceded the fire, she found herself believing them. She dipped the quill.

If there is truth in them, there may be serious trouble even when the damage of the fire is repaired. Duggan Quinn has been fired. Pelham has taken charge of the offices and put Braxton in charge of the shop. He is not well liked, nor is he competent to handle the job he has been given. Our employees will be happy if a Sullivan is in charge again. And it is Mother's wish that we carry on the Sullivan Company as it used to be. James, I beg you to return with all haste. Jeb can carry on there in your absence.

Your loving sister,
Maura

She blotted the page then folded the paper and slipped it into an envelope on which she wrote her brother's name and his Pittsburgh address. She laid the letter aside to be posted in the morning, then returned to her mother's room.

Pelham was just emerging, and she stood aside silently to let him pass. He said nothing as she entered. Maura dismissed the servant and took her place on a small bedside chair. She reached for her mother's hand and stroked it gently. Under the coverlet, Francine's breast rose and fell like a leaf in the wind, each breath a meager gasp.

The minutes lengthened into hours. Maura was aware of the servant's return, but she waved the girl away when she would have relieved the watch. Mother had not stirred, but her face had grown paler, her breathing more shallow.

Near evening Lenore brought hot tea, drew the curtains and lighted the lamps; Francine roused slightly but was too weak to sip from the cup Maura offered. The doctor returned, and when he took the patient's pulse, he shook his head. He looked at Maura with a sad expression. "Has she wakened?" he asked softly.

"No."

He fiddled with his watch chain, then moved to the door, beckoning to Maura with a finger. She joined him in cold dread of what he would say.

"Thare's nothing I can do anymore, Miss Sullivan. She's in the Lord's hands now."

Tears rushed to Maura's eyes and she choked back a sob.

He said, "I must tell you the truth, girl."

"She cannot die!"

The doctor grasped her shoulder firmly. "The truth is, she probably will not last the night. You must prepare yourself."

Maura pulled away and went back to the bed. She buried her face in her hands and let the tears come. Nothing could be done—nothing could be done! The words hammered in her brain.

There were voices behind her, Pelham's querulous and the doctor's low. She turned and saw Pelham in the doorway. Beyond him, a disheveled Braxton scowled as he peered into the room. Then the door closed the faces away.

Lenore came with more tea and a tray of biscuits, but Maura could not eat. When she shook her head, Lenore left the tray and withdrew.

A few moments before midnight her mother's breathing became so shallow that Maura could not detect it. Then her hand grew cold. Alone in the silent room, Maura bowed her head and wept. Francine Sullivan Turk was dead.

For Maura, the next days were strangely devoid of feeling. It was as if her emotions were in limbo, suspended because she had no one to share them with. Pelham made arrangements for the funeral after asking Maura's wishes in the matter. She was adamant on one thing: that her mother be laid to rest beside Patrick Sullivan in the small cemetery at St. Patrick's Church. Much to her surprise, Pelham offered no resistance to the idea. She had prepared herself for a fight if necessary, thinking that her stepfather would be perverse to the last, but he seemed preoccupied, though he was properly grief-stricken when callers paid their respects.

She saw little of Braxton but several times was aware of his stumbling through the house late at night after a drinking bout alone in the study. The night before the funeral, he and his father sat in the library talking in low tones over a bottle of brandy. Occasionally their voices raised in disagreement but were quickly subdued as they recalled they were in a house of mourning. Their seclusion continued until well past midnight when both walked unsteadily to their bedrooms. A chair crashed as Braxton knocked into it, then the upper floor fell silent; Maura stared at the dark sky outside the window until at last weariness overcame her.

The morning dawned clear, with the tang of autumn. A fitful wind rustled gray-green leaves that suddenly seemed ready to give way to winter. Massive cumulus clouds trailed across the sky, sometimes gathering to cast shifting patterns on the streets below. The funeral was set for eleven but people began to gather before the house as early as nine. The factory had been closed since the fire, and it seemed every employee had come to pay last respects to the deceased and to walk behind the black-draped carriage that would carry Francine Sullivan Turk to her final resting place.

Maura wore a dark gray gown with plain lines and no ornamentation. Lenore drew her hair into a soft bun at the nape of her neck as Maura watched in the glass. Her gray eyes looked back with tearless sorrow. Lenore brought a black bonnet with long black ribbons for Maura to tie under her chin.

"'Tis time," Lenore said and held a dark cape to Maura's shoulders.

Downstairs, six men stood by the coffin in the parlor, which was heavy with the aroma of gardenias. Pelham nodded as Maura entered. She watched solemnly as the casket was taken out, then walked stiffly behind it, ignoring the arm Braxton proffered. She had to sit with him and Pelham in the coach, but it was as if they no longer existed. She drew herself into a corner and stared from the window as the carriage slowly followed the hearse. To the rear were the other coaches, along with dozens of men and women, even some children, who walked in solemn procession.

The cortege circled the park then turned onto Rutgers Street. After two blocks, they turned west on Frankford. Maura realized that Pelham had ordered the undertaker to go crosstown rather than follow the more commercial Queen Street downtown. How like him to consider his own prestige even at a time like this.

The line of carriages turned again on William Street and rolled slowly south. People hurrying about their business paused to stare, and men doffed their hats in respect. Proprietors of small, elegant shops stood in doorways, and faces appeared at house windows. Other vehicles drew to the curb to wait until the funeral party had passed.

Maura saw a thousand faces without seeing any of them. Her vision, like her life, was dulled by the heavy ache in her breast. It was hard to believe her mother was gone. Her conscience rebuked her for the lack of understanding and sympathy she'd felt for her mother since her remarriage, but she could not bring herself to look at the two men seated beside her.

As they passed Wall Street, she glimpsed the fenced common of City Hall Park with its four marble pillars topped by massive stone balls that were said to have been dug from the ruins of Troy. At last they turned into Prince Street.

The church bell tolled mournfully as the cortege approached. Inside the church, Maura sat with Pelham and Braxton in a front pew and listened numbly to the mass. Behind them, the Rothingwells, the Riders and David Walton occupied the second pew. The rest of the church was filled with workers from the factory, neighbors and friends. Maura was wrapped in a peculiar loneliness amid the crowd. She had no one, only James who was so far away.

The priest's words droned on without touching her mind. When the mass was over, she filed with the others into the churchyard to stand by a newly dug grave and watch the coffin lowered. She dropped a handful of dirt atop the wooden box. It was finished.

On the way to the carriage, many people spoke words of condolence. Maura accepted hands offered in sympathy. Just a few days ago, these same faces had been smiling and expectant at the regatta. Now they shared a common grief.

No one spoke of the fire, but she knew it was uppermost in every mind.

Near the gate, she saw Duggan Quinn standing apart from the others and went to him.

"I have not thanked you for saving my life."

He looked at her tenderly. "I could do no less." His gaze shifted to the line of people emerging from the churchyard. "It pained me to hear of your mother's death."

Many had spoken the same words, but she felt a special sincerity in his. Their differences were temporarily erased by the need to have someone to talk to. She mumured her thanks.

"I have not spoken with Pelham or Braxton," she said. "Is the damage from the fire severe?"

He nodded. "The main shop is a total loss, but the storehouses were saved and the boatyard was not touched. As soon as the rubble is cleared, temporary arrangements can be made so the men can go back to work."

Remembering the fight with Braxton that had precipitated the fire, she asked, "And you? What will you do?"

"I've not yet decided." His voice was low, and his eyes never left hers.

"My father had many friends among the businessmen of the city. I would be glad to speak to them on your behalf."

His gaze was steady. "I've no need of charity."

She colored. "I intended none. A good workman is an asset to any firm."

"Braxton Turk thought otherwise."

"Why must you twist everything I say?" Her irritation surfaced and she looked away. She was relieved when Lenore touched her arm. "Mr. Turk says the carriage is waiting."

"Good day, Mr. Quinn."

"Good day, Miss Sullivan." He watched as she crossed the walk and was handed up into the carriage. Pelham was glowering. When Maura was seated, he swung himself up and sat, still staring at Duggan, as the footman closed the door and lifted the step before climbing to his place beside the driver. The black coach, its mourning ribbons fluttering in the breeze, moved down the street and out of sight.

Pelham scowled at his stepdaughter. "On the day of your mother's funeral, it is unseemly for you to engage publicly in conversation with the man who was responsible for her death, Maura."

She gaped in astonishment. "Responsible!"

"In essence, yes."

She could not believe her ears! "Your humor is in poor taste."

Pelham snorted. "It is the truth, not an attempt at humor. The facts of the incident which led to the fire have been related to me. That blasted Quinn is clearly to blame. I am considering bringing criminal charges against him."

"He was *not* to blame!" She turned to Braxton, who tightened his mouth and pulled at his mustache. "This is your doing. You have distorted the truth to your own advantage," she accused.

He shrugged carelessly. "I was present, and I am well aware of the events as they took place."

His face was blotchy and bruised where Duggan had pummeled him, and the sight gave Maura a certain satisfaction. She looked at her stepfather. "I don't know what you've been told, but Duggan Quinn was severely provoked and did only what any man would have done."

"He struck the first blow," Braxton said in a sharp tone. "I had to defend myself."

Maura said bitterly, "I saw how you defended yourself with a crowbar! You couldn't stand up to him man to man, so you resorted to underhanded methods. *You* caused the fire by knocking down a lantern!" She was surprised at the calm coldness of her tone. Enforced proximity with the two men she hated most in the entire world left her filled with disgust. To hear Braxton blame Duggan for his own actions infuriated her.

Braxton shrugged off the accusation though his eyes blazed. Pelham thumped his cane impatiently on the floor of the coach. "Nevertheless, the matter cannot be ended if you continue to accept the man publicly. Do not speak to him again."

Maura's eyes flashed dangerously. "Not speak to him! Am I to consider that an order?"

"It *is* an order!"

"By what right do you presume to dictate my life?" She could no longer keep her anger under control.

"I am your guardian, dear Maura." Pelham's dark eyes

moved languidly to sweep her face. "Your welfare is my responsibility now that your mother has passed on. I am not a man to take my responsibilities lightly, I assure you."

"My guardian!" The words were drawn from her like a last breath. Such a thought had never occurred to her. Mother had not spoken of any such arrangement, or indeed of any legal matters at all. Was it possible? Pelham was a lawyer. If he said it was so, in was undoubtedly true!

"The papers were drawn up some months ago. Your mother was concerned about your welfare. She feared her death would leave you quite alone." He smiled. "As indeed it has, except for Braxton and me. I am your guardian until you come of age, unless, of course, you marry before that time." His glance met Braxton's and the atmosphere seemed charged with the hidden exchange between them.

Maura's flesh crawled. She felt choked with loathing. Her stepfather was hinting at a marriage between her and his son! How very convenient for them! To have her wed to Braxton would insure Pelham's control of the Sullivan Company. He was not content with the portion that had been her mother's, he wanted *hers* as well. It was a union that would take place over her dead body!

"I have no intention of marrying in the near future," she said vehemently.

The supercilious smile lingered on Pelham's lips, and Braxton seemed to be appraising her and judging her worth as a bride. Suddenly the occasional remarks and advances he'd attempted since moving into Meadowfield took on hideous new meaning. The thought of him touching her made her ill, and she resolutely turned her face to the window to watch clouds of dust and debris scattering before the rising wind.

CHAPTER FIVE

The day passed in fragments of hollow silence and subdued activity. The house was strangely empty without her
mother, and Maura felt the loss keenly. Francine had been
a buffer between her and Pelham, she realized now, a
bridge across the gulf of silence that separated them. She
assiduously avoided him and his son. In her room, she sat
by the tall window and watched the desultory activity
about the yard and stables. She was glad she could not see
the street where life went on as usual. Her life would never
be the same. The fact that Pelham was her legal guardian
gnawed at her mind like a persistent rodent. Had he
pressed her mother into signing the documents that made it
so? Despite her mother's foolishness in many things, Maura
could not believe she wouldn't foresee the disaster that
might result. Pelham would have full legal control of
Maura's life. She would have no money except what he
doled out to her, and he would supervise her every activity.
He might even force her into marriage!

Maura shuddered. It was more imperative than ever that
James return. With his help, she might find a way out of
this terrible predicament.

Dinner was a strained hour during which Pelham and
Braxton consumed great amounts of brandy and Maura
barely tasted her food. She excused herself early, pleading a
headache, and retired to her room. At Lenore's insistence,
the slipper-shaped bathing tub was set up and filled with
steaming water brought upstairs by a retinue of maids and
houseboys. When it was ready, Lenore supervised her mistress' undressing and climbing into the water to relax and
ease her tense muscles and troubled mind. And when she

emerged. Lenore wrapped her in a soft woolen nightgown and tucked her into the ornately carved teakwood bed that had been hers since childhood.

"A good night's rest will put a different color to the world, pet." The servant brushed a damp curl from Maura's forehead.

"I'm not sleepy."

"You'll soon drift off if you give yourself a chance. I'll leave the lamp low and look in on you after a bit."

Maura did not protest. Lenore's compassion was comforting after the arduous day. She let her thoughts wander but tried to keep them from depressing paths. Even in the warm cocoon of the bed, she felt a cold foreboding that would not be shaken.

Unbidden, her thoughts went to Duggan. His future was as uncertain as her own, except that he was a man, and men had distinct advantages when it came to controlling their own lives. Would he remain in New York? She wondered if she should speak privately with some of her father's associates. Duggan need never know. She felt a stirring in her breast at the memory of his tender lips and his strong body. No matter how much she denied it, she had wanted him in those exquisite moments they were together. She'd been enmeshed in emotions that were strangely new and wondrous and impossible to tame. She sighed and hugged her arms across her body. It was better that Duggan go out of her life—not for the stupid reason Pelham cited but because he had the power to unsettle her completely. No other man had ever affected her this way, and she was unsure of herself. She was determined to fight it, yet she felt herself being drawn deeper into a turbulent sea of emotions. Besides, Duggan was brash, outspoken, and far too arrogant for his own good. Despite his claim of close ties with her father and James, he was a man set in his ways and too eager to do battle with his fists. It was senseless for her to concern herself further. It was quite possible she would never see him again.

She extinguished the lamp and resolutely wooed sleep. It came reluctantly and was filled with somber nightmares of black-garbed figures filing past the bed where she lay. She woke slowly, aware of a soft sound that came from reality, not dreams. She sat up and looked about. The room was bathed in moonlight from the window where the draperies had not been pulled. She sensed a presence and peered toward the door.

"Lenore?"

There was no answer, but a whisper of sound betrayed a figure that moved in the shadows. Maura threw back the covers and put her feet over the edge of the bed to grope for slippers. She was frightened but there was something more, something she could not define.

"Who is it?"

Heavy breathing, then a soft laugh.

"Braxton!" She saw him clearly in a splash of moonlight. His face was contorted in a grin, his eyes bleary and heavy-lidded. His mouth opened, but instead of speaking, his tongue rolled across his lips as though he were relishing the moment.

"Get out of my room!" She reached for the robe Lenore had laid across the bottom of the bed. Awkwardly, Braxton lurched and grabbed for her. As she pushed him away, she realized he was very drunk. She struggled with the robe, but he was at her again, tearing at the green wool and wrenching it from her grasp.

She let go as the material rent. She backed away, arms raised to strike out if he tried to touch her again.

"Beautiful," he said thickly. "You know damned well how beautiful you are!"

She stepped sideways and tried to rush past him, but he spread his arms and would have caught her except that she ducked and darted back out of reach. His breath became a rasping menace. Maura retreated as far as she could until her thighs pressed against the marble top of the night table.

"Get out of here!" Anger overcame fear. She groped on the table and found the hairbrush Lenore had left there. She raised it threateningly, as Braxton came at her again. She struck out and the brush hit him on the side of his head.

"Damn—" He stumbled back momentarily, then charged in rage. "I'll teach you to hit me!"

His weight was overpowering. She was thrown back to the bed and he fell on her, pinning her arms. His mouth searched wetly. When his lips brushed her cheek, she twisted away. His sour breath sickened her and the intimacy of his body on hers was obscene.

He muttered her name hoarsely as he tried to kiss her.

"Maura . . . I cannot wait until you are my wife. You've driven me mad!" His words were a hot iron pressed to her brain. His hands tugged the neckline of the gown and his fingers crept across her naked flesh.

"You are insane!" She shoved with all her strength and succeeded in pushing him off balance so that he toppled sideways with a startled grunt. She swung blindly and felt her hands strike his head, face and shoulders. She was aware for the first time that he wore only a dressing gown which had come loose in the struggle. She recoiled from the touch of his bare chest, and stumbled to her feet.

Instantly he leaped after her. Her nightgown ripped, then his hands were on her. For a moment she thought he would drag her to the floor and climb on her, so wild was his fury. She fought by battering his face; she kicked and raked at him in a frenzy, uttering not a word as she saved her strength to fight.

The door flew open and a puddle of light spilled from a lamp held high. "Holy Mother!" Lenore rushed in and set down the lamp, her face a mask of disgust and anger.

"Get out of here!" Braxton snarled. "You've no damned business—"

Lenore reached for him with the fury of a mother lion protecting her cub. She drummed fists on his broad back so that he scuttled away in surprise and exploded with rage. He struck savagely and sent her reeling. Lenore cried out and crumpled against the wall.

Maura was up, screaming at Braxton. "Leave her alone!"

But he was beyond reason. He caught up a poker from the fireplace and rushed at Lenore as Maura's voice shrilled:

"Stop it, stop it! Put that poker down!"

She hurled herself at Braxton so his arm could not deliver the blow. He muttered as Lenore edged away, her eyes round in horror.

"What is going on?" Pelham's voice thundered from the open doorway. "Have you all gone mad!?"

Braxton slowly lowered the poker, then tossed it to the hearth. Maura ran to Lenore to help her onto a chair.

Pelham's forehead furrowed as he took in the scene: his son disheveled and panting, eyes wild as a madman's, Maura with her torn gown exposing creamy pale flesh and taut, high breasts, the servant with a smear of blood at her temple.

Pelham pointed the cane at Lenore. "Get out," he commanded. When she did not move, he sliced the air with the stick. "Go, woman. Get to your bed and do not show your face till you are summoned."

Lenore edged past him and scuttled from the room.

"Take your filthy son, too," Maura said contemptuously. She pulled at the torn gown, trying to hide her nakedness.

Pelham chuckled and leaned forward with both hands on the cane. "You two must pursue your pleasures in a quieter manner. You'll raise the entire house."

"Pleasure?!" Maura hissed. Were they both insane, their brains addled by brandy? "This pig has crawled from the slime to force himself on me. Do me the kindness of removing him. He is drunk and I find him even more disgusting than usual!"

Braxton looked from her to his father with a leering half-smile. He swayed slightly and put a hand to the table to steady himself. Maura averted her gaze from the shadow of his naked body beneath the open robe.

"She invited me," Braxton said thickly. "She's been tempting me for weeks by flaunting her nakedness."

"You're a liar!" she spat.

Pelham sighed. "A man is driven by his desires, but there are some proprieties, Braxton. She'll be yours soon enough with no interference from anyone. You might keep that in mind and be more discreet."

Maura could not believe her ears. They were bartering her like a load of lumber, discussing her fate as though it were signed and sealed. And not for the first time, she realized. They had discussed it over their brandy and made plans! She shuddered with revulsion.

"I will never marry him!" She shot a disdainful glance in Braxton's direction.

Braxton scowled, but Pelham merely shrugged and walked out of the room. Braxton stood for a moment with a confused expression. It was difficult for his sodden brain to absorb his father's meaning. He'd expected rage, but had detected . . . what? Approval? Not quite, but tacit agreement. He turned to Maura, who stood defiantly glaring at him. She was beautiful with her hair disheveled and her breasts heaving with anger, even though he had little liking for her evasion and fight. He took a step toward her. She retreated like a wary animal.

"Stay away from me!" she snapped.

It was like trying to turn back the sun. He burned with lust. He moved slowly, in a guarded stance, in case she flew at him again. The sight of her set his pulse racing anew, and he was aware of the throbbing desire in his loins.

Maura eyed him with cold hatred. She would kill him if he laid a hand on her. She glanced about for a weapon. If she could get to the poker he had dropped—

But he recognized her intent before she could dart to where the tool lay. He grabbed it up and hurled it under the bed.

What else? There was nothing except the lamp. Braxton seemed to read her thoughts and moved between her and the hypnotic flame. He shook his head and grinned while edging toward her. He was stalking her like a cat with a mouse, playing a game with high stakes. Her only hope was to reach the door and escape into the hall. How she hated him! And Pelham, who had left her to a fate he considered inevitable! She would die before she gave in to either of them!

She measured the narrowing distance between them. Braxton had relaxed to an easy pursuit, thinking her boxed into the corner once more. Prickles of fear rose along her spine as she looked at the walls and the corner of the armoire that blocked her way.

Braxton lunged. She darted under his outstretched arms, and he pitched headlong. Cursing, he stumbled up, but she had already gained the few precious moments it took to get

the door open. The cool air of the hall bathed her fevered
naked flesh. Too late, she remembered the robe that had
fallen to the floor. She could not go back! With a hand on
the railing, she flew down the steps on silent feet. Moonlight streamed through the tall windows flanking the door,
and her shadow leaped along the wall. Behind her, Braxton
stumbled and swore as he thundered in pursuit.

Maura fumbled with the night chain, but it seemed to
tangle hopelessly. When at last it slid free, she yanked the
door open. A rush of cold air hit her. She hesitated long
enough to grab a cloak from the coat tree. In that instant,
Braxton fell upon her, wrapping his arms around her and
pinning her to the wall.

"Let me go!" She beat at him as his fingers bit cruelly
into her flesh and he tried to cover her mouth with his.
"Let me go!"

"Only when I am finished with you, you witch!"

She scratched his face and tore at his robe, but he was a
madman bent on a single purpose. Despite his drunken-
ness, he possessed the power of a bull. He locked his arms
around her and began dragging her back up the stairs.

"Let me go!" Her scream echoed in the empty hall and
her arm ached where his fingers dug into it. She bumped
on the treads, and her legs rapped sharply as she tried to
gain a foothold. She was numb with horror.

All at once, there was a splash of light below the stairs.
Her brain registered it sluggishly. From the rear hall two
figures darted like shadows, and Maura cried out as one of
them bolted up the steps. In the lamplight, she saw Duggan
Quinn's face twisted in black rage. Before she had time to
wonder at his presence, he grabbed Braxton. She fell free
and quickly clutched the railing so she would not topple.
Braxton's grunting and panting filled her ears. She scuttled
away as the two men fought on the stairs, their twisting
shadows grotesque on the wall above. Duggan swung a fist
that landed at the side of Braxton's head. Braxton yelped
and went down but managed to grab the handrail and pull
himself up. He braced his weight and kicked out viciously.

"You damned bastard!" Braxton snarled. He released the
rail and rushed at Duggan. "I'll kill you!"

101

Duggan hit him solidly and spun him around. Before he could fall, Duggan hit him again. Braxton crumpled.

Duggan turned toward Maura, his eyes blazing, but showing concern. "Are you hurt?"

"I—I'm all right," she said breathlessly as she hugged her arms over her naked breasts. She pointed as Braxton got up and prepared to spring.

Duggan crouched. "You'd kill me then, Braxton? Come on, try it!"

Braxton jumped, but Duggan ducked low and came up with several powerful blows to his middle. Braxton's agonized breath was a series of quick grunts as he fell to his knees. Duggan yanked a fistful of the silk robe to jerk him up, then hit him with all his strength.

Braxton moaned as he struck the steps hard and rolled. In the next instant he went down, heels over head, bumping and slamming all the way to the bottom. He crashed to the hard floor and was still, one leg on the steps, the other folded under him.

Maura peered over the rail; she felt dizzy and sick. Lenore rushed from a corner carrying a lamp and bent over the sprawled figure. A dark stain was forming under Braxton's head. His face was waxy in the wavering light, but he was breathing.

In the upper hall, a door opened. Pelham Turk cursed and thrashed about as he came to investigate the disturbance. Several servants hung over the bannister of the third floor, peering down in stunned horror.

Duggan grabbed Maura's hand and raced down the stairs. He led her around Braxton's still form, pausing only long enough to grab Maura's cloak, which Lenore had fetched, and wrap it about her. She was shivering with the cold and shock. Duggan kept his arm around her protectively.

"What the hell is going on?!" Pelham Turk's voice thundered above them.

Lenore motioned. "Go quickly. I will delay him."

Duggan led Maura along the hall to the back of the house. When she tried to talk, he shook his head and whispered, "Wait."

They moved past the dark sitting room, the morning

102

room, then out the back door to the yard where a carriage stood close to the steps. Duggan swept Maura off her feet and lifted her to the seat as easily as he would a child. She was keenly aware of his strong arms and his protective closeness. What would she have done if he had not come? Muffled shouts from the house made Duggan leap to the seat and take up the reins. He slapped the horse's flank. The carriage wheels crunched on the hard-packed earth as they turned toward the gate, where a pale-faced stable boy stared as they raced past. Then they were racing through the dark streets. The wind rushed at Maura's face and she huddled in the silk cloak.

When Duggan glanced at her, she asked, "How on earth did you come to be there?"

He concentrated on maneuvering the carriage around a corner before he answered. "Lenore sent for me."

Bless her, Maura thought. She had believed herself helpless except for her own efforts, but Lenore had not been daunted by Pelham's orders.

Duggan peered at her, becoming aware of her disheveled appearance and her near nakedness under the cloak. She tried to curl her icy bare feet under the seat, and she shivered uncontrollably.

He caught the reins between his knees and quickly slipped out of his coat. He put it over her. When she protested, he would not listen.

"I'll not have you with your death of cold. You've endured enough."

What had Lenore said to bring him so quickly? She flushed at the thought, yet there was no hiding the truth: he had witnessed her struggle with her stepbrother. Her mind was filled with questions that could not be shouted above the noise of the wheels on the cobblestones.

The small chaise rocked as it went sharply around a corner. For a moment, Maura was pitched against Duggan, and his hand steadied her. The strength of his touch was reassuring, and she breathed a prayer of thanks for his quick, unquestioning response to Lenore's summons. He slowed the carriage as they turned onto Broadway. The wide thoroughfare was relatively quiet because of the late hour, but coach lanterns still gleamed in a steady flow of

103

traffic, restaurants were still open and couples were emerging after late suppers following the theater. She recognized Thomas Downing's Oyster House where she had gone with the Astors after the opening of Plumbe's Daguerrian Gallery. How long ago it seemed. In a year's time, her entire life had changed.

They crossed westward on streets that were unfamiliar to Maura. The neighborhood slid into shabbiness, and the houses crowded together like huddled refugees. There were no pleasant parks or spacious yards to break the monotony of the rows of gray stone buildings. After two blocks, they drew up before a house. Maura peered at it curiously. It was tall and narrow, one of a row that lined the entire block. Tiers of cast-iron balconies on three levels gave the buildings a unified look and offered a measure of privacy to the tall windows that opened onto them. The houses themselves were set back from the street and had small bare yards enclosed by wrought-iron fences. Lights glowed at several windows, but most were dark It was obviously a workingman's neighborhood, and few enjoyed the luxury of late nights.

Duggan stepped down, tied the reins, and lifted Maura into his arms.

"I can walk," she said. The feel of his encircling arms flooded her with warmth.

"In bare feet? The paths here are not as spotless as those at Meadowfield. It would be easy to cut a foot on a shard of glass or a bit of metal lying about." He grinned at her. "Besides, you're as light as a wisp. I hardly know I've got you in my arms."

Nothing was further from the truth. He was all too aware of the soft, feminine bundle he held against his chest. Her breath whispered at his bare neck and sent tingling waves of longing through his body. He hadn't stopped to put on a collar or button his shirt when the boy had come with Lenore's frantic message. It was lucky he had been out of bed and dressed, he thought, recalling his other unexpected visitor a few minutes before the lad had arrived.

He took the steps two at a time, crossed the porch, and shouldered the door open. The entrance hall was unlit except for a hazy glow that filtered through the curtained window. He managed to extract a key without relinquishing his precious cargo, then entered a long hall lighted by a single lamp. He climbed the stairs to the second floor. Maura glanced around the gloomy hall. A rooming house—she'd never seen one before. Half a dozen doors opened off the wide hall, each shut now against intruding eyes. The steps were bare, and Duggan's footfalls were loud as he carried her along the second-floor corridor. At a door in the rear, he used another key to let himself into a dim room. He set her down and turned up the wick of a lamp.

"It's not what you're accustomed to, but it will have to do until we figure out what's to become of you. Here now, you're shivering again. I'll put coals on the fire." He crossed to a grate and busied himself with a shovel and coal scuttle.

She glanced around. The room was small and almost bare. There were only a round table, a ladder-back chair, a heavy oak bureau topped by a graying mirror, and a brass bed with the sheets and blanket in disarray as though it had just been vacated. So shabby was the furniture, not one stick would have been tolerated in the servants' quarters at Meadowfield. Without realizing it, Maura shrank inside her cloak as though disdaining to touch anything. Then she realized Duggan was watching her. The fire flared behind him and shadowed his face so she couldn't read his expression, but she had the uncomfortable feeling that he was reading her thoughts.

"I'll fix you a cup of tea," he said abruptly. He took a kettle from a shelf in the corner and brought it to the grate. While it heated, he readied a pot, generously spooning pungent black tea from a small tin.

"Sit, I won't bite you." He indicated the chair.

She settled herself and watched him curiously. He was as comfortable preparing tea as he was handling a sailboat or working on a carriage frame. He moved with a grace that belied his size and strength. The same hands that had beaten Braxton savagely such a short time ago were incredibly gentle when he carried her. She was unable to understand fully the glow of pleasure she'd experienced when he held her against his chest or how easily she put aside the anger she'd felt toward him only a few days ago. But that had been before he rescued her first from the burning factory, then from Braxton's hateful attentions. Was she always to be in his debt? When he glanced at her, she looked away to hide turbulent thoughts. She did not want him to think her ungrateful.

Duggan saw how she huddled in the silk cloak and raised her feet from the drafty floor. She was a perfect blossom suddenly cast into a patch of thistles. Despite the cloak, a vision of her womanly curves under the torn nightgown was etched in his brain. Only his hatred for Braxton curbed the sweeter emotions that would have filled him. Thank God Lenore had the presence of mind to send for him! Duggan's blood churned. He should have killed Braxton in their first encounter at the factory! He hoped the bastard lay dead in his own blood now. If he ever laid a hand on Maura again—

There wasn't time for blind rage. It was dangerous to bring Maura here, but there hadn't been time for anything else. It was a stopgap measure. As soon as he found a safe place, he'd vacate the room without a trace. There was a possibility that Pelham would secure the address and come looking for him tonight. At best, they had until morning. When the kettle hissed, he wrapped a blue cloth around the handle to lift it from the fire. The aroma of strong tea filled the room.

"I've no milk, only a bit of sugar," he apologized.

"That's fine." Maura watched as he crossed to the shelf and returned with a green bowl. He wore a blue shirt, open to the waist so that a shadow of dark chest hair was exposed. Under the snug sleeves, his thick muscles rippled sensuously. An unbidden memory of lying in his arms on the riverbank made her pulse quicken, and she felt a tide of color stain her cheeks. She wondered if Duggan realized the predicament in which he'd placed himself by rushing to her assistance tonight. Pelham would be livid! He had already threatened to prefer charges against Duggan because of the fire. Now with Braxton injured—possibly dying—he would certainly do so.

What would she have done if Duggan had not come? She was no match for Braxton's brute strength, spurred by liquor and lust. He'd meant to have his way with her, and though she would have fought him with every ounce of strength, he might have succeeded. She shuddered at the thought.

Glancing at Duggan, she saw a calm countenance and blue eyes which were unreadable. She sipped the steaming tea.

"I cannot stay here," she murmured.

"You cannot return to Meadowfield," he said vehemently.

She knew he was right. She could not go back to Meadowfield as long as Braxton and Pelham were there.

Duggan regarded her with a wry smile. "Nor can you go very far garbed in a tattered nightdress and without slippers on your feet."

She flushed. Even with the cloak around her, she felt unclothed under his gaze.

He saw her shiver and came to her at once. "You're cold—here, let me move the chair closer to the fire." He took her hand and drew her up. As he did, the silken cloak slid from her shoulders and cascaded to the floor. His gaze was irresistibly drawn to her full breasts where the tattered nightdress did not hide the creamy flesh. Her bosom rose and her breath caught; her hands fluttered in a vain attempt to cover her nakedness. A warm tide of desire swept him, and he could not resist taking her in his arms and claiming her lips. The interval since their last embrace was swept aside in a swelling passion that refused to be contained. Her body was no longer cold but incredibly warm and alive; her mouth was intoxicating.

Maura felt swirling heat engulf her. The hard leanness of Duggan's body stirred her senses and caused her pulse to race. He whispered her name as his hand caressed the high curve of her breast. Delicious shivers of pleasure made her tremble when his lips blazed a velvet path to the thudding pulse beat at her throat. She tried to tell herself she could not give in to the feverish desire. She tried to tell him. . . .

"We mustn't—"

"You don't mean that. You want me as much as I want you." His lips trailed on her burning flesh again, and she shivered uncontrollably. Then his callused hands were

107

pushing aside the tattered nightgown and stroking the shivering length of her body. He drew her to the bed. The hunger that had come to life on the riverbank swelled, and her mind reeled. She managed to whisper weakly, "No—let me go. You are no better than Braxton—"

In answer, he buried his face in her breasts. His lips and tongue drew fiery patterns on the naked flesh. Every muscle of her body grew taut, yet was somehow drained of strength. She pushed at him helplessly.

"You would compare me to him when I can teach you the true meaning of passion? No, Maura, I am better than Braxton, have no doubt of it." He teased her mouth with a kiss that was endless, exquisite torture. It was like being caught in the eye of a hurricane. She struggled for breath as she felt herself drawn deeper and deeper, swirling, eddying . . . She sobbed and pleaded, "Let me go—"

"You do not want that." His voice was gentle, yet sure, and his hands did not relent in their sensuous quest.

"Stop—" It was a thread of sound, lost in a whimper of delight as he stroked the silken flesh of her thigh.

"You forget I know the promise of your body. You welcomed me once. Do it again." His fingers nibbled at the intimate joining of her thighs. "Your body tells me you share my desire. Let your lips tell me the same."

She shook her head and her amber hair fanned about her shoulders. Her throat was arid with a scorching heat that came from the depths of her soul. Then he was kissing her again, and her lips parted greedily to welcome his tongue.

His clothing rustled and was discarded quickly. Maura saw his powerful maleness released from the restraining garments. Her blood pounded like a storm-driven surf. Her breath caught as he took her in his arms once more. When their flesh met, there were no more words of protest, only willing acceptance and eagerness as he resumed the lingering journey of his lips at her throat, her rounded breasts, and the sweet-scented valley between. When his hands parted her quivering thighs to brush at the most erotic spot of all, she was swept into a chasm of desire.

A remnant of guilt impelled her to try to draw away, but he petted until she fell back, helplessly ensnared. He teased her with his tongue which had become an excruciating, delightful weapon. She moaned softly, and tears spilled over her lashes. He kissed them away as he moved over her.

Her breath caught. When she tried to speak, Duggan covered her mouth with kisses. Then there was the gentle fire of his body entering hers, a momentary pain quickly erased by aching delight. She was lost in heady pleasure that made her body move with a will of its own, welcoming him fully and meeting his masculine demands. It was as though she had waited for this moment a very long time. She claimed it breathlessly as they soared to a pinnacle of bliss. She cried out softly, no longer in protest but in joyous fulfillment.

He lay holding her close until her heart slowed its mad pace. He stroked her eyelids, and she pressed against him in wonder as he murmured her name over and over.

At last he released her and rose to begin to dress. Maura lay sated, unwilling to end the intimacy. Duggan stirred the fire to reheat the kettle. She wanted to call him back, but her lips were silent as he occupied himself brewing another pot of tea. When he brought her a cup, she pulled the cape to cover herself, awkward now that the intimacy was shattered.

He studied her with a pensive stare. How tempting it was to hold her and banish the outside world, but he could not. They had already tarried dangerously long. He steeled himself against his tender emotions and forced himself to speak not from his heart but from logic. "We cannot stay here, it is too dangerous. We'll have to find you some clothes and a place to stay. Do you have relatives you can go to?"

She felt a stir of annoyance at his easy dismissal of what they had shared. Did she mean so little to him? With effort, she controlled the tremor in her voice. "James is all the family I have."

"No cousin, or trusted friend? Perhaps someone from the factory? Your father was well-liked."

She frowned, her displeasure forgotten as she considered her plight. She would be uneasy asking favors in a situation as grave as this. Pelham was capable of extending retribution to anyone who aided her.

"No one," she said at last.

Gazing at her, he knew that she did not want to endanger others by drawing them into her quarrel with her stepfather. He longed to hold her close and protect her, but he had no illusions about his own immediate future. She was in more danger being with him than she would be alone. Pelham Turk would set the police on him for sure. There'd be thirty days in Jefferson Market Prison if they caught him, or a longer sentence in the Tombs if Pelham could convince the courts that Duggan had been responsible for the factory fire, or if Braxton died. Lacy Marsh had come unexpectedly to his rooms earlier that evening to tell him her uncle had been asked to draw up papers filing formal charges against Duggan. He could offer Maura nothing but misery, at a time when he longed to give her love. He had already succumbed to passion and allowed precious time to slip away. He must get her to a safe place as quickly as possible.

"Then you will have to go to James in Pittsburgh," he said. "I'll make arrangements."

She had recovered her composure to a degree. "I will not run!"

"Would you stay and return to Braxton's company? You might not be as fortunate in escaping him next time. In Pittsburgh, James can arrange for a lawyer to look into your mother's estate and take action against your stepfather."

"Action?"

"Surely you are not going to allow him to take over Meadowfield and the Sullivan Company? They were your father's, and now they belong to you. Your mother will have left her share to you and your brother."

Her heart plummeted, and she stared fixedly at the cape string she was twining around her fingers. "Her share goes to Pelham," she said.

Duggan's face darkened. "She made no provision—?"

"I have only what my father left me, and Pelham is my legal guardian now that Mother is gone."

Duggan was astonished. "Your guardian?!" He swore, then took a deep breath. "I should have expected—and there's no undoing what's been done, at least not without expert advice. A good lawyer will be able to find a way.

110

But first things first. Drink your tea, then rest. I'll be back shortly."

"Where are you going?"

"There are things to be done. It's best you know nothing about them for now." He crossed to a hook and took down a blue work shirt. It was clean, though somewhat worn at the sleeves. "You can use this for a nightshirt." He tossed it to her, and as she released the cloak to catch it, the wrap fell open from neck to waist. When his gaze went to her breasts, her face flushed and she tugged the garment closed.

"I have no intention of sleeping," she said angrily.

Was she upset with him—or with herself? She did not know.

Her spirited answer made him smile. "Suit yourself." He slipped on his jacket and said, "Don't open the door to anyone. I'll let myself in with a key when I return."

She listened to his footfalls in the hall, the opening and closing of a door, then silence until she became aware of distant voices, laughter and a few bars of a song sung off-key. She finished the tea and let the cloak drop so she could slip her arms into Duggan's shirt and button it to the throat. It hung so loose she was almost lost in it. She scowled at the image reflected in the glass as she rolled up the sleeves. Her cheeks were bright and her eyes smoldered with an inner fire. She was furious with herself for succumbing to Duggan again and with him for taking advantage of her momentary weakness. Yet had she really struggled against his advances? With Braxton, she'd clawed and fought as though her life were at stake. In comparison, she had acquiesced eagerly to Duggan. Even in anger, she could not deny the pleasure she'd experienced. She had never known a man like Duggan. His physical presence was overwhelming, yet her conscience struggled with the realization that they were worlds apart. He was a factory laborer, a brawling, rough man who relied on his fists to settle everything. A man who took what he wanted. Was it because he was so different that he attracted her? She sighed, unable to answer her own questions.

She had no idea when Duggan would return. She had told him she did not want to sleep, but weariness weighted her eyes and her body was numb. She wandered about the room, examining it more closely. In a corner was a small locked trunk, but there were few other personal articles. Over the bed, a shelf had been built to hold books. She lifted one and saw it was a volume of Thackeray. Returning it, she noticed a scrap of paper beside the pillow. Thinking it had dropped from the book, she retrieved it and idly unfolded it. It was a note, written in a spidery hand.

My dearest Duggan—You are heartless to run off and leave me! I should be furious, but I will forgive you. I will learn what I can of the matter Uncle Theodore was discussing. Come to the house after he's left for the factory in the morning. I'll be waiting for you.
Your own loving L.

She stood thunderstruck, staring at the paper as a sudden, trembling anger filled her. L . . . ? Uncle Theodore . . . ? Lacy Marsh! She dropped the note, then picked it up again and threw it to the table. How dare Duggan seduce her in the bed where he had entertained another woman! She tore off the blanket and sheet furiously and tossed them in a heap, then grabbed up her cloak and spread it on the floor in front of the grate. Curling up her body, she pulled it to cover herself. She was so angry her whole body shook. She bit her lip until tears came to her eyes. She hated Duggan Quinn—she hated him! She closed her eyes and tried to blot him from her mind.

She woke with a start some time later and discovered that Duggan had returned. She had not heard the door, but he was standing at the table with Lacy's note in his hand and a puzzled frown on his face. He turned as she sat up. His curious look toward the bed evidenced questions he did not put into words.

"I found it on your pillow! I am sorry to have disturbed your dalliance, and regret that you felt compelled to come to my rescue at the price of leaving someone who finds you so irresistible!" She arranged the cloak over her bare legs.

He would have laughed except for the anger in her smoky eyes. The glow from the grate lighted her hair to burnished gold, and her beauty aroused an ache in his

112

heart. He carelessly tossed the note aside and looked at the heaped bedclothes, then back to her.

She tossed her head and set her jaw. Duggan smothered a grin, then lifted a bulky package he'd dropped on the chair and threw it to her. She let it fall to the floor.

"Clothing," he said, "unless you've become so attached to my shirt that you cannot bear to part with it."

"I am not attached to anything belonging to you!" She turned away from his infuriating smile.

He went on as though her anger were insignificant. "I have seen Lenore. Unfortunately, Braxton is not dead, though his injuries will cause him a devilish headache for a bit. Pelham is in a fair temper but lulled by whiskey. I hope he is too preoccupied to search us out at the moment. By morning it will be a different story, and we must put as much distance between you and him as possible."

His grave tone alarmed her, and she forgot her annoyance.

"Lenore agrees that you must go to James. Pelham will blunder about and raise a storm, but when he cannot find you, he'll settle down. Even if it occurs to him that you've gone to Pittsburgh, he won't know your route and won't be able to overtake you before you reach James."

"He will punish Lenore." She could not leave the servant to face her stepfather's wrath.

"With you safely away, Lenore will not stay on at Meadowfield. She has little liking for Turk."

"She must come with me!" Maura's hopes soared.

He smiled. "I said that very thing, but she says she's too old to make such a journey. She'll go to her sister in Brooklyn until you return."

She looked at him. "And what of you?" He had spoken only of her going.

"Don't worry about me."

"I wasn't worried," she snapped. She knew immediately it wasn't true. He'd risked a great deal to help her, and she knew he was in danger.

In an easy tone, he said, "Turk will have the devil's own time trying to find me, never fear."

"You will not go with me?" She realized suddenly that she did not want to leave him.

113

"It would not add to your safety. Perhaps by following me, Pelham will be sidetracked."

He was trying to set her mind at rest. She felt confident that he would outwit Pelham—and the police, if it came to that. Still, she did not want to relinquish the comfort of his presence.

He glanced at the window and the black sky. "We've lingered too long. Every moment counts if you're to be away from the city by sunup. Dress quickly while I see to the carriage." He indicated the bundle which lay on the floor beside her. "Lenore is packing a small trunk and will send it here within the hour." He left without giving her a chance to comment.

Lenore had sent a dark blue gown of soft chambray, with a jacket that would protect her against the night air. There were undergarments, stockings, black kid slippers, a hairbrush and tortoiseshell pins. There was also a small black velvet reticule and, in it, a handful of silver dollars and bills. Probably every penny Lenore was able to collect about the house, bless her!

Maura spread the clothing on the bed and slipped out of the coarse work shirt. Her nightgown was torn beyond salvation, and she discarded it in a heap. She had drawn on the silk chemise and was sitting down to pull on stockings and shoes when the door opened without warning. Snatching up the gown, she started to berate Duggan for his unexpected entrance, but the look on his face stopped her.

"Quickly, we must go at once!" He was already scooping up the remainder of her clothing. He glanced about for other evidence of her visit, saw the crumpled nightdress and grabbed that. He snatched up her cloak and pulled her to the door and out into the dark hall. The lamp at the landing flickered as a pounding sounded at the front door. Duggan swore under his breath and urged her into the shadows. There was a back stair, narrow and black as pitch. He held her hand tight. "Step easy, put a hand to the wall. Here, just another step . . ."

Behind them, they heard the front door open. A gruff voice demanded, "We've come for Duggan Quinn. Which room is his?"

Maura's heart thudded so she could scarcely breathe. It was beyond belief or imagination that she could be stum-

114

bling down back stairs in the middle of the night, barely a breath ahead of pursuit! Her life was suddenly tumbled about like a cabbage in a basket! She stumbled and felt Duggan's arms slide about her. His face was so close she felt his warm breath.

"Not a sound," he whispered.

Silently she let him lead her through the blackness, once again finding comfort in his closeness and forgetting her anger.

CHAPTER SIX

They slipped out into the cool night air. Duggan quickly fastened the rear door and propped a length of wood against it so it could not be opened from within.

"That'll give us another minute," he said.

Darkness blanketed the unfamiliar yard, but Duggan seemed able to determine their way readily. He pulled her along at a faster pace than she had thought possible in the blackness. Shadows shifted and merged as the moon left a film of clouds to bathe the yard in a pale, ghostly light.

Duggan headed for a high, pitch-roofed stable some distance back. A horse nickered and bumped his stall. Maura smelled the acrid odor of dung. Duggan's hands worked the latch, then slid back the heavy door with only a faint rasp of protest from the rusty hinges. He cocked his head toward the house. Hearing no outcry, he drew her inside and told her to wait. She listened to his steps on the dry straw. There was a metallic rattle, then a squeak of hinges and heavy footfalls. Duggan's voice whispered, "Easy, now . . . easy . . ."

Maura smelled the strong animal odor, and the horse snuffled softly. "Can you ride without a saddle?" Duggan whispered.

"Yes." It meant straddling the horse's back, but she had ridden that way many times as a child. She breathed silent thanks that there had not been time to encumber herself with skirt and petticoat.

His hand searched for hers and pressed the leather reins into it. "She's a gentle mare and won't give you any trouble. Wait here another moment."

He was gone again. The horse nuzzled her shoulder and

she rubbed its nose. Then Duggan was back, leading a second animal.

"We'll walk to the alley nice'n slow. The police will be coming round to the back soon, but we'll see their lanterns."

He moved through the open door. Lights had come on in the house, and shadows moved behind the curtained windows. Snatches of muffled voices drifted to them.

Duggan pointed. "This way."

They were on a path that led to the rear of the yard. It was uneven and dipped slightly as it neared the fence. When he unfastened a gate and swung it back, they came out into a deeply rutted alley. Duggan paused to fasten the gate again and bend the hasp so it would be hard to open. The ground was soft from the recent rains. Their tracks would be plain as far as the gate, but in the well-used alley it would be hard for the police to tell which way they'd gone.

Duggan bent a knee for Maura to climb on the horse. The mare tossed its head restlessly, and Maura spoke softly to it as she settled onto the animal's strong back. It was a gray, full-bodied animal that was accustomed to drawing a rig rather than having a rider, but it accepted the situation docilely as Duggan had predicted. Maura took the bundle of clothing Duggan handed up.

Duggan mounted and signaled her to follow. They walked the animals to the mouth of the alley. Then Duggan took the lead as they increased their speed and turned into a paved street.

The cold air made Maura shiver under the thin cloak. She wished it were possible to stop long enough to dress, but there would be time for that when they were safely away from the house and the police. Almost as though divining her thoughts, Duggan looked around and she saw the gleam of his smile. It was cut short by a loud shout behind them.

Duggan nudged the horse to a gallop, glancing around to be sure Maura was directly behind. Hooves thundered on the pavement and echoed along the street. There was a clatter and shouts as men scrambled for horses to set out in chase. In moments the entire night erupted with the sounds of pursuit.

118

Maura concentrated on keeping her seat as the horse raced under the pressure of her drumming feet. Thank heaven she at least had donned her shoes. Was she destined to rush through the night in a state of dishabille? It would have been amusing if the situation were not so perilous.

The horses loped through the darkened city. Maura lost all sense of direction in the unfamiliar neighborhood; she had no choice but to trust Duggan completely. He seemed to have a destination in mind. What arrangements could he have made before discovering the police were at hand? No matter how many twists and turns they made, they eventually headed west again with the humpbacked moon directly before them.

She was breathless and her heart was thundering when at last he slowed, raised a hand, and stopped. She reined in the mare. "What is it?"

He shook his head, listening, and she found herself wondering if running from the police was commonplace with him. He seemed to enjoy it. There was a devil-may-care expression on his face as he grinned at her.

"I think we've left them behind," he said with a twinkle in his eye.

"Where are we going?"

"To the river." He nudged his horse to a walk. "There's a stage leaving Hoboken for Pittsburgh at six this morning. We'll have plenty of time to cross and book your passage."

Maura said nothing. How could she argue when she had no choice? Her earlier anger with Duggan gave way to practical need. She had no means to undertake her own welfare at this point. She had only the few garments Lenore had sent and the small purse. Duggan had already made arrangements of some kind. She'd be a fool to toss them aside. She glanced at him sidelong as they rode. His face gave no hint of his thoughts. He might have been out for an afternoon's pleasure instead of fleeing from the authorities.

They came at last to a wide, cluttered street with long, low buildings that housed the ferryboats and offices. Alongside were warehouses and moored ships. Maura had been here many times to meet people coming home from cruises or from Jersey, but never in the dark of night when each shadow took on a sinister appearance. She was not fright-

119

ened, though she felt a sustained excitement and her hands were trembling. It seemed unlikely the police would guess the direction they'd taken, but in the morning a more thorough search would be made. Pelham would leave no stone unturned, trust him for that.

The ferries on the Hudson ran frequently during the day but only one each half-hour in the evening, and then only till midnight. It was well past that now. The broad, bulky boats were tied up, sedate and silent, waiting for the morning rush.

Duggan studied the dim waterfront where a few distant lights bobbed. Luck and the fact that Maura had done his bidding unhesitatingly had enabled them to evade the police. Now he prayed that the boatman with whom he'd struck a bargain to row them across had not wandered off with a bottle and forgotten the tryst. It had been too close a call, the police arriving just as he returned. Thank heaven they'd not been a few minutes sooner, or they'd have found Maura alone in his room. Pelham Turk would have made the most of that, to be sure. Maura would have been dragged home and guarded carefully until he was sure she could not upset his plans. He did not suppose for a second that Turk would pass on any of her parents' estate to Maura, any more than he had honored Patrick's intention to take Duggan into the company. Turk would see to it that full control was in his own hands, and he would bleed the accounts to suit his needs, if he hadn't already done so.

Spying the customs sheds, he motioned Maura to halt. He slid down and stepped into the deep shadow of the building. Beside it, rough steps led to the water's edge where there was a large square float to which several fishing boats were tied. The smell of tobacco drifted to his nostrils. He peered down and made out the figure of a man hunched over a pipe as he sat in the stern of a boat. Duggan retraced his steps to where Maura waited.

"Come, there's a boat waiting."

Maura drew back into the shadows. "I'll not go another step until I've dressed!"

He relented and turned his back to keep a careful watch on the street behind. It would not do to be careless now.

Maura huddled in the dark perimeter of the shed, her back to Duggan but glancing over her shoulder every few

120

moments. She was still breathless from the headlong flight, and her hands fumbled as she hurriedly drew on the blue chambray. The air was icy, and she buttoned the jacket with shaking fingers, then pulled the silk cloak around her again. There was no time to do more than brush quickly at her tangled hair, which had not been combed since her wakening to Braxton's intrusion. It seemed so far in the past—was it possible only hours had passed?

When she rejoined Duggan, he slipped a hand under her arm and led her down to the float.

The boatman swiveled his head. "There you are. I'd begun to think you wasn't coming." He stared at the girl. "You two runnin' off t'get married?"

Duggan gave a careless shrug and grinned broadly. Let the old man have his romantic notions. They might make him less likely to divulge information if he were questioned.

"Thought so," the old man said with an answering smile of conspiracy. "All right, get in—watch your step, miss. Here, gimme your hand."

Maura stepped gingerly into the boat as the boatman grasped her arm with strong fingers. He indicated the rear seat and she sank onto it. The wide boat rocked, and the smell of river, fish, and rotting vegetables, as well as other indefinable odors assailed her.

Duggan crawled past the boatman to seat himself close to Maura. The man grunted as he threw off the painter and pushed with an oar. The boat swung around slowly. The interval of black water between it and the float widened. He ran out both oars, then tugged with one to straighten the boat before he began to row.

Duggan whispered close at her ear: "Across the river you'll be in another jurisdiction. Pelham will eventually be able to influence the Jersey authorities to continue the search if he's determined, but it will take time, no matter how much he fumes. By then you'll be safely away."

Glancing back, she saw the retreating shoreline of New York. From a distance, the city sparkled with pinpoints of light. How long would it be until she saw it again? She wondered, too, if Duggan was going out of her life forever. She realized how painful the idea was. She owed him a debt of gratitude, even though she was annoyed at him for being so sure of himself and of her. He had not voiced a word of regret at the role he'd played in her life, nor had he referred to their lovemaking. It was as though she had casually shared a bed with him, and he could put the interlude from his mind completely—just as easily as he had dismissed his earlier assignation with Lacy Marsh. The fact that he had neither denied her accusation nor made any attempt to explain filled her with seething jealousy. She resolutely turned away from him and watched the old man row. The pipe in the corner of his mouth puffed white smoke now and then. Once, he glanced around and said, "Bundle up, lass. It'll be cold out on the river."

The cloak offered little protection against the sharp wind as she sat staring ahead to the shadowy, distant shore of Jersey. Moonlight streaked the water, casting up bits of light then covering them. A mist drifted by and swirled between her and the boatman so he seemed momentarily lost in a fog. The old man seemed to accept the midnight journey as though it were commonplace. She wondered what he would say if the police questioned him. Despite Duggan's assurances, she knew they could be caught and taken back. Pelham would never allow either of them to draw a free breath.

It was much colder than on the shore, and she dug her hands into the depths of the cloak. Duggan put an arm around her to shield her from the wind, and Maura did not pull away. She watched the boatman move the long oars effortlessly as the boat glided across the current at a steady pace. The sound of the oars rocking against the thole pins was a monotonous song. Distant boats hooted now and then, and once someone's shout was answered by a wail, but the boatman was oblivious. He glanced around every few moments to guide himself, changing course twice as though directed by some instinct. Maura peered and tried to pick out the landing he was making for, but she could not tell one bit of shoreline from another. There were yellow lights and a few red, most in buildings but some that bobbed slowly up and down. The shadows gradually began to take the shape of buildings and the masts and yards of ships at mooring.

The old man was certain of his destination now and looked over his shoulder frequently as he made for shore. He rowed along a patch of inky water between a pier and a tall-masted ship with a dark tangle of rigging, then swung the boat around a small wharf so he could throw out the painter and encircle a post.

"We're at the foot of River Street," he said. "There's a preacher 'bout a mile north. Seamen's church, but it's always open." He grinned at Maura and she smiled as though they shared a wonderful secret.

Because the old man was watching, she stayed in the shelter of Duggan's arm as he helped her out. The boat pitched dangerously and banged against a piling as Duggan pulled her to the wharf. When he turned to pay the boatman the rest of his wage, the old man pocketed the money, released the line, and immediately settled to the oars. The boat quickly became a shadow against the dark water.

Duggan took her arm and led her to the steps angling up to the pier. He was aware of how easily sound traveled over the water, and was silent as he guided her upward with a firm hand on the damp metal railing. At the top, she paused to take a deep breath and look back.

"It will not be long until you can return," he said softly.

She gazed at him. "Do you really believe that?"

"Of course I do, and you must too. James is sure to know a lawyer who'll see you through the legal course."

She did not argue, but somehow he made it seem too easy. Pelham would never relent. He, too, was a lawyer and would know a way to handle any attack. But at least she was free of him for a time. It was as if a great burden had been lightened, if not lifted; she was still bitter about leaving her home, the *Sullivan* home, in Pelham's hands.

"You're tired," Duggan said. "Don't let your thoughts dwell on problems that cannot be solved tonight. Come, maybe we can find a place to ease our cold bodies and spirits with a cup of hot coffee."

With a last look at the winking lights, Maura gathered her skirts and fell in step beside him. She refused his hand and held her head high. She would not let morbid thoughts drive her to despair. She was safe for the moment and would hold positive thoughts about the future. She stifled a sigh as she thought about the trunk Lenore had packed but which had not come in time.

The narrow streets were deserted and there were no lights. Duggan seemed to know exactly where they were

123

going, each corner to turn. He insisted that they walk in the center of the roadway rather than on the narrow sidewalk.

"It's better," he said in answer to her question.

She found out why quite soon. Two figures detached themselves from a dark doorway ahead. The men were dressed in rough work clothes with caps pulled low over their heads. They separated from each other and waited as she and Duggan approached. When they saw that she was a woman, they exchanged a few quick words and leered.

Duggan made no sign that he noticed them. Under his breath, he said to Maura, "Keep walking, no matter what happens."

He fished under his coat but she could not see what he was after. Did he have a gun? In spite of his confidence, she felt a tremor of fear.

Without warning, the two men jumped, one from each side. Duggan pushed Maura hard to shove her out of the path of the attack. She stumbled but did not lose her footing, then was mesmerized by Duggan's sudden movement. He ducked to the right, his hands thrust out. The man who had been crouched to strike was stopped in his tracks, then rolled sideways to the hard-packed dirt, clutching at his midsection, his breath exploding in pain. The second man growled and went for Duggan with a vicious swipe of a heavy fist. Duggan pivoted and sprang. His arms moved with blurring speed and his feet kicked out. The second assailant fell like a dead weight and lay without moving.

Duggan rushed to Maura. To her amazement, he was not even breathing hard. She stared at the two disabled men. "What did you do?"

He took her hand and pulled her along. "A trick I learned in China. They call it a martial art." He rubbed the short bit of smooth wood before tucking it into his belt and buttoning his coat over it. "Maybe it will teach them a lesson about setting upon travelers."

Maura took an amazed breath. She had a lot to learn about Duggan Quinn! She realized he could have killed Braxton easily but had not done so: he'd preferred to fight on even terms. Duggan became more of an enigma with each new facet she glimpsed.

They turned onto a wide avenue and went two blocks. Near the corner they came to a two-story building with offices at the front and a wall with a wooden gate around the barns. On the glass window was the legend in gold leaf: HARNDEN & CO. EXPRESS. A single lamp glowed inside the station, but it was not yet open for business. There was a Harnden office in New York; Maura recalled seeing it on Wall Street. She realized that Duggan had taken yet another precaution to insure her not being traced. Pelham would naturally inquire at stage and train offices in Manhattan; a young woman traveling alone was a rarity that would be readily recalled.

Alongside the building, a low wooden bench with the Harnden name painted in yellow letters squatted in the shadows. She dropped onto it gratefully. A milk wagon clattered past, the heavy barrels rocking on the wagon bed. The sky had begun to lighten, and the street became visible in the gray dawn. There was an auction house across from them, with every sort of goods and material in the window: casks, pictures, rugs, furniture and even wagon wheels. Next to it, a gently swaying sign over a door proclaimed: HOTEL.

"You'll be in Pittsburgh in a few days," Duggan said. "James will arrange a place for you to stay. I'll send him a wire as soon as the telegraph office opens."

He reached into his pocket for a brown leather pouch, which he pressed into her hand. She felt the hard outlines of coins.

"Take this. You'll need food and lodging during your journey. It's not much but—"

She shook her head. "I don't want it. I have the money Lenore sent."

"Please, set my mind at ease." He folded her hand around the pouch. Nothing would stop him worrying, he thought, but knowing she had a bit of cash would help. It disturbed him that neither he nor Maura had heard from James for so long. Pelham surely knew how the new Pittsburgh business was faring, but the few times Duggan had asked after James, Turk had clearly indicated that Sullivan affairs were none of his business. Duggan wished he did not have to send Maura off alone now, but there was no other way. He'd made dangerous enemies in the Turks, and he would be a hunted man for a while. Worse, Pelham would surmise that Maura was with him. With luck, Duggan hoped to lay a broad trail that would lead pursuit away from her. That done, he'd follow her to Pittsburgh and confer with James.

"Very well," She took the money. "But I shall pay it back." She tucked the pouch into her reticule.

"If you wish." Why did she persist in putting him at arm's length each time he tried to help? She was too determined to stand alone. Well, maybe it was to the good; it would be hard enough for her to win back what was hers. A generous helping of spirit might tip the scales in her favor.

They sat in silence as he searched for something to say that would be more than a triviality, but words would not come. The sky was streaked with rose and yellow in the east, and suddenly the street was more than a dim alley. He could pick out the wood grain on an armoire in the auction window across the way. An old man appeared, shuffling along on the opposite side of the street, looking into trash bins as he went. A wagon clattered past, and a man came down the steps of a house half a block away and hurried off buttoning his coat.

"The savage dawn," Duggan said softly. "When I was a boy this was the time of morning I had to carry water from the well into the house. Five pails of it . . ."

Maura thought of her father getting ready to go to the factory. When she was small, he had carried her on his shoulders as far as the carriage every morning. It seemed a lifetime ago.

Duggan fished out a turnip watch, flicked open the case and tilted it to catch the light. Then he got up and walked to the door. "According to the sign, they open soon." He peered through the glass, using both hands to shut out reflections. "There's a lunch counter and someone's making a fire in the stove. You'll have something in your stomach before long."

Again he was speaking only of her. She walked the length of the window. "You need some coffee as much as I do."

He smiled and nodded. "But I don't think it's wise for me to be seen with you. We must part company now." He sounded reluctant.

126

Maura did not want him to go. "I don't think we've been followed."

"I hope not. Still, it's better not to take chances." He came close and took her hand, pressing it between both of his. "I'll watch until the stage is underway with you safely aboard."

They stood gazing at each other for several moments. His eyes were shadowed pools. He had looked at her that way as they lay on the narrow bed in his room, entwined in each other's arms. Only then there had been expectant joy in the look; now there was sorrow. She wondered what her own expression mirrored, and lowered her gaze abruptly. His hand cupped her chin and raised it. Then she was in his arms, held close as he kissed her with an ardor that stirred more than memories. All anger vanished and she clung to him, eager for the demand of his mouth. Her lips moved beneath his of their own accord. She did not want him to go, not now . . . or ever. When he released her, she tried to speak, but the words faltered on her tongue.

He grinned disarmingly. "Think of me when you climb into your warm bed tonight. How I wish that fate had dealt the game differently so that I could share it with you. Perhaps—" He broke off with a shake of his head. He could not sustain the pretended levity. "I must go. It'll be light soon." He turned, strode across the street and vanished in the gloom between two buildings.

Maura watched until she could no longer pick out his figure. A warm flush spread along her neck to her cheeks. She had misread his expression and almost made a fool of herself by begging him to stay! To him, she was merely another link in his chain of conquests, nothing more! And now, whatever duty he fancied he owed the memory of her father was paid. He could walk away with a good-bye kiss and only mild regret that their acquaintance had to end so quickly.

Maura raised a hand to her burning face and turned back to the window. If he was watching, she did not want him to know she cared one way or the other. Let him do as he pleased, it was nothing to her. Yet her glance moved across the reflection in the glass, searching the gray outlines of the buildings on the opposite side of the street.

127

The sound of voices made her look around. Two men were approaching, both middle-aged and dressed in dark suits and bowler hats. One sported a fringe of gray whiskers, the other had a definite paunch. The man with the whiskers produced a key and unlocked the stage company door. When he noticed Maura he lifted his hat.

"Good morning, miss. Are you waiting for the morning stage?"

"Yes, I am." She nodded to the other man who also lifted his hat.

"Perhaps you'd like to come inside out of the chill."

"Thank you."

"You must be going to Pittsburgh. The stage leaves in about an hour." He glanced toward the lunch counter. "That coffee smells good. I'm glad Darcy woke up on time today." He extended an arm. "The waiting room's right over there. If you'd like breakfast I'm sure Darcy will accommodate you."

"Thank you again. Where do I get my ticket?"

The paunchy man answered her. "I'll have the booth open in a jiffy." He indicated a row of ticket booths near the lunch counter, then unlocked a narrow door and went inside to remove his coat and put on a gray jacket with the name of the stage company sewn on a pocket. He pulled on paper cuffs and fussed with something behind the grill. Two other men came in, and after surprised glances at Maura, entered the office and began to ready their own ticket booths.

"One way to Pittsburgh, miss?"

"Yes." She opened her reticule.

"That will be twenty-two dollars." He punched several holes in the ticket and slid it through the grill as she pushed the money to him.

She thanked him and went to the lunch counter. It was a long plank much like a bar, with a row of leather-covered stools bolted to the floor in front of it. It was still damp where it had been wiped clean. A youngish-looking man was working behind a partition, slicing something with a long knife. He saw her and nodded, "Be there in a minute, ma'am."

She sat on a stool and noted that the station was filling up. A drayman halted a team in front of the door to deliver several heavy boxes. Two yardmen loaded them on a hand-cart and rolled it away toward the rear. A gangly youth in overalls wandered in and took a seat at the counter with a quick, interested look in Maura's direction. She glanced at the big clock over the double doors of the waiting room. There was plenty of time before the stage. She ordered eggs, toast and coffee from the cheerful Darcy.

"Comin' right up, ma'am."

The delicious flavor of the coffee surprised her, and she drank greedily. As the chill from the night's adventures began to dissipate, she relaxed a little. Her gaze went to the window to search along the street for Duggan. He'd said he would watch until the stage departed, but she could find no sign of him. If he was there, he was well hidden.

Then her eye was taken by a tall, lean man of about thirty, very correctly dressed in a morning coat of dove gray and well-fitting trousers. A black boy trotted behind him with two heavy bags, his shoulders bent under the weight. The man was so handsome, and so startlingly different from the others in the station, it was impossible not to follow him with her gaze. At the window he bought a ticket. When he walked past Maura he smiled and touched the brim of his plantation hat in a courteous gesture before pushing the door into the waiting room.

She had seen and known a great many wealthy men because of her family's position, but none of them had the easy grace and charm so evident in this stranger's every movement. At first glance she had assumed him to be a business executive or a professional man, but as she studied him she had the feeling that he did not fit any mold her mind created.

Two other men entered and crossed to ask in loud voices for tickets to Pittsburgh. Each carried two heavy bags and she recognized them as traveling drummers. She had seen countless like them in various stores on Broadway ever since she had been a child. In line behind them was a man in a worn and wrinkled suit. His wife and two small children waited as he counted out the exact money for four tickets.

Maura finished her coffee and pushed the cup away. These people were to be her companions on the stage. She was glad for the simple blue gown and dark cloak that

129

would not draw too many stares and allowed her to blend with the crowd. She paid for the food and went into the waiting room to stand by a window facing the yard.

It was a square room with polished benches and a clock on the wall. Three theatrical posters were the only decorations. The benches were almost empty. The well-dressed man in the wide-brimmed hat stood by the last window. His luggage was piled behind him, and the boy sat on a suitcase. Maura knew he was watching her, but she kept her attention on the yard where several hostlers were examining the harness of a six-horse coach.

A man in blue uniform with brass buttons and a visored cap put his head into the waiting room. "Ten minutes till stage time." He closed the door.

She watched a driver climb to the box of the coach, sort the reins, and get the team moving at a walk. The carriage rumbled over the gravel and cinders and halted in front of the station door. One of the hostlers opened the waiting-room door. "Folks going to Pittsburgh, I'll take your stowing baggage."

The family had a number of valises and packages which they hurriedly placed outside. The black boy carried the gentleman's bags out, and when the man tossed him a coin, disappeared at a run. Maura went out as the luggage was packed into the boot. The agent held the door open and collected tickets.

"Allow me, miss . . ."

She turned as the man in the plantation hat offered his hand. His polite smile showed perfect white teeth. Maura gave him a fleeting smile as she let him take her hand and stepped up. She thought he released it reluctantly when she seated herself facing forward by the far window, but his face was impassive as he also helped the young mother and said a few words to the children. The coach rocked gently as they clambered aboard. Maura pulled her skirts aside as the woman slid beside her.

"I'm so glad we're finally getting started." The woman tugged at one of the children. "Sit down and be quiet. There'll be plenty to look at in a moment."

The man in the plantation hat took the place directly opposite Maura, and she felt his eyes on her. The woman's husband took one of the children on his lap. The two

130

drummers ran from the waiting room, each with two bags to be deposited in the boot. They climbed aboard and took seats, smiling and tipping their hats to the women.

"We's lucky the stage ain't filled to the brim," one said, "I seen it when you had to ride on top or be left behind."

Still grinning, the other said, "You travelin' alone, ma'am?"

"Yes," Maura acknowleged. Their stares made her uncomfortable, and she lifted her chin and looked away. She wanted to make it clear that she was not interested in their eager attentions. One averted his gaze and whispered to his companion. They were both lean, tanned young men, one with a ridiculously large nose, the other tow-headed with a sloping chin.

The uniformed man with the brass buttons leaned in. "Everybody set?"

There was a chorus of assent, and the agent slammed the door, then called, "Have a good trip, Zack. You can take 'er on out."

The driver shouted to the lead team, then the coach bucked and the iron tires gritted as they bumped into the road. Maura settled back and her eyes swept the street for a glimpse of Duggan, but he was nowhere to be seen.

Duggan shifted his weight and leaned against the brick wall of the hotel. The early-morning light did not penetrate the alley, and he knew he could not be observed from the stage station. He felt a melancholy ache when Maura appeared at a station window and gazed out as though searching for him. He longed to rush back and take her in his arms, but there was no sense in prolonging his pain. Maura would be safe with James, and he prayed that it would not be long before she could return to Meadowfield.

Each time he thought of the Turks, his blood boiled. He wished passionately that he had killed Braxton instead of leaving the job undone. It would insure that the swine never laid hands on Maura again! Thank God Lenore had not wasted any time in sending for him. If Braxton had succeeded in dragging Maura upstairs . . . he smothered his rage. He had enough troubles without bringing a murder charge on his head, despite the satisfaction it would give him to beat Braxton's brains out.

131

And Pelham Turk was no better. He'd made sure Maura had no means to fight him. The bastard would convert everything to his own name and leave Maura and James out in the cold unless they took quick action. Duggan worried again about why he had not heard from James.

The coach rattled around to the front of the station, blocking sight of Maura. He heard the driver call out and saw the passengers filing from the waiting room. With a quick glance along the street, he moved to where he had a view of the stage door just in time to see a man in a gray coat and a wide-brimmed hat take Maura's hand and help her into the coach. As she seated herself near the window, her profile caught the light and her hair glinted like a halo. She glanced out, and he pressed back into the shadows, though he was sure she could not pick him out of the gloom.

Ah, Maura, he thought. *You are going out of my life too soon, but I pray it will not be for long.* He sighed and savored the sweet memory of her surrender to him. He would never forget those gray, challenging eyes and the determined lift to her chin, nor the warmth of her flesh and her honeyed lips. He sighed as the hostler slammed the coach door and the driver shouted to the team. The stage rocked as it turned onto the street, and moments later it was out of sight.

Pelham Turk woke groggily. A pulse in his temple throbbed and his head was a heavy mass of dull pain. The stale taste of too much brandy lingered in his mouth.

He glared at the servant. "What the hell do you want?"

The valet spoke hesitantly. "You asked to be wakened when the police sergeant returned."

Pelham grunted. The events of the previous night came into focus. He struggled to sit up, but when the valet offered a helping hand, he shoved it away impatiently. "Lay out my clothes, damn it! Do you think I can greet callers in my nightshirt!"

The servant laid out dark trousers and a black brocade smoking jacket. When Pelham was dressed, the man handed him the malacca çane.

Downstairs, Pelham scowled at the burly sergeant who stood uncomfortably before the fireplace in the small parlor. Pelham knew instantly that the news was not good.

"Well?"

"I'm sorry, sir, Quinn was gone when we got to his room. We picked up his trail for a bit, but he lost us in the dark."

"And my stepdaughter?" He could not mask his impatience. Duggan Quinn was secondary now that Maura was gone.

"No sign of her, sir."

"Damn! She's been kidnapped, and you stand there like a fool telling me there's no sign of her! What kind of men do you have working for you?!" Pelham's cane thudded with a muffled staccato sound on the carpet.

The policeman cleared his throat. "No one saw Quinn take her into the rooming house and there was no sign of her there. We can't be certain he took her to his room at all."

"*I* am certain!" Pelham thundered. The policeman cringed at the force of his words. "If any harm comes to her, I'll see that you are held accountable!" The angry explosion made Pelham's head throb dangerously. He closed his eyes until the wave of pain passed. He spoke more quietly when he said, "You say you picked up his trail?"

"My men spotted two riders on a street not far from the rooming house. There were two horses missing from the stable, according to the landlord."

"Two? So Maura *was* with him!"

"My men had only a glimpse of the pair and couldn't tell if they were male or female. They eluded us in a matter of minutes. It might not even have been Quinn. . . ."

Pelham muttered a curse and thumped the cane again. He had half a dozen servants who'd seen Quinn and Maura leave this house, and he had Braxton's declaration that it was Quinn who'd beat him savagely. Less than two hours had elapsed before Pelham had the presence of mind to summon the sergeant from the precinct and send him after the pair. And this idiot was saying there was no trace of them! He glowered at the man.

"What is being done now?"

The sergeant seemed relieved to escape renewed attack. "We are asking at every train and stage station in the city. Every man on the force has a description of your daughter. If they try to leave the city, we'll find them."

Pelham was not convinced. "You questioned the maid, Lenore?"

He nodded. "She swears she knows nothing."

She was lying, Pelham was certain. Why else would she have been packing Maura's clothes last night? The stupid woman was not even afraid of the police, it seemed.

"Very well," Pelham said. "I want to be informed the moment you uncover any lead, is that clear?" He would go after Maura himself so there would be no opportunity for her to tell a story to the authorities.

"Yes, sir."

Pelham rose and limped from the room. Damn Braxton. This was his fault. If he hadn't gone after Maura in drunken lust, she'd still be here. Well, when she was back, Pelham would arrange the wedding immediately so that nothing she did would matter. In time, Braxton would tame her. If not, it would be her husband's worry, not his.

Upstairs he entered Braxton's bedroom and stared at the puffy, bruised face below the white swath of bandage. The doctor had given him a draught to make him oblivious to the pain, and he was snoring with a soft, guttural sound. On the table beside the bed, a small brown bottle contained another dose of the narcotic. Pelham picked it up and dropped it into his pocket.

CHAPTER SEVEN

The woman beside Maura clutched her husband's sleeve as the coach slewed around a corner and hit a rut.

"Oh, my goodness!" She looked at Maura apologetically. "I've never been on a stagecoach before."

"The horses are frisky, ma'am," the big-nosed drummer said. "They'll settle down directly."

"The damn driver is showin' off," the other commented. "These drivers is all the same. Why, some of 'em's so uppity they won't even talk t'you. Ain't that right, Harry?"

"You bet," Harry agreed, still looking at Maura.

They rode along a narrow, crowded street, where a hodge-podge of brick and wooden buildings shouldered for space near the river. Hoboken's shipping industry rivaled New York's, and there was speculation that the town would soon be chartered as a city. Already, dozens of factories had sprung up to produce the goods the community needed or that could be exported in trade. They passed a clattering foundry; despite the early hour, the smell of molten iron and the clang of hammers dominated the air. Workmen carrying lunch buckets hurried along the streets, heads bent against the brilliant sunrise. The coach horn blared, and the driver bawled at a pair who didn't move quickly enough to suit him.

The roadway was rough and the coach bounced on inadequate springs. Maura tried to settle herself on the leather seat and longed for the comfort of a Sullivan carriage. This was her first ride on a public stage, and it did not promise to be a pleasant trip. But she'd have to make the best of it.

She glanced at the woman beside her and smiled at the two children. The woman was not much older than Maura, but her face had already lost the bloom of youth and her hair was drawn back severely in a style easy to care for but not very becoming. There were tiny wrinkles at the corners of her eyes and she had a perpetual worried frown, even when she smiled. Maura was sure she did not realize it.

Her husband was busy pointing out things to the boy on his lap. The woman turned to Maura. "Have you been to Pittsburgh before?"

"No, this will be my first time." Maura felt the man in the gray coat glance at her. She kept her eyes on the woman.

"Mine too, though Sam has been. I've never lived anywhere but New Jersey. We had a farm. Goodness, I've never even been to New York City. Do you come from New York?"

"Yes."

The woman's glance swept over Maura's silk cloak. "I thought so." She smiled nervously. "We're going to live in Pittsburgh."

"I'm told it's a pleasant city."

"That's what Sam says." She seemed relieved. "Our name is Loganhall. I'm Stella."

"It's very nice to meet you, Stella. I'm Maura Sullivan." She wondered instantly if it had been wise to give her name, but it was already out. It seemed to mean nothing to anyone in the coach, which was reassuring.

"I'm Harry Judkins," one of the drummers said quickly, "and this here's Irving Robb. He's in ladies' ready-to-wear and I'm in shoes."

Everyone glanced at the tall man opposite Maura, who nodded pleasantly. "The name is Fontaine. A pleasure to meet you all." He lifted his hat. "Charmed, ladies."

"What do you do, Mr. Fontaine?" Mr. Loganhall asked.

Fontaine's voice was low and well modulated. "Do you hope to farm in Pennsylvania now, sir?"

"No, I'm done with farmin'." Loganhall did not notice his own question had been avoided.

Stella said eagerly, "Sam's brother lives there. He's found a place for us. Sam's to be a partner in a hardware emporium!" She glanced at her husband quickly as though afraid she'd said too much, then fussd with a ribbon in the little girl's hair.

"Excellent business," Fontaine said. He smiled at Maura.

"Do you expect to live in Pittsburgh, Miss Sullivan, or are you passing through?"

Maura hesitated. "I'll be staying for a while." She'd forgotten how interested people were in each other, how nosy. It would be noticeable if she avoided answering, but she had to be careful not to divulge too much. The Sullivan name was well known and often mentioned in the New York *Herald* and even Mr. Greeley's new *Tribune*. Patrick Sullivan's obituary had been a glowing tribute to one of New York's most prominent citizens. Only last week, the Sullivan regatta was written up on the society page, as were their Thanksgiving balls and other gala affairs each year. Until she was safely away, Maura dared not risk calling attention to herself, lest she make it too easy for Pelham to trace her. She glanced out the window. Farmhouses and red barns dotted the turnpike route, replacing the business and industrial buildings as the city fell behind.

Fontaine said, "I'd be happy to recommend a hotel, Miss Sullivan. I know Pittsburgh well."

"Thank you, but I'll be staying with relatives."

"That is convenient," Fontaine murmured.

"My brother," Maura said stiffly. She didn't care for Fontaine's lifted eyebrows, though his smile remained pleasant.

"Is he in business?" persisted Stella.

"Yes." Were they going to draw her out forever? She had no desire to pursue the subject, and she was uncomfortable under the stares of the drummers, who seemed to smile at some hidden joke. She knew it concerned her, and it irritated her to guess what they were thinking. They were on the road constantly and met all kinds of travelers. No doubt her traveling alone gave them a wrong impression. The same wondering look was in Fontaine's dark eyes.

The turnpike bent to the south and Maura studied the mountains in the distance as Stella chattered on. Maura only half listened. Stella Loganhall was the kind of woman settled in the placid, uneventful life offered by the half-dozen suitors whom Maura had spurned. No wonder her father had declared that no man was good enough for her. Her brow furrowed as she thought of her father's last jest that someday she'd find one who met her expectations.

What were her expectations? As she tried to define them,

Duggan Quinn intruded on her thoughts. He was the first to bring her alive and to kindle the fire of passion. He had also roused her temper more than once with his stubbornness and self-assurance. There were tender moments when she thought she loved him, but there were also times when her anger was proof that she did not. She had longed for excitement, yet when it came, it did so with overtones of calamity.

She thought about the factory fire and her mother's death. She would miss her mother; the loss would be an emptiness added to the void caused by her father's passing. Maura had shared herself and her dreams with her father, and from that had come a deep love and understanding. She wondered if there would ever be a man as good and kind for her to love.

She realized Stella was talking to her. With effort, Maura brought her attention back. "We'll be living on Fourth Street," Stella said. "Is your brother's business near there?"

"I'm not sure. I don't know the city. The address is on Chancery Lane."

"Pittsburgh is very large," Fontaine said. "The two streets are a considerable distance apart." The two drummers looked at him. Harry opened his mouth but closed it without saying anything.

Stella looked disappointed, but before she could pick up the thread of the conversation, the little girl claimed her attention.

"Do you travel a lot, Mr. Fontaine?" Sam Loganhall asked.

"Some, but not as much as these two gentlemen." He indicated the drummers.

Fontaine seemed to be smiling behind his grave façade. Maura let her gaze drift across him, but looked away as he spoke again.

"Pittsburgh is a city where a beautiful woman can find many things to amuse herself and while away the hours. There are tea gardens, theaters, riding paths—whatever suits your fancy."

Maura's eyes met his briefly, and she could not read his expression. His gaze slid to Stella, who was obviously entranced by his words. Even Stella's husband and the two drummers were fascinated as Fontaine went on to describe

138

places that were only names until he gave them character.

"I've been to Pittsburgh five times," Harry Judkins said. "Seems like we're talking about two different cities. I ain't seen nothing but smoke and dirt."

"You gotta admit they're building some right nice places since the fire back in '45," Robb said.

Harry shrugged carelessly. "Sure, and they been peeling Grant's Hill so's you can durn near see across from the Allegheny to the Monongahela. But I still ain't seen none of them fancy places Mr. Fontaine is talkin' about."

"That's because you hang out in saloons," Robb said. Everyone laughed.

"Gimme Philly anytime. Now there's a city with plenty to see and do." Harry nodded. "Wisht we were stoppin' there this trip."

The two drifted into a discussion of places they knew in Philadelphia. The others fell silent, listening or content with their own thoughts.

At midday the coach halted in the dusty yard of a tavern for a scheduled rest. "Ever'body out that wants to stretch," the driver bawled, jumping down from the box. He slammed back the door, and the passengers climbed down gratefully, glad to be able to walk about.

"Don't go fur," the driver said. He blew a quick toot on his horn and went to see to the horses. Two hostlers were bringing fresh animals, while others unhitched the teams. The driver finished his task and stomped into the tavern.

Maura turned as Fontaine spoke. "Shall we find ourselves a bit of lunch, Miss Sullivan? I'd be honored by your company."

"Thank you, Mr. Fontaine."

"My friends call me Beau. It's short for Beauregard." He bowed almost formally and took her arm to steer her toward the inn. He was so charming she could not take offense.

The tavern was small and crowded and smelled strongly of cabbage and cooked meat; the low ceiling was grimed with smoke. The two drummers were talking boisterously in the taproom, and from time to time, raucous laughter boomed. The Loganhalls gathered at one end of the serving room to find places at a long table scarred and cut with initials that marked countless travelers who had used it.

139

Fontaine steered Maura to the opposite end of the room.

He said lightly, "I'm sorry about the accommodations, but it's the best the house can afford." His engaging smile made light of the situation.

Maura took up the pleasant banter. "I'll think of it as a picnic."

"A wise decision." Fontaine studied the chalked menu on the wall. Maura saw him smile warmly at the serving girl who came to their table first, obviously attracted by the handsome traveler. The girl smiled boldly and stood closer to his shoulder than necessary. Fontaine gave no sign that he noticed as he asked Maura her preference. She ordered boiled beef, simple fare that the cook was unlikely to ruin. Fontaine related both orders to the girl, who brushed against his shoulder as she retreated.

"I deplore coach traveling," Fontaine said. "The train is much cleaner and faster. I've heard that rails will be laid the entire distance between New York and Pittsburgh by next year. Is your home in New York, Miss Sullivan?"

"Yes. Do you know the city?"

"I have just come from there as a matter of fact." He looked at her curiously. "I did not see you on the ferry."

Maura felt her throat catch. "I came across the river with friends."

"I see." He did not press the matter. "In which part of the city do you live?"

She hesitated, but it was difficult to ignore a direct question without seeming rude. "St. James Park."

"Ah, a pleasant neighborhood. Do you come from a large family?"

"No, very small." She saw him smile again, but she could not guess his thoughts. She searched her mind for a subject that would lead him away from the line of questioning he was pursuing. She was relieved when the girl brought their food.

"I've been in New York for several months," he said. "I enjoyed it, but I'll be glad to see Pittsburgh again. I have many friends and acquaintances there." When she did not reply, he added, "I'll be very happy to show you the city, Maura. May I call you Maura?"

Surprisingly, she found herself nodding. He rewarded her with a captivating grin. "And you must call me Beau. It's foolish to continue formalities among friends, don't you think?"

In spite of her determination to remain aloof from her fellow passengers, she nodded and returned his smile. Beau's pleasant manner made it easy to accept his overture of friendship.

The beef was tastier than she had dared hope. The spicy aroma filled her nostrils, and she concentrated on the plate. The serving girl brought a teapot, and Beau poured for each of them as he launched into a discussion of food and drink in New Orleans, another place he'd been. He'd spent years there, he said, and preferred it to New York and even Boston.

While he talked and ate, Beau studied Maura openly. Maura Sullivan, if that was her real name, was a beauty. He had known a great many women in his lifetime, but she was one of the most provocative, even though he could measure their acquaintance only in hours. Her striking beauty softened her boldness to something compelling rather than brassy. That she could so easily pass for a lady of position and breeding testified to the cleverness behind her studied manner. He'd known courtesans who graced the most distinguished drawing rooms, and even they could not match Maura's poised, innocent demeanor.

But Beau had seen the man who sat with her in the early-morning shadows of the stage depot in Hoboken, and who'd scurried off at the arrival of dawn's first light. And he'd seen their kiss. The man was not an uncle or brother wishing her *bon voyage*. Theirs had been an intimate, lingering kiss of passion. Beau wondered where they'd spent the night. Like as not, the man was a respected businessman who could not afford to have his assignations discovered, so he had taken Maura across the river. With dawn, he was on his way back to his home and business, and she was off to greener pastures. Or had she been paid to leave town? That, too, was possible. A wife too suspicious . . . a business associate double-crossed . . . Beau could not imagine Maura having any trouble replacing one lover with another.

When they finished lunch, Maura excused herself to seek the necessary. Beau wandered into the taproom where he bought half a dozen cheroots and ordered a whiskey from

141

the barman. He knocked the drink back quickly, then went out to the door to wait for Maura. When she appeared a few minutes later, he said, "The driver is still inside. Would you like to stroll a bit before he blows the horn?" He took her arm and they went down the steps into the yard. The coach was standing in the shade of the building, the horses drowsing while two men squatted near the boot talking in low tones. Beau turned toward the gate. Maura pulled the silk cloak around her shoulders against the sudden gust of breeze.

"Tell me about your family," Beau said pleasantly.

"My family?" She looked at him in surprise.

"You have a small one, I believe you said. One brother, no sisters?"

How readily he stored bits of conversation to piece together facts! "Yes, just the two of us."

"And he is in business in Pittsburgh, yet you have never gone to see him before. I'm sure he's looking forward to your visit. What line is he in?"

She let out her breath. "Does it matter?" Why was he so persistent?

He laughed with an engaging grin. "I was only making conversation. You've told me so little about yourself, I have to search for a subject. Are you always so reticent, or is it just your brother's occupation you don't want to discuss?"

Maura couldn't take offense at his banter. She found herself smiling. "He is in the boat business."

"I see. I imagine that would take a bit of capital to get started." Beau's face was shadowed under the wide-brimmed hat.

"Yes, my—" She stopped, then took a breath. How easily he coaxed more information from her than she intended to reveal. She admonished him gently. "Must you pry, Mr. Fontaine?"

"Forgive me. I meant no harm." His dark eyes held a spark of laughter, though his face was properly solemn.

"Why do we always talk about me?" Maura asked. "Tell me about yourself, Mr. Fontaine. What takes you to Pittsburgh?"

He regarded her with a cool, dark gaze. "Business. I'm in investments and real estate. I have clients in the Pitts-

142

burgh area and find it prudent to visit them from time to time. Besides, I enjoy a change of scene. I'm not a man to settle and put down roots like Loganhall and his hardware store."

"Do you disapprove of roots?" Maura asked pertly.

"Not at all. Every man to his own taste." He glanced at her. "What are your tastes in the matter, Maura?"

There was an intimacy in his voice that made her vaguely uncomfortable, yet when she looked at him, his expression was guileless.

"I have always had roots."

He smiled. It was the answer he had expected, though probably not the truth. She was amusing herself by telling him about a mythical brother in Pittsburgh. Probably it was her most recent lover who was actually a boatbuilder. She was inventing lies with the smoothness of long practice, but he was used to equivocation. Didn't all men lie when they sat at a poker table? Dealing with them, Beau had learned to sift the truth from pretense. This woman was skirting the truth, or else why would she be traveling alone without a snip of baggage? She was running from something.

They halted across the road from the tavern. He studied her exquisite profile as she gazed at the sunlight-hazed hills. The swaying trees dappled the ground with shade, and a swarm of large brown birds came swooping from an aerie to gossip and argue above their heads. Beau spied the driver emerging from the tavern. The man reached for his horn.

"I expect we'd better go back."

The Loganhalls were first into the coach; both children were yawning and irritable. Maura sat with Beau once again across from her. The two drummers ran from the inn at the last moment, just as the driver was ready to slap the reins.

Maura pulled the shade partway down. The window had no glass, and dust sifted in. She could see it in the folds of her dress and at times it gritted between her teeth as clouds boiled up behind the wheels. She leaned back as the drummers encouraged Beau to discuss various cities they knew.

By midafternoon, the road became steep. The horses strained on the grades, and the downhill runs were terrifying when the highway fell away sharply to an incredibly green valley below. The thin thread of a river wound among verdant woods and splashed over rocks. Maura's eyes were weighted with an aching tiredness. She'd had little sleep before Braxton burst in on her, and less than that on the hard floor of Duggan's room. She closed her eyes and savored the warm memory of Duggan holding her and loving her gently. As the conversation dwindled, she drifted into sleep. Even the jolting and swaying of the coach did not waken her. When at last she opened her eyes, several hours later, the sky had turned mauve with sunset and they were only a short distance from the inn at Norristown where they would spend the night.

CHAPTER EIGHT

Duggan took a devious route from the stage office back to the waterfront. It would be foolhardy to take chances now. The fewer people who saw him, the fewer there would be to recall his face.

He stood at the forward railing of the squat, broad-beamed ferryboat with his face turned to the spray-laden breeze. The other passengers were mostly workmen headed for the docks of New York. Duggan's dark trousers and coat were not out of place, and no one spared him more than a casual glance. When the ferry bumped into its slip, Duggan hurried away in the rush of departing people.

The neighborhood near the waterfront was familiar to him. It was one where men minded their own affairs and asked no questions. The high-stooped, narrow-windowed brownstone houses bore the indelible stamp of poverty. Duggan glanced up as the curtains at a window pulled back. A young girl in a nightdress raised the sash. Seeing Duggan, she stared boldly. He touched his cap and smiled without slowing his stride.

Near the corner, he went up the steps of a house and pushed open the heavy carved doors. The dark hall smelled of sweat and garbage. A narrow flight of stairs hugged one wall. Duggan went up, past the first two landings to the top. The hall had only a cracked skylight to dispel the gloom. He tapped softly at a door.

There were faint sounds inside. The door eased open a crack, and a face peered out. Then the door was flung open.

"Duggan!" The little man grabbed Duggan's arm and pulled him inside. His gaze swept the hall momentarily before he shut the door. "You're a sight for sore eyes!"

145

"It's been a long time, Sean."

The little man shook his head. "Aye, I've missed you, but I know how busy you're kept. What brings you here before workin' hours of a mornin'?"

"There are a few laddies watching my regular haunts in hopes of catching me unawares," Duggan said with a wink. "I've a need to stay out of sight for a while."

"You can stay here as long as you want," Sean said quickly. "Name any favor I can do for you."

Duggan clapped a hand to his friend's shoulder. Sean was a wizened gnome, barely reaching as high as his own chest.

"There's never been a time I couldn't count on you, Sean. If a man could have only one friend in this world, I'd choose you."

Sean beamed, then peered at Duggan. "Is it the law you're running from?"

"In a manner of speaking. But what kind of hospitality is it to keep a friend standing at the door and not offer him a cup o' tea?"

Sean's head bobbed and he scuttled across the room. He scooped up the kettle and shook it, listening with head cocked. Satisfied it was full enough, he set it on a small gas ring, then struck a sulfur and held it close. Blue flame sprang up around the kettle, and Sean searched for cups among the litter on a table.

Duggan sat on the cot, pushing aside the rumpled blanket. "Have you heard from Kerry?"

Duggan was at ease in the untidy room. His friendship with Sean and his younger brother Kerry was one of understanding and trust. They'd met on a seamy waterfront dock where, as raw immigrants, they'd been beset by a gang of thugs bent on stealing their meager purses and the clothes off their backs—except that Kerry and Duggan were not the stupid country louts they'd been mistaken for. The two fought like lions to protect the older, crippled Sean, and they made short work of their attackers.

Sean dumped soggy leaves from a teapot and poured water to rinse it. "He's still in Washington City. And he's still asking for trouble. He'll never learn to keep his mouth shut and control his temper." He emptied the pot into a sink piled with dirty dishes, then spooned fresh tea from a tin.

Duggan said, "Kerry's a good lad. He stands up for what he believes is right. The world can do with more like him."

"He thinks everything can be settled with shouting or with his fists."

Duggan grinned. "The same's been said of me."

Sean shook his head. "You held your tongue and your job when Turk made his changes. Kerry said his piece— and he got himself fired, and Turk saw to it he couldn't get another job here. If he's not careful, he'll be booted out of Washington as well."

Duggan gave Sean a reproving look. "He's only asking for a union that will put an end to the unfair practices used by men like Turk."

"Asking?" Sean scowled. "No, he's demanding—and he's not making himself very popular in the doing. They're calling him an agitator."

"Maybe it's come time to demand. . . ."

The kettle hissed, and Sean poured the boiling water. As the tea steeped, he regarded Duggan quizzically. "You didn't come to pass the time o' day about Kerry. I thought your days o' brawlin' were past. What is it this time?"

Duggan winked. "The honor of a beautiful Irish lass."

A grin split Sean's face and he clucked. "I might ha' known." He waited for Duggan to go on.

"I have to leave New York for a while," Duggan said. "I need help arranging it."

Sean nodded.

"I want to go by railroad."

"Tim McCleary works in the yards over at Charles Street. He can put you aboard the freight car of yer choice, lad."

Duggan shook his head. "I want to travel by coach." He reached into his pocket and counted several bills onto the gray blanket. "*Two* tickets to Boston on the Harnden Railway Express. Wait until the office is fairly crowded so people will notice you and remember your destination."

Sean looked surprised.

Duggan winked. "And if you can manage to mention in the hearing of others that you're buying the tickets for your old friend Duggan Quinn, it would help."

Sean's surprise gave way to a wide grin. "Am I to say who will use the second ticket?"

"Hint that it's a lady. You know nothing more."

Sean poured the tea. "If the law is lookin' for you, I may be followed from the station."

Duggan shrugged. "If they question you, say only that I said I'd return for the tickets here."

Sean sipped the steaming tea. "And what about the tickets?"

"On your way back, stop for a beer at Paddy's Tavern on Broadway. Slip the tickets under a dollar bill as you buy a round of drinks for a few friends. I'll pick them up there."

"It's done," Sean said. "Now drink yer tea and make yerself comfortable."

The hot tea chased the chill Duggan had felt since leaving Maura. "I cannot stay," he told Sean. "There's someone I must see before I leave. One more thing: I'll need to know exactly what time the trains depart. I'm told Harnden has a schedule chalked on a board."

Sean puckered his brow. "The first is at six-thirty— ye've already missed that one. There's another at eleven and one at four o'clock. They leave on time unless the weather is bad. That's not likely to be a problem today."

Duggan cocked an eyebrow, amazed at his friend's convenient knowledge.

Sean grinned. "Tim McCleary sets store by his knowledge o' schedules. I've heard him recite them so often, I know them by heart."

"Buy Tim a beer on me, then," Duggan said with a grin. He finished the tea and put the cup aside.

"Will it be long until I see you again?" Sean wanted to know.

"If all goes well, it will be only a few weeks."

Sean extended a gnarled hand, which Duggan grasped. They said no more as Sean opened the door, peered along the hall, then let his friend out.

When Duggan reached the quiet, elegant neighborhood near Lafayette Place, he slowed his pace and stayed close to the high hedges surrounding the stately homes. Theodore Rothingwell's house was set well back from the street, with an iron fence bordered by clumps of white birch and evergreens. Rothingwell had been with the Sullivan Company a long time, and there was little he did not know of its operation. He hadn't liked the change of management under Pelham Turk, but he was too weak a man to risk losing his job by openly voicing an opinion. His marriage to an ambitious woman fifteen years younger than himself kept him on the edge of debt, so the regularity of his pay envelope was more important than from whom it came. Still, he had liked Patrick Sullivan. Because of that, Rothingwell often spoke at home about Pelham Turk's troubling decisions.

When Lacy came to Duggan's room last night, she'd overheard a conversation between her aunt and uncle. It ended abruptly when she entered the room, but she was sure it boded trouble for Duggan. She had come to warn him—and to flirt prettily as she scolded him for not calling her since the picnic. She mentioned, too, that there was something concerning Maura that might interest him. Before he could coax more information from her, the message from Lenore had come unexpectedly, and Duggan had raced out.

Now, Lacy's crumpled note was in his pocket. If there was a chance that her information might help him fight Turk on Maura's behalf, he had to know it.

He slipped around a corner where a bed of late chrysanthemums provided a riot of color. He glanced toward the house, though he knew he could not be seen from the windows. At the rear gate, which was used by servants and tradesmen, he slipped the latch and hurried to tap on the back door. A maid appeared.

He waited impatiently, standing where he was shielded by a laurel bush, while the maid delivered his message to Lacy. A few minutes later, he was shown into the morning room.

Lacy was seated in a wing chair near the window The curtains were drawn back, and sunlight splashing through the pane made her hair look like spun gold. She wore a yellow gown with a full skirt and a wide ruffle at the bottom. The bodice was pale lace with a wedge-shaped neckline that was kept from being indecorous by a brown silk rose tucked between her breasts. The sleeves were tight at the top, then billowed over snug cuffs. A brown silk sash with long streamers accented her waist. She had chosen the

149

dress and the setting with care, and with full knowledge that she was strikingly beautiful. The gown whispered as she rose.

"I knew you would come!" She flung herself into his arms and lifted her lips for a kiss. When he gave it perfunctorily, she frowned. "Perhaps I shall not forgive you for your dreadful behavior last night if that's the greeting I must satisfy myself with this morning!" She pouted prettily.

He grinned. "Would you have me ravish you while the servants watch?"

She tossed her blond curls. "It would be preferable to such a chaste, brotherly kiss!"

"Your eyes are the color of amber when you are angry."

"You are impossible!" But she was smiling. She grasped his hand and pulled him toward a brocaded sofa.

"Your note promised news."

"Is that the only reason you came?"

"If the news concerns my welfare, it may affect the time we can spend together—now or in the future." He looked at her somberly.

She hesitated, then abandoned the coy game. "Aunt Nancy was reluctant to tell me details, since she knows that I've been seeing you, and Braxton too, lately." Lacy's eyes flashed with momentary triumph, and Duggan knew he was supposed to be jealous. When he scowled dutifully, she went on. "Uncle Theodore has learned that Pelham is drawing up formal charges against you for assault and arson! Braxton swears that you swung the lantern that caused the fire in the factory."

"It sounds like the kind of thing he would say."

"You're not surprised?"

He shrugged. "Only that he waited this long. You said there was something about Maura—?"

Lacy's eyes smoldered. "I believe you came out of concern for her, not any desire to see me!" She lifted her chin and turned away from him.

Duggan had experienced her bouts of temper, and he had little patience with them. He also knew that to spar with her was a waste of time. The quickest way to bring her out of her snit was to pretend he did not care. He rose, and she jumped up.

"Don't go—I'm sorry. But I am a woman, after all. It's

150

hardly flattering to know that a man prefers someone else's company. There, I'm being unfair again. It was Maura who demanded to ride with you the day of the regatta. You could scarcely refuse." Smiling, Lacy drew him back to the sofa. "Besides, it would seem that Miss Sullivan is about to be married and will be forced to abandon her flirtations with every man who crosses her path."

Duggan could not hide his astonishment. His blue eyes searched Lacy's face for a sign that she was lying, but she was confident and delighted with the truth.

"Who is she to wed?" he said carefully.

"Braxton Turk. Uncle Theodore was told in the strictest confidence. With Mrs. Turk's death, there will have to be a suitable mourning period before the announcement can be made."

"Pelham Turk told him this?"

"Yes." She fussed with the brown sash, smoothing it over the daffodil-colored skirt. "I must say, the way Braxton was carrying on the day of the regatta, one would hardly think he was practically engaged. But I suppose a man must sow the last of his wild oats before he settles into marriage."

Duggan could not forget the look of loathing on Maura's face as they skirted Braxton's body in the hall at Meadowfield last night. Nor could he forget the warm delight of her in *his* arms, the yielding willingness with which she had clung to him. If Pelham was announcing Maura's engagement to his son, it was without her consent or knowledge, Duggan was certain. It was to be a wedding of convenience for Pelham and his aspirations to gain total control of the Sullivan Company.

"Duggan?" Lacy's voice was petulant, and he realized that she had been talking. When he looked at her, she said, "I haven't a thing in the world to do all day. Everyone is still moping about the fire and Mrs. Turk's funeral. Really, there hasn't been a bit of laughter in this house for days! Will you take me for a ride? I cannot bear this mausoleum another moment!"

A refusal sprang to his lips, but it was quickly silenced as an idea began to form. He had hoped to convince the police that Maura was traveling with him to Boston by buying two tickets. How much better actually to have a companion! Someone who would be remembered, and who might pass for Maura if only vague questions were asked.

"As a matter of fact," he said, "I have some business that takes me to Peekskill today. I was planning to travel by the new Harnden Railroad Express. I've heard they've added passenger cars that are excellently appointed and the latest fashion in travel comfort. Would you like to go along with me?"

"I would love it!" Her eyes danced.

"My business will only take an hour or so. We can find a pleasant place to lunch, then hire a carriage to drive back."

"Oh, Duggan, it sounds wonderful! I'll run up and get my cloak—"

"There's something I must do first," he said quickly. "And with your uncle involved in drawing up warrants against me, it might be better if we met at the Harnden station. You know where it is?"

She nodded.

"The train leaves at eleven. If I come at the last minute, don't worry. I'm not about to miss the train when I have the chance to spend an entire day with you."

Lacy's pink tongue showed at her lips. "I'll be there."

He squeezed her hands. "It would be prudent to wear a bonnet and cloak, unless you want every ruffian in the station crowding around. I would hate to miss the train because I was forced to knock the teeth from a lot of leering smiles."

Lacy laughed softly. "You would do that on my account?"

"I would, but I hope it's not necessary today. There isn't another train until late afternoon, and we would lose precious time."

She tried to draw him into an embrace, but he released himself gently. "It would be best for you to arrive as close to departure time as possible. Wait near the boarding platform, and I will swoop you up and whisk you aboard."

"You make it sound very romantic. . . ."

"You put romantic notions in a man's mind."

She smiled, pleased with his return to the ensnaring fold of her charm. "I will remind you of those words later today."

Grinning, he took his leave as she blew him a kiss from the tips of her fingers.

The locomotive belched smoke, and a misty cloud of steam spurted into the hazy autumn morning. Freight doors slammed and bolts were fastened. The whistle screamed.

Duggan was hidden behind a cluster of carts piled with crates. He'd been watching the station for some time. It was bustling with activity, passengers arriving and freight being loaded. Duggan studied those milling about the station, counting men in railroad uniforms and not surprised when the number grew. Two men dressed in dark suits had arrived without baggage more than an hour earlier. They conferred briefly with the stationmaster, then disappeared into his office. Ten minutes later they emerged wearing peaked caps with the railroad insignia.

Now one of them was patrolling the length of the train as though inspecting the wheels and tracks. The other was standing on the rear platform of the last passenger coach. The conductor hovered behind him, obviously unwilling to entrust his duties to anyone, regardless of his authority.

A carriage rattled to a halt on the road. When the door opened, Lacy stepped down, pushed money into the driver's hand, then hurried across the platform. Duggan grinned. The bright dress was covered by a brown fitted coat with fur at the collar and hem. She also wore a wide-brimmed hat with a veil that covered her face and tied under her chin.

The conductor leaned out to look along the station. He had already started to signal the engineer when he saw Lacy hurrying toward the train. Duggan waited until she was abreast of his hiding place, then stepped out.

"Perfect timing," he said over the piercing sound of the steam and the clank of metal as the wheels began to turn. Before she could answer, he was lifting her so the conductor could pull her aboard. The train was picking up speed as Duggan jumped onto the step. The detective squeezed past and avoided looking at Duggan as he tried to attract the attention of his partner, sure now that he had their man cornered. The conductor opened the coach door and ush-

153

ered Lacy inside. Duggan stood a moment, brushing imaginary cinders from his coat. The detective grabbed the rail and gave a hand to the man running alongside the train. Duggan turned abruptly and planted a swift kick on the detective's backside. The startled man fell forward, arms waving. The other could only spread his arms and break the man's fall as the two tumbled to the ground. There was a mad scramble as they untangled themselves and ran after the coach, but they were too late. The train had gathered enough speed to outdistance them easily. Grinning, Duggan opened the door and entered the coach. He slid into the seat beside Lacy and fished for the tickets.

"And now," he said when the conductor finally left, "we have the rest of the day ahead of us."

"I have not forgotten your promise of romance, Duggan," she said softly. Her lashes swept her cheek as she glanced at him sidelong. "There is no need for us to leave Peekskill until late."

He looked askance. "What would your aunt say to your arriving home in the middle of the night? Or to your spending the day with a fugitive, for that matter?"

"Aunt Nancy does not know I'm with you."

"You lied to her?" he teased with a mocking look.

"I avoided the truth. If I were to tell my aunt everything I do, I would have been sent home long ago." Her smile was intimate and inviting.

Duggan had been with her often enough to know that she was on equal terms with lies or truth as her fancy struck or need dictated. At first he'd found her amusing, but he had long ago decided she was not a woman he would wed, despite her efforts to coax him in that direction. Since the day of the picnic, he had had thoughts for no one but Maura. A twinge of guilt assailed him for taking advantage of Lacy's eagerness, but it could not be helped. As he glanced around the coach, he was glad to see it was filled. The Harnden Express was one of the most popular trains going north. Passengers would be getting off and on at every stop, but the conductor would remember that their tickets were to Boston.

Lacy settled cozily beside him and chattered about some of the things she hoped they'd see in Peekskill. He listened, smiling and nodding from time to time as he let her ramble. His greatest worry was that the police would wire ahead and try to intercept the train at one of the early stops. The longer he could keep them believing it was Maura Sullivan at his side, the safer for her.

His peace was short-lived. As the train neared Yonkers, Duggan glimpsed a police wagon, drawn by two magnificent bay horses, racing toward the station. Quickly, he drew an envelope from his pocket and pressed it into Lacy's hand.

"What is it—?"

"Keep it," he said without explanation. It contained enough money for her return ticket, a farsighted precaution he'd taken in case of just such an emergency. He smiled reassuringly at Lacy's puzzled look, and patted her hand. "Wait here."

"Where are you going?!"

He did not answer, but hurried the length of the car to the rear platform. A tall, portly man was standing at the rail puffing a black cigar. He looked up genially.

"'Morning, friend. A pleasant trip. You going all the way to Boston?"

Duggan cursed the luck that put a witness to his hasty departure. But there was no time to lose. He squeezed past and descended the step on the side of the train away from the platform.

"Hey—!" The portly man looked as though his fellow traveler had gone mad. The train was still moving, although it was slowing as it neared the station.

Duggan flexed his knees, released the rail and leaped out. He hit hard and rolled sideways, tucking his arms and head close to his chest. Cinders bit through his clothing, and he felt the sharp edge of a rock cut his knee. Then he was up and running across the right-of-way, into an open field, toward a vista of golden-leafed birches. The ground sloped sharply downward, a disadvantage, since anyone on the train would be able to follow his progress clearly. The rumble of the wheels eased, then faded until there was only the persistent chug of the steam vents.

Then a shout went up. "There he is!"

Duggan did not slow down or look back. Gaining the trees would give some cover. A moment later he plunged into a dense grove of mulberry. He forged ahead as the

155

cool greenness closed around him. He couldn't see any break in the foliage ahead, and he prayed the woods were deep and thick. It would not take long for the police to organize a search.

Damp leaves were a carpet underfoot. Except for the crackle of twigs, he made his way quietly. After several minutes, he paused, holding his breath to listen. There was no mistaking the shouting progress of the men who were after him. The sounds came from several directions—they were trying to surround him. He began walking more slowly. They could close a ring and squeeze him in it unless he found a bit of the circle left unguarded. He momentarily considered doubling back toward the railroad tracks. It would be unexpected, but by now everyone on the train would be gawking and watching the search. It would be impossible to slip through unnoticed.

He came to the edge of the woods and ducked behind a thick oak bole to survey the countryside. Before him was a field scattered with dry cornstalks that lay every which way on the dark, moist earth. He could see a fence in the distance and, beyond it, the pointed roof of a barn.

He skirted the woods just within the fringe of brush so he could keep a sharp watch for his pursuers. If they'd gone around both sides of the copse, they might converge on this spot soon. He moved as fast as he dared until he came over a small rise. He halted abruptly. Near the porch of a weatherbeaten house, a man was climbing into a wagon. He slapped the reins, and the gray mare moved down the lane slowly. Duggan watched until it reached the road, then he raced across the clearing.

The barn smelled of dung and sweet hay. Sunlight filtered through cracks in the walls, and dust danced in the shafts of light. There were several empty animal stalls and a hay loft piled high with a recently harvested crop. A ladder nailed to a support beam led up to it. On a peg hung a dusty jacket.

Grabbing the jacket, Duggan climbed quickly to the loft. The air was hot, and the dust that rose from the disturbed hay made him wrinkle his nose so he wouldn't sneeze. He crawled toward the loft doors that looked out across the yard. Lying flat, he peered about.

The wagon was out of sight. The narrow road stretched

past a pasture where a dozen cows grazed and lost itself in the golden sea of a grain field. Duggan studied the woods. A fly droned and settled on his hand, but he did not move. He saw a flutter of motion in the trees, then a policeman emerged from the woods. Two others came directly behind him. One of them looked toward the barn. A moment later, the man was crossing the clearing with a shotgun in the crook of his arm.

Duggan scuttled crablike away from the doors. Pulling on the jacket, he rumpled his hair and smudged his face with his grimy hands. Then he grabbed a pitchfork from a rafter and began to toss hay down to the animal stalls.

"Hey! You up there!"

Duggan paused with a forkful of hay and peered over the top of the ladder.

"Huh? Who're you? What you doin' here?" He frowned and rubbed a hand across his chin.

"You been here long?" the man with the shotgun asked.

Duggan rubbed his chin slowly. "Been working here 'bout a month now." He hoped the man was not personally acquainted with the farmer.

"Damn it! I mean have you been here in that loft all morning?"

"Only since I finished my other chores. Somethin' wrong? You the police, ain't you?" He pretended to study the uniform.

"Yes, and you'd better give me some straight answers now. You seen anybody don't belong around these parts?"

"This morning?"

"Yes, of course, this morning, you idiot!"

Duggan scratched his temple. "One fella come outta the woods little bit ago."

"Where'd he go?!" The tall man almost danced with excitement.

"What's he done?"

"Damn it! Where'd he go?!"

Duggan shrugged. "The wagon was just going down the lane. He hopped on the back."

"Charlie Evans took him to town?"

Duggan was relieved he had not tried to guess at a name for his absent host. "Dunno. Saw them talking, but the wagon didn't stop. What's he done?"

157

The policeman didn't bother to answer as he turned and ran out. He shouted to his companions who were still circling the woods, pointing toward the road and gesturing. The others seemed to understand. Someone blew sharply on a whistle. There was a rush of activity as men appeared from the woods and orders were shouted back and forth. The man near the barn set out at a brisk walk toward the road. Those at the woods cut across the field and were lost to sight.

Duggan scrambled down the ladder, hung up the jacket and slipped from the barn. Grinning, he headed in the opposite direction.

CHAPTER NINE

The inn at Norristown was larger and better appointed than the small country place where the stage had stopped for the noon meal. It was in the heart of town, on a broad street lighted by gas lamps at the corners. The driver blew a blast to announce their arrival as the coach rumbled into the yard and pulled up by the side door. Two husky lads ran to unload baggage, and the passengers climbed out stiffly.

Maura's head ached and she was tired, despite the nap. She wanted nothing so much as a hot bath and a change of clothes, but she knew the chances of getting either were slim. The fact that she had no baggage was looked on as suspicious. The landlord glowered and muttered until Beau took him aside and talked with him. Maura saw the tableau but was too tired to care. She wanted only for the matter to be settled.

"I want a room alone," she told the clerk. He looked aghast. "I insist." She fixed him with a steely gaze. "And I want a bath."

"Really, miss, may I remind you that you are only staying the night. The bath is reserved a full day in advance. Arrangements cannot be changed at the last moment."

Maura glared at him. He was a fussy, skinny man with spectacles and a prim mouth. "Damn your arrangements!" she said.

His eyes popped wide. "The tub has been spoken for. I cannot change that. You'll have to do without. It does happen that I can give you a single room. Please sign the register." He swung the book around and she took the proffered pen. Half a victory was better than total defeat.

The room was at the rear of the second floor. It was a

159

tiny cubicle with a narrow bed, a washstand with basin and pitcher, and a lamp. There was one straight-backed chair under a minuscule window with yellowed curtains. As she entered, a maid came with a bucket and poured hot water into the pitcher. She was a big farm girl with round eyes and arms like a wrestler.

Maura gave her a coin from the pouch in her reticule. "Come back in ten minutes with more hot water."

The girl pocketed the coin with a smile, and nodded. "Yes'm."

In the lamplight, Maura surveyed the room, determined not to be depressed by its meagerness. She was a long way from home. For the time being, she had to put aside her notion of comfort as she had always known it. She undressed down to her chemise and began to wash.

The girl returned and poured out the cold water before filling the basin with steaming fresh. "I got it hotter this time, miss."

"Thank you." Maura rewarded her with a smile. When she was gone, Maura stripped naked and quickly finished her bath, then dried with the large, soft bath blanket the girl had left. It was chilly in the room, and she slipped into her underclothes again as goose bumps raised on her flesh. She laid the blue chambray dress on the bed and brushed it with the wadded-up towel. It looked only slightly better, but it was the best she could do. Next she used the towel to brush the heavy layer of dust from her shoes. She combed her hair, dressed as carefully as possible, and went downstairs.

The common room had a beamed ceiling and a massive stone fireplace at one end. Lanterns that hung on hooks along the side walls gave off the smell of hot oil to mingle with that of cooked food. As she entered, Beau came toward her.

"I was beginning to think you'd retired without supper." He smiled and indicated a small table. "Come sit with me."

She allowed him to seat her. He'd changed his shirt and coat, and the faint stubble of beard that had blued his chin was gone.

"The food is quite good," he said. "The chef cannot provide us with *poulet en croûte,* but his striped bass is completely digestible." He signaled a waiter. "A wineglass for the lady."

"On your recommendation, I'll try the bass." His light tone put her at ease and made some of her weariness vanish. She buttered half of a hot bun. "You've already finished. You mustn't let me detain you."

"On the contrary, I apologize for not waiting," he said with a lazy smile. "And I assure you, I have no pressing matters in Norristown to take me away from such charming company." The waiter brought a glass, and Beau poured wine from a tall bottle. "This is palatable stuff for this part of the country, but I fear Americans will never become appreciative wine drinkers." He lifted his glass. "To the most beautiful woman in the inn."

"Flattery runs away with you."

"I speak the deepest truth." He leaned forward earnestly. "And if you notice the glances your presence evokes, you'll know it."

She sipped the wine. Any woman liked to hear such compliments, and she was no exception. She looked around to find the eyes of several men on her. Perhaps Beau was right, but then she was only one of three women in the room. Stella and a stout matron in a baggy dress were not much competition.

As she ate her supper, Beau ordered another bottle of wine, once again deploring its quality, but drinking it with relish. The two drummers were laughing and drinking at a nearby table with two other men. Once she thought she heard her name mentioned, but she told herself that was ridiculous and she did not look around.

The fish was quite tasty, but she could not finish it. Her weariness returned in full force, and her eyes grew heavy in the warm, stuffy room. So much had happened in the past few days; the mental strain was as great as the physical.

Beau pleaded with her to stay to finish the bottle of wine with him, but she refused. "Tomorrow will be another long day, Mr. Fontaine."

"I forbid you to call me that." He scowled over an enchanting smile.

She laughed softly. "Then good night, Beau. I'm sure you need a bed as much as I do."

161

His dark eyes were momentarily puzzled. He smiled curiously. "You're not like any woman I know, Maura. . . ."

She bid him goodnight again and went upstairs. Strange, she'd thought similarly of him. She could not fit him into any slot or mold. He was urbane, charming, and quite the gentleman, yet unlike any of the well-brought-up men she'd known all her life.

She put him from her mind as she dropped to the chair in her room and pulled off the black kid shoes. She rubbed her stiff, cramped feet. If only she could call Lenore and order a deep basin of steaming water! She sighed. No good dreaming idly.

She unbuttoned the blue chambray. Despite the brushing, it was not clean. The thought of putting it on again in the morning repelled her, but she had no choice. She hung the dress carefully over the chair. When she reached Pittsburgh, she would shop for a wardrobe to tide her over until she returned to Meadowfield and her own life. How good it would be to see James and have him to talk with! Never before in her life had she felt so alone.

Clad in her chemise, she blew out the lamp and crawled into bed. The sheets were icy, and she rubbed her flesh to warm herself. The window showed a glimpse of the moon's cold disk as it slid behind the branches of a tree. The view turned her thoughts to Duggan and the frantic ride they'd made across the city by moonlight. Was it only twenty-four hours ago? She hugged her arms to her breasts and felt a delicious shiver of pleasure as she recalled Duggan's strong arms around her, the power of his maleness claiming her. But when she was with Duggan, she was not in control of her emotions, and the thought was frightening. He swept aside her protests as easily as he brushed tendrils of hair from her cheek. All her resolve fled under the expert caresses he lavished on her flesh, and she was lost in sensuous pleasure. Yet she was still as uncertain of his feelings as she was of her own. That afternoon in the solitude of the clearing on the riverbank, he'd said he could love her. She thought it foolishness at the time and made light of it. They hardly knew each other. She had not been able to comprehend the physical attraction that swept them into intimacy. She hadn't been ready to speak of love—or anything else.

Yet the second time they lay together, the joy was no

162

less, even though the interlude had not been followed by declarations of love. They had talked only of the danger surrounding them and her flight from New York. Necessary, of course, but hardly romantic. Still, he'd kissed her with fervor at the stagecoach station before he vanished into the shadows, and he'd been more worried about her safety than his own. She sighed, wondering where he was now. She closed her eyes as weariness drugged her brain until she was unable to hold a thought. The sounds from the common room below became indistinct. The walls were not thick enough to keep out the noises from other rooms along the corridor, but her mind blanked them out. Any other time, the lumpy, hard mattress and unfamiliar surroundings might have made her restless, but she drifted quickly into sleep.

Maura half roused from deep slumber, struggling with wakefulness before letting it slip away. The warm cocoon of sleep was comforting, and she did not want to be released from it. She dreamed and burrowed deeper into a pleasant fantasy of arms slipping about her, a lean male body drawing close. Hands caressed her flesh, pushed down the thin chemise and teased her breasts. She sighed in the dream and opened her thighs to a tender touch.

Consciousness came abruptly and frighteningly. It was not a dream! Someone was beside her in the bed, touching her intimately and expectantly. She pushed savagely at the head nestled at her bosom. She pummeled her fists at the man and opened her mouth to scream. The head jerked up abruptly and there was a startled exclamation.

"What—?! Maura, for God's sake—"

Beau Fontaine! Maura was so surprised that for a moment she fell back. Against the pale glow of the moon at the window, she saw his smile as his lips moved over her. His tongue teased her mouth, and his body slid over hers. She felt the length of him burning against her flesh, felt his hard, probing maleness at the joining of her thighs. In panic, she twisted and tried to push him off, but his grip was like iron as he pinned her beneath him. Her mouth was forced open, and his tongue tormented hers. One hand cupped a breast and found the soft nipple, which quickly grew taut under his skillful fingers. She tried to cry out, but

163

her breath was trapped by his eager mouth. Then he was entering her. Her head spun in panic as she struggled and beat at him. He raised his head and breathed heavily as his passion mounted.

"Stop! Let me go!" Her words were as ineffectual as the blows she rained on him. She felt the swelling pressure of his masculinity, followed quickly by the scalding surge of his pleasure. He collapsed atop her, gasping for breath.

Maura gathered every ounce of her strength and shoved him aside so that he sprawled to the floor.

"What the hell—!" He sat up, holding his head.

Maura leaped off the bed and yanked up the blanket to cover her nakedness. Glaring at him across the interval of moonlight, she had trouble controlling the trembling in her voice.

"Damn you! Get out of here!"

He shook his head and began to rise. Maura backed to the table and picked up the heavy pitcher.

"If you come near me again, I'll crush your skull!"

"Maura, for God's sake—"

"Get out!" She was shaking with rage.

"All right, all right." He stumbled to his feet. His hair was disheveled and his arms hung limply at his sides. He seemed confused as Maura threatened him again with the pitcher. "At least allow me a minute to dress." He indicated the chair where his clothes were. He did not shift his gaze from the pitcher she was holding aloft as he edged toward the chair.

The sight of his nakedness made Maura want to turn away, but she dared not take her eyes from him. He pulled on trousers and shirt and bent to slide his feet into the boots.

"I have never known a woman to welcome a man to her bed, then threaten to kill him for complying with her wishes," he said huskily. He reached for his coat and hung it over his arm while he fastened the buttons on his shirt and tried to hook the collar.

"Welcome you?! Are you demented?" She held the blanket tightly, afraid he might see how badly she was shaking.

He frowned and peered at her. "You are serious. . . ."

"I'm hardly in the mood for jokes!"

"My God! You're not— I— Lord, if I've made a mistake, I apologize profusely!"

"I'm not interested in your apology. Get out of here!"

He slipped his arms into the coat, straightened it, then brushed back his hair with a quick sweep of his hand. "Care or not, I must apologize for mistaking you for a—"

"A harlot?!"

"My God, I'm sorry. Please forgive me."

"Just go!" A new fit of trembling shook her, and she bit her lip.

He walked to the door and turned the knob. A glow of light from the hall bathed him. "Good night, Maura." His voice was gentle, his expression puzzled. The door shut behind him. Maura listened to his footsteps fade.

She sank to the bed and sat staring at the door until the trembling ceased. Beau had believed that she wanted his attentions, that she had actually extended a veiled invitation! She'd been aware in the coach that the drummers were entertaining idle thoughts about her virtue because she was traveling alone and without baggage. But she had convinced herself that Beau was different. She thought he was a gentleman who recognized her breeding and background. How could she have been so wrong?

After a long time, she rose and poured water into the basin. It was cold, but she scrubbed her face and body as though to rid herself of the memory of Beau's lovemaking.

Pulling the door shut behind him, Beau cursed himself for ten kinds of fool. The wine had stirred his passion and dulled his senses, else he would not have approached her so crudely. He'd been sure of her purpose and invitation—but mistakenly so! If she was not a strumpet, why in the world was she traveling alone, in obvious flight? He couldn't be blamed for his error. Even the two drummers believed her a woman of shady virtue. Beau suspected they would have sought her out themselves if he had not made it clear that he was staking a prior claim.

Damn! It was a stupid mistake, no matter how much he had enjoyed her warm, delectable body. He went downstairs to the taproom and ordered a bottle and glass at the bar.

Beau drank off the first shot and refilled the glass before glancing around. Only a few tables were occupied, though several stages had put in for the night. Passengers tended to retire early, to rest for the day ahead.

Several men were huddled over drinks, laughing as stories and gossip were exchanged. At a table near the door, three men were playing poker.

Beau took his glass and strolled over to watch a hand. He found it difficult to concentrate because Maura kept interfering with his thoughts.

One of the men looked up. "Want to take a hand?"

Beau hesitated. It was a low-stakes game that might divert his mind. He took the vacant chair and settled himself. The man opposite him was a cadaverous-looking stranger with long, bony fingers and small eyes. He could be a gambler, Beau decided; he'd be the one to watch. The other two introduced themselves as Willis and Snyder. The gambler was Kincaid.

Snyder said, "I seen you come in on the Hoboken stage, Mr. Fontaine."

"That's right, I did." He watched Kincaid deal smoothly, without tricks. He picked up two sevens, nothing else.

"There was a pretty little wench on that stage. They tell me she's got no baggage," Snyder said with a knowing wink. Willis laughed.

"You're wrong," Kincaid said in a flat voice.

Beau had been about to speak. Now he looked at Kincaid with surprise.

Willis said, "Gimme three cards. What do you mean, wrong?"

The dealer picked up the deck. "You're wrong that she's a whore. Sorry t'spoil your fun, but she's a lady."

"How do you know that?"

"Because I've seen her before." Kincaid motioned with his finger. "How many cards, Snyder?"

"Four. Where'd you see her?"

Kincaid dealt. "I came from New York City on the stage yesterday." He glanced at Beau. "How many?"

"Three." Beau picked up a pair of Jacks and a trey. "Did you meet her in New York?" he asked Kincaid.

"Not likely. She's a society gal. I saw her at an outing of the Sullivan Carriage Company. I went along as a guest of one of the clerks. She never even noticed me."

Beau scowled. The Sullivan Company. It was a famous

name. Kincaid was studying him. Beau smiled. "That's mighty interesting, Mr. Kincaid."

"Every word true."

"You mean she's part of the Sullivan family?" Willis said.

"Daughter of the owner," Kincaid said, with a nod. "Her father died some months back, and the mother was just buried a few days ago."

Snyder threw in his cards. "Then why in hell is she travelin' alone like that?"

"Who knows?" Kincaid said. "Rich women are peculiar. How you gonna figure 'em?"

"Bet a quarter," Snyder said, placing a coin in the middle of the table.

Beau followed. "Raise you a quarter."

Kincaid sighed and threw in his hand. "Nothing."

"Call you," Snyder said. "Well, she's a goddam beauty. She can have me anytime."

Beau laid down the two pair, face up. Snyder grunted and tossed in his hand. "You win, Mr. Fontaine."

Willis gathered up the cards, sorted them and began to shuffle. "I never figured her for a whore anyways. She ain't got the look."

"I read about the family in the papers," Kincaid said as he fished for a cigar. "Kind of a scandal the way the old man's widow married herself off so quick to that lawyer."

"Jesus, lawyers!" Willis exclaimed. "Bad as politicians."

"Well, this one took over the company right quick. Name of Turk. Maybe that's why the girl is running off."

"What d'you mean?" Beau asked. Kincaid seemed well informed.

Kincaid struck a smelly match and puffed at the cigar. "According to the papers, now that the mother's dead, the company is owned by the girl, her brother and Turk. Maybe Lawyer Turk is pushing her to sign away her share."

"Goddam lawyers," Willis said, dealing the cards around.

Beau scooped up his hand absently; he was seeing Maura's face instead of the cards. So she was part-owner of one of the largest firms in the nation. He studied Kincaid covertly. Undoubtedly the man was telling the truth as far as he knew it. Maura's name *was* Sullivan, and she was certainly different from the rest. He groaned inwardly at his own stupidity in thinking she was a high-class prostitute. He'd never associated her with the upper level of society. He thought she'd been imitating. He'd been off on the wrong track from the start.

"Fontaine?"

They were all looking at him. Beau forced his thoughts back to the game. He studied his cards. "I'll open for—"

"It's already open. Are you in?"

"Yes." He tossed his coins into the pot. Had he ruined his chances with Maura by the drunken invasion of her room? It might take some doing to win back her confidence, but he was sure he could do it.

Snyder won the pot and Beau rose. He couldn't concentrate. "Excuse me, gentlemen, I'm going to check out."

CHAPTER TEN

In the morning, Maura went downstairs to breakfast filled with misgivings. She was still angry and shaken, and she had no desire to face Beau Fontaine. She considered waiting for a later stage, but decided the delay would be foolish and dangerous. It would give Pelham an edge she'd fought hard to prevent.

Besides, the entire incident had been Beau's fault. *He* was the one to be ashamed. She would not hide like a prim schoolgirl. She would ignore him completely, even if it was impossible to avoid him.

He was in the common room, which was crowded with passengers getting ready for the day's journey. Maura took a seat as far from him as possible, but she felt his eyes on her throughout the meal. Immediately after breakfast, the innkeeper announced the departure of the Pittsburgh stage. Maura once more found herself seated across from Beau. She could not escape the conversation but she took no part in it. She thought she detected a subtle difference in the attitude of the drummers; for a moment, she wondered if they had somehow learned what had happened last night. That was impossible. Fontaine was not fool enough to discuss such a delicate subject with talkative traveling companions.

Beau was flawlessly polite, but he did not attempt to engage Maura in conversation. She felt his gaze on her several times, and when she challenged it, he did not waver. It was she who looked away.

Outside Norristown, they were stopped frequently at tollgate houses where the grumbling driver paid over sixteen cents for the pole to be lifted. Then the road narrowed, and they crossed several stone bridges and began to climb again. There were long stretches between farms and houses here. The road was rutted and occasionally had large rocks that might catch an unwary driver. The coach seemed to pitch and shake more than ever.

Before midday, the Loganhall boy became queasy. He turned pale and perspiration broke out on his forehead. His father shouted for the driver to pull over. Growling, the driver pulled the team off the road and halted at the edge of a meadow. Sam jumped out and carried the boy toward a stream. Stella scurried behind.

Maura noticed the little girl was also looking pale. "Let's walk a bit," Maura said to her. She took the child's hand to climb from the coach. They went toward a grove of swaying willows where they could not see the retching boy at the stream. Maura tried to keep the girl's mind occupied by pointing out a few late-blooming meadow flowers and a fat squirrel that darted from their path.

The day was cool, with low clouds that threatened rain. Maura wandered slowly, picking green leaves from dipping branches and crushing them between her fingers to inhale the fresh, sharp aroma. Glancing back, she saw that Beau had left the carriage and was watching her. She deliberately turned away as he began walking toward them. She called to the child and grasped her hand.

"It's time to go back."

When she turned, Beau was blocking her path.

"I'd like to say again how sorry I am about what happened last night," he said softly.

"I don't want to discuss it."

"Nor I. I assure you, I am desolate at my mistake in judgment and the embarrassment I caused you. I want to forget the incident completely, and I want you to say you forgive me."

She tried to move past him. "They're bringing the boy back."

He reached out and his fingers came to rest lightly on her shoulder. "I beg you to forgive me. I was drunk and acted stupidly. It will never happen again, I swear it."

"Do you think that all you need do is apologize to right the terrible thing you have done?" She was angry, but at the same time felt a warm blush creep across her neck as she recalled his body against hers.

"Please, in God's name, don't castigate me. I am miserable and would do anything to erase it all. Would it help if I were to slash my wrists and bleed my sorrow?" He held his hands out as though offering them to her knife.

In spite of herself, she felt her anger dissipating at his mock-tragic face and his laughing eyes. She looked away. "We have to return to the coach."

The pressure of his hand increased as he touched her shoulder again. "Say I am forgiven."

She took a deep breath, wondering if she was doing the right thing, but becoming increasingly helpless in the light of his persuasiveness. "You are forgiven. . . ."

He heaved a huge sigh and grinned roguishly. "Life has become worth living once more. I thank you, Maura Sullivan, for the sunshine you have brought me."

"But it's starting to rain," the little girl piped as she frowned at Beau with frank curiosity.

Both Maura and Beau laughed, and the tension of the moment was gone.

"So it is," Beau said cheerfully. "Best we get you back to the carriage." He scooped up the child, and she giggled as he carried her back and settled her in the coach. The Loganhalls had returned. Stella bundled the boy in her cloak against the chill and dampness. The others settled and the driver yelled impatiently at the team.

The window at Maura's side became an instrument of torture as the raw day turned suddenly cold. Damp wind knifed past the flapping shade to sting her cheeks. She wedged herself into the corner and thought of the dozen warm cloaks and coats in her wardrobe at Meadowfield. The thin silk one she wore was little protection against the growing cold.

The steady drizzle continued. It was a blessing only because it settled the clouds of dust. It made the interior of the coach as cold as a tomb. By the time they pulled into a stable yard for the noon stop, Maura was half frozen. Teeth chattering, she was last out of the coach.

In the common room, Beau pulled a chair up to the roaring fire. "Sit here. I'll get you a hot drink," he said to Maura, then vanished in the direction of the bar.

Maura threw off the icy silk wrap and held out her hands and feet to the leaping flames. Would she ever be warm again? Beau was back in a minute with a heavy mug.

He put it in her hands with the command, "Drink." It was steaming, and she sipped gratefully. She felt the warmth slide down to her stomach and begin to spread. Beau went away again and returned with a blanket, which he spread over her shoulders and tucked around her solicitously.

"You're beginning to look a little less frozen." He smiled gently.

"Thank you." She was grateful, and her mistrust was banished completely. She sipped the tea. Nothing had ever tasted so good. Maura closed her eyes wearily. As the warming effects of the drink seeped through her, her feet began to tingle in the black kid slippers. Slowly the numbness was passing. She was already beginning to dread the return to the cold, uncomfortable coach. If only she could stay right here where it was warm.

Beau stood looking down at her. He was relieved to see the color returning to her cheeks and some of the strain easing. It was a grueling trip for anyone. A delicate woman like Maura, who was unaccustomed to discomfort, would find it exceptionally tiring. He wondered again why she had chosen the inconvenience of public transportation rather than one of the elegant coaches her family manufactured. She was running from something, he was sure. He hated to rouse her, but she had to have food to sustain her for the rest of the day. He went for a tray. When he returned, he touched her arm.

"Here you are." His voice was cheerful. He took the mug and gave her a fork, then settled the tray on her lap. He'd brought a bowl of hot stew, thick with cubes of meat and boiled vegetables, and a plate of warm, fresh bread with creamy butter melting into it.

The strong, meaty aroma made Maura realize how hungry she was. How thoughtful Beau was. How could she harbor any resentment toward him? Everything he did proved his contrition. She smiled to thank him.

"You dropped off to sleep," he said with a look of concern. "I'm sorry to wake you, but you'll be glad of the food before the day is out. And I fear our driver is not the man to wait patiently while ladies nap." He pulled another chair close. "Feeling better?"

"Much." She attacked the meal while he sipped coffee

172

he'd brought for himself. As she ate, he watched her with a smile.

"Aren't you following your own advice?" Maura asked, breaking off a piece of bread and putting it in her mouth.

"You dozed longer than you think. I've already eaten. The others are still in the dining room."

She realized the room was empty except for the two of them. She concentrated on the stew and, in minutes, had cleaned her plate. Beau went out again and returned moments later with another cup of steaming tea for her and coffee for himself. He also had a pair of woolen boots tucked under his arm. To her astonishment, he knelt in front of her to pull them on over her shoes.

"I got them from the landlord's wife," he said with a grin. "Just the thing for a chilly coach journey, don't you think?"

They felt wonderful, and she protested very feebly. "I can't accept—"

"You *can,* and you will. They are a birthday present from me. It would be terribly rude to refuse a birthday gift." He made it sound so comical, she laughed. It was hard to refuse him.

"It's nowhere near my birthday," she said impudently.

"It's for the one already past. I missed it, since I had not met you then. Now let's hear no more about it. Come along, the driver is getting surly. He's had his rum and is eager to be underway again. He prides himself on his schedule."

She walked with him to the door, and suddenly felt a heavy cloak being pressed around her shoulders. She turned to find herself staring into Beau's solemn, dark eyes.

He put up a hand. "Before you say anything, remember that my feelings can be hurt very easily."

She rubbed the wool of the cloak. It was thick and serviceable, and it felt delightfully warm.

"I know you came away from New York too quickly to bring baggage, and I ask no questions. I will only say that it has happened to me." He rolled his eyes. "Heaven forbid it ever does again."

She smiled and snuggled into the thick wool. "Where did you get it?"

"The same place I got the overboots." He pulled the cloak closer under her chin and tied the drawstrings. "Let's say no more about it. We're friends, and friends do not fuss over small favors."

She smiled, amazed at how completely she had forgiven him. It was as though the incident of the previous night were only a haunting but disturbingly pleasant dream. She let him take her arm as they crossed the muddy yard.

"It should take us that far," the driver was saying. "Long as we don't do no racin'."

The two hostlers stood staring at a rear wheel of the coach, and one said something Maura did not hear. The driver swore sharply. Beau helped her into the coach and she settled with the woolen cloak to shield her from the rain and the wind. When Beau took his seat, one of the drummers asked what the trouble was.

"Something about a wheel, but the driver wouldn't say much," Beau answered.

It was raining hard by the time the coach rolled from the yard, doubletrees jangling, and turned onto the rutted turnpike. Maura retied the heavy window curtain, but the rain still slashed through now and then, and the wind was icy on her cheek. She pulled the hood of the cloak around her face. She was grateful to Beau. She had been wrong about him last night. He was telling the truth when he declared he had invaded her room with a completely mistaken idea about her. She rejected the possibility that she had encouraged him to think he was invited, but she had to admit that a man might view the situation differently.

Rain drummed on the roof. Far off, thunder began to rumble. The driver shouted to the horses and cursed one particular lead animal.

"Damn horse must be afraid of the rain," Harry said. "Some horses is crazy. You never know what they're going to do."

The coach clattered over a wooden bridge. Thunder boomed and crashed in the sky. A jagged sliver of lightning brightened the interior of the coach with eerie light, and the two children wailed.

What had been an uncomfortable journey now became a horrible one. The carriage swayed and jolted as the wheels dropped into unseen ruts. Despite her efforts to brace herself, Maura was constantly thrown against the hard wooden edge of the window. The strain tired her muscles until she felt bruised. The coach creaked and rattled, and the whimpers of the Loganhall children added to the riot of sounds. Soon the lightning was close enough to make everyone jump. Harry joked about incidents he'd witnessed where people had been hurt during storms until Beau curtly told him not to frighten the children.

After it had done its worst, the storm rolled off behind a mountain ridge, taking the eerie lightning with it, but the rain continued in a steady patter. The driver was forced to slow the teams because the ruts in the road became still deeper, and the coach slewed at every turn. His swearing and steady barking at the horses were audible over the drumming of the rain.

Finally the storm began to let up. The rain dwindled to a faint drizzle, then stopped altogether. The countryside seemed to steam as mists rose. Low clouds rolled and tumbled, shredding as the sun broke through. Golden shafts filtered through the mists and a rainbow shimmered over the horizon. The sky cleared miraculously as the breeze washed it clean.

Maura unfastened the curtain and welcomed the sun on her face. The view from the high road was spectacular. Below lay an undulating green valley, with deeply weathered rail fences separating fields where red cattle grazed. The chimneys of isolated farmhouses sent trails of smoke upward. The idyllic scene restored Maura's humor. She returned Beau's quick smile and rearranged herself on the seat.

Abruptly the driver yelled. The coach swerved, then slowed. Maura held aside the curtain and looked out as the teams halted.

"What the hell—you tryin' to git run down?!" The driver was shouting at a woman with a thick red shawl over her head and shoulders, who was standing in the roadway. Her skirts were soaked and her boots were muddy. She gasped as the driver raised his whip as though to send the horses trampling over her.

"Please—let me ride as far as the village," the girl cried. The shawl slipped back from her head. She was young and pretty in a full-blown way. "My father is ill. If the doctor

175

doesn't come quickly——" She broke off with a sob and hid her face in her hands.

The driver grumbled, but the two drummers had already pushed open the door on their side of the coach. They smiled and beckoned to the girl, who ran toward them. "C'mon, can't leave a lady in distress."

"Can't pick up ever' damn stray along the road," the driver muttered.

"We'll pay her fare," Harry said magnanimously. "Ain't that right, gents?" He glanced around at the others, demanding chivalry. He and Robb leaned to give the girl a hand up. The shawl fell to the crook of her arm, and their gazes were fully occupied with the tight blouse that strained across her breasts. The girl fluttered her lashes and smiled to show a flash of teeth.

Maura caught a ripple of movement in the trees and looked around as three horsemen galloped from cover. They wore long ponchos and slouch hats pulled low over their foreheads. Each carried a pistol.

"Hell's fire——!" The driver realized he had been tricked. He lashed the horses and the coach jerked forward. Stella Loganhall screamed. The abrupt motion pitched the two children across the seat. The strange girl struggled to free herself, sudden fury flashing in her eyes as the two men did not release her. Robb and Judkins were still holding her wrists, and in what they considered a gallant move, they pulled her into the coach with her feet and skirts flying.

"Fool driver!" Robb shouted over the clamor. "You all right, miss?"

In answer, the girl kicked him viciously in the shin with a booted foot. He howled and sat down hard. Judkins' eyes went wide as the girl bent and bit his hand, forcing him to release her. The coach rocked and pitched. The door slammed against the side with splintering crashes. Outside a pistol fired. Stella shrieked again.

Maura gripped the edge of the window as the coach gained speed. Mud spattered wildly from the wheels. The driver was bawling at the teams steadily. A second pistol shot blasted slivers of wood from the side of the door only a hand's reach from Maura's face, and she flinched. For a moment, everything seemed unreal. The three horsemen thundered behind them, and the driver's whip cracked. It was a miracle that the stage kept the road in its wild careening. Everyone was jounced and tossed like potatoes in a sack. The attempted holdup happened so quickly, it was several moments before Maura realized the girl was part of it.

Beau recognized it too. The girl was gripping the door frame as though she would leap out the instant the coach slowed.

"Hang on to her!" Beau shouted to the startled drummers. Robb and Judkins grabbed for the girl again, but she fought them off like a wildcat. Loganhall was torn between trying to shield his wife and children and helping subdue the struggling woman.

"Get down!" Beau ordered Maura as another shot rang out. He yanked a small Colt from his vest and glanced out the window. One of the bandits was only yards away and was aiming his pistol at the driver. Beau snapped a shot and missed.

The driver's shotgun blasted. The bandit's chest became a red, bloody ruin. His horse stumbled and went down, and the dead rider sprawled in the mud. The shotgun roared again, and the coach swerved dangerously. A fusillade of shots cracked. Several hit the coach with loud raps as though someone had struck it with a hammer. Suddenly the carriage lurched. There was a loud, splintering crunch, and it tilted to a steep pitch. The teams were dragging it around while the driver strained to halt them. Maura was hurled like a toy across the aisle into Beau's lap, then slid to the floor. The Loganhalls tumbled along the seat amid the children's screeches of terror. The two drummers fell in a heap with the captive girl. Robb's head cracked against the seat and he groaned and went limp.

The coach dragged to a stop, leaning at a crazy angle. For a moment, everything was still. Then the children began to cry. The bandit girl recovered first. Shoving and pushing Robb and Judkins aside, she grabbed for the pistol that had fallen from Beau's hand. He saw her move and dived for the gun, but he was not fast enough. With a triumphant smile, the girl cocked the pistol and pointed it.

"Stay where you are—git your hands off me—" She scrambled around, trying to face them all. Outside, the two horsemen galloped up.

Maura glimpsed a bearded man's snarling face as he pointed his gun into the coach. Before he could pull the trigger, the driver's pistol barked. The bandit slumped and at that moment his horse reared and threw him off.

The third man shouted and the girl turned her head. Instantly, Beau jumped for the gun, but again the girl was too quick. She jerked back and lashed out with the barrel. It slammed into Beau's temple with a sickening crack, and he fell heavily. Maura gasped. The girl clicked back the hammer and warned her away. Maura moved back cautiously. The girl's face was taut and her eyes were too bright. It would be dangerous to cross her—she might begin shooting at any moment.

Another shot cracked and the driver yelped. Maura's heart missed a beat, then raced furiously. If the driver was dead, they'd be at the mercy of the bandits. After losing some of their men, they might not want to leave behind live witnesses.

Outside a man shouted, "Penny? You all right in there?"

The girl answered, "All right, Jim."

The man dismounted and peered inside. He had a thin, lined face and needed a shave. "Git their valuables. Hurry it up." He glanced at each of them as though estimating their worth, and his eyes lingered on Maura.

The girl made a pocket of her skirt. She moved the gun slowly from one head to another. "Gimme everything—money, jewelry—that watch—" She poked the gun barrel at Beau's vest where a gold watch chain was draped. Harry Judkins pulled out the watch and dropped it in her skirt. He turned out his own pockets glumly.

The Loganhall children had fallen into subdued weeping. Their eyes were round and their lips quivered. Stella was clutching them so hard they could scarcely breathe. When the girl barked at her, Stella opened her reticule and shakily removed a small coin purse. Samuel drew out his wallet and tossed it into the girl's skirt.

Beau did not stir. A thin, ragged line of blood oozed along his cheek, and his face was pale.

The girl stabbed the gun toward Maura. "What you got, missy?"

Maura was wedged into the corner of the leaning coach. She felt the hard edge of the door along her spine, and her

178

legs were folded under her. Before the crash, her reticule had been at her side, but she had no idea where it was now. She felt for it, shaking her head.

"Don't pretend you got nothing," the girl snapped. Her voice was a snarl. "A fine lady like you."

Maura feigned confusion. "I can't find my purse. It was here—" She glanced around and tried to pull herself up. The girl watched closely.

Outside the man yelled at her to hurry. "Someone might come along, dammit!"

On all fours, Maura felt along the floor. Then without warning, she grabbed the girl's ankles and jerked her off her feet. The move was so swift it took the girl by surprise. She toppled backward with her skirt flying and her arms waving. Maura flung herself on top of her and wrested the gun from her hand. Without hesitation, she struck out with the gun butt and hit the girl's forehead. She quickly raised the gun to strike a second blow, but there was no need. The girl fell into a heap with her mouth sagging open. Maura's breath escaped in a huge gasp.

"My Gawd!" Harry Judkins stared, then quickly began to pick up the things that had fallen from the bandit girl's skirt.

Outside, the man called, "Penny—?"

Maura crawled over the downed girl and peered through a window. The driver was sprawled across the top of the seat with his arms dangling and his coat bloody. The bandit on horseback was leaning over him emptying his pockets. Maura aimed the pistol and fired.

The bandit jerked around with the force of the bullet. Blood began to stain his poncho at the shoulder. He swore as he saw Maura, and he tugged out his gun, at the same time trying to steady the horse. Maura fired again before he could aim. The bullet grazed the horse's rump. The animal reared and the bandit's shot went wild. The horse raced off with the wounded man clinging to the pommel. Maura fired after him, and the bullet ripped into a tree.

"My Gawd . . ." Harry Judkins gaped as Maura lowered the Colt. "Are you all right?"

She nodded and sank onto the tilting seat. Now that it was over she was shaking from a combination of relief and fright. The gun fell into her lap from now-limp fingers.

She saw Beau stir. He touched a hand to the lump on the side of his head and winced. Robb groaned and tried to open his eyes. The Loganhalls huddled together like peas in a pod, all of them pale with shock.

As Beau struggled to sit up, he saw the bandit girl slumped on the floor. He looked around dazed.

Harry Judkins whistled and shook his head. "You shoulda seen her! She walloped that damned girl, then shot the other'un outside. I never seen anything like it." He gazed at Maura admiringly.

Beau squeezed onto the seat beside her. "Are you all right?" He picked up the pistol.

"I—I'm fine now."

"You're sure?" He peered at her, searching for any injury. When he had reassured himself, he went to the door and looked out.

"She chased off the last one," Judkins said. "He was swearing a blue streak. He'll be a long time nursing that wound. I don't think he'll be back in a hurry."

"Let's see to the driver," Beau said. He jumped down from the coach. Judkins was right behind him. Beau turned to help Maura out as Harry clambered up to the driver's seat and examined the man.

"He ain't dead," he called. Beau quickly helped lift the driver down. They laid the big man on the wet grass and Beau pulled aside the coat to look at the wound. The driver stirred and grimaced with pain.

"Went through the flesh. We'll need something to staunch the bleeding," Beau said.

Leaning against the broken wheel, Maura reached under her skirt to undo a petticoat and hand it to Beau. He folded it and knelt beside the driver again to press the soft cloth to the wound.

The driver groaned and opened his eyes. Beau pulled the shirt and coat over the makeshift bandage. "That will have to do until we can get to a doctor."

"Don't need no fool doctor," the driver grumbled.

"Suit yourself." Beau got to his feet and turned back to the coach.

The Loganhalls were sitting on the ground. Irving Robb was near them, still pale, his head in his hands. Beau put an arm around Maura's waist and led her away from the others. He spread his coat on a flat rock and seated her.

"You are a constant wonder, Maura. I would not have thought you the type to be a crack pistol shot."

She saw the earnest expression on his face and the wonder in his eyes. "I'm hardly an expert," she said truthfully.

"You wounded a highwayman and drove him off. That takes a bit of fancy shooting," he insisted.

She shook her head. "I caught him by surprise, that's all."

"Our fate might not have been pleasant if you hadn't acted so heroically. Not many women could have done it." He looked at her with warm admiration. Maura lowered her gaze. To think she might have killed a man left her shaken.

Beau started to say something, but a shout from Harry Judkins interrupted.

"She's getting away!"

The girl in the coach had regained consciousness, crawled out, and was running pell-mell toward the woods. She held her skirts high and leaped like a deer over the ditch. Judkins pounded after her, but in moments she vanished among the shimmering wet leaves. Judkins floundered through the slapping branches for several yards, then gave up. He came back shaking water from his coat.

"Let her go," Beau said.

"But dammit, she's just as much—"

"We've got enough problems," Beau said, indicating the broken axle and wheel. "Besides, we've killed two of her men and wounded the other. She's not likely to come back. We can report the holdup at the next town and let the law handle it."

The driver had managed to sit up and lean against the front wheel. "Gonna need a new axle. There's a stage stop four, mebbe five miles ahead."

"Then I suggest we unhitch the horses. I'll ride to bring back help." Beau slipped the Colt from his vest and handed it to Maura. "An added precaution," he said with a grin.

CHAPTER ELEVEN

Pittsburgh lay swathed in a dense cloud. At first, Maura thought a thunderhead had blown in from the river, but to her dismay, she quickly realized the pall was from smoke and dirt. Harry Judkins had been right.

The coach slowed on the crowded Federal Street bridge. Passengers peered out to glimpse the destination they'd waited so long to reach. Stella's face fell, and Maura watched her with a twinge of sympathy. The city was not much at first glance. It seemed a helter-skelter architectural maze. Small demure-looking cottages nestled in the shadow of larger stone buildings, many of which had cumbersome cornices and ornate façades. There were gray, boxlike, multistoried commercial establishments, and tall, thin spires of churches. Everywhere, buildings and trees alike had a gray, lifeless hue.

When the coach came off the bridge, another fact quickly became apparent. Many of the streets were seas of mud from which the stench of pollution rose as densely as the black strata over the city. Maura put a handkerchief to her nose and looked at Beau.

He smiled encouragingly. "This is the part Harry sees."

Judkins grunted good-naturedly as he pulled his watch out and flicked it open. "I may have time to make one call," he said, shaking his head. "Can't afford to lose a whole day."

They had been delayed overnight after the incident with the bandits. The local sheriff, a laconic, slow-moving man, had questioned each of them about the holdup. Satisfied with their stories, he had dispatched deputies to pick up the dead bandits. The others were probably long gone, he pre-

183

dicted, but if they showed their faces in those parts again, he'd nab 'em. Maura did not voice her skepticism.

The next afternoon, the passengers from the ill-fated stage had crowded aboard a stage from Scranton to finish the journey. The driver had stayed behind to wait for the repairs on his coach.

Beau, seated beside Maura, smiled. "Stage stations are located for convenience, not scenic beauty. I assure you, all Pittsburgh is not so grim."

Maura hoped fervently that he was right. Even a brief sojourn in such depressing surroundings would be unpleasant. But there were unappealing sectors in New York, she supposed, and in every large city. Beau was right, convenience seemed the most important concern.

The stage came into a square ringed with hotels and taverns. Three awkward-looking Conestoga wagons stood in the center of the common, their curved frames and canvases resembling sails in a sea of mud. In front of the Spread Eagle Tavern, a pack train of mules stirred restlessly as the stage rumbled by. The driver bawled curses and cracked his whip to scatter pigs and dogs that crowded the roadway. Several street urchins danced alongside the coach begging and offering to carry bags in exchange for nickels. From the opposite direction came a covered wagon drawn by six horses with their saddlebows mounted with jingling, clanking bells. The wagon bed was piled high with bales of rags. It drew up at a shop door lettered: JOHNSTON & STOCKTON.

The stage passengers began to gather their belongings and ready themselves for the arrival. The driver jerked the teams to a halt beneath a tall pole bearing the sign: THE GOLDEN CROSS KEYS.

"Pittsburgh, on time!" he shouted. He swung down as several hostlers ran out to unharness the horses. Without a backward glance, he ambled toward the high, arched entrance to a walled courtyard across the common, where half a dozen drivers were quenching their thirst and engaging in the spirited swapping of stories. The air was blue with oaths and laughter.

Maura let Beau help her down from the coach. She was stiff and cramped from the jostling ride. It was a relief to have the long wearying journey over. She'd slept badly the last few nights, since she'd been forced to share a room with Stella and the little girl. And the six-day trip seemed like an eternity. She wondered how people survived the long journey all the way across the country. She gazed at the bustling activity around them. It was possible that some of these wagons were going all the way to California. She shuddered at the prospect, though she knew that there were thousands of people lured by gold who were willing to endure any hardship to go in search of it.

"Let me see you to your brother's house," Beau said, taking her arm to guide her past a muddy puddle. "Wait here. I'll find a carriage."

She stood on the wooden verandah of the hotel, well away from the doors so she would not block the steady flow of traffic that moved in and out. Her traveling companions on the stage nodded as they passed. The two drummers hoisted their bags from the rack and started across the square. Irving Robb kicked out at a dog that nipped at his boot. The animal snarled as it cringed away. Then Robb and Judkins were out of sight around the corner of a square brick building that housed several stores with warehouses above.

The Loganhalls were met by a florid man in coarse homespun, who greeted them without emotion. Maura wondered idly if Sam's brother had met every stage until they appeared. Stella turned to wave briefly to Maura as her husband helped her into the wagon. She did not look back as it rattled off.

The square was enveloped in activity and seemed to be a hub of the city. Another stage arrived with noisy clatter and the shouts of the driver. The moment it stopped, two men climbed out and helped down a woman in a scarlet gown that was much too daring for daytime wear. Maura realized that she was a whore, and studied her with curiosity. She was buxom and flamboyant. A short cape over her shoulders was thrown back to reveal the low neckline of her dress and the cleavage between her breasts. The dress was silk, accented with rows of jet beads and black lace. Her waist was tightly corseted, and the gown cascaded over well-rounded hips. Her eyes were bold under a mountain of golden curls on top of which perched a tiny black hat. She favored the men with a dazzling smile as they set her safely

185

across the muddy walk. She did not pull away when one of them slid a hand to her waist and squeezed her.

A small buckboard drawn by a chestnut horse came to a stop. Beau looped the reins around the brake and swung down. He helped Maura up, then shouted to a ragged child of about ten to toss up his baggage. Flipping the child a coin, Beau settled himself in the driver's seat and slapped the reins against the chestnut's flank.

"Now, you said your brother's address is in Chancery Lane?"

She nodded, surprised that he recalled a fact mentioned so casually.

"Then I suggest we go immediately. I imagine the sooner you are settled comfortably in a house with the conveniences you are accustomed to, the happier you will be." He smiled as though her comfort and happiness were the most important things in the world.

When they left the square, they rode along a wide cobblestoned street filled with shops. Women with baskets paused to study window displays or haggle over prices. Children rolled hoops and skipped rope amid barking dogs that had to be fended off. Shopkeepers lounged in doorways, smiling at customers or gossiping. There were greengrocers, butcher shops, dry goods and hardware stores. Carriages and wagons were drawn up so every hitching post had at least one set of reins through it. The air hummed with voices and the sound of wheels and hooves on the stone. It might have been a New York street, except for the gray pall of smoke. But if the good people of Pittsburgh noticed it, they did not let it interfere with their lives.

"This is Fourth Street," Beau told her.

Where Stella's brother-in-law lived and had his shop. Maura glanced about as though half expecting to see the Loganhalls, but they had vanished into the sea of the city. A shop located here should prosper. Maura hoped Stella would find the happiness she sought.

As they rode, Beau identified prominent landmarks: the distant fort which loomed black against a gray sky to the west; the county courthouse standing like a domed sentinel atop Grant's Hill in the opposite direction. On the block past Fourth Street, Beau indicated a wooden structure which housed the Post Office and, upstairs, Philo Hall, which was used for public gatherings.

He turned the buckboard at the next corner. The street was narrower, and three scarlet-leafed maples gave a welcome splash of color. Tall houses with low stoops faced the street; a sidewalk of planks had been laid over the cobblestones. After one block, Beau turned the wagon south again.

"Chancery Lane," he said with a twinkle in his eye.

"But you said it was miles from Fourth Street!"

He grinned conspiratorily. "I thought you might prefer to be unencumbered by visits from the wife of a hardware store merchant."

"What a terrible thing to do!" But she had to smile at how easily his lie had been accepted. "Why are you so sure I would not welcome company in this strange city?"

He gazed at her with dancing eyes. "I am hoping that you will welcome mine, for I do not intend to let you go out of my life. Will you allow me to call?" He looked hopeful. "To show you the city, of course. I give my word that I will behave with the utmost decorum and be the best guide you could hope for." He held her gaze as though to convince her by his own will.

She could not deny that she wanted to see him again. He would be a friendly face in a strange place, and his pleasant, easy manner would be cheerfully welcome. "I'd be delighted to have you call," she said honestly.

"Would this evening be too soon?"

She laughed. "Gracious, yes! Haven't you seen enough of me these past days? Besides, I must shop. This dress is barely fit for the rag bag."

"You look as beautiful now as when I first met you. But if you insist, I will postpone the pleasure. Tomorrow, then?"

His easy banter amused her. "You are very persistent. All right, tomorrow."

He rewarded her with a roguish wink. "And now we must locate your brother. Do you have an address? Thank heaven the city has been farsighted enough to number its houses."

She told him, and he frowned in concentration. "That would be close to the river, I think."

It seemed to her that nothing in Pittsburgh was very far removed from the river. The city was a triangle nestled at the fork where the Allegheny and the Monongahela rivers met. The distance between the two across the central city was only a matter of a few blocks.

Once away from the common, she began to catch glimpses of pleasant houses and some of the charm Beau had mentioned. Despite the pall of smoke, homes were well kept. Small patches of gardens fronted the street, and window boxes were bright with fall blossoms. Occasionally a large house stood apart from its neighbors, fenced by iron railings that did not hide the view of tended yards with stone paths and overhanging trees.

The address on Chancery Lane was only a short distance from the Monongahela River. The house was a pleasant, unpretentious frame structure of three stories, with tall, narrow windows and black shutters. Beau's knock was answered by a plump woman with a frilled cap on her head and a white apron over a gray poplin dress.

In answer to his query, she shook her head. "Mr. Sullivan moved away several months ago."

Maura could not hide her surprise. "Where has he gone?" Why hadn't James written to tell her?! She felt a surge of annoyance at his thoughtlessness.

"I don't know, miss."

At Maura's crestfallen look, Beau said, "Perhaps we could speak with the lady of the house?"

The servant nodded and disappeared inside. Beau reassured Maura. "Don't worry, he has probably found other lodgings for convenience sake. Most of the boatworks are situated upriver a distance."

A thin, angular woman with gray hair came into the hallway. "Maggie tells me you are asking after James Sullivan."

Beau bowed. "This is his sister who has come from New York to see him. She was not aware that he had moved."

"I'm sorry. There is not much I can tell you. It was June, I believe. I have not seen him since."

Despair washed over Maura. "But why did he go? Did he leave a forwarding address?"

"He said it was business that necessitated the move. I

188

have forwarded letters to him at the boatworks. If you inquire there, I'm sure they'll be able to help you."

"Can you tell us how to reach it?" Beau asked.

The woman gave instructions, to which Beau nodded his thanks.

"I'm only sorry I can't help more," the woman said. "Your brother is a fine young man. I was sorry to see him go. When you see him, please give him my regards."

Maura and Beau thanked her and returned to the wagon. Maura gnawed at her lip. She had the worried feeling that something was wrong. James had not written of the change. Was it because something had happened and he didn't want to worry her?

"It won't do a bit of good to fret before you know the whole story," Beau said gently.

She let out her breath and forced a smile. Beau was right, but still . . .

"I'm sure it's exactly as I said. Your brother wants to be closer to his work. The location the landlady gave is several miles from here. From what you've told me of your brother, he is not one to waste time driving back and forth if he does not have to."

Still Maura's fears did not ease completely. Beau tried to distract her with bits of information about various houses they passed. One on the corner of Chancery Lane at the river had been built only the previous year, he said. It was on the site of the original home of John Ormsby, one of Pittsburgh's outstanding citizens, which had been destroyed in the conflagration of 1845. Ormsby had come to Pittsburgh with General Forbes in 1758, Beau told her.

"It was General Forbes who built the new fort and called it Fort Pitt after the English statesman. Ormsby owned the first ferry across the river. It ran to his estate on the south side of the Monongahela. He built an elaborate mansion so he could summer there with his sizable family—ten children, I believe!" He rolled his eyes in mock despair until Maura smiled. He was working hard to raise her spirits. "One day I'll take you to see it. There are lovely unspoiled hills for miles around, perfect for picnicking."

From the riverbank, Beau pointed out the steamboat landing a few blocks to the west. Even from a distance, the bustle was apparent. There seemed to be a constant cross-current of loading and unloading. Slaves burdened under bales and crates labored up and down gangplanks. Black smoke rose from the twin chimneys of several boats, and out in the river, a large paddlewheeler let off a blast of steam.

They followed the river east. Beau indicated several vacant lots not yet built up again after the great fire. Most of the area along the river had been restored, though, and the houses ranged from modest to stately. They overlooked the water and the opposite shore where rolling, green forests stretched against the gray-blue sky. Sunlight danced on the distant hills and brushed fall foliage with gold. On the river, steamboats, small sailboats, pirogues and a few ugly, flat barges loaded with coal and iron ore moved like water beetles.

Past Grant's Hill, Water Street ended. Beau took a narrow, unpaved track that followed the shoreline. When they came to a large boatyard, Maura looked around expectantly, but Beau shook his head.

"This is the Greenaugh Shipyard. It's one of Pittsburgh's oldest. For the past decade, Pittsburgh has enjoyed the reputation of being the leading boatbuilding center on any river in the country." He smiled. "But you probably already know that, since your brother has wisely chosen the city for his venture."

"I admit I have heard him say it," Maura said. "But I had no idea—" She spread her hands to encompass the scene of the river and the sheds and machinery of the Greenaugh yard. It was twice the size of any she had seen in New York. If this was a sample of the boatbuilding industry here, James was up against formidable competition.

Another mile or so along the river, homes grew sparse and the city turned industrial. Factory smokestacks gave off black residue that drifted into the cloud hovering overhead. A strident clatter of metal came from a foundry. Nearby, a huge rolling mill sprawled near the water's edge. A monstrous pile of coal dwarfed the grimy-faced men who shoveled it into small railcarts which quickly vanished into the gaping maw of the furnace shed. Beyond, the open doors of another shed showed tons of boiler plate and bar iron ready to feed the city's hungry industries.

If the landlady at Chancery Lane had not given such

190

detailed instructions, Beau might have missed the Sullivan Boatworks. The yard was comprised of a few small buildings, a storage shed, and a single paddlewheeler on the ways. A small, hand-lettered sign on the closest building identified the company office. Beau halted the chestnut horse just inside the gate.

"We'd better leave the carriage here," he said, glancing around the littered yard where pieces of lumber and metal were scattered everywhere.

Maura took a deep breath and tried to hide her disappointment. It was so small! Compared with the Greenaugh yard, it was a pathetic, dingy sore on the waterfront. Yet in spite of that, Maura felt a stir of excitement at inhaling the familiar wood odors and hearing the sing of hammers and saws. Men supported by scaffolding were working industriously on a partially completed structure. She studied the riverboat with interest. It was quite different from those built in New York. It was shallower in draft and more ornate in design. Several workmen were adding the square wheelhouse to an upper deck. Several others were finishing the huge paddlewheel housings at the sides of the boat.

Maura lifted her skirt and stepped out of the buckboard.

"It's an excellent sidewheeler," Beau said as he studied the boat appraisingly. "Your brother knows his business."

Maura knew little about Western riverboats, but she was willing to accept Beau's judgment. "Then let's find him so I can introduce you to the finest boatbuilder in Pittsburgh." Laughing, she slipped an arm through his and they started for the office, picking their way around debris, wood, and tarpaulin-covered machinery.

The building was unpainted and plain. The door opened directly to a large office where a man in shirt-sleeves sat at a desk with his head bent over a ledger. A shoulder-high partition separated two small areas in the rear. On one, a gold-lettered sign read: JAMES SULLIVAN.

The clerk looked up. "May I help you?"

"We've come to see Mr. Sullivan," Beau said.

The man frowned and glanced at the partition behind him. "One moment, please . . ." He got to his feet and walked quickly to the rear office.

Maura heard the murmur of voices. The thought of seeing James overwhelmed her, and she rushed across the

191

room. She could not wait another moment! She felt as though her heart would burst with excitement.

"James—!"

She halted abruptly. The clerk and a short, wiry man in a black frock coat looked around with startled expressions. The short man gave her an unctuous smile. He was middle-aged, with a touch of gray in his brown hair, and pale eyes that had a washed-out look. But there was a hard edge to his expression and in his voice.

"I'm sorry, Mr. Sullivan is not in. May I help you?"

Maura regained her composure. "I am his sister. I have just arrived from New York."

"His sister? *Maura?*"

"Yes." She was only mildly surprised that he knew her name.

The man bowed deferentially, smiling. "James has spoken of you often. Welcome to Pittsburgh. If I had known you were coming—" He motioned the clerk out.

"Please, sit down." He indicated two wooden chairs facing the desk and glanced at Beau. It was a sparse office, with only the desk, chairs, and a table piled with blueprints, drawings and assorted papers.

Maura was impatient. "Thank you, Mr.—?"

"Denfield. Richard Denfield. I am your brother's assistant."

"Will James be back soon, Mr. Denfield?"

"I'm afraid not. He has gone to Cairo."

"*Cairo?*" Her heart sank.

"Yes, down the river in Illinois," he explained as though she might not understand.

Maura sat down abruptly, all the strength gone from her legs. James gone—after the long journey here and the expectation of seeing him again.

Beau sat beside her and folded her hand into his. The pressure was reassuring, as was his smile. He turned to Denfield. "Miss Sullivan is surprised and disappointed. She has come a long way. Has Mr. Sullivan been gone long?"

Denfield sat back and tented his fingers. "Let me see, it must be almost two weeks now. I am astonished he didn't write you." He gave Maura a slightly patronizing smile.

"I have not heard from him for several months."

Denfield scowled. "But we send a mail packet to New

York every week. Surely your brother includes some personal letters as well as the reports to Mr. Turk?"

"None since early summer."

"I don't understand. Of course, he has been very busy. As you can see, we're nearing the completion of the steamer. There has not been a spare moment—"

"Where is Jeb MacDonald?" If she could not see James, at least she could assure herself of his well-being by talking to Jeb. And Jeb's familiar, friendly smile would ease some of her disappointment.

Denfield's face grew somber. "He was taken ill last week. Cholera. It's a constant menace here. I pray the current eruption doesn't match the magnitude of those of other years. It's the first outbreak since the fire." He stopped, realizing he was rambling.

"Jeb—ill? I must see him!" Maura's heart wrenched. Jeb was like family.

"I don't think that would be wise, Miss Sullivan. Cholera is—"

"I must!" Maura was irritated with the man, who shrugged imperceptibly and laid his palms on the desk.

"He is at Mercy Hospital. We could not allow him to stay here."

Maura frowned. "What do you mean, *here*?"

Denfield cleared his throat. "Both he and your brother have been living on the premises for several months."

"Living *here*?" That was impossible! Maura wondered if the man was sane.

"James said it saved time. He was anxious about the production schedule."

"It seems strange that he would go off to Cairo under such circumstances." Maura felt instinctively that something was wrong. The behavior Denfield was describing was unlike James. In fact, the man was making her very uneasy.

"He said it was a trip necessitated by pressing business." Denfield did not look at her.

Maura let the subject drop. Unaccountably, she wanted to get away from the boatyard. She rose and gathered her reticule. "Is there an address in Cairo where I can reach him?"

"Ah, the New Carolina Hotel, I believe, on South Street."

"Thank you, Mr. Denfield."

"Where can I get in touch with you—in case I hear from your brother?"

Maura realized suddenly that she had no place to go. Beau answered for her. "Miss Sullivan will let you know when she is settled. Now, if you'll excuse us—" He inclined his head and ushered Maura out. The clerk nodded civilly as they crossed the outer office and left.

When the door closed, Maura's lips tightened ominously. "I don't believe a word he said!" Her anger drove away the despair she'd suffered on hearing Denfield's startling news. "I want to talk to Jeb. Do you know where Mercy Hospital is?"

"Yes, but I don't think you should go, at least not right now. You're tired and you've had a shock. A good night's rest will restore your energies. Morning will be time enough."

He was looking at her so earnestly, she forced herself to reconsider. He was right. Her nerves were frayed and she was bone-weary.

"Let me settle you in a hotel. You're too tired to make important decisions. After you've rested, you can write to your brother. Then if you insist, you can visit the hospital, though I advise against it. Cholera is not a pretty sight."

She smiled wearily. "All right. You're being very kind. I do appreciate it, Beau."

"Then let me continue a bit longer. I know an excellent hotel I'm sure you'll find comfortable." He guided her back to the wagon. As soon as she was seated, he turned the horse and started back along the river road. Maura glanced at the steamboat on the ways. The *Patrick*, James had said it would be called. It would be ready soon, and she would ride on its first voyage as James had promised. She could not imagine what had taken him away from his work here, and her disappointment was not relieved by Denfield's casual assurances. Certainly if James knew Jeb was ill, he would return at once. Had he been informed?

She frowned and stared toward the river, which danced with silver flecks as the sun lowered toward the horizon. Duggan had promised to telegraph James. Surely he would have sent the wire to the boatyard; or if it had gone to the house on Chancery Lane, it would have been forwarded.

Why hadn't Denfield received it? She was annoyed with herself that she had not demanded more satisfactory answers from the man. She was his employer as well as James! It was just that everything had taken her so completely by surprise and her expectations had been dashed so abruptly. She sighed inwardly, thinking of the confidence she and Duggan had placed in this journey to Pittsburgh. For a moment, her thoughts lingered on Duggan. The past few days had been such a confusing turmoil, she'd scarcely thought of him. Warm memories flooded her mind now as she recalled the strength of his arms around her, the sweeping passion that dispelled all else when she was encircled by them. How strong he was, and how easily he seemed to make things right, at least temporarily. But he was not here now, and she had to fend for herself. Except for Beau's help . . .

Beau drove through an area of the city she had not seen. It was newer, with buildings not yet grayed by the smoke. There were large estates, with rolling green lawns and autumn-painted oaks and maples, and white stone paths that led in and out among the gardens. He turned onto a boulevarded street that afforded a view of the river. After a block, he drove under the portico of a red brick hotel with white columns. A brass plate was engraved: LAFAYETTE HOUSE. A liveried doorman waited as Beau tossed the reins to a boy who jumped up to claim the horse. Another lad in a scarlet coat unloaded Beau's baggage. The doorman offered Maura his hand, then threw open the doors.

"Aftanoon, Mista Fontaine."

Maura was surprised at the man's knowledge of Beau's name. She was beginning to realize that Beau was indeed well acquainted with the city, as he'd said. She had relied on him heavily since her arrival, and for the moment, she was more than content to go along with his decision. The hotel looked excellent—and expensive. She thought guiltily of the small amount of money in her purse. It would not last long.

The boy with the valises followed them across the foyer. The reception desk was tucked into a small alcove formed by an ornate archway. In the lobby, sofas and chairs cushioned in red velour were arranged in small groupings, each with a pink marble table where drinks or coffee could be set. The floor was carpeted in an intricately patterned Persian design. Any bit of debris that found its way to it was quickly brushed up by an elderly man in a gold coat and cap, who moved about with a broom and dust pan.

The reception clerk said, "Mr. Fontaine . . . I am delighted to see you again. I was not informed that you were arriving."

"An unexpected trip. I trust you have space for me?"

"Of course." The man glanced discreetly at Maura.

"Miss Sullivan will need a comfortable room. One facing the courtyard, I think."

The clerk dipped a pen in an inkpot and turned a ledger. "Room 210 is very pleasant. I'm sure you will find it satisfactory, Miss Sullivan."

She wrote her name and saw the man's quick glance at the bags as he handed the pen to Beau.

"Will suite 306 be satisfactory, Mr. Fontaine?"

"Excellent." Beau scrawled his name and pushed the book back.

"How long will you be staying with us, Mr. Fontaine?"

"That depends, Harrison, that depends."

The clerk made a quick notation on a card, then tapped a bell that brought a bellman running. The clerk handed over two keys with heavy brass tags. Beau slipped an arm under Maura's.

A number of people were sitting about the lobby. A few glanced up as they passed. Maura felt conspicuous in the wrinkled, spotted blue gown and the shabby cloak, but she held her head high as they followed the bellman up the wide, curving stairway. On the second floor, the man unlocked a door near the end of the hall. When he would have carried in the bags, Beau stopped him with a gesture.

"Take the bags to 306. I'll be along shortly."

"Yes, sir."

Beau smiled at Maura. "Would you like a tea tray sent up? You look tired."

"I'm more grimy than anything else."

"A bath, too. Then a nap will restore your energies. When you waken, we can tackle some of the problems that have befallen you the past few hours."

"You've already spent a great deal of time helping me. I can't impose on you further."

"Impose? Nonsense. It's a pleasure. You can repay me by having dinner with me tonight."

"You would be ashamed to be seen with me in any public place until I have a chance to buy a decent dress to replace this!" She fingered the blue chambray.

"There are some fine shops close by where, I'm told, ladies can find ready-to-wear gowns that compare favorably with those sewn by the finest dressmakers."

She thought of the few bills in her purse. But she could not go about looking like a ragamuffin. She smiled. "If that's true, I'll be delighted to join you for dinner."

"Excellent. I will stop by about eight. Until then, pleasant dreams, Maura." He lifted her hand to his lips and kissed it.

Maura closed the door and unfastened the heavy cloak. What a remarkable man. She was grateful for all he had done. She would have managed alone, but he'd made her way much easier. Hanging the cloak in the wardrobe, she realized how completely she had forgiven him for the incident at the inn in Norristown. Her fury had become a hazy memory that was no longer disquieting. It was far easier to think about Beau's delightful smile and the touch of amusement that seemed ever present in his brown eyes. She was looking forward to seeing him again.

Beau strode along the hall whistling softly. Unexpected events sometimes had a way of turning advantageous. Instinct told him this was one of them. The more he learned about Maura, the more puzzling—and intriguing—she became. When she discovered that her brother was gone, she'd shown only fleeting discouragement, which was quickly banished by hard resolve and a lift of the chin. She had not even considered returning to New York. Interesting . . . perhaps he was not mistaken about her running away from something or someone. But whom? Ah, a delicate question, but one he would find an answer to eventually. He would not make the mistake of trying to rush Maura into sharing confidences.

He was startled by a woman's voice. "Beau!"

He blinked, then smiled with pleasure. "Irene, what a lovely surprise!" He took her outstretched hands and glanced along the hall behind her. She was alone except for two personal maids dressed for an outing, but farther down the hall, an elderly couple had just emerged from a room.

Color suffused Irene's cheeks as she looked at him with wide blue eyes that danced with excitement. Her blond hair was carefully coiffed in the latest bouffant style, and she wore a scarlet hat with a short veil and a large red rose. Her afternoon dress of red linen trimmed with rich brown fur, indicated she was on her way out. She held his hands as though restraining the impulse to throw herself into his arms.

"I didn't know you were in town! Why didn't you let me know?" she breathed.

He laughed softly. "Because I have only this moment arrived. I was on my way upstairs to pen a note to send around to you."

"Liar . . ."

"Would you prefer me to say I had no thought of you at all in my head?" He pressed her hand to his lips and she sighed.

With a sharp glance that sent the two maids several steps back out of earshot, she said, "No. I am so happy to see you I can scarcely think. Must we stand here so everyone can witness my confusion?"

He raised an eyebrow suggestively. "I can hardly sweep you off your feet and carry you upstairs, Mrs. Zachary."

She colored and darted a glance along the hall. The elderly couple was approaching at a maddeningly slow pace. Irene bit her lip. Beau bowed formally as the couple started down the stairs.

In a soft undertone, he said, "I have suite 306. I would be delighted to entertain you as soon as you can elude the eyes of the curious and make your return upstairs seem proper."

The blush on her cheeks deepened, but the quick glance she gave him told she would lose no time in joining him.

In a voice meant for the ears of the descending couple, he said, "I do hope I have the pleasure of seeing you and the Senator very soon."

"Of course, Mr. Fontaine. Thomas will be delighted to know you are in Pittsburgh. You must come to Hagenstead for a visit before you run off again."

"My pleasure." He bowed and smiled back at her as he

began to climb the stairs. She stood several moments, unable to tear away her gaze, then quickly turned and continued downstairs.

The third-floor suite was large and had windows that gave a view in two directions. The bellman had set his bags on a rack in the bedroom and was kneeling to strike a fire in the grate. He rose and dusted the knees of his trousers.

Beau flipped a five-dollar gold piece, which the man caught expertly. "Have a bottle of the finest champagne sent up immediately."

"Yes, sir!" The man beamed as he made a last survey of the room to be sure everything was in order, then left, pulling the door shut.

Beau went to the window and looked out across the river and the streets where he'd ridden with Maura a short time ago. And now she was right here, barely a minute away. He smiled and turned to inspect the suite. He always stayed at the Lafayette House when he was in the chips, and he was always given one of the finest rooms. This one was no exception. The walls were papered in a soft green, stenciled with vines climbing bamboo. The muted colors were picked up in the chairs and the two long sofas with their high, curved backs. Marble-topped tables were arranged for convenience, and a polished cherry-wood writing desk stood at one side of the big windows.

The bedroom was almost as large as the sitting room. It was tastefully decorated with a mahogany four-poster bed that had a cream-colored satin quilt, an inlaid cabinet of rare woods, and a huge armoire with a carved door. At one corner, a washstand held a basin, pitcher and an oval-shaped bar of Pears soap in a mother-of-pearl dish. Several towels were stacked on a shelf, ready for use. Perhaps he should have gotten a suite for Maura as well. This was the kind of luxury she was used to. But he'd pushed too hard and fast once, and he did not want to make another mistake in that direction. The room she'd been given was pleasant, well appointed and within Maura's present limited means. He had an idea she'd react with anger if she knew he'd looked inside her purse as she slept beside the fire at the inn.

Whistling, he removed his coat and went into the bedroom. He tested the water in the pitcher and found it cold.

He yanked the bellcord. A few minutes later a knock sounded, and a maid curtsied as he handed her the pitcher. When she returned with hot water, Beau gave her an appreciative pat on the rump before she scurried out.

By the time he'd washed, another knock sounded. The moment he opened the door, Irene Zachary rushed into his arms, lifting her lips. As she clung to him, her slender fingers raked across his shirt trying to find a way under the cloth. Her body moved sensuously against him.

"How wicked you are to surprise me that way!" She pressed close. She was a tall woman, and her head was almost at a level with his. She drew back and regarded him with bold blue eyes. "I almost fainted on the spot!"

"Did you, my dearest Irene?"

She laughed because they both knew that she had never fainted in her life nor was she likely to. "I would have preferred it to having to stand there pretending you were simply an old friend of the family!" She slid her hand into the opening at the front of his shirt. Her fingers began to work across his warm chest, tangling and teasing in the coarse hair. He took her in his arms and kissed her again until she sighed and went limp.

"You are a devil—"

"Mmmm, and you are an absolute angel." He nibbled at her ear.

"Were you really going to send a note?" she demanded.

"Of course."

"What a stroke of fortune that Thomas has business in the city this week! We can spend every possible moment together. Oh, Beau, I have missed you."

There was a tap at the door and she jumped away guiltily. He grinned at her discomfort. As he opened the door, she moved back so she would not be seen.

"Your champagne, sir."

Beau took the tray and closed the door. "Now let's drink a toast to our reunion," he said as he crossed to the table and set down the tray. He lifted the chilled bottle from a silver ice bucket and wrapped a towel around it. He worked the cork loose, popped it and poured the glasses full. He held one out to Irene.

"To you, my pet."

She shook her head as she lifted the glass and came to

200

stand very close to him. "To *us* and our reunion. May it be as delightful as all our times together have been."

Beau's gaze strayed to the window. Irene set her glass aside. "You have something on your mind," she said in gentle accusation.

"Only you, my sweet."

"I think not, but I can be persuaded." She smiled devilishly and glanced at the bedroom.

"You are a brazen hussy."

"I am a woman." She came into his arms again and sought his mouth. She sighed and probed at his lips until his tongue met hers. Her hands were insinuating, and when she tried to find the buttons on his trousers, he pulled her toward the bedroom.

He watched her undress. They had been together too many times to pretend anything but the desire they felt for each other. She never failed to arouse him, and though his mind was still partially distracted with thoughts of Maura, he had no wish to pass up the opportunity of the moment. She dropped her chemise and stood before him in naked splendor, her arms outstretched in welcome. When he removed the last of his garments, her eyes went quickly to the dark triangle where his maleness sprang.

Then they were together, hands exploring, mouths tasting, until their bodies met in passion. She clawed at his flesh and writhed, moaning and speaking his name as she arched to meet his body. His hard muscles moved under her hands and his mouth stopped her cries until all thoughts were blanketed by exploding pleasure.

He lay beside her and they were silent for a long time. His eyes were closed and his mind lulled for the moment. Irene leaned so one full breast rested on his chest.

"I have never known you speechless, Beau Fontaine."

He opened his eyes. Her face was very close and her lips were pouting prettily. "You forget I have just come from a long stage trip and have had little rest for several days."

"I have known you to play poker all night and dine and dance through ten days without being tired." She frowned and curled a finger in the dark hair at his chest.

"Perhaps I am slowing down," he said with a smile.

She regarded him with a curious look. "It has been four months since I last saw you. What has happened?" She sat

201

up suddenly and her eyes narrowed. "You've met some-one!"

"I've met many people." He was tired of her badgering.

"A woman!" she accused.

He shrugged and, rising from the bed, found a cheroot in his coat pocket and bent to hold a taper to the fire. He inhaled deeply before returning to the bed.

"You are the only woman in my life at this moment. Content yourself with the thought, Irene."

She started to say something but thought better of it. It would do no good to anger him. She'd seen displays of his temper in the past, and she knew it was the fastest way to drive him away. And she had no desire to do that. She nestled against him and watched him smoke.

"We are returning to Hagenstead in two days. Can you join us there?" she asked at last. She did not look at him but kept her face pressed against his chest.

"I'm really sorry, but I can't. I have business here in the city."

She bit her lip. "We are giving a ball on Saturday. Will you come to that?" When he did not answer immediately, she said, "Thomas has invited a number of people you may find interesting. There's talk of his being renominated for the Senate. A dozen people from Washington will be there, including Obediah Cromwell."

He was glad she could not see his surprise. He raked his hand through her hair. "Obediah Cromwell of Massachusetts?"

"The same."

Beau blew smoke thoughtfully. Cromwell was a Boston politician with power and influence that kept his pockets lined with gold—and he was a gambling man. Beau had never been in a game with him, but he had anticipated the prospect for a long time. He twirled a lock of Irene's hair around his finger.

"I will be delighted to come," he said.

She curbed a smile. "To see me or Cromwell?"

"Both." He bent to kiss her, but when she would have pulled him close again, he eluded her and rose to dress.

When she was ready to leave, she came into his arms again at the door. "We have a theater engagement tonight, but I can plead a headache and escape early. Thomas will not suspect."

He frowned. "I am engaged this evening. Tomorrow night?"

"There is a dinner party in Thomas' honor." She shook her head in annoyance.

"Slip away."

"I cannot—"

"Ah . . ." He looked disappointed.

"All right," she said quickly. "I'll find a way."

He kissed her lightly, then let her out of the suite. When the door closed, he refilled his champagne glass and stood at the window to stare at the river and the imposing walls of the Fort.

His luck was turning, no doubt about it. First Maura Sullivan, and now Obediah Cromwell. Yes, his luck was turning.

CHAPTER TWELVE

Night fell swiftly, and a batting of gray clouds hid the moon. This sector of Washington City had no street lights, and there was only a pale glow from a window at the end of the alley. Kerry Flannigan pointed, then led the way.

Duggan followed him into an office at the back of the Gunnerson Carriage Works. The room was crowded. Men sat on desks and the few chairs and boxes they'd brought from the shops. Duggan was aware that he was being scrutinized carefully. Several men greeted Kerry and reached to shake his hand. None of them was especially young, and although they were dressed in work clothes, each had the stamp of the skilled craftsman. Kerry had called them together because they were the most influential workers in the plant.

Kerry raised his hands and the men fell silent. "Thanks for coming," he began. He looked around and his smile faded. "It's a sorry fact that we've waited so long to hold this meeting. And even sorrier that our courage now is spurred by knowing Gunnerson is out of the city and won't find out about it!"

There was a restless murmur. They had not come to be accused, but the truth hit home. Kerry's tone softened as he leaned forward earnestly.

"But we're here—and that's what counts. Or at least it will be if we make it." His gaze shifted around the room, pausing briefly on a man here or there. "The only way we're going to get anything out of Gunnerson is to work together. Some of us've tried alone and gotten nowhere. When Tony Packorski asked for more money last week, he was fired. He'd been out sick too many days, Gunnerson said." A discontented buzz rippled. Kerry nodded. "Sick

205

without pay! Not one cent did Tony collect while he was flat on his back with influenza. Gunnerson isn't interested in a man's health, only how fast he can work!"

The murmur swelled until Kerry held up his hands again. "I'm not going to waste time going over ground we've already covered. I think we're ready for action. We're tired of everything being Gunnerson's way—right?"

There was a chorus of agreement.

"I've brought someone to talk to you." Kerry clamped a hand to Duggan's shoulder. "This is my good friend Duggan Quinn from New York. He's been working in the Sullivan Company for a long time—was a foreman there, in fact, just like you, Willie." He singled out a burly, sandy-haired man with a glance. The man pursed his lips and nodded. "Some of you may remember that I worked for the Sullivan Company before coming here—until I tangled with a sonofabitch named Pelham Turk."

A man in the rear said, "Don't tell us about Pelham Turk. We've got Walter Gunnerson!"

There was laughter, and Kerry joined in. When it quieted, he continued. "I'll never make excuses for men like Turk and Gunnerson, but *we're* the ones who are letting them get away with it! We're making it easy for them to do what they're doing because we don't fight back!" He glanced at Duggan. "Duggan and I go back a long time, since we came from the old sod. He's been like a brother to me, and I'd trust him with anything I've got, including my life."

The room had fallen quiet. Kerry went on in a softer tone. "You all know why we're here. I've talked to you privately. Now it's time to bring the idea out into the open. I'm talking about forming a union right here at Gunnerson."

A thickset man seated on a desk said, "It costs money to form a union. Gunnerson won't pay for it, that's sure."

Kerry nodded. "If the company supported the union, they'd own it. We don't *want* it that way!"

"You want *us* to pay for it?"

Kerry nodded again. "It has to be that way, Frank."

"That means less money in my pocket on payday."

Duggan spoke up. "Everything needs a start. It won't

206

cost each man much. Most of the work can be done by volunteers at first—"

"At *first*?" Frank asked. "What about later?"

"Hear me out," Duggan said. "As things are, you work for the company as long as Gunnerson wants you and at the wages he wants to pay, right?"

Heads nodded and a few men muttered.

Duggan went on: "If one of you wants more money, he goes to Gunnerson alone. One man against the weight of the company. How many times does he get what he asks?"

Someone said, "He's more likely to be fired like Packorski."

"If you have a union, the union does the asking. No man has to buck Gunnerson alone. All of you together ask for more money, and you've got bargaining power."

A gray-haired man seated on a box scratched his chin. "What if the company says go to hell?"

"I'm too old to find a job somewhere else," another said.

Duggan raised a hand. "If you're all together, do you think Gunnerson is going to fire the lot of you? Can a carriage company make rigs without wheels? Or without bodies? How many expert wheelwrights are there in the country? How can he keep the plant open if he has no craftsmen?"

"They need us!" Kerry shouted. "Gunnerson can't build coaches with ditchdiggers!" He swung his arm. "Every man in this room is a master craftsman. It would take months—maybe years—to train others to do your jobs. Gunnerson knows that!"

Duggan said quietly, "He'd lose more money than he can afford, and the company's reputation would suffer beyond repair. Believe me, he'll think twice before he cuts his own throat. And that's exactly what he'd be doing if he went against *all* of you."

There was silence for several minutes. Then a ruddy-faced man leaning against the wall spoke. "Suppose Gunnerson says no without firing us. He's the one holds the pursestrings."

"Then we refuse to work! We strike!" Kerry shouted. "It's the same either way. He can't turn out carriages without us!"

"I've heard o' some that struck and was tried for combin-in'."

"Hell, Joe, that was a hundred years ago! Gunnerson ain't fool enough to try something dumb like that. What would it get him? We still wouldn't be working, and he'd have no carriages to sell. Anyhow, it would cost money to bring suit—and we all know how stingy he is about spending a dollar!"

Laughter rippled, and the tension eased. Kerry said, "Does that answer your question, Frank?"

Frank looked surprised. "What question?"

"About the dues we'll have to pay to get the union started and keep it going. It'll cost each of us a few dollars, but the union will get us higher wages so we'll take home more money each week. And we'll demand better lighting—"

"And shorter hours!"

"And something if a man is sick—"

Kerry smiled. "If the union does that for you, Frank, are you willing to pay a few dollars in dues?"

"Hell, yes," Frank shouted with a grin.

"That's the way it'll work. All of us together can be as strong as the company."

"But it's not all one-sided," Duggan shouted as the men began to laugh and talk among themselves. When he had their attention, he said, "We have a responsibility to work our best so the company makes money. Without the company, none of us has a job."

"When did Gunnerson ever worry about any of us?"

Duggan was about to reply when the door burst open and a dozen club-wielding men spilled inside. There was a scramble as everyone tried to avoid the swinging sticks and grab up whatever was at hand to fight back. Duggan picked up a chair and jabbed the legs at a man rushing toward him.

"Gunnerson's thugs!" someone shouted.

"Duggan—!"

He turned just in time to ward off a blow. Kerry jumped and wrested a cudgel from the attacker, pummeling the man with his fist, then cracking the stick hard against his head. Frank was swinging viciously with a weapon he'd taken, but most of the others were unable to counter the

208

surprise attack. They fell back under the raining blows. Someone opened a door leading to the factory, and the men began to scatter. The attackers didn't follow but converged on the front of the room. Duggan realized they had one objective—to get him and Kerry. Somehow Gunnerson had gotten wind of the meeting and sent his thugs to put an end to it, and to permanently silence the men who had called it. In all likelihood, Kerry had been lulled into thinking he was safe with his employer out of town, when all the time he was being set up.

Swearing, Duggan whirled and struck at a man in a heavy coat and cap. From the corner of his eye, he saw Frank take a wicked blow to the head. Duggan leaped to a desk and wrenched down the lamp. With a heave, he hurled it through the nearest window. The glass shattered and there was a momentary whoosh of flames in the alley outside as the oil ignited and quickly burned. The flare died quickly and the room was plunged into darkness.

"Duggan! Here—" Kerry's hand found his and he was pulled toward the door.

"Get a lantern!"

"Don't let them get away! The door—!"

Kerry changed course abruptly. In the blackness, Duggan could only make out vague shapes, but cool air told him Kerry had opened a door. As they rushed into a hallway, a figure loomed, and Kerry fell to one knee, coughing and sputtering for breath as the man struck him. Duggan kicked out sharply and sent the man sprawling. The figure tumbled head-over-heels. A club clattered to the floor. Duggan scooped it up as he helped Kerry to his feet. Half carrying him, Duggan rushed to the end of the hall. A shout went up behind them and light flickered as someone found a lantern. Duggan hurled the club, end over end, at the men who rushed into the hall. He didn't stay to see it find its target. He pulled the door open and rushed out.

Kerry said thickly, "The bastard tried to choke me—"

"Save your breath for running!" Duggan hustled him along. They were on a side street, and Duggan recognized the way they'd come earlier. When they were a safe distance from the factory, he let Kerry catch his breath.

Kerry massaged his neck and swallowed experimentally.

With a grin, he said, "That's another debt I owe you, friend."

"And another score to settle with Gunnerson. What about the others?" He glanced back along the quiet street.

"Most got out all right. I think those bastards had orders to put the fear o' God in the men but not inflict much injury. An injured man can't do a full day's work, Gunnerson knows that. But they were out for my blood—and yours, my friend."

"They didn't get much." Duggan grinned and wiped a hand across a small cut at the corner of his eye.

They began walking more slowly, since there was no sign of pursuit. Kerry breathed harshly. "I hope this demonstration gives the men something to think about. Gunnerson's had his way too long. Soon the power will be on our side, and Gunnerson will be taking the licks."

"*If* the men don't run scared. That's happened before," Duggan said thoughtfully.

The blanket of clouds had not lifted, and the air was heavy. The fetid odor of the canal drifted with the fog. They had a brief glimpse of the dome of the newly finished Capitol through the trees along Virginia Avenue as Kerry turned into the street where the rooming house was. They went up the stairs wearily.

As they washed up, Kerry said, "I've someone else I want you to meet, Duggan."

"Do you have another fight in mind?"

Kerry laughed. "Not with fists. This is a man who fights with words."

Duggan toweled his neck, peering at his friend.

"A United States Senator," Kerry said.

"You know a Senator?" Duggan let his brows climb in amazement.

"He's a man sympathetic to our cause, and he's got influence in Washington. Senator Elias Jerome of Pennsylvania," Kerry said. He winked. "I know a lass who can wangle an invitation to a party he'll be at. Will you go?"

Duggan grinned and held up his coat. "If I can wash the blood out of this sleeve . . ."

When the tub was filled, Maura sent away the maid and stripped off the dress she'd worn for almost a week. She

210

would have been overjoyed to discard it, but she laid it over a chair. She had to don it once more in order to go shopping. She thought of her limited funds and dumped the contents of her purse on the bed. She counted the bills and coins. Hardly enough to outfit herself and pay for the hotel room as well. The cash from Lenore had been consumed by expenses during the journey. Except for the money Duggan had given her, she had nothing.

She slid out of the chemise and tested the steaming water before lowering herself into it. The heat stung her flesh, but at the same time she felt the tingling abatement of her fatigue. She soaked luxuriously, inhaling the faint fragrance of the lilac oil the maid had added to the water. It seemed an eternity since she had enjoyed the comfort of a hot bath.

How drastically her life had changed in a short time. She was suddenly in a strange place, without a familiar face or loved one nearby. It was bewildering to realize that she no longer had Father, Mother, Lenore, not even James at the moment. Or Duggan . . . Her breath quickened with a rush of sensuality. When she was with him, the moments were a beautifully tuned harmony. But they'd been over too quickly. He had awakened a need that surfaced now and caused her body to ache with wanting. She rippled the water with her hand. Would she see him again? In spite of the anger Duggan often roused in her, she could not deny that she missed him. And she desired him. She wanted to lie in his arms, feel the heat of his body claim her, feel the fulfillment of passion. How expertly he tempted and tormented her before bringing her to ecstasy. He was experienced . . . with women like Lacy Marsh as willing partners for his lessons! Her cheeks flamed as she thought of the note left on Duggan's pillow. What did he see in Lacy? Was she more skilled in the ways of love? For that matter, did experience count for a woman as it did a man? She began to lather her body with smooth, sensuous strokes. She did not believe that Lacy was better than she—in any way!

I'm younger . . . and my body is firmer and slimmer . . . my mind is sharper so I can talk to a man on his own level instead of simpering and fawning. . . .

Her brain conjured a picture of Lacy clinging to Duggan's arm, and the vision sickened her. Perhaps men liked that sort of foolishness. Her own tongue was often too

211

sharp, she knew that well enough. Could she learn to act differently? She sighed with the knowledge that it was impossible.

The water was cooling quickly, and she finished her bath, then poured water from the pitcher to wash and rinse her hair before wrapping a heavy towel around her head. She stepped from the tub and wound herself in a large bath blanket, feeling restored and relaxed . . . and very sleepy. She'd dismissed Beau's suggestion of a nap, but now it was a deliciously attractive thought.

Still wrapped in the blanket, she went to the window and looked out. The room faced a courtyard decorated with vine-covered trellises. At small café tables, couples sat over drinks. The courtyard was sheltered by the building and looked pleasantly warm in the late-afternoon sun. A man glanced upward, and Maura drew back quickly, although she knew he could not possibly see her through the lace curtain. She drew the velour draperies and plunged the room into pleasant gloom. Dropping the bath blanket, she looked at herself in the long glass beside the dresser. Was her body exceptional? Average? She'd never given the matter much thought, but it was obvious she did not lack for roundness where curves should be. Her breasts were firm and high, her waist slim, her hips smoothly rounded. And her face was pretty. She'd heard it often enough to believe it. She thought her eyes a bit widely spaced, but she accepted the beauty of her features without question. They had a combination of her mother's delicacy and her father's strength. The boldness in her eyes bespoke an eagerness for life, and the thick amber hair, tousled now from the bath, gave her a hoydenish look. She looked ready to do battle. What was it her father had said? "It's no wonder no man has ever asked you for his wife—you'd drive him crazy with your challenging ways and your need to win!"

Perhaps it was true. The gray eyes stared back at her. But she could not pretend to be what she was not. Not for any man . . . not even for Duggan Quinn. She turned away from the mirror and climbed between the cool sheets.

Maura woke with a start at a tap on the door. Glancing at the ormolu clock on the mantel, she saw that she had slept two hours. The room was dark, and it had grown chilly. The knock sounded again.

"Yes?"

"It's the maid, miss. I have some packages for you."

Puzzled, Maura flung back the covers and, realizing her nakedness, quickly wrapped the bath blanket around herself. She opened the door a crack and after peering out, stepped back so the girl could enter. It was the same girl who had brought the bath; her arms were laden with parcels so she could hardly see over the top of them.

"There must be a mistake—" Maura closed the door and went to light a lamp.

"The gentleman said I was to bring them at seven o'clock."

At Maura's puzzled frown, the girl added, "Mr. Fontaine, miss. He said he'll come by in an hour." The girl deposited the packages on a chair and straightened her apron. "Will there be anything else, miss?"

Maura shook her head dazedly. The girl curtsied and departed as Maura lifted the top package. The soft muslin bag was closed by a drawstring which she quickly untied. She took out a bonnet of gray silk with brown ribbons forming a ruffle across the crown and brim. It was the latest fashion—she'd seen illustrations in *Fraser's Magazine* and in advertisements for Stewart's on Broadway. Amazed, she set it aside and opened the next parcel, then the next, and the next. In minutes she had laid out an entire ensemble, from silken undergarments to an exquisite dress of russet wool, so light that it scarcely had any weight at all. The skirt was full, with rows of velvet ribbon that gave it a layered effect. The bodice was pleated in tiny rows edged with pale gray lace. The sleeves were snug at the wrists and had two rows of velvet ribbon and five pearl buttons for accent. There was also a gray wool cape that swept the carpet as Maura placed it about her shoulders. The satin lining was smooth on her bare shoulders as she stared at herself in the mirror.

The towel fell forgotten to the floor. Hugging the cloak to her, she went back to the bed. She examined each of the garments in turn, marveling at Beau's perfect choices, but at the same time she knew she could not accept them.

213

Spots of color warmed her cheeks as she lifted a beige silk chemise trimmed with wide lace. Beau had overstepped the bounds of propriety. No near-stranger had the right to send such intimate gifts. It was another measure of the boldness she'd seen the first night of the stage trip, another attempt to seduce her. Far more subtle this time, but seduction nonetheless.

She started for the bellcord but paused with her hand in the air. The clothes were a peacock of color on the rumpled bed. Her own garments on the chair were a sorry bundle of dirty, mud-spattered rags.

She walked back to the bed slowly. She lifted the silk chemise, slipping it on and feeling it whisper against her bare flesh. Then she sat to draw on the silk stockings, two satin petticoats, and finally the rust-colored gown and soft, brown kid slippers. Viewing herself in the glass, she knew that she could not have chosen a more suitable outfit had she shopped herself. The fit was excellent and the color one of her favorites. It seemed impossible that Beau had selected them but she knew he had.

Crossing to the dresser, she found the hairbrush and began to work at her tangled hair. Soon it lay in shimmering waves across her shoulders. She caught it back and twisted it to a soft bun at the nape of her neck, fastening it with the tortoiseshell pins. Too severe . . . She fluffed it and pulled loose a small curl at the temple. Glancing in the mirror, she knew she had never looked prettier. And she knew that she was not angry with Beau. He had saved her the trouble of shopping. She would reimburse him for the purchases, she told herself; she could not accept them otherwise.

When a tap sounded at the door, she realized the hour had flown. With a last look in the glass, she bundled up her discarded garments and tossed them out of sight in the wardrobe before opening the door.

Beau stood smiling at her. He had changed to gray trousers and a darker coat with gleaming pearl buttons. His waistcoat was navy blue silk, embroidered with tiny flowers. The gold watch chain across it caught the flickering light of the hall lamps. He shook his head in amazement.

"I knew you'd be lovely, but I couldn't have imagined such a vision! Here, let me look at you!" He stepped inside and put a hand to her shoulder to turn her slowly. "The color heightens your complexion and deepens your eyes. Yes . . . excellent, excellent!"

"You are embarrassing me." Her eyes danced.

"Does it embarrass the nightingale to know its song is lovely?" How charming she was with her hair soft around her face. The tired lines were gone and her color had returned. He'd chosen well with the shade.

"The nightingale does not have its song delivered while it sleeps! I was more exhausted than I thought. You've saved me the time and trouble of shopping."

"The dress pleases you then?"

"I am delighted. If you will tell me the cost—"

"Let it be a gift."

"No, I cannot accept."

"Very well. I shall find the receipts and calculate the cost, though I warn you, I have little head for mathematics. I would make a poor shopkeeper." He smiled and his gaze swept her again. "And now I'm sure you must be as hungry as I am. We've had nothing since that dreary lunch at the noon stage stop. Have you ever tasted mutton so unappetizing? Thank heaven I know an excellent restaurant where the wine and cuisine will erase the memory from our palates. May I help you with your cloak?"

CHAPTER THIRTEEN

The carriage Beau hired was a handsome rockaway, with leather seats and curtains that could be drawn to close out the night air. Beau gave instructions to the driver perched in the canopied seat, then spread a woolen robe over Maura's lap.

"The nights turn cool quickly. If you're chilly, I can pull the curtains."

"No, it's perfect. I prefer being able to see."

They drove away from the heart of the city and through a suburban district. The smoke cleared miraculously, and the moon and stars glistened overhead. Many wealthy Pittsburghers were moving out to escape the congestion, Beau told her. The population was burgeoning. It seemed as if every level lot were being cleared for a house or business enterprise. There was talk that one day Grant's Hill would be as flat as the rivers.

They rode out Centre Street, past the Schenley farms where late wheat rippled like a sea of pale gold. Even the farms were being squeezed out of the city, Beau said, but he supposed progress was inevitable.

They came to a vast estate bordered by miles of white fence dipping and rising with the contours of the land. A large house with its windows shining with lights stood atop a rounded knoll.

"The Negley home," Beau told her. "Alexander Negley was one of the first white settlers in this region. The family has not parted with any of the land, except to allow a widening of the Pittsburgh–Greensburg turnpike where it crosses over there." He pointed, and she saw the wide road and a cluster of buildings. "He planned an entire town to keep him company."

"Planned it?" Maura looked questioningly.

"Yes. He encouraged people to move out by building a school, a church, and everything a town needed. The town is still thriving today, as you see."

"Mr. Negley was a man of vision."

"And a man of sufficient capital to purchase thousands of acres of land to do with what he would."

"A man should expand his holdings and build his dream. My father always encouraged James and me to set goals and work toward them."

"Your father was a wise man. Have you followed his advice?"

She looked to see if he were teasing, but his face was hidden in the shadows. "Not always as strongly as I should, but for the most part." She thought of how she had allowed herself to be driven away from the Sullivan Company by her stepfather and Braxton. She had not held to her convictions there. She recalled, too, the promise she made her mother to keep the company in Sullivan hands. She would keep *that* promise, no matter what.

"Ah, here we are," Beau said. The carriage had drawn up at a large stone house set well back from the road. At first glance, it seemed to be a private dwelling, but as they alighted, a doorman stepped forward and pulled open the wide oak doors to admit them.

"The Blue Horse Inn," Beau told her. "One of the finest in western Pennsylvania. The chef is from Paris and does not speak a word of English. The proprietor prefers it that way so the man will not be lured away by some other inn-keeper. Good evening, François. . . ."

The maître d' bowed and greeted Beau by name. They were shown to a secluded table where a waiter hovered discreetly while Beau selected from the wine list.

Maura was impressed with the restaurant. It seemed that after a long string of disappointments, she was finally comfortable and cheerful in her surroundings. Pittsburgh was as delightful as Beau had said it would be. She glanced around with interest. The decor of the dining room was elegant, with blue velour upholstery and gold and crystal chandeliers that danced rainbows against the ceiling. A thick, midnight-blue carpet was soft underfoot; the tablecloths were sparkling white. Maura recognized the china as Limoges and the flatware as sterling.

"George Washington is said to have dined here," Beau said. "The house was originally the home of a man who was killed in the fighting at the Battle of Brandywine. His widow was forced to sell the property, and the new owner converted it to an inn. And very profitably, as you see. There have been several owners, and the Blue Horse has never lacked for customers. Its reputation is the finest." He leaned close and whispered, "It is said that if one were to dine here often enough, he would see every famous person in Pennsylvania society come through those doors."

"And have you tried it?"

He shrugged, and the smile lingered. "Enough to believe the prediction would be valid if I spent more time. Look, there in the corner. Do you know who that is?"

She dared a glance, then shook her head.

"It is William Johnston, governor of the state. And there, with the woman in the hat with the enormous cabbage rose? Peter Michaels, owner of the Pittsburgh Mercantile Company." He pretended to study other faces, then continued to give her names—the mayor, a banker, a newspaper publisher. It was a few minutes before she realized he was inventing lies to amuse her.

"You are incorrigible," she scolded.

"I consider that a compliment as long as I have made you laugh." He gazed at her lingeringly until she looked away.

They sipped the wine and talked about many things. No matter what the subject, Beau was eloquent and well informed. Maura was enjoying herself thoroughly. When it came time to order, he asked permission to make the selections for both of them.

"The specialty of the house is magnificent. People travel great distances to sample it. I envy you that you will be tasting it for the first time."

He glanced up, and the waiter was beside him instantly. "We will have the *Consommé Julienne, Escalopes de Saumon* with *Sauce Tartare, Côtelettes d'Agneau et Petits Pois, Jambon au Madère*—" He glanced over the top of the menu. "Shall I order dessert?"

She shook her head. "Perhaps some cheese later."

When the waiter left, Beau said, "I'm delighted you accepted my invitation, Maura. I hope it will be only the first of many pleasant evenings."

"I may not be in Pittsburgh long," she said, thinking of her unexpected predicament.

"Surely you'll stay until your brother returns?" He fingered his sideburns.

"I don't know. A great deal depends on his reply to the wire I send." And on her finances, she thought. She did not have funds to continue on to Cairo if James were staying on there. Nor did she have enough money to live here unless she could secure an advance from Denfield.

"The man with cholera, is he a relative?"

She shook her head. "He has worked for the Sullivan Company since it was founded. He was a close friend of my father's and to both James and me."

He nodded, then switched to a more pleasant subject. He didn't want her mind to dwell on dreary paths when such a delightful evening lay ahead. "I'm sure your brother is enjoying Cairo. It's a pleasant town."

"You've been there?" It seemed he traveled a great deal, and Maura was amazed at his knowledge of the country.

"Many times. Cairo has become a hub of the nation since the westward expansion and the tremendous growth in river traffic. It lies at the junction of the Ohio and Mississippi rivers, you know. It's a lively, interesting place with many kinds of amusements."

"You said much the same about Pittsburgh," Maura said with an indulgent shake of her head.

He looked askance. "Did I? Perhaps all cities are nice. Do you suppose that can be it? I must admit that rural living does not agree with me." He grimaced. "Very bad for my digestion."

"M'sieur . . . ?" The waiter looked shocked.

"Ah, I was not speaking of the cuisine at the Blue Horse, Henri," Beau said with a reassuring laugh.

The man looked vastly relieved and began to serve the first course. As they ate, Beau chatted on amusingly. Maura could not recall when she had enjoyed a dinner more. When at last they were sipping coffee, Maura let her gaze roam about the room. The restaurant had filled and there was a steady stream of trays to and from the passageway that led to the kitchen. She noticed the maître d' suddenly hurry toward the entrance where a tall, portly man in evening clothes was removing his gloves. A blond woman, considerably younger than he, joined him. After greeting the maître d', they were led to a table in the center of the room. The woman swept through the dining room with an engaging smile. The man nodded and occasionally paused to exchange words with someone.

The woman was very attractive, with an oval face and large blue eyes framed by sooty lashes. Her blue gown emphasized the fairness of her skin, and the décolletage revealed a startling amount of full bosom. She was aware of the attention her entrance occasioned. As she took her place, her eyes canvased the room. The man seated himself and his gaze brushed Maura's. To her surprise, he rose and came straight to their table.

"Beau Fontaine! What a nice surprise. Irene mentioned that you were in the city."

Beau pushed back his chair and put out his hand. "Hello, Senator. Good to see you again." At the Senator's meaningful glance toward Maura, Beau said, "Maura, may I present Senator Zachary, one of our eminent lawmakers. Senator, Miss Sullivan."

The tall man bowed over Maura's hand and held it slightly longer than necessary. "Charmed. How is it that I have never met this beautiful lady before, Beau? I thought I knew every pretty woman in the state!" His smile said he had every intention of correcting the oversight.

"This is Miss Sullivan's first visit to Pittsburgh," Beau conceded.

"I sincerely hope you are enjoying the best it has to offer, my dear. Do you come from these parts?"

"New York." Maura rescued her hand.

"Ah, New York. I am astounded that they would allow such a beautiful creature to escape. Well, you could not have chosen a more knowledgeable guide than Beau, Miss Sullivan. Are you staying long?"

"I'm not sure, Senator."

"I hope you won't rush away. You must bring her to Hagenstead, Beau."

Beau merely smiled.

"We're having a gathering on the twenty-fourth. I'd be honored by your company, both of you."

"We'd be delighted," Beau said with a trace of a smile.

Zachary grinned broadly. "It's settled then. But of course I'll be seeing you in the interim." He inclined his head at Beau. "Are you coming in to the tables?"

Beau's fingers drummed silently on the tablecloth. "I hadn't planned to." Most evenings he availed himself of the gaming in the private rooms, where many of the best people of the city slipped away for a fling at the tables. Pittsburgh did not condone open gambling parlors, but if a man knew his way around, it was not difficult to find a game of chance.

"Why not? You owe me something, you know. Even in a house game, I'd take great pleasure in beating you."

"I don't understand," Maura said as she looked from one to the other.

"Why the gaming tables, Miss Sullivan. Hasn't Beau told you? The gambling rooms of the Blue Horse are famous." He leaned toward her and lowered his voice conspiratorially. "Beau's losses have kept the place solvent many a night, and his winnings have bankrupted it, too. I'm looking forward to matching wits with him." He nudged Beau and laughed heartily. "Not lost your famous luck, have you?"

"I'm afraid you'll have to do without me tonight, Senator."

Zachary produced a thin cigar and rolled it in his thick fingers. "It's not like you not to give a man a chance to win back a dollar, Beau. I haven't forgotten our last encounter."

"Perhaps another evening. Miss Sullivan has had a tiring journey—"

"Please don't refuse on my account, Beau," Maura said quickly. She felt almost trapped into saying it because of the Senator's coaxing.

"There," Zachary said with an expansive smile. "All your objections are overcome. I daresay Irene will welcome having someone to chat with while I play."

"You're certain you don't mind?" Beau said to Maura.

"Of course not. I'm sure I'll find it fascinating." She was

222

not sure at all, but she already felt guilty at how much of Beau's time she had usurped.

"Of course you will." Zachary put the cigar away and clasped Beau's shoulder. "Though not as much as Beau does, I'll wager. I'll see you in back after a bit then." He bowed to Maura. "A delight meeting you, my dear." He nodded to Beau and made his way back to his table.

"A compelling man," Beau said with an apologetic smile.

Maura sipped her coffee, noting that the Senator's wife was staring at them curiously. If Beau saw, he gave no sign.

"I wouldn't have thought you interested in gambling," he said wonderingly.

"I don't intend to play, only to watch you. Your friend would have been very disappointed if you had refused, and I think you would have been, too." Maura studied his handsome face.

He chuckled. "Am I so transparent?"

"On the contrary. I believe this is the first time I have been able to tell what you are thinking by the expression on your face." She gazed at him over the rim of the cup. "You are almost a complete enigma to me."

"Aha! A man of mystery!" The corners of his mouth twitched in a smile.

"Well, intriguing," she admitted with a smile.

He glanced across the room. "Very well, then I shall grant the Senator his wish. I have the feeling you'll bring me good luck tonight. Would you like more coffee?"

When she refused, he pushed back his chair. "Then I suggest we stroll into the gaming rooms and I'll show you around." He took her arm and guided her to the rear of the restaurant. There was a short hall, decorated with pictures, and an oak-paneled door that gave no indication of what lay beyond. A man in a frock coat and striped trousers came from an alcove as they approached.

"Good evening, Mr. Fontaine."

"Hello, Fritz. Are the rooms crowded?"

"Not yet, sir." Fritz opened the door and bowed them through.

The change from the quiet dining room was startling. The gaming room was noisy and busy, with men at round tables chatting and playing cards. Others stood around roulette tables and discussed bets as the wheels turned and the little white balls were flicked by impassive, tailored croupiers. Maura was surprised to see a number of well-dressed women with glittering jewels betting as eagerly as the men. Others sat at gilded tables along the wall, sipping coffee and wine.

It was an opulent room, with thick, rich red carpeting and heavy draperies at the tall windows. Despite the cool weather, half a dozen ceiling fans were operating, swirling the gathering cloud of blue cigar smoke. Beau leaned close. "This is called a carpet joint," he explained. "A slang term, of course. It's anything but a joint. It gets the name from the decor and the clientele. In many places, gambling is confined to squalid rooms or secluded alleys." As he took a cheroot from his pocket, a boy hurried over with a flaming taper. Beau puffed and blew smoke. "Although gambling has gained a modicum of public respect, in many places the law still frowns on it."

She looked around at the well-dressed patrons. "It certainly seems a gentleman's game."

"It can be a ruffian's game as well, but not here, of course." His smile said he would never expose her to anything that was less than perfect. Slipping his arm under hers, he led her toward a table where a faro dealer was turning cards from a box. They watched for several moments, then Beau drew her back so he could explain the game in a low whisper. Maura listened in fascination, amazed at the willingness of men to wager huge amounts on the turn of a single card. Beau pointed to a bearded man in a beautifully cut gray coat who stacked five gold pieces on a number as casually as if he were dropping pennies in a collection plate. Another player quickly placed a copper penny on the same number. Beau explained that he was betting against the number and the other man's wager. Around the table, the men fell silent as the dealer slipped a card from the box and turned it over. The man in the gray coat did not even blink as his gold was swept away.

New bets were placed, and the man stacked another five gold pieces on his selection. The winner stayed with his luck and coppered the bet once more. Maura was astounded at the seemingly inexhaustible supply of money that changed hands without a murmur. At Beau's touch on her arm, they moved to a roulette table where a glittering wheel spun and the ball clicked and rattled until it fell into a slot. Beau detailed the method of betting as Maura watched a woman in a black gown lose a stack of chips in two spins of the wheel.

"Do you want to play?" Beau asked.

Maura shook her head, thinking of her very meager finances. "It seems unprofitable." And foolish, she thought. She wondered how Beau could find it so intriguing.

Beau pursed his lips. "Not always. Here, I'll place a bet for you." He slipped a five-dollar gold piece from his pocket and before she could protest, laid it on number fourteen. When she tried to admonish him, he put a finger to his lips, then took her hand. "The date that I met you," he whispered with a sly wink.

Other bets were placed and the croupier spun the wheel, his eyes scanning the table as last-minute wagers were put down. Then he called, "No more bets!" The white ball chattered and dropped off the back track. "Fourteen, red," he intoned, indicating the number on the betting board as he scooped in the losing bets.

Beau smiled eagerly at Maura. "I knew you were lucky. The house pays twenty-seven to one." The croupier pushed chips toward them as people began to place new bets.

"But I did nothing!" Maura was incredulous at his sincerity.

He laughed boyishly. "That *proves* you're lucky! Now, what number would you like to bet next?"

She shook her head adamantly. "No, the money is not mine and the thought of another wager makes me nervous." It would be foolish to let herself be convinced by his high-spirited banter.

Still laughing, Beau picked up the chips. "Then we'll take these to the bank and cash them in."

She followed him across the room to a table where a thin-faced man sat with a cashbox and a mountain of chips of various colors. When Beau spilled the winnings before him, he counted out one hundred and thirty-five dollars and pushed them across. Beau immediately gave them to Maura. She tried to refuse, but he shook his head with grave certainty.

"I merely placed the bet for you. The winnings are yours. You'll ruin my reputation as an honest man if you

225

don't accept." He pressed the bills into her hand. Looking up, he said quickly, "Ah, the Senator has arrived. You're sure you don't object to my playing a hand or two of poker with him? He has his heart set on winning, though his skill with cards does not match his eagerness."

"It will be interesting to see if you're as talented at poker as you are with women," Maura said.

He smiled beguilingly. "Only if you bring me luck." He drew the white lace handkerchief from her sleeve. "A talisman to keep you close to me."

She laughed at his foolishness as he slipped the handkerchief into his pocket and folded his hand over hers. His grip tightened intimately for a moment, then relaxed. "Now I cannot lose," he declared. "Come along, I'll introduce you to Mrs. Zachary, though I warn you she's a terrible gossip and a cat to boot." He drew back his lips and hissed as he extended the fingers of one hand like claws. "Definitely feline . . ."

She suppressed a smile as the Senator and his wife approached.

"There you are, Beau. Miss Sullivan, may I present my wife, Irene," the Senator said pleasantly.

Irene Zachary studied Maura with an appraising look. Her gaze took in face, figure, gown. . . .

Maura smiled, trying to put aside the judgment Beau had planted in her thoughts, but she found it difficult under the woman's critical scrutiny.

The Senator said, "Miss Sullivan is from New York."

Irene's gaze flashed at Beau for an instant. To Maura, she said, "How delightful. You must find Pittsburgh quite dull in comparison."

"On the contrary, I am enjoying it very much." Maura was surprised at the hostility in Irene's eyes.

"Irene's been badgering me for months to take her to New York." Zachary smiled indulgently. "You can regale her with news of the latest fashions and entertainments while Beau and I find ourselves a game."

Irene looked at Beau with an unreadable expression. "Maybe Miss Sullivan would prefer to gamble. I'm sure Beau has explained some of the fine points of the table games to her."

Beau regarded Irene with a wry smile. "Maura has had

incredible luck with her first bet. I'm hoping some of it rubs off on me."

"Let's hope not!" Senator Zachary declared with a booming laugh. "You've got enough already." He glanced about the crowded room. A page in a gold coat with a blue horse embroidered over the heart veered toward them. "The ladies require a table," the Senator said. With a questioning glance at Maura, he amended, "Unless you plan to continue playing, Miss Sullivan?"

"No. I do not have the faith in my luck that Beau has," Maura said with an easy smile.

The Senator laughed and took his wife's arm as the page led them to a table. Beau pulled out a chair for Maura. He bent to say softly, "I'll only play a few hands. I'd prefer to spend the evening with you."

He bowed to Irene. Her mouth was a tight line as her gaze followed him across the room where he and the Senator joined a card game already in progress.

Maura was amused by Irene's pique. The woman regarded Beau with a proprietary air. What were they to each other? Beau had warned her of Irene's nature, yet Maura could not resist baiting the other's animal instincts.

"He's very handsome, don't you think?" she asked sweetly.

Irene's gaze came around abruptly. The glint in her eyes was icy. "Yes he is. He's the talk of the city each time he favors Pittsburgh with one of his visits. He has so *many* women flocking about, it's hard to keep track of them." She looked at Maura insinuatingly. Maura met the look boldly and their eyes locked. Irene said, "My husband tells me this is your first trip to Pittsburgh. Are you visiting relatives?"

Direct and prying. Devilishly, Maura said, "No. It is simply a pleasure trip. One ought to see something of the country, don't you think?"

Irene ignored the question. "Are you traveling with your parents or with friends?"

"I am traveling alone, though I've made friends during the journey."

The arrow found its mark. Irene's eyes flashed and a tic of annoyance worked at the corners of her mouth. Maura's smile did not waver.

227

Irene said archly, "I have never accustomed myself to the idea of *ladies* traveling without proper escort. But then I was brought up in the Southern tradition. My father would not permit me to go out without a maid in attendance. It was not until I married Thomas that I realized some women actually spend evenings alone with gentlemen."

Maura gave her an amused smile. "How fortunate that Thomas rescued you from such a dreary fate."

High spots of color stained Irene's cheeks, and she looked away toward the poker table. Maura sipped a glass of champagne and thought what a small-minded, petty woman Irene Zachary was. Did she engage in barbed remarks with every woman she met, or only women who were seen with Beau? She suspected the latter, and wondered if there had been some romantic attachment between them. Irene claimed to have led a sheltered life. Maura tried to picture Beau sitting in a drawing room courting a young lady while chaperoned by family and servants. The thought brought a smile to her lips.

"How long have you known Beau?" Irene asked when she turned back.

"Not long."

"Did you meet him in New York?"

"At a gathering near there." A stage station might be called that. Maura was enjoying fencing words with the woman.

Several emotions fought for control of Irene's pretty features, and Maura succumbed to the temptation to add fuel to the fire, "We became friends quickly. He's very charming and persuasive, as I'm sure you know."

Irene's eyes blazed and her knuckles were white as she clenched her fists. "As a married woman, I only hear of his charms secondhand. He has broken many hearts in this city and elsewhere as well. Tell me, Miss Sullivan, are you staying long in Pittsburgh? I am surprised your family consents to such adventurous travel for one so young." She regarded Maura with a supercilious air.

Maura was both amused and annoyed at having her personal affairs questioned so closely. Irene was typical of the bored, wealthy women Maura had known and disliked all her life, empty-headed gossips who pried and poked. Even

Beau saw through her. Maura smiled with feigned innocence.

"My plans are not definite."

Irene struggled to control her anger. She had the ominous feeling that Beau was involved with Maura Sullivan. He *had* been distracted this afternoon, and despite his denial, she knew it had been because of a woman. Had fate brought Beau and Maura here tonight, or had he planned it deliberately, knowing that she and Thomas would stop by after the theater? She would not put it past him! She was shaking with fury. She saw that Maura had turned her attention to the gambling, and she let the conversation die. It shook her that Beau would flaunt his latest conquest so brazenly! She studied Maura covertly. Beau found her attractive; that was obvious from the way he looked at her. She was pretty, of course, with that milky white skin and flaming hair, and she wore her clothes with the unconscious grace and elegance of one who had always been accustomed to the best. That was something that could not be imitated. Maura's every movement proclaimed a moneyed background. It didn't improve Irene's temper to have to admit it. She cooled herself with a silk fan painted with a Chinese lion. Damn you, Beau Fontaine!

Maura saw that the stack of bills and coins in front of Beau was growing steadily. As she watched, he raked in another pot. The other players grumbled and shook their heads. One threw in his cards and pushed away from the table. The Senator's face was pensive as he shuffled. The players were silent except to call their bets. The hand was over quickly, with Beau winning again. The Senator shook his head in disgust.

"Not a bit of luck! I haven't held a decent hand all night. Beau seems to have the Lady in his pocket."

"Luck is fickle," Beau said with a careless smile. "She may sit on your shoulder with the next deal."

Zachary pushed aside the cards and rose. "I'm smart enough to know when the cards are against me. It was my misfortune to insist on playing tonight." He sighed. "Gentlemen, if you will excuse me, I shall rejoin the ladies."

"And I," Beau said, pocketing his winnings. "I have a woman more beautiful than Lady Luck waiting for me." He inclined his head at the murmur of protest from the men who hoped to recoup their losses, but he did not give in to their urging. "Another time . . ."

The Senator signaled for more champagne as he and Beau joined Maura and Irene at the table. "Damnedest rotten luck I've had in a month," he proclaimed, producing a cigar and rolling it in his fingers. "Beau is the only one who comes away with full pockets."

"You exaggerate, Senator," Beau said. "Anyone can have a good night."

"Maybe he has a secret," Irene suggested maliciously.

Beau regarded her lazily and cocked an eyebrow. "I do. Maura has given me a lucky charm." He plucked the lace handkerchief from his pocket and held it aloft. "It's a well-known fact that beautiful red-headed Irish lasses have stolen the secret of the leprechauns. Everything they touch turns to gold."

Maura was delightfully outraged by his audacity, and a twinkle came to her eyes. Irene shot her a murderous glance, but the Senator laughed loudly.

"It makes losing a little more palatable to know you are the cause of it, Maura," he said. The waiter arrived with the wine in an ice bucket, showed him the label, then unwound the wire from the cork. "I should know better than to gamble with Beau," the Senator went on as the man filled the glasses. He held his to the light. "To Lady Luck and the secret of the leprechauns."

"To my Lady Luck," Beau said with an intimate smile at Maura. He sipped the wine. "Thomas has invited us to your party on the twenty-fourth, Irene. We're looking forward to it."

Irene's gaze was coldly intense. "A party at Hagenstead would not be complete without you, Beau. But I understood Maura may not be staying that long." She let her gaze slide to Maura with wicked implication. "I'm sure her family is anxious to have her home as soon as possible. Imagine traveling alone . . ."

Beau grinned disarmingly. "Perhaps I can change her mind."

Irene's mouth twitched and she fussed with the diamond clasp on her beaded purse. "Let's hope so. . . ."

She was jealous, Maura decided, consumed by pure, base jealousy. There *had* been something between her and

Beau at some time. It was impossible to tell from Beau's expression what his feelings were, though: he seemed unperturbed.

They finished the champagne, then Beau insisted it was time to leave. Maura did not protest, although she felt exhilarated and not the least bit sleepy. It was a relief to escape Irene's sharp glances and tongue.

In the carriage, they sat close on the leather cushion. Maura was aware that Beau was watching her, and she marveled at how perfectly at ease he was. If Irene Zachary's jealousy disturbed him, he gave no sign. Maura was curious to know more about the woman.

"Have you known the Zacharys long?"

"Several years. Thomas was in local politics before he was elected to the Senate. Even with a Washington post, he prefers to live at Hagenstead as much as possible."

"Where is Hagenstead?"

"Several miles outside the city. It is a magnificent place, as you'll soon see."

"I have not said I would go to the party," Maura reminded him.

He reached for her hand. "The party is only four days off. You won't have heard from your brother that soon. Please, say you'll go. It will give you something to look forward to."

Maura enjoyed the warm pressure of his fingers. "I think Mrs. Zachary would prefer to have you attend without me."

"Bosh." He sounded genuinely amazed. "The Senator himself invited you. Did Irene say something?"

She could not see his face clearly in the dim carriage, and his tone was casual. Still, Maura was convinced that Irene would miss no opportunity to make her uncomfortable if she went to Hagenstead.

"I got the feeling she didn't like me."

Beau laughed gently. "The feline characteristics I described. Irene is jealous of every beautiful woman she meets, especially those in the bloom of youth who remind her that she is passing her prime. You mustn't let her influence you. If you don't go, I won't either."

"You promised the Senator," she chided.

"I promised for both of us." He leaned close and the

231

moonlight played shadows across his face. "You cannot run away now that I have found you. Say that you'll accompany me to the party." His voice was softly insistent.

For a moment, she was silent. She had no real reason to refuse, and she realized how much she enjoyed his company. "I'll go," she said finally.

He squeezed her hand, then turned the conversation to other subjects, making her laugh and putting troublesome thoughts from her head.

The Lafayette House had settled to dim quiet. Flambeaux along the drive cast leaping shadows as the carriage came to a halt. The doorman saw to paying the driver as Beau helped Maura out.

Several lamps had been left lighted, but most of the lobby was in thick shadow. The night clerk glanced up and, recognizing Beau, nodded. Near the stairs, a silver-haired man had fallen asleep over a newspaper. His head drooped forward and he was snoring softly. Beau pointed and went by on tiptoes in exaggerated silence. Maura wagged her head and stifled a laugh.

Then they were at her room. The long hall was dim and hushed. Beau unlocked the door and solemnly handed her the key. He was standing very close, his eyes veiled and his lips smiling.

"This has been one of the pleasantest evenings of my life," he said in a near whisper. "I hope it will be the first of many."

Her heart skipped a measure. She was sorry to have the evening end. The light banter they'd engaged in seemed out of place now, and she could think of no appropriate reply.

He did not expect one. He gazed into the dark pools of her eyes and put his hand on her shoulder. Holding her gently, he brushed his lips across hers. For a moment, there was a fleeting disturbance mirrored in the gray pools. The sooty lashes fluttered, but she did not pull away. He drew her close and kissed her again.

Maura felt her reserve swept away as she surrendered to his kiss. There was none of the aggressive crudeness that had marked the encounter at the inn. Beau's lips were gentle. One hand played softly at a tendril of hair at the nape of her neck, sending irrepressible shivers through her. The

232

kiss was filled with gentle passion that roused no fear. A pulse throbbed in her temple and her desire stirred.

Beau looked at her longingly. "You are the most desirable woman I have ever known," he whispered. He brushed a curl that had fallen against her cheek. "Sleep well, Maura, and thank you for coming into my life." His lips closed the interval between them for another brief moment. Then he released her and walked down the hall without looking back.

Maura closed the door and leaned against it. Her legs were trembling and her breath fluttered. She pressed her hands to her face and found it burning. She forced herself to take several deep breaths. She was not a schoolgirl to swoon at a kiss!

The bed had been turned down and a lamp lighted. Maura glanced around. Was it because she was so far from her former life that everything seemed so different? Beau's kiss should not have aroused her. Yet she had not pushed him away. She had welcomed him, had not wanted the kiss to end. She pressed her hands to her face again.

Sighing, she hung away the cape and hat, then undressed and sat in front of the glass to brush her hair. Beau was charming and entertaining to be with, that was all. He had rescued her from gloom and despair. He was a pleasant companion and a perfect gentleman.

No . . . it was more than that. She stared at her reflection in the glass. Her eyes were bright and her cheeks delicately tinted with pink. She had enjoyed his kiss. She'd experienced a stirring of sensuous, womanly pleasure at being in his arms, pleasure filled with expectation. Her lashes lowered over reproving eyes. It was not possible that she wanted him that way! Not after what he had done in Norristown! She was allowing loneliness to color her judgment and discretion.

She rose and crossed to the glowing coals in the fireplace. A warming pan lay atop the grate. She grasped the long handle and slipped the pan into its thick flannel cover, then slid it between the bed sheets. Finally she blew out the lamp and climbed into bed.

She lay a long time with her eyes closed to the faint glow of the fire, trying to put Beau out of her mind. It was as hopeless as trying to forget his kiss. She had called him an enigma, and it was true. He was a man of many facets—like a perfectly cut prism that threw off a rainbow of color, depending on how the light struck it. He seemed to thoroughly enjoy gambling, but so did the Senator and many other men. The difference was that Beau won.

She smiled at his story of the leprechauns. He had the knack of turning any conversation to laughter with a twist of words. He'd even made the winning at the roulette table seem part of a game. It was impossible to take offense at anything he did or said or to stay angry with him for long.

She wondered about his business. Investments must be profitable to support his expensive tastes. The Lafayette House was on a par with the Astor House in New York. It did not lack for a single amenity and obviously was patronized by the wealthiest people. Senator Zachary suggested that Beau gambled extensively. That pastime required a good deal of money too, unless Beau really did win as often as the Senator claimed. Maura had never known a gambling man before. Her father had been against it in principle, though he would occasionally place a wager on a horserace. That was sport, he'd always said, and a man risked only his opinion of horseflesh.

She sighed and burrowed her head in the pillow, trying to woo sleep. Beau's kiss haunted her, and the longing it stirred would not be banished. When at last she fell asleep, she dreamed of a smiling, laughing Beau.

CHAPTER FOURTEEN

In the morning, the maid gave Maura a note from Beau. It said he was sorry but business demanded his attention. He had arranged for a carriage to take her to Mercy Hospital if she had not changed her mind. It was signed simply, "Until later . . . Beau."

She hummed softly as she dressed, recalling the pleasant evening and Beau's goodnight kiss. He was right—she felt refreshed after a night's sleep. She would see Jeb, then wire James. Yesterday's disappointments seemed less formidable, and she felt confident as she went down to breakfast. Several people were seated in the large sunny dining room with its green plants and sparkling white linens. Maura achnowledged their courteous nods and sat down to an excellent breakfast. Reluctantly she declined a second cup of dark, aromatic coffee.

The clerk said the carriage would be brought around immediately. Thanking him, she walked outside. The smoke had not yet settled, and the day was delightfully fresh. As she climbed into the coach, a couple emerged from the hotel. With surprise, Maura recognized Irene and Thomas Zachary, but the carriage was underway before they saw her. She'd assumed they would have returned to Hagenstead the night before. Of course, a dozen reasons might account for their staying in town. She shrugged off the thought. She was a bit bored with the Zacharys and was beginning to regret her promise to attend their party.

The carriage was a small closed landaulet with glass windows. At first she wished it were an open carriage so she could enjoy the lovely morning, but after a short time she was glad to be enclosed. The clear day hazed rapidly. They were traveling east and north, toward the Allegheny River and the central city where, she decided, the smoke never lifted as it did in the outlying districts. She did not recognize any streets, though she was sure they could not be far from the stage depot. Narrow thoroughfares were flanked by shops and houses. At intervals, pitch pots and coal fires, lighted in the hope of preventing cholera, trailed smoke and noxious odors to mingle with the stench of garbage and stagnant water. Maura pressed a hand to her face and turned away.

They crossed Liberty Street. They were only a few blocks from the river, but there was no refreshing breeze to clear the air. The streets grew shabbier and more industrial. Factories huddled like refugees, black smoke spewing from chimneys. The coach turned on Penn Street and headed east again.

Maura's spirits sagged. What a dreary location for a hospital. She had no firsthand knowledge of cholera, for New York was not as prone to outbreaks as many other cities, and she had never seen a victim. However, she knew that most who were stricken died. She uttered a quick, silent prayer for Jeb's recovery. She wondered if she might be able to take him out of the hospital and care for him in more pleasant surroundings. She could— She reined her thoughts abruptly. She could do nothing. She barely had enough money to survive. How could she assume responsibility for Jeb as well?

"The hospital, miss," the driver said.

Maura realized the carriage had come to a stop. She climbed down and told the man to wait. The building was three stories high, with wide steps leading to an oak door. Over it were carved the words: MERCY HOSPITAL, SISTERS OF MERCY, 1848. Even though it was only a year old, its red brick was already covered with soot. Maura went up the stairs and pulled the bellcord. Several minutes later, a young nun in a loose-sleeved black robe and a white hood with black veil opened the door.

"Good morning, Sister. I have come to see Jeb MacDonald."

"Please come in." She led Maura into a wide hall with high ceilings and walls paneled in dark wood. Two doors led off to the right. At the rear, double doors opened onto a corridor that went both directions into the building. The air

236

was close and heavy and tinged with the faint odor of chloroform. The nun indicated a bench against the wall. "Please sit." Her robe whispered softly as she disappeared behind one of the doors. A few moments later she was back, accompanied by an older nun.

"I am Mother Mary Veronica. How can I help you?" The woman's face was serene and unlined, despite her advanced years.

"I was told that a man named Jeb MacDonald was brought here last week. A cholera patient . . ."

"We understood that he had no relatives." Mother Mary Veronica's smile was placid.

"I am a friend. Jeb has no family." Maura felt a chill. "He—he is here?" She could not bring herself to consider that he might be dead.

"Yes," the Mother Superior said gently, "but he is still very ill. The miracle of cleansing perspiration occurred only last night. It will be some time before he regains his strength."

"Thank God!" Maura breathed a sigh of relief. "May I see him?"

"Yes, but you must not tire him. Sister Catherine will show you the way."

Maura followed the young nun through the wide doors and into a corridor where a stairway led upward. Near it, a door opened onto an operating room where Maura could see three rows of benches placed around a red plush operating chair. Beside it, a table held forceps, knives, hammers and a cautery iron. Maura averted her glance.

On the second floor, the nun led her into a long ward. Beds were arranged along the walls with only a narrow passage between them. Above each hung a heavy wooden crucifix. Every bed was filled. Several nuns were feeding patients or dressing sores. One, a cherubic-faced girl barely out of her teens, sponged a skull-like face with staring eyes and a mouth twisted in agony. The odor of sweat, putrefaction and waste was overpowering.

The nun indicated a bed in the center of the room. Maura gasped. This could not be Jeb! The man in the bed was a skeleton who bore no resemblance to the hearty Scotsman she had known all her life! His white hair was matted to his skull, his eyes were sunken, his lips swollen.

237

His skin resembled coarse, blue-red leather. He lay rigidly on one side as though his body were seized by viselike cramps.

Sister Catherine said, "He sleeps a great deal. This morning he took the first nourishment he's had in several days." Her glance at Jeb was full of love and compassion. "The Lord has seen fit to spare him, praise be."

Jeb stirred as though aware of the voices. Maura moved to his side quickly.

"Jeb . . . It's Maura." When he did not respond, Maura glanced at the nun. "Can he hear me?"

She nodded, and Maura turned back at once. She stroked Jeb's head, brushing back the damp hair. His skin was dry and parched, but no longer feverish. He seemed aware of her touch, and at last his eyes focused.

"It's Maura, Jeb. I've come from New York to see you," she said gently.

Surprise misted his eyes. With great effort, he whispered, "I thought I was dreaming."

"No, Jeb, I'm here."

The cracked lips smiled and his eyes closed momentarily. When he looked at her again, he said, "I'm glad to see you, lass."

"You must save your strength to get well."

"Aye, I'm devilishly tired." His breath fluttered in a tremulous sigh.

Maura blinked back tears. "I'll come again soon. Then we can talk."

He frowned as though trying to capture an elusive thought, but the effort was too demanding. He sighed again and his eyes closed. Maura bent to kiss the leathery cheek and pat his hand.

"He's asleep," Sister Catherine murmured.

As Maura followed the nun downstairs, she sought reassurance that Jeb would recover. Sister Catherine allowed that he had been one of the fortunate few whose fever had broken; the grip of the disease had loosened. "He will be all right."

As soon as she arrived back at the hotel, Maura sat at one of the Chippendale writing desks in the lobby and drafted a telegram to James, telling him she was in Pittsburgh and that Jeb was ill. She pondered a long time over how much to say of Pelham Turk's treachery and finally decided that it was a matter best discussed privately. She said only that he must return as soon as possible. Sighing, she slipped the message into her purse. She would have Denfield send it as soon as possible.

There was no message from Beau, so Maura ordered a carriage and set out for the Sullivan Boatyard. Richard Denfield was surprised to see her again, and even more surprised by her request.

"I have seen Jeb at the hospital," she told him. "It will be some time before he can return to work. Under the circumstances, I will take over the management of the company. Please bring me the records and work schedules so I can familiarize myself with them."

"But Miss Sullivan—" Denfield's eyes popped. "It's not—it's not necessary." He smiled unctuously. "I assure you, everything is proceeding smoothly. There is no need to worry yourself."

"I want to see the records, Mr. Denfield. You forget that I am a Sullivan." She fixed him with a hard gaze until at last he went to do her bidding. Maura settled herself at Denfield's desk—James' desk!—and began to pore over the ledgers and account sheets. She could hear Denfield and the clerk, Smith, whispering in the outer office.

As she immersed herself in work, she felt exhilarated. She hadn't realized how much she missed an intimate knowledge of company affairs. And Pelham could not stop her now. Even if Denfield had wired him of her arrival, it would be at least six days before he could get to Pittsburgh—if he cared enough to pursue her. It was quite possible that he was glad to be rid of her. If not, by the time he found her, James would be back, and Pelham would be powerless against the two of them.

She spent an hour studying the brief history of the boatyard. James had built several small boats which were sold at a profit, enabling him to take on the larger project of the *Patrick*. The boat was two hundred and seventy-five feet in length, with a beam of forty-six feet. Her hold would have a depth of nine and a half feet and would be capable of carrying fourteen hundred tons of freight. There would be eight boilers, each twenty-eight feet long and forty inches across. Maura realized it would be one of the larger boats on the river. No wonder James was excited! Maura went through a sheaf of work orders and supply requisitions. The *Patrick* was supposed to be completed early in November, less than three weeks away.

She rose and walked to the window that overlooked the yard where the boat was on the ways. Would it be ready on schedule? The hull was completed and her superstructure framed in, but the cabins and deck housings were not yet enclosed. The twin chimneys were black fingers pointing skyward. A few men were working on the wheelhousing, and a half-dozen others were building the pilothouse. She counted less than a dozen men in all.

She frowned and crossed to the outer office. "Mr. Denfield, why are there so few men at work?"

He looked up from the corner desk where he had retreated with a pile of letters. "It's our regular crew."

"How do you expect to meet the deadline with only a handful of workmen? It's ridiculous. Hire more immediately. Don't you realize we have less than three weeks?"

"Yes, Miss Sullivan, but—" Denfield gaped as though she were asking him to deliver the sun in golden slices at her feet.

She sighed impatiently. "Mr. Denfield, when my brother left you in charge, I'm sure it was with the understanding that production was to be kept on schedule. That is impossible if a dozen men are attempting to do the work of fifty!"

Denfield fiddled with some papers on the desk. His cheeks took on bright spots of color, and Maura wondered if it was from anger or embarrassment at being caught derelict in his duties.

"There are difficulties," he murmured peevishly.

"There will be a lot more if this schedule is not met!" She thrust out James' estimates. "There is at least a month's work left for a full complement of laborers. The work has slowed down abysmally since James left, and *you* will have to account to him for your inefficiency!" Maura tried to control her churning anger.

Denfield cleared his throat and his lower lip jutted forward. "Men will not work without wages, Miss Sullivan."

Her back stiffened. "Then pay them!"

Denfield looked triumphant. His voice regained some of its timbre. "We cannot afford to pay the twelve who are still here," he said coldly. "They are already owed for two weeks and threatening to leave. If they go—" He shrugged, and his eyes gleamed maliciously.

Maura stared at him. She had not studied the financial records of recent months, but the company was definitely in the black when work on the *Patrick* had begun. The building materials were paid for, and there were sufficient funds to meet the payroll. What had gone wrong—or was Denfield lying?

The office manager was watching her smugly. Maura met his gaze without displaying her wavering confidence. "Bring me the account book," she demanded. Without waiting for an answer, she turned back into the office and seated herself at the desk. When Denfield brought the book and wordlessly laid it before her, she did not look up. She waited until he had retreated from the office before she opened the ledger.

After an hour, she knew that what Denfield said was true. It was all there—the actual costs far exceeded the proposed ones. The unfinished riverboat was already showing a deficit of $4,000. The original work crew of forty had been cut to fourteen, and there was an outstanding payroll of several hundred dollars.

How had it happened? Maura fought growing dismay as she studied the figures. When she could find no answer, she took out the office reports and memos she found in a drawer of the desk.

A fire in a storage shed . . . twelve hundred board feet of finishing lumber destroyed. A cracked boiler plate which had to be replaced. Faulty timbers under the texas that resulted in a collapse . . . lost work hours and money. The *Patrick* seemed to be under a cloud of misfortune.

She stared thoughtfully out the window. Did James' trip to Cairo concern these catastrophes? Perhaps he was trying to raise additional capital on his own rather than ask Pelham for it. Matters were getting worse. The Sullivan Boatyard was sinking deeper into debt. She watched a workman

241

scramble across the texas deck as he fastened a guy wire. How long would this handful of men work if the payroll could not be met?

She spent several hours trying to learn all she could about the faltering company. The troubles seemed to have begun several months back, shortly after her father's death. Until then, James had been in no danger of failing to reach his goal. What had happened? Had he lost faith or heart? He was stubborn and sometimes reckless, but she had never known him to show faulty business sense. She could not imagine him gambling or becoming so engrossed with women that he neglected his work. And Jeb had been on hand to oversee the yard even if James *were* negligent.

She sighed and finally pushed aside the books and papers. She was going around and around in circles, getting nowhere. She needed time to think in order to come up with some kind of plan of action. It seemed impossible to do anything in James' absence—and Jeb's—but she had to try. Telling Denfield she would be back the next day, she left and returned to the hotel. The sun was lowering behind the Fort and the air had taken on a decided chill. She entered the lobby and threw back the hood of her cloak.

Beau strode toward her with a relieved smile. "I was beginning to worry. Did you see your friend?" He tilted his head and peered at her as though inspecting her for signs of illness or injury.

"I'm sorry. I should have left word. I did not expect to be gone so long." She had been so preoccupied she hadn't even thought to leave a note telling Beau where she'd gone.

"It doesn't matter, as long as you're all right. You *are* all right?" He looked at her intently.

"Yes. And thank you for arranging the carriage. I saw Jeb, and to my vast relief, he seems to be recovering. I've spent the afternoon at the boatyard."

"Tell me about it over tea," he said. He slipped a hand under her arm and led her to a small dining room where tea was being served. She realized she had not eaten lunch, and she attacked the tiny sandwiches with gusto as she related the events of the day to Beau.

"And so my situation seems to become more hopeless by the hour," she said finally. "I've wired James. In the mean-

242

time, I will not let Denfield close down the yard, even though it's on the verge of financial ruin."

"Has Denfield suggested a shutdown?"

"No, but his attitude plainly indicates he is considering it."

He regarded her pensively. "You cannot expect men to work without wages. They have families to feed."

She set her jaw. "And we have a boat to build! I'm sure James has gone to raise the money he needs." Even as she said it, she knew that the rest of the workmen might walk off before James returned. Worry gnawed at her.

Beau took her hand with a comforting gesture. "I don't want to pry into matters that are not my concern, but it seems to me that an appeal to your stepfather would be logical. After all, he has a stake in the success of the Sullivan Company." With the fire that had disrupted the New York factory, Pelham Turk would definitely be interested in recouping his loss from another source. Beau saw the quick, tight lines bracket Maura's mouth. Mention of her stepfather did not please her. Was it he who had caused her to run from New York?

Her voice was knife-edged. "I will not beg from my stepfather!" Too late she realized she was revealing too much. "I'm sorry, I'm taking out my temper on you, the person who deserves it least. Your suggestion is excellent, except that I do not get along with my stepfather. There is no way I can appeal to him."

"I understand." He squeezed her hand reassuringly. She still had not told him anything of the circumstances that had made her leave New York, but the bitterness in her voice said more than words. Her hatred for her stepfather was unbridled.

She finished the last of the sandwiches and wiped her fingers on the white linen napkin An idea had been forming as she talked. It was a slim hope, but it was something. "Beau, you've already done so much, I hate to ask a favor."

"Anything I can do," he insisted quickly.

She took a breath. "Are you acquainted with any bankers? If I talk to someone—"

"You may be able to borrow money, is that it?"

She nodded hopefully.

He was thoughtful a moment. "There is one man. I don't know him personally, but I've heard Thomas Zachary speak of him. It would do no harm to see him. I'll take you in the morning. But only if you consent to have dinner with me again tonight."

The thought of refusing never crossed her mind.

They ate in a pleasant restaurant only five minutes' ride from the hotel. It was not as elegant as the Blue Horse Inn, and much quieter. Again, Beau was greeted cordially and seemed to know all the staff by name. They shared an intimate table in a secluded corner and dined on pheasant, rice and tender sweet corn. Over coffee, Beau delicately brought up the subject of finances.

"If your brother is delayed in his return to Pittsburgh, you cannot possibly get along with only one dress to your name. Let me arrange credit for you at one of the shops. You can purchase what you need or have fittings—whatever it is women do. Then when your brother comes back, you can settle the bills."

She had never been in debt before, but he was right. She couldn't get by with a single outfit. It might be weeks until she returned to New York. With a heartfelt smile, she agreed. Beau clasped her hand warmly and said no more.

Later when he saw her to the door, he again took her hand and held it lingeringly. The flickering gas lamps in the hall gave a dim yellow light. His face was bathed in shadow as he drew her into his arms and brushed her lips with a gentle kiss. For a moment, her breath fluttered and a sigh escaped. Then Beau released her and whispered, "Good night . . ."

Maura felt a strange disappointment as he left her. Was it possible that she was falling in love with Beau?

The following morning, he was waiting for her. They ate a hearty breakfast in the cheerful, sun-splashed dining room. Immediately afterward, they rode to the boatyard so Maura could collect the necessary papers that would help her cause at the bank. Denfield protested, then retreated into angry silence when Maura reminded him that she was in charge and he would do well to remember his place.

Beau hid a smile at Maura's forcefulness as he carried the small satchel back to the carriage.

The Pittsburgh Bank was a large, square building in a busy section of the city. The inside consisted of a cavernous room with stone pillars and an arched ceiling of dark wood. Five tellers' cages were along one wall, each with a grilled front and glass partition. The tellers were impeccable in black suits, stiff white collars and black cravats. They smiled and frowned in exactly the same manner, and Maura wondered if even the smile had been part of their training. Several knots of men stood here and there discussing business or passing the time of day. The bank seemed to be a clearinghouse for the city's businessmen.

The far side of the room was fenced behind a waist-high oak railing. At half a dozen neatly spaced desks, clerks were occupied with ledgers or letter-writing. Beyond, the heavy steel door of a vault stood open, and another oak door was lettered: NATHAN COPPERFIELD, PRESIDENT.

Beau accompanied Maura as far as the clerk stationed immediately outside the president's office. After telling the man her name and mentioning that Senator Zachary had sent them, Beau gave Maura a reassuring smile.

"I'll wait outside," he whispered in a sepulchral tone lightened by a wink. "You'll want privacy for your business."

Before she could demur, he'd taken his leave and she was being shown into Mr. Copperfield's office. The banker rose from behind his desk and rubbed his hands with a papery sound as he smiled benevolently. He was a small, round man with a balding head and pale eyes. He wore a dark suit with a gold watch chain across his vest.

"Please sit down, Miss Sullivan. It is not often that I have the pleasure of seeing such a beautiful young lady in these offices. Please—" He indicated a large leather chair across from his own.

Maura sank into the chair and was almost swallowed up by it. Although she was easily as tall as Copperfield, she felt dwarfed as he seated himself behind the desk. She wondered if the arrangement had been designed to put customers at a disadvantage.

"And now, what can I do for you? My clerk tells me Thomas Zachary recommended your visit. . . ."

Maura did not correct the misunderstanding. If it would help to have the banker believe that, so much the better. As briefly as possible, she explained her quest, opening the satchel and laying out cost sheets, receipts and schedules on his desk.

Copperfield tented his fingers and listened, occasionally leaning forward to glance at some item Maura pointed out. His smile faded slowly and was replaced by a studied frown. At last he cocked his head and held up a finger.

"The name did not jog my memory until now. Sullivan, yes—James Sullivan. Is he related to you?"

"My brother . . ." Maura's elation ebbed quickly as Copperfield's frown deepened.

"Of course. The Sullivan Boatworks. Forgive me, Miss Sullivan, but I am not accustomed to young women taking an active part in business dealings. But surely your brother must have told you?"

Her jaw tightened. "My brother is away on business. I have not seen him since my arrival in Pittsburgh."

"I see . . ."

"Is something wrong, Mr. Copperfield?" The worry had become tangible. The banker's gaze fastened momentarily on a point beyond Maura's head, then came slowly back to her face.

"Your brother came in to see me three months ago. He secured a loan for two thousand dollars at that time. I'm afraid it is quite impossible to consider advancing further sums until the present encumbrance is paid off."

Maura sank into the warm leather. Copperfield shook his head and rubbed his hands again in a nervous gesture that added to Maura's feeling of defeat. She frowned and tried to recall the accounts she'd studied yesterday. There was no record of the loan. She could not have missed it if it were there. Why hadn't James recorded it properly? She realized the banker was staring at her, and she drew herself up determinedly.

"It seems I have wasted your time, Mr. Copperfield. I apologize." She began to gather her things.

"Not at all . . . not at all. It does no harm to reassess one's position now and then."

Hope flared. "You mean you may reconsider my request?"

246

The banker shook his head quickly and looked away. "No, dear me, I'm sorry. I didn't mean to give that impression. Purely for business reasons, of course. Tell me, Miss Sullivan, does your brother plan to return soon? I'd think he would regard his business obligations as paramount. As I recall, his note falls due very soon. I'm sure he doesn't want to be in default."

Maura dropped the last of the papers into the bag. "The Sullivan Company always meets its obligations, Mr. Copperfield. You can be sure my brother will be, in touch shortly." She rose and turned to the door. "Thank you for your time, sir."

The banker nodded as he showed Maura out. She was still shaken by the news of a debt in addition to the problems she already faced. Two thousand dollars! She prayed that James had gone to work a miracle in Cairo. They certainly needed one.

Beau was solicitous on hearing of her failure, and he tried to cheer her with an offer of a pleasant ride in the country. It was a temptation to forget her problems, at least temporarily, but Maura declined.

"There is another matter I cannot postpone," she declared firmly.

At his curious look, she offered only a partial explanation. "I must consult a lawyer on a matter that requires immediate attention." With James away, she dared not waste precious days before taking action against Pelham. She considered asking Beau's advice, but she hesitated to involve him in her fight with Pelham, not only because he'd already been so kind to her, but because this was her own battle.

He asked no more questions. "A lawyer . . . hmmm . . . There are many, of course. Give me a moment to think." He ran a thumb along his sideburn. "Fulleron, yes. Davis G. Fulleron. His offices are nearby. Shall we stop?"

He helped her into the carriage. Giving the driver an address, Beau settled back and chatted about inconsequentials. She marveled at how willing he was to help her without prying.

The law office was on the second floor of a gray stone building that faced the Fort. Beau spoke to the clerk at a wide desk behind a wooden railing and was told that the lawyer was in. The clerk vanished into an inner office to relay the request for an appointment and returned a moment later to usher Maura into the lawyer's office. It was a dark room with tall, narrow windows that faced a courtyard and offered meager light. It was almost austere, with a rolltop desk, several uncushioned chairs and a glass-doored bookcase full of faded volumes with matched bindings. Davis Fulleron smiled perfunctorily and showed her to a seat before folding his long, thin frame into the wooden armchair at the desk. He swiveled to regard her with solemn, pale eyes.

"How can I be of service, Miss Sullivan?" he asked in a silky voice.

Maura chose a direct approach. "I am Maura Sullivan, Patrick Sullivan's daughter, from New York. I'm sure you're acquainted with my family's name and reputation."

The lawyer knit his brows. "The Sullivan Carriage Company and Boatworks?"

"Yes. When my father died last winter, the business came to my mother, my brother and me. A short time ago, my mother also passed away. Although it was expected that her share of the company would be divided between James and me, to my astonishment I have learned that it has gone to her second husband, or so he claims. It was never my father's intent that the business he worked so hard to build pass into the control of persons outside the family. I am of the opinion that considerable pressure was brought to bear on my mother, who was weak and ill, to agree to this arrangement. I would like to engage your services to look into the matter and set it to rights."

Fulleron hooked his thumbs under his chin. For several moments he was silent. His expressionless eyes never left her face. At last he said, "I'm well acquainted with the Sullivan family reputation. Mrs. Sullivan married a prominent New York lawyer, I believe, Pelham Turk?"

"That's correct." Maura would not let her mind dwell on her hatred for Pelham. "I have reason to think Mr. Turk intends to usurp control of my share as well as my mother's, and I will do everything in my power to prevent this."

The scowl etched deeper between Fulleron's brows. "How does he plan to do this, Miss Sullivan?"

248

"I would put no underhanded methods beyond him," she said bitterly.

"I see . . ." Fulleron was silent again, and he leaned back in the chair so that it rocked slightly on its springs.

"Will you handle the matter?" Maura demanded impatiently.

The lawyer pursed his lips and settled deeper into the chair. When he spoke, his tone was flat. "Do you have documents to substantiate your claim that you are one of the New York Sullivans?"

She drew back as though slapped. "You doubt my word?"

He shrugged impassively. "The Sullivan family is well known. Details of their personal lives are printed in newspapers and gossiped about widely. I have never met you before. It's a natural precaution to want your identity verified."

She was dumbstruck. It had never occurred to her that she would be questioned about something so . . . so obvious! "I have no legal documents, but anyone in New York can attest to my identity!"

"And in Pittsburgh?"

Denfield had accepted her, but he was not likely to come to her aid. She shook her head.

Fulleron lifted his mouth in a wry smile. "There are a thousand people named Sullivan in the country. It's a common enough surname with the influx of Irish during the last fifty years. In my profession, one sees many opportunists who hope to take advantage of someone else's name and fortune."

Maura's mouth fell open and fury flashed in her eyes. "I am not accustomed to having my veracity doubted, Mr. Fulleron!"

"Miss Sullivan, legal proof is absolutely vital. I can scarcely go into court without it. You mentioned your brother—is he able to back your claim?"

"Of course!"

"Then I suggest we make another appointment when he can come with you—"

"He is out of the city on business." Maura began to realize the futility of her position. She had no choice but to wait for James' return.

"I see." Fulleron's smile faded.

"Mr. Fulleron, this is a matter of greatest urgency," Maura pleaded. "Every day it is delayed reinforces my stepfather's position. The Sullivan Company assets are considerable. I only want what is rightfully mine. If it is impossible to undertake action in the matter of my mother's estate, will you at least take steps to ensure that my share of the company profits is not misdirected? I have had no accounting from my stepfather since he took over the company."

His lips worked in and out. At last he shook his head. "I regret that any action at this time is impossible. If you can provide verification—"

Maura rose abruptly. "I'm sorry I've wasted your time, Mr. Fulleron!" Anger made her hands tremble, and she clutched her reticule. She felt foolish for not realizing she would need proof to convince anyone of the truth of her story, especially a lawyer. "I am staying at the Lafayette House. Please send your bill to me there. Good day." She marched from the office.

Beau sensed that she had met another failure. "Is there anything I can do?"

She shook her head. She was too upset to discuss the fiasco, and the knowledge that she could do nothing until James returned left her feeling helpless. Beau insisted her spirits needed reviving and he ordered the carriage driver to take them across the river.

"An outing is exactly what you need," he declared. "Autumn will soon be gone and I will never forgive myself if you have not seen its splendor in the hills. And when we return, I know a lovely place where we can relax over dinner. Your problems will seem less formidable, even if I cannot erase them."

When she tried to thank him, he shushed her and clasped her hand. "Being with you is all the thanks I need."

The next day, Maura grew increasingly impatient for a telegram from James. She asked half a dozen times at the hotel desk, but each time she was told there was nothing, and her irritation changed to worry. She would have set off in search of him except for her impoverished state. Her meager supply of cash was almost depleted and she had no hope of replenishing it until the Sullivan Company was out of debt. Beau reassured her by reminding her that the telegraph was a very recent invention and service was not as reliable as might be hoped. Often wires went down or equipment failed, and there was a distinct shortage of trained operators. She must not worry. He tried to cheer her in a dozen small ways. He kept his promise to introduce her at several shops where proprietresses were willing to extend credit. She purchased several ready-made gowns and had fittings for half a dozen others which would be tailored from fabrics she chose.

She also spent hours at the boatyard reviewing the books but found no mention of the loan from the Pittsburgh Bank. At last she concluded that James had not wanted Denfield, and more specifically Pelham, to know about it, so she did not question Denfield on the subject. She was certain that anything Denfield learned would be quickly passed on to Pelham.

The dilemma seemed more hopeless than ever. Four workmen quit, and the progress on the *Patrick* was almost at a standstill.

Her only ray of hope came from Jeb MacDonald.

On her second visit to the hospital he was sitting in a chair near the window. He was dreadfully thin and weak, but the sickly, bluish hue had faded from his skin. His eyes lighted up when he saw her.

"I thought it had been a dream after all, lass."

She sat on a low stool and clasped his hand. It was so thin she could feel the sharp knuckles through the papery skin. "How good it is to see you up!"

"Aye, it's good to get out of that bed. I've never had anything drain m' strength so. But it's over. Let's talk of pleasant things. I dinna know you were coomin' to Pittsburgh. Is yer mother with ye?"

Sadly Maura told of her mother's death and her own flight from Meadowfield and the Turks.

The Scotsman's eyes went hard. "The man's insane. Whippin's too good for him and that Braxton!" He shook his head wearily. "Poor Francine . . . she's better off with Patrick."

"And I'm better off in Pittsburgh—or so I thought. Only I arrived to find you ill and James gone. Why did he go? He should be here running the yard."

"We've had trouble, lass. Jamie's gone to try to borrow money. Without it . . ." He frowned and his eyes clouded.

"I've been to the office and seen the books," she said.

"You've met Denfield?"

Maura nodded. "I am not impressed with the assistant James has chosen. The man seems barely competent."

"Assistant?! Did he tell you that?" Jeb was incredulous.

"Yes, isn't he—?"

"The man's nothing but a clerk! He'll have everything mucked up."

For a moment, Jeb thrashed about. The thin blanket covering his legs slipped off and Maura rescued it. She tucked it around him. "The nurse will put me out if you become excited and have a relapse," she scolded. "Now, tell me the story from the beginning, then perhaps we can figure out what to do."

Jeb sighed. His voice was reedy. "Pelham Turk refused to advance a penny for 'Jamie's folly,' as he calls it. Not one penny even though Jamie is only weeks away from completin' the best damned boat on the river!" He shook his head angrily. "At first it was only a few hundred dollars—because of the rain. Two weeks' downpour put us behind schedule. Jamie needed men to work overtime to make up for it."

Pelham had never even mentioned that James had asked for help! In fact he'd never admitted *hearing* from him—not even when he knew Francine was worried sick! Maura's neck corded and warm anger seeped across her face. How needlessly her mother had been made to suffer! Not only needlessly, but with deliberate intent on Pelham's part!

Jeb said, "We struggled along until the accidents began. Small at first, then worse. One damned thing after another until Jamie and me moved ourselves into the storehouse so's we could keep an eye on things."

He was suggesting deliberate sabotage! "Did you discover anything?" she asked.

He shrugged and the effort seemed to weary him. "The accidents let up, but the damage was done. We're behind

252

schedule and in debt. If Jamie doesn't manage a healthy bit of cash—" He sighed, and his bony fingers plucked at the blanket.

Maura laid her hand over his and tried to sound cheerful, even though she shared his despair. "He will. You know for a fact that James can charm the birds out of the trees. He won't have any trouble coaxing a few thousand dollars out of some intelligent businessmen."

"Aye . . . but he may have to sell the boat to do it, lass." Jeb's eyes misted with tears of weakness and frustration. "It would break his heart."

Maura drew a hard, deep breath. It couldn't be! James would not consider selling the dream he'd cherished so long. But even as she told herself she would not believe it, she knew it was possible. What other course was open to him? None, unless they could finance the completion of the boat and get it in the water.

She saw that Jeb was exhausted, and she rose to go, patting the blanket around him and smiling with more cheer than she felt. "You must get well quickly and come back to help me run the yard. Denfield is impossible, as you well know. I need your expert guidance. Rest now, and don't worry. The Sullivans are not beaten yet."

His eyes closed as she kissed his cheek and left him drowsing in the sunlight.

CHAPTER FIFTEEN

The day of the party at Hagenstead was clear and bright, with a westerly wind that held a whisper of winter. Maura found herself looking forward to the event, despite her early misgivings. During their dinners together, Beau occasionally talked of the Zachary estate and praised the magnificent stables the Senator kept. His prized horseflesh included Arabian stallions and a Kentucky Walker that had been sired by the famous Greenbriar Dandy. He told her, too, that the house itself had an illustrious history dating back to when British troops occupied it during their battles against the French.

In a fit of recklessness, Maura purchased a ball gown from Madame Courbon, the fashionable dressmaker Beau took her to. It was full-skirted, deep green satin that shimmered and rustled softly with every movement. The low scooped neckline was edged with black lace that lay against Maura's creamy skin like a delicate cobweb. The bodice was lightweight velvet, with full sleeves that ended just above the elbows, and there was a diamond-shaped inset of satin covered with lace at the front. With it, Maura wore black lace gloves and carried a small beaded reticule.

Beau smiled approvingly as he held the gray wool cape for her. "You are a vision! Men will turn green with envy at my luck in being your escort."

Maura smiled at his extravagant praise. Because of the mourning period following her father's death, it had been a long time since she had enjoyed a social affair. Maura suffered a pang of remorse at the thought of how inadequately she had mourned her mother's so recent death. But with her world turned upside down by Pelham and his son, such a formal observance was scarcely possible. Now, with Beau at her side, she knew it would be a pleasant evening, and grim thoughts must not spoil it.

Beau was resplendent in a black tail coat and trousers. His cravat was tied under a stiff white-collared evening shirt with ruffles that cascaded to an embroidered gray silk vest. A thick gold chain anchored his watch to a pocket, and he wore a high black silk hat with a rakish flair. He was in top spirits and provided excellent company.

Hagenstead was set among the hills east of the city, amid towering pines and oaks. It was a ride of less than an hour, but Beau insisted they start early so Maura could see more of the countryside. Since her arrival in Pittsburgh she had barely been beyond the city limits; Beau was determined that she see some of the more attractive sights. He hired a landau and driver, and provided a thick woolen lap robe to ward off the chilly air.

The road wound through the hills like a meandering stream. The journey took on the air of a summer's outing as Beau pointed out little things that delighted Maura—a ruffled grouse strutting in a meadow, a rabbit sniffing the air as it listened to the sound of the carriage, a flaming maple forecasting the season. When they arrived, Maura was sorry the ride had come to an end.

Hagenstead was vast, with miles of white fence rails enclosing fields and forests. The gatekeeper tipped his hat and waved them into the long, twisting drive to the house set far back from the road.

The drive was bordered by sycamores which were black as the last rays of evening sun vanished behind a hill. Golden shafts spiked through leafy branches, and the wind whispered like a prayer at day's end.

The house stood on a rise against a backdrop of thick forest, with a breathtaking view of the valley below. In the distance, a silvery ribbon of river etched its way across the landscape, disappearing now and then among the steep hills and wooded basins. The sun was below the horizon now, and the shadows were thickening.

The driveway ended in a sweeping turnaround where several carriages were halted. The house was ablaze with lights. Large and rectangular, it stood three stories high, with a dormered attic and five dark chimneys silhouetted against the sky. Steps led up to a portico with magnificent fluted columns. The wide front doors were attended by two liveried footmen in blue velvet coats with silver buttons and ornate froggings.

Beau and Maura were ushered into a hall that ran the full depth of the house. It was lighted by crystal chandeliers with hundreds of candles reflected in shimmering prisms. Strains of music drifted over the murmur of voices as Thomas Zachary greeted them.

"Ah, Beau! And the delightful Miss Sullivan. How nice to see you again." He clasped Maura's hand as a servant took their wraps. "Did you have a pleasant ride? Irene was worried that a cold snap would chill the gaiety of her party."

Maura smiled and made some suitable comment as Irene Zachary detached herself from a group and came toward them. Her eyes caressed Beau for a moment, but her glance at Maura was guarded.

"I'm delighted you were able to come after all," she said. She was wearing a dress of ice-blue silk that matched her eyes and highlighted her fair complexion. The voluminous skirt was gathered in pleats to a bodice covered with a scrollwork of seed pearls. The neck and sleeves were un-adorned except for self-piping; the skirt was caught up at intervals with tiny satin bows to give the effect of draped layers. Maura knew at a glance that it had been fashioned in Paris. Irene linked her arm through Beau's and smiled enchantingly. "I have warned Thomas that I intend to spirit you away to show you the new gelding he bought last week. It's a gorgeous creature."

"Beau and Maura have come to enjoy the party, not view the stables, my dear."

Irene tossed her head. The blond curls, arranged in clusters at the sides of her head and held by sapphire-studded clips, danced. "I'll only detain Beau a few minutes. And I wouldn't dream of taking Maura away from the festivities. Thomas, you must introduce her to some of the gentlemen so she can dance. The musicians are already tuning up. Come along, Beau, we'll be back before we are missed." She smiled innocently and tugged at his arm, propelling him down the hall. Beau gave a suggestion of a bored sigh and winked at Maura.

Maura hid her annoyance rather than give Irene the sat-

257

isfaction of knowing she was ruffled. It was going to be a wretched evening if Irene continued to exhibit this possessive jealousy. Maura began to regret coming—and the evening was just beginning.

When Thomas offered his arm, she let him lead her into the ballroom. Several dozen guests were already gathered. The strains of a lively quadrille wafted from the musicians' alcove. The room was festooned with garlands of greenery and hothouse flowers so the air held the mild aroma of a forest. Six huge chandeliers blazed with light, their crystal prisms shimmering and tinkling softly in the breeze from an open window. The room was papered in pale green and silver, and the woodwork had been rubbed to a gleaming luster that reflected the lamps.

Senator Zachary headed for a group near the window. Maura became the focus of attention as he introduced her. She memorized the names quickly: Mr. and Mrs. Schneider, a middle-aged couple with stiff backs and stern faces; Senator Elias Jerome, a portly man with sleek black hair; Barth Coles, tall and slender with pale eyes that lingered on Maura with suggestive intensity; Rachel Morrison, a pretty, fluttery woman in red; and a bald man with a hawk nose and a courtly manner who was introduced as Obediah Cromwell.

Cromwell and Coles vied for Maura's attention, plying her with questions. In moments, she was relaxed and fell into easy conversation.

"If this is your first visit to Pittsburgh, I would be delighted to show you some of the sights," Coles said, taking her arm possessively.

Zachary chuckled as Maura slid deftly from the man's grasp. "I don't think your wife would appreciate your being seen about with such a lovely young lady," he said.

Coles was not embarrassed in the least. He shrugged impassively, his smile lingering expectantly on Maura. "Besides," the Senator continued, "Miss Sullivan already has an escort. None other than Beau Fontaine."

Coles' eyes widened. "I didn't know Fontaine was in town."

"Fontaine!" Obediah Cromwell glanced about as though expecting Beau to materialize. When his gaze settled on

258

Maura again, his expression had altered subtly. "Mr. Fontaine's eye for beauty must be commended. I trust he'll be joining us soon?"

Maura said glibly, "He is looking at the Senator's new gelding."

"Irene couldn't wait to show the animal off," Zachary explained with an indulgent air. "She's quite taken with it. I must confess it's a superb specimen."

Cromwell ignored the remark and watched Maura keenly. "I've heard so much about the fabled Beau Fontaine, I consider it a stroke of luck that I am to meet him at last."

"I had no idea he had a reputation," Maura said pertly.

"I'm told the man is incredibly lucky at poker. If the cards fall to him as fortunately as does the company of beautiful women, I expect the reputation is well deserved."

Maura smiled at the compliment but wondered that Beau's gambling merited such widespread acknowledgment.

Cornelia Schneider was obviously bored with the attention Maura was receiving and diverted the conversation. "We've been hearing rumors that the Chilton Ironworks may close down, Barth. Is there any truth to them?"

"None whatsoever," Coles said peevishly. "We are producing more than a thousand tons of pig iron a year. The boom in boatbuilding has expanded the market and encouraged us to double our quota."

"The stories imply you're having labor disputes," Joseph Schneider said.

Coles bristled. "That sort of rumor always flourishes. It's nonsense. This business of unions has everyone agitated. We've barred the union people from our plant. They stir up trouble and make our men think they'll get something for nothing. They're appealing to the rabble."

Maura's interest perked. "I didn't realize that unions were widespread. I heard of them in New York."

Barth Coles forgot his flirtation in momentary pique. "Local organizations have existed since the Revolution, but they've never gained power. And with good reason. If shoemakers in Philadelphia want better ventilation and lighting, it's between them and the shop owners. It's foolishness to

259

think that shoemakers all across the nation should band together, for God sakes!"

Elias Jerome pursed his lips. "Your viewpoint isn't as widespread as it was a few years back, Barth. There's talk at the Capitol that unions should become national. There are half a dozen groups lobbying Congress right now."

"Government has no business interfering," Coles declared.

"Union advocates claim it's time someone interfered on behalf of the working class. It may be a point well taken." Jerome glanced around the group.

Maura said, "What can unions promise workers that the men cannot get by direct negotiation with their employers?"

"Power, Miss Sullivan," Cromwell answered brusquely. "A thousand men have a louder voice than ten or fifteen."

"Do they intend to gain their objectives by shouting?" she asked.

Barth Coles laughed, and Cromwell gave him a hard look.

"If need be," Cromwell replied. "Management rarely listens to the workers who put money in their pockets. They demand production but are deaf to the cries of those who do the producing."

"You're speaking in very broad terms. No one can believe management is as insensitive as you paint it," Maura protested.

"Enough people do to create a surge in pro-union sentiment, Miss Sullivan."

Maura did not like Cromwell, but she wanted to hear more of his views. Duggan had talked about unions. "If workers have free rein to make demands, it can result in confusion and nothing will be accomplished," she said. "Every group needs someone to speak for it. Who will speak for the unions?"

"The unions will be run democratically," Cromwell answered. "They'll hold elections and choose spokesmen."

Barth Coles looked incredulous. "Do you really believe that every man will be polled on his opinions? It's more likely that a few will force their convictions on the rest. It will wind up being a few hotheads biting the hand that feeds them. No company can operate profitably with dissent fomenting."

"Management has been in the driver's seat too long," Cromwell said sharply.

"But management is the backbone of business," Maura insisted. "If men with vision, ability and money did not establish factories, there would be no work."

Cromwell glared at her as he would at a child who had forgotten her manners.

Senator Jerome altered the direction of the conversation. "If unions go national, they'll be a powerful voting bloc. No Congressman can afford to ignore that factor. The State of Pennsylvania already has the Workingman's Party."

"You forget that management also makes up an important contingent of voters," Senator Zachary said churlishly. "I have to consider them in any balloting on a bill. *They* are the people who put me in office and keep me there. I'm not interested in unions."

Jerome extracted a cigar from a silver case and clipped the end. "I was hoping you'd listen to the other side, Thomas. I took the liberty of bringing along someone who hopes to enlighten you before we return to the Senate and consider the bill against national unions."

Maura realized that Jerome shared Cromwell's viewpoint but was much more tactful. She turned her attention to the Senators.

Zachary was trapped between duty and bias. "Any friend of yours is welcome in my house, Elias."

"Even if he espouses the union cause?"

Zachary laughed. "I hope you have brought him to enjoy my hospitality and not bend my ear to his pleas. Who is the chap?"

"A very persuasive young man who was introduced to me in Washington a few days ago. He convinced me that his issue is worth listening to and doing something about. He's trying to organize a union for the building trades—carriage-makers, shipbuilders and the like."

Maura looked at him with a startled expression. "Shipbuilders and carriage-makers, Mr. Jerome?"

"Yes. He has recently come from New York, where he says conditions have reached a point that demands action.

261

We've had several incidents in Washington as well. It bears looking into."

"Nonsense," Zachary said. "Most carriage-makers are small businessmen. And as to boatyards, it's ridiculous. There are hundreds of them. We've a dozen right here in Pittsburgh that have sprung up in the past two years, not to mention the big outfits like Greenaugh or Fitzsimmons. How can they be expected to join under a single banner? They're competitors, not a social club."

Jerome was unruffled. "The companies are competitors, Thomas, not the workmen."

Maura was still staring at him. She could not shake the numb feeling that overwhelmed her. She heard herself asking, "Who is this man, Mr. Jerome?"

"A fellow by the name of Duggan Quinn."

The blood drained from Maura's face and her heart went on a rampage. Duggan! Here? Her glance darted in search of him. The thought of seeing him took her breath away, and her legs felt suddenly weak. Had Duggan come to Pittsburgh because she was here? She tried to concentrate on his connection with the union, but the memory of their last hours together set her pulse racing. She struggled to regain her composure.

"Are you all right, Miss Sullivan? You're very pale." Senator Jerome was solicitous.

"I—I'm all right," Maura said shakily. "It's a bit warm—" She accepted a glass of wine Zachary took from a passing servant. Jerome was staring at her curiously, and Barth Coles stepped to open the French windows. The breeze restored the color to Maura's face.

Rachel Morrison fluttered a lace fan. "It *is* close in here."

"More likely it's the dull talk of management and labor problems," Senator Zachary said. "Gentlemen, I fear we've been boring the ladies."

Barth Coles put a hand to Maura's elbow. "I prescribe a stroll on the terrace to revive your spirits, Miss Sulivan. Will you allow me? The view this time of evening is spectacular."

He led her through the doors that opened to a circular terrace. Several couples stood near the balustrade, and others strolled toward the gardens.

The rear of the house faced west, and the city lay far below in the distance. Lights twinkled and glittered like fallen stars, and hazy reflections shimmered on the twin ribbons of the Monongahela and the Allegheny. To the south, a smokestack of a factory spewed fire against the sky, obliterating the stars.

Coles pointed. "The Chilton Ironworks lie beyond that ridge. You must allow me to show it to you one day soon." He smiled gallantly. "Unless, of course, you have an aversion to noise and dirt. A lovely young lady—"

She slipped deftly from his hand which had strayed to her waist. "Do you have an interest in the company, Mr. Coles?"

"You must call me Barth, because I already think of you as Maura. Yes, I am the manager. It has been in my wife's family for more than fifty years. It was one of the first ironworks in Pennsylvania, and it's the largest in the county."

Maura moved away from his arm again and strolled along the terrace. She glanced through the open doors of the ballroom, still searching for a glimpse of Duggan. How long had he been in Pittsburgh? How long was he staying? It was difficult to pay attention to what Barth Coles was saying.

"Our tonnage last year exceeded that of our closest competitor by more than five hundred. We plan to start building another smelter before the year is out." He kept pace with her, walking close so his arm brushed hers.

"The Schneiders mentioned labor disputes. Have they been serious?" She tried to divert his attention from persistent amorous thoughts.

He expelled his breath with a touch of impatience. "It's much too lovely an evening to occupy ourselves with talk of labor disputes. Tell me, will you be staying long in Pittsburgh? We're having a hunt and a masked ball in two weeks. I'd be delighted if you would come."

They had reached the end of the terrace. Barth would have continued down the stairs into the garden where shadowy paths wound under swaying Japanese lanterns, but Maura turned back toward the house.

"It's growing chilly," she said. "Perhaps we should go in."

"Only if you'll dance with me."

It was preferable to being alone with him here. The musicians had struck up a waltz, and the floor was crowded. The pressure of his hand at her waist was insistent, but she ignored it. She glanced at couples dancing by, looking again for Duggan, but she did not see him. Belatedly she wondered what had become of Beau.

Irene clasped Beau's hand as she pulled him through a back door. The night air was cool on her flushed face, and she shivered as she slipped her arms around him and drew him into an embrace. Her lips searched eagerly for his, and he kissed her.

She drew back and stared at him in the leaping shadows of the coach lamps. "Why did you bring her here?" she demanded.

Beau gave her an amused smile. "I assume you're referring to Maura. Your husband made a point of inviting her."

"You've spent an inordinate amount of time with her this past week! Why didn't you tell me she was staying at the Lafayette House?"

Beau held her off at arm's length. "You seem to know a lot about my activities."

"I have made it a point to learn. You don't fool me for a minute, Beau Fontaine. You've been seen all over the city with Maura Sullivan."

"I wasn't aware that I had to account to you for my movements," he said with a shrug.

His detachment infuriated her. "I won't be treated this way! I came to your hotel room and you weren't there. If you recall, it was your suggestion for me to slip away from the dinner party in Thomas' honor so we could spend a few hours together!" She glared across the interval of dusky light.

"I'm afraid it slipped my mind."

Rage made her speechless. She jerked away and walked toward the lighted stables where the guests' carriages and horses were quartered. Beyond, a smaller stable was dark. Irene veered toward it. She called out to a stableboy for a lantern. The boy hurried toward them, but when he would have led the way, she took the lantern from him and ordered him off. She held the light aloft as Beau pushed open the door.

The stable smelled of hay and dung. The air was warm and dusty, and a horse whinnied. Beau took the lantern and raised it in a slow circle to cast light on the stalls; Irene pointed to the farthest one.

The sleek Morgan was a prize bit of horseflesh, as superb an animal as Irene had claimed. Beau stroked the horse's cheek and ran a hand along its taut neck.

"Magnificent . . ."

Irene had no interest in pursuing the subject. The horse had only been an excuse to get Beau away. She took the lantern from him and hung it on a peg, then slipped into his arms.

When he hesitated, she admonished, "Don't turn me away. I've been longing for you since the afternoon in your suite." She lifted her mouth. Their breath mingled and quickened as their lips met. Irene's hands found their way under his coat and kneaded his flesh.

Beau shook his head. "I don't fancy Thomas sending someone to look for us if we are gone too long."

"We are safe——"

"We were seen coming in here, my dear. If you do not value your own reputation, please consider mine."

She flung herself away. "You are insufferable!"

He laughed and stroked her cheek. Her anger vanished instantly, and she returned to his embrace. He kissed her fervently. When he released her at last, she lay her head on his shoulder.

"Are you bedding her?"

"Who?"

Irene reined her annoyance. "Maura Sullivan."

"No."

She looked at him, trying to detect deceit. She could read nothing in his face. "Are you saying that to placate me?"

"It happens to be the truth."

She chewed her lip, then sighed and demanded his mouth for another kiss. "Will you come upstairs later tonight? It won't be difficult to slip away."

"All right."

"Do you promise?" She was pushing too hard again, and

265

she saw the quick retreat in his eyes. She tried to bring him back with a gentle tone. "Thomas has hired a troupe of entertainers."

"Ah, the perfect time." He brushed her lips hurriedly. "And now we must return to the party. You promised me an introduction to Obediah Cromwell. Has he arrived yet?"

Irene smothered an irritated sigh and brushed a bit of straw from her arm. There was a smudge of dirt at her wrist. She saw the corner of a handkerchief at Beau's pocket and pulled it out. He tried to reclaim it, but she wet a corner with her tongue and scrubbed at the smudge. Then she realized it was a woman's handkerchief, the same one Beau had at the Blue Horse Inn—Maura Sullivan's. Her back stiffened, but she smiled disarmingly.

"Cromwell has been our houseguest for two days. But I have forbidden Thomas to spirit anyone off for poker tonight. You'll have to do your gambling another time."

"Of course. May I have the handkerchief back?"

She stuffed the lacy cloth into her décolletage. "I will return it when you come to my room. Perhaps it will ensure your keeping your word this time."

Her silly game angered him, but he was in no mood for a scene. "Shall we return to the party?" she said, smiling.

CHAPTER SIXTEEN

Obediah Cromwell approached as the waltz ended, and Barth Coles relinquished Maura reluctantly. She was eager to learn if Cromwell knew Duggan. When she asked him, he regarded her with a smile.

"I've met him, and I'm wholly in agreement with him. The man has a good head and he's willing to go after what he wants. Unions need more fighters like him," he said emphatically.

"Taking power by force shouldn't be condoned," Maura said. Cromwell had a brusque manner and seemed easily persuaded to a violent stand. She thought of how easily Duggan too had been goaded into physical combat, for his own cause *and* for hers.

"Labor and politics call for strong action and strong men," Cromwell declared.

"Are you a politician?"

"Yes, but not like Zachary and Jerome. I'm with the Democratic Party in Boston. I spend a lot of time in the Capitol seeing how my boys are managing, though. We don't consider the Whig President a serious threat. We wield more influence in Congress than Clay and his people can buck. Our man will be back in the President's Mansion in '52. And when he is, the unions will have a friendly ear."

"You favor national unions then?"

"Absolutely. They'll become the backbone of industry in this country. It's time for the workingman to be heard, and we're gaining the voice to do it."

Again, she was put off by his brusque manner. He caught her quick frown. "But a pretty little lady like you shouldn't worry her head about such things. Business and politics are for men."

"I disagree, Mr. Cromwell. Women have an excellent sense for business and can manage as capably as men." She considered telling him of her connection with the Sullivan Boatyard, but decided against it. Cromwell would more than likely use their casual acquaintance as an excuse to intrude at the boatyard, and she was not sure yet how she felt about the union he and Duggan proposed.

He chuckled and looked at her with amusement. "A foolish idea, but you make it sound plausible. A man would be insane not to leap at the opportunity to work with you." He gave her a suggestive look and his hand strayed intimately to her waist. She drew back, but he held her.

"Have you ever been in Boston, Miss Sullivan?"

"No." She longed for the dance to be over so she could get away from him.

"You must come and let me show you the city. Are you returning north soon?"

"I'm not sure." She suppressed a shudder as his fingers slid toward her hip.

"I have business down the river, but I'll be going back to Boston by way of New York within the month. I will certainly look you up so we can continue our discussion."

"It's impossible for me to make plans just now," Maura said evasively. Cromwell seemed to think she'd leap at the chance to become better acquainted. The thought repelled her, and she was relieved when the music finally ended. She excused herself quickly and left him standing in the middle of the floor.

She spied Beau in the doorway and made her way to him.

"I apologize for being gone so long," he whispered as he whirled her onto the dance floor in the circle of his arms. "Are you enjoying yourself?"

"Very much, now that you have rescued me from a dull partner."

"The gentleman seems quite taken with you."

She made a face. "He was disgusting."

He stared across the room over her shoulder. "I don't think I know him."

"Obediah Cromwell, a politician from Boston who believes he controls—or at least should control—the nation."

Beau laughed. "He talked politics while dancing with the most beautiful woman in the room? I am astounded!" He glanced over the heads of dancers and studied the man. So that was Obediah Cromwell. . . .

"Now you sound exactly like him!" Maura said. "And besides, is that any worse than abandoning me as soon as we arrive?" she asked devilishly.

Beau looked contrite. "Irene is aware of my weakness for good horseflesh. The gelding is everything she claimed. Perhaps you and I can slip outside later so I can show it to you. Right now I find it intoxicating to hold you in my arms." He smiled and for a moment pressed his face to her hair.

His good humor was contagious and Maura could not be annoyed. She was beginning to enjoy the party, though she could not put Duggan from her thoughts. It was almost unbearable knowing he was nearby yet not seeing him.

The waltz ended and the musicians began a lively quadrille. Irene Zachary and a handsome young partner helped form the square. Irene's gaze met Maura's with a hint of triumph. What had occurred between her and Beau? Irene's expression made it seem less innocent than Beau claimed.

When the dance ended, the four joined a group near the punch table. The circle widened to admit them.

Senator Zachary smiled at Maura before continuing the story he was telling. Beau winked surreptitiously, then turned his attention to the Senator.

". . . so I agreed to a race. My gelding will give Clinton Henry a surprise or two, I'll wager."

"Have you seen the filly run?" a red-faced man asked.

Zachary shook his head. "No need. I've watched the gelding, that's enough."

"The gelding is my horse, Thomas. You promised." Irene pouted prettily and fluttered her lashes.

"And so it is, dear, so it is. But surely you will not deny me this chance to even the score with our neighbor who boasts that his horse can beat any challenger."

Irene sighed with exaggerated resignation.

Elias Jerome said, "I've heard that Henry has accepted several matches for the filly. There's word of one tomorrow morning."

Zachary made a show of boredom. "If he tires the horse, so much the better for me."

The others laughed, and the conversation drifted into fragments. Elias Jerome glanced toward the French doors and called out.

"Duggan—here, you haven't met your host and hostess. Let me introduce you."

Maura turned and found herself looking into Duggan Quinn's eyes. He might have left her only minutes ago . . . or never at all. Her pulse fluttered, then raced, and her strength ebbed away. She'd forgotten the breadth of his shoulders, the strength in his face. She was assailed by the memory of his arms about her and his naked flesh against hers. A rush of longing made her breath catch.

Duggan could not believe his eyes. Maura, here—! He stared at her to be sure he wasn't dreaming and scarcely heard Jerome's droning introduction.

Maura returned his smile with more courage than she felt. The blood was singing in her ears, and the room seemed to shift out of focus. She could not tear her gaze from Duggan. He was dressed in a dark suit that was slightly out of place among the satin waistcoats and silk cravats, but he held his head high as Jerome completed the introductions.

"And this is Miss Maura Sullivan from New York," Jerome said, "and Beauregard Fontaine."

"A pleasure." Duggan finally relinquished Maura's eyes and smiled around the group.

Irene gave him a captivating smile. "Elias tells us you have come from Washington City, Mr. Quinn. With so many social functions every week, how is it the Senator and I have never had the pleasure of meeting you before?"

Duggan's face was serene. "I met Mr. Jerome only a short time ago. And I was in Washington only a few days—I was not invited to many parties."

Irene gave him a saucy look. "You must let me rectify that oversight as soon as we return to the Capitol. Are you going back soon?"

"I had not intended to," Duggan said glibly. "But with such an offer, a man could easily change his mind."

"I will look forward to it." Irene's smile was seductive.

Maura felt a twinge of rage, though she was unsure at whom it was directed. She deliberately looked away as Senator Zachary spoke.

"Elias tells me you are a man with a cause, Mr. Quinn. Have you come to our party to plead it?" His tone was condescending, and Irene noted it instantly. So her husband was in disagreement with this man. She studied Duggan with interest. He was hardly the usual guest, which made him all the more intriguing. He was different from most men she knew—there was an earthiness about him. . . .

"I came because it afforded me an opportunity to meet you, Senator. I hope to have a chance to speak my views."

Zachary was taken aback by the direct answer. "A social affair is hardly the place to discuss politics," he said stiffly.

"But it is done all the time, Thomas," Irene chided. "Why should Mr. Quinn be denied the privilege you claim for yourself and your friends?" She smiled winningly at Duggan. "Tell me, Mr. Quinn, what are these views my husband wishes to suppress?"

Duggan did not hesitate. "They concern unions, Mrs. Zachary. I am striving for the formation of protective organizations for workers."

"But there are unions already, aren't there?" Irene frowned.

"Yes, and they have proved their worth a thousand times over. All the more reason to expand into fields that don't have them, and to fight against legislation that would inhibit their growth." He glanced at Zachary. "There is a bill before Congress now to do just that. I'd like to enlist your aid in defeating it."

Zachary said, "It seems to me that if we must have unions, they should operate at a local level. Problems vary from area to area. It's impossible to make blanket decisions that will benefit everyone. Besides, I hold with the idea that national unions would be illegal."

"The Massachusetts court ruled otherwise," Duggan said drily.

There was a quick flash of anger in Zachary's eyes. "The decision was made at the state level. It may be contested in the Supreme Court." Then with what seemed like a sudden burst of good humor, Zachary chuckled. "Next thing we know, someone will try to control horseracing with union laws."

There was an appreciative laugh around the group. Duggan was unsmiling. Maura saw a tic of anger at the corner of his mouth.

"Sport and men's livelihoods can hardly be compared, Senator. If you spent ten hours at a forge or climbing the hull of a ship on the ways, you'd know the difference."

There was an awkward silence. Maura mentally berated Duggan's lack of tact. He was a hothead . . . he would accomplish nothing if he lost his temper and alienated Zachary completely. Why couldn't he learn that simple truth? She paused in her thoughts, wondering if she wanted Duggan's crusade to be successful. She was still not sure how she felt about unions.

Barth Coles said disdainfully, "Local organizations would be better able to keep in touch with problems than a national group. If necessary, the state can oversee their operations, but I say the less interference from national government the better. No offense to our eminent lawmakers, of course, gentlemen." He grinned at Zachary and Jerome.

"Hardly Yankee sentiment," said a sparse man with a Southern accent.

Coles shrugged. "Like Henry Clay, I subscribe to compromise. As long as it doesn't interfere with my individual rights."

"And your rights to manage the Chilton Ironworks as you see fit?" Duggan said pointedly.

Coles glared. "That too, Mr. Quinn. The company has operated successfully for almost half a century. Neither the state nor the federal government need concern themselves with it. *Nor* any union."

"If an ironworkers' union is formed, you may be forced to accept it," Duggan said.

"That day will never come!" Coles' face was suffused with growing anger.

"It's inevitable when men are treated no better than slaves." Duggan's gaze did not waver.

"Are you an abolitionist, too, Mr. Quinn?" Beau asked with a lazy smile.

"I'm in favor of political and economic equality for all men. No man should be master over another."

"Ah . . . *strictly* a Yankee sentiment," Beau said wryly.

Zachary was still piqued at Quinn's insult. "Slavery has unfortunately become a national issue, Mr. Quinn, but many of my constituents feel that labor unions should not. I intend to vote in favor of the bill that is pending."

Jerome cleared his throat and tugged at the satin lapels of his coat. "Will you do me the honor of coming to dinner soon, Thomas? We can discuss Mr. Quinn's ideas more fully. Like you, I pride myself on hearing all sides of an issue before I vote."

Zachary's face was mottled. It was obvious he would prefer to end the matter there and then. Irene smoothed the troubled waters.

"I think it's an excellent idea—on the condition that I am included in the invitation, Elias. I would enjoy hearing more of Mr. Quinn's opinions. It's refreshing to listen to one so devoted to a cause." She looked at Duggan sidelong. He gave her a conspiratorial wink.

Maura's fingernails dug into her palm. He was shameless! He would use any means to further his cause! She almost hoped Senator Zachary would refuse, despite his wife's acceptance. But he did not.

"Very well," Zachary said with forced politeness.

Irene flashed a triumphant smile at Duggan. "I shall look forward to it." She glanced at the mantel as a heavy gold clock under a glass dome began to chime. "We must see to the entertainment, Thomas. I know you will all be delighted by the performers. They have never before been seen in Pennsylvania. Please, find seats—" She nodded and Thomas followed her toward the curtained stage at the far end of the room.

The group began to drift away. Duggan stood smiling at Maura. "It's very good to see you again," he said softly.

Beau looked at him. "I had no idea you two were acquainted." His inquisitive gaze went to Maura.

"We're old friends," she said, hoping her voice did not betray her emotions.

"I see." Beau's calm was unruffled. Was it coincidence that Quinn was advocating a union for carriage-makers and shipbuilders and Maura's family was engaged in these businesses? He thought not.

"Did you have a pleasant journey to Pittsburgh?" Duggan asked. His tone was polite, but the look in his eyes set Maura's heart thudding against her ribs.

"It was fine." She was barely able to speak with his blue gaze unsettling her.

Beau did not miss the exchange of glances. And he had not missed the quavering note in Maura's voice. They were more than old friends. He studied Quinn and realized suddenly that this was the same man he'd seen with Maura at the stage station in Hoboken, the man who had passionately kissed her good-bye.

"Maura's family is in the carriage and boat business in New York and Philadelphia, as you know, Mr. Quinn," Beau said. "I'm afraid you have trod on more than one toe with your talk of unfair working conditions and labor striking back at management."

Duggan smiled tolerantly. "Maura knows my views. We've discussed them before."

Beau prodded. "And do you agree with them, Maura?"

She refused to be baited. "I'm not sure. There seems to be more to the matter than one would think at first. I'm still gathering information so I can make an intelligent decision."

Duggan's eyes danced. "Perhaps I can acquaint you with details, if Mr. Fontaine will relinquish your company for a while."

Beau regarded him coolly as a musical fanfare called attention to the curtained dais. "Perhaps later, Mr. Quinn. The entertainment is about to begin. Maura, shall we find seats?" He was damned if he would let Quinn walk off with Maura and leave him standing alone. The man was too cocksure.

Duggan bowed. "Perhaps later." He sounded unconcerned, but Maura saw the glint in his eyes.

"I'll look forward to it," she murmured. Then Beau was leading her toward the seats that had been arranged to afford a good view of the stage. Maura stared ahead as an expectant hush fell over the audience. She resisted the impulse to look around to see where Duggan was. Her cheeks

274

were flushed and her eyes too bright. She felt Beau's gaze on her and pretended to be absorbed with the stage.

The curtains parted, and there was a murmur of approval from the audience. The backdrop of the stage was a shimmering, billowing, yellow silk cloth that seemed to change color subtly as the lights dimmed. A gaudily dressed minstrel strolled out strumming a mandolin. At the spatter of applause, he bowed, then began to sing a ballad in a clear tenor voice. At the end of the song, he cavorted about the stage in an acrobatic dance that brought gasps from many of the watchers. Then he introduced a juggler who kept ten sticks circling over his head like darting birds. There were pantomimists, musicians, and singers. Act followed act, each more compelling than the previous one.

Beau glanced up and saw Irene in the doorway. She shot him a silent signal before disappearing into the hall. Beau leaned forward to whisper to Maura.

"Can I bring you something to drink?"

She shook her head. "Nothing, thank you."

"I'm going to slip away for a glass of champagne."

"You'll miss the entertainment—"

"I'll be back shortly." He squeezed her hand. "Besides, I can see quite well from the other side of the room. You're sure I can't bring you something?"

When she shook her head again, he slipped out of the row, ducking low so he would not block anyone's view. Maura watched sidelong as he headed away from the refreshment table and toward the door. A minute ago Irene Zachary had been standing there. With furious certainty, Maura knew that Beau was meeting her. A prearranged rendezvous would explain the triumphant look in Irene's eyes when they'd returned from the stables—if they'd ever gone there at all! Maura's fists clenched. Was Irene so important to Beau? So irresistible that he'd risk an assignation here in her own house? A lovers' tryst . . . Irene would welcome him boldly in her bed, Maura was certain. She thought of the night at the inn in Norristown when Beau had come to her room. He'd been powerful and dominating, despite her struggles. And she'd played the part of virgin instead of woman. Now Beau undoubtedly held her in contempt and was trying to deceive her with a transparent excuse. He *wanted* Irene. He wanted a robust bed partner who would not play childish games. Maura felt her face flush and was thankful for the lowered lights that kept anyone from witnessing her humiliation.

Irene had already vanished. Beau glanced in both directions along the hall, then headed for the wide, carpeted stairs. The door to the library opened abruptly, and Senator Zachary intercepted him.

"Ah, Beau, I've been looking for you." Zachary took his arm with a glance toward the ballroom. "I have someone who is anxious to meet you."

Beau's brows raised questioningly.

"Obediah Cromwell insists on learning for himself if you deserve the reputation you've earned at poker. The man fancies himself an expert and wants to match wits with you."

"I've heard of him," Beau said with an easy smile. And wanted to meet him for a long time, he added silently.

"Then come along before Irene discovers what we're up to." He ushered Beau into the paneled library. Three others were already there: Elias Jerome, a local politician named Stanley Meriam, and Cromwell.

Cromwell extended a fleshy hand. "I've waited a long time for this pleasure, Fontaine. You do me an honor by accepting my invitation."

"The pleasure is mine, Mr. Cromwell."

Beau was already studying the man's movements and facial expressions, the quick shift of his eyes that betrayed inner tension. Cromwell drew a cigar from an inner pocket, rolled it between his fingers, then sniffed it. He put it between his teeth and struck a match.

"The Senator has been telling me you're riding high, Fontaine. He thinks you'll win the city away from the founding fathers."

"If the city fathers are foolish enough to wager it, I may at that," Beau said good-naturedly.

Everyone laughed. Thomas Zachary motioned to a table where cards were laid out and a tray of drinks had been set on a nearby cart.

"Shall we, gentlemen?"

Maura concentrated on the stage with a determination to put Beau's deceit from her mind. What difference did it make? He was free to do as he pleased; she had no claim on him. Hadn't she made that clear when she threw him out of her room at the inn? She stared at the stage, barely seeing the tumblers and marionettes. Then, suddenly, she was aware of someone sliding into the chair beside her. She turned quickly.

It was not Beau but Duggan. Her heart stopped, then bounded at a riotous pace.

"Come outside with me—" Duggan grasped her hand and was already out of the seat.

His touch was a vibrant shock and she could not move. Duggan beseeched her with a look. Numbly she rose and followed. Several people glanced up as they eased past the crowded chairs. Duggan closed the door as they stepped outside.

The terrace was empty. Behind them, a burst of applause indicated the end of the act and the introduction of another. Duggan was still holding her hand. His strength seemed to drain hers. He drew her to one side of the terrace where the shadows were deep and the scent of wintergreen clung in the air.

They stood looking at each other for several moments. It was as if they had been parted forever, yet never apart. Duggan's lips formed her name, and his hands moved along her arms to pull her close, as gently as though she were a fragile butterfly. Then she was in his arms and he was kissing her with need and passion that had been reborn at his first glimpse of her in the ballroom. For a moment, she was unyielding, then she answered with blind hunger. His hands explored the curve of her shoulder, the soft, silken hair at the nape of her neck. Her flesh was warm and enticing, and his longing surged like a tide.

Maura clung to him breathlessly. Her lips parted under the pressure of his, and she welcomed his tongue. The blood sang in her ears. The cool air was a welcome balm on her fevered cheeks.

"Maura . . . Maura . . ." His whisper sent shivers along her spine, and she pressed her face to the rough cloth of his coat.

277

"You're trembling—" His arms enfolded her, drawing her to him as though he would never let her go.

All her strength ebbed. The trembling came not from cold but from the joy of seeing him, of being held. . . . His fingers entwined in her hair and played at her ear. She raised her face, lips quivering, and he claimed her mouth again. She felt the hard leanness of his body against her breasts. An ache filled the core of her belly. When at last he released her, she looked at him numbly. He smiled.

"Are you glad to see me?"

The spell was shattered and sanity returned in a rush. Maura drew apart from him, but he did not release her arms. He watched her closely.

"Is it so difficult a question to answer?" His soft voice held a lilt of laughter.

"Of course I'm glad to see you. I—" Emotion welled, and she swallowed. "I'm relieved to know you escaped the police and Pelham. You—you didn't have any trouble?" She wanted to know everything that had happened, every danger he had faced, how he came to be here now.

"None I couldn't handle." He'd felt for a moment that she was experiencing the same desire and emotion as he, but she'd quickly drawn a curtain of reserve between them. Was it the man—Beau Fontaine? She'd lost no time in finding an escort. "You're not glad for any other reason?"

She brushed a curl from her flaming cheek. She wanted to throw herself into his arms and tell him of all she'd endured since they parted. But the recollection of how easily he'd left her in Jersey, how unperturbed he'd been at her accusation of his affair with Lacy Marsh made her hesitate. He had not spoken of love or asked her for anything.

"From what Mr. Jerome said, you seem to have kept busy since I last saw you." She could not meet his gaze.

He saw her lashes lower. Was she deliberately avoiding personal matters? He could not believe she didn't care—

"I left for Washington very soon after your departure," he said. "I was introduced to Jerome there. When he invited me to come to Pittsburgh, I leaped at the chance." He put a gentle hand to her chin and raised her face. The sooty lashes fluttered as she looked at him. "I hoped I would find you. I could not believe my eyes when I saw you tonight."

"Your surprise could not equal mine." Her gaze wavered.

"And my pleasure? Do you share it as well?" His tone was caressing. For a moment he was sure that she wanted him. Then she turned away. The words of love died on his lips. He drew back and leaned on the balustrade. Muted applause came from the ballroom, and he glanced toward the doors. The lights did not go up. They were still alone on the terrace.

When he spoke again, his emotions were under control. "I must talk to James. Is he here tonight?"

She shook her head and misery flooded her with sweeping power. "I haven't seen him. He went to Cairo two weeks ago."

Duggan's heart lurched. "You've been alone?!" He thought she was safely in James' care!

A rush of color stained her cheeks. "I've managed," she said.

He knew almost to the penny how little cash she had had when she boarded the stage. It was barely enough to keep her a few days, yet she was wearing an elegant gown and had slipped into Pittsburgh society as easily as she had belonged in New York. A picture of Beau Fontaine's smiling self-assurance and possessive manner blazed in his mind. Surely she had not turned to him? The man had money and superficial charm but he was unworthy of Maura's consideration. She couldn't be so foolish as to consider these things important.

He forced his voice to be steady. "The steamboat's finished then, and James has gone down the river with it?"

"No." At his astonished look, she related the details of the troubles at the boatyard, James' quest for financing and Jeb's illness. Duggan's face grew grave.

"Who is seeing to things at the yard?" he asked when she paused.

"A man named Denfield, but Jeb does not have any faith in his ability."

"If Jeb says it, it's fact," Duggan said flatly. "And all the accidents and setbacks?"

Maura spread her hands. "There have been none since I arrived, but the work is almost at a standstill. Denfield says the men will not work without pay, and there's no

279

money in the company account. I went to a banker for a loan, but it's no use. He not only refused, he informed me that a loan James secured is now due."

Duggan's jaw tightened. Sharp rage was building in his chest. If only he'd known sooner—!

"Have you taken legal action against your stepfather?" There was a slim hope it was not too late to stop Turk.

Maura heaved an exasperated sigh. "I saw a lawyer but he would do nothing. He had the temerity to demand proof of my identity to substantiate my claim."

Duggan swore softly. Of course a lawyer would hesitate going against Pelham Turk without evidence. If James were here— No use crying over what couldn't be changed. He rubbed his square chin and studied Maura's face in the shadowy light. He didn't like to add to her burdens, but she had to know how serious the matter had become. "I've heard disturbing news," he told her.

Cold fingers of fear pressed along her spine. His tone was so grave. . . .

He chose his words carefully. "Your stepfather has begun the work of rebuilding the factory." Her momentary relief vanished when he went on. "He is claiming that the entire business belongs to him."

"That's impossible!" Outrage shook her. She grabbed the edge of the balustrade to still her trembling hand.

"Nevertheless, he's doing it, though not publicly. He can't risk anyone delving into the truth of the matter before he's ready to play his hand."

"There are too many people who know that James and I hold shares in the company. He cannot get away with it!" she said vehemently. If Pelham were there, she would have throttled him. He was an underhanded thief who would stop at nothing! She looked at Duggan scornfully. "You are a fool to listen to such prattle."

Duggan's eyebrows arched, and his mouth lifted to a suggestion of a smile. "And you are a fool to think Pelham has given up his fight because you left New York. You've caused him inconvenience and delay, but he has not abandoned his plan to have you marry Braxton."

"Never!" The sound exploded from her lips.

Duggan smiled. "I'm glad to hear you haven't lost your spirit. You'll need it—and a generous amount of courage—

280

to beat your stepfather. Never underestimate him, or you may discover how wily and persistent he is." He cocked his head and studied her blazing eyes. "He has announced your engagement to Braxton."

Maura was speechless with rage. Duggan must be insane—even Pelham would not dare such a thing.

"He is saying that the marriage has been planned for months, and that it is being delayed because you are distraught over your mother's death and have gone off for a rest. The wedding will take place as soon as you return."

She felt as if a huge fist had gripped her and was squeezing the breath of life from her. Her throat grew tight with horror. "I would die before I'd marry him!" she whispered hoarsely.

He was silent, still staring at her intently. The pain in her face made his heart ache. He reached to take her in his arms. She was stiff and unyielding, but he drew her close and stilled the shuddering of her body. "And I would kill him before I let him touch you," he said gently. The sweet scent of gardenia from her hair intoxicated him. He felt her tremble again, and he stroked the high curve of her breast. "Maura . . . Maura, I love you."

He spoke so softly she thought she imagined the words. She wanted to look at him to see if there was mockery in his eyes, but she did not move. The roughness of his broadcloth jacket against her face was comforting, warm and soothing. His hands gentled her with caresses. Love . . . he loved her! She knew she'd been waiting a long time to hear him say it. Once before he had toyed with words of love, but she had refused to listen.

Slowly she raised her head. She could not read his expression in the shifting shadows cast by the rustling birches bordering the terrace. Then he was kissing her. She pressed against him, taut and expectant. When his tongue tormented her, her lips moved beneath his of their own accord. The kiss was an eternity of fire. She wanted to stay in his arms and never leave. She wanted his lovemaking, tender, bold and demanding. She wanted to be loved and love in return.

"Maura, marry me," he whispered, nibbling gently at her ear and teasing it with his lips.

The words were so unexpected her breath caught. Marriage—to be with him forever—! Joy surged through her. He did love her! He wanted her as she wanted him. She tried to speak, but her lips could only form his name in silent ecstasy.

He stroked her cheek and pressed his face to hers. She welcomed the faint stubble of his beard against her skin.

"If you are married to me, Pelham will be forced to abandon his insane plan. We can fight together to take the Sullivan Company away from him."

The words struck her like a physical blow. She pulled back to stare at him.

"What is it?" He tried to take her in his arms again, but she would not be drawn back.

The mention of Pelham had dashed her euphoria and brought reality into cold focus. "How can you speak of Pelham and your love for me in the same breath?"

He laughed, and the sound grated on Maura's senses. "They were not exactly in the same breath. I meant only that I love you and want you and you should not be alone."

"And that you can assure yourself of a comfortable future!" She was being unreasonable, but she was angry and didn't care. Love was not something to be weighed and balanced against practical needs.

"Don't be a fool!" Did she really believe what she was saying?

His sharp tone infuriated her. "Perhaps I would be a fool to believe your declarations of love." She twisted away, but he grasped her arm and would not let her go. A cold lump formed in his stomach.

"Do you think I'd pretend love for personal gain?!"

"You used Lacy Marsh to get information from her uncle!" The words were out before she could stop them.

Duggan's chin lifted and his eyes hardened. What she said was true, but not in the way she believed. Lacy had given him valuable information, and he'd used her shamefully in his escape from the city because that too would help Maura. But nothing more. Lacy couldn't hold a candle to— He inhaled sharply and let go of Maura's arm. With a cruel smile he said, "You told me yourself you'd never believe an Irishman, so there's no point in denying your accusations."

282

It was true then! He'd bedded Lacy and murmured the same sweet lies he told her now. She fought back scalding tears, and the ache in her breast became acute pain. She could scarcely breathe, but she would not show him how much she cared.

He said sarcastically, "Fortunately, being an Irishman does not hamper my skill at menial work. It's possible that I may be able to help at the boatyard. I'll be there tomorrow—unless you forbid me entrance?" He cocked his head and regarded her with a tight smile.

She clamped her teeth to bite back the quick angry retort that sprang to her lips. She'd be worse than a fool to turn down his offer. Duggan had been an excellent foreman in New York. Maybe he could help.

"There's no money to pay you—" she began.

"Damn your money!" How could she persist in such warped thinking? "Am I welcome or will I be sent packing?"

Maura swallowed the hard lump in her throat. "Any help will be appreciated." Her hands were trembling and she felt a churning in the pit of her stomach.

"Thank you." He bowed with mock formality and turned on his heel. He strode across the terrace and vanished into the house.

Maura could not stem the stinging tears that spilled down her cheeks. She buried her face in her hands and choked back a sob. Minutes ago she had been ecstatic thinking she loved Duggan. Now she was miserable with the conviction she did not. She sniffled and found a handkerchief in her sleeve. She wiped furiously at the tears as she heard a tremendous burst of applause from the ballroom. The entertainment was over.

Dabbing at her eyes again, she tucked the handkerchief away and walked to the French doors. They opened as she approached and several couples strolled out, chattering about a magician whose act had closed the entertainment. One woman looked curiously at Maura as she hurried past.

Guests were gathering around the long buffet tables. Maids in frilly white aprons and caps were serving from steaming platters and iced bowls. A waiter uncorked champagne and filled glasses on a huge silver tray.

Maura saw Irene Zachary a few feet away, her lips tight

283

as she scanned faces. The knowledge that Beau had been with her was too much. Maura tried to slip into the crowd, but Irene put out a restraining hand.

"I just saw Mr. Quinn come in from the terrace. Judging from his expression, he did not enjoy your tête-à-tête." Irene smiled maliciously. "I had no idea you two were acquainted. Or is it a friendship that developed quickly under that irresistible moon?"

Maura's temper exploded. "My friendships are none of your concern, Mrs. Zachary!"

Irene's eyes glinted. "You must call me Irene. After all, we have so many interests in common. Tell me, have you seen Beau?" She let her gaze sweep the room before settling on Maura with infuriating deliberation.

Contemptuously Maura said, "Perhaps he has gone to look at the gelding again."

Irene's smile did not waver. "I don't think so. No one is permitted in the stables without my permission, even my most intimate friends."

Maura was sick to death of dueling with words. "Excuse me, Mrs. Zachary." She brushed past and Irene's gaze followed her across the room.

CHAPTER SEVENTEEN

Thomas Zachary puffed a cloud of gray smoke from a nearly spent cigar. The air was hazy, and his mood was considerably less jovial than it had been earlier. He glanced across the table.

"Your luck seems to be holding, Beau. I swear, I've never known a man with a larger share of it."

"Obediah has taken his share of pots." Beau glanced amiably at Cromwell, who fingered a stack of coins and bills in front of him. The stakes had been high from the start, and Cromwell was a good player. Despite Beau's scrutiny, he had no idea what was going on behind Cromwell's pale eyes. The hint of tension that had been present earlier had given way to a watchfulness that would have unnerved most opponents, but Beau did not let his concentration be disturbed. He was winning steadily and had given up only a few pots to Cromwell and the others.

"I am amazed that the tales of your luck are not exaggerated, Fontaine," Cromwell said. He folded his hands over his paunchy middle as Beau began to shuffle.

"I never thought my reputation worth discussing." Beau hid a smile. Cromwell's eyes did not leave his moving fingers. For all the man's scrutiny, it had been simple to manipulate the cards and ensure strong hands for himself. Most of the time, it had not even been necessary, since his luck was excellent indeed. But a man could use the protection of a sure thing.

Cromwell picked up his hand and studied it. "I have friends who travel to New York frequently to gamble," he said, apropos of nothing.

"I'll open." Jerome tossed out a ten-dollar bill. He laid down two cards. His eyes were bright, and Beau surmised

285

he had three of a kind. Jerome didn't have the face to succeed at gambling.

It went around the table without anyone dropping out. "How many cards, gentlemen?" Beau dealt, noting that Cromwell took three. No more than a pair then . . . "Dealer takes one." He dropped the deck and picked up his hand.

"I am told you were in New York recently," Cromwell remarked to Beau. "Did you happen to visit the Harlem Club?"

"I've been there several times," Beau conceded reluctantly. Was the man making idle conversation or was he after something? Beau's last night at the Harlem Club was enlivened by a quick retreat across the river ahead of a chap who had lost not only at the tables but in the bedroom.

They were silent except for the bets. Jerome stayed in, but the nervous tic at the corner of his mouth indicated to Beau that he'd drawn little or nothing to his openers. Meriam folded. Zachary raised fifty dollars. Cromwell saw it and raised another ten. Beau tossed seventy dollars in the pot. "Raise ten more."

Zachary hesitated, then saw the bet. Cromwell raised another ten, which Beau doubled. Zachary called. Beau turned up a straight flush, Jack high.

"Damn!" Zachary watched Beau rake in the pot. "Most phenomenal luck I've ever seen!"

"Or trickery with the cards," Cromwell said casually.

Beau's expression did not alter, but he sensed the sudden tension around the table. Senator Zachary looked uncomfortable and cleared his throat. "Perhaps we should call it an evening, gentlemen. Irene will be wondering where we've vanished." He pushed back his chair. "The entertainment must be over. I hear the music has resumed. Shall we?"

"I think Fontaine owes us an opportunity to win back our losses," Cromwell said with a sharp edge to his voice.

"I would be happy to, but if Thomas thinks the ladies have missed us and will be wondering—"

"You occasion a great deal of wonder in some quarters, Fontaine."

Beau scowled. "What is that supposed to mean?"

Cromwell raised his jaw pugnaciously. "A comment on your *incredible* luck. I have never seen its match, except for a riverboat gambler named Devol, who has been thrown off more than one vessel."

"Are you accusing me of cheating?" Beau gave him an amused look.

"I am."

The silence was strained. All eyes went to Cromwell as Beau measured his words. "If we were not in the home of a respected friend, Mister Cromwell, I would consider that an insult that must be answered."

"There are other times and places," Cromwell said threateningly. His face was mottled with anger.

Zachary got to his feet quickly. He put a hand on Cromwell's shoulder. His surprise at hearing Fontaine called a cheat was overshadowed by Cromwell's foolhardiness in openly making the accusation.

"Obediah, I gave my word that I would introduce you to Leah Wilson. Irene is determined to match-make, and though I usually oppose such feminine wiles, I think you will enjoy the lady's company. Shall we see if we can find her?"

Beau swept up his winnings and could not resist a parting jibe. "I hope your luck is better with women than with cards," he said lazily.

Cromwell sputtered and his face flushed. He leaped up and took a quick step toward Beau, who stood immediately, his hand poised close to his waist. Zachary glanced nervously from one to the other as Jerome and Meriam stepped away from the table.

"Your luck with the ladies is also frequently remarked upon, Fontaine!" Cromwell's voice climbed and his hands doubled into fists. "It's said that you are in league with the Devil. How else can you stay two steps ahead of the men you've cheated and the husbands you've cuckolded?"

Beau's hand went to his vest but stopped as it touched the butt of the Colt. It would be stupid to start anything here. Zachary and the others might sanction his calling Cromwell out, but not shooting him in cold blood. He lowered his hand slowly.

Zachary looked relieved and took Cromwell's arm in an attempt to divert him to the liquor tray. Cromwell balked and stood his ground. Thomas had heard rumors of Beau's trouble in New York, but he hadn't paid much attention. That kind of story was always around for gossiping tongues. Besides, his own relationship with Beau had always been pleasant. Still, Fontaine did win with remarkable regularity. Did cheating account for it, as Cromwell implied? The idea was not impossible. Irene had met Fontaine at some party or other and begun to include him on their guest lists. The Senator had never inquired too closely into his background. There had seemed no need—until now. He'd look into it. There'd be people to talk to in the city.

Beau straightened his coat. "I regret that Mr. Cromwell is taking his losses with such bad grace. I expected a challenging evening where men did not cry over the loss of a few thousand dollars, but—"

Cromwell jerked free of Zachary's restraint and rushed at Beau. The Senator was between them instantly.

"For God's sake, Obediah—"

At that moment, the door opened and Maura looked around with a startled expression. Cromwell sputtered and dropped his hands. Beau's gaze was steely for an instant, then he smiled disarmingly at Maura.

"Forgive me for being gone so long. Our game has just ended. I was about to look for you." He inclined his head toward the four men. "Thank you for a pleasant evening." With another smile, he took Maura's arm and led her from the room.

Maura felt an uneasy prickle at the nape of her neck. The atmosphere in the library crackled, yet Beau was unperturbed.

"Did I interrupt something?" she asked as he closed the door.

He shrugged. "It was only a minor disagreement, nothing important." He glanced toward the ballroom and saw Irene excuse herself from a group and start toward them. Her mouth was a tight line, and she opened and closed her fan with angry little snaps. He sighed inwardly. She was not going to let his broken promise go unremarked.

Smiling, he spoke before she did. "We were just looking for you, Irene. I'm afraid we must leave. Maura is not feeling well, and even though she protests, she should go home and rest. Will you forgive us?"

Maura hid her surprise and arranged an apologetic smile on her face. Irene did not look convinced. Beau was talking too fast, Maura thought, as though he were afraid to give Irene a chance to speak. She was sure his sudden eagerness to leave had something to do with the scene she'd witnessed in the library.

Irene's eyes blazed. She started to say something, but the library door opened and the four card players emerged. Cromwell's face was still suffused with rage. Zachary looked disturbed; he'd obviously been hoping to find Beau gone.

Irene looked at Maura with a hard smile. "Perhaps you should lie down," she said with forced sweetness. "I can have one of the maids prepare a room upstairs. I would never forgive myself if you were taken ill in the carriage. The night air can be treacherous." She turned to Thomas. "Maura is not feeling well," she explained.

"I'm sorry to hear it. Is there anything we can do?"

Maura put a hand to her brow in feigned delicacy. "It's nothing serious, but Beau is right. I should go home." She gave Irene a pert look. "Actually, I find the cool air stimulating. I'm sure I'll feel better by the time we reach the hotel."

"How fortunate," Irene murmured with a murderous sidelong glance at Beau. Damn him!

"Well, if we can't dissuade you, I'll have your carriage brought around." Zachary spoke quickly to a servant.

Maura said good-bye to her host and hostess and the others. Obediah Cromwell nodded, watching Beau with undisguised malice. Elias Jerome clasped Maura's hand warmly and said he hoped to see her again. She wondered where Duggan was, but refrained from asking. She had not yet conquered the tumultuous emotions that came from seeing him again. Her purpose in blundering into the library had been to ask Beau if they might leave so she would not be trapped into a second confrontation with Duggan. Now she felt a keen disappointment at leaving without another glimpse of him.

The maid held Maura's cape and handed Beau his hat. After final farewells, they went out to the portico to wait for the carriage. Maura wondered if she only imagined that everyone seemed relieved to see them go. There was a low

289

mutter from Cromwell as the door closed. A moment later, the landau rattled on the drive.

They were silent as the carriage, wrapped in a haze of pale moonlight, went down the long drive. Beau seemed preoccupied. In the darkness, Maura was overwhelmed by the vivid memory of Duggan's kiss. Anguish stabbed as she tried to put him from her thoughts. His face seemed to dance in the shadows, and his words of love echoed in her mind. She had been glad to see him—and all the time he must have been laughing at her. How could he be so cruel?

Beau reached for her hand and smiled. "You were magnificent to fall in with my story. I have never known a woman so quick-witted." He pressed her hand to his lips.

"Do you always leave parties so abruptly?" she asked lightly, determined not to let haunting thoughts of Duggan assail her. Her earlier annoyance with Beau was forgotten.

"Only when I run into people like Obediah Cromwell, who cannot abide losing at cards. The man was positively livid. I think that if Thomas had not restrained him, he would have taken revenge with his bare hands." He shook his head as though the entire incident amused him beyond words.

Maura wondered how much Cromwell had lost. It surprised her that Beau would play cards in the middle of the party, but like the other men, he seemed to find nothing extraordinary about it. She flushed as she recalled her own petty jealousy in thinking he'd gone to meet Irene.

Beau was still holding her hand as though it were the most natural thing in the world. She knew he found her attractive, but he had kissed her affectionately, without passion, these past evenings when he left her at her door. She wished he would take her in his arms now to ease the aching despair she felt over the rift with Duggan.

But Beau talked of trivialities as the carriage clattered over the narrow road. He pointed out a neighboring farm which he said was built before the Revolutionary War.

Maura was glad of the small talk that kept her mind from more troubling thoughts. By the time they reached the hotel, she had put the scene with Duggan from her head.

Beau unlocked her door and stood looking at her tenderly. Maura's pulse quickened as he drew her into his arms.

His lips were gentle, and her hesitation quickly gave way. For a few breathless seconds, she was caught in a spiral of desire, spellbound by surging passion that was a flight from reality. She met the kiss with growing intensity.

Beau felt her tremble as he released her slowly. Her eyes were closed and her lips parted. She was totally desirable. "Will you have dinner with me tomorrow? I find your company more enchanting than words can describe," he murmured.

When she nodded, he brushed her lips again. "Good night, Maura. Sleep well." Softly closing the door, he went down the hall smiling.

His touch burned at her lips and her emotions whirled as she realized she had not wanted the embrace to end. With heart racing, she flung off her cape and undressed by the light of the fire. Then wrapping herself in a robe, she went to stand at the window and stare out into the darkened courtyard. Only the feeble glow of a lamp behind the lobby doors disturbed the darkness. The vine-covered trellises traced black fingers against the whitewashed walls, and the bare tables were ghostly silhouettes.

She examined each facet of her friendship with Beau like a jewel under a loupe. He was attractive and charming, perhaps more so than any man she'd ever met. Was she falling in love with him? How could that be possible, when only hours before she had longed to hear Duggan's words of love? She pressed her face to the cold glass. She had not known a dull moment in Beau's company. He had a zest for life that banished gloom and made her feel light-hearted. But he was an enigma as well. She knew very little about him. He seemed well liked by everyone but Obediah Cromwell, and Cromwell's outburst was difficult to understand. Most men who gambled learned to live with their losses as well as their winnings. Was there more to Cromwell's anger than Beau had indicated? The two might have disagreed on some other subject.

Sighing, she crossed to the bed. Climbing between the sheets, she stared at the ballet of shadows on the ceiling. What she felt for Beau was quite different from the riotous emotions she felt for Duggan. The shock of seeing him again had unsettled her terribly. Yet her overpowering joy and desire had been quickly dashed by their angry quarrel.

Duggan was an opportunist. She did not believe for a moment that he really loved her. How different the two men were. Beau was slim and smooth, always soft-spoken and gentle. Duggan was hard and strong in appearance and manner. Yet both aroused her passion. But Beau would not fulfill it because he believed she did not want him.

She pressed her face to the pillow and shut her eyes. A dimly remembered core of heat filled her belly, and she wondered if it would ever be quenched. At last she fell asleep.

She was wakened abruptly by a tap at the door. Sitting up, she stared around the dark room. The last embers of the fire glowed like feral eyes, and the moonlight touched only a small corner of the room. The urgent tap sounded again.

"Who is it?"

"Beau. Open the door!"

She was on her feet instantly, scooping up the robe and thrusting her arms into it as she ran across the room. She slid the bolt back. Disheveled and breathless, Beau rushed inside and pressed the door shut. He clutched her arm and put a finger to his lips as he listened for sounds outside.

Maura felt the warmth of his hand through the soft material of the robe. The only sound in the room was the soft rasp of his breathing as they stood in the darkness. Finally he guided her away from the door. The room had grown cold, and Maura hugged her arms to her body as the chill seeped through her.

"Thank you," Beau said with a grin. "You've saved my life."

"Your life!" She thought he must be joking, but his eyes were somber.

He had dressed hastily in gray trousers, a shirt still open at the throat, and a dark jacket. His hair was tousled as though he'd been wakened from sleep, but he somehow managed to look well groomed. He searched his pockets for a cheroot but found none. Crossing to the fireplace, he stirred the dying embers and tossed on a scoop of coal. The fire hissed and sputtered as flames licked upward. Maura was still staring at him as he came back to her side.

"It seems Cromwell's rage has been fanned by a few late

brandies, and he's come gunning for me. He has the foolish notion that I cheated him at poker."

Her astonishment at the accusation did not match the shock and fear of hearing that Cromwell would seek violent revenge. "But to kill—?"

Beau shrugged, and with his fingertip worked away the frown that creased her brow. "Many a man has been killed over cards, but I do not intend to be one of them. My friendship with the clerk downstairs spurred him to inform me that Cromwell was on his way. He was able to detain him while a boy ran to warn me. I came down by the back way." His easy smile made it all sound like a game.

Maura could not believe he could be so casual about the danger. For a fleeting moment, she thought he *was* playing a game. He was watching her with a dark, unreadable gaze, and she was suddenly aware of her disheveled appearance.

Just then, the sound of heavy steps came from the hall. Beau gripped her arm and darted a glance toward the door. They stood listening and holding their breath until the steps faded.

Beau whispered, "I would not put it past Cromwell to try every door. If Thomas could not dissuade him from his folly, he must be spoiling for blood."

Maura was still incredulous. "Did he lose so much?"

"No more than he can afford. A man has no business gambling if he cannot stand his losses."

He was very close to her, and the pressure of his hand was warm and exciting. Though the danger was past, Maura's heart was racing. When Beau looked at her, her pulse leaped.

"You have rescued me from what could be a very nasty situation," he said softly. The firelight played across his face, and tiny flames danced in his eyes.

Maura's heart thundered. "I did nothing. . . ."

A smile turned up the corners of his mouth. Behind them, the fire flared suddenly and cast an eerie yellow glow. Maura's face was bathed in gloom, but her eyes, dark as the night sky, never left his face. He raised a hand to stroke the lustrous softness of her hair, which was loose across her shoulders and gleamed with burnished red. She was more beautiful than he had ever seen her.

"You gave me sanctuary, the thing I needed most," he said.

Her lips parted and moved silently. She put a hand to her hair to smooth it. He caught her wrist gently.

"No, that is not true." His voice was barely audible over the hiss of the fire. His fingers traced the curve of her cheek. Staring deep into her eyes, he said, "It is not sanctuary I need most . . . it is you."

For a moment, the room was so still Maura could hear her own heartbeat. Beau's gaze seemed to draw her into the fire of his eyes, and she felt his warm breath brush her face. Her gaze faltered as he bent close. Her eyelids fluttered and closed when his lips met hers. The kiss was a tremulous breath, sweet and heady. Then passion burst. Beau's mouth bruised hers and his arms tightened around her. Maura shivered and pressed against him. From the moment he'd entered the room, she'd been aware of an inner trembling his presence stirred. The wild rush of emotion now was like a breathtaking ride astride a sleek horse with the wind at her face. Sensations welling deep inside her went madly out of control. His lips molded hers, forcing them back and parting her teeth. She accepted his tongue and tasted the lingering flavor of fine brandy. The faint night stubble of his chin was rough against her skin.

His hand found its way beneath her robe, and the silk gown whispered as he surrounded the contours of her breast and touched the nipple. Under his fingers, it grew taut. Radiating shivers made Maura gasp.

"I want you. Do you want me?" he whispered against her lips.

When she tried to answer, the words were swallowed up in another sweet, heady kiss. She was mesmerized by the hardness she felt at his loins. Her breath was a hot flame in her throat, and heat seemed to sear her eyelids. She heard a whimpering sound and slowly became aware that it was she who made it. Beau drew her to the bed and lowered her gently as he pulled away her robe and gown. His warm, searching lips found the pulse at her throat, then moved along her flesh until they captured one taut peak of a breast. Maura felt the quick, warm, moist response of her body. Her back arched and her hands reached to hold him close. The torment was a delight she wanted never to end.

Her hand insinuated itself beneath his shirt to his warm, naked back.

Beau's hands moved possessively, exploring, seeking . . . and he renewed his kisses at her breast. Shuddering with pleasure, Maura stared at the pulsing patterns of firelight on the ceiling. His touch crept across her belly with a slow, gentle kneading. A steady throbbing began inside her, and her hips moved as though controlled by the motion of his hand. Her warmth flared to white heat. The breath rushed from her lips as Beau's fingers whispered across the thicket of hair at the joining of her thighs. Her whimpering became a low keening sound. She wanted him shamelessly and wantonly.

He raised his head to claim her lips once more, and she pressed against him. Her arms encircled his broad shoulders and held him so the fabric of his coat grated at her naked flesh. He seemed to become aware of it, and he drew away and quickly divested himself of his clothes, dropping them heedlessly where he stood.

Maura was trembling when he came to her and once again renewed her passion with a fiery kiss. His nakedness was hard and unyielding, yet so incredibly welcoming that it took her breath away. His hands teased her breasts, her belly, found the soft mound of sensitive flesh between her thighs. Maura's breath escaped in a pleading sigh. Beau moved over her slowly, parting her legs and pressing his maleness against her with slow sureness.

Without pretense, Maura welcomed the probing thrust with raised hips. Her fingers pressed into his back, urging him closer and demanding him totally. His weight was a welcome burden as he became part of her. His quick breath blended with the wild pounding in her ears. Maura's body arched. His weight shifted and he thrust deeply. The flooding delight made her moan softly, and she clung to him as he began a rhythmic stroking inside her. A corner of her mind recognized that he was expert in the ways of pleasing women, but there was no condemnation in the thought, only savoring pleasure.

Beau caressed her silken hair, burnished gold by the firelight. It seemed incredible that his headlong flight from danger had brought him to such a delectable reward. Maura's lips glistened as her tongue slid across them to

295

savor a remembered kiss. She was beautiful beyond belief, and she roused his excitement beyond bounds. The response of her body belied the innocence he had mistakenly attributed to her. She was wild with desire, eagerly meeting his demands, her eyes begging for fulfillment.

Maura felt a flooding warmth spread through her. She heard the startled sound of her own cries of ecstasy and Beau's wordless answer. She was swept headlong into a rushing torrent of pleasure and catapulted to its lofty peak.

His movements slowed and finally ceased. He kissed her lips gently as though they had grown more sweet by their lovemaking. When at last he moved to lie beside her, she could not find words to describe her serenity. She fell asleep with his arm across her naked breasts.

CHAPTER EIGHTEEN

Beau woke with first light and gazed at Maura. The business with Cromwell last night still rankled, but it had put him in Maura's bed at last. And she was as hot-blooded as any woman he'd known, perhaps more so for her inexperience. She responded to his lovemaking like a flower unfolding in the warm, sensuous spring. And there had been no recriminations afterward to spoil his pleasure.

It was a temptation to rouse her with renewed ardor, but he slipped from bed without waking her. Dressing, he examined the fat roll of bills he'd won last night. Cromwell had astonished him. The man's eyes were sharp indeed if he suspected a stacked deck. Beau had played with Zachary countless times without a whisper of suspicion. Cromwell was apparently more experienced with professional gamblers. Damn! There had never been a word of scandal attached to Beau's name here in Pittsburgh. Now he'd miscalculated. He hoped Cromwell would be disinclined to talk about the matter when he sobered up.

He bent and brushed a gossamer kiss on Maura's cheek before he let himself out of the room. He took a carriage from the hotel, slipping the doorman a five-dollar bill. The man beamed, and Beau knew he would be as loyal as the clerk who had warned him about Cromwell. Dollars spent on hotel employees were a good investment.

The carriage took him over the road they'd traveled the night before and turned in at a farm less than five miles from Hagenstead. A black lettered sign on the gatepost read: TWELVE OAKS. The carriage slackened its speed as it wound along the tree-bordered drive. A freshly whitewashed rail fence enclosed a huge meadow where a dozen or so horses grazed. Beau alighted and walked down a gravel path toward a stable in a flat basin between rolling hills. Several men standing near a paddock looked in his direction as he neared.

"Beau Fontaine—I should have known no horserace could escape your attention. I heard you were in town."

"Good morning, Clinton. I only learned last night that you were racing today. I took the liberty of driving out. I'm told your filly is a high-stepper."

"That she is, as fine a piece of horseflesh as ever ran in these parts." Clinton Henry was a tall, wiry man with leathery skin that evinced his love of the outdoors. His interest in horses extended to riding as well as racing, and he kept a large stable of animals for hunting, polo, and the pure pleasure of ownership.

A groom led a chestnut filly from a stall and stopped before the group. Henry studied the animal critically, running a hand along its withers. He spoke a word to a slim youth who came from the stable.

Beau looked at the horse with an appraising eye as the lad swung himself up and walked the filly into the sunshine. The animal was lively and responded perfectly.

"I hear she's running against Blackmail," Beau said, falling into step with Henry and the others as they headed for the track behind the stables. Blackmail was a two-year-old with a reputation for speed and dependability. The horse belonged to one of Pennsylvania's leading breeders, Russell Paxton, who prided himself on owning the fastest animals in the state. Any new horse was immediately challenged so he might hold his well-deserved reputation.

Paxton was already at the track. A two-year-old black filly pawed the ground in restless anticipation as the rider patted its neck and spoke calmingly.

"We're ready when you are," Paxton said, eyeing the chestnut. There was frank admiration in his gaze, but it did not undo his pride and confidence in the black filly.

At Clinton Henry's nod, the two jockeys led the horses onto the half-mile oval track. A boy in checked cap and knickers ran out to mark the starting line as the riders steadied their mounts.

"What odds are you giving?" Beau asked.

"Three to one," Paxton said.

Clinton Henry looked amused. "I think you're trying to undermine my confidence."

Paxton shrugged. "I know Blackmail can win handily. I'm not afraid to back the knowledge with a thousand dollars." He took a wallet from his pocket and counted out ten hundred-dollar bills and handed them over to one of the men who had come with Henry. The man glanced at Henry, who nodded.

"Is the action closed or will you entertain outside bets?" Beau asked.

Paxton looked at him quizzically. "You would bet against my filly?"

Beau shrugged. "Purely a sporting gesture. I am told the filly shows an early foot and has no inclination to run for an airing."

Henry laughed. "If you weren't convinced before, Paxton, you should be now. Beau Fontaine is betting my horse."

Paxton shook his head. "I'm surprised you'd be taken in by track tales, Fontaine, but I'm only too glad to relieve you of your cash. It's something I've never managed to do at the poker table. I'll take his bet, Bunting."

The man holding the money extended a hand for Beau's bet. Henry grinned. Beau's contribution was as large as his own. There was a flurry of conversation as other small bets were placed, and the men gathered at the rail. The boy who'd marked the starting line drew back, raised a pistol, then with a glance at Henry, fired. The horses broke evenly. Puffs of dust rose under pounding hooves as the riders leaned forward to coax speed, each intent on his own mount but very aware of the animal beside him. The men at the rail were silent. For a time, the horses were neck and neck. At the quarter-mile turn, Henry's filly began to pull away. The rider on Blackmail kicked and hunched forward, but the gap could not be closed. When the horses reached the finish line, the chestnut was ahead by two full lengths.

Henry congratulated the rider before turning to an amazed Russell Paxton. The big man shook his head in wonder.

"What will you take for her?" he demanded.

"She is not for sale."

"I'll pay five times what you gave for her."

"She is not for sale, but anytime you would like to race against her again, I'll give you a chance to recover your losses." Henry was enjoying his victory and the other man's discomfort. Bunting counted out each man's winnings.

"Your trip out was well worth the time," Henry said as Beau pocketed the money.

Beau grinned and fell in step beside the horseowner as they walked back toward the stables. "During my last visit to Pittsburgh, I was unfortunate enough to lose heavily betting against one of Paxton's horses. I couldn't forego the opportunity to even the score."

"Your confidence in my judgment of horseflesh is touching," Henry said wryly.

"A man is an expert when he devotes his life to a subject."

Henry laughed. "I am well enough acquainted with your expertise at the gaming tables." He regarded Beau curiously. "It surprises me that you have returned to Pittsburgh so quickly. There've been persistent rumors of a dark cloud accompanying your departure after your last visit."

Beau looked surprised. "What kind of rumors? I considered it one of my most pleasant trips." He'd had no glimmer of such stories.

"Always a winner, men begin to wonder."

They had reached the stable where the groom was walking the horse in slow circles around a dirt enclosure. A stableboy waited with towels and brushes to rub down the animal. The saddle had been removed and the animal's body glistened with sweat; it tossed its head and neighed as though aware of its accomplishment.

When Beau was silent, Clinton Henry turned. "A word of advice, Fontaine. It would not be wise for you to put in an appearance at the Tagston Club. Several members there have not forgotten your last visit and the empty pockets with which you left them. *If* you manage to gain entrance, you might find yourself escorted to a back room where some of the members would be undisturbed while they took their revenge out of your hide."

Beau whisted softly. "I see. . . ."

"Personally, I have always enjoyed my games with you

and have never found your playing suspect, but there seems to be a growing number who no longer share my views. There's gossip this morning about an incident last night at Hagenstead. I believe you attended the Senator's party."

Beau was amazed that the news had traveled so quickly, but he said nothing. Henry's wealth and background gave credence to his words. They had shared many a friendly evening over poker, and it was Henry who had introduced Beau to the Zacharys.

"It was nothing of consequence," Beau said.

Clinton Henry shook his head. "Obediah Cromwell feels differently."

"You've heard details?" A scowl was etched between Beau's brows.

"Only that he lost heavily and refuses to credit it to luck alone. He found ready support from two gentlemen who had met you at the Tagston Club last spring. It might be wise for you to avoid them until tempers cool."

Judging by the incident at the hotel, Henry might be right. But it was something that would die quickly; it had happened before and Beau Fontaine was still on top. Still, it might be wise to follow his friend's advice.

Beau cocked his head and watched the groom with the horse. "If you continue to acquire such magnificent animals, I'll have no need to stay up nights over cards, my friend."

Henry laughed heartily. "That would be changing the spots on a leopard, Fontaine. An impossible feat." He saw that the groom was bringing the horse into the stable. He turned to Beau. "I'll be racing the filly at the Rotsner track this season. Will I see you there?"

"I'm looking forward to it. And now, thank you for a pleasant morning—and my winnings."

They shook hands, and Beau crossed the wide drive to where the carriage waited. As the driver swung the coach around the circle and headed back down the drive, Beau leaned forward to call instructions.

"Turn east to the next estate." He had some unfinished business with Irene.

As the carriage approached Hagenstead, Beau told the driver to take a narrow lane that led to a rear gate used by tradespeople and servants. There was no gatekeeper; en-

301

trance was gained by ringing a bell to summon a servant. The rear gate had come in handy more than once when Beau visited Irene secretly.

He told the driver to wait while he rang, then stood in the shadows of the ivy-covered wall until a fat black woman in striped calico and a white apron appeared.

Her eyes rounded and her mouth opened in surprise. "Mistah Fontaine, what you doin' here this time o' mo'ning?" She cast a hurried glance toward the house. "Miz Zachary, she still sleepin'." She opened the gate and let Beau slip through. In the kitchen, the aroma of coffee, bacon and fresh doughnuts made Beau's mouth water.

"Charmaine, send a girl up to tell Mrs. Zachary I must see her." He winked.

Charmaine shook her head in despair but did not argue. "You gonna get yo'self in big trouble one o' these days. Big trouble . . ." Muttering, she went through the pantry and called to a girl who was filling a serving tray with small bowls of jam, honey and butter. "Louella, run upstairs and wake Miz Zachary, tell her someone here to see her. And if the Senator catches you, I'll whip yo' hide so's you cain't sit, understand?"

"Yes'm." The girl scurried off with a curious glance in Beau's direction. The black woman poured a steaming mug of coffee and placed it in front of Beau, who had seated himself at the worn block table. Charmaine put a plate of doughnuts before him.

"I heared 'bout the trouble las' night, Mistah Fontaine. You crazy comin' back here. Mistah Cromwell find out, he gonna come afta you—"

Beau favored her with a smile. "We won't let him find out then, will we, Charmaine?" He slapped her broad bottom as she leaned to refill his coffee cup.

She shook her head but could not hide a huge grin. "You the Devil, Lawd bless me if you ain't."

The girl returned a few moments later and stood on one foot then the other as she told the cook that Mrs. Zachary wanted the caller to be shown upstairs. She could not keep her gaze from Beau, who bit into a doughnut and finished his coffee before rising. Charmaine peered along the back hall, opened the door wide, then hurried Beau through. The rear stairs led directly to the bedrooms upstairs.

At the upper hall, he paused and listened before walking to Irene's door and tapping softly. It opened immediately and he was inside. Irene slid the bolt before she turned to him. Her cheeks were pale and her eyes were blazing.

"Your conceit astounds me! You leave me cooling my heels last night and now you come as though nothing had happened!" She glared at him with arms akimbo. Her hair, not yet done up, tumbled about her shoulders and stained the blue robe with gold.

"You are the most beautiful creature I have ever seen," he said smoothly. His smile lingered as he brushed his hand over the silken hair.

Irene felt herself wavering. "Why didn't you come up last night?" she asked petulantly.

"I was on the way when Thomas waylaid me. If I had refused to play with Cromwell, your husband would have suspected that something was amiss." He slipped an arm to her waist and drew her close, still stroking her hair. "You know I would prefer to spend my time with you." He threaded his fingers into the golden mane and forced her head back gently, then kissed her slowly and intimately. For a moment she was stiff and unyielding, but her pique quickly vanished under the expert ministrations of his lips and tongue.

When at last she was able to speak, she said, "You are wicked beyond words."

He grinned. "Shall I go then?"

"No!" She pressed against him, molding her willing body to his angular lines and lifting her mouth for another kiss. It was long and satisfying.

Irene led him to the bed that was still rumpled from her sleep. She let the blue robe fall away to reveal her naked splendor. Beau watched her arrange herself on the pale satin sheets like an ivory statue on display. He undressed and lay beside her, covering her body with kisses that drove her to a frenzy. His hands ranged the creamy flesh, readying her expertly until she was oblivious to everything but her own swelling passion. Then he moved over her. Irene's flesh burned against his as she strained toward him, moaning and lifting her hips to demand him. She was like a wildcat, and their passion exploded quickly and satisfyingly.

When it was spent, Irene lay with her eyes closed. She was aware of Beau moving away, but she was too content to stir. When at last she opened her eyes, he was brushing a bit of lint from his vest and pulling on his gray morning coat. She watched him lazily, reluctant to have him leave but knowing it was dangerous for him to stay longer. Finally she roused herself and donned the blue robe.

"When will I see you again, darling?" She tried to slip into the circle of his arms, but he busied himself with the fastenings of the coat.

"It is difficult to visit Hagenstead unobserved. I would not want Thomas to begin questioning my presence."

"I'll come to the hotel. I've done it before." She regarded him closely. "You're not leaving town, are you?"

He kissed the tip of her nose. "Nothing could induce me to go as long as you are here." He picked up his wide-brimmed hat and brushed at it. "Send me a note telling me when you will come. And now I must go. Ah—one thing, the handkerchief you took last night. The lady has missed it, and I promised to retrieve it."

Irene's eyes flashed dangerously. With tight lips, she went to the chaise longue and found the scrap of lace amid the clothing she had discarded the night before. She thrust it at him. "The lady be damned! I would wish her in Hell if I were not so sure that you too are destined for that place and would find a way to enjoy it with her!"

Beau laughed and tried to kiss her again, but she turned away and pouted. Beau Fontaine was the most maddening man she'd ever known, and she vowed for the thousandth time never to see him again.

"I must slip away before your husband finds out I'm here. It would not be a simple matter to explain, eh?" Beau straightened his coat and put his hand to the doorknob. Relenting, Irene came to him for a kiss.

"I'll send a note soon. Thomas is due back in the Capitol in a few days, but there's no reason I can't delay my return. Maybe we can spend a few days in Philadelphia or Baltimore?" She looked hopeful and expectant.

Beau kissed her and stroked her cheek. "That's a wonderful idea. And now I must go. I've already stayed too long. The household will be stirring. Glance along the hall and see if the coast is clear."

Irene opened the door a crack and poked her head out before motioning to him that it was safe. He slipped out and walked quickly and quietly to the back stairs. He turned to blow her a kiss from his fingertips before he descended. He did not linger in the kitchen but slipped out the rear gate to where he'd left the carriage.

Maura woke, stretching languorously as she banished sleep. The pillow beside her was empty. Beau's clothing was gone and there was no sign of him. She felt a keen disappointment, then indulged herself by recalling the exquisite pleasure of being in his arms. She sat up, hugging her knees to her chin, and watched the errant sunlight steal between the curtains. Tiny particles of dust drifted in lazy, shifting patterns. How wonderful it had been. She felt no shame, only wondrous satisfaction and elation at being fulfilled as a woman.

Abruptly, Duggan intruded on her thoughts. He'd been the first, and it had been even more exquisite with him. Perhaps it had been the wonder of discovery and her lack of experience. Or perhaps her memory served her falsely.

Sighing, she rose from the bed. She saw a paper propped against the lamp and hurried to retrieve it. Belatedly she recalled the reason Beau had come to her room last night. She read the note quickly.

I would have wakened you wtih kisses, but I could not bring myself to disturb your sleep. My desire is tempered only by the knowledge that we will share many nights. . . .

Cromwell fell victim to the brandy and was forced to abandon his search after tumbling in a heap on the stairs. I am told he was carried off by friends who promised to see him home. Morning's light—and the hangover he is sure to have—will subdue his temper.

I regret that I must attend to some business this morning. I am already longing for the feel of you in my arms and the taste of your lips. . . .

Until this evening, yours, Beau.

She breathed a sigh of relief that Cromwell had given up his pursuit and that Beau was safe. She hummed softly as she bathed and dressed.

Duggan was already at the boatyard when Maura arrived. He was in James' office with the account ledgers spread before him on the desk. She halted in the doorway and looked at his bent figure and wide shoulders. His hair was rumpled as though he had been running his hands through it absently, and his blue work shirt was open at the throat. He had rolled his sleeves to the elbows. He was so intent on what he was doing, it was several moments before he became aware of her presence and glanced up.

"Good morning. I must know exactly where matters stand before I can begin asking men to work," he said. "No wages have been paid for three weeks. Except, that is, for Denfield and Smith, who have drawn their pay regularly. Suppliers are demanding cash, but the machinery that's already been installed is paid for, that's something at least." He shuffled through a stack of papers and came up with notations he'd made. "Two thousand dollars owing to suppliers and another three hundred or so in back wages—and five or six hundred to pay for the work yet to be done. Three thousand dollars would let us squeak by."

Maura felt a small ripple of impatience. He made it sound so easy. "You might as well ask for ten thousand. We cannot borrow a penny." She dropped her reticule on the long table under the window and unpinned her dove-gray hat.

"If you believe that, why do you come here to the office every day?" he challenged.

Her cheeks flushed. "Because I will not stand idle while everything James has worked for is destroyed!" Why was it he had the ability to make her angry so readily?

Duggan grinned. "The Sullivan spirit. That's more like it. Now I suggest we stop bickering and set to work." He found another list he'd made. "These men were laid off when James and Jeb first ran into problems. We'll need them back if we're to get the work done. James was a fool to let them go. Might as well be hung for a sheep as a lamb."

She was irritated that he found fault with James' management, but she could not argue with the logic. "How will we get men to work if we cannot pay them?"

He regarded her with a solemn look. "That is my con-

306

cern. Yours is here. You'll have to manage the office. Denfield cannot be trusted."

He made no effort to lower his voice. Maura flushed when she realized it carried clearly to the outer office where Denfield had resumed his desk beside the clerk, Oliver Smith. Maura was furious with Duggan's high-handed manner and with his lack of tact. For a moment she was ready to do battle, but she forced herself to swallow her pride. If Duggan believed he could get men to work, she could not afford to challenge him.

He rose and gathered the materials on the desk into a pile, taking one sheet and handing it across to her. It was the list of men who'd been laid off.

"Tally each man's back wages so he can be paid as soon as he comes in tomorrow morning." He lifted his coat from the rack and slipped it on. Raking his fingers through his already disheveled hair, he turned and strode from the office, leaving Maura to stare after him speechlessly.

The consummate arrogance! She was shaking with rage. How dare he give her orders and take over so boldly! She sank into the chair that was still warm from the heat of his body. How dare he! Her body sagged. Oh God, she thought, I don't care about his presumptuousness as long as he does what he says he'll do!

Elias Jerome had loaned Duggan a small runabout with a dapple-gray to pull it. As he climbed to the seat and snapped the reins, Duggan expelled his breath in a heavy sigh. He'd been churlish with Maura. How easy it was for her to goad him to anger when he wanted nothing more than to be gentle and loving with her! But she'd made it clear last night that her feelings toward him did not extend to marriage. Well, they'd see about that. The young lady had a strong will, but it could be worn down in time. Scowling, he turned the runabout onto the road and trotted the gray. He was not a man to give up easily.

And Maura was not a woman to be given up easily. He'd tried once before in New York, but she was hopelessly enmeshed in his every waking thought—and his dreams as well. Seeing her again brought the passion and longing back in a rushing tide. Her kisses lingered on his lips long

307

after he'd stormed away from her. He laid awake until the early morning hours tortured by the memory of her in his arms and the eagerness with which she'd met his lovemaking. The need to hold her again, to feel her warm flesh and to share his love was overpowering.

But there were more immediate problems to be solved now. Affairs at the Sullivan Boatworks were worse than he had anticipated. How had James let himself get into such a fix? He was too good a businessman to make the kind of mistakes that showed in the records. Denfield claimed that James had sole authority, that every decision was his. But despite Denfield's avowal that his own responsibilities began only after James departed and Jeb took ill, Duggan was sure there was more to it than that. During the first few months when the business was at its most vulnerable, James had consistently shown a profit. How could the picture change so abruptly? And the fact that there had been no accidents or incidents this past week, since Maura's arrival, also merited consideration. Had her presence made the difference?

The maid who answered the door at Hagenstead showed Duggan into a small sitting room. He stood at the window looking out over the rolling lawns and neat flower beds vibrant with fall blossoms. He wondered how many men it took to keep the yards looking so perfect. As many as it took to run the Sullivan Boatworks, he imagined. This was the kind of life Maura was used to. Would he ever be able to offer it to her?

"Mr. Quinn." Obediah Cromwell entered the room and extended a hand to Duggan. "I'm glad to see you again. I was hoping to have a chance to talk with you last night, but—" He shrugged, indicating a Chippendale sofa where they could be comfortable. He settled himself gingerly. His head was still throbbing and there was a heavy burning behind his eyes. He didn't recall getting home or into bed last night. His last memory was of exploding rage when he didn't find Beau in his room at the Lafayette House.

He peered at Duggan. "What can I do for you? No man undertakes a morning visit after a late party unless he has something on his mind."

"Senator Jerome tells me there's a strong labor movement in Boston and that you're largely responsible for its

308

establishment. You've been able to marshal strength and get results."

Cromwell cocked an eyebrow. "How does this affect you?"

Duggan hunched his wide shoulders and met Cromwell's gaze. "I need fifty men to work a job, and I need the money to pay them."

"I like a man who's direct, Quinn, but what gives you the idea I can help, or would? Pittsburgh is a long way from Boston." Cromwell studied Duggan with interest. He knew Jerome had brought Quinn here to gain Zachary's support if possible.

"I don't think you'd be in Pittsburgh unless there was something in it for you," Duggan said candidly.

Cromwell guffawed. "You are direct!"

"There's been union talk in all the major cities from Norfolk to Albany," Duggan said. "Every town with industry is going to be facing the question soon. Steelworkers here in Pittsburgh are already agitating for the means to get better working conditions and higher pay. They're ripe for unionization, and I suspect you're playing a part in the action." Duggan had heard gossip, no more, but it was not hard to draw conclusions.

Cromwell was thoughtful before answering. "Suppose I am?"

"I say more power to you. It's time the steelworkers and a hell of a lot of others had their say. I'm acquainted with both sides of the picture, Mr. Cromwell, and I believe labor and management can work together for their mutual benefit. I want to see labor unions in every industry."

Cromwell grunted. "What is this job you need men for?"

"Construction of a riverboat. The hull and superstructure are up and the engines in. She's almost ready to be put in the water, but none of the finishing work has been done. I need joiners, shipwrights, cabinetmakers and a few steamfitters." Duggan mentally recounted the list he'd made earlier. He would also need carpetlayers, and craftsmen to finish the cabins and salons, but that could come later.

Cromwell puffed his cheeks. "It will take several days to line up the work force you described."

"I have two dozen men who may be willing to start tomorrow if I can pay them the wages they're owed."

Cromwell inhaled deeply and leaned back. His head still ached horribly, but his physical discomfort didn't diminish his interest in the proposition Duggan was outlining. "So we come to money."

Duggan nodded. "I need three thousand dollars immediately, and a guarantee of more before the end of the month."

Cromwell's eyes went wide as he chortled. "*You* want a guarantee? I'm the one who should be asking for that. What's in this for me—other than a little help in organizing men. And that's something I can get without you, as you well know."

Duggan was prepared. "There's your money back with interest, and five percent of the net of the first trip down the river."

The room was quiet. Cromwell's gaze never left Duggan's face. Duggan masked his anxiety. Cromwell had to be handled with cool detachment and not be given any advantage that might become a wedge.

"You indicate you're in favor of unions, Quinn. Can I assume you want to see one in the shipping industry?" Cromwell watched him with a curious expression.

"The need is there," Duggan said cautiously. Cromwell wasn't chatting idly, he was certain. The need was present in any industry where men could be hired and fired.

"Agreed. I'll get you fifty men if you give me your guarantee that they'll have a contract for a year's work."

Duggan pursed his lips. So that was it. Cromwell would put men into jobs in exchange for an on-the-spot nucleus of a union. He rubbed his hand across the shadow of beard that had already begun to show at his jaw.

"I'll have to talk to the Sullivans. A contract signed by me would be useless."

"Sullivan? There's a Sullivan Carriage Company and Boatworks in New York." Cromwell scowled.

"The same. They've established a new boatyard here."

Cromwell's eyes narrowed distrustfully. He didn't like being played for a fool. With all the money behind the Sullivan Company, why the hell was Quinn begging for a few thousand dollars?

Duggan saw the questioning look and explained briefly. "If you're familiar with the company, you know that Pelham Turk has been controlling the New York interests. The boatyard here is James Sullivan's project, and Turk wants to see it fail. He cut off financial support and is trying to force James into bankruptcy."

His neck corded as he thought of the evidence he'd discovered to prove that Turk was behind James' problems. The monthly allotment Patrick had set up was cut off, and Pelham Turk refused to put another penny into the boatyard. "We're spreading our resources too thin," Turk had written. If James proved beyond a doubt that the boatyard could be self-supporting, Turk would welcome the expansion.

"How do you fit into the picture?" Cromwell said.

"I worked for the Sullivans in New York until I came to loggerheads with Turk. I want to see him pushed out. James and Maura can do it if they meet this contract."

Maura Sullivan? The woman with Beau Fontaine last night? She had not revealed her identity when they discussed unions. An unusual woman . . . perhaps he should not have dismissed her professed interest in business so summarily. Obviously Quinn was bargaining with her sanction. What had she been doing here with Fontaine last night?

"All the more reason to guarantee themselves the strength to meet future contracts. We can draw up an agreement for their approval. Bring it back signed and you'll have your men."

"James Sullivan is out of town. I need the men tomorrow."

Cromwell worried his lip between his teeth. "Miss Sullivan's signature will do for now. You can get her agreement?"

Duggan did not hesitate. Neither of them had a choice. It was possible that Denfield had already notified Pelham that they were in Pittsburgh.

"If you can have the men there in the morning," he agreed.

"They'll be there." Cromwell reached into his pocket to bring out a fat wallet. Opening it, he counted out a handful of large banknotes and laid them on the table. Rising, he pulled a bellcord to summon a servant to bring pen and paper.

The desk clerk stared at Duggan with a haughty expression. "Miss Sullivan is in room 210. I'll send someone to announce you."

"That won't be necessary," Duggan said. He strode across the lobby and was aware of the man's gaze following him. Several people cast curious glances in his direction, and Duggan forced himself to slow his pace. He was not forging into battle but seeing the woman he loved. He went up the stairs at a more sedate walk.

His gaze encompassed the embossed wallpaper, thick carpets and crystal chandeliers. He should have known Maura would stay at an elegant hotel. Fancy trappings like this were her natural setting. He wondered idly how much a room here cost. More than most men earned in a day, he suspected. How was Maura managing to pay for it? Her supply of hard cash was used up by now and there was no money in the company account to be tapped. The nagging worry that had begun at Zachary's ball returned with hot fury. Was Fontaine keeping her? Disgust made him shudder and reject the idea. Maura was not fool enough to be taken in by an easy smile and a glib tongue. Surely she saw Fontaine for what he was. Still, there was the fancy ballgown . . . and the attractive outfit she'd worn to the office today. . . . No! He would not believe that of her!

He hesitated at the door of room 210 and straightened the blue wool frock coat with an impatient tug. When at last he rapped, the sound was loud in the hushed hallway.

Maura glanced at the ormolu clock. Beau was early. With a final peek in the looking glass and a pinch of her cheeks to heighten the color, she went to the door. She opened it, smiling eagerly.

"Duggan!" What was he doing here? Her smile became a nervous one and she tried to still the pounding of her heart. "I did not expect to see you again today."

"You were already gone from the office when I returned. Denfield was sulking and muttering. He's not accustomed to having a woman oversee his duties, especially one who's proved her efficiency so handily." He grinned and tilted his head to give a rakish air to the compliment.

Maura flushed. The praise was totally unexpected and left her in confusion. This morning he'd seemed barely tol-

312

erant of her presence in the office; now he was calling her indispensable.

"May I come in?" he asked. "I have something to discuss with you."

The color in her face deepened but she stepped back. As he moved past, his sleeve brushed her arm, and a tremor shook her. His physical presence had the power to befuddle her no matter how angry she was with him. She used the seconds it took to close the door to compose herself.

Duggan glanced about. The room was pleasant and well appointed, the kind of surroundings that set off Maura's grace and beauty. The door of the wardrobe stood ajar and he glimpsed a neat row of gowns. Another unbidden thought of Beau Fontaine crossed his mind, and his jaw tightened.

"What is it you want to talk about?" She hadn't intended to sound curt, but the words rushed out.

He gave her an amused smile. "I suggest we stop nipping at each other's heels and be friends. If we're going to work together, it will be more pleasant."

She hid her embarrassment. Seeing him unexpectedly had given her a turn, and despite her stern self-admonitions, her heart had not slowed its mad race.

"I'm sorry. It's just that I'm surprised to see you. Has something happened? Did you get the men to return?" It was much safer to discuss business than personal matters.

"I did."

She clapped her hands and laughed joyously. "That's wonderful! Will they be on the job tomorrow? If the boat is in the water by—"

"Easy, love, easy." He smiled indulgently. She was like a child at Christmas.

Maura pressed her lips together to halt the flood of words. How calm he was, how sure of himself. The very qualities that sometimes annoyed her were completely captivating now. And she had not missed the familiar endearment—the word "love" sang inside her head like a bell.

She forced herself to speak calmly. "Tell me about it. I want to hear everything."

"Most of it is dull and uninteresting. All that need concern you is that we'll have men at work tomorrow, and every day until the work is completed. Seventeen of the

313

men James laid off are returning, and they'll be able to act as foremen."

"But how——?" She shook her head. "I can't help but ask questions. You've wrought a miracle!"

"Hardly. I've spent the afternoon searching out and talking to the men who worked for your brother. Every one of them had a good word for him and was sorry to leave."

"But the money they're owed?"

Duggan walked to the window and looked out into the secluded courtyard. "It's in the safe at the office, awaiting distribution in the morning." He turned to meet her incredulous stare. "I would prefer you handle it rather than Denfield. You made the list?"

She nodded, dumbfounded. Duggan had kept every extravagant promise he made! It seemed too good to be true. She would gladly handle whatever tasks he delegated. But there had to be more . . . where had the money come from? Mr. Copperfield at the bank had refused her flatly, and even James had been unable to borrow the amount he needed. Yet Duggan . . .

He turned toward the window and a frown was etched between his brows. He seemed to be pondering some important question, wondering whether or not to share it with her. Some of her joy began to dissipate.

"Duggan." She waited until he turned to look at her. "Where did the money come from? I have a right to know since James and I will be expected to repay it."

He was reluctant to tell her about the union since the subject had already caused harsh words between them. He hedged. "The money is coming from Obediah Cromwell. He is willing to underwrite a loan to see us through the completion of the boat."

Her enthusiasm cooled as she recalled Cromwell's amorous advances and his penchant for violence. "Cromwell is a politician. What interests can he have in the Sullivan yard?"

"He is interested in a profit on his investment. The loan must be paid with interest and a small percentage from the *Patrick*'s first voyage." He hesitated. "According to James' records, the first trip downriver offers a chance to carry freight and passengers to the tune of a handsome profit for the company."

Maura's shock was beginning to ease. "And you promised some of this to Cromwell?"

"It got us the loan when we had nowhere else to turn," he reminded her. "A starving cat cannot demand cream."

She knew he was right, but that knowledge did not lessen her distaste for entering into any kind of agreement with Cromwell. It surprised her that Duggan found it easy to deal with the politician. She sighed. "Well, I cannot find fault with your miracle." She managed a smile. "Is that all of it, or does Cromwell demand a pound of flesh elsewhere?"

Duggan avoided her gaze. He'd hoped to delay the discussion about the contract until he could lay the groundwork for her acceptance of it, but now she was watching him with a puzzled expression.

"There is something else then," she said hesitantly.

"Yes, one other point. But it will benefit the company in the long run as surely as meeting the contract does."

She waited for him to go on. She was trying to suspend judgment, to believe in him as totally as she had a few minutes ago; but a slow, insidious dread was building. If anyone but Cromwell were involved . . .

Duggan removed a slip of paper from his pocket. It crackled loudly as he unfolded it and held it out to her. She read it quickly. The company was guaranteeing the men a year's work. She reread the lines to be sure she understood every word and that no hidden implications escaped her. At last she looked up.

"I expected something much more demanding. A year's employment doesn't seem unreasonable. When this boat is done, James will have no trouble financing others."

She amazed him. He'd expected an argument, at least a protest, but she saw the wisdom of the arrangement instantly! He grinned at her.

"If you have a pen, you can sign it now. I'll get it to Cromwell and we can put our minds at rest."

Maura crossed to the writing desk and dipped a quill. She quickly scrawled her name at the bottom of the page and handed the paper back to Duggan with a huge sigh. His quick smile showed he shared her relief.

"Will you have dinner with me to celebrate?" he asked, holding her eyes with compelling force.

Longing assailed her. She wanted so much to be with him— She reined her wild thoughts. Beau was coming. She looked away from Duggan's intense blue stare and felt her cheeks warm. "I have already made plans."

"Change them." He took her hands. They were soft and smooth in his callused palms. "There are a million things I want to tell you, and a million others we should talk about." He slipped an arm about her. "We've been apart too long. I was fool enough to let you go last night, but I do not intend to make the same mistake twice." He gazed at her, and she was swept into the deep blue sea of his eyes.

Her breath caught and her throat felt dry. Heat engulfed her and robbed her of breath as Duggan bent toward her. For a moment, his wide shoulders were all she saw, then the heat of his breath caressed her lips and closed over them. The tumult that had been building since their angry quarrel was washed away by swift, intense pleasure as his tongue traced the outline of her mouth. Her arms encompassed his broad chest, and she pressed herself to the strong planes of his body. Her gnawing doubts and fears vanished. She knew that she wanted to be his, never to let him go. Her flesh craved his with terrifying need as heat swelled in her body. She loved him. She was as sure of it as she had ever been of anything in her life. Now that they were together again, nothing else mattered.

"Don't send me away," he whispered as he released her mouth and buried his face in the warm hollow of her throat. "Let me stay with you always. . . ." His lips burned at her flesh and she shivered delectably. When she was silent, he raised his face and gazed into the gray pools of her eyes, searching for the answer he wanted to hear.

Maura swayed on a precipice of longing. Her lips parted to tell him that she would never send him away, that she returned his love tenfold. Life was meaningless without him. Her brain reeled as she searched for words.

Before she could speak, a tap sounded at the door. For a moment, it was a disquieting ripple in the wonder of their discovery. When it came a second time, she tried to draw out of Duggan's embrace, but he held her close.

"They'll go away," he whispered. He kissed her ear. His breath fluttered the soft hairs at the nape of her neck and sent a shiver of delight through her.

The tap sounded again and more loudly. Maura tensed. It was Beau. Guilt flooded her at how easily and completely she had forgotten their engagement. She darted a sidelong glance at the door and tried to quiet her thundering heart. Even in the overpowering awareness of her love for Duggan, she could not be cruel to Beau. He'd done so much, she owed him at least an explanation.

"I must answer," she whispered as she extricated herself from Duggan's arms with a nervous smile.

Reluctantly he let her go and watched her smooth her hair before she opened the door.

A worried frown vanished from Beau's face the moment he saw her. He bowed formally, then straightened with a jaunty wink and drew his hand from behind his back. He was holding an exquisite yellow rose, which he presented to her with a flourish.

"Only a shadow of your beauty, but the best I could find in a world of mere mortals." His eyes danced with high humor, and his hand closed around hers as he pressed the flower into it. The intimate touch of his fingers made Maura bite her lip guiltily.

Beau stepped inside with a careless assumption of welcome. He stopped short when he saw Duggan, and a momentary look of surprise crossed his face, but his smile did not falter.

"Mr. Quinn, nice to see you again." He extended a hand which Duggan shook without enthusiasm. Beau turned to Maura. "If you and Mr. Quinn are discussing some important business, I can wait outside." He glanced at the clock on the mantel. "We have a few minutes to spare before the theater." His tone intimated that any seconds they were apart were wasted.

Both men were watching her, and confusion engulfed Maura. She wanted to be with Duggan, but could not bring herself to hurt Beau. And after last night . . . She glanced at Duggan, then at Beau.

"Duggan stopped by with some very good news," she said. "He has convinced the men to return to work at the boatyard and has secured a loan so we can pay them." Her eyes glowed with pride.

Beau's expression flickered. "That is good news!" he said heartily. "I know how deeply concerned you've been." His

317

gaze dismissed Duggan and settled on Maura as though her happiness were the only important thing.

Duggan struggled with a bristling annoyance. "I've asked Maura to have dinner with me in celebration," he said flatly.

Maura hid her dismay at his boldness. He'd mentioned nothing of the sort. But she did want to be with him. . . .

Beau smiled patronizingly. "Maura has already promised to have dinner with me." He gave her a warm, possessive glance. "I've gotten tickets to *Of Age Tomorrow* at the old Drury Theatre and made reservations for dinner at the Golden Triangle Inn. I know you'll enjoy both." He flicked a glance in Duggan's direction. "Perhaps Mr. Quinn will ask you another time."

Maura was torn between gratitude and desire. She had not agreed to Duggan's invitation. In his brash way, he'd plunged ahead, assuming she would fall in with his plan. And she *had* promised Beau. It was not that an evening with him would be unpleasant; until a few minutes ago, she'd eagerly been looking forward to it. But that was before Duggan swept back into her life.

Duggan's irritation swelled. He liked Fontaine less with each passing minute. He didn't like the idea of Maura being with him, or the way Fontaine's gaze lingered on her. The thought of Beau touching Maura—kissing her—made his blood boil. How could she look twice at such a cheap gambler? Elias Jerome had related the account of the card game at Hagenstead and Cromwell's accusation. Duggan didn't doubt the truth of it for a moment.

He set his jaw. "Maura is capable of making her own decision." He glanced at her and a pink flush tinged her cheeks.

Maura battled with her conscience. The memory of Duggan's lips, sweet on hers, pulled her into the current of his will. She *did* want to be with him.

Beau's eyes flashed but his smile was confident. "I'm sorry, Maura. I didn't mean to sound as if you were obliged to accompany me." His wounded expression stabbed her conscience. He reached to his pocket for a cheroot, then bent to strike a match on the hearth. He puffed the cigar and smoke wreathed his head. Tossing the spent match into the grate, he went to retrieve his hat from the chair where he'd dropped it.

Maura was filled with chagrin. "But I *am*! Please don't go, Beau." She turned to appeal to Duggan. "Can we postpone the celebration until tomorrow? My gratitude will not be any less—"

Duggan's sapphire eyes mirrored pain, and Maura could have bitten her tongue. She spoke of gratitude when it was love she felt—love he wanted to claim. If only he had discussed the invitation with her before flinging it at Beau like a gauntlet.

Duggan scowled. "Is that your answer?" he demanded. His jaw was set and a corner of his mouth twitched. Beau was watching Maura, who looked from one to the other in indecision.

"Is it?" Duggan demanded again as he met her gaze.

Maura pleaded for understanding as her own confusion overwhelmed her. "I must be fair. Beau has already made plans—"

Duggan's neck corded and a vein throbbed in his temple. Fontaine blew out a stream of smoke and cocked his head as if he'd known all along what her answer would be and wondered why it had taken Duggan so long to catch on. Without a word, Beau moved to the door and opened it, stepping aside to show Duggan his welcome had worn out.

Fuming, Duggan marched across the room. As he reached the door, Beau gave him a contemptuous smile. Rage blinded Duggan. Without warning, his fist shot out. He realized the stupidity and futility of the gesture in time to hold back much of the power of the punch, but it caught Beau on the chin with an impact that made him stagger.

"Duggan!" Maura rushed toward them. She took Beau's arm and looked at him solicitously. "Are you all right?"

He looked dazed as he touched his jaw gingerly. "I'll survive." He tried to smile but winced with pain.

Maura whirled on Duggan. "Must you always react so violently?! Whatever has gotten into you?!"

"A man fights for the woman he loves." Duggan's tone was icy and his eyes were blue steel.

Her heart wrenched, but she could not condone such impetuous behavior. She bit her lip and looked away. Duggan whirled and marched down the hall.

Maura started to call out to him, but Beau took her arm. He grimaced as he moved his jaw experimentally, then gave her a lopsided smile. "He packs a mean wallop. If he's that belligerent in his push for unions, it's no wonder no one will listen to him. Senators are not accustomed to dealing with rowdy bastards. I think you'd be advised to discourage any further social calls from the man. He's nothing but a common laborer. You have nothing in common with a ruffian like that."

"He is not a ruffian!" Maura jerked free of Beau's grasp. He stared at her in complete astonishment. Tears welled in her eyes and her lip quivered.

"Maura, you saw what he did!"

Blinded by tears, she denied everything but the burning truth in her heart. How could she explain how she felt about Duggan? Nothing mattered but that he loved her—so much that he would fight for her in every way. The tears spilled and she pulled away from Beau and raced into the hall.

Duggan was no longer in sight. She raised her skirt and raced to the stairway. She could just glimpse his broad back descending.

"Duggan!"

He turned, poised for a moment with his hand on the railing. The terrible scowl was still on his face but he did not resume his descent. Maura went down slowly until she was just above him. The coldness of his eyes was unrelenting. She moistened her lips with the tip of her tongue.

"Please don't go," she murmured. "I would be delighted to have dinner with you."

He was silent, but his eyes betrayed a flicker of churning emotion. "You're sure?" he said at last. His voice was a whispering caress.

She smiled and lifted her chin. "I'm sure. . . ."

When he grinned, her world was set right all at once. He took her arm and held her close.

"I'll need a cloak. . . ."

"Of course."

Together they went back up the stairs. Beau was gone when they reached her room, and neither of them mentioned him. The small pang of guilt that Maura felt vanished as Duggan drew her into his arms and kissed her tenderly.

He watched as she put on the gray cloak and a green bonnet. Thank God she had come to her senses . . . thank God she was his.

They dined in a quiet, small restaurant on a side street. Maura barely tasted her food or noticed her surroundings; she was completely engrossed in being with Duggan. They talked about the boatyard and the work that had to be done. Duggan's confidence rekindled Maura's own, and she listened eagerly as he sketched plans that would bring them closer to the reality of James' dream.

Maura voiced her concern over not hearing from her brother. "It's not like him to be so thoughtless. I sent a telegram four days ago and have not heard a word."

He disguised his own fears to soothe hers. "Worry is a luxury for those who have naught better to do." He clasped her hand in his strong grip.

"Is that another of your Irish poems, Duggan Quinn?"

He laughed softly. "You put a man in mind of poetry and all that is beautiful. Do you know how much I've missed you these past few days, not knowing if you'd had a safe journey or where you were? It was a trial I don't want to go through again." His voice was as gentle as a summer breeze and seemed to whisper across her flesh.

She was warm, then shivered with a sudden chill that rose from an inner trembling. He clasped her hand more firmly and lifted it to his lips. His touch was soothing but it also roused a sweet yearning. The room seemed to blur so there was nothing but his smiling face and his soft voice.

"Now that I've found you again, I will never let you go," he said.

She was entwined in the golden thread of his words. She dared not speak, lest the wondrous moment be shattered like a fragile crystal goblet struck by a high-pitched note. She seemed to be floating on a cloud alone with Duggan, and she wanted the moment never to end. In a daze, she felt his coaxing hands draw her to her feet and wrap her cloak around her shoulders. Then they were on the street and the cool, damp air was bathing her fevered cheeks.

"I'll find a carriage."

321

She stayed his arm. "Let's walk." She wanted to prolong every moment with him and savor it to the fullest. Smiling, he tucked her arm in his and held it against him as though it were part of him. Maura raised her face to the cool mist that was rolling in from the river. Once before they'd walked together on a dark street. How long ago that early morning in Hoboken seemed. She smiled inwardly. They'd been parting then, but now they were finding each other.

They were silent as they strolled. Only the clatter of an occasional carriage disturbed the quiet of the nearly deserted street. Their footsteps echoed on the pavement and, nearby, a cat sang a night medley. Maura felt at peace for the first time in a very long while.

When they reached the hotel, her heart took on a faster tempo as Duggan climbed the stairs with her and held out his hand for the key. She gave it to him with trembling fingers.

Inside, Maura hung away her cloak carefully, spending more time on the simple task than it merited. But she was suddenly shy now that the outside world had been shut out. The wonder of her longing filled her as she turned to find Duggan smiling at her. He had taken off his coat and loosened his collar and tie as though he could not bear the restriction any longer. He came to her in a single step and gathered her to him. The firelight played shadows on the angles of his face and made dark, unfathomable pools of his eyes. A soft smile lingered on his lips as he bent to kiss her. His mouth brushed gently at first, then claimed her fiercely. Maura gave herself up to bliss, letting her lips be molded under his and feeling the warmth of his tongue as it forced past her teeth and spoke silently on hers. She was not aware that her arms had gone around him until she felt the taut muscles of his back beneath her palms. His flesh seemed to scorch through the cloth of his shirt as her fingers kneaded gently and she shivered with rising desire. His hands found the fastenings of her dress. A moment later it fell away from her satiny shoulders. He murmured her name and pressed his lips to the pulse beat at her ear, still holding her so close that she felt each rise and fall of his breath. Even through the silk chemise, the cloth of his shirt was rough against her breasts. Then her gown fell away and her body molded to the hard planes of his. She closed

322

her eyes and was swept into a warm tide of tingling excitement.

Duggan lifted her from her feet and carried her to the bed. He swept back the covers and lowered her to the sheets. Then he was kissing her with fierce abandon . . . her lips, the silken curve of her shoulder, her breasts. . . . Maura took his head between her hands and laced her fingers in the dark curls. His lips nibbled at a tumid nipple and his tongue caressed its contours before releasing it at last and sweeping to her belly. And when she thought she could not stand the exquisite torture a second longer, he taught her a new meaning of the word with delicate, warm kisses at the joining of her thighs. Her head spun in whirlwind frenzy and her body arched.

Then he was over her, his bronzed silhouette naked in the firelight. The incredible heat of his flesh seared along her length as he parted her thighs with a gentle knee. Her craving was so sweet, she welcomed his thrust and raised her knees to embrace him and pin him to her fevered body. He entered her with a fierce claim, and again she arched to meet him, giving what was hers to give and taking his surging power. Together they soared to spiraling heights of rapture and, after an eternity, were washed up on the calm shore of bliss.

And this time, there was no parting. Maura fell asleep curled against Duggan's strong, naked body.

Pink threads of dawn streaked the sky and a breeze tapped at the windowpane with insistent fingers. Maura stirred and reached for the comfort of Duggan's warmth. He kissed her eyelids and held her so the tangled hairs of his chest etched delicate patterns on her sleep-warm face. She nestled against him. As though part of a half-wakeful dream, he touched her flesh wonderingly, gently. She murmured and would have opened her eyes except that he kissed them shut again. Beneath the cover, his hand reached for her intimately, and her quick flood of desire surprised her. Still in the hazy shadow of sleep, she was aware of him moving over her, entering her to quickly kindle the fires of her love. He was gentle yet strong, and he controlled his passion surely until he had brought her to the brink of yearning need. Then he carried her in the sweep of his ardor to a summit of sweet, fulfilling joy.

She slipped once more into the warm cocoon of slumber to dream she was wrapped in a cloud that drifted slowly in a sky the color of Duggan's eyes. She burrowed in its solace where no cares could touch her. When at last she woke, the room was flooded with sunlight and she was alone in the bed. Smiling, she hugged her arms across her breasts and marveled at the joy she'd found in Duggan's arms. How right it was, how perfect. She shivered with the memory, and sighed.

At last she threw back the covers and rose. Pouring water from the pitcher, she washed her face and studied it in the mirror. There was a new sparkle in her eyes and her cheeks glowed. Love was a tonic to her drained spirit, and she was completely renewed. Her whole body was alive and vibrant. Secure in Duggan's love, she felt her life had new purpose. Humming softly, she donned a robe and rang for hot water.

When she arrived at the boatyard, several horses and wagons were tied at the fence and a small knot of workmen were clustered outside the office door. They touched their caps politely and stepped back to let her enter. Duggan was seated at a desk that had been pulled to the center of the room where the men could file past. As each gave his name, Duggan checked the list Maura had prepared and paid out the back wages due. Denfield sat in a corner, scowling as he bent over a letter; he pretended to have no interest in the proceedings, but now and then cast venomous sidelong glances at Duggan.

Duggan smiled and relinquished his seat to Maura, introducing her quickly to the men.

"This is Miss Sullivan, who is in charge until her brother returns. You'll find her as fair as he and as deserving of your loyalty."

There was a murmur of surprise but to a man, the workers nodded. Duggan left Maura to finish the payments while he went outside with the men. She heard him assigning various tasks as they walked toward the boat on the ways.

By noon the ring of hammers and saws was joyous music

to Maura's ears. She counted fifty-seven men at work, half again as many as James had employed. She marveled at the miracle Duggan had wrought. For the first time since her arrival in Pittsburgh, she began to believe that the *Patrick* would be done on schedule.

She stood at the window watching the scene. Three men carried a boiler pipe up the temporary gangplank that spanned the gap between the yard and the deck. Appearing from behind the superstructure, Duggan shouted an order and the men disappeared behind the furnaces. Then he leaned over the rail to talk with several workers who were lifting a heavy beam. Maura felt a swelling pride at how quickly he had assumed responsibility. She had not even guessed he knew the first thing about building a steamboat, yet he had taken charge of the entire operation without difficulty. The men clearly respected him, even though they had not met him before today. He was a man who commanded respect.

She rubbed her cheek guiltily. How could she have accused him of using the company for his own ends, or claiming to love her for the same shallow reason? In spite of the many times she'd turned him away with angry words, he persisted in both his love and his efforts to save the Sullivan Company. Smiling, she turned away from the window to resume her work.

CHAPTER NINETEEN

Work on the *Patrick* progressed swiftly, and Duggan made plans to test the boat's seaworthiness. Once in the water, only two weeks would be necessary to add the elaborate gingerbread fretwork, the furnishings for the cabins, and then the *Patrick* would be ready for its maiden voyage. Provided James came back with the money they needed. The loan from Cromwell would not stretch far enough to pay for the sumptuous stateroom and salon decors, and Duggan was reluctant to bind the company more deeply to the politician. If he had to approach Cromwell again for money, he knew Cromwell would be damned sure he exacted more than the nucleus of a union. He'd tie the Sullivan Company into a knot that could never be undone. Duggan was already walking a tightrope between his own faith in the union cause and Cromwell's powerful ambitions. It would be well not to ally himself still further with the politician's point of view.

Duggan's concern over not hearing from James had increased each day, though he said nothing to worry Maura. Either something had happened or James had not gotten the wire Maura had sent. When Duggan learned that she'd delegated the responsibility of the telegram to Richard Denfield, he was convinced of the latter. In fact, he was becoming increasingly suspicious that Denfield was working for Pelham Turk, not for the Sullivans. He would have sacked the man, but until Jeb was able to return to the office, he needed someone who knew the names of the suppliers James had contacted. Untrustworthy as he was, Denfield could save them hours of searching for information that would normally be taken for granted.

Duggan had sent off another wire to James, telling him

they'd finish the *Patrick* and have her in the water on time, but that it was vital for James to accomplish his business and return before the last of the suppliers demanded their money. Another week's grace was all they had.

Irene Zachary glanced at Duggan from under lowered lashes. She had been looking forward to seeing him again. Now, at the dinner party at Senator Elias Jerome's house, she was piqued that Thomas and the others were so determined to talk of nothing but unions. It was obvious that Thomas had not changed his mind, despite logical arguments from Duggan and Elias. Thomas could be very stubborn, especially if he had been bested. And he had—not by Quinn or Jerome, but by Beau.

Every time she thought of Beau, her anger churned. She had not seen or heard from him since their tryst the morning after the party. She'd sent a message to the hotel, but Beau had not replied. She knew he was still in town, and being ignored put her in a foul temper. He was probably with Maura Sullivan! She'd been a fool to believe his lies even for a moment. He'd found a new playmate and was discarding her like a paid whore. Thomas' inquiries into Beau's gambling had uncovered the fact that there was growing suspicion of his cheating. Half a dozen men who'd lost heavily to him were eager to join Cromwell's crusade for revenge. If she got her hands on Beau first, Cromwell and the others would have to satisfy themselves with what was left of him! She would tear him apart with the greatest pleasure—the lying, cheating devil!

Duggan noticed the smoldering fire in Irene's eyes and wondered what was on her mind. She wasn't receiving enough attention, that much was clear. Irene had flirted covertly with him ever since the evening had begun, and each time the conversation turned to the subject of unions, her concentration drifted. She was an attractive woman but hard lines were already etched at the corners of her mouth: spoiled and accustomed to having her own way.

He had considered begging out of the engagement so he could spend the evening with Maura, but she wouldn't hear of it. The union bill before the Congress was important to him, and she felt he owed himself a last try at changing Senator Zachary's mind. Besides, she told him with a teasing kiss, they would be all the more eager for their reunion after being apart for the night. He'd agreed, but that did not ease his torment now at being away from her for the first time in two days, and sweet thoughts of holding her in his arms slipped unbidden to his mind.

Their nights had been spent in a bliss of discovery, learning a thousand ways to please each other. And Maura . . . Maura was like a flower budding in the lambent spring sun, kissed by the warmth of his love, and slowly unfolding to display the delicate shadings of maturity. He nearly laughed aloud, thinking how she'd tease him if he voiced that poetic image. With difficulty, he brought his attention back to the conversation.

"Times are changing, Thomas," Elias Jerome said. "A representative of the people can't afford to set his mind against progress."

"Progress is a matter of definition," Zachary said. "I fail to see any substantial argument for national unions. The more I hear, the more convinced I am that they can be a dangerous foothold for those who would garner power for their own ends."

Jerome snorted deprecatingly. "If you base your opinion on the hopes of men like Obediah Cromwell, I suppose that's a natural conclusion to draw. But if the unions are formed and controlled by men who are the true voice of labor, they'll be able to keep out the despots."

Zachary reverted to his former argument. "You're asking for trouble as soon as you legislate away a businessman's rights."

"What of the workingman's rights?" Duggan asked. Irene shifted her champagne glass and smiled.

Thomas scowled. "He has the right to quit any job he doesn't fancy. If he can improve his lot elsewhere, let him do it. His rights aren't curbed."

Duggan felt a band tighten around his chest. "And if he can't improve his lot? Is he to starve and let his family beg in the streets? Laborers have as much pride as the most esteemed senators." He could no longer mask his impatience with Zachary's pigheadedness.

"Come now, Quinn, you paint a grossly exaggerated picture. Most factory workers are well treated and content.

329

You may have experienced that miracle in some job or other yourself," Zachary said sarcastically.

"I have," Duggan replied stiffly. "But conditions change. I have seen a complete upheaval because the management of a plant changed. Men too old to begin again were caught between loyalty and survival. If they had a union to protect them, that could not happen."

"Most factories do not change management often," Thomas scoffed. He settled back in the chair and pushed away his empty plate. Wiping his hands on the linen napkin, he sighed.

Jerome masked his exasperation. "I thought you'd find Duggan's arguments convincing, Thomas, but you seem to have your mind set. Is there nothing that can be said to change it?"

"I doubt it." Zachary was tired of the conversation. He'd been out of sorts ever since discovering that suspicion of Beau Fontaine's cheating was commonplace. And if that wasn't enough, all the talk about Beau's affairs had made him almost certain that Fontaine was carrying on with Irene. He was accustomed to her indiscretions, but this was too much. He cast a warning glance at her every time she displayed a flicker of interest in Quinn.

"Then I suggest we retire to the drawing room for coffee," Senator Jerome said. He nodded to his wife, Frances, who immediately rose and led the way from the dining room.

Irene lingered so she could walk beside Duggan. She slipped her arm through his and smiled as though they shared some marvelous secret. "My husband is in a bad temper," she said *sotto voce*. "He's hardly in a mood to listen to any opinion that doesn't coincide with his own. You mustn't take his remarks as final. Perhaps if I talk to him . . ."

Duggan grinned. "I'm sure you can be very persuasive." He saw the pink rise in her cheeks and her eyes danced as she interpreted the remark to her liking.

She flirted openly. "Will you be returning to Washington soon?"

"No, there's nothing more for me to do there. I've talked to everyone who will listen—and some who did not want to." He winked conspiratorially, and Irene laughed.

"*I* think you are very forceful. . . ." She looked at him wide-eyed. "Will you be staying in Pittsburgh then?"

"For a while."

"Then you must come to Hagenstead again soon." Her gaze devoured his powerful frame and broad face. His azure eyes were laughing one moment and solemn the next. His thoughts seemed to be distracted without warning. She slipped her hand into his with a beguiling smile, determined to win his full attention.

"The more I know about you, the more convincingly I can present your arguments to Thomas," she said.

He had no illusions about the price Irene would expect for her help. She was a woman who knew the bargaining power of her body. Her flirting amused him, though he had thoughts for no one but Maura. He pretended to consider her invitation.

"Nothing would please me more, but if your husband is not convinced of the soundness of my views by now, I'm afraid there isn't much hope of changing his mind in the time that's left. The vote on the union bill comes up very soon. I presume the Senator is returning to Washington shortly?"

She was nonplussed. "But I am staying on at Hagenstead." Her voice dropped to a whisper as they reached the library.

"Ah, there you are," Jerome said.

Duggan let Irene's remark go unanswered. The others were already seated, and Elias Jerome was pouring brandy into large snifters. Irene settled on a small Louis XV sofa and arranged the skirt of her violet-colored *mousseline de soie* so there was ample room beside her for Duggan. Fanny Jerome offered her coffee, and Irene balanced the cup delicately. She sipped and watched Duggan sidelong. Despite his size, he carried himself with easy grace, and was as self-assertive as any man she'd ever met. His dark suit, the same one he'd worn to the party, had not come from a fashionable tailor, but he wore it without embarrassment. He was—she searched for the term—earthy. He intrigued her. She wanted to know a great deal more about him.

She realized with a start of irritation that the brandy had loosened Thomas' tongue and he was talking about Beau.

331

"To think I welcomed him into my home without a qualm. The man is nothing but a jackleg gambler. All his talk of business holdings in the South is so much hogwash. He's never earned an honest dollar in his life. He was actually caught cheating at the Tagston Club last spring, yet he has the gall to return and pretend nothing happened! There seems to be mounting evidence that he was also run out of New York because of an affair in one of the leading clubs there."

Duggan's hand tightened around the brandy snifter, and his face clouded. Sleek, fawning Fontaine—a professional gambler! Duggar had taken him for a dilettante—this was even worse.

"Are you sure of your facts, Thomas?" Jerome asked. "It's a serious thing to accuse a man of dishonesty."

Zachary quaffed the brandy, enjoying the sensation he'd created. "No question. A dozen men will testify if he's brought up on charges. And that's exactly what's going to happen if he tries his tricks again here." He smiled smugly. He'd joined Cromwell in making it known that they had a personal score to settle with Fontaine.

A pulse pounded in Duggan's temple. Recalling Beau's lordly airs and his smug conviction that Maura would not be interested in a common laborer, he wished he had smashed in Fontaine's sneering face. If the bastard ever went near Maura again, he wouldn't be fool enough to hold back.

Irene listened to the conversation with growing vexation. She was sick to death of Beau Fontaine! She hoped he got all the trouble he deserved and more. If there were any way she could ensure that happening, it would give her great delight to do so. With the tarnished reputation he had suddenly acquired, she wanted no part of him. Thomas wouldn't allow him in the house, and she did not want to see him elsewhere. Still, she would miss him. Unless . . . unless she found someone to take his place to amuse her and help pass the time. She glanced sidelong at Duggan, wondering what it would be like to feel his brawny arms hold her and his sensuous lips stir her desire.

Richard Denfield clasped his hands and stared at the Turkey-red carpet. He'd been summoned from his dinner by

a brusque message from Pelham Turk. He still hadn't overcome his surprise at learning Turk and his son were in
Pittsburgh. Denfield expected only instructions in answer
to the telegram he'd sent his employer telling of Maura's
arrival. Instead, the Turks had set out for Pittsburgh immediately. Now they were here, and he was forced to give
them the news personally of Duggan Quinn's presence at
the boatyard.

Pelham's face mottled with rage. "You let him bring in
workmen?! You were ordered not to let the work resume!
Damn it, man, can't you be trusted to carry out instructions? Sixty men working fifteen hours a day!" His eyes
bulged and his breath hissed.

Denfield swallowed, not bothering to correct the exaggerated figures. "Miss Sullivan made it quite clear that she
was my employer in her brother's absence. I could
hardly—"

Pelham's cane stabbed the air with an angry thrust.
"You take your orders from me! What the hell do you
think I'm paying you for?"

Denfield bristled and did not answer. He had not been
hired for physical violence. Since Quinn had come to the
yard, he'd amassed a loyal following among the workmen.
Even without them, the thought of going up against Quinn
made Denfield's stomach knot. He'd seen Duggan lift a
crossbeam single-handed. Those powerful fists could flatten
him with a blow. Turk wasn't paying him to risk getting
himself killed.

"You are an imbecile," Pelham jibed. The cane bit into
the carpet with staccato thuds. He sucked in a huge, shuddering breath that did nothing to calm his rage. "Can I
assume you had the sense to prevent her from getting in
touch with James?" he asked sarcastically.

Denfield nodded. "I destroyed the telegram she asked to
have sent." He did not add that Maura could have written
or wired outside the office without his knowledge. Turk
was furious enough without adding fuel to his anger. Denfield watched the Malacca cane chop at the carpet.

At the table, Braxton poured whiskey and drank it in a
gulp. His father had been in a foul mood ever since getting
Denfield's wire. He'd stormed and fumed and finally insisted on accompanying Braxton to Pittsburgh to ensure

333

that Maura did not get away again. If she reached James, she would no longer be a defenseless woman who could be forced into relinquishing her share of the Sullivan Company.

Knowing that Quinn was here did not improve either his father's mood or his own. Braxton had not recovered completely from the beating Quinn had given him. There were still tender spots on his jaw where the bone had been fractured. He didn't relish the idea of coming up against the bastard again. Not alone . . .

"Very well," Pelham said at last. "I will handle everything from now on. Is there a fence around the yard?" When Denfield nodded, Pelham said, "Go to the office in the morning as though nothing had happened. Not a word or hint to Maura or Quinn, or I'll have your hide, is that clear?"

"Yes, sir."

"That's all." The cane slashed between them, dismissing Denfield. He rose and quickly left, breathing a sigh of relief as the door closed behind him. Whatever Turk was planning, he was glad he knew no more. He rushed down the stairs and out into the cool air.

Beau handed over his hat and overcoat to the pretty dark-haired girl who ushered him into the entry hall. The velvety carpet deadened the sound of their footsteps, and their images were reflected by a large mirror over a pink marble table on which stood an alabaster statue of a nude woman. Overhead, a crystal chandelier glowed with the soft light of a hundred tiny candles. A musky smell of incense wafted through the open door of a parlor. The tinkling sound of a piano mingled with voices and laughter.

He hadn't seen Maura since she went off with Quinn, nor had he dared make an assignation with Irene while Cromwell was still visiting at Hagenstead. Better to let sleeping dogs lie. Besides, a bit of novelty would provide a welcome change.

He let his gaze linger on the girl's full, ripe figure. She wore a scarlet dress that showed every curve to advantage; the rosy crescents of her nipples were exposed by the décolletage. The scent of gardenias seemed to rise from the warm, shadowy haven between her breasts.

334

"You are a mirage to the hungry eyes of one who has crossed the wasteland of the city," he said glibly.

The girl gave him a saucy smile. "If it's only your eyes that are hungry, you've come to the wrong place, lovey."

Beau chuckled and studied her with an admiring eye. "I don't recall seeing you here before. Either you're new, or I've been away too long."

"Maybe both." She hung his coat on the rack and took his arm possessively. "I'm Kate. I hope we're going to be friends a *long* time." She pressed close so her breasts touched the bare flesh of his hands. Beau's fingers deftly found the warmth between the surging mounds. Kate smiled and did not move away.

"Well, bless me, it's Beau Fontaine! I didn't know you were in town."

Standing in the hall was a small woman with a full bosom straining at the neckline of her lilac satin dress. Her ebony hair was tightly curled except for twin swirls that lay carelessly at her cheeks to frame her heart-shaped face. Her rouged lips were crimson in contrast to her powdered face, and her nearly lavender eyes glittered like jewels.

"Cora, you're more alluring each time I see you. When you decide to exploit the fountain of youth you've discovered, promise me you'll give me first opportunity to buy into the business." Beau took her hand and pressed it to his lips.

Cora laughed. "The only fountain of youth I've got is right upstairs, and you can buy into it any time you've got the inclination. God, it's good to see you! Let me look at you—" She held him at arm's length and let her gaze take in the length of his tall frame. "Nobody's taken any of your hide yet, least not so's one would notice. Where've you been keeping yourself?"

Beau shrugged. "Here and there. But now I'm here, and I'm sorely in need of some of that fine whiskey you keep."

"That's *all* you need?" Cora winked suggestively.

Beau grinned and looked at Kate again. "My needs are complex but solvable." Kate played her fingers along his arm.

"I can send a bottle upstairs," Cora said with a knowing look.

Kate's fingers trailed along the back of Beau's neck, toy-

335

ing with wisps of hair that fell over his collar. She measured the end of his sideburns with a painted fingernail.

"An excellent idea, Cora, excellent." Beau put an arm around the girl's waist, and she rested her head on his shoulder intimately as they moved toward the stairs.

"I'll have a game going later, Beau. If you're in the mood, stop down," Cora said, winking and rubbing her hands together in a gesture that told him the game was something special.

He cocked an eyebrow. One of Cora's games was the reason he had come. His hands itched for the feel of cards. He had not played since Clinton Henry had warned him away from his favorite haunts. It paid to be cautious. He had no hankering to encounter a lynching party or to be tarred and feathered and run out of Pittsburgh on a rail. But there had been no further incident since Cromwell's drunken rampage. It was all a dust storm on the prairie, quickly blown out.

He put an arm around Kate's slender waist and went upstairs.

Beau poured whiskey from the amber bottle without taking his eyes from the table. Three players had folded, and only Randolph Tobias and he were still in. Beau had been surprised to see Tobias here; he usually played at the Tagston Club. It was a damned bit of bad luck running into him. Beau was uneasy, but when no mention was made of past games or present rumors, he breathed more easily. Lady Luck had not abandoned him after all.

He drew a third card. Tobias had raised, but Beau was sure he was bluffing. He had a King and a deuce showing. Beau had Jacks back to back. His third card was the Jack of hearts. Sweet Lady Luck . . . Tobias turned up a deuce. His expression didn't alter, and Beau hid a grin. The man was a fool.

Beau raised again. Tobias' fifth card was a trey, and he threw in his hand disgustedly.

"That does it," Tobias declared. "I haven't a dollar left in my pocket. I swear, Fontaine, you've got some kind of hoodoo on those cards." He shoved away from the table and called out to Cora. "Can I put the rest of the night on my tab? Fontaine has left me without carriage fare home, as usual."

Cora laughed and signaled one of the girls, who came from the round sofa at the opposite side of the room. She slipped an arm through Tobias' and whispered something at his ear that made him guffaw. He slapped her bottom as he led her toward the stairs.

"Gentlemen?" Beau glanced around the table.

The others shook their heads.

"Another time, Beau."

Beau pushed back his chair, picking up his winnings and slipping them into a pocket. A decent streak of luck. All in all, a very pleasant evening. He pulled a gold watch from his vest pocket, snapped it open.

"You're not quitting already, Beau?" Cora's hand slid across his shoulder in a friendly manner. Beau was a good customer, upstairs and down.

"The gentlemen have called an end to our game. I have no choice." He grinned and put his hand over hers, slipping a five-dollar banknote into her palm. It vanished in a quick motion.

"That's a shame. What's your hurry, gents?" She smiled around the group. They were already on their feet. When she saw that they would not reconsider, Cora escorted them to the door, chatting and extracting their promises to return soon. When she came back to Beau, she made a moue. "Now, I'll think I've lost my touch if I can't talk you into having a drink with an old friend and maybe going upstairs again. Kate's free now, or if you have a hankering for a little variety, I've taken on a little mulatto from New Orleans. . . ." She rolled her eyes and showed a pink tongue tip between her teeth.

"Yes to the drink and no to the rest." He indicated one of the vacated chairs and tipped the bottle to the light. Cora signaled a bar girl, who brought glasses and set them down with a smile at Beau. He poured.

"Beau, you ought to know there are some stories making the rounds."

He raised an eyebrow. They tapped glasses and drank. "What kind of stories, Cora?"

She shrugged. "A little bit of this and a little of that, only

337

they're beginning to crop up regularly. For instance, last night Senator Zachary and a man named Cromwell were asking about you." She finished the whiskey and pushed the glass toward him.

Beau masked his surprise as he refilled her glass. So Cromwell had not given up. And Thomas was taking the accusation seriously enough to look into it. A muscle twitched in Beau's jaw, and he slammed the cork in the bottle.

Cora went on: "Cromwell's a cocky bastard who's too impressed with his own importance. Most of my girls would run and hide when they see him coming if they thought they could get away with it. God, last night he kept up a nonstop chatter about some fast deal he's pulled all the while he was upstairs with Bessie." She shook her head in disgust.

Beau's interest perked. If he could get something on Cromwell, it might prove handy.

"I've heard of him," he said without betraying his interest. "I thought his politics kept him up Boston way."

Cora snorted. "His kind is always fast-dealing everywhere. Seems he's weaseled into some local boatyard so's he can get one of his power-grabbing unions established, and he'll rule *that* with an iron fist, you can be damned sure. He'd been looking for a way to get started in the building industry. I'm surprised Tom Zachary has anything to do with him, but they were cavorting around like old buddies last night." She wagged her head again. "But the point is, Beau, the two of them asked me and my gents if you'd ever been caught cheating." She cocked her head and looked at him askance.

"What'd you tell them?"

She sipped the whiskey, still watching him. "I told them that you don't have to cheat. We've been friends a long time, Beau. I run an honest house."

"Cora, I wouldn't . . ."

"I know. I just wanted to put my cards on the table. They talked to a lot of people last night. Cromwell said he was willing to pay for information about you. I finally told him to do his muckraking elsewhere." She smiled. "Not everyone finds you quite as irresistible as I do, though. Just remember that."

338

When he laughed, she patted his arm. "Remember it," she repeated sagely.

"I will."

She sipped the whiskey and looked at the glass thoughtfully. "There are plenty of men who would take pleasure in helping Zachary pin something on you. A hell of a lot of men are jealous of you, Beau."

"I haven't survived all these years by being careless, Cora. But thanks for the word—I'll keep it in mind." He glanced around. "But now I must be going."

"Will we see you again soon?" She stood and walked with him to the door. "We've got a Saturday night regular who claims he can conjure up a royal flush by staring at the backs of the cards."

"As long as he doesn't do it by passing his sleeve over the deck," Beau said with a roguish wink. "I'd love to meet the gentleman."

"Good-bye, Beau."

He let himself out, descending the wide gray stone steps with a jaunty air. It was a dark night with no stars. Far down the street near the corner, someone had built a crackling fire on the cobblestones. He could see figures huddled about the flames. He went out to the street and peered both ways for a carriage. There were usually several in the vicinity, with their little oil lamps flickering like lively fireflies. Cora's house drew a large clientele from among the best names in the city. It amused him that Zachary apparently frequented the house. He wondered if Irene knew—or cared.

He whistled under his breath as he pulled on his gloves. A carriage came down the street toward him with its single horse's hooves clip-clopping steadily. Beau raised his arm to hail it. As he did, he heard a soft grating step behind him.

He turned quickly but had only an instant's impression of an arm and fist before the force of the blow spun him back. Dancing colored lights dazzled him and pain welled. Footpads! He stumbled as he tried to move away from his attacker, but another blow made him grunt as the air whooshed from his lungs. His hat went spinning off and he felt himself grabbed and pulled around to receive a third punch. There were two of them!

He was dazed, and the pain of the blows made his head throb. Instinctively he fell against the closer of the attackers. At the same time, his fingers worked at the buttons of his coat to get the Colt, which would even the odds. Before he could grab it, he was paralyzed by a punch to his middle that sent him to his knees, gasping. Velvet blackness closed about him, then the pain returned with a reddish haze. Blows rained on his head, and bile rose in his throat. He vomited suddenly. Someone swore, and Beau was flung aside. His head hit the paving stones and blackness scooped him up once more.

"Search his pockets."

Beau heard a blur of sound and felt hands pulling at his clothes. His head was splitting, and his mouth tasted of sour whiskey. Then someone was slapping his cheek. "Wake up!"

He focused his eyes with difficulty and realized he was on his back in the street. Something huge loomed over him. It was the carriage, with a bright diamond of light from the lantern that seemed to throb and glow. A man was kneeling beside him, going through his pockets methodically.

"—a pistol . . . and a wad of bills."

The thick roll of money went from the searcher's beefy hand to someone standing behind him. Beau's gaze followed it painfully. The man in the shadows was Obediah Cromwell! Cromwell was dressed in evening clothes, with a red waistcoat and black jacket that stretched across his full middle. He puffed lazily on a long cigar, blowing smoke into the misty night air. He tucked the money away with a jarring laugh

The two thugs jerked Beau to his feet. Staggering, Beau licked his swollen lip and tasted blood. Words came painfully from his throat. "You bastard—!"

Cromwell chuckled and blew smoke in his face.

Beau managed a breath. "So you're a thief as well as a bad loser."

"An eye for an eye," Cromwell said flatly.

"There's more there than your losses—" Beau's chest ached from the pressure of the arms gripping him. Each breath was a painful stab. Cromwell was turning over his Colt in his thick hands. Was the man going to kill him?

"Interest on the money you won by cheating," Cromwell

340

said coldly. He reached up and opened the door of the carriage, then motioned to the two men.

They lifted Beau and heaved him into the coach like a sack of meal. He moaned as his head slammed the iron foot warmer on the floor. For a moment, he lost consciousness. When he came to, Cromwell was yanking his head up by the hair.

"Be out of town by noon, Fontaine," Cromwell snarled. "And if our paths ever cross again, you'd better see me first and start running. Otherwise you're a dead man."

CHAPTER TWENTY

When Maura woke in the morning, her fingers strayed to the pillow beside her before she remembered drowsily that Duggan had stayed the night at Senator Jerome's. She stretched languorously, thinking how much she missed the feel of Duggan's warmth and his tender, loving presence to begin the new day. He had laughed at her fears that her reputation would be tarnished if it became known that a man stayed the night with her. He devoured her protests with kisses until she clung to him and begged him never to leave her. And then he whispered that her reputation would never suffer since they would be married as soon as possible. She would be bound to him forever in love as well as in name.

She wondered if he had missed her last night? Smiling, she thought of his reluctance to be gone even for so short a time. She had coaxed, then finally insisted that he go, because she knew his hopes for pro-union legislation. They had not talked about it; they'd been too busy at the boatyard, too engrossed in their rediscovery of each other. But Duggan was not a man to relinquish a cause dear to his heart. She had still not come to any conclusion of her own about unionism. It was not something that had to be decided immediately, and she was content to let the matter drift. One day she would have Duggan explain it all and try to see it through his eyes.

With a glance at the clock, she rose and rang for hot water. She was eager to get to the boatyard. This was the day the *Patrick* was to be launched. It still seemed a miracle. Duggan had driven himself and the men relentlessly, and the steamboat was ready to be put in the water for her seaworthiness to be tested. There were still a few days' work to be done on the basic structure, and another two weeks or so to complete the finishing touches and furnish the cabins. In spite of James' absence and unforgivable silence, the *Patrick* would be done on schedule. Her maiden voyage would take place before icy winter lashed across Pennsylvania, and by the rush of spring trade on the Ohio, the Sullivan line would be well established. A dream would be reality . . . someday the Sullivan Company would dominate waterways as well as highways.

The maid came with water, put it on the washstand, then curtsied to Maura as she waited.

"Lay out my green wool, please, and the black shoes with the pearl buttons." Maura unbelted her robe and dropped it to a chair. The girl retrieved it and hung it up before fetching the gown. She seemed particularly nervous this morning, Maura thought, and wondered what had gotten into her. It was the same girl who'd brought the mound of packages from Beau on Maura's first night here; Celeste was assigned to regular duty in this wing of the hotel and often answered Maura's bell. The girl laid the green wool on the bed and smoothed it carefully. Then she stood wringing her hands and staring at Maura.

"Whatever is the matter, Celeste?" Maura asked at last. The girl was round-eyed and solemn. Maura tested the water and wrung out the facecloth.

"Oh, mum, it's terrible. How could anyone do such a thing to a nice man like—"

"What are you talking about?" Maura motioned impatiently toward the shoes the girl had forgotten. The maid quickly reached to take them from the shelf and put them near the bed.

"Ohh, it's just awful. I've never seen anything so horrible. Poor Mr. Fontaine."

Maura frowned in puzzlement. "Beau? Has something happened to him?" The way the girl was carrying on— She felt a wave of guilt that she had not seen Beau since the night she stormed out after Duggan. She supposed she would have apologized or at least tried to explain.

The girl's head bobbed like a puppet on a string. "Ohh, mum, he's been beat somethin' terrible. His poor face—" She pressed a hand to her mouth.

Maura dropped the washcloth and grabbed the towel.

"Beau's been beaten?" Good Lord! No matter how angry she was with him, she didn't wish him any harm. "When? Who did it?" The girl stood wringing her hands, startled at Maura's swift reaction, and Maura demanded, "Where is he now?"

Celeste gulped and wiped a tear with the back of her hand. "In his room, mum. I took some fresh cloths and water to him not half an hour ago." She shook her head again and looked ready to burst into tears. Maura dismissed her and finished washing, then dressed hurriedly. Who in the world had Beau had a confrontation with now? She sighed. He seemed to have a talent for rousing the violent side of men's natures. First Cromwell, then Duggan, now this. It seemed strange since he was so gentle and had a completely different effect on women. In spite of her annoyance with him, she would be uneasy unless she saw for herself that he was all right. Taking her cape and bonnet so she could go directly on to the boatyard, she went upstairs and tapped at the door of his suite. She was answered by a cautious voice.

"Who is it?"

When she gave her name, the door opened instantly. Her mouth fell open in horror. Celeste had not exaggerated. Beau's left eye was swollen and there was an ugly purple bruise around it that extended over his cheekbone. An angry red line slashed along his lip where it had been cut, and another thread of dried blood stitched across his temple.

She shook her head sympathetically. "What happened?"

He gave her a weak smile that caused him to grimace with pain. "I underestimated the length of time it would take Obediah Cromwell's wrath to cool," he said as he glanced along the hall, then stepped back to usher Maura inside. "I must confess I'm surprised but delighted to see you."

She stood staring at him. "Cromwell came after you again?" She knew Cromwell to be a violent man, and had submerged her dislike of him because he was willing to lend money to complete the work on the *Patrick*. But to beat a man so savagely!

Beau managed a lopsided smile. "He had some of his thugs do the job while he stood by enjoying the show. And he took care to ensure there were no witnesses who might come to my defense." He shrugged as if the incident were no longer important. At the moment he was more interested in learning what had brought her to his suite. He'd counted her lost after she'd run off with Quinn. But she was here, and not a minute too soon. He'd been just about to leave in search of transportation to greener pastures. He was not taking lightly Cromwell's ultimatum of a noon deadline.

"Please don't look so pained," he said consolingly. "I assure you, I'm very resilient. The bruises will heal, and in the meantime the maid has gone to the chemist to bring a powder that will cover the worst of my sins so I can present my face in public."

Maura shuddered, still overcome with horror at Cromwell's cold-bloodedness. "I had no idea the man would stoop so low."

"Cromwell does not forgive or forget easily. He is not a man I would care to involve myself with in a business transaction. I hear he can be as ruthless there."

A sudden eddy of fear caught Maura and she paled. Beau saw the shadow cloud her eyes and was instantly solicitous. "Here, what an oaf I am, talking about vengeful politicians and business dealings. Forgive me. I have already confessed my delight in seeing you. Can I assume I am forgiven for my callous and careless remark about your friend Quinn?"

She nodded absently; her mind was still troubled over this new facet of Obediah Cromwell's nature. Beau had met him only a few nights ago at the Hagenstead party, yet he spoke of Cromwell's business dealings. Did he have more deals in Pittsburgh than the one with the Sullivan Company? She gnawed her lip until Beau asked her what was troubling her.

"Has something gone wrong at the boatyard? You said Quinn had secured a loan and you were saved from disaster."

She sighed and tried to still her fears. "It's true, but he secured the loan from Obediah Cromwell."

"What?!" Beau was thunderstruck to hear it was Cromwell who had played the part of savior to the Sullivans. His mind dredged up the chance remark Cora had made. Cromwell had used skulduggery to worm his way into a

346

boatyard for the purpose of setting up a union. The Sullivan Company? Of course! There could not be another. Cromwell had met Maura and Duggan at Irene's party, and he'd sized up Quinn as a man who might prove useful to him.

Maura nodded. "The money came from Cromwell."

Beau's eyes narrowed. "What is he to get out of it?"

She told him the conditions she'd agreed to. He scowled and crossed to the table for a cheroot, then spent several moments lighting it. When he turned back to Maura, his expression was thoughtful.

"It would seem we both underestimated Cromwell," he said at last with a wry grin.

"What do you mean?"

He raised an eyebrow and studied her again. Did she know nothing of the arrangement Quinn had made with Cromwell? No . . . Quinn had dealt behind her back, he was sure. The grubby laborer reverting to type while he let Maura think he was a knight in shining armor. The memory of Quinn's punch still rankled.

"Maura, my sweet innocent, I think you've been duped."

Dread filled her, and unreasoning anger. "What are you talking about?" Now that ugly suspicion had crept into her calm bliss, she was driven to know the truth. "Please explain yourself."

Beau made a deprecating gesture. "Obediah Cromwell is chortling over his most recent coup. He's bragging all over town that he's bought his way into your boatyard as a means of setting up his labor union. He says it's giving him the foothold he needs to control the entire building industry."

"That's ridiculous!" Her face flushed, and she was swamped with guilt because she could not refute his statement.

"Is it? You admit that Quinn secured the money you needed. Quinn is rather partial to the union cause, as I recall. Who better to aid Cromwell in a private arrangement? By joining forces with Cromwell, Quinn gains his objective while lulling you into the belief that he's championing your welfare. By the time you realize the truth, it will be too late to do anything." He shrugged carelessly and puffed at the cheroot. The aroma of the tobacco eddied around his head.

347

Thunderstruck, Maura sank to a chair. It couldn't be true! Duggan wouldn't— No! Her brain refused to accept it. Duggan loved her! The past few days had been so happy—they could not be pretense. A cold core settled in her belly and she sent Beau an appealing glance. He had to be mistaken!

"Maura, you're far too intelligent to be blinded by Quinn's deceit any longer. The man's an opportunist. He saw the chance to get what he wanted and he took it. Don't you see that he used you? God only knows what kind of pact he's made."

Maura moistened her dry lips. "I signed an agreement." Her voice was small and distant in her ears.

Beau looked at her in astonishment. "With Cromwell?"

She nodded. "Duggan brought it to me." She related the terms of the agreement.

He whistled softly. "That's it, then. Duggan has guaranteed him the nucleus of a union on the premises, and he tricked you to putting your name to it. Cromwell's banking on the honor and reputation of the Sullivan Company as well as the advantage of time he expected to have before you found out." Beau shook his head regretfully.

Maura rose, trembling with anger. The truth of Duggan's perfidy lay like a dead weight in her heart. How could she have been such a fool to believe the sweet lies that fell so readily from his treacherous Irish tongue? She had once accused him of the very deviousness Beau was describing, but she had let her doubts be swept away by kisses and murmured promises. And she had signed away the future of the Sullivan Company!

Beau watched hatred take shape in Maura's eyes, and a warm glow of satisfaction filled him. Whatever romantic notions she'd entertained about Quinn were dashed now. Beau was sorry he would not be around to soothe her wounded pride and let her find solace in his bed. He'd enjoy it all the more, knowing he'd evened the score with Quinn.

"I regret being the bearer of such bad tidings, Maura. You know how fond I am of you." He smiled engagingly. "If there is anything I can do, you need only ask."

"Thank you, Beau." She gathered her cape and hat. "You're always offering to help, even when you have prob-

348

lems of your own. I'm really sorry about the beating. You're sure you'll be all right?"

He grinned. "Of course. It's over and done with. I'm not one to dwell on the past."

"A laudable attitude," she said. She wished she could shut off the past as easily, but it would haunt her forever. Her anger bubbled like a cauldron, but she forced it beneath the surface as she smiled at Beau. "I must be going. Perhaps I'll see you again soon?"

He frowned and fingered a sideburn. "I may be going out of town on business for a few days. I have an appointment this morning that will influence my decision." Did she look disappointed, or was he reading too much into the brief flicker of her gaze?

"Maybe when you return, then," she said.

"I shall look forward to it." He opened the door for her and clasped her hand warmly before she took her leave. He watched until she reached the stairs, then chuckled softly and closed the door.

Excitement crackled in the air like a banner. Work on the *Patrick* had slowed as preparations for the launching got underway. Men with buckets and mops were greasing the long slipways that hugged the keel and ran down to the river. Others were laying the sliding ways and building poppets at the bow and stern. The launching cradle was almost complete. Lines were already strung over pulleys to ease the heavy keel blocks from under the hull. Most of the work on the boat was done; it would not take long to complete the painting and interior work and furnish the cabins.

The joy with which Maura had anticipated the day was overshadowed by her roiling anger. She climbed from the carriage and marched into the office to confront Duggan.

"Where is the agreement with Cromwell that I signed?" she demanded without preamble.

Startled, he looked up from his work and his smile of welcome waned. "Cromwell has it. But is that any greeting for the man you love?" The smile turned up his mouth again as he rose from the chair and came to take her hand. She jerked away and flounced across the room. Glaring at him, she unfastened her cape and bonnet and threw them onto the coatrack.

349

Duggan stood his ground, watching her curiously. "I knew you would miss me, my sweet," he said, "but I had no idea that one night apart from me would put you in such a temper. Come here now, love, and tell me what has upset you so that you refuse me the kiss I've been waiting for all morning."

Her cheeks flamed at the thought that Denfield and Smith in the outer office might hear. Twenty-four hours ago she would not have cared if the whole world knew she loved him, but now . . .

In spite of her determination to control herself, her voice rose. "You speak of love, when all the time you've been plotting behind my back? If you had any decency you would grovel and beg forgiveness!" She lifted her chin and tried to fight back the sting of tears.

With a bewildered scowl he took a step toward her, but when she drew back, he halted. His eyes took on the hue of a stormy sea. "What is this foolish notion you've taken?"

She clenched her fists. "I have learned the truth of what you have done. You have made me a laughingstock and held me up to contempt. You have—"

With a quick stride, he was at her side and grasping her arms. "What the devil are you talking about?" His face clouded with angry confusion.

"The agreement with Cromwell!" The words lashed with the sting of a whip. "You have pledged the Sullivan Company to his union. Have you so little honor that you had to stoop to trickery to gain your ends and betray me in so base a manner?" She trembled as she tried to free herself from his iron grip. When he would not release her, she met his bold gaze with a scornful look.

The warmth was gone from his voice when he said, "I have neither tricked you nor betrayed you, no matter what idiotic prattle you've listened to that has driven away your common sense."

She drew a sharp breath. "Do you deny that Obediah Cromwell intends to form a union here at the Sullivan Company?"

A moment of silence passed, and his fingers released their hold. His dark brows pulled to a V over his troubled gaze. "I do not deny that that is what he hopes to do."

"You've known from the start!" She had demanded his

answer, but having received it, she knew the last shred of hope had been torn from her. How desperately she had wanted Beau to be wrong, to find that Duggan had some explanation for what he'd done, a reason that would soothe her fears and make her world right again. But he did not deny it. He did not even pretend it was a mistake or a misunderstanding. She was sick with disgust and loathing.

"I divined his intent," Duggan said coldly, "but I did not plot against you in any way. A union can be a benefit to everyone."

"You said nothing of a union when you presented his paper to be signed." Her voice was as icy as her contempt.

"Would you have signed it if I had?"

Her rage exploded. "I would not! I don't care a whit for your damned union! I am interested only in the best interests of the Sullivan Company!"

His face darkened. "Where would the Sullivan Company be if I had not agreed to Cromwell's conditions? Do you think some miracle would have gotten the men to work? Are you so accustomed to your life of luxury that you give no thought to where it comes from? Men must work if the Sullivan Company is to stay solvent!" He wheeled about and slammed a fist on the desk to vent his fury.

Maura trembled under the force of his indictment, but the outburst pricked her pride. She pulled back her shoulders. "I have given a great deal of thought to keeping the company financially sound and its reputation as unblemished as when my father was alive, while you have tried to undermine everything!"

He whirled and his face was livid. "I have done nothing except finish the *Patrick* in record time! Your father would have commended me for that, not condemned me!"

Maura laughed cruelly. "You want my thanks for selling me out?"

"I have *not* sold you out! I didn't tell you about the union because it would only have upset you. When the times comes, I can handle Cromwell."

She fumed with indignation. He thought her too naïve to understand the implications of the agreement and had counted on her gratitude to convince her to sign. And he had ensured her cooperation by using his compelling masculinity to bind her to him. Like a fool, she'd listened to his words of love and believed them.

When she was silent, he drew a shuddering breath and set his jaw. "Where did you get the foolish idea that I am a wild jackal to be held at bay?"

She bristled. "I'm told that Cromwell is boasting all over the city that he will soon control the building industry through the union *you* helped him establish."

Duggan's eyes narrowed. "Who told you this?" He was still stunned by her attack and wanted a direction for his fury.

She lifted her chin and gave him a frigid glance. "A friend showed me the kindness of telling me."

"Kindness?" he jeered. " 'Tis a questionable friend, I think."

She tossed her head. "At least I can trust Beau—"

Duggan let out a whoop of rage. "Beau Fontaine?!" As soon as he had left her, she'd turned to that knave!

Maura's eyes widened. "He has heard the story from more than one quarter."

"The man's a lying, cheating scoundrel—a jackleg gambler! Maura, for God's sake, don't listen to his stupid poker-table gossip!" Duggan's hands clenched to fists as he fought his disgust. Didn't she see what Fontaine was? Was she still attracted by his thin veneer of charm?

"You are a fine one to call another a liar! What have *you* been doing these past days with your damned union and your pretense of loving me? Did you hope to keep me blind to the fact that you are insinuating yourself into the Sullivan Company by any means you can devise? Beau was right—you're an opportunist who sees a chance to climb above his station!"

Duggan recoiled as though slapped. "Is that how you see me? A grubby laborer who's forgotten his place?" His fists were so tight the fingernails dug into the callused palms. He flexed his hands to relieve the rigid muscles. He was seething with a rage that had climbed to the edge of violence. If Fontaine were here . . .

Maura clamped her lips and lifted her chin disdainfully. When Duggan reached out and grabbed her arms, she twisted away from the cruel pressure of his fingers.

"Do you?" he demanded. "Or are you parroting the words of a man whose reputation has less value than his honor at the card tables?"

"Let go of me!" She beat at his broad chest with her fists, but Duggan shook her until her hands fell limp at her sides. She stared at him coldly. "Would you beat me as you do any man who angers you? Is violence always your answer?" she asked in a scathing tone.

He pushed her away in disgust. "Forgive me, Miss Sullivan. I have forgotten my station again." His jealousy was a caged beast tearing at the bars of its prison. "Beau Fontaine would not act in so base a manner." He made a mock bow, pressing one hand over his heart and smiling sardonically. When he stood, he collected his jacket and cap from the coatrack and pulled them on. With a last savage look at her, he strode from the office, leaving her alone with her trembling anger. She started to call after him, then quickly bit the back of her hand to quell the impulse. Let him go! Let him go out of her life forever! She never wanted to see him again!

The outer office was deathly still as the door slammed behind Duggan. Maura listened for the sound of his rig, but instead his footsteps stomped on the heavy planking that had been laid as a walkway between the office and the *Patrick*. Maura hurried to the window in time to see him striding down the bank. As he reached the boat, he shouted to several men, then lifted a coil of rope and carried it up the gangplank. A moment later, he had pitched into work with maniacal fury.

Maura let out a shuddering breath. Duggan intended to stay on the job. She gave a vast sigh of relief. She would not have begged to bring him back, but she realized how relieved she was to have him still in charge of the work. She could not deny his value as a foreman, no matter how much she resented his intrusion in affairs that were none of his concern. She tapped a knuckle against her teeth in concentration. There had to be a way to undo the commitment to Cromwell. She would show them she was not the simpleminded female they mistook her for! And she would do it without Duggan Quinn!

The flurry of activity caused by Duggan's arrival settled

353

as men took places along the rails and lifted the heavy lines that would moor the boat once it was in the water. Others on shore readied the thick ropes slung over the pulleys.

Maura's body tensed in anticipation. The boat was going into the water! She grabbed up her cape and flung it over her shoulders as she ran from the office. She had waited a long time for this moment, and she would not let her annoyance with Duggan diminish the pleasure of seeing the *Patrick* glide down the ways triumphantly.

Standing at the head of the plank path, she tugged the cape close as a biting wind lifted dust and leaves in its wake and whipped her hair in feathery tendrils. The mild days had given way abruptly to crisp autumn that was denuding the trees and browning the hillsides. She shivered and folded her arms over her breasts.

She spied Duggan on the top deck. For a moment his rugged profile was clear against the gray sky. The knit cap was pulled back on his head, and a forelock of dark hair blew errantly in the wind. His broad shoulders hunched in his seaman's jacket as he shouted instructions to two men near the wheelhouse. Maura steeled herself against any weakening of her resolve. Duggan Quinn would never again find quarter in her heart.

"Excuse me, miss, can y'tell me where I'll find Duggan Quinn?"

Maura glanced around with a start as a man's voice broke into her preoccupation. He was an old man with sparse yellow-gray hair poking out in spikes from under a cap with a cracked visor. His face was weathered to the texture of worn leather, and his eyes were the color of ripe pecans. A brier pipe was clamped between his yellowed teeth, and he squinted as smoke curled past his face.

"Why yes, but he's busy now. I'm Miss Sulivan. If you tell me your business, perhaps I can help you." She wondered if it was safe to have such an elderly man climbing about on the boat.

The man nodded. " 'Scuse me, miss, I should have known you'd be the owner. Quinn mentioned you."

"Do you have business here, Mr.—" She smiled to remind him he'd neglected to give his name.

"Tolly Jeffries. Quinn's hired me to take yer boat into the water." He cast an appraising glance at the *Patrick*. "She's

354

got a solid foundation, all right, and her wheels are set right to hold down heat loss from the engine. There'll be less vibration with the shorter pitmans. . . ." He sucked at the black pipe. "Ye've picked the best design for speed and handling, Miss Sullivan."

She was pleased and surprised at his candid judgment. "The credit goes to my brother. I'm helping out at the office while he's away on business."

"You'll not go wrong sticking with this design, not until something better comes along," Jeffries said sagely. "And now if ye'll tell me where Quinn is, I'll get to work."

"I'll take you to him."

The old man shuffled as they crossed the wide planks that had been laid as a walkway across the rough river-bank. He seemed too old and frail to handle a huge river-boat, but Maura knew Duggan had confidence in his ability or the man would not be here.

"Have you worked on the river long, Mr. Jeffries?"

He grunted. "Born on a flatboat on the Delta. The river's my home. Ain't a boat afloat I can't handle. Been north far as the Falls in Minnesota and clear up to Fort Benton on the Missouri." He glanced at her and seemed to pull back his shoulders. "Piloted the *New Orleans* back in '10 for the Roosevelts."

Maura gazed along the river where a small steamer moved lazily with the current, its chimneys spilling black smoke. Small wonder that Duggan had chosen Jeffries. He spoke of the river and of boats with the tenderness of a lover. James would have picked him, too.

They reached the gangplank. "Duggan was on the top deck just a few minutes ago," Maura told him.

"The texas, miss. If ye're going to own a riverboat, ye better learn to call her right," Jeffries said sternly. Touching his cap politely, he went up the gangplank. Maura watched his spare figure disappear up the stairs leading to the second deck—no, boiler deck, she admonished herself silently. A moment later she heard Duggan call out to Jeffries.

A gust of wind caught her cape and flapped it about her legs. There were still a dozen things to be done in the office, but she stood a while longer, gazing at the *Patrick*. She shivered with excitement . . . if only James were

355

there to share it. How good it would be to see him—and
have him put an end to the necessity of keeping Duggan
on. Close by, a workman shouted and gestured as a timber
was swung into place on the poppet. Maura moved out of
the way, glancing back over her shoulder as Duggan and
Jeffries came into view in the pilothouse. The old man nodded and sucked his pipe as Duggan talked.

A foreman directing the clearing of the ways came toward Maura. His frown gave warning that owner or not,
she was in the way. With an apologetic smile, she lifted her
skirts and picked her way along the boards. When she
looked back, the gangplank had been lifted and the carpenters were drawing back from the cradle. Half a dozen of
the burliest men took places at the aft end of the boat with
sledgehammers poised.

Maura hurried up the bank where she could watch the
magnificent sight of the boat sliding down into the water.
On the texas deck, Duggan was making sure everything
was in order. He glanced toward the pilothouse where Jeffries was at the wheel. A burst of steam jetted from the
escape pipes with a shrill, hissing noise. Black smoke
spilled from the chimneys with a shower of sparks. Duggan
lifted a hand.

Maura shivered with anticipation. She held her breath as
Duggan took a final look around, then sliced his arm
downward in a signal. The men at the chocks swung the
hammers. Dull thuds tolled like bells. A shout went up as
the blocks fell away. The boat began to slide slowly down
the greased ways. A cheer exploded over the noise of scrap-
ing wood as the *Patrick* moved majestically toward the
river. A huge splash sent a wave of water over the after-
deck. The *Patrick* rocked, then settled like a dowager
queen. The men yelled and waved their caps. On the texas
deck, Duggan grinned broadly and pulled off his cap to
return the salute. Tolly Jeffries yanked the bellcord and
whistles shrilled. The yard erupted in activity once more as
men rushed to catch the lines being tossed by deckhands.

As the excitement began to settle, Maura's heart was still
racing. It seemed a very long time since she had seen anything so glorious. If only James were here to share the moment. The *Patrick* was his vision, but even so she knew
that his delight could not be any greater than hers. The

launching was not only a financial victory, it was a personal one over Pelham as well. It would mean his defeat, and it would put the Sullivan Company back in Sullivan hands.

She stood a moment longer, watching the bustle aboard the boat. Carpenters and pipe fitters doubled as crew, readying lines and inspecting the hull while Jeffries manned the wheel and brought the *Patrick* around parallel to the shore. Reluctantly, Maura turned back to the office. The blood sang in her temples, but her spirit was heavy. This was a day to be shared with loved ones. How proud Father would have been to witness the triumph. She recalled how intimately Duggan had spoken of her father and brother. Had they been fooled by his hypocritical friendship? She would not believe it possible, except that Duggan had hoodwinked her so completely. Well, let him stay on and work if that was his intent. She would use him as he had used her. Then when the steamboat was finished, she would send him packing.

As she reached the office, a shiny black landau with the top up and the windows closed slowed near the gate. Maura paused as the driver pulled at the reins. The pair of bays tossed their heads and snorted as they came to a halt. Maura glimpsed two men in beaver hats inside the coach. They seemed to be studying the yard, but they did not climb down. Instinctively she drew back into the shadows of the office building. Her hands were suddenly cold.

Who were they and what were they waiting for? She tried to convince herself her imagination was racing heedlessly, but a growing dread crept along her spine. She peered cautiously as she heard the sound of wheels again. Three flat, open wagons drew up behind the landau, and twenty or thirty men leaped down. They wore heavy coats and had caps pulled low on their heads. Most were carrying thick clubs or lengths of pipe. Fear hardened in Maura's stomach as the door of the landau opened. She jerked back as a tall, thin man with a stiff, awkwardly swinging leg climbed out. Pelham Turk!

It couldn't be! Her palm was sweaty as she pressed it to her mouth to stifle a startled cry. In panic, she darted back into the shadows. What was he doing here? But even as she voiced the silent question, she knew he had come for her!

Denfield had written—and Pelham rushed to Pittsburgh before she could flee again. She shuddered, and retreated deeper into the gloom as the blood thundered in her head. She dared not let him see her!

Duggan—!

She glanced quickly toward the steamboat, but Duggan had vanished from the wheelhouse. The workmen on the launching cradle were not yet aware of the menacing group clustered near the landau. Maura realized suddenly why Pelham had brought a contingent of men. He was not going to be satisfied with her—he planned to complete his revenge on James as well!

Behind Pelham there was a flutter of motion and Braxton stepped out of the carriage. Maura's heart lurched. A sickening memory of Braxton's pawing hands tearing at her clothes and clutching her body made her shudder. For a moment she reeled, and a sour taste rose in her throat. She pressed a hand to her mouth as Pelham and Braxton advanced toward the office, Braxton with long angry strides and Pelham limping and stabbing his cane into the hard earth. Maura turned quickly and ran to the end of the building. What were her chances of getting away before she was seen? There was no way! Pelham's men were already spreading out to cover the yard and converge on the waterfront. She would be seen immediately if she tried to retrace her steps to the *Patrick*. And Pelham and Braxton were blocking the way to the road.

Dear God!

The workmen became aware of the intruders, and the sounds of construction dwindled, then ceased. Faces turned toward the advancing group. Several workers climbed down from the launching cradle they were dismantling and faced the newcomers defiantly. Someone shouted Duggan's name. He appeared on the hurricane deck of the *Patrick*. With a quick appraisal of the situation, he vanished and appeared a moment later on the main deck. Two deckhands put a small dinghy over the side, and Duggan jumped in and rowed quickly to shore.

Maura watched his foolhardy, bold approach. Pelham had already spotted the boat and was watching it fixedly. He'd halted on the path only a few yards from her. Maura shrank back against the wall, her heart pounding and her throat brassy with fear. If he saw her, a shout would bring his men to run her down. She would not have a chance.

Neither would Duggan.

The dinghy scraped onto the mud, and Duggan leaped out and strode up the bank. One of Pelham's men stepped out to block his path, but Duggan shoved him roughly out of the way. By the time the man regained his feet, Duggan was halfway to the office. Pelham and Braxton stared at him with openmouthed wonder.

Duggan's path took him close to the side of the building where Maura was hiding. She took a step, but when he spied her, he warned her back with an imperceptible motion. She hesitated, then at another urgent glance from Duggan, withdrew into the shadows and hugged her cape around her, hiding in its folds.

Two of Pelham's men split from the mob and moved behind Duggan, but he ignored them as he confronted the Turks. His fists were tight and he balanced his weight on the balls of his feet, like a cat ready to spring.

Pelham's voice carried the sting of a whip. "What the hell are you doing here?!" His face mottled as he recognized the brawny Irishman. He sputtered futilely, then found his voice. "This boatyard is private property!"

Duggan hunched his shoulders and his muscles tightened. Braxton took a quick step back. "It *is* private property," Duggan said menacingly, "private *Sullivan* property. Get out of here before I throw you out!" He could barely restrain himself from leaping at the man.

Dear God, he can't take on the lot of them! Maura glanced toward the waterfront. The workers were gathered in a ragged line near the launching cradle, their gazes fixed on the confrontation. Pelham's toughs halted and shifted their clubs, waiting for orders.

"The police will have something to say about your trespassing, Quinn!" Pelham raised the cane, motioning to the two men behind Duggan. "Seize him! You, Higgins—grab him!"

Duggan jumped aside, sure as a cat, and his fist shot out to catch the heavyset man squarely. The man staggered and fell back into the arms of the fellow behind him, who quickly pushed him aside and rushed at Duggan. Duggan sidestepped and shot out a foot to trip him. He sprawled in the dirt with a thud. But a third man was already running up, brandishing a length of pipe.

Maura's heart leaped to her throat and she smothered a scream. But Duggan saw the man before he could deliver a blow. In a quick move, he scraped up a fistful of dirt and flung it in the man's face, then ducked under the swinging pipe and wrested it from the other's grip. He shoved the thug atop the other two who were struggling to their feet. All three tumbled in the dirt again. Maura watched helplessly. She wanted to scream at Duggan to get back, but it was too late. Pelham signaled again with the cane.

The hired toughs surged forward with savage yells, heading for the moored *Patrick*. They met Duggan's men head-on with wild shouts and wicked blows of fists and weapons. Maura searched for Duggan in the violent melee. She couldn't pick him out, but she heard him shout, "Keep them off the boat! Keep them off the boat!"

Half a dozen men fell under the bludgeoning clubs and dropped heavily. A burly steam-fitter sent one of Pelham's toughs sprawling. Duggan rapped another on the knees with the pipe, and the man howled like a wounded animal. Pelham and Braxton backed up the path and fled into the office. Duggan swore and ran for the building, but he came up abruptly as he caught a glimpse of Maura hiding in the shadows.

"Get out of here—get away now!" he whispered hoarsely.

She shook her head numbly. She had to fight for what was hers.

"Don't be a fool!" He stepped close and grabbed her arm. "It's *you* he's after!"

"I won't—"

"You've got to go—and don't come back! Get away quickly before he sees you." He turned her roughly. "Get on a boat and go to James. You'll be safe with him."

Shouts erupted near the waterfront as the battle raged. A length of wood hissed close by, and Duggan shoved Maura aside. "Maura, for God's sake, go before it's too late! You can't let him win now!" He pushed her toward a weedy path behind the office. She stood numb, filled with pain and confusion. For a moment, Duggan's eyes were soft with tenderness. "I've got to go back. Don't let Pelham find

360

you, no matter what." He pulled her to him and kissed her savagely, his lips bruising hers, his chest crushing her breasts. Then he pushed her toward the path and quickly turned away.

Rushing back toward the melee, he uttered a quick prayer that none of Pelham's toughs stumbled across Maura and brought her to their boss. But they were hired to fight, and they would not expect her here. He glanced back to watch her scramble toward the road, holding her skirts out of the dirt. If Turk found her, he would haul her off like a sack of grain, and the police would be on his side. A legal guardian had the right to take charge of his ward even if she protested.

Near the road, Maura halted and looked back. Duggan was heading toward the fight but halted as Pelham ran out of the office, his face twisted with rage. Maura's heart thundered as Pelham raised a long-barreled pistol, but at that instant Duggan broke into a run and zigzagged toward his men. Pelham tried to take aim, but he could not single out his target among the crowd.

For a moment, the men drew apart like savage dogs licking their wounds. Duggan burst through a line, knocking aside anyone in his path. Pelham shouted and waved the pistol. A swirl of men leaped after Duggan. Pelham made his way quickly down the hill as Duggan was surrounded.

Maura put her hands to her temples and held her breath. Pelham was insane! *Dear God, don't let anyone be hurt!*

The knot of men separated, and Maura watched with frozen breath as Pelham took aim. She screamed as the shot rang out. A tall figure in a dark jacket twisted and collapsed to the ground. His companions swarmed around him and vicious cries rent the air. Fear turned Maura to stone as she searched the milling crowd for Duggan's familiar face.

Not him—oh God—! Not Duggan!! No matter how much she despised him, she could not bear it if he fell under Pelham's bullet. Then she spied Duggan bending over the wounded man, pulling back his jacket to examine the injury, then quickly giving orders to the others. Maura heaved a shuddering sigh of relief that quickly gave way to concern for the downed man.

If he were dead, Pelham was a murderer, she thought

ruthlessly. He had fired without apparent provocation. Duggan and the others would swear to it and Pelham would be charged. She herself could testify to his murderous intent. For a hesitant moment, she was torn between flight and staying to savor the sweet revenge that would come with her stepfather's defeat.

But the fight was not over. Duggan's men were swinging out with wicked blows and hurling stones to stay the attackers. A rock smashed against the office and a window shattered with a tinkling of glass. Pelham viewed the melee, then fled to safety inside. His ruffians knotted and began to move slowly down the hill. The others held them off long enough for two of their number to carry the wounded man out of the battle area, then they closed ranks and stood to fight.

Maura became aware of another sound above the tumult. A wagon with a clanging bell was racing along the road. She pressed into the tall, dusty weeds and watched a black police wagon rattle by and halt behind Pelham's carriage. When it jerked to a stop, uniformed men spilled out and raced into the boatyard. Several warning shots were fired into the air. There was a flurry of confusion, then the two groups of fighters drew apart slowly, eying each other warily.

The policeman in charge shouted for the mob to throw down their weapons. Clubs and pipes thudded to the hard ground. The men milled restlessly, muttering and swearing, as the police formed a line to seal them off. Maura scrambled farther up the path. The police were sorting out the fighters, letting Pelham's men cluster near the office while they corraled the Sullivan workers and herded them up the bank. Maura came to the sickening realization that the arrival of the police had been arranged in advance: Pelham *wanted* the men to be caught in the midst of fighting. It was all part of a devious, well-timed plan. And she knew with dread certainty that no matter how many men swore to the truth, it was Pelham who would be believed. He had bought influence and protection. He would have Duggan thrown in jail in order to settle old scores as well as new. And he would take over the Pittsburgh boatyard!

She spun on her heel and raced up the scrubby hillside

to the road. Her only hope was to get to James as quickly as possible.

Duggan had turned in time to see Pelham level the pistol. He had dodged instinctively as the shot rang out, then swore in shuddering rage as the bullet splatted with dreadful force into the man beside him. The tall man gave an agonized moan and clutched his bloody, spurting chest. Duggan grabbed him quickly, but the man's falling weight toppled them both. The warm blood soaked Duggan's sleeve as he lowered the man to the ground. Hands quickly reached to pull Duggan up. He shook them off and bent over the wounded man.

"It's Boyce," someone said. "Is he hit bad?"

Duggan tore open the man's shirt and examined the wound. Around them, the men hurled sticks and rocks to drive back Pelham's men. There was a momentary lull, then the thugs renewed their attack.

Boyce grimaced with pain and his eyes opened. Duggan said, "The bullet went through the flesh under your arm. I don't think it's hit anything vital, though you'll not be lifting a hammer for a while." He patted Boyce's shoulder and grinned. "Don't worry, man, you'll collect your wages while you're healing." He motioned quickly to two of the others. "Take him out of the way. We have to get him to a doctor."

The two picked up Boyce, and Duggan looked around as a new sound intruded. A police wagon clanged into the yard. Pelham rushed out of the office to yell instructions as police swarmed from the wagon with drawn guns. As though expecting the intrusion, Pelham's men began to fall back. Duggan signaled his own men. They were brave, tough fighters, but they could not stand against bullets. He wanted no man to lose his life.

A red-faced sergeant yelled, "Line up, you scum, line up where I c'n see all of you! Throw down them clubs!" He leveled a pistol. "Throw down them clubs!"

"Do as he says," Duggan ordered.

"All right." The sergeant motioned his men to surround the group. "Now you file up here one at a time and git yerselves outta this boatyard. I don't want no trouble from anyone——"

"What about our pay?" a man demanded.

"You don't git paid fer trespassin'," the sergeant yelled. His face deepened in hue. "You all's trespassin' on private propity. Mr. Turk here is willin' to let you go scot-free, long's you don't make no trouble. But don't try comin' back. First one sets foot in this here boatyard goes to jail, y'hear?"

A wave of muttering rippled as the men began to shift and shuffle up the hill. Duggan hung back, slipping behind the crowd. He shook his head and whispered to several of the men. "Don't worry, you'll have your pay. And you'll hear from me—tell the others. Someone see to it Boyce gets to a doctor."

The men nodded and moved away slowly.

Duggan had no plan in mind, but he'd be damned if he'd stand by and let Turk take over. Sidling toward the launching cradle, he gave a quick look back. The police were frisking his men before passing them one at a time through the gate. Pelham's men were still clustered near the office and formed a human screen between him and Turk. There was no sign of Maura, and he thanked God she had gotten away.

He crouched and swung himself over the heavy timbers of the skeletal cradle. Pelham would be eager to get his hands on him. He'd have men searching the moment he realized Duggan was not among the others. He might even offer a reward for information. *Well, you'll not see me until I'm ready for you, Turk. The Devil take you!* Turk might convince the police that he owned the Sullivan yard, but Duggan knew better. It belonged to Maura and James, and one day soon, everyone would know it! Even the police.

He crawled over the greased slipways and crept to the water's edge. Gritting his teeth against the cold, he slid in. His flesh was instantly numb, and the heavy coat pulled him relentlessly down. Stroking slowly so he would not splash, he swam downriver away from the *Patrick*.

Maura hurried along the road. She was bristling with fury and a renewed determination. Pelham had planned well and moved swiftly in the hope of catching her unawares and whisking her off before anyone could come to her rescue. But he had not counted on the strength of the men in the Sullivan yard. Her mouth was bitter with nausea as she thought of the one who had fallen under Pelham's shot. It was a high price to pay for loyal service. None of them had bargained for violence. She prayed that the man was not seriously wounded.

The wind bit at her face and made each breath a raw pain in her chest. Her hair tangled about her face and dust gritted between her teeth. She'd been so engrossed in getting away, she hadn't given a thought to how she was going to accomplish the purpose she had set for herself. Now she tried to take stock of the situation. Cairo was a thousand miles away. How in heaven's name was she going to get there? Her purse was in the office—or in Pelham's hands by now, she supposed. Even if there had been time to rescue it, the fare down the river was far more than the small amount of cash she had. That had vanished long ago except for a very few dollars. She was living on credit. It hadn't occurred to her to replenish her funds from the money Duggan had secured from Cromwell. Every dollar was desperately needed elsewhere, and the matter had not seemed urgent until now. If only there had been time to think a plan through! She sighed. No use longing for the moon. This was a time for practical thinking.

A carriage rattled on the road behind her and she quickly pulled up the hood of the cape to hide her face and her coppery hair. There wasn't time to run—and no place to hide! Trembling, she stared steadfastly ahead, not daring to look around lest she find herself face to face with Pelham or Braxton.

A small black chaise drawn by a strawberry roan came abreast of her. The bespectacled driver peered in astonishment and yanked the reins. The chaise rocked to a halt as the driver glanced around trying to determine where Maura had come from and where she was headed.

"Are you all right, ma'am?" he asked, touching the brim of his low-crowned black hat. His eyes were owlish in his round face and his cheeks were bright with the cold. He wore a black suit, a white shirt with a boiled collar and a string tie looped under it. His plump white hands threaded the reins nervously.

Maura hesitated. He looked respectable and anything but dangerous. She invented a quick lie. "I foolishly did not tie my horse securely enough when I dismounted to pick some wild flowers." She gave an exaggerated sigh of dismay. "That shrieking bell on the wagon that went past a few minutes ago made the animal bolt." She smiled and pretended embarrassment. "I find myself without transportation back to my hotel."

He glanced around again, then smiled paternally. "I am Reverend Ludlow of Linden Grove Parish." He touched his hat brim again. "Please allow me to offer you a ride. I am going right into the city." He held out a hand, which Maura took as she scrambled up.

"You're very kind, Reverend. I'm staying at the Lafayette House."

He slapped the reins and the horse set out at a slow walk. Maura resisted the impulse to glance back, and settled herself on the hard leather seat, listening distractedly to the minister's chatter. She answered his questions as briefly as possible without divulging anything of herself. After a few minutes, Reverend Ludlow was content to ramble on about his flock and his ministry. Maura occupied herself trying to figure out a way to secure passage to Cairo. By the time the chaise pulled under the portico of the Lafayette House, she had fixed on the hope that Beau might once again save her from a dilemma. If he was still in Pittsburgh!

Thanking Reverend Ludlow profusely, she rushed upstairs, pausing long enough in her room to clean her grimy face and comb her hair. When the image in the mirror looked presentable, she went upstairs to Beau's room. Summoning her courage, she knocked on the door. At first there was no answer and her heart sank. Finally, she tapped again and said, "Beau, it's Maura."

The door opened. Beau smiled. His bruises had been covered so they were much less noticeable, but his eye and lip were very puffy.

"I didn't expect to see you again so soon," he said. "I'm delighted that I have the chance to say good-bye." He brought her in and closed the door.

She felt a strange disappointment as she noticed the open bedroom door and the suitcases on the bed. "You're leaving, then?"

He nodded. "The business I spoke of has become urgent.

I must leave within the hour." He went to the table and poured two small glasses of whiskey and brought one to her. "Will you share a farewell drink?"

She sipped the whiskey, smarting at its bite as it slid down her throat. It would be pleasant to relax, but her problem was urgent. The longer she delayed, the closer Pelham might be in pursuit.

Beau saw the shadow veil her eyes. "What's wrong, Maura?" He looked at her solicitously. Twin lines of a frown were etched between her brows and her gaze was troubled as it searched his face.

She plunged recklessly into her quest. "I need money," she blurted.

He thought his ears were deceiving him. The Sullivan Company was in full operation. She'd told him herself that the loan Quinn had obtained had put the men back to work. Her problems were solved.

"You said the boatyard was doing well," he said guardedly.

She sighed. "The work is going fine but there is no extra cash for other needs. I didn't have the foresight to take an advance for my own expenses. Now it's too late." A vision of the melee at the boatyard filled her mind, and her heart went cold.

Beau took her arm as he saw the paling of her cheeks. "What is it?" He led her to the settee and sat beside her.

In a quavering voice, she related the events of Pelham's unexpected appearance at the boatyard and the fight that ensued. She could not bring herself to speak of Duggan, but that was the only part of the story she omitted. When she finished, she appealed to Beau.

"I must go to my brother so we can stop Pelham before he destroys us all. Will you help me get to Cairo?" She lowered her gaze. "I seem always to be imposing on your generosity, but I have nowhere else to turn."

"You did the right thing, of course!" he chided. "Now we must concentrate on coming up with a solution."

At her hopeful expression, he grinned wryly. "We seem to share a common predicament. Though I do have business elsewhere, it is not that which takes me away in such haste. Cromwell has given me until noon before he comes after me again. Even though the man's accusations are a

367

stupid pack of lies, I have no desire to be shot down disproving them." He noted the flicker of fear that tightened her face. Did his safety matter to her? Maybe he had not lost her after all. He reached to smooth her creased brow. "Here now, it's not that bad. I've endured worse."

Her breath trembled as his hand lingered at her cheek. She felt a strange pang of regret at the thought of not seeing him again. "Where are you going?"

He cupped her chin and lifted it. "It so happens, Miss Sullivan, that I am going to Cairo," he said with a roguish smile.

"Cairo?! Then—"

He nodded and his eyes sparkled with humor. "We shall travel together so I can keep an eye on you and make sure you are delivered safely to your brother."

The power of his gaze trapped her, and she felt herself drawn into an inexplicable web. He took her gently into his arms and brushed her lips with a gossamer kiss. A haunting image of Duggan reared in her mind, but the knowledge of his treachery veiled it so it was shrouded in mist . . . a part of the past. His kisses had been as false as his words; she meant nothing to him—nor he to her. That was the way it must be. She yielded as Beau kissed her again and stroked her hair. When he looked at her, his smile was warm and comforting.

"The *Ohio Queen* leaves in an hour. Can you be ready?"

An hour . . . salvation so close . . . and the security of Beau's strength. "Will you lend me the money for passage? I was forced to leave my purse at the office—I have nothing."

He laughed softly and bent to kiss the words from her lips. When he released her, he stood and scratched a sideburn thoughtfully.

"Ah . . . money. It has been a day of mishaps all the way around. Lady Luck seems to have abandoned us for the moment. When his thugs finished with me, Cromwell emptied my pockets of every dollar I had." He reached into his trousers and brought out a few coins. "My total wealth is here in the palm of my hand." He clamped his fingers shut and the coins clinked dully. He grinned at Maura and winced as pain pricked his lip. "It seems we *are* in the same predicament."

Maura's hopes crashed and she rose to go. How could he talk so glibly of traveling down the river if neither of them had the price of passage? Had he raised her hopes only to dash them? Was Beau playing a cruel joke?

He blocked her path and held her at arm's length to peer at her. "How easily you grow solemn! Smile, darling, we can still go."

"How?" she asked incredulously. "I don't have the cash to settle my bills or buy a ticket on a barge!"

He chuckled softly, then threw back his head and let his laughter burst into the room with complete abandon. Startled, Maura tried to draw back but he held her fast and began to whirl her around. She was too surprised to do more than hang on so she would not fly into space like a bird taking wing. The room spun around her and her head reeled. She tried to tell him to stop, but the sounds became an irrepressible laugh. The dam of tension burst and her relief was an uncontrollable flood. Tears coursed down her cheeks as the noise of their merriment crowded back at them until they sank helplessly on the sofa, locked in each other's arms. Maura buried her face in Beau's shirtfront while the laughter subsided slowly. He stroked her hair as he pressed his lips to her jasmine-scented cheek.

"Any problem is easier to solve if you don't clutter up your mind with dire thoughts." He chucked her under the chin until a smile lifted the corners of her mouth again. "That's better. Now, to our immediate problem. Neither of us has the price of our boat passage, and the management here is apt to take a dim view of our departing without settling our accounts. Still—" He rubbed his chin and wrinkled his brow. "If you are willing to undertake a small adventure, there is a way."

"How? We must pay—"

He regarded her with an amusingly villainous leer. "Yes, if you cannot pay your bill, it's jail for you, my pretty little miss! The management will not be swindled by beautiful women without funds!" He cocked his head and peered at her. "Perhaps we can have adjoining cells . . ."

She could not suppress a smile. How readily he made light of the darkest situation!

He took her hand and pressed it between his own. "So you will know what kind of a scoundrel you are traveling with, I confess that I am acquainted with ways of leaving hotels unseen and unhounded by dreary managers who want their money. Trust me, and I shall remove us from these premises with no one the wiser."

For a moment she was horrified at the thought of running off like a thief, but this was no time for delay. Besides, she had no choice.

Beau sensed her reluctance. "We can settle the amount due as soon as we have wooed Lady Luck to our side once more. Now the sooner we're off, the better. Are you packed?"

"I don't even own a valise."

He strode to the bedroom, dumped the contents of one case, snapped it and brought it to her. "I can manage with the other. Now hurry, I'll be at your door in fifteen minutes." He drew her into his arms again and gazed at her. "You must not worry anymore. Fate has a great deal of happiness in store for both of us."

"I'll be ready," she said, as he released her gently.

A quarter of an hour later, Beau tapped at her door. He lifted the valise and looked both ways along the hall before leading her to a narrow, dark stairway at the rear of the building. His bag was at the landing, and he hefted both pieces of luggage and started down. Maura followed with a guilty conscience and a thudding heart. Beau made it seem like a game, but if they were caught— She pushed away the thought. She had to concentrate on getting to James. Nothing else mattered. Her emotions had settled to numbness that barred Duggan from her mind.

The stairs led to an alley where trash was piled in boxes and spilled to the ground. A rat scurried from one dark mound to another as they passed, and Maura hugged her skirts. She fixed her gaze on Beau's back and closed her ears to the soft, scuttling sounds.

They came out into a back street where a high fence shielded the hotel from neighboring houses. A gust of wind rustled the flaming red ivy that was ready to shed its leaves for the winter. Beau grinned and set down the cases behind a high hedge that surrounded a private yard.

"Don't look so guilty, love," he chided as Maura glanced over her shoulder. "Here now, set your bonnet right and let's have a smile." He adjusted her hat and nodded approval as he set it exactly at the angle he wanted. His fingers gently touched the corners of her mouth until she found herself smiling. "That's better. Now, it will never do to be seen toting our baggage like common folk. I will secure a carriage. Wait here."

He vanished around toward the front of the hotel, leaving her to marvel at his daring. After sneaking out the back way, he boldly marched to the front entrance! She would not believe it except that she was seeing it with her own eyes. Beau was not like anyone she'd ever met, that was certain.

CHAPTER TWENTY-ONE

Pittsburgh had a brisk river trade in three directions: the Allegheny from the north and the Monongahela from the south, and, the mighty Ohio winding westward to connect with the great waterway of the Mississippi. Tall-masted sailboats glided past squat coal barges towed along by tugs like recalcitrant children. Steamboats with colorful banners and gaudy fretwork crowded the levees to unload cotton and take on crates of machinery and manufactured goods and huge bins of coal. A bouyant air pervaded the waterfront, despite the back-breaking labor and fierce competition as captains and mates haggled with ships chandlers.

Beau instructed the driver to deposit them at the end of Liberty Street. Almost at the tip of the city's triangle, the broad thoroughfare spilled across the waterfront like a funnel. The gently sloping bank had been leveled at the top for a width of about fifty feet. Along it, market houses and stalls formed an irregular line of red brick and bright canvas awnings. Children had spread bits of cloth and set up shop wherever they could find a few inches of space. Farmers were selling produce directly from the backs of wagons, blocking the roadway so that pedestrians and carriages had to weave past. The smells of garbage and freshly butchered meat overwhelmed the pleasant aromas of charcoal and hot roasting chestnuts. Hundreds of voices bid loudly for attention as vendors cried out their wares and bargained raucously. Every conceivable product was for sale: shiny red apples from large baskets; potatoes in burlap sacks or individually, according to a customer's needs; fresh fish, corn, meat and poultry, and an assortment of trinkets, tinware, dry goods and tools. Bales of unloaded cotton from the South awaiting transport to warehouses and

373

factories, formed a barricade on the levee. A thin Negro in ragged pants and a shirt torn off at the sleeves leaned against a bale and played a lively tune on a harmonica. His bare feet, immune to the cold, tapped the rhythm. When a passer-by tossed a penny, he scooped it up without losing the tempo.

Beau lifted down the bags and flipped the driver a coin. Then, settling Maura on a wooden crate, he told her to wait. He would see to their tickets and be back shortly. His conspiratorial wink cut short her questions. A moment later he was swallowed up by the crowd.

Maura looked around with growing interest. The waterfront was different from New York's, though the bustle and noise were similar. Somehow the gaudy riverboats gave the scene a carnival air that was fostered by the intermittent sound of calliope music. Maura found her foot tapping as she watched the milling crowd.

There were numerous well-dressed men and women, as well as seamen, ragamuffins and tradesmen. An elderly man and a young woman dressed in a bright blue coat with bear tippets paused at a market stall. The vendor in striped shirt and black trousers, with dark hair that fell past his shoulders, held up a gold necklace for the woman's inspection, swinging the locket like a hypnotist's pendulum so that it caught the light and sparkled. The woman clapped her hands and whispered to her escort. He laughed and reached for his wallet. Near Maura, a mongrel dog with visible ribs barked furiously as a child teased it with a stick.

Maura gazed at the river and tried to pick out the *Ohio Queen*. There were a dozen boats at the bank, their sloping hulls nosed to the shore, their jackstaffs spiring upward like a row of sentinels. Tall black chimneys with fluted tops towered over the decks, and guy lines wove in intricate spiderwebs. Maura tried to make out the lettering on the nearest vessel. *Jennie*. Beside it was the *Nantucket*, its deck piled high with cotton. The third was the *Ohio Queen*. Maura studied it.

It was not as large as the *Patrick* but a good-sized boat nevertheless. The gilt-lettered name boldly painted across the front of the pilothouse glinted as the sun broke from behind the clouds. A huge brass bell mounted forward of the texas was being rung by a Negro lad who seemed to dance at the end of the rope. The *Queen*'s main deck was already piled with cargo—boxes, sacks and crates of all sizes. Deckhands were lashing it and pulling tarpaulins over anything that might be damaged by moisture. Roustabouts chanted as they carried heavy coal boxes aboard and disappeared toward the furnaces. Black smoke roiled from the chimneys, and steam puffed from the escape pipes with a shrill whistle.

The boiler deck was crowded with passengers who leaned on the rail to wave and shout to friends on shore. Well-dressed, smiling women and men in silk hats strolled among the crowd. On the main deck, the captain stood beside the clerk at the head of the gangplank greeting new arrivals. He was a tall, imposing man with a tanned face, a shock of black hair and a flowing mustache. He had a word for everyone and a special greeting for those he singled out as important.

Maura glanced about for Beau. During the carriage ride to the levee, Maura had asked how they would get tickets without money. Beau had winked and told her to leave it to him. She wondered now if it was as easy as he thought. The *Ohio Queen*'s departure seemed imminent. Was there time for Beau to secure the money they needed? She didn't know what passage cost, but it was far more than the few coins Beau had. Perhaps he planned for them to stow away? The idea made her smile, but it would not be any more ridiculous than running from the hotel by the rear exit.

Then she saw Beau weaving through the crowd. He was smiling, and Maura's breath quickened. He looked well-pleased with himself. His shoulder accidentally brushed a woman who turned to glare at him indignantly. When Beau gave her a dazzling smile and touched the brim of his silk hat, the woman's scowl turned to a smile as she stared after him.

How easily he brought smiles to women's lips, Maura thought. He seemed able to charm any female from the darkest mood. She'd discovered it was almost impossible to stay annoyed with him for any length of time. Even her rage over Duggan seemed easier to endure with Beau's cheerfulness to lighten her mood.

"It's all arranged," he said as he reached her. He glanced

375

around and snapped his fingers for a lad to take the bags. The boy hefted them and staggered under their weight as he scuttled down the sloping footway. Beau made a small bow to Maura. "And now, Miss Sullivan, the *Ohio Queen* awaits the most beautiful woman who ever trod her gangplank. May I offer my arm?"

"How did you manage the tickets?"

"It was a simple matter once I put my mind to it." He winked audaciously. "You have taken up with a very clever fellow, my dear. But the Captain is impatient to be underway. Shall we?"

He took her arm affectionately and led her up the gangplank. The Captain bowed to Maura and shook Beau's hand.

"I don't believe I've had the pleasure. . . ."

"Mr. and Mrs. Fontaine," Beau said smoothly. He felt Maura stiffen and turn, and he squeezed her hand in urgent warning.

Maura managed to mask her indignation with a tight smile as the Captain said, "Delighted, Mrs. Fontaine. I am Captain Dance. Welcome aboard the *Ohio Queen*. She's one of the finest boats on the river. We're proud to say she's never had an accident. If there's anything I can do to make your voyage more pleasant, don't hesitate to call on me. How far are you going?"

"To Cairo." Beau produced the tickets and gave them over to the clerk, who inspected them and nodded.

The Captain's smile broadened. "I hope you'll do me the honor of dining with me one evening."

Maura felt Beau's insistent pressure on her arm and forced another smile. "Thank you, Captain Dance, we'd be delighted," she said. The introduction as Beau's wife had taken her by surprise and unleashed a sweep of resentment. He was taking too much for granted! He had no right to put her in such a compromising position just because she had turned to him for help and he had given it willingly. She recognized the folly of creating a scene in front of the Captain, but as soon as they were alone—!

The Captain was smiling again. "The *Tennessee* stateroom is at the rear of the main salon. I'm sure you'll find it very comfortable. We'll be casting off shortly. If there's anything you need, the room steward is available twenty-four hours a day."

Maura murmured her thanks and moved on with Beau. He guided her past the twin anchors drawn up on the forward deck. Maura glanced around eagerly. Up close, the riverboat was even more exciting than from the shore. She smelled the dusty, dry heat of the fires. Beyond the stairs, their red glow flickered like winking eyes as the stokers shoveled coal to get up steam. The lower deck was crammed with cargo. Near the starboard rail, several small areas were penned off for squealing, bawling pigs, and cows that complained mournfully. A short distance away, a handsome bay, its eyes shielded by blinders, was tethered to the rail. The horse stomped restlessly and nickered. Several deck passengers lounged against boxes or sat on rolled blankets wherever they could squeeze into a space.

The stairs to the boiler deck were carpeted in red. They ascended halfway in a broad, straight line, then divided toward either side of the passenger deck. A mahogany railing gleamed in the lights of the fires below. Maura glanced down at the huge coal bins that took up much of the space under the roof housing. It seemed enough fuel to take them to the ends of the earth, but she knew the ravenous furnaces would consume it quickly.

The boiler deck was crowded. Passengers wandered in search of their cabins or pressed to the forward railing to view the departure. Beau and Maura followed the boy with the baggage. It was necessary to push past a group of men who stood with drinks in hand as they laughed and chatted. Heads turned as Maura passed.

The boy scurried aft, clearing a path as he found the cabin. Beau handed him several coppers, then closed the door as the lad went out. Beau spread his arms as though putting the cabin on display for her.

"Will this do, Mrs. Fontaine?" He grinned as he pulled off his gray kid gloves and tossed them and his hat to a chair.

Maura looked around in amazement. It was as elegant as any room she had ever seen. Though she was accustomed to luxury, she had not expected to find it here. Underfoot, a thick brown wool carpet was like a bed of forest moss.

377

The walls were papered in a gold fleur-de-lis pattern with ornate borders of braided gold cord. In the center of the ceiling, a crystal chandelier could be raised and lowered on a pulley by a cord fastened near the door. Eight small lamps with etched crystal globes were arranged in a circle, and prisms of Ravenscroft flint glass reflected the light in tiny rainbows. Every bit of woodwork was hand rubbed mahogany that gleamed in the diffused light from three stern windows at which brown velvet drapes were pulled back to admit the gentle breeze. There was a broad bed with a velvet throw and a down quilt, two upholstered chairs, and a small table under the windows. On a larger round table in the center of the room, a cut-glass decanter of whiskey and two glasses had been set out.

"It's very nice," she admitted, "but it's impossible for me to stay here. It would be best to speak to the steward immediately."

He looked at her in astonishment, then glanced around the cabin. "This is the finest stateroom the *Queen* has to offer!"

"That may be, but you had no right to engage it for *Mr. and Mrs.* Fontaine!" Her displeasure at his deception surfaced quickly. "I will not travel as your wife! You might show a little regard for my reputation. After all, my family is very well known. If anyone should recognize me—"

He took her hands. "Maura . . . I would never do anything to disgrace or upset you, you must know that!" He tilted his head and gazed at her solemnly. "It was the only cabin left. The *Ohio Queen* is one of the finest boats on the river, as Captain Dance claims. It is often booked weeks in advance. We were fortunate that there was a last-minute cancellation and this cabin was available, else we would have been obliged to wait for a later—and slower—boat. You indicated that your stepfather would search for you as soon as he realized you were gone." His eyes showed a pained expression. "I did what I thought was best. Of course if you want me to ring for the steward, there is still time for us to disembark."

It had not occurred to her that his reason would be so practical. It *was* urgent that she leave Pittsburgh with all haste, but nagging doubts still assailed her.

He lifted her hand to his lips. "It was a matter of necess-

378

ity, but I admit I do not find the idea of spending several days with you unpleasant." His lips nibbled the back of her hand intimately. "I have not been able to put our one rapturous night from my mind." He glanced up and saw her reluctance wavering. "My every concern is for your wellbeing and happiness. I would marry you this instant—" He sighed and shook his head despairingly. "Forgive me. My emotions make me too bold. If your good name is endangered, I would never forgive myself. But I would never ask you to enter such a sacred union for base, practical reasons alone. I care very deeply for you, Maura. If you will give me time to woo you properly . . . ?" He gazed at her with longing and hope.

Maura's annoyance evaporated instantly. How could she chastise him when he was so kind and unselfish? A warm blush stole along her neck when he spoke of love after the shameful way she had treated him. But marriage . . . ? She extricated her hand from his warm clasp and busied herself removing her hat and cloak. He took them from her and hung them in the wardrobe.

"I apologize for my ungratefulness," she said softly. "You have wrought the magic of getting me on my way to Cairo, and I am in your debt." His talk of love and marriage quickened her pulse, but she was not ready to commit herself to matrimony, even though she was strongly attracted to Beau. And even though he had proved a dozen times that she could trust and rely on him. She had believed herself ready to marry Duggan, only to discover that she had plunged headlong into an emotional entanglement that clouded her judgment. To ease the strained moment, she spread her hands to indicate the room.

"The cabin is lovely. How in the world did you manage when you had no money?"

He grinned and pulled from his pocket a leather wallet bulging with banknotes. He tossed it to the table with an impudent wink. "That was a half hour ago, pet. Things have changed for the better." He lifted the decanter and poured himself a whiskey.

Maura picked up the wallet and riffled the bills. There were several hundred dollars! She shook her head, dazed. "Where did it come from?"

He grinned and tapped his coat pocket. At her puzzled

frown, he reached into the coat and took out a deck of cards. "I found several pilots who had just come ashore with their wages and were eager to play a few hands of poker," he said.

"You gambled?!" She was incredulous.

"What quicker way to get the cash we needed?" He drank the whiskey and refilled the glass. "I don't propose to take you to Cairo as a deck passenger. I want you to have everything that is within my power to give."

She still found it difficult to believe. With only a few coins in his pocket, he'd won hundreds of dollars! She shook her head and smiled ruefully. "Suppose you had lost?"

"Ah, but I didn't. How could I when I had my lucky charm?" He pulled her lace handkerchief from his pocket and closed his hand around it as though it were his most precious possession. "When you are not at my side, it brings me luck. I cannot lose." He reached into his pocket again and drew out a gold heart on a slender chain. Moving behind her, he reached around to fasten it against her throat. "For the one who has changed my destiny . . ." He pressed his lips to the pulse beat below her ear and heard her sigh.

When he turned her to face him, she fought the racing of her pulse. "Are you always so willing to risk your fate to chance?" she said.

"Only when the prize is as precious as you." The room was very quiet for the space of several heartbeats. Then Beau picked up the whiskey glass and sipped, studying her wondering face over the rim. "Besides, I don't see it as a risk but as an opportunity for advancement. More than once the direction of my life has been changed by the turn of a card or the smile of a beautiful woman."

"I would think a man in the investment business would do better to depend on knowledge and experience." Her chiding was without sting. She could not be upset with him when he had done so much.

Beau's humor was too good to be spoiled. He finished the whiskey and took her in his arms. "I forbid you to concern yourself with such trivialities. We are leaving our cares behind. It will do no good whatsoever to worry about anything until you reach Cairo and your brother, isn't that so?" He raised her face and looked deeply into her eyes. A tremor rippled through Maura as his gaze held hers. "This journey is to be pleasant and full of joy. Now, let me hear you laugh."

He was like a coaxing child who would not give up his quest. Maura smiled, but he was not satisfied. He gave a huge sigh of resignation and lifted her off her feet before she could protest. Coaxing and demanding, he pressed kisses to her face.

Maura gasped for breath. "Put me down—"

"Not until you promise to banish your foolish fears and somber thoughts."

"Stop—I'm breathless—!"

"Promise?"

"Yes, yes—ohhhh!"

He lowered her gently to the bed and lay beside her. Then he was kissing her, and the spinning of her brain was intensified by the hot demand of his lips. The long, possessive kiss left her breathless, and her heart thundered. Beau's hands lingered at her breasts, then worked at the fastenings of the amber-colored gown.

Maura tried to deny the response of her body. A vision of Duggan impinged on her conscience. "No—" she whispered.

He kissed her again, and his tongue brushed an invitation across her lips. She hovered on the brink of a sensuous abyss, trying to resist, to draw back before she was helpless. But his hand searched under her chemise and touched her bare flesh. Undulating waves of pleasure tormented her, and she shivered helplessly. Her lips moved to protest but instead welcomed his kiss. How strong he was . . . how desirable . . . She was alive with sensations that muted the din of voices and the waterfront. Beau captured her in a growing fervor. Nothing else seemed to matter. Her arms went around him and pulled him close so the spell would not be broken. It was safe and secure having him close and hearing his comforting words. Problems vanished miraculously. She sighed as his hands worked magic at her clothing. Taffeta whispered as the bodice fell open and her skirt was undone. For a moment, cool air bathed her fevered flesh, then he was covering it with kisses. Overhead, the richly paneled ceiling and crystal chandelier blurred in the intensity of her desire. Nothing else mattered. . . .

Her flesh tingled as his hands caressed and parted her thighs. Then his body was probing gently, thrusting into her. Flames of aching need swept her. She strained to accept the rhythmic pressure of his manhood. She was caught in a firestorm of longing and swept heedlessly in his engulfing path. Then she was climbing to a tumultuous frenzy that was met by the warm rush of Beau's pleasure.

She lay panting softly with her eyes closed, though she was aware of Beau moving away and pulling on his clothes. Her eager response to his lovemaking confused her. How was it possible to experience such pleasure when bittersweet memories of Duggan's ardor rippled insistently beneath the surface of her conscience? Only yesterday her entire life had been centered around him. Now he was a painful reminder of how easily her emotions had betrayed her. She was determined to guard against such folly again. She had berated Duggan once for balancing love against practical needs, but she knew now that the words had been blurted with the rashness of a starry-eyed romantic. That delicate balance *was* necessary, for on it hinged the stability of a relationship. Out of it grew the love and trust needed for marriage. Beau understood that. He was not the carefree lover he appeared on the surface, but a deep, kind and understanding man.

The *Ohio Queen*'s whistle shrieked. Maura sat up abruptly and reined her wandering thoughts. Beau grinned as he tied his cravat.

"We'll be underway in a few minutes. Everyone gathers at the rail to watch the departure. It's an excellent opportunity to meet our fellow passengers." His gaze lingered on her naked breasts and he smiled.

Blushing, she rose and began to dress, still puzzling over her volatile emotions. Whistling softly, Beau brushed his hair and studied his reflection in the glass. From time to time she felt his gaze on her, but he left her to her thoughts.

By the time they walked to the forward deck, Beau had to press through the crowd to find them space at the rail. Several men stepped back smilingly, as though pleased to relinquish their places to a beautiful woman.

The bell on the hurricane deck clanged with resonant peals that overrode the clamor. The escape pipes spurted steam shrilly, and the mate shouted to the deckhands to get the gangplank in. A few roustabouts hurried on board as the hands strained on the lines and the heavy planks swung inboard slowly.

"Cast off!" the Captain shouted. The order was echoed by the mate on the main deck.

Crewmen tossed off the lines from bollards, and the paddlewheels began to turn. Smoke belched from the chimneys and showers of crimson sparks erupted into the sky. The crowds on shore cheered as the *Ohio Queen* backed from the levee with her buckets threshing and her whistle blowing. Last good-byes were shouted back and forth.

Muddy water roiled and splashed as the big paddlewheels reversed and the boat began to move forward. Waves rolled up on the levee; the black smoke swirled and sank like a heavy cloud to make the onlookers ashore cough and fan themselves. The brass bell tolled as the *Queen* moved ponderously into the current and showed them her stern.

They were underway.

Beau watched Maura and marveled at his good fortune. A few hours ago he believed their paths would no longer run a parallel course, and now she was standing beside him. Fate played a capricious hand. Maura's presence was a breath of summer warmth to what otherwise might be a dreary trip. Cromwell had cleaned out every dollar he had, and the prospect of recouping had seemed dim until Maura came on the scene once more. It was likely, of course, that his luck would have taken a swing for the better anyhow, but he could not discount the part she played as a lucky omen. It had been that way since he first met her. And now they were sharing a cabin. Her indignation over her reputation was amusing, but it had given him an opportunity to plant the notion of marriage in her thoughts. The Sullivan holdings represented a considerable fortune, and he would not be adverse to acquiring a share of it by taking her as his bride.

It was another stroke of luck that a good cabin on the *Ohio Queen* remained unclaimed at sailing time. It was a fitting setting for Maura and conducive to romance. He grinned inwardly at the delectable memory of her eager response to his advances. She was not the untutored virgin she had pretended when he met her on the Hoboken stage. She was a delightful, robust bed partner. That suited him. He liked women with spirit and verve, and he especially liked the absence of recriminations or pretended remorse. It was going to be a very pleasant journey. And when they reached Cairo, the Sullivan Company would belong to Maura and her brother. Could he woo her to the altar by then?

A couple beside them caught Beau's eye. There was something vaguely familiar about the man, though Beau couldn't recall ever meeting him. He was of medium height and heavyset, with thinning blond hair under a black silk hat. He wore a red-and-white-checked waistcoat which emphasized his bulk, and a thick gold watch chain hung across his middle like a glittering crescent. He glanced at Beau from under hooded eyes as he rolled a cigar to the opposite corner of his mouth. It was an appraising glance, the kind a gambler gives his opponent before a hand is dealt. Beau nodded almost imperceptibly and let his gaze slip to the woman. She was a whore, he could not be mistaken about that. She was buxom and pretty, with a trifle too much rouge and white powder. The soft lights of a parlor or bedroom might take ten years from her age, but the bright sunlight was not kind. A webbing of lines showed beneath the carefully applied powder, and wattles threatened under her chin when she was distracted and did not hold her head high. Under the short cape of dark fur, her dusky rose gown was tight and provocative. She wore black lace fingerless gloves that exposed three gaudy rings set with diamonds, rubies and opals.

Beau realized the man was watching him. He smiled and extended a hand. "If we are to be fellow travelers, we should be acquainted. I am Beauregard Fontaine."

The blond man shook his hand. "Paul Giraud of St. Louis." The woman turned with a haughty look which relented as soon as she saw Beau. Giraud said, "Miss Ellie Wyatt of New Orleans."

Beau masked his surprise. Paul Giraud! The name was known the length of the Mississippi. He'd never met the man but his reputation was something else. Tales of his gambling were told in every bar from St. Louis to the Delta. Giraud . . .

Recovering, Beau took the hand Ellie Wyatt offered. "Delighted, Miss Wyatt. New Orleans is my home, too, at least by birth, though I rarely spend enough time in that belle of Southern cities these days." He took Maura's arm as she turned from the rail. "My wife, Maura . . ."

Maura felt a momentary start at again being introduced as Beau's wife, but realized she must accept the situation gracefully. Ellie spared Maura a brief, disinterested glance. Giraud touched his hat brim and gave an indication of a bow. "Will we have the pleasure of your company all the way to Cairo?"

"Yes." Beau patted Maura's hand lovingly. "This is our honeymoon. A second one. Our first was cut short by some pressing business that delayed us." He looked at Maura with a twinkle in his eyes.

How glibly he lied, she thought. Still, he had a relaxed, confident manner that put people at ease. Ellie Wyatt was smiling as though she'd known him for ages. Giraud was suggesting that they retire to the grand salon where they could find whiskey and tea.

The salon was crowded with passengers who had come in from the deck or who had chosen to enjoy the departure surrounded by luxury. Maura had only seen the bare skeleton of the *Patrick*'s lounge, and she was amazed at the elegance of the long, narrow salon. The decor was ornate, with a bold red carpet and twin rows of white columns stretching the length of the room at either side. Cornices were carved with scrollwork and scallops, painted white against a pale-blue ceiling. At intervals, magnificent-globed chandeliers dispelled the gloom. The room was windowless except for those facing the front deck. These were open now to let a cooling breeze into the otherwise stuffy room. Beau found an empty table among the dozens with their sparkling white cloths. At a square grand piano, a man in a fawn-colored suit played sprightly music. Maura recognized a popular Chopin waltz. A festive air pervaded the room, and voices buzzed over the tinkling music. Half a dozen black-coated waiters served tea and drinks.

At the center of the salon, a large silver samovar was set up on a marble table, with trays of tea cakes and tiny biscuits surrounding it. At one side, a tall cake frosted with white icing, bits of chocolate and colored candies was a replica of the *Ohio Queen*.

Beau and Paul Giraud fell into conversation about the river. Traffic had more than doubled in the past year, and the volume of cargo along the waterway seemed to increase daily. Every boat going in either direction was loaded to capacity, and passenger travel was on a definite upswing. Giraud made frequent trips, he said. Maura puzzled over the way Beau and Giraud eyed each other and weighed their words while pretending nonchalance. The woman puzzled her, too. She made no effort to engage Maura in conversation, but her glance settled on her frequently. She seemed to be judging an opponent, yet not with the air of a rival. Without knowing why, Maura decided she didn't like Ellie Wyatt.

A waiter brought tea for the ladies and whiskey for the men. Giraud's enthusiasm for his subject continued. The Ohio was enjoying as much activity as the Mississippi, he declared, though he preferred the Big Muddy. It was the lifeline of the nation, and Cairo was its hub. Hundreds of families a year passed through Cairo on their way west. The recent gold strike in California had started a westward push that would alter the history of the nation.

Beau seemed vitally interested in everything Giraud said. They talked of places that were familiar to both of them: the Galt House in Louisville, the new Golden Sun Hotel in Cairo. It was as if the two were renewing an acquaintance. For the most part, the women remained quiet, but when Beau spoke of New Orleans, Ellie smiled and wondered aloud why she had never met Beau since they came from the same city.

"My misfortune," he said gallantly. "My family owns a large cotton plantation north of Lake Pontchartrain. My father is still active, though he expects me to take over the management one day soon. He's getting on in years."

Maura hid her surprise. Beau had never spoken of his family's holdings, and she wondered why he did so now. Was he trying to impress Giraud and the woman? Was he lying? She glanced at him, but he was as sure of himself as she'd ever seen him.

He went on. "I've spent a number of years traveling and

386

seeing to other investments. The river gets in one's blood."

"And once it does, a man never settles on dry land," Giraud added.

Beau finished his whiskey. "Perhaps you're right. There are many things a man cannot get out of his blood."

"Do you play cards, Mr. Fontaine?" Giraud removed the spent cigar from his mouth, examined the ash for a moment, then tossed it into a nearby spittoon.

"Occasionally," Beau answered without a flicker of expression. Did Giraud know, or was he fishing? Beau couldn't claim the same kind of reputation as the other gambler, but his name was not unknown along the river. It was surprising that their paths hadn't crossed before this, but there were hundreds of boats on the Ohio and the Mississippi.

"Perhaps we might engage in a friendly game," Giraud said with a lazy smile. His hooded eyes studied Beau.

"That would be pleasant." The hook baited for a sucker . . . So Giraud did not recognize him! The offer was one made to any friendly passenger who happened along. Beau contemplated dropping some clue to his own gambling habits but discarded the thought immediately. It would be a challenge to beat Giraud at his own game. Risky, though. Giraud had killed half a dozen men over a card table.

"Several men are gathering in the barber shop after the evening festivities. Join us if you're free." Giraud's gaze flicked at Maura.

After the lie Beau had told about their honeymoon, Maura expected him to decline, but he nodded. Maura was relieved when Giraud and Ellie Wyatt declined a second drink and excused themselves. Beau watched them cross the room. Giraud paused to talk to several people as he headed for one of the starboard cabins which opened off the salon.

When Beau turned his attention back to Maura, she said, "You are full of surprises. Why is it you've never mentioned your plantation or family before?"

He laughed softly. "Because I invented them for Miss Wyatt. I've never been closer to a bale of cotton than we were on the levee in Pittsburgh. But most women find it disarming to realize a stranger might be a neighbor one has never met."

387

Maura shook her head. "You have a hopeless disregard for the truth."

He winked and lowered his voice. "Would you prefer I confess that we have run out on our creditors and are barely one step ahead of the law?"

She had to laugh. "I don't think I would want to change you even if it were within my power."

"Good," he said. "Nor would I change you. I bless the lucky stars that put me on the stage in Hoboken that morning. It was the most fortuitous journey I have ever taken." He reached for her hand and held it tightly in his slender fingers. "Except for this one. I predict that it will be not only more interesting but far more comfortable than the miserable stage." When she smiled, he looked around the salon, his gaze sweeping as though searching for someone. At last he turned back to her. "Without a doubt you are the loveliest and most charming woman aboard. Will you do me the honor of accompanying me to the Captain's ball tonight, Miss Sullivan—or Mrs. Fontaine?"

Maura smiled. "I would be delighted."

CHAPTER TWENTY-TWO

Duggan swam with the current, keeping his head low in the water. His boots and coat were lead weights dragging him down, and it was a struggle to stay afloat. His teeth were chattering and his body was numb when he finally reached a thicket of rhododendrons overhanging the bank about two hundred yards downstream. He pulled himself ashore and lay panting on the muddy bank. When his breath was no longer a knife in his chest, he crawled into the thicket and peered toward the boatyard.

The last of his men were climbing to their horses or wagons. Pelham Turk's men still milled about the yard, but they too had begun to disperse when the others went. Pelham came out of the office and spoke to one of them, who immediately delegated five others to row out to the *Patrick*. To search for him, Duggan thought. *Well, they'll not find me, you miserable devil. And you've not beaten me yet.*

Pelham conferred briefly with the police sergeant, shaking the man's hand and walking with him as far as the gate. As the police van drove off, he paused to watch the continuing search.

Duggan heaved a soft, sighing breath. Thank God Maura had gotten away. Pelham surely knew by now that she'd been in the yard; Denfield would have seen to that. Damn Denfield . . . he should have sacked the man as soon as he suspected his allegiance to Turk! But all Denfield could tell him now was that Maura was staying at the Lafayette House. Pelham would go around to the hotel, but it would be another blind alley. Maura already had a good start. He prayed she'd be miles down the river before Turk realized she was gone. There were half a dozen riverboats leaving the levee every day, and he hoped Maura picked the fastest one afloat.

He smiled as he thought of her sweet lips in their parting kiss. Despite her anger, she'd yielded and clung to him for an instant. Maybe with a few days to cool her Irish temper, she'd realize he was not the villain she imagined. A wave of jealous rage flared when he thought of Fontaine spewing half-truths to poison her mind against him. How could Maura even listen to a man like that? He shuddered as a chill gripped him. When this rotten business was over, he'd never allow anything to come between them again. There'd be no room for pride or anger when he was done loving her.

Duggan sighed and hugged his arms across his chest. His sodden clothes were icy on his flesh, and he clenched his teeth to stop the shivering. With difficulty, he forced his thoughts to the urgent problem at hand. He glanced at the boatyard where Pelham was pacing impatiently as he waited for the rowboat to return from the *Patrick*. The man had to be stopped, but it would not be an easy task when the police were convinced that he was acting within his rights. Duggan cursed himself for underestimating Turk's wiliness and determination. He should have been stopped before he gained a secure foothold in the company. But who was to blame? Not James, who had work and problems of his own to contend with here. And certainly not Maura. It had been hard enough for her living in the same house with the Turks. Pelham would never have allowed her to delve deeply into company affairs, even if she had tried.

A picture of her slender figure bending over James' desk, with the sun gleaming on her coppery hair, made Duggan's heart skip. He was delighted by the interest she'd taken in the office and the keen grasp of business she had shown. She handled the work as efficiently as any man—more competently than Denfield. Duggan was sure now that Turk had been paying Denfield all along to muck things up in order to thwart James. No wonder the man had panicked when the yard began operating again and he hadn't been able to lift a hand to stop Maura's orders. It was he who had notified Pelham of Maura's whereabouts, and

Turk had lost no time in getting there. Duggan muttered an oath.

He glanced back at the boatyard in time to see the skiff nose into the bank. The men climbed out and went quickly to Pelham, who listened, then pounded his cane in rage. Finally he turned on his heel and limped back to the office. Duggan grinned and eased his cramped legs. What would Turk do now? The only avenue open to him was to try to trace Maura's movements.

And I'll not let you out of my sight until I'm sure she's safe!

The office door opened again. Pelham and Braxton emerged. Pelham signaled the burly man called Higgins, and the three climbed into the landau and rode off. Denfield stood in the doorway and seemed to heave a sigh of relief before re-entering the office and closing the door.

Duggan eased himself upright. He slowly worked the stiffness from his muscles. Skirting the yard and the guards Pelham had left, he made his way to where his rig and the dapple-gray were tied. He climbed up and slapped the reins, turning the runabout to follow the settling trail of dust the landau left.

By dinner hour, Pelham's temper had curdled. The idiots on Maura's trail had found nothing! She'd left the hotel and no one knew where she'd gone. A woman could not simply vanish into thin air, damn it! One as pretty as Maura would be noticed wherever she went. And Duggan Quinn had vanished too.

He swore as he remembered how Quinn had aided Maura's escape once before. He wouldn't let it happen again. No, this time Quinn was going to jail. Pelham had instructed the police sergeant to arrest the man on sight. There were charges enough to hold him. Denfield would swear that Quinn had taken over the boatyard by force and brought in his rabble to finish the steamer so he could use it for his own profit. He would do twenty years in prison before Pelham was finished with him.

Pelham paced the length of the sitting room and glared at Braxton, who had settled into an armchair with his whiskey bottle.

"Keep your wits about you, damn it!" Pelham snatched away the bottle. "I'll not have you sottish when I need you."

Braxton laughed caustically. "If you could force enough whiskey into Maura, maybe she wouldn't fight so hard."

"Shut up, you fool!" Pelham's cane raised. Braxton cowered and his smile vanished. His father leaned over him. "When they find her, the wedding will take place at once. There's a justice of the peace three blocks from here. I've already talked to him."

Braxton nodded. It would give him the greatest satisfaction to force Maura into marriage. The she-devil had tortured him long enough. He'd show her he was not to be made a fool of. He didn't give a damn about the company—that was his father's concern. Braxton's only interest was to have revenge on Maura. Feverishly he downed the liquor in his glass, ignoring his father's angry glare. Most women found him desirable—in fact, he'd had his pick. Ex-cept for Maura. Soon . . .

A knock sounded and Pelham bounded to the door and yanked it open. Higgins came in holding his cap in his beefy hands.

"We've found her, sir."

"Where is she?" Pelham peered into the hall.

"We don't have her, but we know where she's gone." Higgins twisted the cap in thick fingers.

"If you let her get away—!" Pelham's face grew purple.

Higgins said quickly, "She was already gone when I learned she'd been on the waterfront. She took a boat down the river this morning."

"Damn!"

Higgins went on quickly before Turk's anger could be directed at him. "She went aboard the *Ohio Queen* posing as the wife of a gambler named Fontaine. He's well known along the levee. Poker, faro—"

"There was no sign of Quinn?" Pelham didn't care about the gambler.

"No one's seen a man fittin' his description, and I know for certain he weren't on the *Ohio Queen*. Every cabin was taken. Fontaine got the last one. She's headed for Cairo, Illinois."

Pelham let out his breath slowly. At least Quinn had not

gotten away. And without his help, Maura would be on her own. The gambler could be bought off or disposed of readily. Pelham dug in his pocket and extracted a banknote, which he handed to Higgins.

"That will be all."

Higgins looked astonished. "Don't you want me to follow her? I can hire a fast sternwheeler and catch up with the *Queen* before she reaches Louisville."

"You know of such a boat?" Pelham demanded.

Higgins nodded. "A man named Sharp runs a profitable trade by beating every other boat on the river. For a price—" He smiled and shrugged.

"Where can he be found?" Pelham's cane tapped impatiently.

"At the end of Graves Street. He's got a shanty—" To Higgins' surprise, Pelham cut him short and dismissed him with an imperious wave of his hand.

As soon as the man was gone, Pelham turned to Braxton who was peering at his father with a curious expression.

"Why didn't you send him after her?" he asked in amazement.

Pelham gave him a vexed look. "Because *you* are going after her! And as soon as you find her, you'll take her ashore to the nearest justice. I don't care if you have to chloroform her to get her there, she's to come back as Mrs. Braxton Turk!"

For a moment, Braxton was too stunned to speak. His father crossed to a small satchel, dug in it, and came up with a vial of pills. He handed them to his son.

"These will keep her docile enough on the return trip. Now go, and be quick about it!"

Braxton smiled as the prospect began to take shape.

Duggan was puzzled when Higgins emerged from Pelham Turk's hotel and immediately headed for O'Meara's Tavern. Turk had not sent him in pursuit of Maura. Why not, he wondered. He watched until he was certain the man had settled to an evening of ale, then slipped from his hiding place and crossed to the hotel.

Higgins had made a careful investigation of the waterfront, questioning every roustabout, shipping clerk and ticket agent. The man was obviously well known along the levee and docks, and there had been no chance for Duggan to catch up to him unexpectedly. Nor had he been able to intercept him when he rushed from the office of the Nelson Packet Line and made tracks back to Turk. The reason for such haste had to be that he'd discovered which boat Maura had taken.

Duggan was both relieved and concerned. Maura had gotten safely away, but now Turk knew where she was headed. And if Higgins' services were no longer required, it could mean only one thing: Turk was going after her himself.

The hotel clerk studied Duggan's damp clothes with obvious disdain. He started to order him out, but Duggan assumed a humble attitude and asked for Turk's room number.

The clerk, still scowling, hesitated.

"Have ye no mercy, man?" Duggan whined. "Mr. Turk will order me sacked if I don't bring him the news he's waiting for. Isn't it enough I've already been beaten and tossed into Hogg's Pond while trackin' down the man he wants? If ye doubt m' story, send someone up to ask him if he's not after a man named Quinn—a black Irishman if one ever drew a breath!" He shook his head and raked his fingers through his tousled hair, looking back over his shoulder as though afraid he might still be followed.

The clerk hesitated, then relented. "Mr. Turk is in room 204—but use the back stairs." He sniffed contemptuously.

Duggan thanked him, then scuttled toward the rear stairway before the man could change his mind.

He peered along the upper corridor, then made his way to 204. He listened but heard no voices inside. Was Pelham alone? Duggan recalled the gun Pelham had used. More than likely he still had it, but there was no time to hunt for a weapon for himself. He'd have to rely on his hands and his wits. He rapped loudly on the door.

Pelham's querulous voice answered. "Damn it, Braxton—!"

The door jerked open. Duggan pushed inside before Pelham could recover from his shock. He tried to raise the malacca cane, but Duggan wrenched it away and flung it across the room.

Pelham's breath hissed between his teeth. "I'll have you killed for this—"

"Not if I leave you dead when I go." Duggan stepped toward him and Pelham backed away in terror. His face paled and the loss of his cane seemed to make him shrivel. He eyed Duggan's massive fists and a thin sheen of sweat formed on his brow.

"What do you want?"

"Your man Higgins was here. Why?" Duggan demanded.

Pelham's glance shifted, and he drew himself up, no longer as frightened as he had been. Duggan realized that his question had relieved Pelham's fear on some score.

"The man's an employee. There's nothing strange about his coming—"

"The man's one of your hired goons, and if you've turned him onto Maura, the two of you will be swimming in a pool of blood before another hour passes!" Duggan grabbed Pelham's jacket and shook him like a dustcloth.

Pelham's teeth rattled and fear shadowed his eyes again. "Let me go!"

"Not until you tell me what I want to know." He punctuated each word with a vicious, bone-jarring shake. Pelham's head jerked back and forth like a broken puppet's.

"There's nothing to tell!"

Duggan sprawled him into a chair and stood over him, pushing up the damp sleeves of his jacket and flexing his arms. Pelham's eyes went wide.

"Wait!" When Duggan eased his stance slightly, Pelham swallowed hard and sat up. He tugged at his coat where it was bunched under his armpits.

"Am I waiting for my health or do you have something to say?" Duggan demanded.

Pelham held up a placating hand. "Higgins came to tell me he'd learned where Maura was. That's what he was paid to do." A glint of triumph erased the fear in his eyes.

Duggan's heart missed a beat. "Where has she gone?" It was difficult to talk past the sudden thickness in his throat.

Pelham's eyes narrowed. "She's gone back to New York—"

Duggan pounced like a cat, pulling Pelham out of the

chair and striking him with the back of his hand. Pelham's head snapped and his eyes glazed. Duggan lifted his hand again. It would be easy to beat Turk to a bloody pulp and kick his carcass aside like a dead rat.

"That blow was for your first lie," he said threateningly. "Which of us will tire of this game first, do y' think?"

Pelham gulped and shook his head in defeat. A trickle of blood oozed from his lip, and he wiped at it nervously.

"She's taken a steamer downriver."

"Just any steamer?" Duggan's voice was like a coiled spring.

"The *Ohio Queen*. It left this morning."

Duggan flung him back into the chair. Pelham lay like a rag doll, but his bloody lips curled into a smile. "She's not alone. She's gone with a gambler named Fontaine."

Duggan's torso swung about like an angry bull's. For a moment, the air seemed trapped in his lungs like a fiery bellows. It whooshed out painfully. "If that's another of your lies—"

"It's the truth!" Pelham felt a surge of glee at the pain in Quinn's eyes. The fool was in love with Maura and had risked his life for nothing!

Duggan's emotions tangled hopelessly. If Pelham was telling the truth, what did it mean? Had Maura gone with Fontaine by choice? No! He could not believe that! *Easy, man,* he told himself. *Don't make judgments without facts.* Maybe Fontaine had secured passage for her. The man knew his way around the levee. Duggan could understand Maura turning to him for help. Anyone who could expedite her departure would have been a godsend.

Pelham saw that the news had shaken Quinn, who seemed to be wavering between another attack and rushing off on a foolhardy quest in search of Maura. Pelham drove the knife deeper.

"Higgins says they're sharing a cabin as man and wife."

A cry of rage exploded from Duggan, but before he could move, Pelham leaped from the chair and rushed toward the desk where he kept his gun. Duggan tried to close the gap, but Turk had the pistol out, the hammer pulled and his finger on the trigger.

"Now you've lost your chance, Quinn. Move away from

the door while I ring for someone to call the police. Don't look so pained. Maura is not married to the tinhorn. But she *will* be married to Braxton soon!"

Duggan halted. At such close range, Pelham's shot could not miss. He watched as Pelham sidled toward the bellcord and yanked it imperiously. Braxton had gone after Maura! That was why Higgins had been taken off the job. Duggan's blood pounded in his temples. He would be of no use to Maura dead. He estimated the distance between him and Turk and knew he'd never make it

He stood with his arms loose at his sides. The sound of Pelham's breath was harsh in the silence. When a tap came at the door, Pelham's gaze did not flicker from Duggan as he moved sideways to unlatch it. The maid's mouth fell open when she saw the gun.

"Tell the manager to call the police and have him send up someone to assist me immediately!"

"Yessir—" The terrified girl moved back with her hand pressed to her mouth.

Duggan lunged before Pelham could swing the door shut. He was past Turk, pushing aside the maid and running down the hall. The girl screamed and clamped her hands over her ears as though waiting for the sound of the gun. Pelham swore and tried to get past her, but she was so panicked she grabbed at him and went on shrieking as though the Devil were after her. Duggan wheeled around a corner and plunged down the stairs. Along the corridor, doors opened and voices demanded to know the cause of the commotion.

He reached the dark landing that led to the lobby but turned instead toward a door leading to a back hall. The mingled smells of cooking assailed him. Breathlessly, he groped along the wall to another door, then let himself out into the alley. The night was suddenly quiet; he gulped air as he oriented himself. He started for the street but stopped in his tracks as the piercing cry of a police van filled the night. The station was only a block away!

Quickly, he retraced his steps, then scrambled over a fence and lost himself in the darkness.

By the time the *Ohio Queen* had been underway a few

hours, some of Maura's tension began to ease. She'd seen no one she knew on board. With each passing hour, the chance of being recognized seemed more remote.

When they finished their refreshments in the salon, Beau took her on a tour of the boat. Since it was to be their home for the next few days, he wanted to show her everything it had to offer, all the amusements she might fill the hours with if she tired of his company. He made it sound as if he would make no demands on her. Maura told herself again how considerate he was and how fortunate she was to have him at hand.

Stewards had arranged chairs on the deck, and passengers settled in small groups to watch the panorama of the shore. That was a favorite pastime, Beau said, and some spent their entire days at it. Riverboat travel was a very lazy way of life.

Beau showed her the library. It was hardly more than a tiny alcove amidships, but it boasted a shelf of books and copies of the most recent Pittsburgh newspapers. The supply of newspapers would be replenished at every town where they were available, clear down to Cairo. People were extremely interested in the debates going on in the Senate. John C. Calhoun of South Carolina was waging a veritable war against the Declaration of Independence with his statement that nothing could be more unfounded than the prevalent notion that all men were born free and equal. The North had to stop agitating the slavery question, he said, and he also held that the admission of California as a free state was clearly illegal. A man had the personal right to hold slaves, and there were many in the newly admitted westernmost state who were being denied that choice.

The talk of slavery made Maura's thoughts return to Duggan. He'd vowed that all men were free and equal, yet he condoned a violent organization that would enslave the Sullivan Company!

Beau saw the shadow cross her face and realized her mind had settled on disturbing thoughts. Skillfully, he guided the conversation from politics to lighter subjects.

"Ahhh," he said with an exaggerated wink, "here is the ladies' salon." His voice dropped to a conspiratorial whisper. "If you crave excitement, this is the place to find it. Look there—see the wicked tapestry that overweight ma-

398

tron in blue is embroidering!" He rolled his eyes. "A satyr and nymph!" He clucked his tongue and indicated a mousy woman in gray poplin, then looked away quickly. "I believe she is knitting a baby's cummerbund! I am shocked at her daring!"

A quick burst of laughter bubbled in Maura's throat. She ducked her head as the women looked up. If they only knew what Beau was saying! But they only nodded and smiled placidly before returning to their needlework. Maura looked around the room. It was comfortably furnished with small settees and chintz-covered chairs that might have come directly from any Peekskill summer home. Only in Beau's fertile imagination did it take on any sinister qualities.

Beau was pleased at her restored good humor and led her to the railing so they could watch the river. When he asked if she wanted a chair, she shook her head. They found a spot apart from others where they could talk quietly or be silent if they chose.

Dozens of small boats were scattered along the shoreline. Two had bright sails that were splashes of orange, blue and red against the fading green of autumn. A small sternwheeler pushed a heavily laden barge with its cargo covered by a weathered canvas. Men on the boat shouted and waved as it passed, and a skinny lad with wheat-colored hair came out onto the top deck playing a violin. The strains of the lively tune drifted over the water until they were drowned out by the heavy thrashing of the paddle buckets.

The river made great snaking turns through heavily wooded countryside. When the *Queen* passed a farm or a town on the riverbank, bells tolled to salute her. Beau told her it was a custom practiced the length of the river, and the louder the racket, the more esteemed the passing boat.

As they moved southwest, Ohio was on the starboard side and Virginia on the larboard. The river was like a twisted ribbon, wide at points then suddenly funneling to a narrow channel so that it seemed possible for Maura to reach out and touch either shore. There were dozens of tiny islands and some larger ones where smoke drifted against the afternoon sky, bearing evidence of the existence of houses or factories.

When Maura commented on the irregularity of the river's path, Beau declared it was a straight thoroughfare compared to the Mississippi. Now *that* was a winding, twisting river that couldn't make up its mind, he said. River pilots left notes at landings to apprise each other of how the Big Muddy had eaten into one bank or the other with her shifting currents; new channels were constantly being made. Legal complications often arose because of the river's changing habits, he said. Slavery was legal in Missouri but not in Illinois. When the river capriciously presented Illinois with a piece of Missouri, or vice versa, it freed slaves or bound them so that river-town lawyers had a steady stream of clients with appeals.

The day that had begun cloudy turned magnificently clear, with only a gentle breeze and a faint nip in the air. The sky hung like a blue Dresden bowl over the constantly changing scene, and Maura was drawn into the lazy, carefree attitude Beau had predicted would overtake everyone sooner or later. The afternoon passed in idle conversation and quiet strolling. Beau didn't suggest they join their fellow passengers or seek out company, and Maura was grateful. Gradually her taut nerves relaxed and smiles came readily in response to Beau's chatter. Pittsburgh seemed a long way behind.

By evening, everyone was looking forward to the Captain's party. It was the most popular topic of conversation during dinner, which was served in the main salon. It was transformed to a dining room by pushing together the small tables to form larger ones that sat eight. These were spread with sparkling linen, fine china and glistening silver. The menu, printed on a large pasteboard decorated with a picture of the *Ohio Queen* at the top and with a garlanded border of *fleur-de-lis*, was overwhelming. There was a selection of soups, boiled meats, roasts, fish, and vegetables. Pastries, puddings, cakes, fresh fruit and ice cream were available for dessert, and there were wines and spirits in abundance. The menu was as grand as that of any fine hotel she'd ever visited. When she commented on the fact to Beau, he smiled and said the riverboat was the floating palace of the rivers.

They sat with several people they'd met casually, and conversation was sprightly. Maura noted that Paul Giraud and Ellie Wyatt did not attempt to join them, although there were vacant seats at their table when the pair entered the dining room. Several times during the evening, Maura caught Giraud's eyes on them.

The room grew stuffy and Maura was glad to leave as soon as the meal was over. Lights along the riverbanks flickered and winked. A pale moon crept over the horizon and hung in the dark sky like a white disc trapped among the branches of the trees. Here and there on the dark deck, couples whispered in the shadows. Beau slipped an arm around Maura's waist as they strolled toward the stern.

"It's good to see you happy," he said tenderly.

She looked at him in surprise. "Have I been so somber?"

"You've had worries." He touched her cheek lovingly. "I'd like to think I'm partly responsible for relieving them, at least for the moment."

"You are." She felt a rush of warmth and gratitude. She returned the pressure of his hand and saw the quick smile he gave her. "You're always saying I'm your lucky charm, but I think it's the other way around. You've been there to help me every time I've reached a point of desperation."

"Is that the only reason you care for me? I was hoping you felt . . . love. . . ." His voice was barely a whisper over the steady splash of the slow-moving paddlewheels.

Maura's pulse quickened. How could she define her feeling? Affection? Yes . . . and passion, too. But she was still stung by the treachery of the love she'd known with Duggan. The thought of it was bitter. Would she ever plunge into a roiling sea of breathless, heady emotions again? It might be easy with Beau. . . .

"You are very quiet all of a sudden. Never mind, my question does not require an answer." He tucked her hand under his arm as they went through the dim inner passageway that bypassed the wheelhousing and led to the stern cabins. The creaking and splashing of the wheel made conversation impossible for several moments, and Maura used the time to collect her thoughts. She wanted to right the impression she'd given by her silence, but there seemed no easy way to do it. An explanation might only make things worse, since her own feelings were still a murky, dark pond that would not settle.

When they reached the cabin, Beau paused and took her in his arms. There were no other passengers on the stern deck. They were alone in a splash of moonlight filtering through the fretwork of the deck cornices. Soft whispering shadows played over Maura's face, turning her gray eyes to black pools. Beau kissed her lingeringly and her breath escaped in a soft sigh.

"No matter what your feelings are, I will always bless the day we met," he whispered. He traced her lips with a fingertip and felt them quiver. Smiling, he released her so he could unlock the door. "Now you must put on your prettiest gown for the Captain's party. I want to show you off!" He tossed his coat on the bed and began to unbutton his collar, whistling a soft tune and smiling each time their gazes met.

The curtains at the windows had been drawn and the lamps lighted. The chandelier reflected a million dancing rainbows to give the room a warm cheery look. Fresh hot water had been brought in large pitchers. Beau pulled off his shirt and bent over the basin.

Maura hung up her cloak and inspected the meager array of dresses in the wardrobe. She decided on a lemon-yellow silk which she had purchased at Madame Courbon's shop near the hotel. And never paid for, she recalled guiltily. As though sensing her thoughts, Beau flashed a smile as he dropped a damp towel and slipped off his gray pants. He chose pale buckskin trousers, a white shirt with a soft collar and a satin cravat the color of a midnight sky. Adjusting the cravat, he watched Maura readying her creams and lotions. She was still a bit uncomfortable with him, he thought; despite her eager responses in bed, she was not accustomed to living with a man. It amused him, but he thought it wiser not to chide her about it. At times he was sure he could read her thoughts like a book. At others, she was the enigma she professed him to be. He buttoned an embroidered silk vest and slipped on a cream-colored frock coat with dark brown velvet lapels. With a last look in the glass, he slipped his wallet into his pocket.

"And now I shall leave you to whatever it is women do to stay so beautiful. I'll wait for you in the salon." He blew her a kiss from his fingertips and let himself out.

As his jaunty whistle faded, Maura undressed and poured steaming water from the pitcher so she could wash. Beau had an extraordinary knack for putting her at ease;

402

she wished it was not necessary to rely on him, however. Her own emotions were so volatile, she was constantly at war with herself and with others. She splashed water on her face and scrubbed her cheeks with the soft cloth. Would she ever be different? Were patience and serenity virtues that could be learned, or were they bestowed on some with a lavish hand while denied to others? Or did they come magically at some point in one's life when happiness was achieved? Despite his drive and ambition, her father had found inner peace as he grew older and had his loved ones around him. Perhaps love was the answer. With a catching breath, she savored the memory of Duggan's strong arms and gentle caresses, his powerful maleness compelling her to eager submission, the tenderness in his kisses. . . . With an impatient sigh, she reached for the towel. Even though Duggan had worried about her safety at the boat-yard, not his own, she would not be fool enough to trust him again after what he had done.

She sat before the glass, unpinned her hair and began to brush it out. When it was smooth and silken, she lifted it and studied her reflection. The humidity had curled the amber tresses to soft waves. She decided on a simple style in which her hair was drawn softly from her face on either side, so that curls fell over her ears. It was a style that Lenore had often arranged on summer evenings.

She wondered if Lenore was happy at her sister's. She sighed. How much life had changed. She tilted her head at the reflection in the glass. The past weeks had been filled with excitement, adventure and tears, yet she had gained maturity and independence. She was no longer a restless captive of a meaningless life. She'd become a woman who would never again be satisfied with less than the most life had to offer. Serenity would come when she had fulfilled her father's dream and her promise to her mother—and thwarted Duggan and Cromwell's base plan. The Sullivan Company would grow and prosper, and it would *never* pass into Pelham Turk's hands or be taken over by a union.

The sound of music from the salon drifted over the noise of the engines and paddlewheels. Maura realized Beau would be wondering what had happened to her. Quickly, she put aside the hairbrush and slipped into the yellow gown, struggling to fasten the hooks which went from neckline to hips at the back. The dress was full-skirted, with three tiers of taffeta. Each had a row of embroidered roses at the edge, and the front waistline dipped to a cluster of tiny yellow silk rosebuds. The neckline was softly curved to expose her shoulders, and the sleeves were formed by three narrow flounces of lace that matched the skirt. She tugged at the tight bodice and knew the décolletage was very becoming. She leaned toward the looking glass and pinched her cheeks to heighten the color, then arranged a curl so it fell perfectly. She found short white gloves, a lace handkerchief which she tucked into her bodice, and a black silk and bamboo fan. With a final glance in the mirror, she let herself out and made her way forward.

The salon was already crowded. The musicians were playing a slow waltz, and numerous couples were on the dance floor, gliding and turning in the latest dance steps. Maura's fingers tapped instinctively as she looked around. Beau appeared at her side instantly.

"That gown gives your eyes glints of pure gold. If you had not just spent so much time getting ready for this party, I would whisk you back into the cabin and keep you for myself. As it is, I shall have to content myself with a dance. May I have the pleasure?"

He swept her into his arms and onto the dance floor. Eyes turned toward them as she followed him in a perfectly executed waltz turn. He held her at arm's length, but the pressure of his hand at her waist was possessive. He was an excellent dancer and seemed to know every step Maura had ever seen. And she had no trouble following him, much to his delight. He smiled intimately as though they were alone on a cloud, far above the world of mere mortals.

When the dance ended, Beau led her to a table where a silver tray held a bottle of champagne and two glasses. He held a chair for her, then signaled the waiter to pour the chilled wine. Beau raised his glass.

"To the most beautiful woman in the salon."

Maura frowned and pretended to count on her fingers. At his curious look, she said, "I am wondering how many times you have told me that pretty lie."

He chuckled good-naturedly. "Not often enough. Besides, it is not a lie. You must not be so modest. I find

404

overly modest women a trifle exasperating. It seems I must compliment them a hundred times over in order to convince them! A proud, confident woman should say, 'Thank you, sir, I am pleased that you noticed.' "

"Thank you, sir, I am pleased that you noticed," Maura mimicked.

They laughed and touched fragile champagne glasses, then drank. Once again they seemed to be floating on a delicate, solitary cloud. The spell was broken as the musicians struck up another tune.

The salon had been decorated with garlands of white and yellow chrysanthemums entwined with glossy leaves and red ribbons. Each table had a small crystal bud vase holding a fragrant red rose. Maura wondered where on earth such perfect blooms had been found this time of year.

Beau noted her pleasure and relaxed, smiling often at people who passed. Some of the travelers were prominent citizens from Pittsburgh or Southern cities. Beau had glimpsed the passenger list when purchasing the tickets. Now he remembered bits and pieces of conversations he had overheard, and introductions helped him tie names to faces. He began to identify people for Maura.

"The Ruhls of Cincinnati. German immigrants who have taken over the operation of one of the largest coal mines in the state. And there—the man who looks as if he'll burst his coat buttons if he swallows another mint julep—that's Colonel Farady of Natchez. Cotton." He arched an eyebrow. "It's said he owns seven hundred slaves and ships ten thousand bales a year. A very wealthy man. The young woman with him is his wife, not his daughter." Beau winked. "They were married last spring. The celebration lasted five days, and it's said that the Colonel did not draw a sober breath the entire time."

"How terrible for his bride," Maura said pertly. She was not sure if Beau was telling the truth or inventing stories for her amusement as he had at the Blue Horse Inn.

Beau shrugged. "Knowing the Colonel's reputation with women, perhaps she was glad of the respite." He let his glance cross the room. "Ah, I see our friend Giraud has met Charles Stevenson."

"Is that extraordinary?" Beau was watching Giraud and Ellie at a table across the dance floor. The man with them

405

was short and thin, with a stooped look and gray hair. He was smoking a long, thin cigar and nodding earnestly at Giraud's remarks. From time to time he looked at Ellie, who answered with a bold smile.

"No, merely interesting."

When Beau did not elaborate, Maura asked, "Who is Mr. Stevenson?"

Beau's eyes narrowed slightly. "A freight man who operates the largest river trade north of New Orleans. He knows every riverboat captain on the Ohio and the Mississippi and can recite to the pound the amount of freight any boat carries. He's often called the Baron of the River." And he has a penchant for gambling, Beau added silently. Obviously Giraud had already singled the man out as a target. Beau wondered if he would be in the game Giraud had proposed for later in the evening. A very interesting prospect, very interesting indeed. Realizing he was ignoring Maura, he turned back to her with a smile.

"More champagne, or would you prefer to dance?"

"The music is so lively I cannot keep my feet still."

"Then come. Nothing gives me greater pleasure than holding you in my arms, no matter what the pretext." He rose and held out his hand.

After two waltzes, the musicians swept into a spirited polka. Beau tapped and bobbed, then whirled Maura across the floor. They spun and turned to the quick tempo. Beau's grin was infectious. He was enjoying himself so fully that Maura shared his high spirits. Her skirts flew and her face flushed as they whirled around the room. Lights flashed and winked like a kaleidoscope. Her laughter rang out and was answered by Beau's intimate touch at her waist.

When the last note died and the fiddlers raised their bows, Maura collapsed against Beau in breathless exhaustion. Grinning, he led her outside to the rail. A cool breeze carried the scent of pine, and the night was filled with the shrill call of crickets. Several people were enjoying a respite from the closeness of the salon. A pretty young girl turned to face them. She was wearing a frilly organdy dress that would have been more fitting for a summer lawn party. Her mouth fell open in amazement.

"Beau Fontaine! What a magnificent surprise!" She held out her hands and blocked his path.

Beau looked startled for a moment, then said smoothly, "Anabelle—this is unexpected. I had no idea you were traveling."

She blushed and touched her cheek coquettishly. "Papa had business in Pittsburgh. After all the exciting tales I've heard about the river, I simply *begged* him to let me come along. It's absolutely *sinful* for a girl my age never to have been nawth of Baton Rouge, don't you think?"

"Absolutely sinful," Beau agreed solemnly. Anabelle was staring at Maura, waiting to be introduced. "Maura, this is Miss Anabelle Dumaine of New Orleans," Beau said. "I've had the pleasure of visiting the Dumaine plantation many times."

Anabelle's gaze fixed on Maura, noting the arm slipped through Beau's. "Maura . . . ?" Her questioning tone asked for a fuller identification of the woman at Beau's side.

Maura tilted her head. She had not missed Beau's omission of a last name or the fact that this time he had not claimed she was his wife. It seemed a calculated choice, and she felt a rush of irritation. She smiled sweetly at the fluttering girl and said devilishly, "*Mrs.* Fontaine. Beau and I were married a few weeks ago in Pittsburgh. This is our honeymoon." She cast a sidelong glance at Beau. His face was expressionless.

Anabelle's face fell. For a moment, Maura thought the girl would burst into tears. She was sorry she had played such a petty, senseless joke, but there was no way to undo what she'd done.

Finally Anabelle smiled tremulously. "I had no idea. . . . Congratulations to both of you. I just *know* you're going to be very happy." Her luminous blue eyes fastened on Beau with terrible reproach, and her smile wavered. Quickly she forced herself to talk of something else. "Are you going to New Orleans?"

"I'm afraid not. We can only go as far as Cairo this trip, though I hope to take Maura all the way down the river soon. She's never been to New Orleans and has a treat in store for her." He smiled at Maura and his expression held no censure.

Anabelle recovered from her shock and was flirting girlishly. "The *Memphis Belle* will be in Cairo when we ar-

407

rive. If you change your mind, maybe we'll see you aboard."

"A fine boat," Beau said, "but we'll have to wait for another time. Our business in Cairo is pressing and we'll be several days, I'm sure. Tell me, how is your mother? And your father—you say he's with you?"

Anabelle simpered. "Mama is enjoyin' *excellent* health. She refuses to leave home, though Papa *begged* her to come along. He's so busy talkin' business, I hardly see him." She glanced at the group by the rail. "Deah me, whatevah has become of my manners? I'm so taken with seein' you again, I haven't introduced you to these *nice* people. Colonel and Mrs. Faraday, and Harper Lynch . . ."

Beau shook hands with the Colonel and Lynch and smiled at young Mrs. Faraday. The Colonel grasped Maura's hand and pressed it to his lips with a flourish. Harper Lynch seemed less than delighted at having Anabelle's attention diverted. He was a sallow-faced, nondescript man who looked awkward in an expensive cutaway coat and a ruffled shirt. To Maura he suggested a partridge that had suddenly found itself surrounded by peacocks.

Colonel Faraday offered Beau a cigar from a silver case. "Fontaine . . . I've heard the name. Are you in cotton, sir?"

"In trading, sir," Beau answered smoothly. "I deal in many commodities. I must say your name is known to me also." He gave the man an admiring smile. "The Cotton King of Natchez."

Faraday chuckled appreciatively and puffed a cloud of blue smoke that drifted like a genie from its magic lamp. "How is it we haven't done business? I thought I knew every trader on the river."

"My misfortune," Beau said smoothly. "Perhaps we can rectify that in the near future. I know several boat owners eager to do business. I may be able to get you an excellent price per ton. Do you ship only on the river or around the Gulf as well?"

Faraday beamed. "I have two textile mills in Massachusetts that want to buy as much cotton as I can send them. There were years when I was glad to sell them my entire crop, but times have changed. We're no longer dependent on New England for cloth. Why, in the past year, seven new mills have opened up between Cincinnati and Paducah! They can't keep up with the demands of people heading west to California. They're pouring through Cairo faster'n anyone can count them. And every man jack, woman and child is buying clothes and linens to see him across the country. Booming market for cotton, booming! My darkies can't bale it fast enough to keep them happy." He puffed his cigar a final time, then arced it over the railing toward the glassy calm of the water. A trail of sparks followed until it hit the surface. "I'm thinking of investing in a riverboat of my own. Another profitable business. It doesn't hurt to diversify one's interests."

"I am acquainted with the owner of an excellent boatyard in Pittsburgh," Beau said with a quick glance at Maura. "When you're in the market for a boat, Colonel, I'd be glad to put you in touch with him."

Faraday gave a noncommittal shrug. There were plenty of brokers who'd like to arrange business deals. Beau sensed the dismissal. The Colonel wanted only to boast and applaud himself.

Glancing past Beau, Faraday's face lit up. "Mr. Stevenson—!" He hailed a gray-haired man who had just emerged from the salon. "Good to see you again. We met in Cairo several months ago. Colonel Faraday, Natchez." He shot out a beefy hand.

"Of course," Stevenson said. "And Mrs. Faraday. Nice to see you again."

Faraday made introductions, and for several minutes the men engaged in conversation about shipping cotton and machinery. When the band struck up a tune, Anabelle fluttered her fan at Beau.

"Will you ask me to dance, Beau? I'm sure the others will excuse us. We have so *much* to catch up on. It's been an *eternity* since I've seen you. Imagine, you getting married!" She smiled forlornly at Maura, who nodded as Beau looked at her questioningly.

Beau accepted Anabelle's hand and led her into the salon. But his gaze drifted back to Maura as he whirled the other girl onto the dance floor.

How transparent Anabelle was, Maura thought, and determined to have Beau to herself for a little while. There was no doubt that she was terribly disappointed to learn

409

that someone she considered an eligible bachelor had suddenly claimed a wife. Maura regretted succumbing to the spiteful impulse to announce her fictitious marriage to Beau. She was even more amazed at the jealousy she felt because of Anabelle's flirtation and the way Beau had accepted it so matter-of-factly. Was there no woman who did not find him irresistible?

With a start, she realized Harper Lynch had spoken. He was holding out his hand, and waiting for her response as he glanced at the dance floor. She forced a smile and put her hand in his sweaty palm. He'd said so little, Maura had the impression he was only an image, with nothing substantial underneath—not a real person at all. He led her through a series of dance steps without flair or imagination. Maura began to look forward to the end of the dance and finding Beau again.

CHAPTER TWENTY-THREE

The waterfront was dark and quiet. The moon climbed above the gray cloud hanging over the city, and its pale light filtered through in intermittent patches. Here and there, a dusting of stars was visible in the black sky.

Duggan drove past the yard without slowing. To anyone inside, it would be just another wagon heading toward Squirrel Hill, hardly worthy of note. There was a light in the office and a lantern hanging on the forward rail of the *Patrick*. No telling how many men were in the office, but he could count on at least two or three more scattered about the yard and aboard the boat, which had been tied up to the bank. Duggan made out a faint haze of smoke drifting from the chimneys. The fireboxes had not gone out. He grinned.

Behind him in the wagon, stokers and deckhands craned to look at their destination, appraising the boat as Duggan did. The *Patrick* would not be difficult to take. Pelham Turk had not foreseen the need for a large armed guard. That much was in their favor, though Duggan had warned them to be prepared for anything.

Duggan halted the rockaway a quarter of a mile beyond the boatyard. He slid from the seat and tossed the reins to the stableboy, who had a silver dollar in his pocket to ensure the return of the wagon to the depot. Behind Duggan, Tolly Jeffries climbed down. Eight others—stokers, deckhands and engineers—slid to the ground and formed a knot.

Duggan had briefed them before they were hired; each man knew the job of taking the *Patrick* down the river depended on first getting it away from the mooring without being detected. They were expert boatmen all, men who were willing to work hard and who refused to pay the scavengers who controlled the waterfront and demanded a third of a man's wages for a job. Like many others, they preferred to deal secretly with captains who refused to pay blood money to the crimping masters. They considered the crimps a scourge brought from the ports of Baltimore and Philadelphia, and the sooner they were driven from the river towns, the better for all.

Duggan motioned the men to follow, and they moved along the road in silence. No man had to be told what to do as they reached the fence surrounding the Sullivan yard. In minutes, they were over the barrier, edging toward the *Patrick*. At intervals, Duggan halted and cocked his head to listen for telltale sounds that would betray the whereabouts of Turk's guards. As they neared the partly dismantled launching cradle, a soft cough alerted them. Duggan pointed, and three men broke off to slip around the other side of the scaffolding that was stark against the gray sky. There was a scuffling sound, a groan, then silence. Moments later, the three rejoined the group. Their grins were all the answer Duggan needed.

Another man was leaning against the railing at the head of the gangplank. Duggan saw him silhouetted when the moon broke through its cloud cover. He waited until the light was obscured once more, then advanced up the plank.

"That you, Logan?" the guard called softly.

Duggan grunted and hunched his chin into his collar. The man started to speak as Duggan reached him, and Duggan struck him with a short, heavy stick. The man gasped and fell to the deck.

Tolly and the others came aboard. Two of them lifted the unconscious man and carried him down the gangplank, tossing him onto the bank like a sack of garbage. They returned carrying long poles. Duggan signaled them to wait before pulling in the gangplank: there might be others.

He found one on the hurricane deck, dozing against the texas. A moment later, the unconscious man was slung over his shoulder, being toted ashore. Two of Duggan's men made a quick survey of the boat and came back grinning. Except for the men on shore in the office and the unconscious forms stacked like cordwood under the launching cradle, they were alone.

Every man knew his job. Tolly Jeffries went immediately to the pilothouse. The stokers hurried to the fireboxes as the deckhands unfastened the lines and began poling the boat out from the bank. The *Patrick* was moored parallel to the shore, headed downstream. They could drift with the sluggish shoreline current while the engineer was getting up steam. And with the forward deck at a right angle to the shore, there'd be less likelihood of the fires being spotted. The moment the firebox doors were opened and the embers fed, the rosy glow would be visible for miles. But if the men in the office were as inattentive as those on the boat, the *Patrick* would be gone before they realized anything was amiss.

Duggan made sure the running lamps were in place. They wouldn't be lighted until the *Patrick* was safely away, not unless the unpredictable current dragged them into the main channel where they'd be a danger to others. Duggan posted a man aft on the hurricane and another on the forward texas deck to stand watch.

The moon spilled from behind a cloud, and Duggan glanced apprehensively toward the building on the bank. The dim light at the window had not changed, and there was no sign of anyone coming to investigate. He breathed a prayer to the Blessed Virgin. If their luck would hold a bit longer . . .

He ducked past the main staircase and made his way among the stacks of wood that had been loaded in preparation for the launching. There was enough to see them through the night, but they'd have to wood up soon after daybreak.

Heat from the boilers and pipes had already warmed the passage to the engine room. It was a hot blast after the breeze on deck. Macalister, the engineer, had removed his coat and was leaning over the engine in shirt-sleeves, a peaked cap pushed back on his head so curly red hair fell across his forehead. Nodding to Duggan, he turned a valve and adjusted a gauge-cock.

"With the escape valves closed, we should have enough steam up in twenty minutes, thirty at the outside. Can you soak the logs in coal oil?"

"Haven't got any," Duggan said.

Macalister shrugged, then grinned. "Tell Tolly Jeffries to

clean his specs and stay awake. This boat is going to move like a hound after a polecat."

Duggan slipped out and climbed the aft ladder to the cabin deck, making a quick half-turn on the starboard side to have a look at the shoreline. The *Patrick* was drifting like a sluggish beetle and had gone only a few dozen yards downstream. He could still see the lighted window of the Sullivan Company office much too clearly to suit him. But the biggest danger was past. Even if they were seen now, the guards would waste precious minutes spreading an alarm and trying to round up enough men to attempt to halt the *Patrick*. Maybe it wouldn't occur to them to ride into the city and alert Pelham Turk. Another boat setting out from the levee at Liberty Street, several miles below them, might intercept the *Patrick* and force it to shore—but not without a hell of a fight, Duggan vowed silently.

In the pilothouse, Jeffries was working by moonlight. A lantern on the floor, covered by a piece of tarp, cast just enough light to see his footing. He glanced sidelong at Duggan but did not turn from the wheel. He held a spoke with one hand, while his other rested lightly on the wheel rim. He looked completely at ease, as though steering a boat without steam up, on a pitch-black river, were an every-night occurrence.

"Twenty minutes, Macalister judges," Duggan said.

"That'll put us close to Sukes' Run. We'll need our running lights." He leaned forward to have a better look at the patterns of the water. He pulled the wheel down and the boat's prow eased to larboard.

Duggan glanced again at the darkened yard behind them. The light in the office was obscured momentarily as the *Patrick* rounded a small bend overhung with weeping willows. Then the light winked back into view. All at once, a larger splash of light poured out as the door opened. Two figures were outlined against the doorway. They stood a moment, then turned back inside quickly, appearing in a moment with lanterns. Then they were running toward the bank.

"That tears it," Duggan said. "Take her into the main current, Mr. Jeffries. You'll have your lights and your steam!"

Duggan leaped down the steps and shouted to the men on watch as he raced to the boiler deck.

"Show the running lights!" The *Patrick* was already nosing toward the main channel. The lights of other boats could be seen in the distance.

Now that the need for quiet was past, Duggan's feet pounded on the deck like a drumroll. He covered the length of the boat to the main staircase in seconds and vaulted the rail, dropping to the main deck. From shore, he heard a shout and a shot exploded. So Pelham's men were armed. Small good it would do them now—the *Patrick* was well out of pistol range.

The heat of the fires washed over him as he neared the fireboxes. The stokers were throwing logs in, pushing them back with long poles, as fast as the flames could eat them. Flames leaped and swirled. A thin stoker named Waco wiped a grimy hand across his sweating face, leaving a trail of soot.

"We need more steam!" Duggan shouted over the roar. When the man frowned, Duggan pointed toward the shore. "We've been seen!"

Waco nodded and nudged the man next to him. A wordless message exchanged between them, and a deckhand named Poge, who'd been helping with the woodpile, picked up a bucket and passed it forward.

"Heave it in, Collier!" Waco yelled.

The stoker stepped back and flung the contents of the bucket into the firebox. Grease spattered and hissed, and hot orange flames licked upward ravenously. Collier shielded his face with an arm and cringed, and Poge was already passing up another bucket. A moment later, flames roared again.

Waco grinned. "Grease from the slipways. Brung it on wi' us. Thought it might come in handy."

Duggan grinned and clapped the man's shoulder, then made his way to the engine room. Macalister had rolled up his shirt-sleeves, and his face was filmed with sweat. The insulation between the furnace walls and the engines had not been completed, and heat crowded into the room and reflected from the heavy metal. The doctor engine pumping water to the boilers chugged steadily as Macalister peered at a water gauge.

415

Duggan watched the needle creep up. Macalister gave him a nod and tilted his head to watch the steady progress of the needle. He adjusted a cock with a small twist of his wrist. "Climbing fast. 'Nother five-ten minutes."

"We don't have that long!"

Macalister shook his head and tightened his mouth. "I'm an engineer, Quinn, not a miracle worker. You tell them blackguards at the fires to give me steam and I'll get your engines started!"

He pulled a lead weight from a hook and hung it on the safety valve. The needle jerked, then settled to its steady climb.

Duggan returned to the stokers. The four men were shoving logs and tamping them back as fast as the fires could take them. Seeing Duggan's frown, Waco tossed in the empty wooden grease-buckets.

"Can't make them burn any hotter!" he yelled.

Duggan returned to the upper deck. Running lights had been strung along the rails, and Bainbridge, a broad-shouldered, middle-aged man with a bald pate, was busy lighting lanterns in the texas. Duggan made his way to the dark pilothouse.

"We've got twenty-three pounds of pressure, Mr. Jeffries. Can you take her out on that?"

Jeffries grunted and sucked at his pipe. "I can try, Mr. Quinn. She's riding light."

"Then let's get out of here!" Duggan said.

Jeffries grabbed the speaking tube and blew sharply. "Look alive, Mr. Macalister! Give me enough steam to steer a course! Give me all you've got!" He jerked a bell-cord, and the gong sounded. The huge paddlewheels began to turn with agonizing slowness. Below, the deckhands swung their signal lanterns.

The shoreline began to glide by. Duggan stepped out onto the texas deck as the chimneys sent showers of sparks and smoke against the sky. The glare overshadowed the moonlight for a few moments, then the soft velvet night wrapped around the *Patrick* once more.

Behind him, he heard Jeffries ring down to the engine room again. "Give me full steam, Mr. Macalister, full steam ahead!"

Beau and Maura spent most of the evening with Anabelle Dumaine and her father, a bantam of a man who seemed to watch Beau as though afraid he might try to snatch his daughter from under his nose. Obviously he did not share Anabelle's enthusiasm at seeing Beau again, but he was polite and devoted most of his conversation to Maura.

Several times, Maura saw Beau glance about. She thought his gaze rested on Paul Giraud more than once but she could not be sure. Giraud did not join them or even acknowledge Beau's presence by more than a nod.

Many of the older couples were beginning to drift toward their cabins, willing to end the festive evening. To her surprise, Maura felt weary and lethargic, and realized the day had taken its toll on her energies. She was relieved when Beau noticed her stifle a yawn and got to his feet. He smiled at the Dumaines.

"I see the musicians are putting away their instruments. It has been a charming evening, but if you will excuse us now . . . ?" He offered his hand to Maura.

She rose, glad to leave. Mr. Dumaine stood and bowed. Anabelle gave Beau a pouting smile as he led Maura from the salon.

The air outside had cooled considerably, and Maura shivered. Beau put an arm about her.

"You should have brought a heavier wrap." He drew her into the curve of his arm.

"It's only the sudden change and my weariness. I didn't realize until now how tired I am." She was aware of Anabelle's watchful gaze following them past the windows.

"Will you be too cold if we walk slowly? There's nothing more romantic than moonlight on the river." His arm tightened, and she felt the familiar weakening that came whenever she gazed into his obsidian eyes.

She looked away toward the river, which had become a glistening silver path between black shores. She did not want to talk of romance. She had avoided his earlier attempt to introduce the subject because she was not sure of her own emotions. But more and more, she was beginning to wonder if they did not run deeper than she was willing to admit. Would she react jealously to Anabelle's silly flirtation if she did not love Beau? And she enjoyed his com-

417

pany to a degree she would not have believed possible. And his lovemaking . . .

Beau studied her profile and the faint line that had appeared between her brows. She didn't want to talk about love, that was obvious. He'd been positive she was snared in the delicate web he'd spun. But although she came to him willingly and eagerly, she would not speak words of love. Most women babbled them incessantly. Perhaps Maura needed more time. After all, she was not like most of the women he knew. He smothered a sigh as he thought of Anabelle, who was tiresome, dull and talkative to a fault, and didn't have a brain in her pretty little head. The richest women were so often like that.

Most of the cabin windows were already dark and the boat was quieting for the night. Below, deck passengers had found places to rest their heads, and the occasional creak of a hammock groaned over the low throbbing of the engines. The running lights shone as green and red beacons against the inky water. A path of moonlight wavered in the wake of the paddlewheels, flickering and dancing in a lazy chase of the stern. Somewhere a Negro sang a plaintive melody to the strumming of a banjo. Everything else was still except the soft booming of the steampipes and the splashing of the wheels.

The *Ohio Queen* nosed shoreward as the channel split around the black hill of an island. Beau paused and drew Maura close as he pointed to a cluster of lights a quarter of a mile downstream.

"Drake's Landing," he said.

She looked at him in amazement. "How can you tell in the dark?"

He pressed his cheek against her face and felt the quick intake of her breath. "Because I have traveled up and down this river enough times to know it by heart. There are a half-dozen wood stops between Wheeling and Marietta, but only two on the northern bank. Smith's woodyard is fifty miles below Wheeling and we passed it shortly before dinner. *Voilà*—this must be Drake's!"

She laughed softly, and her beauty quickened his pulse. The moonlight gave her hair the same dark, iridescent sheen it painted on the river, and her moist lips were an invitation.

Beau leaned on the rail and stared at the dark, shadowy shoreline gliding past. Above them, one of five sleeping Negroes under a tarpaulin on the landing stirred and threw it off. On the *Queen*'s main deck, roustabouts hung lanterns along the forward rails, and the mate shouted for hands to man the sling.

"We're stopping," Maura said in surprise.

"It's only a wood stop. We have to take on fuel. The fireboxes consume it at a great rate. We can load only enough coal at Pittsburgh to take us this far." He slid an arm around her to shield her from the freshening breeze and pointed to a huge, dark mass on the landing. "The wood is stacked in cords close to the water so it only takes minutes to toss it aboard."

"Why don't we continue using coal?"

"Wood is much cheaper and more plentiful along most of the river. We'll be making several stops every day from now on." He directed her attention to the landing. "Watch."

Two Negroes lighted pitch torches and ran to place them in iron brackets stuck in the ground. Maura could see the huge woodpiles in the sudden light. The steamboat nudged in slowly, throwing up a froth of waves that pounded against the wooden platform. Maura thought everyone had retired for the night, but passengers appeared out of the darkness to line the rails and watch the excitement. The mate shouted orders. The lines went out and the big boat rocked ponderously as they were tightened to pull her in. As soon as the boat touched shore, roustabouts formed lines to pass the wood from shore to deck.

"Load de wood—load de wood—" The quick chant throbbed in the night.

Deck passengers jumped ashore and pushed into the brush to attend to calls of nature. Below, the mate pounded the deck, "Lively—look lively there—we ain't got all night—"

Maura watched in fascination as, by the flickering light of the torches, the Negroes rushed the wood aboard. They were barefooted, with ragged trousers, and all were stripped to the waist or wearing cowls made of salt sacks. At the end of the gangplank a burly, ebony-skinned giant received each log and passed it along in an effortless

419

rhythm. The men were a symphony of motion, sweating bodies gleaming, oblivious to the chill. Their throaty voices drummed the song, "Gimme dat log—gimme dat log—hunnerd logs, an' a hunnerd days. Load de boat an' load de boat, a hunnerd days till you's done."

The piles of wood on shore diminished like magic and there was a shrill warning blast from the boat's whistle. Those ashore hurried back as the chanters began, "Nine more logs—nine more logs—eight more logs—"

A grimy man in slouch hat and patched homespun coat emerged from a shack and trod the gangplank to be met by the mate. They compared notes, then the mate dipped into his pocket and counted out silver to the woodman.

"De las' log—de las' log—"

The mate shouted for the gangplanks to be swung inboard, and while they were still moving, the paddlewheels began to thresh, backing the steamboat away from the platform.

"The entire thing took about fifteen minutes," Beau said.

Maura watched the Negroes pry the sputtering torches from the iron baskets and toss them into the water. The pine knots sizzled out, and the woodyard was suddenly dark again.

The passengers moved away from the rail and drifted back into the main salon or their cabins. Maura expressed her amazement that so much fuel could be taken aboard so quickly.

Beau smiled. "Captain Dance prides himself on keeping the *Ohio Queen*'s reputation as the fastest boat between Pittsburgh and Cairo. A number of brief wood stops are necessary or she'd be known as an old scow and no one would buy passage." He kissed her cheek. "You're shivering—" He tightened his arm about her and they went inside.

When she had undressed and slipped into bed, Beau insisted she have a small glass of brandy to ward off the chill. "I can't have you taking ill."

She downed it, making a terrible face that caused him to smile and shake his head as he tucked the covers under her chin.

"I'm sorry I agreed to a game with Giraud, but I won't be long. Cards are a major pastime aboard riverboats, and

420

I would be considered less than a gentleman if I disappointed the others. Though I imagine a man's wedding trip might provide an acceptable excuse." He pressed his lips tenderly to hers in a brandy-sweetened kiss.

Maura felt a stir of desire. The liquor had spread a warmth through her body, and she snuggled under the thick quilt. Gazing into his dark eyes, she said mischievously, "Would you stay if I asked?"

His breath caressed her face. "Eagerly." He pressed his lips to the erotic pulse at her throat and his hand slid under the cover and closed over the warm mound of her breast. The silk nightdress was no covering at all, and the heat of his flesh on hers made her tremble.

"*Are* you asking me?" he whispered as his lips captured an earlobe and nibbled it tenderly.

For a moment Maura felt a warmth that did not come from the brandy. She stroked his cheek and sideburns, holding his face close as her pulse quickened. At last she expelled a fluttering breath.

She said softly, "I would not ask that." Did she imagine it or did the tension ease from his shoulders?

He raised his head and regarded her with a loving look. "You're sure? Giraud can always find another player." But his eyes betrayed the lie. His thoughts were distracted and he spoke mechanically, despite the delicate tracing of his fingers at her breast.

Maura smiled and pushed him away gently. "Enjoy your game. I'll be here when it's done."

"Mmmmm." He nuzzled her neck and kissed her a dozen times as though he couldn't bear to leave the sweetness of her flesh. "I'll play only a hand or two and pray that I can keep my mind on the cards. You are a tempting distraction to my concentration." He brushed her lips, then sighed and claimed them in a full and satisfying kiss. "I will return soon—perhaps you'll be awake?" He looked hopeful.

Yet Maura felt his mind was already elsewhere. She nodded and he stood and straightened his coat. Glancing into a mirror, he adjusted his cravat and smoothed his dark hair. With a smile and a kiss blown from his fingertips, he lowered the lamps and went out.

Beau poured whiskey without taking his eyes from Paul Giraud. The others had folded, and only he and Giraud were still in. Giraud gave him a bored look from under hooded eyes as he rolled a Ruy Lopez. Giraud was as skilled at five-card stud as he was at breathing, and he was giving Beau a run for his money.

The game was honest, which surprised Beau. He'd expected a few tricks from Giraud, but the gambler had dealt straight and played his cards well. And the cards had fallen for him. After several hours, Beau had lost nearly two hundred dollars, which he was determined to win back. The other players were no competition or challenge. Occasionally Giraud tossed in a hand with a shrug, letting one of them take a small pot. Just enough to keep them interested and willing to play, Beau suspected. He'd watched every flick of Giraud's wrist, every finger movement, to be sure none strayed to the bottom of the deck. Nothing, he was sure of it! Giraud was giving no cause for suspicion, despite the growing stack of coins and notes before him.

But now the game had settled into a match of wits between the two of them. It was as if Giraud were testing him. Had he been wrong about the gambler not recognizing his name? Was he sizing Beau up, waiting for him to make a foolish move?

Beau fingered Maura's lace handkerchief in his pocket. *Come on, Lady Luck, don't abandon me now.* He had a pair of Queens back to back on the first up-card, and he'd turned a nine and a four on the next two. Giraud had two tens and an ace showing. He'd raised before drawing his second card, but Beau couldn't be sure he wasn't bluffing. It could be a move designed to make Beau throw caution to the wind. Giraud was a master bluffer. For the most part, Beau had been unable to anticipate his moves.

Beau's expression didn't flicker as the fifth card was turned. A Lady smiled at him . . . three Queens. *Sweet Lady, sweet Lady Luck!* Giraud turned himself an ace. Beau's confidence wavered for a moment, then he dropped ten dollars in the pot. Giraud puffed a halo of smoke, matched the ten and added another. Beau smiled lazily as he saw the bet and raised again.

Giraud studied Beau through the thin veil of smoke. The

barbershop was hushed, except for the muted grinding and splashing of the paddlewheels and the hiss of steam.

"Call."

Beau turned up his third Queen and took the pot with a grin. It was a good sign, he thought. He was on the way back.

One of the players pushed his chair from the table. "I'm out."

Giraud spared the man a glance as the dealer looked around the table. "Everyone else in, gentlemen?"

The man at Beau's left pulled out a turnip watch and flicked it open. "It's nearly three in the morning and I have a lady waiting." He winked as he rose and slipped his arms into his coat. "Until tomorrow night?" Several heads nodded.

"Anyone else?" the dealer asked.

When no one answered, he began to deal.

She was curled on her side, with her russet hair fanning over the pillow and her dark lashes brushing her cheeks like the kiss of dawn. Beau eased the door shut quietly and stood staring at her. The sound of the paddlewheels was loud in the morning stillness, and Maura's sleeping form was a soothing balm to his anger.

Giraud had bested every hand he held for the last several hours. Cleaned him out! Damn, he was sure now that the gambler had done it deliberately and with a deftness that came from years of practice. Beau hadn't been able to detect a single false move when Giraud dealt, not one! Yet he knew the gambler had cheated him as surely as he was standing there with an empty wallet. What the hell had happened? Several times he had called for new cards, but without the foresight to bribe the bartender to use his privately marked deck, and a new deck had not changed his luck. Giraud had bested him there as well. And the man had a superior system for marking the cards—Beau hadn't been able to detect a single spot or pinpoint!

He sank to a chair and pulled off his boots, lowering them gently to the floor. Quickly he disrobed and tossed his things over the chair. His wallet slipped from his pocket, and he picked it up and tossed it onto the heap. Silently he cursed Paul Giraud again. There'd be another game before the journey was done . . . and next time the outcome would be different! No man would get the better of him!

With a glance and a smile at the slumbering Maura, he slid into the bed and snuggled close to her sleep-warm body. She stirred drowsily as he stroked the gentle, sweet curves of her breast and hip. His fingers found the edge of the gown and pushed it aside.

Maura stretched with lazy, feline grace as she emerged from the heavy, engulfing sleep. The whispering touch seemed like part of a dream at first, then slowly she realized that she was in Beau's arms and the cabin was drenched in sunlight.

"What time is it?" she murmured sleepily. She tried to move, but Beau's gentle pressure held her under his caresses.

He pressed his face to her warm bosom and murmured, "Six . . . You're as warm as a kitten." His tongue teased her breast and drew the soft peak between his lips to lavish favor on it. Moaning softly, Maura pressed his head between her hands, feeling the silkiness of his hair and the heat of his breath on her flesh. The nipple grew turgid, and she strained toward him, urging his head closer. A core of heat in her belly rippled outward in quivering waves.

Dimly, her mind coped with the realization that Beau had been gone all night, but it seemed unimportant as expectation began to swell. Beau pressed his body along hers and slowly, masterfully closed his lips over hers. She felt his muscles grow taut as the kiss became a hungry demand.

She moved against him impatiently, but his answer was to explore her teeth and lips with his wild tongue, so that her passion surged unbearably. Then he was kissing her body again, blazing a scorching trail down its warmth, pausing at the taut muscles of her belly, then moving with maddening, slow deliberation to the satiny smoothness of her thighs. She writhed and her breasts heaved with a shuddering sigh as she begged him to end her torment. Her fingers raked his lean flesh and tried to pull him onto her so she could feel the hard, savage fulfillment of his entry. It seemed an eternity before he at last moved over her. Her legs, heavy with an aching numbness, parted like leaden weights to welcome him. Then he was entering her, and numbness and heat fused. The unbearable tension became a

424

fiery torment that swirled her deeper and deeper into its pit. Her body arched and begged for release as her legs slid around his smooth hips. She met his thrusts with eager, demanding response, and the pounding of her heart echoed in her ears as she moaned with frenzy. His eyes were dark unfathomable pools as he gazed at her. His lips drew tightly back, exposing his teeth and the tip of his tongue trapped between them. Maura beseeched him to end the exquisite torment. Her words keened into a pagan cry of pleasure as he plunged into her with an exploding, quenching fire. Huge, undulating shock waves rocked her and drew her to the heights of ecstasy before gently and slowly washing her onto the shore. Her breath came in fluttering gasps until at last her body was still.

Beau lay beside her, his arm thrown across her breast as though to claim her forever. Maura savored the aftermath of her pleasure. She was amazed at how completely she had given herself to Beau and how wonderful their coming together had been. It was as though she had no resistance, no desire to examine her innermost thoughts when he could please her so expertly. He drove away logic, wondering and doubt.

A beam of sunlight crept across the bed as the boat navigated a bend in the winding river. Maura felt warmth on her face and opened her eyes slowly to stare at the rich wood paneling of the ceiling. Beside her, Beau's breathing fell to a smooth, regular pattern as he drifted into sleep. She looked down at his face pressed against her breast. His jaw was relaxed and his lips parted so his breath made them tremble slightly. The long sideburns were dark etchings against his pale, smooth skin to relieve the hard line of his jaw.

He'd gambled all night, despite his promise to play only a hand or two. How easily he made and broke promises. His word was given without hesitation and without intent to deceive—at least she wanted to think that. He seemed always to say what others wanted to hear or what would put them at ease. He told pretty lies that flattered and cajoled, and he told outrageous lies to avoid tense moments or awkward scenes. The charm that had attracted her so strongly was largely sham, she realized, but he still had the

425

power to claim what he wanted with little or no resistance from her.

She sighed softly and lifted his arm so she could slide out of bed. Beau did not stir. She gazed down at him with a wondering expression. As much as he amazed her, she was even more amazed at her own willingness to be swept along in the current of persuasion. She'd told him that he was always at hand to rescue her. Was that true? She would have found a way out of her dilemmas through her own resourcefulness, as she had always done before. But his beguiling manner made it easy—and pleasant—to leave the decisions to him and to share his infectious good humor. Perhaps it was because the rest of her life was marked by conflict and struggle that Beau seemed an oasis of calm.

She smiled at the thought. Everything Beau did was attended with excitement and an element of peril! His life was far from placid. Still, he made light of trouble and danger, shrugging them off and dismissing them as though they never existed. He was not one to look back. Perhaps he was wise.

She crossed to where his clothes lay in a heap and straightened them. His wallet was on top of his shirt, and she started to slip it back into his pocket, then frowned and opened the flat leather pouch. The sheaf of bills he'd shown her yesterday was gone. A single twenty-dollar banknote remained. She turned to stare at him.

Had he lost everything at cards?

CHAPTER TWENTY-FOUR

"Why the hell are we putting in to shore?" Braxton demanded churlishly. He was exasperated and miserably cold. The sternwheeler *Pawnee* might be the fastest boat on the river but it was far from comfortable; the night had seemed endless. His temper was frayed and weariness weighted his eyes. He huddled against the rail and tucked his hands under his armpits to warm them. The boat was nothing more than a river tramp, with few accommodations for sleeping.

Elger Sharp was both captain and pilot, and he was not in the habit of taking passengers on his journeys up and down the river. Every inch of space was given over to cargo that would bring him hard cash for speedy delivery.

Sharp gave him a sardonic look. "Ain't no boiler made can run without wood in the firebox. We's just about down to kindlin'." He swiveled his head and spat, mindless of where the tobacco juice splattered. "If'n you think you can do better, find yourself 'nother boat, mister. Ain't nothin' to me."

Braxton clenched his teeth and tried to control his temper. He'd paid cash in advance to hire Sharp to overtake the *Ohio Queen*. He'd disliked the surly boatman from the outset. Sharp asked an outrageous price for his services, saying arrogantly that only a man running or chasing had need of the fastest boat on the river, and a man running or chasing couldn't be too choosy about what he paid. Take it or leave it. Braxton had struck the bargain with misgivings.

The *Pawnee*'s superstructure had been leveled except for a small cabin over the engine room and boilers, with a dwarfed pilothouse atop it. Her stripped decks accommodated an astonishing amount of cargo. Sharp transported produce, grain, machinery and livestock between Pittsburgh and Cairo, promising delivery in a third less time than any of the larger boats. The small sternwheeler had two boilers and an engine with eighteen cylinders and a nine-foot stroke. It was crewed by four firemen, two engineers, and a few deckhands who doubled as roustabouts or anything else that was needed. One was a lumbering, mute giant named Dobie, who had a bald head and the strength of a bull. Braxton mistook him for an idiot until he saw the man's quick comprehension and response to any order Sharp gave. Sharp even entrusted the wheel to him when he wanted a respite. Dobie hunched over the wheel like a hulking bear but kept the boat on course by an inborn instinct that went beyond intelligence. Still, Braxton avoided Dobie assiduously and was uncomfortable under his staring scrutiny.

Braxton peered out at the misty shore. The sky had lightened, but dawn had not yet broken the gray cold. Mist hung in wispy tendrils that swirled and settled like vagrant ghosts as Sharp brought the boat around and nosed it to shore. Her shallow prow slid up the muddy bank, and Dobie leaped ashore with a line. A moment later the *Pawnee* was moored, and the bald giant was running toward the woodpile before the sleepy yard owner roused himself and emerged from his shack. He recognized Sharp and waved laconically as he stretched and scratched his buttocks. He shouted and kicked at a pile of rags near the door. A lanky Negro unfolded himself from a tangle of sacks and went to help Dobie. Sharp climbed down from the pilothouse. Pausing to pick up a box, he jumped ashore and gave it to the yard owner. The two disappeared inside the shack.

Braxton cursed and paced the crowded deck, impatient to be underway but helpless in the face of Sharp's arrogant authority. It was no good railing at the man. He was mean enough to delay the journey out of spite. Still, they had covered a good number of miles already. Maybe before he had to spend another night on this scow they'd sight the *Ohio Queen.* If he didn't have to go past Cincinnati, he'd have Maura to warm his bed tomorrow. He felt the quick, stirring desire in his loins. He'd waited a very long time for that little bitch, and he had every intention of making her pay dearly for the trouble she'd caused him.

428

Damn it, what the hell was Sharp doing? The loading was finished and the deckhands were sitting on the gangplank sharing a companionable smoke. Steam hissed raucously from the vents, and the river seemed unnaturally still without the churning of the paddlewheel.

Where the hell was Sharp?

Maura spent the morning sitting in a deck chair, staring at the river and feeling that her life was slipping past as surely as the scenery beyond the rail. Several people she'd met the evening before paused to pass a bit of time and chat idly. When they asked about Beau, Maura said he was occupied with business. Afterward, she wondered why she had lied.

Beau wakened in midafternoon and joined her in the salon. Even though lunch had already been cleared, a waiter brought him thick slices of roast beef on hot bread, fresh from the oven. Beau ordered whiskey and downed a glass before drinking several cups of steaming coffee. "Just to get my eyes open to the new day," he told Maura with a careless grin.

When he finished they went on deck where people were gathering at the forward rail. Beau craned to see what was causing the ripple of excitement. Another riverboat, the *Robert Welsh*, had drawn abreast of the *Ohio Queen*, and passengers were shouting and waving back and forth from one boat to the other. The *Queen*'s bell rang sharply and everyone turned to see Captain Dance on the texas deck. He cupped his hands and shouted across the water.

"You're a fool and an idiot, Captain Rice! The *Queen* can beat that garbage scow of yours with only one boiler fired!"

There was a roar of protest from the other steamer, and laughter rippled from the growing crowd on the *Ohio Queen*'s decks.

"Ye've more mouth than brains, Cap'n Dance, and I've fifty dollars that says we'll pull into the levee at Ashland before your smoke comes in sight!"

Captain Dance gave a mighty roar, then pulled off his cap and slapped it against his thigh. His hair fell across his face like a black mane. On all decks, crewmen began to scurry about in anticipation of a race, ready to fall in with the Captain's orders in an instant. Races were a relief to the monotonous daily routine, and the rivalry between the *Ohio Queen* and the packet *Robert Welsh* was of long standing. Every time the two boats met, one captain was sure to challenge the other. Captain Dance and Mr. Fenison, the pilot, were still smarting over the last defeat their rival had dealt them, and they itched to even the score.

Beau shaded his eyes and glanced toward the texas deck. Captain Dance's face was flushed as he waved his arms excitedly. "If it's a race you want, you scroungy muskrat, you've got it! Five minutes at the sound of my horn, Rice, and we'll be waiting at the levee before you round the bend at Catlettsburg!"

A roaring cheer went up on both boats, and passengers crowded for places at the rail where they could watch. Captain Dance ran down to the hurricane deck and pealed the *Ohio Queen*'s bell. The crew went into a flurry of action. Deckhands passed the wood to the stokers, and every roustabout was put to the woodpiles to heave fuel. The pilot eyed the interval between the two boats and gauged the river ahead, noting the path of the current and the changing patterns of the river's surface.

Men at the rail began to shout bets to those aboard the *Welsh*.

"The *Queen* will win by half an hour!"

"The devil it will! You'll swallow our whitewater all the way! Ten dollars!"

"Done!"

"Five on the *Welsh*!"

"Taken—who else is fool enough to bet against the *Ohio Queen*?"

For a moment bedlam erupted. Banknotes were flourished; men hastily conferred on who would hold the bets. Giraud stepped forward and offered his services as bookmaker, grinning around as men pressed money on him and shouted their wagers. Giraud marked papers with a stubby pencil.

Beau turned to a mustached man in a high silk hat and gray coat. "What are the odds?"

"The *Welsh* won the last match but the *Queen* took four in a row before that. The *Queen* makes her best speed when drawing five and a half feet forward and five feet aft. I'd say she's balanced near perfectly, if we can convince the passengers not to weight the larboard rail."

"Leave the women and children to gawk here," Giraud said, slapping the stack of banknotes sharply on his palm. "Men, protect your bets by balancing the starboard!" He glanced at Beau impassively. "Are you wagering, Fontaine?" He knew Beau had left the poker game that morning a loser by four hundred dollars. He'd see the color of his money before taking a bet.

Beau pulled out his wallet and extracted a bill. He handed it to Giraud. "Twenty on the *Ohio Queen*."

Maura stared at Beau as he handed over the money. He was betting his last dollar! What in the world was he thinking of?

Giraud's expression did not alter as he folded the banknote with the rest and looked around. "Gentlemen, last call!" A few others hurried up to place last-minute bets.

Then there were two short blasts of the *Queen*'s whistle. A cry rose in its echo. The two steamboats surged forward from their lazy drifting patterns. The race was underway!

When Maura started toward the rail, Beau took her arm and steered her to the opposite side.

"But we can't see the race from here!" she protested.

"The more evenly balanced the boat is, the faster she rides the water." Even as he spoke, Giraud was urging the men to the opposite railing. Several of the women tagged behind, staring over their shoulders to glimpse the *Welsh*. The *Queen*'s whistle screamed over the tumult and black smoke jetted from the chimneys. A shower of sparks shot upward and a tall column of steam burst from the escape pipes. The *Ohio Queen* moved ahead slowly and another cheer went up. There was an endless stream of jibes and insults called across the water as the passengers good-naturedly rooted for victory. For several minutes, the *Ohio Queen* was almost a full length ahead, then the *Welsh* began to close the gap. Captain Rice clanged his bell and blew a long toot on the whistle as the two came abreast once more.

There was an agonized wail from those at the *Queen*'s rails. Several men yelled up to the captain for more steam. Below on the main deck, the clamor of iron fire doors could be heard intermittently. The roustabouts were chant-

431

ing a rhythm as they fed the logs from woodpile to furnaces. A blanket of black smoke spread across the sky in a wide wake behind the two vessels.

For a while they seemed evenly matched, with neither pilot able to gain an advantage for long. They were on a wide stretch of the river where they could easily steam side by side, but not far ahead there were chutes and bends that barely provided room for one boat. Shifting sandbars would ground an unwary pilot who did not mark his course exactly.

Giraud stood apart from the crowd and lighted a Ruy Lopez, puffing gray smoke as he peered thoughtfully at the pilothouse and the chimneys. Captain Dance was doing his damnedest; he was not a man to take defeat easily. Giraud had sat in many a game with him on previous trips, and he'd ridden many a race as well. When the time came, Dance would go all out to win, that Giraud knew. He smiled and let his gaze move across the crowd. It lingered curiously on Maura. She was a beautiful woman. He couldn't help wondering why she'd taken up with Fontaine. Beau had admitted last night that the story of their marriage was fictitious, a simple matter of convenience so they could share a cabin without gossip. He could figure Fontaine's motives easily enough, but what did Maura Sullivan hope to gain from the alliance? Would she really give Beau a stake as he'd claimed last night when his cash was gone? Or was Fontaine betting money he didn't have? He'd been lucky enough to walk away from the poker table with a few dollars while Giraud's pocket was fatter by several hundred. From here on, the color of Beau's cash was the only thing that would get him into a game.

Maura glanced in Giraud's direction, aware of his scrutiny. His hooded stare met her gaze, then slithered away as another shout went up at the larboard rail. Why was he watching her? The flesh crept at the nape of her neck. She didn't like Giraud even though she had scarcely spoken to him. He reminded her of a snake, cold-eyed and emotionless. She suppressed a shiver and forced a smile when Beau looked at her solicitously.

"Are you cold? There's time to get a wrap from the cabin before we reach the chute—"

She shook her head quickly. "It's the excitement."

He accepted the answer with a relieved smile, then looked back to the race as a new shout went up and several of the ladies gasped in horror. The *Ohio Queen* was hugging the shore at a bend where low willows and beeches dipped to the water's edge. Without warning, a small fishing boat glided from a sheltered cove directly into their path. The pilot saw it and screamed a warning on the whistle. At the rail, half a dozen people shouted and waved their arms. The three fishermen looked around and their mouths opened in surprise and panic. They scrambled to the oars and began to row furiously. The *Queen*'s whistle shrieked a piercing series of notes. A woman close to Maura pulled her child away from the railing and pressed his face into her belly.

Maura's breath caught. There was no way the little boat could escape in time! Below on the main deck, several deckhands ran forward and stood helplessly as the *Ohio Queen*'s prow grazed the stern of the rowboat. It rocked dangerously, and the three shouting and swearing men pulled harder at the oars. The boat swerved away, but not soon enough. The churning water of the paddlewheels caught it and spun it like a top in the powerful eddies. For a moment it was suspended on the crest of a roiling wave, then it pitched sharply and flung the three fishermen into the water.

Maura glanced toward the pilothouse expecting to see the pilot stop the *Queen*, but he was eying the *Welsh* and concentrating on the wheel. Even the passengers had returned their attention to the race, except for a few women who sighed with relief as three heads appeared in the water behind the *Ohio Queen*. The fishermen swam to their overturned boat, swearing and raising their fists in futile, threatening gestures.

Maura felt a rush of anger at the callousness of the men who were far more concerned with winning their bets than with the lives of innocent people. Already a spirit of camaraderie and expectancy had returned, and the fishermen were forgotten. For some reason, the incident depressed her. She would have gone to the cabin, but when she suggested it to Beau, he looked amazed.

"The race is far from over. We'll soon be coming to the cutoff at Hanging Rock. If Fenison can get us through ahead of the *Welsh*, our victory is assured." He slipped an arm through Maura's and patted her hand. "Stay and bring me luck."

Before she could answer, his gaze slipped back to the *Queen*'s opponent which had inched ahead so her paddle-wheels were in a line with the *Queen*'s forward deck.

The man in the silk hat and gray coat hailed the captain. "Throw some pitch onto the fires!"

Giraud puffed his cigar and yelled, "Something to sweeten the pot if we win, Captain?" He glanced around at the men. "Shall we pass the hat, gentlemen, and make it worth the Captain and Mr. Fenison's while to see that the *Ohio Queen* does not lose?"

A chorus of agreement went up. A small, stubby man with a large mustache removed his bowler hat and began to pass it among the crowd. Banknotes and silver dollars rained in. Beau released Maura's arm and accepted the hat when it came to him. With a show of high spirits, he pressed it on the others near him.

"Let's give Mr. Fenison all the encouragement we can, gentlemen . . . Ah, excellent, with another round, he'll be able to buy the *Robert Welsh* for firewood when the race is over."

Men pushed forward eagerly to drop their offerings into the hat. If anyone else noticed that Beau had not contributed, Maura saw no sign of it.

Beau glanced around the assemblage. "Last chance, gentlemen—show the pilot your faith in him! Come, come—didn't each of you book passage on the *Ohio Queen* because of her fine reputation as the fastest boat on the river? A reputation worth keeping, eh?"

There was good-natured laughter and a few more silver dollars clinked into the bowler. With a huge grin, Beau passed it to Giraud. Giraud counted it quickly, then called up to the pilothouse. "Nearly two hundred dollars, Captain! You'll retire a rich man tonight if we're first in Ashland!"

Captain Dance had a hurried conference with the pilot, striking up a bargain of their own. Then he rang the ship's bell sharply to signify their acceptance. Steam burst from the escape pipes, and a roiling column of black smoke spilled from the chimneys as the pilot yelled into the speaking tube. In the salon, the band struck up a lively rendition of "Hail Columbia," accompanied by a new wave of shouts and cheers.

Ahead, the river became serpentine for several miles. Fenison followed the fast water and spun the wheel to make a crossing. The *Queen* veered toward the far bank. On her larboard, the *Welsh* was forced to follow suit. If the *Welsh*'s pilot had acted a moment sooner he would have gained advantage, but the delay cost him dearly. The *Queen* nosed into the chute almost a full length ahead. The roar that went up from the *Queen*'s passengers brought a wave and a smile from Captain Dance.

The fast current of the chute carried the two steamboats along like leaves in a spring freshet. The bank loomed close enough to touch, and drooping willow branches scraped the upper deck rails. On shore, a dog took chase, yapping furiously as though warning the intruder that it had ventured into forbidden territory. On a small landing, three children danced in delight at the sudden excitement.

The *Ohio Queen* emerged onto the flat expanse of river below the chute, a length and a half ahead of the *Welsh*. Fenison shouted new orders to the engineer and the chief stoker. Several deckhands came dashing from the housing near the fireboxes and began to run out one of the long gangplanks. As soon as it was suspended over the water, one of the men crawled out onto it and lay on his belly, eyes shielded and his head hanging over to watch for treacherous sawyers. The others ranged themselves at vantage points along the high deck.

One waved and shouted, "Sawyer on the larboard bow!"

The pilot had already seen the dimpled surface of the water and the boat turned away from the danger.

The passengers on the hurricane deck began to mill about. Some returned to the lounge where the bar was doing an active business, and the band continued sprightly music that portended victory. But the race was not over yet.

Beau stayed at the rail to watch the *Queen*'s progress. Behind them, the chimneys of the *Welsh* showered sparks against a puffy white cloud. Giraud strolled over, smiling and touching his hat to Maura.

"Captain Dance and Mr. Fenison are assured of winning their prize," Beau said complacently.

Giraud looked amused. "I never count my winnings until I've raked in the pot. There's a lot of water between here and Ashland."

"If we take the channel at Hanging Rock, there's no way the *Welsh* can close the gap."

Giraud regarded him with a discerning look. "I think we've convinced them it's worth the risk. Barring any accident, I calculate we'll touch the levee within the hour—well ahead of the *Welsh*, of course."

Beau pulled out his gold-encased watch and flicked it open. "Easily," he declared. "I'd be willing to wager it will be no more than three when we put in."

Giraud looked amused. "Three-ten would be closer."

"Twenty dollars says otherwise," Beau said evenly.

Maura knew he did not have a dollar in his pocket and she wondered what recklessness made him push the issue. Giraud extended a hand and nodded. They shook, and with another half-smile at Maura, Giraud walked away.

"Money seems to have little meaning to you," Maura said in a bantering tone that held an undercurrent of annoyance.

Beau shrugged impassively. "The *Ohio Queen* is a certain victor. If I lose the private bet with Giraud, I can pay him out of my winnings on the other."

"Are you always so sure of winning?"

He grinned and placed a quick kiss on her cheek. "Only when I have the luck of the leprechauns at my side. Now, would you like something hot to drink or shall we stay here and see the finish of the race? There's a place at the forward rail that will afford a view almost as good as the pilot's." He looked as eager as a child at a picnic.

She recognized the fruitlessness of anger. She let him lead her to the space at the rail which had opened as a family returned to the lounge. Though many of the passengers seemed to think the race won, the pilot was keeping a wary eye on the *Welsh*. From time to time it would gain a little ground, but never enough to make up its loss. The passengers on her decks had fallen silent except for random shouts. Captain Rice paced the *Welsh*'s hurricane deck like an angry cock, his head thrust forward and his chin jutting.

436

Beau pointed across the water to direct Maura's glance to a long, slanting line on the surface. "A bluff reef," he said. "A solid sandbar below the water, almost straight up and down. If we were to hit it, the bar would tear the bottom out of the boat."

"But we're heading directly for it!" Maura exclaimed in astonishment.

Beau grinned. "But we won't hit it. A river pilot can read the water as well as I can the spots on a deck of cards. Watch—there where the line fringes out at the upper end and begins to fade away. That's the head, where the water is deepest. He'll cross over there." He glanced toward the boat behind. "And the *Welsh* will be forced to go around or follow us at a safe distance. We'll easily gain several lengths."

Maura watched the *Queen* follow the line of the reef until it reached the head. In the pilothouse, Fenison seized the wheel and spun it around until it was hard down and held it. For a moment the boat hesitated, then surged to starboard, across the reef, sending a long, angry ridge of water foaming away from the bow. How magnificently the boat responded to the pilot's commands! For the first time, Maura experienced the awe and excitement that James had whenever he spoke of the river. No wonder it had lured him like a siren of the deep. Maura lifted her face to the breeze as the engine bells jingled and the engines answered the pilot's demand for full speed ahead. The escape pipes shot white columns of steam aloft.

Beau said, "Damn! I should have bet fifty! We'll touch in at the levee before three!" He slapped his fist into his palm. "That's Hanging Rock ahead. When Fenison takes the channel, there's no way the *Welsh* can come abreast again!"

Several other men shared Beau's opinion. From various quarters on the deck, they began to call up to the pilothouse. "Take the channel!"

With a sudden burst of steam, the *Welsh* labored around the reef and began to creep up on the *Queen*. She was heading for the channel, trying to nose in before Fenison could reach it. She had the advantage of the offshore current and a more direct line to the mouth of the channel. Fenison barked furious orders, demanding every pound of pressure the engines could muster. Wood slammed into the fireboxes and two deckhands ran from the galley with buckets of pork fat and lard. The fires sizzled and sputtered as the grease was tossed on. The acrid smell of burning fat billowed, and the *Queen* surged ahead once more and nosed into the narrow channel a whisker ahead of the other boat. Cursing, the pilot of the *Welsh* held his wheel over sharply and steered around the point rather than taste the *Queen*'s wake.

Another tumultuous cheer arose from the *Ohio Queen*. People ran from the salon to see what was happening, and there was general merriment on all sides. A sailor on the gangplank almost toppled into the calm water of the channel when he tried to do a little dance of celebration. A clatter from Fenison's bell sent him back to his perch. The *Welsh* was already out of sight behind the massive rock formation jutting above rich, autumn-touched elms and cottonwoods.

When Beau turned, Maura saw the elation in his eyes. "We've won handsomely! There's no way the *Welsh* can catch up now! We'll be miles ahead as we come out of the channel. Let's join the celebration in the salon. This occasions a drink!"

The *Ohio Queen* came in sight of Cincinnati as the sun vanished behind the horizon in a galaxy of crimson and mauve clouds. Maura stood by the rail watching passengers disembark. Beau had joined the men in the salon after the landing at Ashland to renew the victory celebration. It was still going on. Maura had declined to join him and spent the rest of the afternoon on deck alone. Her amazement at Beau's reckless wagering had not diminished, and it left her with a strange uneasiness. His life seemed to be centered on chance, yet he managed to live extravagantly. He rarely spoke of the investment business he professed to be in, nor had she ever known him to devote time to it. Still, she could not fault his willingness to come to her aid when she needed it most.

The waterfront was ablaze with lights. Half a dozen steamers were tied up at the public landing, which seemed a popular place for sightseers as well as those engaged in trade. Fashionably dressed ladies and gentlemen strolled around the stalls which had been set up under canvas awnings. There were lights in the windows of most of the warehouses and offices fronting the levee. One square brick building had wide doors, with wooden ramps and rails. Next to it, a pen was filled with squealing, snuffling hogs. Maura recognized the sickly-sweet stench of a slaughterhouse. As she watched, several wagons lumbered toward the *Ohio Queen*, and roustabouts fell to unloading. The brawny Negroes hefted the heavy barrels of salt pork and ran up the gangplank, accompanied by a steady stream of profanity and exhortations from the mate.

Maura gazed at the skyline of the city. She was surprised by its size, though she had read various accounts of its boom after the completion of the Miami Canal north to Toledo. Its location midway between Pittsburgh and Cairo made it a crossroads of trade. She could see a dozen church spires and smokestacks of numerous factories outlined against the growing darkness. The dark walls and towers of Fort Washington were dwarfed by multistoried buildings that imposed themselves on the waterfront.

Below the gangplank, two deckhands wrestled with a mound of luggage. A woman's voice called sharply to them to mind that nothing was dropped. Maura looked down and recognized Ellie Wyatt disembarking. She was dressed in a wine-colored gown with tippets of fur adorning the skirt, and a short wool cape was thrown over her shoulders. Her hat, no bigger than a sparrow with wings spread, perched in a mass of dark curls, and she carried a frilly parasol which she tapped impatiently as she waited for her baggage to be taken ashore. Maura glanced around for Paul Giraud, but he was not there. Maura had seen little of Ellie Wyatt since the departure from Pittsburgh, except at the Captain's party where she had basked in the attention of several men who were traveling alone. Even though she had come aboard with Giraud, Maura was not surprised to see another man join her now and take her arm as they went down the gangplank. Maura had surmised she was a prostitute; apparently Giraud no longer found her interesting and Ellie was seeking business elsewhere.

The Captain had informed the passengers that the *Ohio Queen* would lay over in Cincinnati for several hours. The exchange of cargo would take that long, and an important dignitary from Toledo who was coming aboard had apparently been delayed en route; the *Queen* would await his arrival.

Maura suggested to Beau that they go ashore and walk, but his mind was already on a poker game that had been arranged immediately after dinner. Now as she watched the activity on the levee, Maura felt a surging impatience at having to stand about idle. All around her, shouts and laughter were interspersed with the sounds of loading. Nets swung from the forward derricks, lifting crates. A white-haired Negro, his thin legs in ragged pants, his feet bare, sat atop a cotton bale playing a reedy harmonica that emitted a lively tune that inspired foot-tapping. Couples paused at a small pushcart where a vendor was selling roasted chestnuts, and Maura was certain she heard calliope music.

Impulsively, she retreated from the rail and went down the main stairs and then the gangplank with a small knot of departing passengers. She was unaccustomed to the monotony and confinement of an area as small as the boat, and she longed for diversion and a sense of freedom. She wandered along the levee, pausing to look at the various wares displayed in stalls. She had no money to buy anything, and there was nothing she wanted, but she enjoyed the eager pitches of the vendors and their haggling. Some of them were mere children. About a hundred yards from the *Ohio Queen*'s mooring, a bonfire had been built and boxes were piled to form a platform near it. A man stepped up and pulled off his cap, waving it and shouting for attention. A few people paused to gaze curiously at him, then went on. The man was wild-eyed, with spiky yellow hair that stood out like horns from his head and a pale emaciated face with a straggly beard. He began to shout at the crowd that gathered. His arms waved and he pounded his fist or gestured sweepingly. An itinerant preacher. Maura had heard others in New York. The preacher's voice boomed and swelled as he exhorted people to abandon their sinful ways. He shouted a long list of transgressions that made several ladies move away with gasps and averted eyes. A group of children began to jeer and throw pebbles, and the preacher thrust a condemning finger in their direction and thun-

440

dered a promise that God would bring them to their knees. It sent the lads scurrying into the darkness.

Maura realized that the calliope music was coming from a showboat. It was painted gaudy yellow and red. Lanterns strung along the decks and masts made the boat as bright as day. People crowded up the gangplank under a banner that formed an arch: TONIGHT! THE LOVERS' LAMENT!! *Starring the internationally renowned Miss Etta Mays!!*

Sighing, Maura turned back toward the *Ohio Queen*. The merriment left her depressed, and thoughts of Duggan and the boatyard crowded her mind. Was she twice the fool to flee and abandon everything she'd struggled to gain? Despite the threat of the union, Duggan had brought the floundering Sullivan Boatyard to stable ground. But she would never forgive his deceit or his pretense of love. She had exposed her vulnerable heart, and he had wounded it cruelly.

Tears stung her eyes and she dug in her sleeve for a handkerchief. A woman passing by glanced at her curiously, and Maura stepped into the shadows of a building to hide her distress. For an instant, anger overwhelmed her, and she pressed her face to the lacy handkerchief. She was *not* defeated! She would show Duggan that she could win! There was a small scuffle of sound behind her, and she quickly dabbed her eyes. She was making a spectacle of herself in public. Resolutely, she lifted her head and straightened her shoulders.

A dark figure stepped toward her and she stifled a scream.

CHAPTER TWENTY-FIVE

Braxton watched the *Ohio Queen* ease between two other boats at the levee. He had been waiting several hours, not daring to leave the waterfront for fear his quarry would arrive and elude him if he so much as blinked. When the big boat finally nudged the shore and her lines were made fast, Braxton riveted his gaze on the gangplank. He didn't expect Maura to disembark; as soon as the activity subsided, he would board the boat and search her out. He fingered the bottle of chloroform in his pocket. He'd take no chances with her screaming to attract attention.

He'd considered the idea of bringing the boatman, Sharp, to help with the abduction, but his dislike for the man overrode the possible convenience of having him along. Besides, it was better to have Sharp wait ten miles upriver so the eastward journey could be underway as soon as he had Maura aboard. He had a carriage waiting, and the driver had been handsomely paid to refuse other fares. Several miles out in the country, he had even found a judge, a seedy man with the smell of whiskey on his breath and wearing a frayed, shiny black suit and a soiled collar. For the five-dollar gold piece Braxton promised him, the man would have married his own sister to the Devil himself.

Braxton started when he saw Maura at the rail of the *Ohio Queen.* It might be easier than he imagined. And a few minutes later when she disembarked, he could not believe his good luck. He sidled close to the dim warehouses, keeping her in sight as she strolled along the levee. Chuckling, he quickened his step when she ventured into the shadowy recess of a darkened doorway. He ducked out of sight as a passing couple glanced toward Maura. As soon as they were gone, he pulled the small brown bottle from his pocket, uncorked it, and soaked his handkerchief with the volatile liquid that made his palm icy. Then, with a quick movement, he closed in on Maura.

In the instant before he clamped the cloth over her face, he saw recognition and terror in her eyes. She fought like a wildcat, kicking and twisting in his arms, so he had to force her head back against his chest. Her gray eyes were filled with unrestrained hatred. Desperately she summoned every ounce of strength and almost jerked free, but he gripped her arm tightly. He could feel the bone under the soft flesh. His other hand was a molded clamp over her nose and mouth. She retched . . . her eyes glazed . . . finally she slumped into unconsciousness. With heaving breath, Braxton dragged her deeper into the shadows of the alley to the street where he'd left the carriage.

Her head ached with a throbbing pain that caused the gray fog that enclosed her to swirl menacingly. Her mouth tasted like an oily rag and her tongue was a thick mat. Maura could not move. There was something she should recall, but the effort was too tiring. She concentrated on breathing, which seemed a monumental task. Dull sounds penetrated the haze. Gradually she recognized the familiar motion of a carriage. She was slumped against a hard cushion, her face pressed into the leather. Each jolt threatened to explode her head with pain and she opened her eyes slowly. Braxton's profile was etched, black on black, against the window. Memory returned, and she almost bolted up. The wave of nausea and dizziness sent her into the soft fog again.

She was in a speeding carriage with Braxton, traveling through the night. How long had she been unconscious? For a moment, she could hardly breathe. Rage flooded her and she wanted to strike out at her hateful stepbrother, but she quickly realized he would be able to overpower her without difficulty. He possessed the brute strength to subdue her physically. She forced herself to breathe in a steady, shallow pattern as she tried to think. Her only hope was to outwit him.

God! how she hated him! She had no illusions about his intent. He was acting under orders from Pelham, orders that would bind her to the Turks helplessly and forever. Her chances of getting to James would end abruptly.

How had they found her? She hadn't been followed from the boatyard, she was sure. Both Pelham and Braxton had been busy with the battle between their hired thugs and Duggan's men. But if she hadn't been followed, how—?!

She pushed the question aside impatiently. Nothing mattered except that she was here and she had to get away. She opened her eyes cautiously.

The curtains of the carriage were pulled shut, but Braxton lifted a corner and was peering out. A strip of moonlight illuminated his face and made his mustache a dark slash across his mouth. Nausea rose in Maura's throat. He was evil personified. She wanted to lash out at him with every ounce of strength and hatred she had, but she knew it would do her no good. Not now . . .

Think, Maura, think!

She peered about the dim interior of the carriage without moving her head. It was better if Braxton did not know she was conscious. If she could reach the door handle— No, on foot in the darkness, she wouldn't have a chance. She had no idea if they were still near the city, or if they were racing across the countryside. She tried to outguess Braxton's devious mind. Speed would be paramount . . . he would have plans to get her onto a boat to head back to Pittsburgh. He might even have one waiting.

She listened to the sounds of the wheels. Occasionally there was a spit of gravel or the sharp grate of the metal tires on rock. A road that was not too well traveled, she guessed, since no other carriages and horses thundered by. Outside, only the pale moonlight relieved the darkness. Country, then. But where?

She eased her fingers to relieve her stiff muscles. Her hands were not tied, thank heaven for that. Apparently Braxton did not expect her to waken and cause trouble. Were they close to their destination? She strained to hear sounds from the river, but there was only the clatter of wheels and the steady pounding of the horses' hooves. The carriage swerved as the driver took a curve without slowing. Maura almost grabbed the window frame to keep her balance, but stopped herself in time as Braxton turned his gaze toward her. She lay motionless with her face slack and

445

controlling her breathing with supreme effort. When she felt a cool breeze bathe her face, she knew Braxton had drawn back the window curtain. She opened her eyes to glimpse dark trees rushing past outside. The moon danced among branches.

The driver leaned down and shouted something. Braxton jerked the curtain all the way back and poked his head out. He shouted up to the driver and the coach slowed, then bumped off the roadway with a sharp turn that sprawled Maura across the seat. Braxton grabbed her. His touch made her flesh crawl and she bit her lip, forcing herself to submit as he pushed her back into the corner. Her breath choked when his hand lingered intimately at her breast before he moved away.

"Whoa!" The carriage shuddered and came to a halt with a jingle of singletree chains. The horses pawed the ground and snorted nervously. "This be it," the driver growled.

Braxton opened the door and jumped down. He turned to glance at Maura. She was pale and her eyes were still closed, but the effects of the chloroform would be wearing off soon. As long as she could stand—hell, he'd hold her up if necessary. Now if only that drunken sot of a judge hadn't fallen into a stupor. He strode across the littered yard and pounded on the door. There was only a feeble light behind the curtain. Damn. He pounded again.

Maura sat up and peered through the carriage window. She could hear Braxton demanding that someone open a door, but she could see only the corner of a house or shed. She pulled back as the driver's boots scuffed on the box and he climbed down. Cautiously she watched while he walked into the shadows mumbling and cursing softly.

Maura sprang into action. She swung herself out of the coach, lighting on the ground soundlessly. Braxton's back was turned as he continued his demanding summons at the door. The coach was between her and the driver, who was busy relieving himself in the bushes. She had only moments. . . . Finding a footing on the wheel hub, she grasped the edge of the driver's seat and pulled herself up. Her soft slippers made no sound as she clutched the box and scrambled into the seat. The horses shook their heads and snuffled as she groped for the reins where the driver

446

had tied them to the brake handle. She sorted them quickly, then slammed the brake off. She slapped the reins and yanked hard to turn the leaders. Startled, the horses jumped forward. They balked, then swung their heads and clattered into motion. The coach slewed and threatened to tip sideways.

"Hi! Get up there! Get up—yi yi yi!" Maura screamed, slapping the reins.

Braxton spun around and raced for the carriage, his face twisted in fury as he spied Maura on the box. He shouted, but his words were lost in the thundering wheels and hooves. The astonished driver ran from the thicket, shoving his shirt into his pants as he tried to get his suspenders up. He spewed a steady stream of curses and waved his arm frantically in an effort to intercept his team. He fell back helplessly as the carriage gained the road and retraced the route it had taken a few minutes before. In seconds, the horses were in a flat-out run with the carriage flying behind.

The moon disappeared behind the trees and the road became a long, dark tunnel which had no end. Maura could no longer hear the shouts of the two men. The rattle and clatter of the coach and horses filled her ears, and her pulse sang in her temples. They would never catch her now! Even if there were other horses available, she would have a long lead before they could be saddled and ridden in pursuit. She lifted her face to the wind. The memory of Braxton's bewildered look as he realized she had tricked him made her laugh aloud.

She raced the horses as long as she dared. When she finally pulled on the reins, they slowed with mighty tosses of their heads, as though glad to settle to a walk. Maura glanced back, but there was nothing but the velvet darkness. She took a deep breath and shifted on the hard seat. Her chest ached, but she felt an exhilaration that made danger pale. She had escaped, and the road had to lead back to the city and the *Ohio Queen*. A new thought struck her like a blow. Suppose the *Queen* had already left!? How much time had elapsed since she walked down the gangplank? Had she been missed? Beau might be frantic worrying about her.

She set her jaw. If the *Queen* were gone, she would find

447

another boat, even if she had to stow away. She knew with certainty that Braxton's plan had been to get her back to Pittsburgh where she'd be forced to marry him. Pelham was more desperate than she believed, and he would never let control of the Sullivan Company pass from his hands after fighting so hard to get it. For the thousandth time, she rued the day she first heard the name Turk!

She studied the inky forest but there was nothing to indicate her whereabouts. She might be a mile from Cincinnati or fifty. Glancing at the moon, she realized it had not traveled far in its path across the sky—only an hour or two had passed. She wished she could race the horses again, but she knew it would be foolhardy. They were tiring and probably badly in need of water.

The road curved in a wide bend and the trees thinned. Then miraculously, the river was there, shimmering placidly under the silver disk of the moon. In the distance ahead, she saw another glimmer of lights. The city! Her heart leaped as she snapped the reins and clucked encouragingly to the horses.

The *Ohio Queen* was still at her moorings; the loading was finished and deckhands were lashing down the last of the cargo, readying the boat for departure. Maura rushed up the gangplank, oblivious to the surprised glances from the mate and crew at her disheveled appearance. She raced up the main stairs and was trying to slip past the salon when the doors opened and she was trapped in a sudden spill of light. Paul Giraud cocked his head and stared at her, a curious smile on his lips.

"Good evening, Maura. Can I offer you a drink? You look as though you could use one."

She started to refuse when suddenly Beau was there, a whiskey glass in his hand, staring at her as though he were seeing an apparition.

"Good Lord! What happened to you?!"

She drew herself up with a defiant toss of her chin. "I have been out for a leisurely stroll!" Behind him, she could see the card table the two had left. Beau had not even missed her! He'd been too engrossed in his game to wonder where she might be—if he even cared! She tried to push past, but Beau grabbed her arm.

"For God's sake, Maura, what's the matter? You look like you've been in a fight—or worse. I thought you had gone to bed."

She jerked her arm free and faced him furiously. "Go back to your game. Don't let me disturb you!" She whirled and stormed away. As she rounded the corner of the cabins, she heard Giraud's low chuckle.

"The little lady has her dander up about something, Beau. You'd better give her time to cool off before crossing her path, else she'll claw you like a wildcat. Shall we get back to our game?"

A door slammed. Maura sputtered as she fled along the passageway. In the cabin, she collapsed against the door and was unable to stem tears of frustration and rage. Numbly, she staggered to the bed and flung herself across it, beating her fists helplessly. When at last her fury waned, she rolled to stare at the ceiling and a cold numbness penetrated her being. She had been a fool to succumb to Beau's charms, to believe his lies and blind herself to his faults. He was a gambler and a rogue—and he would never be anything more. He was not the tower of strength she had let herself think.

She trembled with a shuddering sigh. She was a blind, weak fool. She'd run to Beau because of her bitter frustration over Duggan's betrayal of her trust. In her misery, she mistook Beau's veneer of charm for strength. And all because her confidence had been eroded by treacherous emotions and an overwhelming sense of loss.

An image of her mother's pallid face surfaced in the pool of conscience. She had castigated her mother for bad judgment and weakness in marrying Pelham. Now, with dreadful clarity, she realized how close she had faltered to the edge of a similar abyss when she sought solace for her wounded pride and rejected love. She had blinded herself to Beau's selfishness because she *wanted* him to be strong. She wanted to lean on him because she'd lost faith in her own inner resources. Because she had lost Duggan.

A tremulous sigh escaped her lips, and she closed her eyes. Tears quivered at her lashes. How easy it was to condemn . . . Never before had she understood a love so deep it could devastate completely. Her mother had shared that binding tie with her father. Their happiness had been

449

in each other so they were one—like the happiness she had shared so briefly with Duggan.

Sniffling, she got up and splashed cold water from the pitcher on her tear-swollen face. It would do no good to weep and bemoan what was done. Thank God she had come to her senses before it was too late. Straightening, she stared at her reflection in the glass and set her jaw.

I am a Sullivan, she told herself proudly. *I have the Sullivan strength and determination. I will not be beaten!*

She crossed to the door to slide the bolt, then she undressed and climbed into bed. Dimly, she heard the throb of the engines and the splash of the wheels as they began to turn. In less than two days she would be in Cairo . . . she fastened her mind on the thought. Nothing else mattered . . . nothing else mattered. . . .

Near dawn, she heard Beau tap on the door and call her name softly. She buried her head in the pillow and did not answer.

Beau was leaning against the rail outside the cabin when Maura emerged for breakfast. Before she could retreat, he pushed a foot into the doorway and forced an entrance. She turned away from him, and he watched her with a scowl.

"Maura, for God's sake, what's wrong? Why did you lock me out?" He shook his head and regarded her as though she were a naughty child playing tricks.

She met his gaze defiantly. "I'm sorry that you were inconvenienced. I should have remembered that the cabin *is* yours. I am only here at your sufferance."

"What the hell are you talking about? You belong here as much as I do. Let's not quarrel, but I find it disconcerting to be locked out in the middle of the night with no idea why." He peered at her, then smiled winningly. "Come on, tell me about it. Obviously I did not do something I should have. Or—"

Her temper exploded and her eyes flashed. "You have done nothing! It is a bit late to concern yourself with my well-being! I have been chloroformed, abducted and almost killed by the man I hate most in this world, and you did not look up from your card game long enough to know I was gone!" The outburst was cathartic, and the words

450

poured from her like the swift flow of a river. Her body trembled and she clenched her fists.

Beau's mouth fell open and his head moved in slow negation, as though he could not believe what he'd heard. "What are you saying?!" He was astonished. He put his hand on her shoulder, and she pulled away as though knifed. His eyes narrowed with a puzzled expression and he shook his head again. "Maura . . ."

She drew a long breath and let it out in a shuddering sigh. "Braxton Turk was in Cincinnati—not by chance, but to find me and take me back to Pittsburgh. He very nearly succeeded." She turned away, drained now that her anger had been released. It would do no good to rail at Beau. She wanted only to be alone.

But Beau would not let the matter drop His astonishment gave way to concern. "He didn't hurt you?" He peered at her solicitously. Kidnapped—no wonder she was furious.

Maura's anger flared momentarily. "It is a little late for your concern! Your gambling has always been more important—" She broke off the tirade, sensing its futility. But the stinging words had found their target.

Beau seemed to retreat though he did not move. His eyes were suddenly hard and cold, pinning her with an arrogant look. "My gambling has kept you quite comfortable these past weeks, or have you forgotten that? Where would you be without the money I've won? Your life in Pittsburgh would have been a little less pleasant, I assure you, although I suppose a woman of your boudoir talents would not have any trouble finding someone to keep her in style. And without my 'tainted' money you would not be en route now to Cairo aboard the finest boat on the river." He glanced around the cabin and gave her an amused smile. "You seem to enjoy the luxuries my gambling is providing—or am I a stopgap until you reach Cairo and have no further need of my generosity?"

A pulse in Maura's temple pounded wickedly and her vision hazed. She lashed out and struck him across the face. The angry red imprint of her hand appeared on his cheek. His hand moved so quickly, she was not aware of it until she felt the pain in her wrist when his fingers closed

451

cruelly. Grinning, he pulled her against his chest, twisting her arm so she could not move away. Maura clenched her teeth to keep from crying out in pain.

"Let me go!" She did not struggle and met his look with brazen courage.

He laughed and bent to kiss her, but she shoved him away savagely. Chuckling, he caught her other arm and pinned her against his chest.

"You are the most desirable woman I have ever known, and I do not intend to let you go." He captured her mouth in a flaming kiss. His tongue probed and caught her by surprise, thrusting hard and demanding a passionate response.

Maura recovered her wits and, with unexpected ferocity, clamped her teeth on his questing tongue. At the same time, she raised a foot and kicked his ankle with a short vicious jab. The double attack startled him and he yelped with pain as he let go. Maura flung herself toward the door, but he was too quick. His fingers clawed into her shoulder and spun her back into the room. She stumbled and fell across the rumpled bed. He lunged at her as she rolled over and tried to get to her feet. Once more he was faster. His strong arms trapped her against the bedcovers and he rolled on top of her. His face over hers was a mask of taunting lust.

"You fight spiritedly, but it only stimulates my desire—" He planted an arm across her shoulders to free one hand so he could tear open the bodice of her gown and expose her naked flesh to his greedy eyes. He licked his lips sensuously as his gaze went to the creamy mounds of flesh. His breath quickened.

Maura felt the hard imprint of his engorged sex organ against her thighs. She struggled, twisting and trying to throw him off balance, but it was no use. Beau's mouth pushed to her breast and his tongue teased the nipple expertly. Maura steeled herself against the tingling desire. She would not submit—she would never let him touch her again!

She shuddered as he tore away her skirt and somehow managed to loosen his trousers without releasing her. Then he was forcing a knee between her thighs, pressing his swollen maleness into the soft haven of her flesh. She felt

452

the sharp pain of his entry, then the hot moist response of her betraying flesh. His arm still pinned her, almost cutting off her breath. His eyes were defiant and ablaze with lust. He took her swiftly, with a fury that bordered on savagery. And when he was finished, he rolled away and lay with chest heaving and eyes closed.

Maura slid from the bed and, numb with revulsion, kicked aside the torn gown. The sight of Beau's half-naked body made her shudder. She never wanted to see him again! She pulled open the door of the wardrobe, took out the first gown her hand fell upon and put it on quickly. She glanced at Beau, but he had not moved. His breathing was harsh and had the even depth of sleep.

How could she ever have thought herself fond of him? Or that he was a gentleman? He'd shown his true colors the night at the stagecoach stop. She'd seen him clearly then for the only time. All the rest was sham. What a fool she'd been!

Trembling, she smoothed her hair, took up her cloak and hat, and let herself out of the cabin.

Braxton whirled at the sound of the carriage. His first thought was that the fool driver had spooked the horses, but then he saw the man lurch out of the bushes. For a moment, as the carriage careened sharply, both men gaped in astonishment. It was Maura! Braxton shouted and raced toward her, but the coach was already rattling onto the roadway, leaving him in its dust. The canopy of trees swallowed it up like a ghostly form dissolving in the gloom. With the sound of the wheels and Maura's shouting still in his ears, Braxton raced back to the door to renew his frenzied pounding.

The driver ran up. "What the hell— You damn well git my horses and rig back, mistuh, else I'll—!"

"Shut up!" Braxton snarled. He thundered his fist on the wood, and the door opened suddenly.

The tousled judge, red-eyed and yawning, peered out. "Oh, it's you. Well, bring the lady in and let's get this over with."

Braxton grabbed the man's shirtfront. "Give me a horse!"

The judge blinked and looked owlish. "Not part of the price—"

"Dammit—where is your horse?" Braxton dug in his pocket and thrust several bills at the man.

The judge looked with bleary-eyed wonder at the money, then grinned. "Out back, mister, in the shed."

The driver caught Braxton before he could escape. "You ain't goin' anywhere 'thout me. That's *my* horses and rig that girl stole."

"She'll leave it at the levee, you fool! She's headed back to the boat!"

"Then I'll jus' stick close t'you till we find it." He stepped aside to let Braxton pass, then followed close at his heels.

"Got a shay, if'n ya'd like to borry that too!" the judge shouted. "Cost another fifty!" He stumbled out into the yard with a lantern.

Swearing, Braxton handed over the money as the driver hitched up the two-wheeled chaise. It would be faster than trying to ride two astride a single mount. He silently cursed the driver for leaving the horses unattended. Maura had been shamming and took quick advantage of the opportunity that presented itself. If the stupid driver had not climbed down—

He exhaled like a surfacing whale. His chances of catching up with Maura before she could barricade herself in her cabin aboard the *Ohio Queen* were slim. She had a good ten-minute start, and she had a fast team that could run circles around the judge's aging sorrel. No, he would lose too much time following Maura that way. There was a better alternate. He'd head directly back to Elger Sharp and the waiting *Pawnee*. He'd have to pay Sharp to continue down the river a while longer before heading back to Pittsburgh.

Maura spent most of the day in the ladies' lounge, going to the dining room for the midday meal and eating quickly before Beau appeared. He might sleep all day; she hoped fervently that he did. She never wanted to see him again.

The *Ohio Queen* reached the canal at Louisville early in the afternoon. Passengers rushed to the rails to view the manmade marvel that avoided the dangerous falls and rapids where the Ohio River descended more than twenty-two feet in only two miles. The *Queen* had to wait its turn because the locks were only long and wide enough to permit passage of a single boat at a time, but the occasion warranted a celebration. Captain Dance ordered the band to play on deck, and children scampered and danced about, weaving among the adults like serpentine ribbons. Once underway again, everyone crowded to the rails to watch the water flow out the dammed cubicles, lowering the *Ohio Queen* as though some giant hand had tired of holding her. And when the gates were opened, the pilot tooted his whistle and rang the bell to mark the passage. The band broke into a lively rendition of "Hail Columbia" which seemed to be their favorite tune for any significant event.

When the *Queen* reached the third lock, Maura saw Paul Giraud come along the cabin deck. Before he spotted her, she ducked out of sight. She didn't like Giraud, and her fury at Beau only intensified her dislike of his gambling companions. She wanted as little to do with Giraud as possible.

Most of Louisville lay on a plain. Low hills rose to the south and east to nestle the city against a sweeping curve of the river. Looking back as the boat came out of the canal, Maura could see the churning, roiling water of the rapids and a fringe of trees that marked islands that seemed to hang above the mists like brooding hawks.

Earlier, Maura had glanced through a book she found in the *Queen*'s library and learned that Louisville was fast becoming Kentucky's most important city. The boom in river traffic made it a center for shipping tobacco, hemp, whiskey, nails and gunpowder destined for use in the westward thrust of the nation. It seemed unbelievable to Maura that families would travel so far to live in the new State of California. If the gold petered out, would they stay? The westward rush might be a fool's chase in more ways than one. So much of the country still lay unexplored.

The levee at Shippingport was as colorful and busy as all the others, but Maura did not watch the activity. Instead she walked to the wheelhousing where the turning of the paddlewheel vibrated the deck. It was not a popular spot with most passengers, and Maura chose it for the solitude it allowed. She recalled Beau's comment that she would soon tire of the many stops and endless wooding and loading. In a way she had, but not through boredom. It was only that she was impatient to reach her destination and James. She felt so helpless cut off from the boatyard.

The sun played on the opposite shore, kissing sycamores with gold and bursting maples into flaming autumn finery. On a hill, the charred skeleton of an isolated tree that had been almost destroyed by lightning cast a long shadow onto the water. The wavering reflection was broken by the ripples of a passing boat. The distorted image was like a mirror of her life . . . shifting and unsettled, a series of endless disturbances. She sighed. The tree's outline would slowly return to what it had been, but her life would never be the same. Her father and mother were gone, and she and James were left to carry on the Sullivan dream. The future that had seemed bright with Duggan was shattered hopelessly. Bittersweet memories assailed her and she realized poignantly how much *she* had lost.

Her gaze was drawn to a building site across the river. At first glimpse of the bare lumber taking form, she thought it was a house, but quickly realized it was a boatyard with a steamer on the ways. Even this far down, the Ohio was booming with boatyards, she realized. The river was truly becoming a highway, as James predicted. How wonderful it would be to see Sullivan boats ply the waters. How her father would have loved it! She smiled at an image of him standing on a texas deck like a king surveying his domain. He would accept the conquest of the river as a glorious achievement.

She was brought from her reverie by a sudden shriek of the steam pipe. The paddlewheel once more began its heavy turning and the departure bell clanged its farewell to the city. Maura was amazed that the stop had been so brief, but after the delay in Cincinnati, she imagined Captain Dance was eager to make up for lost time. She stood at the rail until her head began to throb with the steady pounding of the engines and the slap of the paddle buckets, then retreated to the lounge.

Duggan strode up the gangplank, his face a scowling, angry mask. The *Ohio Queen* had left Cincinnati four hours ago! He'd been counting on closing with her by now. Jeffries had kept the *Patrick* going at full steam, during the daylight hours and most of the night, and he was exhausted, Duggan knew. The old man had gone without sleep, except for a few catnaps he allowed himself on the cot in the wheelhouse. Without a relief pilot, he refused to turn over the wheel to anyone else until he was dropping in his tracks. And then he succumbed only at Duggan's insistence, and it was Duggan who stood the watch. He'd learned enough about the river to be able to hold the boat on course at reduced speed, and to avoid the shoals. He didn't fancy himself being anywhere near a pilot, but he could keep the *Patrick* moving when she would otherwise have to tie up to give Jeffries his rest.

Jeffries outshone even the remarkable reputation that had sent Duggan in search of him in Pittsburgh. Without him, Duggan wondered if they would have come this far. Certainly no other riverman could have made better speed.

He swore and made his way to the pilothouse. Would they be able to catch up with the *Ohio Queen* before Braxton overtook it? He shook his head like a woolly bear. They *had* to! There had been no sign of Braxton but Duggan knew that a small boat like the one he'd hired might easily pass unnoticed or be passed at a crowded levee. He couldn't be sure if Braxton was ahead or behind, but it was a dead certainty that he would not give up his pursuit of Maura.

Tolly Jeffries raised his head when the door opened. He stretched like a bear coming out of hibernation and sat on the edge of the hard cot which had been bought from a ship chandler on the levee at Marietta.

"From the look on yer face, I'd say the news is not good," Tolly observed. He stretched again and reached for his brier pipe, knocking ashes into the cold potbellied stove.

"She's still hours ahead of us," Duggan said. He expected dismay, but Tolly merely shrugged.

"A few hours can be stretched or shortened easily if ye're determined." He tamped fresh tobacco, then put the pipe between his teeth and held a sulfur match to it. Smoke swirled like an eddying current. "Do we stand and beat 'r gums or get underway, Captain?"

Duggan nodded, amazed at the old man's spunk. "We go."

Jeffries leaned to the speaking tube and blew sharply.

"Look alive there, and give me full steam. I want those wheels spitting back water in two minutes!"

Duggan went out to the texas deck to watch the hands cast off.

They came in sight of Louisville at dusk, and there still had been no sign of the *Ohio Queen*. Duggan paced the deck, using the spyglass to inspect the lineup of boats waiting to go through the locks. The *Ohio Queen* wasn't among them. Muttering, he resumed his pacing.

Jeffries didn't have to ask if they'd found their quarry. He studied Quinn's face and sighed. Quinn was a hard taskmaster, but a fair man in every way. Tolly liked him. Duggan had told him enough of the reason for the wild chase so he knew that the pain on Duggan's face was due to worry over the girl. He was in love with her, and not knowing if her bastard of a stepbrother had caught her was worse than death. Tolly had already made up his mind that instead of nosing the *Patrick* into line to wait for the locks, he'd take her straight down the river.

Duggan looked bewildered for a moment, then raced into the pilothouse. "We're going upriver!"

"Yep, gotta go around Corn Island if we're going to go down the falls."

Duggan gaped. "The falls?!" He'd heard of boats smashed to bits on the rocks or torn apart by the rapids. But he also knew that by avoiding the locks they could cut hours off their time—

Jeffries puffed the pipe contentedly. "I was going down the falls long before the first load of mud was dredged for the canal. I'll need steam and lookouts watching for rocks. The river's running only mebbe six inches more'n our draft. If we had cargo, we'd have to jettison it." He grinned at Duggan. "Don't just lollygag there, Quinn. Give the orders for every man to stand by!"

Duggan swung down the ladder and went below. Poking his head into the engine room, he shouted to Macalister. "We're going over the falls! Don't let the pressure slack off!"

Macalister's eyes rounded in surprise, but before he could respond, Duggan was gone. Macalister went forward to the furnaces and shouted to the stokers, "Give them everything y•u've got so Jeffries doesn't have to ask twice!"

"Ain't we gonna tie up?!" The men had expected a leisurely respite as they passed through the canal. Blaze and Delivan were already stretched out asleep near the woodpiles. Macalister roused them with sharp kicks of his boot on their soles.

"We'll need every man for the next hour!"

Duggan found Poge, Vogel and Bainbridge coiling lines. When he told them the plan, they shook their heads and looked astonished.

"Tolly Jeffries is a crazy old man! He cain't take this boat down the falls! Hell, there's rocks bigger'n our engines out there—tear us to shreds!" Vogel said.

Bainbridge swore and Poge looked worried. "Suicide," Bainbridge muttered. "We're riding so light, we'll be tossed like a twig in those rapids."

Poge rubbed his whiskery chin. He was a thin man with rounded shoulders and long arms that hung loosely. "We didn't sign on to git ourselves kilt, Quinn."

Duggan looked at each of them. "There'll be a bonus for every man when it's done," he said. "But if you don't think Tolly can do it you'd better jump over the side now. We're not turning back to put anyone ashore."

There was grumbling again, then reluctant agreement.

"Tolly wants lookouts to watch for rocks," Duggan said. "Get into position. Vogel, take the hurricane deck. Make it quick, man."

Duggan went up to the texas deck. Macalister had pressure up so steam shrieked from the escape pipes. He tied lead weights on the safety valves and the pressure gauges were climbing steadily. By the time Tolly brought the boat into Indian Chute, the placid river became a boiling caldron around the prow of the *Patrick*, sending heavy spray over her bare decks. Without cornices and gingerbread, the boat could have been mistaken for a disabled wreck riding the river, except for the cinders and smoke pouring from her chimneys. Sparks showered down onto the decks but were quickly extinguished by the frothing, lashing water. The current sucked at the hull, pulling the boat into the chute at headlong speed. Cataracts beat at the decks and slapped against the woodpiles that protected the boilers. The stokers stood splay-footed, braced against the twisting and

459

turning motion of the deck. The boat drove into the falls with sickening speed, until it seemed it would break apart under the battering strain. It was as though the devils of Hell were fighting for the right to smash the *Patrick*.

Duggan's feet skidded on the slippery deck and he grabbed the bell standard. He hugged himself to it, thankful that the workmen had not gotten around to installing the iron bell which might batter him now. Water swirled on every side, and a roaring sound filled his head. Spray whipped the decks, and only the piercing scream of the steam valves overrode the tumult. The boat seemed to be plunging headlong into a pit. Walls of water rose on either side, and the boat shuddered and rocked.

Then suddenly it was over. The *Patrick* was spit out into the calm waters below the rapids. Duggan breathed a tremendous sigh and glanced at the pilothouse. Except for the grin behind the brier pipe, Jeffries might have been cruising the widest, safest part of the river.

CHAPTER TWENTY-SIX

Beau saw Maura when he entered the dining salon at dinnertime, but he didn't approach her. He had not yet gotten over her astonishing disclosure that Braxton Turk was following her and trying to take her back by force. Until now, he had not paid much attention to Maura's preoccupation with Sullivan Company affairs. Women didn't have the heads for business. He had not taken seriously her contention that she would wrest control of the company from her stepfather. The man was a lawyer. The thought made Beau smile. Any man steeped in legal knowledge would take all precautions to ensure that *no one* could upset his plans. Maura was only dreaming if she thought she could win over him.

Or so Beau had felt until now.

But for Turk to risk a daring maneuver like kidnapping . . . It could only mean Maura posed a real threat to his plans. And if she *was* a threat, it meant that it *was* possible for her and her brother to take over. The Sullivan Company was well established and profitable. Whoever controlled it controlled a veritable fortune—with potential beyond imagination! From the little he'd seen of the boatyard in Pittsburgh, it too, had the potential to grow into a solid moneymaker. An intriguing thought . . .

Beau glanced casually around the salon again, but Maura was gone. It didn't worry him. It was better to give her temper time to cool. By morning she'd welcome him again. He spied Giraud and inclined his head as their eyes met. The corner of Giraud's mouth turned up in a smile before he returned to his conversation with Charles Stevenson and a tall, portly, balding man with a ruddy complexion and a jovial look. Beau had not seen him before, but he probably had come aboard at Louisville. From time to time, the man's laugh boomed over the chatter. A silver ice bucket had been brought to the table, and Giraud poured champagne frequently. He was setting up a sucker for a game, Beau was sure of it. This was the last night aboard the *Ohio Queen*, which would be in Cairo before dusk tomorrow. Giraud would make his big move now. Tonight's game would have no table limit. The betting could go as high as anyone wanted. Beau hid a smile. Tonight he would make his move as well. He'd been playing cat-and-mouse with Giraud. After losing to him the first night, he'd recouped the second so he was almost even. Tonight he would clean up. Let Giraud set up the suckers . . . Beau would take them all.

When the waiter approached, Beau turned his attention to the menu, then ordered turtle soup, chicken in egg sauce, velvet shrimp puffs, lamb with parsley sauce, sweet corn and Irish potatoes. He asked for a light Chablis to clear his palate without clouding his brain. He wanted to be at his best tonight.

He ate leisurely, enjoying the self-imposed solitude, though he smiled pleasantly as two other latecomers, a young couple who held hands and gazed at each other with mooning eyes, joined him at the table. He made desultory conversation and escaped as soon as he'd finished his coffee and *Charlotte Polonaise.*

He glanced in at the cabin, but Maura was not there. Where the devil was she hiding? He could not believe that she would stay angry much longer. Perhaps it had been a mistake to force her to submit, but she was so damned seductive and desirable, especially with her eyes blazing and her temper roused. He'd never known a woman with such fire! Yet she could be exasperating too, with her determination and single-mindedness. Most women were content to leave moneymaking to men and not involve themselves with business. Still, this instance was special. If Maura and her brother controlled the business, they also controlled the profits. Beau's fortunes rose and fell with the fall of a card, and the thought of having money at hand whenever it was needed was intriguing. Especially if Maura went with it. He had suggested marriage to her to still her worries about her reputation, but now the idea brushed his thoughts persistently. Marriage would solve Maura's problem of her step-father's guardianship as well as enable her to claim what rightfully belonged to her.

It was an interesting idea that deserved consideration. Of course, he'd have to coax her back into loving good humor, but he was confident he could do it before they reached Cairo.

Giraud and three others were already gathered in the barbershop, where a haze of smoke and the smell of mild Virginia tobacco hung in the air. Beau delayed going in so that the game would already be in progress when he arrived. It gave a man an advantage to make an entrance that distracted the others. He'd changed to a russet-colored frock coat over dark trousers and black cravat. Maura's lace handkerchief was tucked in a breast pocket. He cast a quick glance about the room before entering.

Giraud, Stevenson, the jovial chap from the dining salon—and a man with his back to the door. Beau studied the thin shoulders. There was something vaguely familiar about the man, and he hesitated. At that moment Stevenson glanced up and hailed him.

"Mr. Fontaine, are you joining us? I have been hoping for the chance to win back some of what I lost last night."

Beau smiled lazily and sauntered into the room. The table had been set up in one corner under two oil lamps in brackets. On a shelf behind the red plush barber's chair, soaps and lotions had been replaced with several whiskey bottles and a tray of glasses. The barber, a cadaverous man named Opie, was earning the fee Giraud gave him for use of the room by pouring drinks and producing fresh cards when they were called for. Beau had already given him two gold eagles and his own deck.

Giraud rolled a Ruy Lopez between his fingers and cut off the end with a small gold snipper. He gave Beau an impassive look and struck a sulfur on the underside of the table. A puff of smoke veiled his face. Beau pulled a chair out and seated himself, smiling around at the others.

"It's always a pleasure to give opponents a return match," he said easily. "And to meet new—" He broke off and stared at the man beside him whose face he had not seen until that moment. Obediah Cromwell! How the hell

463

had he gotten here?! For a moment Beau thought it was some kind of a trick or a trap. Then he saw that Cromwell was as surprised as he. Beau forced himself to smile casually.

Cromwell's surprise passed and his face was devoid of emotion, except for a cold glint of hate in his eyes. He watched Beau as Stevenson made introductions, not bothering to acknowledge when his name was spoken. The fourth gentleman was Turner Wells of Louisville. He and Cromwell had come aboard at that city and were traveling to Cairo, according to Stevenson. Giraud blew fresh smoke into the gathering haze.

"I suggest we get on with the game, gentlemen. The best way to become acquainted with a man is to play poker with him," Giraud said when Stevenson paused.

The others laughed and Wells asked whose deal it was. Giraud signaled the bartender for a fresh deck and broke the seal. At Beau's inquiry, he was told the game was draw and the table stakes were a hundred dollars unless he had some objection. He did not. Giraud shuffled and laid the deck out for a cut. Beau felt Cromwell's gaze on him but he had recovered from his shock. He remembered Cromwell mentioning travel, but it had never occurred to him that their paths might cross on the river. At their last meeting, on a dark street in front of Cora's place, Cromwell had spoken only of Beau leaving the city. Damn . . . if he'd known Cromwell would not be in Pittsburgh to back up his threat, he would not have run. Still, the politician could pay others to make good his promises. And Cora had warned Beau the word was already out about his dishonesty. *All right, Obediah Cromwell, let's see how good you are when you don't have a couple of hired strong-arms to do your fighting for you,* Beau thought.

They played the first few hands quietly, betting and raising cautiously as each man got the feel of the game and his opponents. Beau knew Cromwell was watching him closely. It surprised him that Cromwell had not reacted more outspokenly to his presence. After the scene at Senator Zachary's and the lengths Cromwell had gone to in order to exact his revenge, Beau would normally expect the man to refuse to play. Or worse, to air his suspicions about Beau's honesty. It amused him that Cromwell was willing to play with

Giraud, whose reputation was known the length of the rivers. Overconfidence was a common failing among men who believed themselves experts with a deck of cards. Cromwell was no better than the rest. He couldn't resist the temptation to challenge any reputation greater than his own.

Very well, Cromwell, let's see how well you do with two of us to watch.

Stevenson took a small pot, then Wells took a larger one with three of a kind. The tension around the table relaxed, and Wells rubbed his fat hands gleefully as he stacked his win in neat piles before him on the table.

"I think this is going to be a very enjoyable night, gentlemen. Obediah, didn't I tell you there was as much action right here on the Ohio as you'd find in Louisville? Yessir, ain't nothin' lackin' 'round these parts no more. Why, just last July when I was down to Cairo, I met the prettiest little Creole gal you ever want to lay eyes on. Her mammy brung her up North to marry some rich freighter who'd made plenty o' fancy promises when he deflowered her in New Orleans. Includin' one o' marriage, except he left town without sayin' good-bye. The li'l miss was downright heartbroken when she discovered her intended already had a wife. There she was, her'n her mammy, a thousand miles from home." He gave a sly wink. "The li'l lady is still badly in need of comfortin', yessir."

Beau glanced at the hand Giraud had dealt. "Three cards," he said, tossing in his discards. He glanced at Cromwell, who was studying his hand with tight lips. He'd learned in the other game with Cromwell that his expression was often deliberately designed to throw others off the track. Cromwell might ponder a poor hand as intently as a good one. After several moments, Cromwell finally threw down and asked for two cards.

"Three," said Stevenson. "I've seen better hands on a muskrat."

Giraud smiled laconically. "Dealer takes one." He put down the deck and looked at his cards impassively.

Turner Wells played a friendly but not very daring game. His thoughts seemed to be still on the Creole girl, and he had to be reminded that it was his bet.

"Ten dollars." He pushed a banknote into the center

and glanced at the bartender. "Let me have one of them rum cheroots, Opie."

Beau debated a moment as he studied his hand. He'd gained another King; three of a kind was an excellent hand, but Cromwell had drawn only two. Even though his expression had not altered, Beau guessed he'd drawn to a full house of four of a kind. He threw his own hand in. A moment later Giraud did the same. Cromwell took the pot with four eights.

Turner Wells shuffled and remarked to no one in particular that he was losing his return fare up the river and he hoped someone would push a little more luck his way. Cromwell grunted and said it was far more likely the little Creole girl would clean out his pockets than an evening at cards. There was a ripple of laughter. Wells chuckled good-naturedly as he began to deal.

They played several more hands, and the betting gradually climbed. Giraud had settled down to serious card-playing, and he ignored the light banter except when some remark was directed at him. He'd picked up indications of Cromwell's skill and he'd also noted Cromwell's close scrutiny of Fontaine. When Fontaine's name was mentioned before he made an appearance, there had been an unmistakable flicker of surprise in Cromwell's face. Giraud would have laid odds that the two had met before. Beau's reaction was well masked, but Giraud sensed a wariness that hadn't been evident before. Fontaine was watching Cromwell unobtrusively. Giraud signaled Opie for a round of whiskey.

Charles Stevenson shuffled and sighed. "Be there this time, cards. You ain't doin' right by me tonight a-tall! You aces, you hear me? Kings? Start comin' my way before these gentlemen see the lining of my pockets!"

Giraud cut. "Perhaps we should remove the limit and give you an opportunity to win back your losses more quickly, Charles."

"That's fine with me. Any objections, gentlemen?"

There was a murmur of assent. Wells brought out his wallet to add a handful of banknotes to his diminished pile. Cromwell did not follow suit, but his expression clearly said the money was there if he needed it.

"I suggest we raise the ante a bit as well," Beau said. "Shall we say twenty dollars?"

The jovial expression on Wells' face faltered, but he snapped two ten-dollar bills from the pile and tossed them in. The others followed suit.

Beau waited until the hand was dealt before he picked up his cards. A pair of treys, nothing else. Giraud opened and no one dropped out. Beau considered throwing the hand in. It wasn't much to go on, but . . . He had the feeling it was time to make his move. Giraud was obviously ready to put the squeeze on. Beau asked for three cards and drew two more treys. He felt a surge of exhilaration. He'd been right! The golden Lady was at his side.

He met Giraud's bet, and Cromwell raised. Giraud raised again. Beau let it go around the table. The double track of a frown appeared between Stevenson's pale eyebrows, and a tic bothered the corner of his mouth. Cromwell raised and the pot swelled to more than six hundred dollars. When the bet came to him, Beau raised another hundred. He sensed a stiffening in Cromwell. The man's eyes seemed to bore through the cards Beau was holding.

Wells twisted his mouth in a quizzical frown. "You took three cards."

Beau shrugged amiably. "I drew a royal flush." It was not his habit to react to baiting, but he could not resist the chance to add to Cromwell's uneasiness. The politician was scrutinizing his every move as though expecting to catch a palmed card or one slipped from the bottom of the deck. The last thing he expected was exactly what Beau was doing—playing an honest hand. Cromwell might have a calm, poker face, but Beau was an expert in probing the slightest weakness a man showed. And he had found Cromwell's—his own cockiness.

"I don't believe it for a minute," Wells said with a huge sigh. "But the hand's getting a bit rich for my blood. I fold."

Cromwell was made of stronger stuff. He met the raise and called. When Beau laid down the four treys, Cromwell grunted and flung his cards down in annoyance. Beau smiled and drew in the pot. Giraud motioned to Opie to refill the glasses, and the game waited until the thin, bent man made a round of the table. Beau swallowed half the whiskey in a gulp. His confidence was swelling mightily. He'd see Cromwell a pauper! It would be a sweet victory

467

after the beating Cromwell's men had given him. The sweetest part of all was that Cromwell couldn't accuse him of cheating. If the politician were not blinded by his hatred for Beau, he'd keep a sharper eye on Giraud! Paul Giraud was playing a close game, a typical gambler's ploy to offset any fears his victims were suffering. Giraud might have stepped directly from a good Baptist prayer meeting, he was playing so honestly—at the moment. Soon he'd call for a fresh deck, and it would be a different story.

At least Giraud thought it would. Beau smiled inwardly with the knowledge that he had given Opie several double eagles to substitute his deck for Giraud's.

The play continued with pots varying from a few hundred to some over a thousand. Giraud reeled his players like fish on a line, letting them grow confident on the bait of lesser pots, only to pull them in on larger ones. Beau studied his system, if anything so unpredictable could be called that, and then played his own game accordingly. The cash on the table seesawed from the pile in front of Giraud to Beau's, only occasionally sidetracked to Cromwell's. The haze of smoke in the room thickened to a cloud that gave the oil lamps a mealy glow. Opie propped the door open to admit a breeze. Wells was beginning to tire, and the whiskey had made him easy prey to Giraud's wiliness. Stevenson dropped out, saying he'd lost enough for one evening.

On the next hand Giraud called for new cards. Beau drew to a pair and found himself holding a full house. He didn't twitch a muscle. The betting began with Giraud at fifty dollars. Wells went to seventy and tossed in his money with a resigned air.

Beau said, "Raise a hundred." Beside him, Cromwell's fingers tightened on the cards. Beau knew he'd been taken by surprise, probably because he, too, held good cards. *Well, my friend, we'll see who has the guts to win now.*

Cromwell held his hand so close his hawk nose seemed to be sniffing the cards. When he shot a sidelong glance, Beau was sure he was running scared.

Cromwell said, "Raise five hundred."

Beau's pulse quickened but his face was impassive. So Cromwell was going to hang in and bluff. But he'd already given himself away.

Giraud leaned back and his gaze was steady. With a slow, deliberate motion, he counted out his bet and dropped his money into the pot. "I see the five hundred and raise another two hundred."

Wells hastily threw in his cards. "Too rich for me, gentlemen."

Giraud turned the hooded stare at Beau. "Seven to you, Fontaine."

Without hesitation, Beau said, "I see the seven and raise another five hundred." His hand was too good to lose faith now. He imagined he could feel Maura's handkerchief burning at his flesh through his shirt. He would have taken it out and held it for added luck, but any move like that might be fatal. Gamblers didn't look favorably on hands in pockets when the stakes were so high. He counted out twelve hundred dollars and dropped it to the center of the table.

Cromwell tapped his fingers on his stack of bills, peeled off several and tossed them carelessly across the table. "One thousand to you."

Giraud folded, which surprised Beau. That left him and Cromwell. A showdown. He examined his cards and reviewed his stand. A full house was a powerful hand. Cromwell was bluffing—he had to be. Giraud had enough to stay in for almost two thousand dollars, and he'd opened with Jacks or better. What the hell did Cromwell have? Whatever it was, it wasn't good enough to bluff Beau out.

He glanced at his depleted supply of cash. Barely a thousand. He tossed it in. "I'll see it and raise five thousand."

Cromwell shifted his gaze from the money to Beau's face. His mouth curled in a hard smile. "You don't have any cash showing, Fontaine."

"I'll give you my IOU."

Cromwell shook his head slowly and the smile became a sneer. "No thank you. I always play for hard cash."

Beau's shoulders tightened. The smug politician was enjoying seeing Beau squirm. Beau would gladly strangle the man on the spot—after taking the pot, of course.

"Giraud, will you accept my IOU? One percent of my winnings as interest."

Giraud's eyes seemed to close as he tilted his head back.

469

"I've seen you lose sure hands before, Fontaine. You'll have to play your own game."

"Then the pot is mine," Cromwell said arrogantly. He folded his cards.

"No!" Beau slapped a palm on the table. He'd be damned if he'd let Cromwell take the pot that belonged to him. With the pretty array of winners he held, it was worth anything— He took a breath and tried to goad Cromwell. "Maybe you don't have the spine for such rich play, Cromwell. Or can't you arrange for any goons to steal back your losses this time?" His voice dripped with contempt.

Cromwell's face mottled. "I have the spine *and* the money—which you do not. Now either put up or quit."

Wells shifted uneasily. "Put up something of value, Mr. Fontaine."

Cromwell smiled icily. "He doesn't have anything worth five thousand dollars, including his life."

A trickle of cold sweat formed between Beau's shoulder blades and his gut tightened. "You are mistaken, Cromwell." The other man's eyebrows arched questioningly. "I have Maura Sullivan. I believe you know the lady?"

Frowning, Cromwell waited for an explanation. A heavy silence fell around the table, and all eyes were on Beau.

"I will put Miss Sullivan up as collateral."

"You're insane—" Giraud whispered hoarsely.

"You can't bet a woman!" Wells looked outraged.

"Hold on a moment, gentlemen," Cromwell said. "You interest me, Fontaine. As it happens, I have an interest in Miss Sullivan's company. Are you saying she will vouch for your losses?"

"She will," Beau declared boldly.

"And if she does not?" Cromwell was skeptical but not closing the door.

Beau reached into his pocket and brought out the key to the cabin. He dropped it onto the table. "I'm sure you'll be able to convince her."

Wells scraped his chair back and started to get up, then sat again, too fascinated to leave. Giraud took a cigar from the silver case and began to work it between his fingers. There was silence around the table for several seconds.

Finally Beau demanded, "Do you accept?" His fingers

twitched and the hairs at the back of his neck rose. He stared unwaveringly at Cromwell.

Cromwell nodded. Beau's breath escaped in a puff. Without looking at his hand again, Cromwell said, "I'll see the five thousand and call."

Beau laid down his hand. Cromwell glanced at the cards, then with a flick of the wrist turned up a straight flush, Queen high.

Turner Wells whispered, "I'll be damned."

Air hissed between Giraud's teeth and he looked at Beau.

Beau's face drained and the sweat traced an icy path along his spine. It couldn't be! Damn it—it had to be a trick! Cromwell had cheated!

He jumped up, spilling his chair over with a clatter and shoving aside his coat to grab for his gun. Cromwell was on his feet instantly, leaping back and pulling out a revolver and firing in the same motion.

Beau's hand closed around the empty pocket where the Colt should have been. Too late he remembered that Cromwell had taken it after the beating in front of Cora's place. Cromwell's slug slammed him with the force of a hundred horses. He spun back and pain flashed in his chest and spread in eddying waves. He crashed to the floor. The chair toppled against the table and the cards and money flew up. Gold eagles clattered to the floor and spun in all directions. The paper money settled slowly over Beau's still form.

Opie leaned against the makeshift bar. "Jeeeez—"

"He was going for his gun!" Cromwell said with a quick look at Giraud and Wells.

Wells nodded. He wanted only to get out. He edged toward the door.

Giraud bent over Beau and put a hand to his chest. After a moment, he glanced up. "He's dead."

Cromwell paled. "He would have killed me if I hadn't—"

Giraud's hands patted Beau's body. "He doesn't have a gun."

Cromwell sucked air noisily into his lungs. His glare pinned Turner Wells near the door, then moved slowly to Giraud and Opie. "You all saw it. It was a clear case of self-defense. Fontaine was a no-good cheat who got what was coming to him." He bent to pick up the banknotes. Counting them quickly, he peeled off two thousand for each of the others and pressed the bills into their hands. Opie and Wells stood staring while Giraud pocketed the gun with unconcerned ease.

"I'll see that the Captain is informed and the body disposed of," Giraud said. "There's no need to concern yourself further." He glanced toward the open door. "It might be better if we disband. The shot may have been heard and raise questions. Gentlemen . . . thank you for a fine game. With the exception of this unfortunate incident, it has been a very pleasant evening."

Wells sidled out the door. With a glance at the prostrate form on the floor, Cromwell scooped up the cabin key Beau had dropped, then left hurriedly.

"I'll close up, Opie, and I'll take care of this." Giraud nudged Beau's body with a shoe tip. He handed Opie half the bills Cromwell had given him.

"Thanks, Mr. Giraud. You sure I shouldn't—"

Giraud dismissed any suggestion with a wave of his hand and a curt shake of his head. A moment later, Opie vanished. Giraud blew out the lamps, plunging the barbershop into darkness. He stood a minute to let his eyes adjust to the gloom and listened to be sure the shot hadn't attracted attention. Fontaine was a fool to try to buy Opie's loyalty, but then Fontaine had been a fool in many ways.

He grabbed the body under the arms and dragged it out on the deck. With effort, he heaved the limp figure to the railing and pitched it over. The noise of the paddle buckets masked the sound of the body hitting the water. Overhead, the steam pipes spit and hissed softly.

Maura was roused by an insistent noise that intruded on her sleep-laden mind. She'd grown accustomed to the steady creak and clatter of the paddlewheels and the intermittent hiss of steam from the escape pipes, but her body tensed as she recognized the persistent scrape of a key in the lock and the rattling of the knob. She glanced at the windows and saw that the sky was still black and moonlight splashed on the river and made dark silhouettes of trees along the shore.

Beau's docile acceptance of being locked out the night

before had lulled her into thinking she was safe in the cabin. She was positive he was playing cards and would be busy all night. What brought him back early? Had he lost all his money again and been forced to quit? She sighed and pulled the pillow over her head to shut out the noise.

All at once a loud crash jolted her. It came again. She sat up as she realized with sickening certainty that Beau was trying to batter the door down. The heavy weight crashed against the panel and the wood groaned. At the next crash, something splintered. The bolt yanked from its screws and flew across the room. The door crashed inward. A figure loomed, outlined darkly against the gray night, then tumbled into the cabin. The door slammed with its own ricocheting momentum.

Maura leaped up as the force of the ramrodding thrust sprawled Beau across the bed, but she was a moment too late. He toppled across her. Furiously, she battered him with her fists and clawed at his face as she tried to push him away. He grunted and shifted to avoid her blows. His hands groped and she jerked away from the scalding touch. He was an animal. She fought with every ounce of her strength. Her sleepiness vanished in an onslaught of fear as she realized he meant to take her by force again! Never! She twisted and struggled savagely as her hands searched for any leverage to free herself. Her fingers encountered his face and crawled upward for his hair. Instead they found a smooth expanse of bald head. Dumbfounded, she fell back.

It was not Beau! Who—?!

Cromwell took advantage of the momentary respite in her fury to right himself and fall across her so she could not move. He pressed against the soft, warm curves of her breasts. His breath rasped and he felt a straining desire building in his loins. He had not intended to act so hastily. The bonanza of "winning" Maura from Fontaine amused him and he planned to use it as an added bit of blackmail to ensure the bargain he'd made with Duggan Quinn. But the argument and the shooting panicked him. His desire for revenge had made him go for his gun too quickly. How was he to know Fontaine was unarmed?

Coming to Maura's cabin was impulse, too. He'd been running from the grinning death mask of Beau's face and Turner Wells' blubbering fear. But now he could not control the masculine urges that became rampant at the feel of her silken flesh. The gown had slipped from her shoulders, and the sweet scent of lilac water clung to her skin. He groaned and stroked her hair.

Fear paralyzed Maura and she drew a breath to scream. The sound was smothered quickly as the man pressed searching wet lips over her mouth. The rough stubble of his beard scraped her face, and the sour taste of whiskey on his breath made her retch. What kind of madman would break into her cabin?! Her heart thudded, and she shuddered as his slimy tongue caressed her lips. One of his hands threaded into her hair and held her fast so she could not get away; the other yanked away the quilt and searched for the edge of her gown. With a sudden jerk, he ripped the cloth from her breasts to hips. His hand mauled the tender flesh.

Maura tried to clear her reeling brain. Her arms were like lead. It was a horrible nightmare from which she prayed to waken. His fingers dug cruelly into her thighs and his kisses swept across her face and throat like scalding water. His breath heaved with an ugly sound in the darkness.

Maura moaned. For a second, his amorous advances halted and he raised his head to peer at her. He laughed throatily. "You once claimed that women could manage any situation as capably as men . . . do you still think so?" He chuckled wickedly again. "Ah, there, I've frightened you. I didn't mean to. It's only that you're driving me wild with your struggling."

Maura gulped air as his hold on her slackened momentarily. She knew the voice, but it took her a second to identify it. When recognition came, she was filled with loathing.

"Obediah Cromwell?!"

"None other, my pet." He closed in on her and planted another wet kiss on her ear as she quickly averted her face.

"This is impossible—what are you doing here—?" She struggled for words as she tried to slide away from him. But she was no match for his strength, and he trapped her with a quick movement.

"I've come to claim my prize. Beau Fontaine was crazy enough to wager you in a poker game, and I was the lucky winner." His sour breath was overpowering.

Maura jerked away in astonishment, pressing her hands against Cromwell's chest and forcing him back. She shook her head in numb horror. "Beau *wagered* me in a poker game?!" She was incredulous. She wanted to laugh, but the sound choked her. Cromwell was here—

"The man's a fool but I've known that since the first time I met him. A smart man never risks any possession he values highly."

Maura struck out blindly. She tried to push him away again, but he grabbed her wrist and forced her arm to the pillow. Her eyes had grown accustomed to the dim light, and she could make out his leering grin. She was trembling with rage, and her wildly beating heart threatened to burst through the bonds of her chest.

"I am not any man's possession!" she exploded. "Least of all, yours!" She renewed her attack until he grasped her other arm and pinned it above her head. His face was over her and his breath had taken on the ragged rasp of lust. His body moved against her insinuatingly, and she writhed.

"Perhaps not, but you cost me five thousand dollars and I mean to have payment on account." He pulled her into his arms and buried her under his eager mouth. His fingers kneaded her naked flesh from shoulders to waist. When they touched the ripped gown, he tore it away completely and stared at her enticing nakedness in the pale moonlight. She was a love goddess. Her breasts strained so the rosy nipples were tumid with excitement. Cromwell felt an anticipatory shiver of excitement. His swollen maleness was strained under his trousers. With a grunt, he released her and struggled to free it.

Maura twisted away instantly. She snaked across the bed and tumbled onto the floor, then scrambled on all fours toward the door before he could recover his wits. The shredded gown tangled around her ankles and tripped her, but she kicked it aside and ran across the cabin. Cromwell was insane! Beau was insane! The whole world had gone mad!

She was within arm's reach of the door when her foot came down hard on the sharp metal of the fallen bolt and she pitched forward. Pain lanced her foot and brought tears to her eyes.

Cromwell lunged. Raising herself, Maura's hand closed

around the doorknob—but not in time. He fell on her like a huge, lumbering bear, his thick arms trapping her against the hard wood.

"You may be worth five thousand at that—!" His hands were all over her flesh and his obscene mouth searched her breast for the nipple.

Every breath seared Maura's lungs. With a strength born of panic, she pulled an arm free and slammed a fist at Cromwell's head. His mouth released her breast with a wet, smacking noise as he shook his head in dazed confusion. Growling like an animal, he came at her again. Maura struck again with a blow that caught the hard ridge of his cheek. Her knuckles screamed with fiery pain, and Cromwell pulled back. Maura grabbed the knob and yanked the door open. Cool air bathed her burning flesh and she shivered with the realization that she was naked. But she couldn't go back—! Cromwell was already staggering to his feet in the open doorway. He reached to grab her, but she darted into the deep shadows of the stern where the deck ended under a canopy of ornately carved woodwork. Too late she realized she had trapped herself in a blind corner. Whirling, she poised for flight, but Cromwell was already blocking her way. He advanced slowly with a smug, evil grin on his face. He spread his arms to snare her. Over the hard, slapping sound of the paddlewheels, she heard his labored breath as his gaze devoured her naked form in the moonlight.

She backed against the rail, her hands and feet searching blindly for a means of escape. They were as far removed from the other cabins as it was possible to get. Her screams would be lost in the churning paddle noises.

Cromwell began to close the gap. Without hesitation, Maura scrambled over the rail. The grin froze on Cromwell's face as he halted. Then he lunged for her. Maura flexed her knees, released her grip and plunged into the moon-bathed river.

The shock of the icy water took her breath away. Her body tingled as she strained upward with the breath bursting her lungs. When her head broke the surface of the water, she gulped air and shivered uncontrollably. The *Ohio Queen* was two dozen yards down the river, its twin wakes spreading like a fan and catching Maura in their ripples.

On the cabin deck, Cromwell leaned over the railing and peered at the inky water. His face was a pale blur for several minutes before he turned and vanished into the darkness.

Maura gasped as her limbs began to numb. She would freeze if she stayed in the icy water long. Damn Beau—and damn Obediah Cromwell! For a moment the fires of rage warmed her. With a quick glance to pick out the bank, she began to swim.

CHAPTER TWENTY-SEVEN

Elger Sharp spat a brown stain onto the deck outside the wheelhouse. He raised a spyglass and focused it on the Kentucky bank half a mile ahead at Paducah. There were three sidewheelers at the levee; he trained the glass on the largest one, which was just backing out into the river. Grunting, he lowered the glass and spat again. He ducked back inside where Dobie held the wheel with iron fists. There was a thin sheen of sweat on the giant's hairless head, and he wore no shirt in spite of the fact that the temperature had dropped well below a comfortable level. He seemed to have some inner source of heat that others were deprived of; even on the coldest days, Dobie never wore more than a thin shirt. Now his muscles bulged and rippled as he turned to look at Sharp. Sharp grunted and poked Braxton Turk, who was dozing on the bench. The damned fool hadn't left the wheelhouse since they resumed the journey at Louisville. Madder'n a wet hen at the fee he had to pay for the continued journey. *Hell, 'twarn't my fault he botched kidnapping the girl,* Sharp thought. *A man's gotta pay for his mistakes.*

Braxton jerked up and rubbed his grimy, stubbled face. For a moment, he scowled darkly but thought better of chewing out the man on whom he was temporarily dependent.

"The *Ohio Queen*'s half a mile ahead comin' outta the levee at Paducah," Sharp said without enthusiasm.

Braxton leaped to his feet. He grabbed the spyglass and ran to the window. He leveled the glass on the big sidewheeler that had made its turn and was churning downriver. He glanced back at Sharp.

"You're sure that's the right boat?"

"I'm sure."

"How long until we overtake her?" Braxton felt an elation which released some of the pent-up anger roiling inside him. Sharp's disposition had gone from bad to foul the past thirty-six hours. But if they caught up with the *Ohio Queen* before it reached Cairo, Braxton had no quarrel with him. He'd done what he promised, overtaking the big boat twice. This time Braxton wouldn't make any mistakes dealing with Maura.

He realized Sharp hadn't answered and he posed the question again. The boatman grunted and shrugged.

"Twenty minutes. But we's missed her last wood stop. She won't stop again till she ties up in Cairo."

Braxton scowled and studied the boat ahead. Smoke spilled from her chimneys as she gathered speed, and white puffs of steam were quickly swallowed up in the black clouds. "Can you come alongside her?"

"Yuh figurin' to jump?"

"Is there any other way to get aboard?" Braxton asked churlishly. He was sick to death of Sharp and his stinking scow.

Sharp ignored the sarcasm. Dobie eased the wheel down slightly to follow the current and threw a vacant, hostile look in Braxton's direction. Sharp grunted and chewed a cud of tobacco before answering.

"Better take that bag o' yers. Once we come even with that boat agin, mistuh, my job's done. Ya got what ya paid fer." He leaned toward the doorway and arced tobacco juice past the cabin roof. "I kin pick up a load o' corn that'll bring a purty price up Louisville."

Braxton went out without answering. He'd be more than glad to quit the boat and never see it again. In the crude cabin that smelled of mildew and sweat, he stuffed his things into his satchel and carried it onto the deck. The *Pawnee* had already gained on the *Ohio Queen*. Slowly the gap was closing. His lips curled in a victorious smile. Maura would not find it so easy to escape this time. He had worked out a story that would satisfy anyone who took her part or tried to prevent him from taking her from the boat—an innocent but willful girl who had been seduced and enticed to run off by a rogue. Yes, it would be totally believable. Maura's protests would be ignored because Fontaine's reputation would speak for itself. She could struggle and fight all she wanted, there'd be many who would come to his assistance. Once he had her safely in a hotel, he would teach her submission until she came with him willingly. He had more than one score to settle with her.

The *Pawnee* moved inexorably closer to the big sidewheeler in the next hour. Braxton could make out the cabin windows across the stern now and see people on the deck. Smoke drifted in a thinning cloud behind the chimneys, and he thought he heard an occasional burst of music over the *Pawnee*'s engines. There would be partying aboard the *Ohio Queen* the last few hours from her destination. He tried to imagine where Maura was and what she was doing at that moment. She'd be anticipating the arrival and full of plans to rush to James for a grand reunion.

Braxton snickered with malicious glee. He would take the keenest pleasure in seeing her face when she discovered he'd caught up with her again after she imagined him cooling his heels in Cincinnati.

Elger Sharp relieved Dobie at the wheel and fetched the *Pawnee* around past the *Ohio Queen*'s starboard.

Braxton stood gazing in all directions along the river. A quarter of a mile behind, a strange-looking heap of unpainted wood was bearing down hard on them. Braxton squinted, then dismissed the unfinished boat from consideration. The Paducah levee was directly across from them, and a sternwheeler chimed her bell and tooted her whistles as the *Pawnee* cut across her right-of-way.

Braxton turned his attention to the river. For a couple of hundred rods, the small sternwheeler hugged the shore in a fast current of shoal water. Then Sharp rounded her to, and the little boat eased back into the channel well ahead of the *Ohio Queen*. Sharp yelled for slow speed ahead. The escape pipe belched a tall column of steam with a piercing whistle, and the *Pawnee*'s engine settled to a morose sighing chatter. The boat drifted slowly and waited for the *Queen* to catch up.

Braxton hefted his valise and poised at the edge of the main deck. Sharp rang a blast on the whistle to signal the larger boat. With cupped hands, he yelled, "Man comin' aboard!" The *Queen*'s Captain shouted permission and deckhands hurried to a clearing between piles of cargo. A mo-

481

ment later they were pulling Braxton up onto the deck. Behind him he heard Sharp yell for full speed. The *Pawnee* veered out of the *Queen*'s whitewater.

The clerk approached Braxton and collected the fare to Cairo. There were no cabins, but since it was only a few hours to the journey's end, he was sure the gentlemen's lounge would be quite comfortable.

Braxton handed over the money. "My sister is aboard, can you tell me her cabin number?" When the clerk frowned and shook his head, Braxton gave him a description of Maura.

The clerk said, "That sounds like—" He looked at Braxton suspiciously.

Braxton quickly pressed a banknote into his hand. "She has run off with a riverboat gambler and our father is bereft. That man will use her shamefully and toss her aside when he tires of her." Braxton assumed a properly outraged attitude. To his glee, the clerk nodded.

"Beau Fontaine has broken a hundred hearts up and down this river. I knew the woman was too fine a lady—"

"She's here then?" Braxton demanded impatiently.

The clerk lowered his voice to a conspiratorial whisper. "Traveling as his wife. *Tennessee* cabin on the starboard side astern."

"I am in your debt. . . ." *And Maura is in my hands!* Braxton could hardly contain his delight as he made his way among the boxes and crates. He'd enlist the Captain's support in getting Maura off the boat. She'd have to be subdued, she'd never go willingly. He fingered the bottle of tablets his father had given him.

He found Captain Dance and the mate on the texas deck. They had just come from the pilothouse, and Dance was holding the spyglass to his eye as he surveyed the river behind them. When Braxton tried to get his attention, he waved him away impatiently and continued to examine the boat that was closing in on them fast. Braxton cocked his head and stared at it. It was the unfinished boat he'd noticed near Paducah. He'd been so intent on the *Ohio Queen* he hadn't paid any attention to it other than to presume it was on some kind of preliminary run. He'd heard of testing the seaworthiness of vessels before the finishing work was

482

completed. . . . James' riverboat had already been launched.

"Damned if that ain't Tolly Jeffries! Couldn't mistake him if he was standing upside down in a barrel of molasses!" Captain Dance exclaimed.

The mate said, "He ain't took a run for three-four years. Heared say he retired to that place o' his in Pittsburgh. Sometimes takes a new boat into the water for its christening, but I never knowed a Pittsburgh launching this far down the river." He shook his head and rubbed the blue shadow of his beard.

"Well, it's him just the same," Dance declared. "Somebody's told him he can't pilot that unpainted skeleton down the river and he's set out to make a liar of 'im. He always was one to do the impossible."

Braxton was impatient with the conversation but intrigued by the boat that was coming closer to the *Ohio Queen* with every turn of its paddlewheels. It was a large boat, perhaps seeming even more so because of the stark lines of its superstructure that were as yet unadorned with scrolls and gingerbread. The pilothouse sat atop the texas like a regal dowager on a throne, and Braxton could see a white-haired man at the wheel. He had a pipe clenched between his teeth and one hand raised to blast the whistle.

"He sees us, Cap'n. . . ."

Dance called up to the pilot. "Give him an answering blast, Mr. Fenison. That's Tolly Jeffries!"

The *Ohio Queen*'s whistle shrieked, and Fenison turned to wave as the skeletal boat drew abreast on the larboard. A tall, broad-shouldered man in a black jacket and rough canvas ducks came onto the main deck and hailed Captain Dance.

"Man coming aboard, with your permission, Captain."

Dance gave him a salute. "Come aboard!" He handed the spyglass to the mate. "That's the second one in the past few minutes, Mr. Nelson. We're getting popular. Put two men on deck to give him a hand."

"Aye, sir." Nelson spied a deckhand coming out of the texas cabin. "Here, you! Man coming aboard from a dinghy. Look lively and see that he doesn't take a spill in this chilly water. Move it, man, stand ready afore his bow touches our shadow!"

The deckhand scampered down the ladder. Braxton watched as two deckhands on the other boat swung a small dinghy over the side and the man in the black sweater climbed in. He shoved off with an oar and settled to rowing in a hard, steady rhythm. A frown worked into the padding of flesh between Braxton's brows. The figure was familiar. . . . He lifted his gaze to the unfinished boat that was heaving to the larboard so the dinghy would clear its wake easily. A hundred boats looked the same before they were completed. Still . . . it *did* look like the boat in the Sullivan yard. He squinted at the man rowing the dinghy. When the man turned to gauge his distance and direction, Braxton saw his face. It was Duggan Quinn! He muttered an oath. Captain Dance turned to look at him in surprise.

"Passengers are not allowed on the texas deck," he said with forced politeness. The man ought to know better. "What is it you want?" He hadn't recalled seeing this man before, but he hadn't taken the time to introduce himself to everyone who came aboard at Evansville and Paducah. Could even be the one taken aboard from the freighting sternwheeler a few minutes ago.

"Don't let that man come aboard!" Braxton pointed at the approaching dinghy.

Dance's eyes widened. "I am the Captain, sir. I'll show you the courtesy of asking the reason for your bold remark before I request you to remove yourself to the cabin deck where you belong!"

Braxton realized he had breached the code of the river and desperately searched his mind for a reason that would be convincing. He'd heard how proud most captains were of their reputations for speed and meeting a challenge. The mate had attributed that quality to the man piloting the unfinished boat. Dance was undoubtedly cut of the same cloth.

Braxton assumed a nonchalant pose. "I took the liberty of coming to advise you that Mr. Jeffries has accepted a large wager that he can beat you into Cairo. The owner of that vessel is determined to establish a new record and win himself several handsome freighting contracts that are presently earmarked for the *Ohio Queen*." He shrugged and refrained from looking at Dance, who was peering at him suspiciously.

"I don't believe it," Dance said darkly, but his glance slid back to the other boat which had completed its outward swing and was chugging at full speed parallel to them. Duggan's dinghy was almost to the *Queen*. Two deckhands had a line ready to throw.

"Nevertheless it's true. As you see, Jeffries is already pulling ahead."

Dance scratched his head and studied Braxton again. "What business is this of yours, sir? I take it you have an interest in the outcome or you would not be here."

Braxton smiled. "Exactly. The man who owns that boat is my rival. If I can beat him out of the contracts he's counting on, I stand to make a handsome profit." He drew out his wallet and opened it so Dance could see the bills. "I would be willing to share my good fortune with you." He glanced at the dinghy that was only a few yards away now.

Dance followed his gaze. "Who's he?" He jerked his head in Duggan's direction.

Braxton lied quickly. "Some roustabout sent to delay you in any way he can, no doubt. I advise you not to let him aboard."

Dance grunted. It was too late. The dinghy had already touched against the *Queen*. Dance returned his attention to the unfinished sidewheeler. Jeffries had increased his lead to half the boat's length.

With a desperate look at Duggan, who was now preparing to climb aboard, Braxton gambled on a final parry. "Unless you act immediately, you may have lost several of your largest accounts, Captain! Order full speed, for God's sake!"

Dance shot another quick look at Jeffries' boat. Then he cupped his hands and shouted to the pilothouse. "Full speed ahead, Mr. Fenison! Tolly Jeffries thinks he can ruin the *Queen*'s reputation with that pile of lumber, and you're in line for a handsome bonus if you prove him wrong! I want to be in Cairo before that floating crate if we have to burn the cabin furniture to do it!"

The pilot grabbed for the speaking tube and shouted orders. A raucous burst of steam drowned out the sound of his voice. The *Queen* shuddered as her wheels picked up speed and foamed frothy water in widening trails. The chimneys coughed, then poured out a shower of sparks and

485

smoke. Dance gave a meaningful look at the wallet in Braxton's hand. With a grin, Braxton pulled out several large bills and handed them over.

"Now sir, if you'll be good enough to get below, I've got another race to win!" He stuffed the money inside his jacket and climbed to the pilothouse.

Braxton glanced at the starboard rail where the dinghy had been. The boat was no longer in sight, nor was Duggan. With an oath, Braxton rushed down to the hurricane deck. Racing across, he went down the steps to the boiler deck. There was no sign of Quinn, but it was possible he was on board. If so—

Braxton swore silently. Several passengers turned with startled looks as he raced past, scanning the names painted on cabin doors. He had to find Maura before Quinn did! He fumed at not recognizing the Sullivan boat when he first spied it. For a price, Elger Sharp would have found a way to stop it before it reached the *Ohio Queen*.

He read off the names of the cabins in gold-leaf scroll. *New York . . . . Ohio . . . Virginia . . .* damn! He pushed past a woman and a child blocking the passageway. The little girl whimpered. The woman gasped and put a hand to her breast.

"My word!"

Braxton didn't bother to glance in her direction. He was behind the paddlewheel housing now, and the thundering noise of wood striking water, lifting and spilling, was earsplitting. On the stern deck, he renewed his search. Finally he reached the last door.

Tennessee!

He put a hand to the knob and twisted it savagely. It gave, and he pushed open the door and slipped inside.

The cabin was empty. He let out an exasperated breath. Damn! The bed wa neatly made and the room in perfect order. Quickly he crossed to the wardrobe and yanked it open. Maura's gowns hung in a row. A man's coats, trousers and vests hung beside them, and two pairs of well-shined shoes were on the rack below. A silk top hat, a pearl-gray derby and a black beavertail hat were on the shelf above. At least they had not left the boat.

He glanced around but there was nothing to tell him where they'd gone. They might be in the salon or anywhere on the boat. As he started out, he noticed the raw wound on the door where the bolt had been torn loose and replaced. He let himself out and headed forward. He'd breathe a lot easier if he were sure that Quinn had not climbed aboard in those few minutes his attention was diverted by Captain Dance.

He hurried through the dim passageway that circumvented the wheelhousing and came out into the bright sunlight again. Passengers had collected along the rails as they became aware that another race was in progress. The pilot of the other boat had seen the *Queen*'s burst of speed and followed suit. The two were almost abreast, and the cheers of the passengers exploded over the racket of the paddles and engines.

Someone shouted, "They're pulling ahead!" A groan went up.

Braxton was thankful for the distraction. With luck, he might spot Maura before she saw him, even whisk her back into her cabin before anyone was the wiser. If not . . . he'd face that problem when he came to it. His father had warned him not to let her reach James no matter what he had to do.

He saw a gleam of red hair under a blue bonnet and hurried toward the woman. But as she turned, he saw his mistake. It wasn't Maura.

Then he saw something else that brought him up short. Duggan Quinn, his face black with rage, was running toward him. Braxton whirled and tried to push through the crowd, but Duggan was upon him, yanking him around and grabbing him by the throat.

"If you've touched her—!" Duggan exploded. His brain reeled with a memory of Braxton grabbing at Maura in the hall at Meadowfield. His fingers tightened on Braxton's throat. A wave of savage pleasure coursed through him as Braxton went limp. Nearby, a woman screamed, and Duggan realized he was throttling Turk. He loosened his hold enough so Braxton could breathe with strangled sounds.

"Where is she?" Duggan demanded. Braxton made a gurgling noise and clawed helplessly at Duggan's hands.

Two men broke away from the crowd and tried to come to Braxton's aid. "Let him go!" one shouted, but he did not venture within Duggan's reach. The other grabbed Duggan's shoulder and tried to pull him off, but Duggan sent him scuttling back with a quick growl and the swipe of a fist. The man bristled but backed away quickly. Then with an unexpected move, Duggan laced his fingers through Braxton's hair and pulled him to his feet. Turk gulped air with a rasping noise and clutched his throat.

"Where's Maura?" Duggan shook Braxton so his teeth rattled.

"Don't . . . know . . ." Braxton's body was shaking as he stumbled sideways and grasped the rail. A large circular area was cleared miraculously as Duggan lunged again. Women hurried out of the way of the ensuing fight. Others were oblivious to everything but the race in progress. Cheers and shouts encouraged Captain Dance to pour on more steam.

Braxton put his hands up protectively. There was murder in Quinn's eyes, and he knew the Irishman was capable of killing him. Hadn't he almost done it already? Terrified, Braxton glanced about for an escape route. The only one was through the passageway he'd just used—and that led to a blind end of the deck.

A pulse drummed in Duggan's temple and his stomach was a hard knot. He'd kill Braxton where he stood if he'd so much as laid a hand on Maura. He loomed over the cringing, sniveling coward and raised his fist.

"This is the last time I'll ask. Tell me where she is or I'll break you into pieces and feed you to the catfish!"

"I—I haven't seen her—I just came aboard. Ask the clerk if you don't believe me!" He glanced supplicatingly at the people who were still edging away. Several were whispering but they made no move to interfere.

Could Braxton be telling the truth? Duggan didn't trust him. Still, he'd just come aboard himself and hadn't had time to search for Maura. The clerk had been strangely reluctant to divulge any information about her. He swore ignorance, but Duggan sensed he was lying. He'd been on his way to the upper deck to ask the Captain's help when he'd sighted Braxton. Now he'd have answers or kill the bastard getting them!

His vision blurred with consuming hate. There was no way to find out if Braxton was lying except to investigate

488

the story and look for Maura himself. He pulled a long draught of air into his lungs to ease the tight band between his shoulders. It would do no good to get himself thrown off the boat and let Braxton remain behind.

He turned at the sound of running feet. Two deckhands were racing toward him. In that instant, Braxton yanked a pistol from his belt and aimed it. A woman's scream made Duggan turn just as the hammer clicked. He leaped and caught Braxton at the hips before he could pull the trigger. They fell back against the rail. Duggan slammed his fist at Braxton's arm, forcing it up sharply. A shot screamed into the air. Bedlam erupted, and the two deckhands jerked up short, afraid of another shot as the two men scuffled. Duggan pummeled Turk in the midsection so that he doubled over and gasped. Before he could recover, Duggan walloped him with a powerful blow that sent him spinning back. For a moment he teetered on the rail like a bird searching for a secure perch. Then with an agonized scream, he fell over into the churning water.

Screams spilled from the crowd, and people rushed to the railing. A man pointed. The women averted their faces as Braxton's head appeared, then disappeared in the rushing water.

"Stop the wheel!"

"There he is—!"

"He's gone under!"

"Oh, God—!"

"Tell the Captain to stop the engines!"

The crowd suddenly fell silent as Braxton's body flipped in the churning whitewater and was sucked under. A loud crashing sound thundered in the wheelhousing. The *Ohio Queen*'s whistle screamed as Captain Dance urged Fenison to widen the lead they had on Jeffries' boat. Duggan's stomach churned as a bloody froth stained the roiling water below the wheel. He had no pity to waste on Braxton, but it was a hell of a way for any man to die. He wiped his hand across his sweaty brow and drew a long, shuddering breath. The two deckhands darted out of his path as he made his way up the stairs to the hurricane deck. This foolish race had to stop before they were all in danger. He'd shout across to Jeffries to end it.

489

"You're moving like crippled old ladies!" the mate screamed over the roar. The firebox doors thudded and clanged as wood was heaved into the maw of the furnaces, sending up hissing sparks. The gloomy area under the main stairs glowed like Hell's pit as orange tongues licked into every corner. Captain Dance would blame him if the *Queen* did not beat Jeffries. Nelson grinned. *Damned wily old river rat, Jeffries. Thinks he can sneak up on a rival and catch her with her pants down, does he? Not while I've got a crew under me!*

"Pitch in that grease!" Huge buckets of grease had been brought from the galley on Nelson's orders. Now the stokers lifted them and heaved them into the furnaces. Flames roared, and the firemen cringed with arms shielding their faces.

"Don't slack off!" Nelson shoved the nearest man back toward the incredible blanket of heat that enveloped the fireboxes.

The stoker's body glistened and dripped with sweat. His eyes glowered. He would have defied the mate except for the beating it would get him and the loss of his job. Wiping his eyes with a grimy hand, he lifted another bucket and sent it whooshing into the fire. Sparks sprayed, and he slapped at a live ember that hissed against his damp, naked chest.

Nelson paced as though willing the fires to burn hotter. He was careful to stay out of the way of the deckhands who passed wood with steady precision. From time to time one of the men glanced at Nelson, but they did not break their rhythm.

In the engine room, Clark Ross had taken off his coat and rolled the sleeves of his blue shirt to the elbows. His collar was loosened and his tie hung carelessly over his shirtfront. He was a slender man, with brawny arms and huge hands that could grip a valve and twist it without effort. He'd been the chief engineer on the *Ohio Queen* for three years, and he took pride in coaxing from the engines every pound of steam the pilot demanded.

But this was foolhardy. Damn it, didn't Fenison realize that the engines were already turning at top speed? What the hell did the man want? There was a limit—

He swiveled his head as his trained ear caught the sound of angry steam hissing through a safety valve. Ross had hung a lead weight on it, but small spurts were leaking out under the metal cap. He glanced at the pressure gauge. A hundred and ten pounds— He brushed his forehead with an upraised arm, and sweat soaked through his sleeve. The boilers wouldn't hold much more.

The speaking tube shrilled. The pilot's voice thundered over the cacophony of the engines and whistling valves.

"Give me full speed, Mr. Ross! This ain't no church picnic! That damn Tolly Jeffries is right on our bow!"

Ross grunted and tightened a valve a quarter of a turn. "You've already got full steam, Mr. Fenison. Ain't nobody but the Devil himself can make those fires any hotter! I got every valve tied down. Ain't one drop of steam goin' to waste!" Hell's fires, the man expected miracles when the *Queen* was already doing the impossible.

Another angry spit of steam made Ross turn. He gnawed at his lip and rubbed his knuckles across his mouth. The pressure had crept up to one hundred and fifteen, and the straining safety valve perked threateningly against the lead weight. The pressure needle edged upward in fitful spurts. The men at the boilers were throwing everything they had into the boxes.

For a moment, Ross cocked his head as he listened to the heavy rumble of the boilers that was an undercurrent to the racket of the engine room. Long ago he had trained himself to hear every noise apart from the others, like a blind man picked out individual smells and sounds to guide him. He hesitated with his hand on the pressure valve. The boilers rumbled and thumped like a dozen barrels going over a waterfall. He didn't like the change in the timbre—

Instinctively he reached to yank the lead weight from the pressure valve. As his hand gripped the heavy metal, the boilers exploded. Sharp fragments of metal and huge clouds of steam crashed through the fire walls. Ross was slammed back by a bulletlike chunk of metal and blinded by the hissing, rolling cloud of scalding vapor. He coughed and struggled to his feet, but the engine room was already an inferno. Through the heavy, hot fog that choked him, he saw a dull glow as flames leaped and ignited the wooden decks.

491

The roar of the fire and echoing explosion filled his brain as Ross sank back against a ripped-open engine. He was not even aware of the sharp, stinging pain where jagged metal cut through his clothing and flesh. His chest was filled with boiling steam and blazing light danced in his head. A sticky warmth seeped across his eyes—blood. With a shuddering sigh, he fell back and closed his eyes.

Duggan heaved himself up the ladder leading to the texas deck. He'd just gripped the top rung when the world exploded in a rush of steam, flames and flying debris. He was dimly aware of screams all around him as he careened through the air like a bit of chaff in the wind. A board struck him aside the head and he fell into darkness, aware of nothing more until the force of the cold water brought him to his senses. For a moment he did not know what had happened. Instinctively he paddled to stay afloat in spite of the sodden clothes dragging him down like an anchor. A chair floated by, and charred, smashed pieces of wood. The word *Tennessee* was painted on one in gilt letters. All around him, debris swirled. Smoke formed a thick black haze that made an eerie spectre of the shattered, burning *Ohio Queen*. Duggan's eyes smarted and he coughed spasmodically. He was moving mechanically, pushing aside flaming pieces of wood and wreckage. Puddles of oil flared with sickly yellow brilliance. Duggan became aware of moans and screams all around him.

The *Ohio Queen*'s boilers had burst! Maura! He looked around frantically as he made out figures clinging to anything that would keep them afloat.

"Maura!"

A red-haired woman bobbed near him, her face slack and her eyes staring in death. His heart gripped with fierce agony. He swam toward her and quickly saw it was not Maura. He grabbed for the woman but before he could reach her, she sank under the surface and an oily slick closed over her. Duggan plunged under the surface, but she was already lost in the jumble of refuse caught in the current. His lungs tortured, he surfaced into the stinging, smoky air.

His brain numbed with terror as he realized he might not find Maura in the confusion. He tried to call out again, but only a hoarse, croaking sound came from his cracked lips. A dozen burns stung his flesh. His shoulder ached where he'd been struck by something in his fall.

A gust of wind cleared the smoke for a moment. Duggan glimpsed the solid outlines of the *Patrick*. Slowly he began to swim.

CHAPTER TWENTY-EIGHT

Maura's teeth chattered and she shivered uncontrollably as she climbed out of the water. Her bare feet slipped on the muddy bank and she fell, too exhausted to move. When at last she tried to sit up, it was with the realization that she would die of the cold if she stayed where she was any longer. She pushed back the heavy, wet hair that clung to her shoulders like seaweed and finally managed to drag herself away from the water's edge. She sat hugging her knees as she stared at the vanishing pinpoint lights of the *Ohio Queen*.

She was still shaking over Cromwell's assumption that she was his for the taking. The ugly old lecher! And Beau—! Oh! She shuddered with a rage that temporarily drove away her chill. *Betting her!* He was insane! His total disregard for her self-respect and feelings strained credibility. He'd put her up as collateral for a gambling wager as though she were some minor piece of property that was his to give away! She uttered a deep growling noise of disgust as another fit of shivering attacked her.

She struggled to her feet and looked around. Where was she? Still a considerable distance from Cairo. The *Ohio Queen* would dock there about dusk. How far? A hundred and fifty, two hundred miles? Her body shook and she hugged her arms over her naked breasts. It might as well be a thousand, but it would not get any closer if she stood here. At least there was a moon. Turning in the direction the *Ohio Queen* was going, she picked her way along the rough riverbank. The moonlight was a hazy glow through the trees that created shifting shadows. A sharp stone cut her foot and she whimpered at the sudden pain. Fighting tears and numbing cold, she clenched her teeth and kept moving. She was between Hell and the Devil. If she waited until daylight so she could see, she might succumb to the cold . . . and if she pressed on, she might easily stumble and break a leg in the darkness. She sighed, then began to tremble with hysterical laughter. She glanced down at herself. Where, in heaven's name, was she going to go clad only in moonlight?! She could not walk into a town or knock on any door in this sorry state! She might escape one menace only to find herself in worse peril. Suppose she happened on a river tramp . . . or a camp of rowdy goldseekers headed west? The integrity she had risked her life to guard from Cromwell might become a valueless commodity. She winced as another sharp object sliced her foot. There were more things to worry about than she had effort to spare, she decided. She would have to manage one thing at a time.

It seemed hours that she walked and stumbled along the bank. The slick mud was treacherous under her bruised feet, and at times her path was blocked by an erosion of the bank or fallen brush. She had to make her way around these obstacles carefully. Her flesh was covered with stinging scratches from brambles that became torturous nets in the dark.

She came to a huge boulder that formed a sheer barrier rising to the treetops. When she tried to get around it, she discovered it disappeared in an impenetrable thicket. Tears scalded her cheeks as she studied the opposite end of the rock several yards out in the water. Bracing herself against the frigid shock, she waded in. Suddenly she stepped off a ledge and was plunged over her head in the icy flow. Sputtering and gasping, she surfaced and began to swim rapidly before all feeling left her body. On the bank, a bullfrog croaked a mocking song.

Maura couldn't still the chattering of her teeth as she finally clawed her way onto the bank at the far side of the rock. The cold had seeped into her bones, and every movement was agony. She forced herself to dance up and down on a grassy flat spot until her limbs tingled and came alive again. Then she set out once more.

She considered trying to find a road—there must be one not far from the river—but she discarded the idea. It would be too easy to become confused and lose her way completely. At least here she had the pale expanse of the river to guide her.

Each step was torture. Her legs were leaden and she had to concentrate on putting one foot before the other. She was beyond shivering except for the inner quaver that was in her marrow itself. Her hair dried to clammy fingers that clutched her neck and shoulders. She forced herself to think of anything that would keep her from sliding into a morass of self-pity and sap her courage.

Meadowfield . . . her father and mother . . . James . . . happier days when they were all together. And she thought of Duggan, but that brought a wave of despair that made her sink to the ground in a sudden burst of tears. She had driven him away and would never know his strength again. He'd protected her from Braxton and Pelham at the risk of his own safety and future—and she accused him of treachery. She'd driven away his love. A vision of his gentle smile made her weep anew, until she forced the image from her mind. What was done was past. Self-pity would not change it, nor would it solve the more urgent problem of staying alive. Resolutely she got to her feet and set out again.

She walked in a daze as she relived the fragile memories of the times she'd spent with Duggan. How wonderful the nights in his arms had been. If only she could turn back time and lie with him again, hear his whispered words and feel his caressing touch. She sighed with longing and regret. She had been on the brink of a new life but had cast it aside in reckless pride. She turned away his love when it was the thing she cherished most. He had been working for her and everything she held dear, but she was too blind to see the truth.

I'd fight for the chance to love you . . . I'd even fight you if necessary, he'd once told her.

Tears overflowed as she recalled the poignant moment on the riverbank. He *had* fought for her. She'd been an idiot to think he was fighting against her. *Oh, Duggan, I can never stop loving you . . . forgive me!*

She blinked and stared at a faint glimmer of light winking through the trees. For a moment, she was afraid to hope. It could be a boat on the river or a reflection of the moon on the water. Her pulse quickened as hope gave her energy. She broke into a run as the light became clearer. It was *not* the river! She sobbed with relief as she came abruptly to a clearing. The yellow glow came from a house outlined on a small knoll above the river. Several acres were cleared around it, and she tumbled into a furrowed field before she recognized it. The cool, damp earth was a balm to her wounded flesh and spirit, and she lay sobbing with relief. Nearby, a flapping noise made her heart skip and she jerked up. The wind whispered past her cheek as the sound came again. About twenty feet away, she saw the outline of a gaunt crucifix in the moonlight. A scarecrow! Laughing and sobbing, she ran to it. In moments she was dressed in the tattered shirt and hopelessly baggy pants that had been set out in some forgotten past to keep away crows.

She raced across the field, immune now to the stings and barbs at her feet. She found a smooth path and fell against the door of the house. She rapped on the rough pine and choked back her sobs.

Shuffling footsteps approached from inside. A querulous voice demanded, "Who's there?"

"I've had an accident," Maura cried. "Please help me!"

The door opened a crack and an eye peered out. Maura tried to smile but a fit of shivering wracked her and left her trembling pathetically. The door swung open. An old man bent over a knobby cane studied her with rheumy eyes.

"Dadburn! A girl!" he cackled, shaking his head and rubbing his whiskery chin in amazement. His thin face was a spiderweb of lines, and his skin was almost translucent. "Where'd you come from?"

Maura gave him a tremulous smile. "The river. I—I fell off a boat." She made a deprecating gesture toward the clothes. "I'm sorry, I had to borrow these from your scarecrow. Mine were ruined in the accident." She hoped he would accept the flimsy excuse. He was obviously very poor, perhaps unable to afford even the loss of these ragged garments.

He peered at her. "Where you goin', gal?"

"To Cairo. Do you have a horse?"

He shook his head. "Ain't got no stock 'tall. Ain't got much o' anythin' anymore. Sorry I cain't he'p ya." His eyes seemed to focus on a distant memory, and he fell silent.

"I must get to Cairo!" Maura's disappointment was so keen, tears welled.

The old man sighed a shuddering breath. "Cain't he'p ya. 'Less ya c'do wi' a cup o' coffee. Got some fresh boiled."

Maura nodded gratefully and stepped inside. The old man shuffled to a brick stove that glowed with a cheery fire. Atop it, a battered blue enamel pot hissed softly. He poured steaming coffee into a mug and handed it to her.

"Ya look plumb froze."

"I am. I have walked miles, and after my swim in the river, it has not been a pleasant experience." She tucked her feet under her as she sank gratefully to the only chair in the room. Evidence of the man's poverty was everywhere: crude, homemade furniture of rough wood, the stove, a few dishes on a shelf, a coat hanging on a peg. A door stood open to a minuscule bedroom where an untidy bed had an open Bible lying on it.

She sipped the hot, strong coffee. Its warmth spread through her body slowly like a seeping tide. For the first time since she'd jumped from the *Ohio Queen*, she began to feel alive and hope returned.

The old man was watching her, half in awe of having a pretty female right before his eyes and half wondering what he could do to help her. He couldn't turn her out into the night again, that was sure. She'd been in the river . . . *tch* . . . cavorting on one of those fancy riverboats, he figured. But that was none of his business. He had no right to judge, that was the Lord's job. She looked like a bedraggled waif sitting there. A pretty one, in spite of the damp hair all blown about and the cuts and scratches all over her. The old scarecrow clothes sure looked better on her than they ever did. She was a mighty pretty one. . . . He sighed for his lost youth.

Maura glanced over the rim of the thick cup. As soon as she finished the coffee, she would set out again. Maybe the old man knew someone—

Before she could ask, he spoke. "That's a nice gold necklace yer wearin'. Ya willin' to part wi' it?"

Her hand went to her throat. She had completely forgotten the tiny heart Beau had fastened around her neck at the start of the *Ohio Queen*'s journey. Did the old man plan to steal it? There was no threat in his voice. She nodded, watching him with a curious gaze.

"Chaim Dawson's got a flattie. He might tek y' down the river if'n y' wuz t' pay 'im smart 'nuf." The old man spoke hesitantly, giving the matter considerable thought. "He's got a shack mebbe half a mile from here. Been there all week, might still be."

She jumped up. "How can I find him? The necklace is gold—he can sell it anywhere—"

The old man grinned and held up his hand. "Have y'self 'nother cup o' coffee. Chaim's mean as a bear if'n he wakes 'fore daylight. Won't be but a half-hour or so. Rest y'rself. I'll find sumthin' to put on them feet." He shook his head in dismay as he glanced at her bruised, filthy feet. Then he picked up the lamp and carried it into the tiny bedroom where he rummaged around for several minutes. Finally he returned with a pair of worn felt carpet slippers and two lengths of twine.

Maura slipped her feet into them and tied the strings to hold them on. Both she and the old man smiled at the picture she made. She was worse than any scarecrow ever hoped to be! But she was grateful, and she told him so. They shared a companionable cup of coffee as they waited for the sky to lighten.

Maura was aware of the astonished stares she drew when she entered the New Carolina Hotel. An astounded desk clerk glanced past her as though expecting someone to rush up and whisk away the tatterdemalion who stood before him. Maura's cheeks flushed with embarrassment but she fixed the man with a bold gaze.

"What room is Mr. James Sullivan in, please?"

The man's mouth dropped and his lips moved soundlessly. Maura knew she was a sight. After a day and a half on Chaim Dawson's flatboat, she had not been able to improve her bedraggled appearance except to wash in the cold river water and knot her hair into a loose bun at the nape of her neck. Her knuckles were grimy and her skin was roughened from the wind and the cold. To make matters worse, she was still garbed in the dreadful clothes that had been relegated to a cornfield.

"I'm sorry, ma'am . . . miss—"

Maura's frayed nerves snapped. She lifted her chin and glared at the clerk. "Sir, I have been in and on the river for the past two days in circumstances beyond human endurance! I have eaten nothing but an abomination called beef jerky and bread that tasted like sawdust. I haven't slept more than a few hours, and I am chilled to the bone. I am exhausted and my temper is short! James Sullivan is my brother and I wish to see him immediately. Now you either tell me where he is, or I shall pound on every door in this establishment until I find him!" She drummed a fist on the desk and blinked away the tears of weariness that threatened.

The clerk swallowed hard and took a step back. "Yes . . . miss—Miss Sullivan . . ." He did not sound convinced, but he lacked the courage to face her wrath again. "He's in room 12 at the top of the stairs. I can send someone up—"

"That's not necessary. Thank you." She turned and marched to the stairway. The soft carpet slippers slapped on the bare floor like beavertails. A man sitting on a horsehair sofa cleared his throat and lowered his newspaper to stare after her. Maura's cheeks were scarlet but she held her chin high as she marched up the stairs. A moment later she was knocking on the door of room 12.

It opened and James stood there. His expression went from puzzlement to surprise to amazement. Maura flung herself into his arms.

"James! It's really you at last!" Maura pressed her face to her brother's shoulder and wept unashamedly. The rough tweed of his jacket was the most wonderful pillow her head ever had.

"Maura! Maura . . . I thought—my God, how did you get here? Look at you—what's happened?" James was incoherent with shock. He hugged her, then held her at arm's length, gazing with loving warmth. He kept shaking his head as though he'd seen the impossible.

Maura tried to smile but succeeded only in sniffling and sobbing. James pulled her into his arms and soothed her as he had when they were children and she'd suffered some hurt.

"There, it's all right . . . you're here now . . . it's all right." He stroked her tangled hair and lovingly pressed a hand to her tear-stained cheek. "Maura, you're safe."

501

Finally her tears waned and she rubbed her cheeks with her rough hands. When she mananged a pathetic smile, James drew her inside and closed the door.

"I'm sorry for blubbering so." She dried the last of her tears and threw herself into his arms again. "I'm so happy to see you!"

He led her to the bed and made her sit. He stood over her, still shaking his head with wonder. Then he laughed. "I have never seen you in such rags, yet I have never seen a more wonderful sight. I was beside myself because I thought I would never see you again—and you appear like a ragamuffin at my door! It's a miracle!"

She blinked and looked at him inquisitively. "I don't understand."

He sat beside her, still grinning in wonder. "How did you escape? Where have you been these past days? When your name did not appear on the list of survivors or the list of the dead—"

"What are you talking about?" He was speaking in riddles her weary brain didn't understand.

"The *Ohio Queen*—you don't know?" It was his turn to be confused.

Maura sighed. "And I never shall unless you stop asking foolish questions and tell me what's going on!"

James took a breath. "The *Ohio Queen* blew up near Paducah. The pilot was steaming at full speed and may have tied down the safety valves, no one is sure. More than sixty bodies have been recovered and a hundred survivors were rescued. When you were not among either group, we were frantic!" He took her hands and pressed them to his face. "But you are safe, thank God!"

Maura went numb with shock. The *Queen* wrecked! She recalled debris and charred bits of wood in the river and Chaim Dawson's laconic comment that a boat had gone to the bottom. It had not even occurred to her to think it might be the *Ohio Queen*. Beau—

"How terrible," she whispered. "I didn't know. I'd already left the boat!"

"Left it?"

She quickly told him the story of Beau's treachery, Obediah Cromwell's odious behavior, and her desperate escape. She gave him a bare outline of the rest of her journey and when she was done, his face was dark with anger and incredulity. Maura sank wearily against him and closed her eyes.

"I have never been more tired in my life. I don't think I can stay awake another minute—and there is so much to talk about!" She thought of Pelham and the reason for her coming to Cairo. But when she tried to talk, James hushed her gently and lifted her swollen, wounded feet to the bed as gently as he would a babe. He slipped off the tattered slippers and drew the blanket over her.

"Sleep now, and we will talk when you wake."

"I mustn't—Pelham is—"

"Hush. Sleep now. There is no problem that cannot wait a few hours now that you are safe." He went to the window and drew the velour curtains to dim the light.

Maura heard him tiptoe to the door and let himself out. As she drifted into unconsciousness, she wondered how James knew she'd been on the *Ohio Queen*. . . .

She woke slowly, coming reluctantly from a very far place. She thought at first that she was at home in Meadowfield, warm and secure in her own bed. Her eyelids were splashed with red and gold patterns where the sun brushed them with morning brightness. She was warm and relaxed, too comfortable to move. She stirred lazily, stretching her body like a cat and sighing softly.

Someone brushed a wisp of hair from her cheek. She smiled as she opened her eyes, remembering that she had found James. For a moment, she thought her mind was playing tricks—that she had dreamed she wakened, while in reality she was still cradled in sleep. Duggan lay beside her, smiling as though it were the most natural thing in the world for him to be in bed with her. He touched her face with whispering fingers.

"Duggan!" She bolted up, and he took her in his arms and held her close against his broad, strong chest. Not a dream, not a mirage, but flesh-and-blood Duggan! She tried to talk and to look at him and to drink her fill of the wonder of his presence. Over and over, she sobbed his name until he lifted her face and covered her mouth with kisses. She clung to him, afraid he might vanish in the same mysterious manner he had appeared. Her lips trembled under his, and she rubbed against the coarse hair of his chest. Her hands explored him, and her heartbeat quickened. He was here, and he was kissing her, holding her. Heady, wild desire rushed through her like a flame before the wind. The agonizing pain in her heart lifted at last, and her pulse sang. Duggan released her mouth and pressed his face to her throat, murmuring her name in a prayerlike whisper as they shared the wonder of their reunion. His hands pulled aside the coarse, grimy shirt and found her breasts. Her aching body strained toward him. When he captured her lips again, she returned the kiss passionately and eagerly.

And then he was meeting the sweet craving of her flesh. The ragged trousers were swept away, and his body found the intimate places that belonged to him by discovery. His powerful maleness entered her with gentle fire. He looked down at her with a knowing smile. Her smile was reflected in the sea-blue mirror of his eyes as she was swept into a consuming tide. They were one, soaring into sensual bliss and finding the pleasure that had been denied them so long. The dimly remembered core of heat in Maura's body fanned to flame, and she clung to Duggan breathlessly. His power filled her and gave her new energy, new desire as they moved in a symphony of love. Its culmination was breathless, wondrous and completely satisfying.

Maura did not realize there were tears in her eyes until Duggan kissed them away. "You must never cry again, love. Horror and evil are behind us now. I'll spend a lifetime making you happy." He raised himself on an elbow and gave her a devilish smile. "Miss Maura Sullivan, will you marry me? Not to save the Sullivan Company but because I love you so much I cannot bear the thought of ever being parted from you again."

The happiness she'd thought complete swelled to overflowing. She smiled joyously and embraced him, unable to form words on her trembling lips. Yes, she would marry him! She loved him with a passion that frightened her by its intensity. Her doubts were gone. Duggan was part of her, and she could not live without him.

He kissed her gently, then more fervently, searching her eager mouth with his tongue. "My own sweet love, my beloved Maura . . ."

Their bodies molded in a new rise of passion, less violent than the first but no less sweeter for it. He brought her expertly to readiness a second time, kissing and caressing her breasts, her belly, the tender, bruised legs. Her hands stole to his flesh and found that he was ready to pleasure her again. Together they climbed to an incredible peak that was beyond time until its dizzy spiral of fulfillment.

She lay in the crook of his arm, her head against his brawny, muscled chest. Softly, he told her of the fight in the boatyard and his pirating of the *Patrick*. As he recounted the events that brought him to the *Ohio Queen* shortly before the explosion, she tightened her hold on him possessively. If she had known he was so close—!

His voice faltered when he told her how he'd searched among the victims and survivors, asking if anyone had seen her or knew her whereabouts. And when the *Patrick* delivered the last of the wounded and dead to the levee at Cairo, he went to James and told the sad news. They grieved together, numbed by their loss and filled with aching pain.

Until she had appeared so wondrously. Duggan grinned. "When James came to tell me of the apparition that had tapped at his door, I thought he'd gone crazy. He could not convince me until I saw you with my own eyes."

"You should have wakened me." The thought of being apart from him one minute longer than necessary seemed a terrible waste. She clung to him dreamily.

"I stared at you all night. I couldn't tear myself away for fear you would vanish like a wraith. I watched the dawn come up over the river. The sky was blood-red, then russet and gold, like your hair. A savage dawn . . ."

She remembered him once telling her of his boyhood in Ireland and the beauty of the early morning. He'd used the same words: savage dawn.

"And when I could not bear it any longer," he whispered, kissing her gently, "I slipped in beside you and waited for the first flutter of your eyelids so I could wake you with kisses."

She returned the intimate smile. "And what of James? Did you tell him your intention?"

Duggan laughed softly. "Any man had only to look at my face to know that I would claim you as soon as possible. I sent James to my room and I took his. One bed is the same as another when there's not a loving woman lying in it." He planted a kiss on the tip of her nose. "You're blushing, my sweet. I never thought you could be embarrassed by something as natural as love. The same girl who scolded me on the banks of the Hudson and told me to take her home because she could do without that tender, precious feeling?" He teased her with a smile and shook his head. "Ah, my lovely colleen. I told James we would be married today. He's out this very moment making the arrangements. Did you think I would incur the terrible Sullivan wrath by doing otherwise?"

"Were you so sure I would say yes?" she asked softly.

His breath fluttered warmly on her cheek. "I have known from the first. I only wanted you to be as sure."

She was sure . . . she was absolutely sure.

Smiling, he kissed her long and leisurely, and Maura recalled her father's prophecy that someday she would find a man worthy of her.

EPILOGUE

Pittsburgh, April 1850

The levee was crowded and noisy with the sounds of a band and last-minute loading. Roustabouts sang a lively chant: "Load de box . . . load de bale . . . gonna see de moon on de riber tonight. . . ."

The main deck of the *Patrick* was piled from its planking to the overhang of the boiler deck. Machinery covered by tarpaulins shouldered crates of clothing, household articles, lumber and wheels for wagons. Barrels of oil from the upper Ohio were stacked deck-high in even rows; bins of coal destined for Vicksburg and Natchez were a hulking mass under the rear deck, as far from the hot furnaces as they could be put.

The *Patrick* gleamed a dazzling white in the spring sun. Her twin chimneys were as black as the smoke that poured from them. Above letters edged in gold that spelled out *Patrick* on the wheelhousing, was the inscription: SULLIVAN AND QUINN PACKET LINE.

Maura slipped her arm through Duggan's and hugged him. "It is one of the most wonderful days of my life!"

"James is as proud as a peacock," Duggan said with a grin. "Captain Harkins has promised he can ride the entire trip in the pilothouse if he's a mind to. Mr. Jeffries says if he does, he'll sign him on as a cub pilot and put him to work."

"James would love every moment of it!" Maura waved as she spied James in the wheelhouse. "He's been looking forward to this day all winter. He's like a child with a new toy."

"I'd hardly call the United States mail a toy. James has the right to be proud of securing a mail contract." The construction of two new vessels had been completed in re-

507

cord time the past winter. With the *Patrick* hauling cargo and passengers daily between Pittsburgh and Cairo, there was enough profit to finance expansion to a hundred men working two shifts. The debt to Cromwell had been paid, and the politician had wisely withdrawn his attempt to organize a union at the Sullivan Company. He realized he had met his match in Duggan, and if he ever dared venture onto Sullivan and Quinn property, it would be at the risk of being throttled. But even without Cromwell, Duggan kept his word in guaranteeing men employment for the year—and beyond for any man who did his job well. James, Jeb and Duggan met with spokesmen regularly to iron out problems and settle disputes.

Duggan was certain that the failure of the Congress to stand behind labor's fight was only a temporary delay, not a death knell for national unions. The local unions at the boatyard and carriage works were examples of how management and labor could cooperate; Duggan vowed that someday they would lead the way for national groups.

He felt a lilt in his heart as he recognized the realization of Patrick Sullivan's dream. Gazing at Maura, he squeezed her hand. "Your father would be very proud."

Maura's eyes misted. "I suspect he's looking down on us right this moment, chuckling a bit, and taking full credit in Heaven for what we have wrought on earth!"

Duggan threw back his head and laughed aloud. Several people turned to stare, then smiled indulgently at the obvious joy of the young couple near the gangplank.

Maura's heart swelled with a wondrous love that had not diminished in the five months she'd been Duggan's wife. She still marveled at their happiness and the complete accord with which they ran the Sullivan and Quinn Carriage Works in New York. Maura preferred living at Meadowfield. It seemed right to be there with Duggan and erase all memories of Pelham and Braxton.

Confronted with the evidence of deliberate sabotage in his effort to ruin James, Pelham recognized defeat and let Maura and James buy him out. With Braxton dead, the fight had gone out of him. James gave a fair price for his stepfather's stock so there would be no legal entanglements to mar the future of the expanding Sullivan and Quinn Company. "Besides," he'd said with a wink and a grin, "with two Quinns now and only one Sullivan, I'd best copper my bets so *I'll* not be voted out one day!"

Maura glanced again at James in the pilothouse. How he loved the river! She didn't think he'd ever leave! She missed him, but when she saw what he had accomplished in Pittsburgh, she could only wish him continued success and happiness.

Duggan folded his hand over hers and gazed into her gray, smoky eyes. "Once a long time ago, you spoke of your father's dream to build a house overlooking the Hudson. If you want it, or one here overlooking the Ohio, you need only say the word, Maura."

She shook her head with a loving smile. "I am as happy as any woman can be. I cannot ask for more."

He cocked an eyebrow. "Not even our delayed honeymoon trip?" he teased.

Maura's pulse quickened. "Yes, that . . . and to watch each new dawn with you."

He kissed her, unmindful of the people watching. Over the quick racing of her heart, Maura heard the shrill call of the *Patrick*'s steam pipes. At the head of the gangplank, the round-faced clerk in a white coat and gold-trimmed cap called a final warning.

"All aboard that's comin' aboard!"

Arm in arm, Maura and Duggan went up the gangplank.